SATAN'S PITCHFORK

Edmund Charles

UK Book Publishing.com

Editing, design, typesetting and publishing by UK Book Publishing

www.ukbookpublishing.com

ISBN: 978-1-916572-53-9

SATAN'S PITCHFORK

DEDICATION

'Satan's Pitchfork' is a fictious novel devoted to the often unsung and anonymous wilderness fire fighters, who annually battle the all-consuming enemy of the American heartland – the great and deadly western wild-fires. Akin to that of a Biblical plague, the wildfires naturally seek to relentlessly consume everything which lies within its path, to include forests, wildlife, houses and sometimes even people. While the wildfires are soulless, those who battle the hellish beast are quite human. These nameless men and women are young, brave, highly spirited and full of adventurism. While the strength of youth is required to fight the wildfires, its passions can also consume the lives of those fighting the blazes. Away from the wild-fires, they often fight an equally menacing foe – the cauldron of their personal lives, which are filled with all the drama that befits young, vibrant souls. For a few brief months throughout the short summer season, the young volunteers leave behind their normal 9-to-5 mundane working routines to become something totally different and special. The majority return back home to live their normal lives and loved ones, sometimes telling tall tales of danger, bravery and sometimes humour; while a tragic minority is left dead, horribly injured, or mentally impaired – with only their family and friends to mourn their spirits. This is a story of those brave youthful Americans from all walks of life who take the annual challenge to fight the wildfires.

TABLE OF CONTENTS

PREFACE

"...we need to get higher in elevation - without working instruments in this weather and terrain, we're dead meat"

"Aspen Control, this is Alpha-Three-One-Whiskey calling for a priority landing approach and weather assessment, Over," the monotone male voice pronounced into his headset mounted microphone. There was only deadly silence, then suddenly there erupted an earful of garbled words accompanied by heavy static. "I say again Aspen Tower, this is Alpha-Three-One-Whiskey, calling for an immediate approach clearance, Over," the elevated voice pleaded in a more urgent and forceful tone. Again, there was only the response of a garbled voice and heavy communications static.

"Switch to alternate frequency four-nine'er-five," a different male voice heralded in a declarative, yet somewhat frustrated command voice.

"Let me try one more time, before switching the frequency, Captain," the subordinate male voice pleaded. Still the radio feedback heard was mere senseless tones and white noise sounds, only one word in ten was coming through the radio static. Both the pilot and co-pilot stared at one another in obvious resignation of the poor air-to-ground communications; they both shook their heads with resigned frustration. Their situation was getting desperate, another comms check was needed with the Aspen Airport control tower.

"Roger that, Captain, changing to alternate radio frequency four-nine'er-five...Aspen Tower this is Alpha-Three-One-Whiskey, do you read me, Over?" the co-pilot uttered in restrained desperation. Once again there was only the eerie silence of an unanswered communication radio check. Silent distress started to fill the cockpit.

Suddenly their headphones crackled to life with the welcomed resonance of an audible human voice bathed in a crystal-clear tone. "Roger, Alpha-Three-One-Whiskey, this is Aspen Tower... I read you '1 by 5', I say again I read you '1 by 5' ...your transmission signal is weak, but your voice is very audible, Break...keep on this frequency, we're experiencing some whiteout and blizzard conditions along with a highly charged ionosphere radio interference... visibility is less than 1,200 yards, Good Copy, Over," barked out the anxious sounding co-pilot and instructing Aspen Control Tower as to signal strength-to-audible communications feedback from the jet to the Aspen airport control tower.

The imperiled plane was methodically circling and using its precious fuel, the aircraft was in a low altitude holding pattern. "Roger, Aspen Control, we have got about 45 minutes of fuel remaining, what's the possibility of landing in the next eight minutes? I need to know whether or not to abort to Denver or try for instrument landing at Aspen, Over?" sounded the stern voice of a rather concerned pilot.

"Roger, acknowledge Alpha-Three-One-Whiskey, Aspen Tower will get you an advisement on your options in one minute, Over" the Aspen Control tower Air Traffic Controller responded back to the circling plane dryly and without a hint of emotion.

"Yeah, I bet it will be more like five minutes, as we burn up valuable and limited fuel, those dip-sticks on the ground have no idea of the pucker factor that the pilots circling up here go through!" the anxious co-pilot remarked to the senior pilot. The reserved senior pilot merely grinned at the slight nervousness of his younger co-pilot.

"Just stay calm, Tom, we'll give them their precious minute, then we'll pester their ground-loving asses again." The slightly greying haired senior pilot relaxingly grinned. Both men nervously laughed, each hiding the inherent danger germane to all aerial activity, especially those which involved foul weather and dangerously diminishing fuel levels during a Rocky Mountain winter storm. Flying was inherently dangerous, yet neither man would have traded it for any other ground job, regardless of the flying dangers and long hours of flying and the long boredom of always being on ground stand-by ready status. The ecstasy and intrinsic danger of flight made the aviation profession very exciting, glamorous and addictive – an excited feeling that no ground-pounder, non-flyer could ever hope to appreciate. Flying was in one's blood and either you had it in you or you didn't. Finally, being a private jet pilot for millionaire and billionaire VIPs was an especially plush flying gig too. It belonged to a small elite set of pilots who flew the private jets of the world's elite and powerful personages. The pay was double that of any airline pilot and it afforded lodging in five-star accommodations; yet the ultimate fringe benefit was meeting the 'movers' & shakers' of the business and entertainment worlds. Few occupations could rival it!

Merely several feet away from the Gulf Stream's cockpit bulkhead, there sat arrayed several modestly, yet comfortably dressed, affluent family members. An older gentleman in his mid-seventies and a pretty woman in her late sixties sat comfortably cuddled next to one another, her head patiently lying against the man's shoulder. A woman in her early thirties and a man in his late-twenties sat facing opposite each other on a comfortable couch, each looking anxiously at one another. "I hope to hell that we land soon, I am sick of being on this flipping plane," complained the young man, in a whining, spoiled tone.

The young woman immediately frowned at the young man and rolled her eyes in a familiar dismissal, then quibbled smartly, "That's all you ever do is complain, instead you could be sitting in coach class aboard one of those commercial flying buses that they call airplanes – you're just a spoiled yuppie brat!"

"Now listen here the two of you, you're not little children any longer, Melissa and Bobby," the elegant and elderly woman named Gloria chastened to her young adult children in a friendly, yet stern motherly tone.

The handsome, elegant older man smiled reassuringly as he lightly padded his wife's hand, "Gloria, you were always the disciplinarian in the family."

She playfully removed her husband's hands with an obvious impatient gesture, then remarked very casually and chided smugly, "Well, my dear husband, someone in the home had to do it, you were forever at the office or away on business travels and I had the domestic oversight at Greystone."

Arthur Hamilton smartly smiled at Gloria, his wife for the past 40 years. He knew and regretted in his heart, that she was absolutely right too! He had given far too much of his life to making money and not enough to the true riches of his life, the precious family-time with his wife and children. Now perhaps in old-age he could redeem some of the lost time from those hectic previous years and devote his remaining earthly time to his adult children and long-devoted wife.

The Hamiltons were part of a dying breed of American royalty – being multi-generational wealthy, sophisticated, pedigreed, well-mannered, very reserved and remarkably non-public. Their family's wealth was counted in the tens of billions of dollars, yet aside from the Boston society pages, their standing in the flashy heinous public press was conspicuously vacant and few Americans ever knew of their power or wealth, let alone that of the family name.

Over the years, Arthur had made increasingly valiant attempts to spend more time with his family and gradually surrender the operations of his private investment banking concern to his elder son – Bradford, who had remained behind to tend the family's investment bank in Boston. Aspen had been an annual family refuge for the past 20 years or so, it was a relaxing break for the family and it abbreviated the dreary Boston winters that befell the psyche between the period between the months of January through April. The younger children always enjoyed the skiing in Aspen, but Gloria was always one to suffer flying anxiety and in her older years, she became increasingly reluctant to take the long journey west; instead, she preferred to stay in the gloomy Boston winter than to face another long, unwelcomed trip to Aspen. Furthermore, the plane's circling made her even more nervous and the routine turbulence over the Rockies made for the plane's pending descent even more annoying. She excused herself to go to the jet's restroom. Soon they would be landing, and her anxiety only made her bladder the more unsettled.

Within the cockpit, the pilot's headsets finally crackled to life after a seemingly endless pregnant pause: "Alpha-Three-One-Whiskey, this is Aspen Tower, please be advised that you have permission to perform an instrument landing on runway 'Charlie' – the approach is on vector 179, ceiling is now only 800 feet with visibility of 800 yards, the runway is clear of snow and ice, Over." The pilots looked at each other with mutual disdain. "Shit, that's one of the worst weather readings that I have ever been given, thank God for modern technology and instrument landing technology," the pilot gasped in audible frustration to his co-pilot.

"Roger, Aspen Tower, we're beginning our descent now to 5,000 feet and then we'll go for the final approach, Over," the senior pilot stated in an almost resigned voice. He and the co-pilot started to push numerous buttons and glowing hues of icons located on the 'glass instrument' panel.

Unexpectedly, the control panel flashed a series of warnings and red panel lights started to flash; this was accompanied by a loud audio emergency buzzer. Both the pilot and co-pilot were confounded and disturbed by the sudden rash of warning lights. Power to both engines suddenly seemed greatly diminished and the plane was losing altitude rapidly. An audio warning signal announced in robotic English that the plane was losing altitude dangerously fast. The pilot quickly announced to his passengers that there was a sudden emergency and that everyone was to buckle their safety belts.

Arthur ensured that Melissa and Bobby had their seat belts adjusted. A nervous Arthur Hamilton struggled to get out of his seat, as he fought the rocking motion of the jet, but finally getting to his feet he tried to get back to the bathroom and assist in seating his wife. He called frantically to his wife, as he tried to grasp the bathroom door handle to open it. Swiftly, he was thrown violently up and back against the bulkhead as the turbulence of the air increased. His right shoulder was badly sprained, and a trickle of blood ran down from his forehead and into his left eye. He had suffered a mild head contusion when his head struck the top of the bulkhead ceiling.

"Fuck me, we just lost our navigation and radar system, we need to get higher in elevation, without working instruments in this weather and terrain, we're dead meat," the co-pilot shouted in frustration and anger. The senior pilot switched off the main circuit breaker for three seconds, then he re-started the main power switch. Amazingly the entire instrument panel was once again working, everything seemed fine and both pilots were relieved as the plane levelled-off its sudden and steep decline. All the passengers were quite relieved too. Just as both the pilot and co-pilot were re-engaging with the Aspen Tower to reconfirm their final approach, before them flashed a fateful sight – a jagged white-capped mountain instantly appeared from the milky-white enveloping clouds that had encapsulated their opaque cockpit.

Their eyes bulged out with an instant doomed resignation. They knew it was too late. In the wink of an eye, the Gulf Stream impacted the mountain and exploded in a ball of flame, disintegrating into many thousands of pieces. Both crew and passengers were killed instantly, torn to shreds by the sudden impact of an aluminum structure travelling 500 mph into solid granite rock formations.

"Alpha-Three-One-Whiskey, this is Aspen Tower - do you read me, Over? Alpha-Three-One-Whiskey, this is Aspen Tower, Over! Alpha-

Three-One-Whiskey, this is Aspen Tower, Over – come in, damn it!",
the tower staff air traffic controller pleaded anxiously as they saw the
aircraft instantly vanished from the radar screens. Like all aviation
veterans, they feared the worst and hoped for the best. The control
tower was muted in utter silence, everyone knew what had happened,
yet no one dared to vocalize their thoughts. After several additional
frantic and failed radio attempts, the alert was signalled for a search and
rescue party to begin at the last known location of the Gulf Stream jet.
An emergency search and rescue team was dispatched immediately to
locate the missing private luxury jet. However, billowing pitch-black
smoke and flames tragically portrayed the obvious spot of the plane
crash to the rescuers. The ragged and fragmented burnt remnants of
the aircraft and its unfortunate occupants were found over the course
of the next several days. DNA forensic analysis was necessary for bodily
identification.

The tragic story received extensive TV and newspaper coverage in
Aspen, the nation and more importantly Boston, the city from which
the wealthy deceased passengers had once called their home. The heart-
rendering story circulated about a wealthy banker and his family who
had tragically died while vacationing enroute to a winter ski trip. It was
also announced that the FAA was investigating, and it was unofficially
suspected that 'human error' was to blame, as was so often the case
when there were no survivors and there were no 'black boxes' on this
private jet for retrieval and study.

The story soon receded from the pages of the media almost as
quickly as it had appeared. Old news had to surrender space for the
newest of stories. For the dead, their fate was fast and final, for the lone
absent family member who was not aboard the plane, however, this
moment was merely the beginning of his agony and ultimately of his
personal life changing crisis. To this sole surviving son, it mattered little
whether the accident was caused by instrument failure, foul weather
or pilot error – all that mattered was that his entire family was dead.
'Lose your parents and you become an adult…lose your siblings and you
become old', so true was this adage which so aptly applied to the sole
surviving son, Bradford Wayne Hamilton.

* *

CHAPTER 1

The Haunting

"Her total appearance was dazzling and almost mesmerizing, denoting feminine power, wealth, and sophistication... she was the iconic woman that other women loved to hate"

Like incessant angelic tears pouring down from the heavens, the translucent speckles of cold rain befell upon the seemingly endless array of marble and granite juxtaposed lifeless figures. This eerie masonry array of assorted crosses, phallic-styled obelisks, and assorted geometrically shaped patterns, all prodigiously inhabited the gated and desolate community of the dead. Row after row of seemingly endless stone edifices populated the lush green cemetery lawn. The unremitting rainfall of an early New England Spring morning fell steadily throughout the passage of a grey and bleak day. The grim weather only served to reinforce an atmosphere of morbidity to the cemetery and to one's personal senses.

The past six weeks had been a living hell, life had taken an indefinite hiatus from his life, leaving him in a constant state of catatonic existence, an anguish from whence neither life prevailed, nor death provided respite. His clear bright blue eyes were constant pools of reflective mist, tinted with traces of crimson. His once broad smile was now camouflaged with a downcast grim mask. He cared little for his personal appearance, the flowers that he now carelessly carried loosely in his left hand were merely a sympathetic veneer of possibilities never to be. Taking life for granted was a preserve of those afforded with a sound mind and body, he now possessed neither.

Sluggishly approaching the dreaded destination, his heart raced with adrenaline, his throat tightened, and his eyes welled up with tides of depressed emotions. The soil and grass were endowed with alternating pools of clear rainwater and of the brown earthen mud from the newly turned graves. He journeyed to this place as much for himself, as for those whom he loved. As to his present prospects, he thought very little and cared even less. The future mattered even less to him. Bradford W. Hamilton was a shell of a man with a rich past, a very bleak present, and possibly a bankrupt future.

His body irrepressibly trembled as he nervously approached a huge, russet-coloured granite monument stone atop of which there graced a massive six-foot tall angel with its extended arms extolled forth unto the heavens. His heart pounded with strong palpitations; immediately he dropped the flowers and fell to his knees, sobbing uncontrollably at the base of the huge tombstone. "Please let me die, Lord! Why them and not me?" he sobbed uncontrollably. In his delirious grieving, he fell into an almost delusional state, being only mildly aware of his physical circumstances. He coughed repeatedly and crudely spat-up phlegm upon the dampened earth.

Bradford lovingly draped his shambled arms around the tombstone upon which was inscribed the surname of 'Hamilton' in big, bold engraved Old English scroll lettering. The ornate and expensive light chocolate-coloured granite stone was newly placed and the freshly turned muddied earth attested to a recent disturbance of the surrounding, and otherwise immaculately maintained, green lawn of the prestigious St. Giles cemetery. St. Giles was an ancient colonial-era cemetery, whose proud departed residents included some of Boston's finest and richest families. It seemed that even in death, the wealthy sought separation from the working classes and publican masses.

Prominently upon the bottom portion of the Hamilton headstone, were inscribed the freshly chiselled names of four persons: Arthur, Gloria, Melissa, and Robert. The birth dates were also aptly indicated, as were the corresponding dates of their deaths. The singular date for all four souls was January 20. Bradford W. Hamilton was the sole surviving son of an ultra-rich Boston family, yet presently he lay cold, wet and alone, prostrate in a foetal position, crying at the muddy base of his family's gravesite.

Precipitously from out of the gloom, there pierced a gravel-throated voice vainly crying out from among the cold stone sentinels, "Is anyone there?... Who's out there?" The old man spied about and caught the horrific sight of a young man lying in the mud at the base of a gravestone.

"Oh my...oh my God...are you all right my boy? Are you injured or hurt?" bellowed out a quivered, rattling inquiry of a quite concerned elderly male voice. Yet there was no immediate response. The old man was unrelenting in both his questions and concern. "I said, are you all right young fellow?" the old man pleaded once again in a tone of genuine concern and gallant inquiry.

"What's that? Who is it? What did you say?" Bradford slowly stammered out, as both his mind and spirit slowly returned to the present reality of everyday consciousness.

"I asked if you are all right, Mr Hamilton...remember it's me, Walter Cromby...I'm the St. Giles groundkeeper...now are you all right, sir?" The aging groundkeeper looked wearily and mercifully into Bradford Hamilton's dishevelled ashen face, which was now quite drenched with rainwater and pieces of muddy earth and sod. Walter was a retired Boston stonemason and carpenter, who now leisurely filled his idle retirement time being employed as a part-time groundskeeper at St. Giles cemetery.

Bradford wearily wiped his eyes with his muddy hands. "I'm...I'm fine... I think. Walter, I just wanted to visit the family and say hello and I guess I just lost myself a little... things have been hard on me lately and I am not quite myself. Walter, I'm sorry for getting you out of the cottage and into this miserable weather," Bradford apologetically explained in a shallow-toned quivering voice.

"Oh no...no, sir, Mr Bradford, it's not you that should be apologizing to me, after all you are the one who has lost all your kin in that terrible and tragic airplane accident, sir. I just got a little nervous and suspicious when I saw the headlights of a car parked outside the gatehouse, but I saw no driver or passengers, so I came out to investigate and that's how I found you! I see you day after day come to St. Giles and my heart breaks at your loss," Walter Cromby elaborated in a fatherly, yet remorseful tone. With the kind aid of Walter's hand, Bradford gently lifted himself up from the soaked, muddy ground and brushed off his fine grey Armani custom-made suit and trench coat.

"Make no worries about any of this nasty business and kindly be assured, Mr Hamilton, that I'll take good care of your kin's plot and I'll call you when the new sod is laid, probably in a few weeks or a month at most, sir," Walter graciously assured Bradford.

"Thanks, Walter, I appreciate your devotion and integrity," Bradford unemotionally replied. "It's my honour to do so, Mr Hamilton, now would you like to come to the caretaker cottage for some hot coffee or tea, Mr Hamilton?" Walter humbly offered.

Bradford was flattered by the offer, but he could not accept it. "I am terribly sorry, Walter, and I thank you kindly, but I have to be at my office; in fact, I'm late already, but perhaps another time, my friend."

Walter could do little more than acknowledge Brad's dilemma and try to assist him to be safely on his way. Bradford Hamilton slowly staggered back to his late-model Bentley sedan. He took a well-worn, white, embroidered handkerchief from the pocket of his trench coat, coarsely wiping away the mud and tears from his sullen face. This sojourn to St. Giles cemetery had been a ritual repeated without fail over the past several weeks; however, the morbid tribute did him no good. He was caught in the grips of a chronic, severe depression, with his psychic redemption being quite uncertain. He slowly and repeatedly drew the fingers of his left hand through his soaking thick wet hair, as in the fashioning of a crude finger comb.

Bradford unfolded the sunshade back-lit vanity mirror; his reflected morbid face was that of bloodshot eyes, pale complexion, strewn wet stringy hair and hallowed, drawn cheeks; he looked akin to that of a vagabond, rather than that of a Boston blue-blood, billionaire executive; however, the reflection bore no lies, just the twisted anguished face of an emotionally beaten man. His attire, though exclusive in design and materials, was rumpled, un-pressed, and now generously soiled with rain and traces of mud. His face was crudely shaven as witnessed by slight razor nicks and uneven stubble patches. Bradford extracted the keys from his trousers and engaged the powerful Bentley Continental V-12 engine. He reached for the temperature controls and activated all the defroster and heat knobs on the highest possible settings. The immediate gushing of warm air was a most welcome respite.

From the lush driver's seat position, he stretched over to open up the passenger side glove box. Therein glistened two onerous, objects: a whiskey flask and a powerful short barrelled .357 magnum revolver pistol. He glanced at the two shiny objects, each object as potentially deadly as the other. A few seconds passed before he finally grabbed one of the objects. He pressed the cold cylinder-shaped object up to his face and then into his mouth. He tilted his head gently back; the cold metal against his lips felt uncomfortable and foreign. There was a sudden gush of warmth into his mouth. An inviting warm liquid generously filled his throat. On this morning like countless mornings before, Brad had chosen the whiskey flask and not the pistol. Yet to continue forth in such a manner would ultimately lead to a similar slow fate – that of death itself! The voluminous mouthful of fine 18-year-old malt scotch was a mere passing mental relief, it temporarily dulled and satisfied the senses, but not the reality of his tormented life.

Ironic it was that Bradford's drinking of distilled spirits was a means of forgetting about the spirits of his lost family. He reached into his right suit breast pocket and withdrew a slender, digital smart phone. He spoke the words 'Margie' and an automated telephone dialling routine was executed. A pleasant feminine voice on the other end of the connection answered, "Hello and Good Morning, this is the office of the Hamilton & MacAlister Investment Banking and Security Trading Corporation, Mr Hamilton's office, may I help you?" Margie DeTagelio answered in a smart business-like and professional tone. "Hello Margie...it's Brad, I'll be in the office in about half an hour or so – okay?" Bradford stated almost apologetically.

"Oh my God, Brad, are you alright? Is there anything that I can do? Katherine is going crazy wondering where the hell you are!" Margie inquired sincerely, as she heard the familiar words of depression in her boss's voice.

"No… I mean yes, I mean …that is to say that I am fine, Margie and thanks for asking, I'll talk to you later when I get into the office… I'm just running a little late again," he poorly feigned in his obvious tepid reply.

"Good, then, we'll expect you in about half an hour then, and please be careful and drive safely," she voiced in a pleading manner. "I'll do my best, Margie, and I'll see you in a bit," Bradford replied as he concluded the conversation and ended the cell call.

Gazing down at his Rolex custom platinum watch, he realized his acute lateness for work and he felt guilty. Others were depending on his presence and performance, but he was letting then down. He had always insisted that his workers seek professional counselling assistance, yet now he failed to follow his own orders. He engaged the silky-smooth Bentley transmission, as his elegant and modern mechanized chariot slowly transported him from the dead fields of St. Giles cemetery to downtown Boston. The heart, or at least the mind, was indeed the den of solitary and singular despair!

* * * * * * * * * * * * * * * *

Mr. Bradford W. Hamilton's privileged life was the essence of which American fables and dreams were woven, he was among the American elite of Ultra-rich. This superlative was informally coined to distinguish the clan from the rising number of mundane multi-millionaires who were popping up across the affluent America of the late 20th and early 21st centuries. This exclusive tribe, sometimes referred to as the 'Ultras Club' was characterized by huge fortunes beginning in the low $100 million range and reaching well into the billion-dollar figures; no mere upstart millionaires were admitted here, nor could they gain easy entry into the 'Club' by mere monetary means alone! One had to possess both a sizable fortune and a lineage of at least three generations of either Boston blood or New England social connectivity, to include the ample 'due paying' for entry into the Club. Each part of the country had its own ultra-rich franchise and a corresponding set of unwritten, but firmly established, mores and practices.

The Club's influence extended directly or indirectly unto the media brokers, the corporate infrastructure, the entertainment industry, and even the gambit of religious institutions. Their .01% of the population either directly or indirectly influenced at least 65–80% of the policies of American society and there appeared to be no end in sight for either their decline or dilution. Some social critics thought that even this magnitude of influence was deliberately understated and that the truer figure was 95%. Even as the government tried to increase taxes upon their wealth, their zeal to maintain and increase their wealth grew even greater, as savvy lawyers and accountants found creative ways to shelter funds throughout the world in a maze of third-party holding companies and intricate trusts. No one ever surrendered power willingly or to disadvantage!

The only prerequisites for remaining in the acceptable 'good graces' of Club membership was the continued financial support of select social activities and, of course, the continuance of having huge sums of money and the unwritten rule of 'living up to one's part.' Scandal and even moderate criminal offences could be either forgiven or at least blindly tolerated and unobserved, if one had sufficient financial resources to shower among the membership elite during the annual social sojourns and charities. Wealth was the lifeblood of the Club and without it, one was soon ostracized from social events and happenings. Continued financial distress, unless alleviated by marriage with the New Money members, frequently meant gradual ostracizing from the Club. Even an established old blue-blood name had its limitations if it was not perpetually monetarily refunded.

Within this singular milieu, Bradford W. Hamilton was born, raised and prospered with no second thoughts of rebellion or self-analysis of either his class or actions. By nature's predisposition of character, Bradford was a man of subdued ego and quiet intelligence. Physically he was a tall, handsome and carefree man in his latter-thirties. His piercing blue eyes, tall athletic frame, and easy-going personality made him a naturally affable man, who had many acquaintances and few enemies.

'Brad', his abbreviated name, was used exclusively and occasionally, by family and intimate friends, was born Bradford Wayne Hamilton into the most socially prominent Boston family of Arthur and Gloria Hamilton. The old money name was not only foremost among the Boston Brahmas, it was among the five wealthiest families in New England and it was among the 30 richest families in the USA. Both of Brad's parents were of exclusive Boston society prominence that originated many generations ago. His father, Arthur Hamilton, was the Co-Executive of the exclusive private capital investment bank in the Boston and Cambridge area, this being the 'family business' profession for the last several generations.

Arthur was a tall and slender man, whose frame one could almost characterize as lanky; this was due to his tall stature and low weight, this being a physiological and metabolic gift of nature that allowed him to continue the same weight and waistline as he had possessed during his university days, some 45-plus years earlier. His personality was demure, amiable, relaxed and tinctured with the tone of honesty and the sincerity of resonance throughout all his conversations and public actions. He kept his personal thoughts and emotions to himself, his wife and family.

Brad's mother, Gloria Theresa Worthington Hamilton, was born unto an equally prominent New England family. The Worthingtons were major power brokers within Boston's inner-most social circles and were members of the Ultra-rich clan. Gloria's father, Jonathan, came from an esteemed Trans-Atlantic shipping family. Jonathan was the family radical who broke from the business ranks of his family, this by becoming a physician. He became a prominent Cambridge physician, whose private family practice clientele included only the most socially prominent members of Boston's elite. An overly generous inheritance and trust fund ensured that he was not a mere 'working-class doctor', rather he had established and headed many clinics, hospital wings, and medical research facilities.

Both Arthur and Gloria were the perfect Ultra-rich stereotypes – this was code for being wealthy, white, properly-educated, socially prominent and being of Anglo-Saxon extraction – a typecast commonly referred to as WASPs. Both husband and wife knew that the bonds of 'sunshine social' acquaintances and friends were composed of a superficial nature when compared to the bonds of friends and family. They made their life and lifestyle fit the needs and attention of their family, and not the exclusive demands and activities of the Ultra-rich.

The Hamiltons had three children, with Bradford being the eldest son, then followed by younger sister Melissa and then by the youngest, a brother and the baby of the family, Robert Paul. Their daughter, Melissa, was an energetic post-graduate student at Brown University, finishing up post-graduate studies in American history. Melissa sat on the boards of the Boston Art Museum, ballet, the Boston Pops orchestra and she had further plans of going on to attend Harvard Law school, specializing in maritime and mercantile law. Melissa had recently developed a keen interest in the sea, its wealth, and its healthy preservation. Her parents heartily approved of Melissa's endeavours because it was a noble pursuit that utilized her talents and it was in keeping with the family maritime tradition which harkened back to her grandparents. The children of the Ultra wealthy had unlimited opportunities to do either good or to bury themselves in their self-indulgent vices.

Being the last-in-line of the Hamilton fold, Robert Paul was the young dynamo and 'trickster' of the family. He was always the one who pulled the most outlandish tricks and he always tried to push the envelope of getting his way with his parents, knowing full well that their best energies had been consumed in disciplining the hides of his older brother and sister. Robert was taking an MBA at Yale with the hope of following in his brother's footsteps and becoming an investment banker, whom he admired greatly. Being the younger son, he sat uneasily in his older brother's shadow of success.

While attending local educational institutions, each child was given chores and responsibilities to perform on a daily and weekly basis for as long as each child resided at the family's Greystone mansion. Neither Gloria nor Arthur was a soft touch when it came to child rearing, they knew that given the proper attention, discipline, and love – the children usually turned out to be well- behaved adults.

* * * * * * * * * * * * * * * *

The Hamiltons were of sound English working stock, originating from the English port city of Portsmouth. They had successfully migrated from England's hard-scrabble, quasi-feudal farm labour system into the more refined urban shopkeeper trades. Their expertise and fondness lay in the journeyman trades that required diligence, intelligence and hard work and honesty, which initially included ship construction, supplying naval ancillary merchandise, and dry-good provisioning; however, the succeeding generations took to the more ephemeral occupations, such as clerking for the merchant trade, bank clerk, and security scribe recorder. However, even these highly prized positions offered only limited opportunities for the ambitious working man, for the common man could never expect to rise to the position of bank manager, security broker, or merchant trader unless one were connected with the upper class or had a royal warrant granted. The only viable advancement option was that of immigration to a new country – primarily to the budding North American colonies, where hard work determined one's destiny, not one's birth name, regal favouritism or ancestors.

Yet the Hamilton family's ambitions were not singular either, as other industrious families in the Old Country also sought self-betterment and riches. The MacAlister clan shared the same rationale for selecting the U.S. Colonies as their country of destination when emigrating from Inverness in the Scottish Highlands – to live a better life for oneself and one's family! In the MacAlisters' case, however, persecution of being a Scot and having inferior rights to those of an Englishman – provided an even greater incentive to leave the yoke of English rule. For them, it figured that anything had to be better than working the fields and herding livestock in the highlands from dawn to dusk only to pay out the majority of one's profit to the English or Scottish landlord and his overseer. Wild rumours and tall tales from the new lands in America promised novel opportunities for those imaginative and bold enough to partake of it. 'If one had to work hard, far better it be to work thusly for oneself and one's kin, than to be handing over the fruit of one's labour to an absentee landowner or landed aristocrat,' the MacAlisters keenly surmised. The MacAlister clan set their sights for Boston and the greater Massachusetts Bay area, due in part to the recent family seafaring experience gained in the service and servitude of the King's Royal Navy. The sea offered ample opportunities in fishing, maritime trading and other seafaring tradecrafts. It would be a rough start at first and a very laborious life, yet so it was for any working-class family no matter where they lived and toiled.

When the MacAlister clan settled in the Boston and Massachusetts area in the early 19th Century, the sea mercantile trade was a thriving business, to include the very profitable whaling trade, which made the MacAlisters extremely wealthy over the course of generations.

Quickly, the MacAlisters also founded, and then dominated, the New England sea mercantile insurance industry, thus becoming very diversified and obscenely wealthy in the process. The U.S. Civil War was an equally very profitable business opportunity for the MacAlisters, as the Union sanctioned trading ships obtained a virtual monopoly with the war trading partners of Europe, Central and South America. National prestige and social lineage befell the MacAlisters when numerous family members volunteered into the Union's war service, mainly as Navy ship Captains and Merchant Marine provisioning officers. Nothing else could be better than that of making money and publicly proclaimed by the government and one's peers as being both patriots and national heroes.

Over the decades both the Hamilton and MacAlister families came to know, respect, and admire one another. Their backgrounds were quite similar, as was their 'rags to riches' success stories. The Hamiltons were vested in the banking and financial business, while the MacAlisters were mainly in maritime shipping, insurance, and mercantile infra-structure enterprises. The two families' business interests often complemented and paralleled each other, but never actually crossed or conflicted with one another.

This unconsummated chasm was finally bridged when Arthur Hamilton and Lionel MacAlister deliberately decided to go into business together in the early 1960s. Lionel and Arthur had both attended Harvard as undergraduates and attended the Naval and Army ROTC programs respectively. When the young, handsome American President John F. Kennedy came into office and challenged the young generation to serve their country, both Lionel and Arthur were all too eager to don their armour and engaged their Cold War nemesis. These were dangerous and yet challenging times, as both the U.S. and the USSR battled for the hearts, minds and resources of the world.

The two men served together in differing, yet complementary, capacities during the Kennedy Administration. Arthur had a natural gift for languages, picking up languages effortlessly. Because of this trait and his native intellectual aptitudes, Arthur was selected for the highly secretive Army Security Agency (ASA) electronic warfare and intercept unit, which intercepted Korean, Russian, and Chinese communications sources. The ASA was organized under the Army, but it reported to and operated under the control of the super-secret National Security Agency. Lionel MacAlister served in the Navy, also in an intelligence specialty as a Naval Signals Intelligence specialist, which aimed to decipher Soviet and Chinese encrypted signals for highly critical intelligence information. Both Lionel and Arthur entered the Service as junior officers and ended their duty three years later as a Navy full Lieutenant and an Army Captain respectively.

Their military service during the Cold War had changed and bonded the two men into a strong friendship that was to last their entire lives. Their military experiences transformed them from being mere peers in the rich man's exclusive club, to being true and lasting friends. Arthur provided the analytical and planning skills so vital for a smooth functioning business staff, while Lionel was the daring, calculating risk-taker and executor of actions – his instincts were keen and sometimes frightening.

Their military duty and friendship became the seeds that quickly formed into a business enterprise that became known as Hamilton & MacAlister Inc. – Investment Banking and Security Trading Corporation. The firm became New England's largest and most profitable corporate and financial underwriting institution. The latest business forays of Hamilton & MacAlister were that of initiating a wealth portfolio management and trust funds custodianships for very select wealthy personages and non-profit institutions such as universities and hospitals. The firm was soon bringing in several billion dollars a year in net profits from this new business venture that was only several years old.

★ ★ ★ ★ ★ ★ ★ ★ ★ ★ ★ ★ ★ ★ ★ ★ ★ ★

The intersection of Park and Bromfield Streets betrayed the heart of Boston's fashionable, but stodgy financial and banking district. It was at 45 Bromfield Street that Hamilton & MacAlister Inc. Investment Banking and Security Trading Corporation operated its corporate headquarters and central office. The classical décor of the weathered ruby red brick accented with ivory white shuttered windows, graced the two-storey American Colonial-era styled building with an aura of refinement. The exterior decor was tastefully accented by elegant black wrought iron enamelled frosted pole lamps, wrought-iron spiked fences, prominent white painted oak window trim, Belgian-block paving stone encrusted streets, manicured common green frontages, and slate grey roofs – were all modern architectural fabrications deliberately choreographed to lead the uninitiated to the conclusion that the 18th Century was alive and well in 21st Century Boston. It also served to advertise competency, trust and reliability.

The Hamilton & MacAlister building was an elegant red brick style, two-storey venue located directly on Bromfield Street. Its generous office space measured some 20,000 square feet, more than adequate for the going concerns of a boutique-sized investment banking and corporate financial securities firm. The lower management, administrative and IT staffs all shared the first-floor offices, while the accounting and executive offices of the senior management were quite appropriately located on the capricious upper 2nd storey. The ornamentation and the ornate walnut and leather furnishings reflected the conservatism and the wealth of both the securities' industry and the firm itself. Special stringent security measures ensured that only 'by-name' personnel could enter the 2nd storey office spaces, to include that of a special access elevator and hidden stairwell. Cameras and biometric scanning devices were tastefully arrayed throughout the entire building, to include a direct panic alarm to the local Boston police station. The charter member officers of the firm all possessed ornate and spacious corner offices, this included the adjacent offices of Bradford Wayne Hamilton and Katherine MacAlister.

Both Bradford and Katherine took to the securities trade and money management business like fish to water and their previous work tenure in the public marketplace placed them in good stead for running the family firm. Since the death of the Hamilton family, however, the once jovial offices of Hamilton & MacAlister had become quite bleak and empty. A spark of vibrancy had been lost. With Mr Arthur Hamilton dead and Bradford frequently not coming into the office until noontime or not coming in at all, Katherine was primarily left to manage the firm, with only a periodic visit from her mother, Faye. With diligent daughterly pleading, Katherine had managed to get her father Lionel to come back into the office on a part-time basis and assist with some of the less stressful executive tasks such as arranging meetings with clients, reviewing financial proposals and signing some contracts.

Katherine needed Bradford back to work as a full man, if only to keep herself balanced and sharp. Being the lone full-time monarch at the firm proved to be quite tiring and dull in a very short time. Her sleep hours were quite minimal, and she was getting grey strands of hairs in her raven black mane. Running a financial firm efficiently of this magnitude required a team, not an individual. Yet her stress could not be delegated.

The firm of Hamilton & MacAlister managed the corporate equity accounts of exclusive regional New England corporations and educational institutions, much in a manner similar to a broker of a 401K account for an individual. Underwriting of corporate debt, new stock issuances and Initial Public Offerings (IPOs) was another specialty of the firm. Hamilton & MacAlister earned only a small charge for these business transactions; however, when the aggregated accounts amounted to many tens of billions of dollars, the annual return was quite handsome and presented minimal or no risk to the firm. The only consumer or retail business was reserved for the by-name, high-end, wealthy investor, who had to have several millions of dollars to invest with the firm. The securities underwriting handling rates were often a modest 2-3% on the face value of the corporate security issuance and a 5% fee for corporate security fund account management. For corporate security dealings amounting in the billions and tens of billions of dollars, the realized profits were of several hundred million dollars of underwriting transaction fees. Annual profits after all expenses and taxes were well over $8 billion and growing. Business could not have been more lucrative. The cherry on the top of the cake, was that there were no public stockholders or non-family board members with which to contend. The business was like a nice fat piggy-bank.

Each of the Hamilton & MacAlister families earned nine figure salaries approximating $250,000,000 annually; this did not include an 8% bonus from the corporate net revenue. The remaining profits were divided and placed into corporate retained earnings accounts for contingency purposes and into the founder's trust fund accounts. The Trust funds of both families was growing by double-digits annually and within less than a decade, each families' Trust fund was projected to generate as much net capital as the firm's primary business. To compound this obscenely rich capital inflow, the Hamilton and MacAlister partners had been achieving this same percentage of profits since the founding of the firm and the money only got handsomer each and every year.

The barriers to entry in security underwriting were most restrictive; however, once there was an established banking business relationship established and the 'Old Clan' connections were liberally 'greased' – the money was virtually guaranteed to pour into the firm in endless streams whether or not the economy was exploding or just puttering along. Global fund indexing investing ensured that the monetary risks were spread evenly across the global funds in multiple piles of investments. This was informally known as 'fortune making without ball-breaking', and all of this was accomplished without contributing a solid, tangible product or even much sweat equity. The business process was the leisurely and brainless type of wealth generation that Wall Street and others dearly loved, but for which most of the American working public and some politicians had developed a definite disdain, if not outright hatred.

Katherine Victoria MacAlister, (the informal name of Kate was used only by her family and close friends), was the sole daughter of Lionel and Faye MacAlister. Katherine was born to Lionel and Faye rather late in their lives, at a time when they feared that Faye could never conceive her own children, yet to these desperate parents, Katherine was finally conceived. Despite their mature years, Lionel and Faye were as proud and nervous as any young couple in their twenties expecting their first child, yet Lionel and Faye were almost twice this age and they had doubts in their abilities to raise a young child.

Katherine was five years younger than Bradford Hamilton and she was a handful of a woman. She was doted upon as a child and was expectedly quite spoiled. Her enemies called her selfish and narcissistic. Not having siblings of her own, Katherine naturally adopted the Hamilton children as her own brothers and sisters, both fighting with and loving them in a sibling fashion. Smitten with Bradford from childhood, she dreamed one day that they would be married and live the lifestyle of their parents.

In her personality, Katherine was a cross between Scarlett O'Hara and Bette Davis, she was destined to be no man's fool or doormat. She could be either fire or ice, depending on the situation or her mood. Her temperament some would call mercurial. She loved and hated with completeness. Any man that married her would be guaranteed of never having a dull moment in his life! Yet when she loved, it was with the fullness of her entire heart.

Katherine, comparable with that of her Ultra-rich 'Clan' peers, attended the most exclusive, old Eastern private educational institutions; she was formally educated at the exclusive Ethel Walker Girls Finishing school, then obtained a BA from Vassar, and finally she went on to obtain a Harvard MBA. She had worked for Morgan Stanley and then First Boston as a security underwriter and trader; this provided her with vital entry-level work security trading expertise, which she used to cultivate the essential personal business connections prior to going to work at the Hamilton & MacAlister family business digs.

To her professional credit, every one of Katherine's peers admired her business acumen, intelligence and sound business judgments, yet she never developed a deep or lasting relationship with any of her co-workers. Like being a King or Queen, a business owner could never really have true friends with their employees, the ability to both reward and punish was incongruent with friendship. Katherine segregated her world into that of business and private, and never did she let the two co-mingle. This made work and life easier for her, yet it kept her most alone. She dated, but very infrequently, as she kept casual sexual liaisons at a discreet distance and to a sheer minimum. Before joining her family's firm, Katherine had managed to marry briefly to socially prominent Bostonian high-power estate lawyer by the name of Thomas Bedworth.

Naturally, Thomas was a charter member of the Ultra-rich Club, yet the marriage was doomed from its wedding vows. Court paper attested that 'irreconcilable differences' caused the divorce, but Katherine and intimate friends knew that it was only a superficial, physical relationship and that she had married only for social convenience. Katherine filed divorce papers only 18 months after her wedding day. Katherine finally acknowledged to herself that she had always loved Bradford since her early childhood and she sought to ignite their relationship from being mere close friends to lovers. Brad was the only man for her and there was to be hell to pay with any woman that tried to get in her way.

True to her Scottish blood, Katherine's physical build was tall and slender, she stood a graceful 5'8", her thick, jet-black hair betrayed only a few hairs of grey, and her dazzling emerald green eyes could stop a charging bull or turn a man's ego to mush. Katherine's elegant appearance was a dual product of possessing good genes and having a disciplined and quite expensive regimen at an exclusive spa. She was the icon of the perfect businesswoman, however, where pleasure and fun were the focus of her interest, Katherine was a powerhouse of vivacious energy. Some of her critics or envious acquaintances would characterize her as being a manic-depressive, while others would scornfully call her the Ice Princess or Ice Bitch. She possessed no close female friends, however with males it was an entirely different matter; men were either seduced by her natural feminine charms, or else they were intimidated by her beauty, intelligence, and power. Katherine coyly used her perfect looks to leverage whatever she wanted from the male clients.

Katherine could employ either the use of her abundant feminine charms or her quick-silver Scottish temper to get her way. She usually employed the former, as she found that she could more easily manipulate men more readily with honey than with vinegar. With women, however, it was an entirely different matter and Katherine used her position, wealth, and viciousness to lash out and defeat any competitors, whether these be real or imagined. In the venue of the boardroom or the bedroom, she was an intimidating lady for both male and female alike.

Katherine's one true female companion and confidante was her mother, Faye. In the course of typical family relationships, mothers and daughters were not typically bonded as either friends or peers, but the strong dependency relationship between Katherine and her mother Faye approached this level of affinity. Perhaps the mutually dependent relationship existed because Katherine was an only child upon whom all forms of attention and devotion were bestowed. Despite the basis of any psychological reason for this mutual dependency, both mother and daughter sought out and fed on each other's emotional needs. It seemed that the need for love and companionship could indeed form strange and convoluted bonding. Faye was as much to Katherine as a sister; a sister that Katherine never had, but which she had secretly always desired.

It had been three years since Katherine and Bradford began their employment at Hamilton & MacAlister in their present capacities as top corporate officers. The necessity of the close work environment drew Katherine and Bradford together, just as the force of gravity draws objects closer and closer together. From the beginning of their partnership, Katherine had set her romantic sights on Bradford. He had proposed to her last year and a June wedding was being planned; however, the dreadful Hamilton plane accident and Brad's subsequent mental instability had placed that date into serious dispute, if not obvious necessary abandonment.

* * * * * * * * * * * * * * * * * *

"Good Morning, Hamilton & MacAlister – Investment Banking and Security Trading Corporation, Mr Bradford W. Hamilton's office, may I help you please?" Margie DeTagelio politely and professionally parroted into the phone.

"Yes, Margie, this is Kent Reynolds from Morgan Stanley, is Mr Bradford Hamilton there please?" inquired the caller in a pleasant, low male voice.

"No, I am sorry, sir, but Mr Hamilton is currently unavailable at the moment, may I please take a message or page him on your behalf?" Margie professionally and pleasantly inquired in her ushered soft feminine voice.

"Well, this is really something of a most critical nature and it's a vital private business matter that I need to speak personally with him about," Mr Reynolds stated in a very serious and business-like tone.

"Mmmm, sir, could perhaps Ms Katherine MacAlister can be of assistance to you, she's the President of 'Hamilton & MacAlister'?" Margie DeTagelio nervously inquired.

"Oh yes, of course! You see, Kate and I are old friends, so please connect us," Kent Reynolds requested in a jovial tone.

"Just one moment, sir, and I'll put your call through," Margie replied eagerly.

Margie deftly placed Mr Kent Reynolds' phone call on hold, then quickly pressed the private line that directed her to Katherine MacAlister's office. "Ms MacAlister, this is Margie, I have a call from a Mr Kent Reynolds from Morgan Stanley and he originally called for Mr Hamilton, but he doesn't want to leave a message and he says it's extremely important... He said that he will be happy to speak with you, Ms MacAlister. With your permission, I'll put Mr Reynolds through, Ms MacAlister?" Margie deftly inquired.

"Kent Reynolds...yes, good old Kent...why yes, please do so, we are old pals from Morgan Stanley, both he and Mr Hamilton were working on a major underwriting sharing agreement several months ago; put him through to me immediately, DeTagelio," Katherine sternly commanded without any artificially contrived pleasantries.

"Yes, Ms MacAlister," Margie meekly replied. Margie was no fool, she took quiet subservient notice and exception to the fact that Katherine MacAlister addressed her by her last name, and in a very demeaning tone at that! 'It seemed that 'respect' was a one-way street as far as 'Kit Kat' MacAlister was concerned,' Margie thought bitterly to herself.

"Kit Kat MacAlister was a hard woman to work for...a real office bitch," Margie mused bitterly to herself. Margie knew that Katherine MacAlister hated her, this she accurately surmised from the spiteful actions that Katherine had made to her in the past. "Oh well, you have to make the best of a shitty situation and this substitution for Mrs Peters was only a temporary situation, after which she would be dealing exclusively with Mr Hamilton's affairs", Margie blissfully concluded. Good paying financial jobs were hard to come by and easy to lose, so she carefully hid any dissent to herself. The Great Recession had left most banking and security firms 'lean and mean', with many staff positions being eliminated. "It was sure one hell of a bitch being one of the working poor amid the inflows of billions of dollars of annual security transactions coming into the firm...it was like working at Fort Knox, you could look all you want, but you could never take any of the big money home with you!" Margie scornfully reasoned with utter frustration.

Katherine's daily routine was to arrive in the office at promptly 9:00 AM; this was after having awoken each day at 6:30 AM. She customarily performed her morning run around her palatial home in the Cambridge suburbs (actually it was the mansion of her parents), performed her bath ritual, had a Spartan breakfast of cereal and fruit, perhaps a croissant with coffee, then it was off to work. Like Bradford, Katherine drove a late model baby-blue Bentley V-12 turbocharged convertible model that immediately bespoke wealth, breeding, youth, and snobbery.

On this particular morning Katherine attired herself in a cream-coloured, eye-catching, attractive and striking two-piece business suit of fine woven Italian cashmere. The skirt was knee length with a matching white double-breasted jacket. Providing the contrast was a black chiffon sleeveless blouse adorned with a 24 carat gold US Eagle coin pendant encrusted with small diamond stones. On her left wrist, Katherine was adorned with a ladies custom-made Rolex pure platinum and diamond encrusted wristwatch. Katherine looked like she'd just stepped from the pages of Vogue or Town & Country magazine. Her total appearance was dazzling and almost mesmerizing, denoting feminine power, wealth, and sophistication. She represented the ideal model of a perfect executive business woman free of flaws or encumbrances, thus she was the iconic perfect woman that other lessor women loved to hate.

"Hello Kate, it's Kent Reynolds from Morgan Stanley, how are you doing?" he cheerfully echoed.

"Well truthfully… it's not good, Kent, it's not good at all. All I can say is that Brad has been a basket case since that damn airplane crash and he's not getting any better and to tell you the full truth, he's constantly depressed and despondent, nothing cheers him up anymore and frankly, I don't see any light at the end of this dark tunnel. I think he may need a shrink, but I know he'll never go see one, he's too proud or something like that!" Katherine unashamedly blurted out in stoic resignation.

Kent was shocked, yet knew that he had to break the ice somehow with Kate. "Well, perhaps this news that I bring you this morning will cheer old Brad up…at least it should tickle your fancy, Kate. You know that Brad and I were working that big stock issuance for a group of select Fortune 500 companies, it was for an elite bundle of companies, and our possible teaming on this was a potential multi-billion-dollar deal for both firms? Well, Kate, hold on to your panties, because I'm here to tell you that Morgan is going into partnership with 'Hamilton & MacAlister' on the mother of all uber-writing deals – the basket of firms include IBM, BP, Facebook, GM, Boeing, Apple, Google, Amazon and Exxon-Mobile and 20 other Fortune 500 companies…it's worth $85.8 billion over a period of 10 years and your cut, or should I say our cut, is a 2.5% underwriting fee per annum for the next ten years! Real easy, steady money, it sure beats working for a living, huh! Now how's that as a wedding gift, Kate?" Kent exclaimed in sheer excitement.

"Wow! Now that's flipping fantastic! Woo… Kent, you sure do know how to say the right words to make a girl happy. If you were here right now, I'd buy you a double scotch and pucker your whistle with a big, wild, wet one and I'm not talking about the drink either, Kent," Kate purred in a teasing sexy tone and accompanied with a gleaming wide smile.

"Now I am really glad that I got to speak with you this morning, Kate! Boy, I never get propositions like that at the Olde Bailey's Tavern, Kate. I'm afraid that I'll have to take a rain check on that drink and I'll redeem that 'wild wet one' at your wedding to Brad in June." Kent sighed with a joyful pun.

There was a sudden dash of silence, as Katherine's girlish smile and exhilaration were immediately dampened upon hearing the words 'June Wedding.' With Bradford's severe grief-stricken depression, a June wedding was now impossible; however, an Autumn wedding was the best that she could hope to salvage and hope for at this time.

"Kate, if there is anything that I can do, please let me know and tell Bradford I'll call him next week to see how he's doing. Is that fine with you, Kate?" Kent inquired in a permissive tone of inquiry.

Katherine could only politely demur to Kent's gentlemanly offer. "Oh of course, yes...that's thoughtful of you, Kent. I hope this news will cheer Bradford up, but I'm not sure if anything can at this point, I've tried everything that I can think of, but nothing lights his fire anymore...thanks, Kent, for the good news and let's meet for drinks soon!" Katherine replied as she politely ended the call.

She was exalted by the magnitude of the new security-underwriting contract; it was far more lucrative than all of the last several years of business combined and it foretold of even greater teaming deals with Morgan Stanley in the future. Big bonuses were in store for everyone at Hamilton & MacAlister from the lowest staff up through the senior account brokers. An initial underwriting fee of over $500 million dollars served to enhance the financial position of both families; however, the new business was merely a fraction of the total package. This deal merely enhanced the wealth that each family had amassed over the generations. Both families were already double-digit billionaires.

Turning away from her temporary despair, Katherine immediately diverted her sorrow away from the Hamilton family death tragedy and instead directed her attention and anger unto Margie DeTagelio, Brad's personal pretty young female assistant. Margie DeTagelio was an defenceless target for Katherine too. Margie was totally dependent on her job for her existence, her position at the firm was not yet established in terms of service longevity, nor was her retirement account fully vested. Margie knew that her career was 'flying in the wind' and that she had to maintain a low profile, especially around the ice-cold, unpredictable and vindictive Katherine.

A quite perturbed and enraged Katherine impatiently lifted her telephone receiver and pushed the button that dialled directly onto Margie DeTagelio's telephone receiver. Margie deftly picked up the receiver and before she had a chance to utter a greeting of any sort, angry loud words thundered from the phone. "DeTagelio, get your fanny in my office now!" demanded Katherine in a harsh tone. Margie's heart sunk as she wondered what new faux pas she had committed to offend 'Her Highness' at this early hour of the day.

Nervously and with great hesitation, Margie reluctantly arose from her desk chair and headed into the adjacent office of Katherine MacAlister. "Yes, Ms MacAlister, how may I help you?" Margie nervously inquired, not knowing the reason for why Katherine MacAlister had so abruptly and harshly summoned her. "That Ice Princess must be on the rag 30 days of every frigging month," Margie crudely swore to herself.

Katherine looked coldly and methodically into Margie's eyes. "DeTagelio, how many years have you been employed with Hamilton & MacAlister?" she sternly inquired.

Margie was now shaking in her modest pumps. "Three years, Ms MacAlister," Margie sheepishly replied.

A slight, scornful frown appeared on Katherine's face upon her hearing Margie's tepid answer.

"Three long years, huh! You're not a novice and that's long enough to have learned some of the protocols and social graces of this office, now wouldn't you say, Miss DeTagelio?" Katherine rhetorically inquired in a most sarcastic and condescending tone. Yet Margie knew better than to try and get smart with Katherine at this point, so she decided to play the subservient little 'mouse girl' once again. She wisely held her tongue and took her verbal medicine from 'Kit Kat' MacAlister. A tongue lashing was indeed forthcoming! Margie dreamed of the day when payback would be all hers. Katherine took Margie's silence for obedient servitude and then she continued her lambaste of poor Margie.

"Let us both think here for a minute, DeTagelio... so in the past three long years of employment here at Hamilton & MacAlister have you ever heard of Miss Katherine MacAlister being addressed in the street vernacular as a 'Ms?'"

Margie was shocked at the question, as it seemed to arise out of thin air. In response, there was only an eerie, evident silence and a befuddled expression reflected on Margie's face.

"You are so pathetic, Miss DeTagelio, I can only surmise from your silence and that funny, dumb expression on your face that your answer is a simple 'no'...so why do you impolitely address me with that publican title of being a 'Ms'? Don't you know, that this form of address annoys the hell out of me? Do you know that it degrades me? Do you know that it is a common leftist and liberal term used by common people who have never earned an honest buck in their lives? Do I look like a 'Ms'? Do I sound like a 'Ms' to you? Do I act as a 'Ms'? ...Well now... do I?" Katherine sternly demanded, while never giving Margie a single chance to answer her rapid barrage fire of humiliating rhetorical inquisitions. Arguments against a raging narcissist tyrant were futile and fatal too!

Katherine took but a short breath before continuing her moralistic browbeating office sermon to further degrade Margie DeTagelio status. "I even despise the sounds that one's lips make when that middle class, phony, feminist acronym is mentioned in my presence, it makes my damn blood curl! I had to put up with all of that nonsense at Vassar and Harvard, but not here in my firm and my office!" Katherine vented with obvious disdain and contempt.

"Well, no, Ms... I mean, Miss MacAlister...I was just using the popular, accepted vernacular term used these days in business and society," Margie despondently struggled to explain before being cut off in mid-sentence by Katherine.

"Now you stop right there, girlie!...Let's get this straight immediately...Hamilton & MacAlister is not a common or popular middle class enclave, nor does it stoop-down to those stupid, government-inspired leftist idiots, whose answer for every concocted and imagined evil is a protest or damned lawsuit – well I'll have none of that crap here and the first employee that tries will be fired or have their legs broken or maybe both! In the future, you will address me as either Miss MacAlister or Miss Katherine...and when I am married, then I will be addressed as Mrs Hamilton. Now is that clear, Miss DeTagelio?", Katherine sternly demanded. She was boiling mad to the point of almost hysteria.

Not waiting for an obedient, cowering answer, Katherine continued her verbal lambaste. "I do not need, nor do I ever want to hear of your Politically Correct validation of my status in this office; you can save that nonsense for the other fools around here, but not to me! I am Miss Katherine MacAlister, holder of two world-class university degrees, daughter of one of Boston's and New England's most prominent families, the President of this firm and I assure you girlie that I can hold my own both personally and professionally against any man or woman in this business or any other area for that matter, without the veneer of any Political Correctness nonsense or civil litigation...those things are for those other phony-baloney people. I have my social image and dignity to maintain in this office and Boston Society and it is definitely not Middle-Class social progressiveness...now is that quite clear? Well, is it? I'm waiting for an answer DeTagelio," Katherine tersely snipped with a heavy tone of disgust and contempt in her voice as she pounded her hand forcefully down onto her desk top. An eerie dead silence filled the room. Kit Kat was making an issue out of nothing just because she had the power to do so and to degrade a woman who she detested. This was clearly an abuse of power and employee harassment at its most foul level of manifestation. Power corrupted certain people horrifically.

"Yes, Miss Katherine," Margie meekly quibbled as she tried in vain to extract herself from the verbal embarrassment and ass-chewing.

"Oh, one more thing, DeTagelio, never address yourself to me by your Christian name ever again to me...we are not on a first-name basis and never shall be...you are the employee and I am your employer. Now, you may leave my office," Katherine dryly and emotionlessly replied as she coldly rendered a false forced smile, as behaved as if the outburst had never happened.

"This lady is crazy! Either Miss Katherine was a manic-depressive or a darn good actress," Margie thought to herself as she quickly vacated the lioness's den.

As Margie quickly walked toward Katherine's office door, she suddenly half-turned and stated in a low tone, "Oh Miss Katherine, I almost forgot to tell you also that Mr Hamilton had called and stated that he will be arriving late this morning and that he's on his way and will be arriving in about 25 minutes." Before Margie even had a chance to exit Katherine's office, she was met with another rage of loud verbal abuse and inquisition.

"Just what in the hell was that you said, DeTagelio? You come right back here!...What in the hell was that you blurted out? ...What did you just say to me?...You come back over here right now, DeTagelio," Katherine roared out to Margie in a voice that was heralded from her office and out into the main office hallway. Caught in mid-step, a cold chill immediately ran up Margie's spine and goose bumps appeared on her arms, both were the sure signs of fear and trepidation. Ever so slowly, Margie turned around in blind obedience and terror as she spied into Katherine's cold and angry green eyes, her eyebrows drawn downward into almost perfect twin horizontal lines.

"Do you mean to foolishly stand there and tell me that my fiancé and the CEO of this firm called here this morning and I am only now being informed? Why was I not informed of this information immediately, Miss DeTagelio? Damn it, girl! I am Brad's, I mean to say that, I am Mr Hamilton's fiancée and I am also the President of this firm, as you are fully aware. I demand to know immediately all messages that he leaves here, especially in his present state of mind and emotional condition.

I just can't believe that you would forget or withhold this information from me; just what in the hell is the matter with you, girl?", Katherine shouted in a hysterical, condescending, and high-toned, shrill voice.

Margie was dumbfounded before she finally found the courage to speak. "I....I....I thought that..." Margie muttered in a frail, mouse-toned voice, as she was instantly cut off again by Katherine.

"Now you stop right there!...You don't think around here, that's for the managers and account executives of Hamilton & MacAlister to do the thinking; you are just a little, non-descript, Personal Assistant and you are to act accordingly! You follow the office orders and rules, and that includes the one that I am making right now."

Margie's entire body and psyche were tensed-up, she knew that she was about to receive a real ass-kicking. Tears started to form in Margie's eyes, but she bravely held back the tears – there was no way in hell that Kit Kat was going to get the satisfaction of seeing her cry.

"Now you listen and listen very carefully, my dear, from now on, you will...I repeat – you will... contact me whenever Mr Hamilton calls into this office and if I am not here, you damn well better find me! You are to send me a message that will be posted to my personal cell phone, voice mail account, e-mail, and a short, printed note written down and annotated with the date and time of the message. Now do I make myself perfectly, frigging clear, Miss DeTagelio?" Katherine sternly demanded in a commanding voice.

Margie stood there silent in red-faced in terror as Katherine shouted forth her insults and she could do nothing but stand there and take it; after all, Margie's job and future were on the line, so she decided it was better to just suck-up the humiliation that she had been taking all of her life. An argument with this type of person was utter futility and filled with folly.

"Well answer me! So, do I make myself clear, DeTagelio?" Katherine repeated in a more challenging and even harsher tone. Margie regained her composure before she spoke.

"Yes, yes, I do understand, Miss Katherine. I will not repeat this error. Is there anything else that you have for me Miss Katherine?" Margie stuttered in humble servitude and outright fear, as she faced Katherine with moistened eyes as she physically bit her tongue to fight back her tears.

For her closing attack, Katherine let out one more piece of sarcasm that personally attacked Margie's personality and womanhood. "Just because you socialize with the firm's executives, wiggle your fanny about, bat your eyes at the men and share a few drinks at Olde Bailey's with them, doesn't make you one of the 'big boys or girls' around here, DeTagelio. Remember that you are as fungible and disposal as trash around here," Katherine crudely sounded-off – this to mock both the overall casual, common fraternization among the employees' class structure at Hamilton & MacAlister and as to her obvious disdain for this unwelcome practice of creeping social democratization. 'I hope this fucking rich bitch dies tonight!' Margie wished, as she subserviently received the verbal abuse and insults.

Katherine was the original control freak, the 'Ice Bitch' had just proven herself worthy of her nick name over this insignificant office munchkin. This episode only served to reinforce this point to both Margie and every other worker at 'Hamilton & MacAlister' of how things worked around this office. Katherine wanted everyone either under her thumb or under her fear, either way it did not matter to her. 'Better to have the workers fear you than to like you,' Katherine crudely and wrongly believed.

Katherine was quite satisfied that she had amply made her point to Margie DeTagelio and that she would soon have Brad's Personal Assistant in the utmost position of servitude, just as she had trained her own secretary and personal assistant, Joan Peters. However, while Joan was like an older meek sister to Katherine, Margie was like a spunky, rebellious, rivaling second cousin. Finally, it did not fortify Margie's position to be young, pretty, and entertaining.

Visibly, Katherine had regained her composure. "Please, just inform me of Mr Hamilton's arrival at his office…buzz me first and then inform Mr Hamilton that I need to see him in my office. Are these instructions clear, DeTagelio, or do you need to take notes?" Katherine tersely demanded.

"Yes, Ma'am, I understand completely, Miss Katherine. Is there anything else, Miss Katherine?" Margie inquired in a tear-cracking voice, as she tried to leave Katherine's chilling presence as quickly as possible. "No, you may go.…just remember our little discussion, Miss DeTagelio and we'll get along perfectly," Katherine responded with another visibly forced perfect smile.

Quickly, Margie made her tactical retreat and closed the heavy oak door before the 'Boston Lioness' found or invented, yet another unfounded excuse to roar again. As she safely made her exit from

Katherine's office, Margie muttered silently to herself what a cold-hearted bitch 'Kit Kat MacAlister' was and that Brad was unfortunate to be marrying such a self-centred and temperamental bitchy woman. 'Katherine was a discredit to her gender and social class', Margie aptly concluded. She speculated that Brad was not going to have a happy or long-lasting marriage with the bitchy Katherine, he was too good and gentile of a man to be cursed for life with a cold, ego-centric witch like Katherine.

Margie knew that she couldn't bear to work for such a cold-hearted bitch for an indefinite period of time and she prayed for Brad's quick mental recovery, as he would restore some degree of normalcy and redemption from Katherine's imposed private hell. His presence would also serve to balance out and tone down 'Kit Kat's' mercurial and sometimes vicious tongue, which was used frequently and viciously against the younger female employees of the firm. Katherine needed to constantly prove her superiority and position among her potential and perceived competitors. Any threats, however, were mere figments of Katherine's over-active imagination and paranoia – both being the telltale signs of an inwardly insecure woman.

Katherine had never warmed to Margie DeTagelio. Margie's sexual threat was illustrated by her beautiful and wholesome good looks, while her native intelligence and street-wise personality was formidable enough to disarm and engage all manner of persons and clients, to include many of the Ultra-rich clients who visited the offices. With keen acumen, Katherine mentally noted Margie's talents and charms, both of which she sought to diffuse, lest her own position tarnish even in a minor way. Given the proper opportunities, Margie could be her potential sexual equal. Equality with another woman had always frightened Katherine and it needed to be defused or defeated.

Margie DeTagelio was 27 years old, single, without children, of small feminine frame – standing about 5'5" in height, slender, and anointed with flowing copper-penny, light-coloured, red hair and beautiful pale blue eyes. Her mother was of Irish extraction, while her beloved father was a third generation Italian American. The DeTagelios were a typical working-class family, they struggled every day for its daily bread, yet always managing to pay their monthly bills on time. There were four children in the DeTagelio family, each of whom fought and jockeyed to get the privileged affection of their mom and dad within the family; of course no child was the favourite of either parent. Margie's father Frank, was a firefighter/auxiliary medic with Boston's Fire Department, being a member of the force for 24 years. Frank DeTagelio was a large-framed man who loved his family, his fire crew and his job.

He had attended weekly Catholic Mass faithfully with his wife, Maureen. Like most parents, he felt alienated by the modern ways and attitudes of his children. He died tragically while fighting a blaze in an abandoned building when Margie was 14 years old. Margie was the oldest of four children, which included two girls and two boys. All the children were now grown and married, save for Margie, who still lived alone with her aging mother in a three-storey, red brick row house located off the Boston harbour waterfront. It was a working- class neighbourhood, where everyone kept to themselves and maintained their modest homes. The house was paid off, a benefit derived from an insurance policy which her father had prudently taken out a few years before his untimely death.

Margie's social time was spent with her married girlfriends and an occasional, non-serious date here and there, which one of her girlfriends had managed to arrange. Like any other child who had lost a parent during their adolescence, neither Margie nor her siblings ever truly recovered from the untimely death of their father. The sudden parental loss caused a mental uneasiness and angst that led Margie to fear long lasting relationships with others. Perhaps this was the reason why Margie had never formed a lasting relationship with a man, or perhaps it was the obligation that she felt to help support her widowed mother. In any event, she kept such fears and counsel to herself and tried to work through her personal problems by herself. It was a characteristic of working middle class people to solve their own personal issues and not seek the advice of professional psychiatrists, psychologists and social workers.

Quite unlike Miss Katherine, Margie did not have a career, she simply had a job – a thankless, menial, laborious routine that grinded away at her soul day after day. This daily drudgery was punctuated with an occasional summer vacation at the crowded seashore or sometimes a bargain package vacation deal to Europe or the Caribbean islands; this modesty was coupled with the purchase of a few personal luxury items that made Middle Class American life comfortably tolerable. Her all-consuming task was simply to stay employed to support herself and her mom, this devoured the bulk of her modest salary earned at Hamilton & MacAlister. She was not yet eligible for the handsome bonuses that the firm supplied until her fifth year of employment vesting, although she did receive a Christmas gratuity and a fractional bonus, both of which provided a very welcomed $10,000 annual supplement to her modest annual salary of $45,000. If she could only hang on until her fifth year, her bonus would be 30% of her base salary plus a $15,000 annual company paid contribution into her retirement account. Staying employed at Hamilton & MacAlister was essential.

Margie had begun work at Hamilton & MacAlister only a few months after Bradford Hamilton and Katherine MacAlister came into the fold of the family business and she was assigned only by random chance to be Mr Bradford Hamilton's administrative assistant and secretary on a temporary basis. Both Margie and Bradford clicked immediately, their personalities complementing each other magnificently. Occasionally, Bradford would meet Margie and the other office workers for a quick drink at Olde Bailey's a few blocks away and there they would all socially mix and discuss the general office events of the day. These office Team-building events were planned by Bradford personally to help improve employee morale and afford a better working atmosphere. Slowly, Margie also became mesmerized and seduced by working around America's power and social elite. If she could never become one of the Ultra-rich, at least she could associate around the fringes of their world and make a nice comfortable living by doing so over the course of her work tenure.

Like Katherine's secretary Joan Peters, Margie's job position offered the potential for making a salary of $95,000 through $150,000 a year, not including the very generous bonuses and matching 401K retirement contributions, although making this salary would take many years for Margie to obtain; nevertheless it was a probable eventuality if she stayed with the firm and stayed clear of Kit-Kat. Joan Peters was doing very well as Miss Katherine's Personal Assistant; however, Joan Peters had worked for Hamilton & MacAlister for 40 years and she was 64 years old. Hamilton & MacAlister compensated its employees well, since it was the proper thing to do and it promoted devoted loyalty. Disloyalty could harm or destroy a wealthy financial institution.

Margie thought of her prospective future and she had to start planning for it now, as life had amply taught her to be independent and prudent. She realized that she had better learn to take care of herself, as the prospect of a Prince Charming sweeping her off her feet and placing her in a gilded mansion were the idle fruitless dreams of every office working girl. All she had to do was work hard, eat some corporate 'shit sandwitches', and avoid any personal conflicts. The only fly in the ointment was the Ice Princess, Miss Katherine MacAlister.

* * * * * * * * * * * * * * * * * * *

"Good morning, Margie, now it is Margie, isn't it, or does my memory fail me once again?" inquired the aristocratic, slightly snobby, and regally dressed woman who was in her late-sixties.

"Yes, Mrs MacAlister, my name is Margie… I'm Margie DeTagelio, Mr Bradford Hamilton's office assistant and thank you for so kindly remembering my name. I'm acting as Miss Katherine's Personal Assistant for two weeks while Mrs Peters is out on vacation," Margie added as she rose from her seat to politely greet this important visitor.

"Oh, and a very good morning to you, sir… Mr MacAlister," Margie stated smartly as she remembered the elegant couple from previous visits. Margie was astonished as to the ordinariness and congenial nature of both Mr and Mrs MacAlister, since their daughter was the direct opposite – Kit Kat being aloof, spiteful, cold hearted, and 100% business.

"Oh please, I apologize, Mr and Mrs MacAlister, for not expecting your visit, I had no idea that either of you were going to be in the office today, I had thought that both of you were vacationing in New York City?" Margie inquired in polite discretion and hoping to confirm that she had not made another tragic administrative mistake.

"Well, yes, your memory is quite correct, my dear, but we grew tired of the City and so we decided to hurry back to Boston and see how you and Brad were getting along," Mrs MacAlister replied as her husband Lionel looked on and nodded in silent approval.

"Well, I hoped you both had a good vacation anyway. I will just ring Miss Katherine to let her know you are here to see her," Margie stated and remembering that Miss Katherine's strict protocols to give her advance notice of any and all visitors to her office, even to include Bradford Hamilton and that of her own parents.

"Oh no… no… no my dear, we'll just go directly into her office uninvited, we always want to surprise Kate just like when she was a child, it also keeps her on her toes." Mrs. MacAlister giggled as they knocked, then burst into Katherine's palatial office.

"Hello, how's our little banking executive doing today? Your mother and I made a bee-line past your polite secretary, I hope you do not mind us showing up unannounced and barging into your office?" Mr Lionel MacAlister voiced as he and Faye MacAlister entered Katherine's office and closed the door discreetly behind them. Margie enjoyed the MacAlisters almost as much as she had liked the Hamiltons; they were sensible, caring, 'down to earth' people, as if such a term could be applied to multi-billionaires.

"How's the younger generation treating the old firm of Hamilton & MacAlister...still keeping your head above water, my beloved daughter?" Lionel MacAlister lightly joked.

"Hey, Daddy, you'll be glad to hear that the younger generation of Hamilton & MacAlister just landed a multi-billion-dollar deal for over a dozen major Fortune 500 companies for security underwriting fees," Kate proudly proclaimed and smiled broadly. "As a bonus, there's more deals in the pipeline too. Daddy, you should welcome your child into the new generation of self-made billionaires! Now how's that for the younger generation for doing business correctly?" Kate stated confidently.

Faye looked on with only mild curiosity, she being more interested in the personal welfare of her daughter and future son-in-law. Like most mothers of a certain age, she pined for grandchildren. Lionel MacAlister continued his inquiry into the state of his daughter's welfare. "Well now, Kate – how are you and my soon-to-be son-in-law doing? How's Brad's personal situation? Any changes in the wedding date, darling?" Lionel MacAlister directly inquired as he held Kate's hand with fatherly affection.

Faye's eyes almost rolled back into her head as Lionel finished verbally polling his daughter.

"Come now, Lionel, how uncaring and crude of you to ask your daughter such pillaging questions in such a crude, direct fashion and only having been in her office these few minutes! Really, Arthur – what has become of your parenting skills?" Faye MacAlister chided shockingly.

As usual, Katherine came to her daddy's defence. "No...no....no... Mom and Dad," Kate interjected, "you both have a right to be concerned and perhaps directness is the correct type of talk," Kate nervously replied, as her parents availed themselves of a conveniently staged, overstuffed plum-coloured Chesterfield styled leather sofa.

Kate quickly walked over to her office wet-bar and poured three generous malt scotches into ice filled leaden crystal shaker glasses. Fay and Lionel looked nervously at one another, knowing that serious talk required a serious drink.

"Oh, my dear, we didn't think that this daughter-parent talk required distilled spirits and this before the noon hour!" Faye MacAlister scorned with a slight air of friendly sarcasm." Without a tint of demur, Katherine directed the conversation squarely back onto the topic of Bradford W. Hamilton.

"Some straight talk demands strong whisky, Mother dear," Katherine coldly chided back to the astonishment of her socially reserved mother. "It's no good…he's not responding, Mother…Brad's simply not getting any better," Kate stated dryly as she sipped her Glenmorangie 18 year-aged malt whisky. "I'll have to distribute our wedding delay notifications to all of the invitees. The wedding is officially pushed back to Autumn; as for Brad, well…I feel that I'm losing him!" she confessed in a tearful outburst.

"He's been totally despondent ever since his family's demise and I fear for my…I mean to say, our future together, but if Brad doesn't improve soon…I just…well I just don't know what the hell I am going to do with my life, Mom!" Katherine sobbed quietly as tears poured down her face, as she slowly sipped the fine aged malt scotch whisky.

Lionel looked over nervously at his wife Faye and hoped that she would say something to their daughter. "Brad needs some time my dear, the entire Hamilton family is gone! Brad's all alone and he needs time to deal with his grief, Kate," Faye's voice pleaded in a reassuring soft tone.

"Yes, I know that, Mother! You think everything is going along great in your life, then wham!…disaster comes up and bites you in the ass. Sometimes I wish that Brad was involved with another woman rather than this mess, I could sure as hell deal with the issue of another woman, but I can't fight a battle against the dead and there are four deceased Hamiltons that Brad is grieving over. If I were Brad, I don't know how in the hell I could wake up every day." Kate was emotionally exasperated and throwing up her arms in utter despair.

Faye tried to console her daughter. "Yes, of course, Kate, none of us knows the depth of Brad's sadness, we just have to do all that we can to help and support him fully," Faye exclaimed in a resigned and heartfelt tone.

"The grieving process takes time, my daughter, we have to give Brad the time that he needs," Lionel counselled gently.

Katherine tried to put forth her strongest smile and agreed in nodding approval to the counsel furnished by her parents. "Well, Brad's going to be here in about 10 minutes and I'll see if I can try again to get him to cheer up just a little and perhaps the Morgan deal will flicker his spirit even if just a bit," she sadly confessed.

Faye slowly walked over to Kate and gently whispered some final motherly advice to her daughter. "Listen to me, Kate, give Brad some time, but not too much time, my dear, your father and I want to have grandchildren soon, we're not getting any younger and we had expected to have a doting grandchild that we could spoil like mad, just like we did with you, Kate," Faye whispered in a low tone to her daughter.

Katherine annoyingly frowned at her mother's suggestive remark concerning future offspring and knowing full well that her peers were well into the child rearing stage; she was behind in her peer-curve on this expected stage of life experience and that situation simply would not do for Kit Kat's ego.

Not letting his wife have the last word on this subject, Lionel lauded one last bit of comforting fatherly advice to his daughter. "You just keep in there, Kate, don't give up on Brad, he's worth your best efforts, darling…well, I guess your mother and I will be heading down to my office and check out the assorted mail and messages that were left during our vacation. Oh, please have Brad stop by my office, we'd love to see him."

Lionel and Faye MacAlister smartly departed their daughter's office and headed down the main corridor of the Hamilton & MacAlister Office building toward Lionel's private luxury suite.

The MacAlisters' marriage was a model upper-class social affair and it was exactly the kind of marriage that Katherine had envisioned for both herself and Brad before the Hamilton air tragedy. She already had one failed marriage to Thomas Bedworth and she was resolute to ensure her marriage to Brad was a storybook success, with the perfect man, perfect children, and perfect social status all to boot!

In her previous marriage, Thomas and Katherine had fought like 'cats & dogs' from day one of their marriage and perhaps this was because they were too much alike: self-centred, possessive, materialistic and jealous. She was resolved to have no repeat of that fiasco. This morning she would try again to slowly bring back Brad's spirit and zeal for life, if only temporarily. The loss of his family would take many years to mend, but she was determined that she was the woman capable of ensuring this, it was her immediate mission in life, in addition to the operation of the Hamilton & MacAlister franchise.

* * * * * * * * * * * * * * * * * *

Finally, Bradford Hamilton had arrived at the Hamilton & MacAlister office just as the rain had ceased its incessant rambling downpour of the forgone morning. He parked his Bentley directly in front of Katherine's identical Azure blue Bentley. Margie was getting a cup of coffee from the firm's break & kitchen area and while walking back to her desk she passed one of the prominent colonial-styled, imposing large front windows that overlooked Broomfield Street below, where she just happened to glance down to the street below and observe Bradford pulling up in his late model Bentley. Margie was both glad and sad, she looked forward to working for Bradford every day and she had a terrible secret crush on him, yet Brad was not in love with her. He fondly thought of and treated her as a younger sister.

Remembering the scolding that she had just received a short time earlier from Miss Kit Kat, Margie quickly acted on her standing orders, as she scurried back to her desk and reported on this news to her office Mistress.

"Hello Miss Katherine, I wanted to promptly inform you that Mr Hamilton has just pulled-up in front of the building, I'll convey your message for him to meet you in your office. Are there any other messages or actions that you want me to initiate?" Margie deftly inquired of Katherine.

"Thank you, Miss DeTagelio, just buzz my office one time right before Mr Hamilton comes into my office and don't go anywhere until you meet him and he enters my office. Don't even go to the Ladies room to take a twinkle, do you understand me?" Katherine sternly ordered.

"Yes, Miss Katherine, I'll give Mr Hamilton your message, I'll buzz you before he enters your office, and I won't take a twinkle until all this is done," Margie stated almost verbatim and most impolitely.

"Great, and by the way DeTagelio, you don't have to talk or act so crudely around the office, this is not your home or a bar," Katherine smartly snapped back and oblivious to the blatant double-standard that existed between employer and employee.

"Yes, of course, Miss Katherine," Margie replied in polite servitude, knowing that any further discussion or discord was hopeless and perhaps career ending.

"Good day, Mr Hamilton, so how are you this morning? Can I get you a cup of coffee or something?" Margie gleefully inquired as

Bradford W. Hamilton slowly exited the richly wood-panelled private executive elevator.

A few pregnant silent seconds passed before Brad reluctantly and slowly acknowledged Margie's morning salutation. "Oh yes, hello Margie." He forcefully frowned in a half-hearted smile of contrived politeness. "Yes, thank you, perhaps a short cup of Columbian Supreme coffee, black and with extra sugar will do me some good this morning, I didn't get much sleep last evening again, I guess that I overslept this morning, it's becoming a bad habit I'm afraid," he awkwardly and poorly lied to Margie.

"Yes of course, Mr Hamilton, and oh by the way – Miss Katherine wants to see you in her office once you get settled." Margie smiled as she quickly got Bradford his sorely needed caffeine.

Silently nodding the acknowledgement of Margie's message, he strayed toward his office with an unenthusiastic trudging walk.

Wearily entering his elegant wood-panelled office, he threw his rain-soaked and mud-stained trench coat onto the coat rack, he straightened out his necktie and rumbled jacket. A sudden knock came on his door, it was Margie again. She was carrying a small, elegant solid sterling silver tray onto which was balanced a small silver pot of black coffee, a croissant, and several small containers of cream and sugar.

"Here it is, boss, piping hot and freshly prepared! Is there anything else that I can get for you, Mr Hamilton?" Margie cheerfully inquired.

Bradford made a sincere, but forced smile. "No, nothing more, Margie, you have done enough already, please tell Miss MacAlister that I'll be in to see her in a few minutes," Brad retorted in a weary voice.

Margie nodded and quietly closed the door to Mr Hamilton's office, she wanted to console her boss in some manner, yet this would be crossing the thin worker-employer relationship line. Mindful of Miss MacAlister's orders to her earlier in the morning, she quickly returned to her desk and gave Katherine a status update call.

"Hello Miss Katherine, please be advised that Mr Hamilton just came into the office, I have just taken him coffee, and he is looking over his mail and reviewing his personal phone messages. He says that he will be in to see you in a few minutes," Margie politely summarized to Katherine.

"That's good news, Miss DeTagelio, just give me a quick buzz right before Brad comes into my office," Katherine requested.

"Yes, Miss Katherine," Margie responded and happy not to have been balled-out again by Miss Kit Kat MacAlister.

* * * * * * * * * * * * * * * * * *

Katherine quickly readied herself for Brad's arrival, as she anxiously checked her makeup, tidied up her outfit, and sprayed a reinforcing dose of Chanel Number 5 onto her neck. She hoped that Bradford would be in a little better mood than he had been over the previous few weeks, but she was not expecting a miracle either. Perhaps the news of the latest corporate stock underwriting with Morgan Stanley would invigorate Brad's mood. It wasn't every day that a multi-billion dollar deal came into the office and Brad had been instrumental in crafting the windfall bonanza.

Within the firm of Hamilton & MacAlister, Bradford was the Chief Executive Officer (CEO), in which capacity he managed the strategic and partner alliance aspect of the business; this position also included the quest for new business opportunities and deal-making, while Katherine gravitated toward managing and implementing the mechanics and daily management of the deals that Brad had consummated, making sure that the business processes and cash flows were maintained and invested according to strict schedule. Katherine was the President and Chief Operating Officer (COO), which equated with the responsibility of managing and running the firm's office affairs on a daily basis, to include personnel issues, chairing weekly and daily executive meetings, and coordinating business activities with the firm's business top ranking staff. Both Katherine and Bradford were equal in the firm's ownership and responsibilities and each one nicely complemented the talents of the other. It was a perfect match of personal and business strengths, much as had been the case for each of their fathers.

Bradford emerged from his office and walked a short distance over to the door that led to Katherine's office. "Oh, please go right on in, Mr Hamilton, Miss MacAlister is expecting you," Margie stated formally, as she quickly and silently buzzed Miss Katherine's office as per Kit Kat's strict instructions.

Katherine took immediate notice of the muted sound of the buzzer and quickly composed her demeanour in anticipation of her co-partner and fiancé.

"Brad, my love, good morning, so how are you doing, my dear? It's so very good to see you up and about this fine Boston Spring day!" Katherine cheerfully exclaimed, as she broadly smiled and beamed to the love of her life. Without uttering another word or awaiting a reply to her greetings, Katherine threw her arms around Brad's neck and gave him a passionate hug, accompanied with a full open-mouth passionate kiss.

Brad's half-hearted reaction was to return Katherine's affections with only a polite peck on the cheek. Katherine was not at all surprised by Brad's lack of passion and affection toward her, or anyone else for that matter, since that February plane crash tragedy.

"Hey Brad, guess what, darling? Guess who has just been awarded the largest financial security underwriting contract in the history of Hamilton & MacAlister? Yes...you did it...we both did it – made it as self-made billionaires, Brad! The Morgan Stanley underwriting deal was just approved this morning...quite a feat when other firms are going bankrupt and laying off staff in this post Great Recession and now we are making billions of dollars...I bet that everyone in the district is green with envy too! We'll have to see if anyone 'key-customizes' the paint on our Bentleys! The boy genius Kent called and gave me the good news. Isn't this terrific, darling?" Katherine exclaimed in a bit of wild enthusiasm that was devoid of any compassion for those less fortunate than herself or the Ultra Club clan.

In his misery, Brad could not have cared less about the deal or money. "Yes, that's great, Katherine. Really good news, I suppose!" Bradford half-heartedly replied without any tint of emotion. Increasing his vast wealth now meant little to him and the deal-making achievement rang hollow too! With the loss of his family, more wealth meant little.

"Well, it's more than good news, my darling. After all, you worked half a year on this deal and it was the passion of your life, besides me of course! This is going to mean great things for the both of us and the entire firm. We might be getting requests to do media interviews! Big bonuses for everyone from the mail boy to the executives, not to mention bragging rights to our competitors!" Katherine exclaimed wildly to Bradford with raw excitement.

"Half a year indeed! A lot can happen to a person's life in six short months!" he muttered softly. "To tell you the truth, Katherine, I'm not feeling too passionate about anything these days, I'm sorry, my dear," Bradford confided as he gave Katherine a terse, cold peck on the lips, as he slowly moved away from her warm embrace and seductive perfumed body.

Dejected, but not deterred, Katherine was not a woman to be robbed of her objective.

"Now, Brad, come on over here, my baby. I have something to show you, something that may perk your interest big boy!" Katherine purred in a toy-full, sexy tone. Taking Bradford gently by the hand, Katherine slowly walked over to the ornate feminine-styled office desk and with a vigorous motion of her hand, she carelessly scattered the papers that were positioned on it, all of these falling generously onto the floor. Katherine then turned her back to the table and deeply looked bewitchingly into Brad's eyes. Wrapping her arms around his neck and pulling Bradford ever more closely toward her body, Katherine seductively laid her body down onto the now empty, polished honey-toned mahogany desktop and kicked her designer high heel shoes off, while Brad's torso obediently followed her body slavishly forward toward the desktop.

Katherine seductively entangled Brad's torso with her long slender legs and embracing arms, carefully moving her appendages up and down his back and buttocks. With her passionate green eyes, fragrant perfume and soft feminine voice, Katherine purred a whisper to Brad, "Okay my strong, sexy, financial genius, why don't you try to underwrite my private offering? Not interested...huh? Well then would you care to check out my credit rating, darling? Too tongue-tied this morning, huh? So, how about a little stock exchange perhaps? A little IPO, as in an 'Intimate Private Offering', then?" Katherine purred and smiled in a devilish passionate manner.

"No to all of these offers? Well then, how about just a little desk sex, my handsome, strong fiancé?" Katherine toyfully giggled, as her long shapely legs slowly moved up and down Brad's thighs and lower back, then slowly straddled around Brad's waist. The full breadth of Kate's black silk stockings and revealing red silk garter belt, richly illustrated the beauty and sensuality of Katherine's voluptuous feminine form. Katherine's fragrant perfume completely scented the office and its aroma finalized the passionate venue. Detached as Brad was from Katherine's immediate sensual advances, the Chanel Number 5 perfume still rekindled pleasant romantic memories that he had with his beloved Katherine.

Brad tried to feign a forced smile that momentarily abbreviated his stoic frozen face, when suddenly and involuntarily, tears moistened in his eye sockets. His spirit ruled over his body and mind. Alerted to his sudden mood swing, Katherine responded immediately to Brad's detracted and distant facial expression.

"Darling what's the matter, honey, what's wrong?" Katherine cried out nervously.

There was an eerie silence, as Bradford said nothing in response to Katherine's inquiry. Her eyes quickly scanned Brad's face, she looked deeply into Brad's tearful eyes, as she remembered back to these same soulless eyes that she had remembered seeing some six weeks earlier at his family's funeral.

"St. Giles cemetery! It's St. Giles, isn't it? You've been to St. Giles again, haven't you, Brad? My dear sweet God, not again!" Katherine cried out with tears in her eyes and a remorse in her voice, as Brad's facial expression betrayed an affirmation of guilt to Katherine's keen accusation.

Katherine slowly, and regretfully, released her appendages from around Brad's torso, knowing that his remorsefulness had made him immune and impotent to her sexual advances. Slowly, Brad moved away from Katherine and turned his back and lowered his head in shame, he felt as if he were a man found guilty of an illicit act.

"Look, Brad, this insanity has got to stop, it's no good, you can't keep doing this to yourself. It does no one any good, least of all you, my darling! Brad, you go to St. Giles cemetery and every damn time it's the same thing: depression, crying, a few drinks of scotch, and then the terrible blues. We can get through this thing together, Brad. I can help you! Will you let me into your dark world, Brad?" Katherine tearfully pleaded.

He struggled to find the words that could convey his emotional dilemma. "Kate, there's nothing you can do for me, it's my problem, and it's my hell. Thanks for the concern, but perhaps you should cut your losses with me; I'm broken, Kate...maybe I'm not the right guy for you anymore. If you don't want me, I'll understand completely!" Bradford confessed dryly and with self-resignation.

Yet Katherine was having none of Brad's self-pity. Brad was her man and not even Brad himself was going to screw that up for Katherine.

"Stop that nonsense, Brad. I'm your fiancée, I love you, and I'm not going to idly standby while you self- destruct before my eyes, damn it! People who love one another, share their pains and problems together, not apart from one another! We're in this mess together, Brad!" Kate shouted, while seeking to add some encouragement and support.

"Perhaps, Brad, you can get some professional advice, I know some professional ..."

Suddenly, Katherine was abruptly cut off in mid-sentence by Brad: "No, I will not go see a psychiatrist or psychologist! I can work this problem out for myself, Kate, and without anyone's help or assistance," Bradford scornfully retorted.

"That's neither fair or logical, Brad, don't be absurd or stubborn, you are unwilling to seek the advice from others and it is precisely this type of professional support that will make you better!" Katherine pleaded with rational clarity, if not also vested self-interest.

"Well then, Kate, show me someone who I personally know who has had their entire family killed, wiped out in an instant and then I'll listen to that person's advice...otherwise any other damn third-party advice or counselling is meaningless bullshit and a sheer waste of time!" Brad scornfully avowed.

"Now, Brad, darling that's a ridiculous position to take, there are many people in your life who love and care for you, namely yours truly and we all just want to help you. What's wrong with this psychological counselling, Brad, I see that nothing else is helping you!" she pleaded.

There was an uncomfortable pregnant pause as Brad pondered Katherine's sage words. "Well maybe you are correct, Kate. You're 100% on the mark. There's nothing wrong with your advice. You're an intelligent woman and a wonderful friend and my fiancée. Perhaps I do need your help and assistance. I know my life will never be the same, I just can't stop thinking that I'll never see my family again. Nothing is the same or can ever be the same again for me, nothing that I previously enjoyed seems very important anymore, Kate. I'm not good for myself, not for you or anyone else for that matter, until I come to terms with my loss. This is something I must do and it must be done on my terms, Kate," Brad confessed openly for the first time and he actually believed his own words.

"You know that I'm always here for you, Brad, whatever you want or need, I assure you. We can start our own family too and have a boatload of children!" Katherine wept softly, as she confessed her own secret future desires.

"Kate, I dearly love you and I know that I have not been the best of company the last few weeks and I'm not a very good fiancé, but I just need some time to pull through; that is, if you still want this run-down wreck of a man?" he muttered to Katherine, smirking with a dry, half

-witted grin on his face.

The clarity of his words were both hopeful and disturbing. Katherine immediately tried to defuse Brad's doubts about himself and their future. "Oh, my foolish and lovely Brad, that's the first time I've seen a hint of your beautiful smile in many weeks. You're a silly, silly boy, Brad Hamilton, what nonsense you are speaking! I am going to feel your forehead for a fever and see if you are delirious. You're my fiancé and I am here 150% for you, day or night. We love each other, Brad. We are made for one another, and as soon as you are yourself again - we are getting married and with God's blessing and a little bit of passionate lovemaking, we're going to start our own family. I dream of having children and living the life that we always hoped to enjoy together Brad. Perhaps a vacation or change of venue will help! We can take a week down to the islands or Paris or wherever the hell else you want to go," Kate hopefully suggested.

"Humm – that's not bad advice, Kate, I'll give your travel suggestions some serious consideration. I'm really not in the mood for a vacation, but a change of venue is intriguing," Brad replied as possibilities of the future raced through his imagination.

Katherine was encouraged by Brad's openness. "You do that, Brad, please do that for yourself and for us," Katherine responded. "Brad, you really do need a wife to keep you straight and proper. You're a mess, it looks as if you had slept in your beautiful suit." She smiled while carefully straightening out Brad's tie. He shyly returned the smile for a brief second, kissed Kate gently on the forehead and then proceeded out of Kate's office.

"Look, Brad honey, you will seriously think about what I said about us taking a break and getting away from Boston? It would help recharge both of our discharged batteries and Daddy can handle the office for a week, all our deals have been solidified and we can afford and deserve the downtime. Daddy also wants you to drop by his office and have a chat with him, okay?" Kate softly whispered.

Brad gave a fainted half smile and nodded his head in brief acknowledgement before walking out of Katherine's office and closing the door gently behind him.

Brad slowly walked by Margie's desk, then suddenly he stopped to say hello. "Hello Margie, how's my favourite secretary and personal assistant doing today?" he inquired in an abnormally low voice and with a slight smile.

"Mr Hamilton, I'm fine, but how are you doing? Is there anything that I can get for you?" Margie inquired politely in a sympathetic tone.

"So, Mr Hamilton is it now!" Brad exclaimed softly and with a refrained devilish smile. "Whatever happened to the name of Brad?" he inquired with some informal jest.

"Oh, I'm just being formal and correct as per Miss MacAlister's guidance, we're in an office setting, Mr Hamilton, we're not at the Olde Bailey's Tavern," Margie smiled while remembering the informal social times that she spent with Brad and the other employees from Hamilton & MacAlister during impromptu social gatherings at the local neighbourhood watering hole.

"Sure of course, Margie… of course anything you say…oh thanks again for the coffee, it really took a chill off my bones," Brad chided as he boyishly grinned at Margie and leisurely walked down the office hallway to the office of Lionel MacAlister.

With a firm, yet hesitant motion, Brad knocked on Lionel's office door and politely waited for a response and permission to enter.

"Please come in," Lionel MacAlister announced in a cheerful tone.

Brad walked slowly into the large and richly masculine arrayed office. The office was decorated in the traditional Anglo Saxon, Edwardian tradition of hard wood panelling, ornate colourful, rich, Persian wool rugs, ornate stone fireplace, and rich leather covered furniture. A huge oak desk was poised at the far side of the room, while two huge reading chairs and a large leather sofa with a complementary leather inlay coffee table completed the major office furnishing ensemble. The entire atmosphere reeked of power, wealth and prestige.

"It's been a little while since we have had a good, long chat, my boy," Lionel exclaimed in a fatherly tone.

"How are you doing, Brad? Is there anything that we can do for you?" Faye pleaded as she gently kissed Brad on the cheek with motherly affection.

Lionel wrapped his arm around Brad's shoulder in fatherly consolation. Brad struggled to paint a contrived smile, as his eyes moistened with tears of appreciation.

"You have both been terribly, terribly kind to me these past weeks. Without your support and that of Kate's, I think I would have…" then suddenly Brad broke down and cried as he clutched Lionel and Faye MacAlister in both of his arms.

"Now, now, it's going to be all right, Brad. In time, it's going to get better...please believe me!" Lionel pleaded comfortingly.

"We are now your family, Brad... I think we always were your family. I always considered you the little son that I never had," Faye cried out as she reassured and warmly embraced Brad.

"You will both always remain members of my family, no matter what happens," Brad emotionally exclaimed as he gently hugged both Faye and Lionel.

"Well, you just let both of us, and naturally Katherine, take care of you, Brad. Over time, you'll have your good days and bad days, eventually we pray that only the good days will persist. Just call on us if you need anything," Faye exclaimed. Brad merely nodded back in dutiful appreciation.

"Oh, how about dinner tonight, Brad?" Lionel welcomingly inquired.

"That's a marvellous idea, Lionel!" Faye exclaimed with excitement. "We can dine at our home or if you prefer, Brad, we can dine out, I know some wonderful little places that are out of this world!" Faye sighed.

"Thanks, thanks both of you for the offer, but I still prefer...I mean I still don't feel up to going out right now... perhaps next week," Brad remarked in an almost apologetic manner.

"Are you sure, Brad, it appears like you have not been eating well and you look a bit thin, now doesn't he, Lionel?" Faye rhetorically inquired.

"Well, yes, Faye, of course I'm doing as well as can be expected and I am eating more regular these days, it's just that I'm not in the mood and my company would be horrendous," Brad only half-joked.

"Well then, next week we have a firm date for dinner, young man, and we will not take 'no' for an answer," Faye threatened.

"Fine, it is agreed, Faye, just give Kate the date and I'll be any place you want me to be." Brad shook Lionel's hand and gave Faye a big motherly hug. "We'll meet next week for dinner then and please give Kate the details. Thank you again for everything," Brad reiterated as he bade farewell to the MacAlisters.

Brad anxiously retreated into his office and closed the door behind him. His office was just the opposite décor from Katherine's, its masculine rich walnut panelling, ornate stone fireplace, and Edwardian furniture all served to reveal an old world aristocratic and conservative nature. Brad wearily slipped back behind the ornate and elaborately carved mahogany desk, onto which was neatly arrayed various sundry and decorative items, to include pictures of his family and those of

Katherine and the MacAlister family. Brad deliberately tried to keep from looking at the painful photos; with an increased frustration he finally turned down the pictures onto the picture frames' faces. A huge stack of unopened mail was piled-up onto Brad's desk. Feeling despondent, he submissively sunk down into the deep leather desk chair and looked blankly around the office.

Unable to focus on the general business correspondence that inconveniently occupied his desktop, he took a short stroll over to his private wet bar, opened up his liquor cabinet, and selected a crystal decanter of highland malt scotch. He opened the small refrigerator and withdrew a handful of ice cubes, placing these into a heavy lead-crystal glass. He took a short sip and gazed about his office again, looking for an activity to excite his overactive and wandering mind. A large pile of correspondence resided on his desk in-box, it captured his immediate attention. 'This was about as good a place to start work, as anywhere else,' he reckoned silently to himself. Brad grabbed a handful of envelopes and started to sort through his mail that had been piling up for several weeks.

Some of the correspondence was of an impersonal or trivial matter – these he threw into a pile to be sorted, filed, and possibly discarded by Margie when she audited Brad's 'to-be-filed' desk container. Brad proceeded to read and signed particular documents that required the approval of the CEO and these he quickly endorsed and arrayed into his desk 'out-going' tray. However, the most moving correspondences were the letters of condolence and support regarding the demise of his family and petitions of prayer for Brad's welfare – it was a universal sentiment expressed within the contents of every letter. His eyes moistened, as friends and acquaintances revealed short fond tales and deeds of goodness performed by all members of the Hamilton clan, which had previously been anonymous to him. After about 30 minutes, a reprieve from these sorrowful messages of sympathy was needed, so he decided to draw his attention to his e-mail account and review its contents.

He touched his keypad and his PC screen magically sparked to life. Brad's e-mail account was revealed, it contained at least 500 e-mails of varying importance and origin. As in the case of the paper correspondence, Brad sorted the important from the unimportant e-mails. He quickly responded to those that were marked 'urgent or reply required', then he quickly closed out these items and proceeded to those marked 'personal-in-nature'. In repetitive manner, Brad read countless events, where his father or mother had performed some act of kindness or charity that was never conveyed or known to Brad before. He sat at his desk and read each e-mail, hoping to learn more about the kindness of his parents. Funny it was that the child never fully knows the details of his or her parents' adult lives and activities, yet such was the normal relationship between parent and child.

He smiled frequently, as he read how Arthur and Gloria had performed numerous large and small favours for numerous people. Each e-mail sender was unanimous in their praise and admiration of Arthur and Gloria; Brad was proud to be his parents' son as he read each word of the 'Good Samaritan' stories and he smiled ever so slightly with each new e-mail opening.

"I suppose many people don't realize how much they are loved and appreciated until after they are gone," Brad mused as he whittled away at the electronic correspondence and sending a polite and sincere reply to each and every one. The process had the strange effect of calming Brad's nerves and allowing him to 'liberate' all the positive feeling that he had for his family. Unknowingly, this was a form of emotional therapy for Brad, even if it was only temporal.

From the numerous correspondences, e-mails, and phone messages, Brad began to appreciate the humane accomplishments of his two wonderful parents, even in their death their personal charity continued to benefit people long after the initial assistance had been rendered. Aside from its altruistic benefits, Brad began to see that there was a kind of immortality in their good deeds and kindness to others. Many of the correspondence related as to how the Hamiltons had been the unheralded benefactors of a family whose home had burnt-down and they had given money to help rebuild the dwelling and provided temporary living expenses, while other stories of gratitude told of scholarships given to recently orphaned children of a Boston fire fighter or policeman. Still others detailed the paying of basic home utilities, medical bills or paying for holiday meals for the needy.

Seductively intrigued, he read more letters. In one instance, a mother related how Gloria had personally paid for the hospital bill of a kidney transplant for her seven-year-old daughter. Another letter related how Arthur had financed a small family grocer, whose small store had been vandalized by local thugs and Arthur not only restored the man's grocery store, but also influenced the arrest and prosecution of the local gang responsible for the terrorism. Still another letter related how Arthur and Gloria sponsored a trip to Disneyland for a dying little girl and her family, months before the little girl was to perish of leukaemia.

Each letter told of a story of desperation, hope, and charity. The letters and stories ran into the hundreds and these began to weigh heavily on Brad's mind. He knew of the public charity events and sponsorships that his parents performed as the co-governors of the Hamilton Trust, but he had never realized the extent of the private Hamiltons' charitable 'invisible hand' of kind intersession. The impact that Arthur and Gloria had on the community was profound, yet these private acts of generosity would never be revealed to the public. Arthur and Gloria were closet charitable benefactors and not merely the public Society Page type.

Both Arthur and Gloria thought it was best to do one's 'prayers and acts of charity' in private, rather than seek public adoration for something that should be kept private. It was a true testament to the character of his parents that all these people remembered and took the time to offer Brad their sympathies. In his deep contemplation, he became emotionally moved by the words of sympathy which he had read. Indeed, charity and good works were the truest forms of immortality. Great fortunes, and the people who made and possessed these, were fleeting things of this world, but one's ability to interact and change peoples' lives for the better – now that was a real form of achievement. Brad wished that his legacy in life could be as rich as those made by his parents.

Up until this tragedy in his life, Bradford Hamilton was merely the privileged son of a very wealthy family, his accomplishments were minor and his life relatively non-descript and filled with conspicuous wealth consumption and personal wealth advertisement. It all seemed as nothing now, a life filled with vanity and privilege. He began to realize that he wanted more from life and also that he owed something of himself to this world. Life was fleeting fast and he now realized it!

Suddenly, the phone rang out and disturbed the tranquillity of his kindred thoughts. "Bradford Hamilton, speaking," he wearily replied. "Yes, good day once again, Brad, it's Lionel, am I disturbing you?" Lionel politely inquired, knowing full well that Brad was having serious emotional and mental difficulties recovering from his family's death.

"Oh, hello Lionel, no…not at all, I was merely catching up on some office correspondence here, it's amazing how much stuff piles up in just a few weeks," Brad confessed with a slight tone of embarrassment.

There was an uneasy lull at the other end of the line, before Lionel once again initiated the conversation. "Well, Brad, I have an uncomfortable, but rather necessary matter to discuss with you and I just wanted to ask you if I could come by and discuss some family-related issues with you, that is, if you are feeling up to it?" Lionel gently inquired of Brad in an almost reverent tone.

Brad thought for a few seconds, guessing correctly that it was his family's estate at issue...something he dreaded dearly, as it distilled his dead family to mere 'dollars & cents'. "Yes, Lionel, please come by my office, I have been expecting this matter to arise, I know that you are a family friend and that you are obligated to do what you must do Lionel," Brad responded almost sympathetically.

"Thank you, Brad, I will be down to your office in a few minutes." As expected, Lionel appeared back at Brad's office, a gentle muffled knock on the door announcing Lionel's arrival.

"It's always nice to have you come by and visit with me, we don't do this this often enough, may I pour you a drink, Lionel?" Brad offered in a friendly manner.

"That's fine, Brad, just a short malt, about two fingers' worth, and neat please," Lionel replied. The scotch drank like liquid velvet, it was smooth and warming. The aroma was like a soft roasted cherry-flavour with a slight hint of vanilla.

Taking a comfortable seat upon an ornate, thickly cushioned, Chesterfield leather reading chair – Lionel dutifully proceeded with his distasteful duty as obligated by personal obligation and legal stature. "I just wanted to let you know that both the First Boston Trust and I are the co-executors of your family's estate and that there are going to be some lengthy procedures to be followed to probate the estate into your name... you being the sole surviving heir. This probate was not the normal and expected progression of events involving multiple wills, trusts, etc. While none of this presents any problems, Brad, it's just a lot of paperwork, accounting and audit certifications, the signing of numerous documents, and the many hours that I will be spending with the lawyers, accountants, and trust executives. In about six months, everything should be fully settled and you will be sole heir of the Hamilton estate without any additional fiduciary encumbrances being outstanding," Lionel sadly voiced in fine sounding legalistic jargon.

Lionel directly got into the gist of Brad's inheritance – it was a sober and staggering summary to say the least. "The successive total of your father's, mother's and siblings' estate that accrue entirely to you, totals approximately $19.5 billion, which does not include the Hamilton Trust assets. The 'Arthur & Gloria Hamilton Trust' is a perpetual, private charity, which is funded at $4.8 billion and which, by law, is obligated to annually divest a certain percentage of its gross principal holdings directly back into charitable functions and acts. As the sole trustee, you simply have to annually donate selected amounts to approved charitable institutions or you may make individual personal donations to needy persons and groups, or conversely you may elect to perform a combination of institutional and personal donations....finally, you can even establish your own trust foundation should that idea appeal to you," Lionel added dryly, as he momentarily paused respectfully to await Brad's reply.

"To make a difference in people's lives! ...Yes, I do want to make a difference in the lives of needy people. You see, Lionel, I am keenly interested in becoming the lead member of the 'Arthur & Gloria Hamilton Trust.' I desire that the Trust will continue to play a key part in the Boston metropolitan area and I want for it to be a true legacy of my parents and for the values that they represented – the investment in human capital for those dearly deserving of it...just as my parents and siblings have positively shaped my life, I also want to help other people as well," Brad thoughtfully expressed to Lionel.

"Thank you, I'm very, very glad to hear you say that, Brad, and I know that Arthur and Gloria would be very proud of their son, just as I am of my future son-in-law," Lionel gleefully stated as he smiled at Brad.

"I think that I can have you ready to act as the Governor Trustee in just a few days and in the meantime, you can start thinking about the possible distributions that you wish to make for this year. When you select or need to make a particular Charitable Trust donation, just contact Mrs Patricia Peet, the Hamilton Trust Administrative Officer, and she will make the appropriate arrangements. Also, any revenues not obligated to specific parties this year will automatically be divided among the established standard charitable institutions as so designated on the standing charity list established by your father and mother. When you are ready Brad, we can meet formally with Mrs Peet and the Board of Trustees," Lionel summarized rather succinctly and dryly.

"Oh, and another thing, Brad, the Hamilton Trust being a private trust charity by law and under existing IRS regulations, must make a donation of 5% of its total aggregate capital base to various charities per annum, which equates to approximately $240 million annually, and as the Hamilton Trust capital base principle grows consistently larger each year from its investments, so too does the amount of money that must be divested. This is a huge sum, may I suggest that the distributions be determined and distributed on a quarterly basis," Lionel concluded in a rather definitive suggestive tone.

There was a momentary silence as Brad consumed the weight of the huge financial figures that had just been conveyed to him and these were staggering to say the least even in the age of billionaires. "I thank you for that information, Lionel, it is never easy discussing money after the deaths of one's beloved friends and distilling the life summary equation in terms of monetary figures," Brad softly replied, as he gently patted Lionel on the shoulder.

Lionel took a healthy mouthful of scotch, finishing off the fiery, peaty nectar of the Highlands and then added, "Yet these final things must be done, my boy, for the dignity of the dead and for the future of the living, please always do good by your parents' legacy and their fortune, Brad." Lionel politely left Brad to ponder in solitude his monumental estate summary.

Brad did a quick mental calculation of his present financial situation and it turned out that his inheritance was to be $19.5 billion, the Hamilton Family Trust $4.8 billion; another $200+ million per annum from the salary and bonuses at Hamilton & MacAlister; and finally, there was his own personal net worth, which was presently about $3.3 billion. This was a vast, almost embarrassing sum of money for someone in his late thirties and he began to realize that he had a deep personal responsibility for the stewardship of this vast financial holding. 'Fate' if you could call it that, had enshrined Bradford W. Hamilton one of the richest, semi-anonymous men in the country.

He vowed to himself to continue the Trust's philanthropic efforts of providing opportunities and benefits to those who needed assistance the most – the individual people themselves, rather than the large established charitable institutions, which often consumed .85 cents out of every donated dollar on overhead and administrative charges. From reading the letters of gratitude and condolences, Brad knew that the most efficient and gratifying form of charitable donation was to make any charity contributions as directly personal as possible to the given recipient, thus encumbering few or no middlemen and the associated bureaucratic overhead expenses.

He discovered from conversations with his parents, that 30-45% of their charitable contributions went to individual people or families. Brad thought that at least initially, 45-50% of the Trust's revenue streams should be divested to individuals or families, while the remaining funds could be devoted to the larger institutional charities and educational institutions. This was a prudent strategy, Brad mused, since people like Margie DeTagelio's family were assisted directly by being a recipient of the Hamilton Trust, this allowed her and her siblings to attend institutions of higher education without assuming the burden of 'needs testing' or administrative ineptitude.

Brad started to assume a very positive attitude, as he envisioned himself assuming a hands-on, pro-active position for himself in the local community. He had finally discovered his purpose to live!

Unexpectedly, there was a short, sharp knock upon Brad's office door – it was Katherine and she was wearing a broad hopeful smile as she entered Brad's office and proceeded to walk over to his desk. He looked up and smiled back at Katherine. It was the first time that she had seen him smile so genuinely since the death of his family; 'something good must have come from his conversation with Daddy,' Katherine pleasantly concluded. She gently placed her arms around his neck. "My darling Brad – I just wanted to come by and see if you wanted to have anything to eat; when was the last time you ate, darling?" Katherine inquired in a friendly and concerned tone.

"Thank you for the offer, Kate, but I'm not too hungry," Brad responded shyly.

"Now look here, handsome, you have to start living and to take care of yourself, Brad, I'm not going to let my future husband waste away on me!" Kate nervously responded with righteous concern.

He knew that Katherine loved and cared deeply for him and he didn't want to hurt her feelings, she was the only person that he was close to after the death of his family. She had stayed loyally by his side while other social grievers had discreetly melted away.

"Oh Kate, I'm sorry about this morning and for the past few weeks. I'll try to get back on track soon, I really mean it this time!" Brad added with genuine affirmation. Kate smiled as she saw that Brad's attitude and demeanour was vastly improved from their initial morning encounter and she needed to encourage this attitude.

"I was just going through some condolences and I was really impressed by my parents' role in the community over the years and Lionel just called me and stated that I was the Governor Trustee of the 'Arthur & Gloria Hamilton Charitable Trust'. I realize now that I want to take an active role in this capacity, Kate, I want to carry on their charitable work, Kate," Brad stated with a voice of determination and authority.

"Perfect, absolutely perfect! I think that's a marvellous idea, Brad, you're going to be a great Governor Trustee of the Foundation, I'm very proud for you Brad!" Katherine beamed as she gave him a huge embrace and tender kiss. She was so very thankful that Brad may have found the catalyst necessary to bring him back from the abyss of his depression and to inspire a worthy cause for his life.

"Is there anything that I can do for you in your capacity as Governor Trustee?" Katherine inquired.

"Not right now, but thanks for asking, Kate. Your dad informed me that my role of Governor Trustee will become effective very soon; however, the Hamilton family probate will take another six months, but you will be playing a major part in the Hamilton Trust after we're married, Kate," Brad added.

Katherine's eyes beamed when Brad mentioned their future wedding. "Brad, you don't know how happy you make me feel when you talk like that, I want us to get married as soon as you're feeling well enough," Kate responded and hoping that Brad could supply some hint of when their wedding day would occur. "Well then perhaps, Brad, we can start planning for an Autumn wedding?" Kate replied with a not-so-subtle nudging hint.

He gently took Kate's hands and tenderly caressed her fingers, then slowly pulled her body toward him. Brad hugged Kate in a prolonged embrace, it was good to feel her warmth and the rapid beating of her heart. He was glad that he was in love with a beautiful, intelligent woman, she was both his lover and closest friend.

"Kate, I'm taking off a little early today, I want to get back to Greystone, get a good meal, get cleaned-up too! I have to think some things over, and get a good night's rest for once...my head is buzzing with the possibilities of being Governor Trustee of the Hamilton Trust," Brad whispered softly into Kate's ear.

"Well of course, my dearest Brad...naturally, go whenever you need to go, my darling. Now do you want me to come over tonight, Brad?" Kate gently inquired.

Brad smiled at the seductive suggestion as he gave his reply, "Kate, you've done more than enough already, I need some quiet time tonight, but I'll see you first thing tomorrow morning, with no lateness, no tears, and no more St. Giles – if that's okay with you?"

Kate smiled back, then smartly replied, "That's a deal, Brad, but if you change your mind tonight, I'm just a call away!" She regrettably realized that Brad wasn't ready for romance, but Greystone was a cavernous and now rather empty 50-room mansion and Brad was probably very lonely being there with just memories and the Hamilton estate caretaker couple. Any dwelling needed human souls to make it come alive.

He decided to quit work at 3:30 PM; and quickly signed the few final documents on his desk. Any errant items that arose, Katherine could sign, since both she and Lionel also possessed executive signature authority for all official correspondence at Hamilton & MacAlister. As a courtesy he bid a nightly farewell to both Lionel and Kate. He vowed to them both, an on-time arrival the next morning and there was a spark of resolution in his voice. This encouraged both Lionel and Katherine, even though they each realized that Brad was far from a complete recovery from his depression. As far as Brad, he was just looking forward to going home to Greystone Manor, consuming a home-made dinner and having some 'thinking time' in more comfortable surroundings than that of a mere workplace environment.

Upon exiting the Hamilton & MacAlister building, Brad was mildly surprised to find that the cool, damp morning had been transformed into a mild, overcast cool Spring day. Before driving away, he placed a brief call to Greystone Manor staff. He drove back home in the hope that this evening would bear no family ghosts to haunt him, nor any black dogs of depression to sullen his spirit.

* * * * * * * * * * * * * * * * * *

Lionel and Faye MacAlister were sitting sedately on an antique 19th century chocolate-coloured Chippendale love seat and sipping on some vintage dry sherry. "Well, Mom and Dad, I need to have a serious discussion with both of you – it's about Brad," Kate nervously confessed, the anxiety was clearly audible in her voice. They were both surprised by their daughter's visit without her first calling them in advance, as this was Kate's usual initial procedure in contacting her parents during their office visits.

"Dad and Mom, what do you think of Brad's condition now? I mean, is he getting any better or do we need professional intervention help?"

Katherine inquired of her parents in a tone of excited concern about her fiancé.

Lionel and Faye looked at one another before answering this loaded question.

"Please, Kate, remember I did tell you that Brad's family tragedy will take serious time for him to work through and I do think that he is on the mend, but I'm no doctor and I can't say exactly when he will fully recover," Faye patiently explained.

While Kate's heard her mother's logical explanation, her facial expression still betrayed a sense of anxiety.

Witnessing the awkward impasse, Lionel decided to add his two cents' worth of opinion to the discussion. "Well for what it's worth, Kate, I spoke with Brad today concerning the Hamilton Trust and he seemed quite excited by this topic and his future in the role of Governor Trustee," Lionel quibbled.

"Oh, please, Daddy, we're not talking business here, we're talking about Brad's mental well-being, I don't see how you could discuss this with Brad at a time like this!" Kate chided back in obvious discomfort of her father's business-related remark.

Seeking only to reassure his beloved daughter, Lionel continued his thoughts, "Now just wait a minute, Kate, what I mean to say is that Brad and I discussed the Hamilton Trust, and Brad was personally excited by the prospect of becoming the Governor of the Hamilton Trust and to assist disadvantaged people just as his parents had done. I think that this means that Brad is still firmly anchored to reality and that he wants to live to do positive things for others, in addition to running the firm. We conversed as a father and son would have talked and I think that Brad just needs some more time to recover, yet I believe that all three of us can get him through this tragic period if we exert support and patience," Lionel exclaimed earnestly to both wife and daughter.

With a brilliant gleam, Katherine's eyes leaped with joy at the positive tone and judgment that her father had just rendered concerning Brad's mental attitude and future prospect for recovery. "Oh Daddy, that would sure be wonderful if Brad could start to become his old self again. Yes, the Hamilton Trust is a good way for him to ease his way back into health and society. You can guide Brad through the Trust details and I can ease him back slowly into the Investment Banking business, these will both serve to keep him busy and improve his mental health," Kate joyfully cried out, as she rushed to hug her parents and glad to believe that her Brad was not a total psychic case.

"Just hold on a minute, my overly anxious daughter, this recovery is not going to be easy for him, Kate, and remember that he will need time in his recovery!" Lionel whispered in his daughter's ear.

"I don't care how long it takes, Dad and Mom, as long as I get Brad back, that's all that matters to me," Kate replied as she gently sobbed in the arms of her father.

* * * * * * * * * * * * * * * * *

CHAPTER 2

'Go West, Troubled Man, Go West'

*"I want to help people and continue to administer the
Hamilton Trust in the manner my parents did."*

W ithin the confines of the steel-grey coloured granite
mansion, the caretakers of the Hamilton estate steadily
worked throughout the day on their methodological tasks
with an almost reverent manner. Over the course of several decades, the
quantity and quality of the servants employed at the Hamilton Manor
had ever steadily declined. It was increasingly difficult to attract high
quality European servants, who had in earlier times eagerly gave their
lives and loyalty to their wealthy employers in return for guaranteed
lodging, subsistence, and a modest salary. It was a symbiotic relationship
which served both parties equally well, yet it was a figment of the past.
The times had changed, and the great pool of European immigration
had begun to ebb just after World War II and the children of the servants
wanted no part of their parents' trade, instead desiring greater upward
opportunities in the world outside of the estate. The full time, on-
demand estate servant had become virtually extinct.

Eventually, the Ultra-rich were relegated to hiring servants from
developing, third-world nations. These foreign workers were either
in-house staff or day labourers. For the majority of the Ultra rich,
the latter alternative of employing daily employees was the preferred
hiring option. The day labourer worked the standard 9:00 AM– 5:00
PM workday and then leaving the estate at the close of each workday,
thus being free to live at their own private dwellings. If cooking was

required or that of the services of a chauffeur, then arrangement and schedules were made accordingly, yet for most domestic staff, the hours were a standard 40-hour workweek. Evening and overtime tasks were compensated accordingly, yet even this practice was the exception to the rule, save for those special holiday parties or rare events such as birthdays or weddings.

It was 35 years ago since the Hamilton family lost their beloved butler, Geoffrey, to a long, but well overdue retirement back to his native England. The Hamilton family felt as if they had lost a lifelong family member. Both Arthur and Gloria chose not to seek a replacement manor butler – in reality, they both realized that Geoffrey was as irreplaceable as a close friend. The employ of a 24 x 7-manor servant to be at the 'beck & call' of the master and mistress of the manor was not a realistic solution. Additionally, the social trends in America were making it exceedingly more difficult to maintain the strict social divisions between an employed resident manor servant with that of the immediate family, without having the relationship deteriorate or morph into a partisan or familiar situation, neither of which was conducive to a healthy employee-employer relationship.

Now only two full-time resident servants remained at Greystone Manor. Along with Brad Hamilton, these three people filled the massive fifty room mansion, with most of these rooms now mostly vacant, save for the ghosts of memories past. The death of the Hamilton family members had served to make an already massive white elephant of a dwelling seem even more cold, detached, and empty. Arthur had inherited the Greystone estate from his father William. Greystone was built in 1915 and like most things in life, it had long ago outlived its utility. Massively constructed, it served only as a vestige of a gilded age long since forgotten. Yet for Brad, Greystone was his life's very foundation, it remained the only thing in this world that he possessed that would not die or betray him.

"Are you done fixing the loose garage handle?" resounded the petite and well-toned Philippine woman. There was no immediate answer to the woman's question. Again, she inquired, this time quite a bit more loudly than her first iteration, "Juan are you deaf? I said, are you done working on the garage door problem?"

A loud and obviously annoyed verbal response echoed back in a well-toned masculine voice that respired with the ever-slightest kiss of a Philippine accent. "What in the devil are you shouting, Carla, I didn't quite hear you?" responded the low gravel-toned masculine voice.

The woman continued her lament to her husband. "It has been like a graveyard around here since that terrible day in February," Carla sighed. "When I think back and remember those early days of children screaming, playing, and running around here....it just makes me want to cry," Carla muttered out in a sudden burst of tears. Juan gently, yet firmly hugged his arms around his wife and threw through back in deep despair as well. Juan and Carla embraced each other, as they both dreamed of happier times, back to their early lives when they had both emigrated from the Philippines several decades ago.

Carla continued her verbal grieving to her husband. "I think that I can no longer love this place of Greystone. I think that I am actually starting to hate this place... I hate it for the memories ...it holds nothing but sorrow for me now. I can just close my eyes and I see Mr Arthur Hamilton in his study reading, I remember Mrs Hamilton dressed like a Queen and entertaining all those fancy rich people, I see Robert and Melissa arguing about the latest school gossip and events...it's all just memories now!" Carla sobbed.

Juan's eyes welled with tears upon hearing and remembering these fond memories.

"Yes, my dear wife, I feel the same way too, but we are old now and this is our home too, it's been our life," Juan pensively reflected. Carla thought about the past 40 plus years, which she and Juan had spent at Greystone Manor. Even her children had enjoyed the amenities of Greystone Manor and the philanthropy of the Hamilton family, a luxury that could not be matched by even the income and lifestyle of an upper middle-class American family. The almost cloistered thoughts came flooding back to Carla of those fond times of the Hamilton children playing on the lawn swings on a hot summer day, of the children sledding down the huge estate hills on a wind gusted winter retreat, or of the elegant Spring lawn garden parties that Arthur and Gloria sponsored for their wealthy friends and neighbours each year! All these fond memories only served to agonize the Lopez's hearts.

Both Juan and Carla knew that Greystone would always be their home, this despite their servant status. The Hamiltons were like blood relatives to them and they felt that this sentiment was a mutual, if unspoken attitude shared by the Hamilton family. The Lopez and Hamilton families traced their mutual roots back to the Cold War, when Arthur Hamilton was serving as an Army ASA Voice Intercept and Linguist specialist and later as an Army Security Agency (ASA) Company Commander. Juan Lopez was a 16-year-old Philippine Army linguist, who was fluent in English, Chinese, and Korean. Juan was under-aged for even the Philippine Army, but he had lied about his age and he looked older than his youth.

Duty in the Philippine Army was a much better choice than begging in the streets of Manila, he wisely calculated. The Philippines after World War II was an impoverished nation and the post war governments had robbed the national treasury for many decades, leaving the country in utter poverty, yet the people were industrious and they sought out foreign work employment whenever this became possible. There was little practicality to staying in school, especially when everyone needed work to support the family, so entire families made their livelihood by out-sourcing their human capital to the Middle East, Asia, Australia and America.

The Lopez family consisted of Juan's aging mother and six other children. Juan's father had been taken prisoner by the Imperial Japanese Army and forced to work as a construction labourer. The Lopez family never saw their father again, nor learned of his fate. They objectively summarized that he was worked to death as a slave labourer, one of the countless and undocumented casualties of World War II. When the Cold War arose from the ashes of World War II, Juan volunteered for military service, as this afforded him extra hazardous pay for the family needs and he got additional opportunities for rank and training. Juan served as a Korean and Chinese translator and transcriber - working on intercepted communication reports from voice radio sources. Arthur Hamilton and Juan crossed paths and Arthur was so impressed with Juan's language skills and judgment that he requested Juan's support for operations involving his own Company unit. Due to security concerns, Juan was not directly part of Arthur's ASA unit; however, he did provide dedicated linguistic and transcription support for certain other critical administrative tasks. The two men developed a lasting and mutual respect for one another, Juan seeing Arthur as his missing father figure and Arthur seeing Juan as the younger brother he never had.

After his military service obligation was completed, Arthur promised Juan that he would assist him immigrate to the US, provided that Juan return back to school and finish his education. In addition, Arthur obligated Juan to promise to send back a percentage of his future US wages, this to help support his mother and siblings. Juan eagerly accepted the offer – he admired Arthur Hamilton and it was an excellent opportunity to immigrate to the land of opportunity, the United States of America. Both were men of sound moral character. Juan continued with his military service and he took the opportunity to take various night school classes. It was while attending one of these night classes in Manila that Juan met his future wife, Carla. She was studying to become a nurse. The two fell instantly in love and each of them wanted to get married, yet each knew that education was their key out of poverty and the Philippines. They each concentrated on their schooling and they had both completed it during the mid 1960s.

Over the years, Juan stayed in contact with Arthur Hamilton, who was also pursuing his higher education by finishing his MBA at Harvard Business School. Arthur was also thinking about his future and that of marrying the wealthy socialite Gloria Theresa Worthington. Arthur knew that eventually he and his new bride would need domestic staff and who better than Juan and his nurse wife Carla? Both Juan and Carla were very industrious and trustworthy, besides they all liked one another and got along remarkably well. With the formidable help of Arthur Hamilton and Juan's past military assistance to the US Army, the couple easily immigrated to the USA. The Hamiltons and Lopezes became an intangible team, as both Juan and Carla quickly adapted to the prosperity and good life of the Swinging American 1960s.

Over the course of the years, Juan was to become a jack-of-all-trades to Arthur Hamilton, to include chauffeur, chief auto mechanic, manor handyman, and finally chief groundskeeper. Carla was a trained nurse and occupied herself by working a full workweek at Boston General Hospital's peadiatrics department. Over time, she supplemented her modest income by working part-time as Gloria Hamilton's personal cook, baby-sitter, and even housekeeper. Some 15 years ago, Carla retired from her increasingly demanding nursing position and devoted her later years by attending to Gloria Hamilton's personal affairs, to include that of becoming de facto 'social supervisor' of the Greystone Manor. Carla mainly performed minor cleaning tasks and prepared the personal meals of Arthur, Gloria, and the entire Hamilton family. Eventually, Carla took her formal education at the Culinary Institute of America in Hyde Park, New York, where she had learned to prepare and serve the finest of Classical French and American cuisine, all of the Hamiltons became especially fond of Carla's blending of Oriental and American style of cooking, especially her exotic and delicate use of spices and marinating.

The high-table fancy French cooking was mainly reserved for special social events and parties, while traditional hearty American fare filled out the normal family dining menu.

Juan and Carla initially lived in the massive carriage house upper floor area of the Greystone estate's spacious 14-car garage. It was a most adequate space with bathroom, kitchen, and modest living quarters. It was here that they raised their three children: John, Hector, and Mary. The Lopez children often played on the estate lawn with both the Hamilton children and 'Katie' MacAlister. All of the children got along together famously and the large number of children made for the playing in the tree house and volleyball games, a lot more fun, especially as all the children lived close to one another and were of the same age groups. The winter sledding was especially joyful with everyone getting their sleds and ploughing down the steep Greystone manor snow covered hills like little daredevils.

The inherent social disparity among the children never seemed to matter very much, that is not until the later teenage years, the consciousness of social peer pressures and possessions suddenly seemed to drop like an 'Iron Curtain' over the children's relationships with one other. Mary Lopez and Kate MacAlister became distant, as Mary's ethnic Philippine background and physical appearance distanced her socially from wealthy white Boston adolescent elite. Indeed, it seemed that innocence and fun belonged to the domain of the young or naive.

The passage of years brought the knowledge and self-consciousness of wealth and social disparity. Suddenly, it began to matter what other people thought, especially in the small community of the Ultra-rich. It was an invisible prejudice, nothing was ever openly spoken or announced, the prejudice was of the ugliest kind: unseen, unspoken and quietly enforced. The prejudice was evidenced in its subtle actions, social manifestations, and unspoken exclusions. Among the Hamilton children, Brad retained the closest links to the Lopez children. It broke the hearts of Juan and Carla to know that their children were being treated as second-class children just because of their background, physical appearances, and social standing, yet they were realists to the raw facts of the world and they compensated for this external prejudice by devoting even more time and love to their children.

The Lopez family retreated into a cocoon of mutual love and close family – a trait so often found to be missing in post-modern white American families. Neither Gloria nor Arthur approved of the Ultra-rich prejudicial treatment, yet they were powerless to change it. The Hamiltons sought to practise their own form of 'social democracy' – this through the establishment of the 'Arthur & Gloria Hamilton Charitable Trust.' With this powerful charity tool, Arthur and Gloria changed the world, one person and one family at a time. This personal method was more gratifying and useful than merely throwing a wad of cash at a huge institution.

Over the course of the years the bonds between employer and estate employee had grown strong, Arthur and Gloria keenly appreciated the goodness and devotion of Juan and Carla Lopez to the entire Hamilton family and especially the Hamilton children. Juan and Carla presented the perfect opportunity for the socially sheltered Hamilton children to learn the ways and attitudes of a working American family. Both Arthur and Gloria sternly reinforced the notion of respect of all the Hamilton children to adult authority figures and this especially included the Lopezes. Even the aloof and class-conscious Katherine thought of the Lopezes as her kin.

Gloria had always insisted that her children address Juan and Carla as 'Mr' and 'Mrs' and the Lopezes in turn addressed the children in-kind. The Lopez's acted as the domestic 'Uncle' and 'Aunt' for the children and as parent figures when Arthur and Gloria were absent due to travel or other adult obligations. Arthur and Gloria showed their gratitude to the Lopezes in many generous ways. When the Lopez children reached college age, Arthur and Gloria provided a full scholarship fund and stipend for each of the Lopez children. John went on to attend MIT and became an electrical engineer, he was now living on the 'left coast' in San Jose near Silicon Valley, located just outside San Francisco, where he was the co-owner of a prosperous electrical engineering firm. Hector attended Haverford University in Philadelphia and he became a secondary school science teacher at a private boys' school in the Philadelphia bedroom suburb of Valley Forge. Mary commuted to and studied at Boston University, specializing in chemistry and she was now in her final year of residency at the Georgetown University's School of Medicine.

Without question, both the Lopezes and Hamiltons were quite proud of all the children they had raised. Immediately following the death of the Hamilton family, the entire Lopez family returned to Greystone to lend their support to Brad, and for this, he was eternally grateful. Although all the Lopez children kept in e-mail contact with

Bradford Hamilton, they seldom saw him in the flesh anymore. The Lopez children now had their own families and career obligations and each of them returned back to their homes, careers, and lives. Time, distance, and eventually death had all conspired to separate the Hamilton and Lopez children, yet Brad still maintained a warm and devoted relationship with all of them. Juan and Carla remained and served as Brad's Rock of Gibraltar.

* * * * * * * * * * * * * * * * * *

Brad slowly pulled up to the estate's main wrought iron gate, a massive affair that consisted of an 8 foot, tall black painted, highly spiked wrought iron rods, surrounded by the edifice of a huge 10-foot-high, thick solid stone wall. The wall and massive gate definitely presented a serious physical barrier to any innocent intrusions and preying public eyes. Mounted atop and out of reach on each of the stone pillars, there was located a diminutive pair of small electronic cameras, each to which provided both visual and infra-red observation of all persons and vehicles entering and exiting the Greystone manor estate. Located on both sides of this seemingly ancient stone and steel edifice, was located an ultra-modern electronic scanning device and keypad entry board and remote TV camera. This scanning device mandated that the visitor to the gate present either a coded card accompanied by a secret code or that the visitor push a large red button and request permission for entry and exit from the manor security staff, in this case, this was to be either Carla or Juan Lopez.

The massive Bentley sedan creeped up to the main manor gates and stopped, Brad flashed his magnetic ID card, then rapidly entered a secret 8-digit code into the security pad. A surveillance camera also recorded his vehicle's details into a computerized data bank that was archived and updated every 30 days automatically by a private security service.

The old massive wrought iron gate slowly creaked open and Brad drove the sedan up the winding tree lined driveway, then into the cavernous garage. The garage door had been automatically activated for opening when Brad had entered his secret code into the cipher pad and this saved him the problem of opening the garage door with another remote device. It also signalled to the Lopezes that Mr Brad Hamilton had arrived home for the evening.

Upon exiting the Bentley, he activated the garage door and alarm, then walked slowly to the side door of Greystone manor, not wanting or needing the formality of a grand main door entrance. Instead, Brad most often used the manor's kitchen-pantry side door entrance, as it was more intimate and natural for him to do so, especially these days when the only manor companions he could rely upon was that of Carla and Juan, and this was a natural area where either of them tended to congregate. A large, empty manor was not a very inviting venue. Ever since he was a small boy, Brad loved the kitchen-pantry area of the manor most, and what child wouldn't, the kitchen was where all the food and goodies were stored. As the oldest Hamilton child, he was assured 'special treats' from the kitchen staff and even the stoic old Geoffrey turned a blind eye to the favouritism afforded to Brad.

As a child, his character was that of a shy, introverted, highly intelligent child, who always aimed to please the expectations of his parents and elders. Some would consider this to be passiveness in a child, but to Brad it illustrated good manners and obedience to authority. Rarely a quarrelsome child, Brad sought consensus and cooperation to 'get his way'. By the time that Brad was a young adult, he was a master of his congenial-self; conversely, this amiable trait served him exceedingly well in the business community.

"Hello Carla? Juan? I'm back!" Brad confidently announced as he unlocked the pantry door and peered into the kitchen area. He heard no acknowledgment.

"I'm home! Hello, Juan... Carla?" Brad repeated as he looked around the kitchen and finding no one present. However, he immediately smelled the delicious and rich scent of a seafood casserole cooking in one of the huge stainless-steel Viking ovens that were recessed and encased in a deep red brick kitchen enclave. The delicious cooking seafood aroma, of which he was quite familiar and singularly fond, quickly rekindled fond memories of his childhood and adolescent days. His appetite was abated by his daily depression and the visit to St. Giles earlier that day. Yet this evening for him was more upbeat and his mood was more relaxed and sedate than in days past and this was definitely a good thing for Brad Hamilton and those who loved him.

Carla was just returning with some old laundry taken from the second-floor laundry bin; when she thought that she heard someone in the manor kitchen area and she suspected that it was either her husband Juan or Mr Brad Hamilton. The manor was very well alarmed and only a few select members now possessed access keys and passwords for unfettered access to the manor and its property.

"Oh, hello, Mr Brad, how nice it is to see you this evening and how was your day?" Carla inquired and with the maternal concern of a mother for a child.

"It was quite good, Carla. I just wanted to come home a little early from the firm, there was not too much happening there for me today, so an early day was in order," Brad jested in an upbeat tone.

"I have placed all your mail on the desk in the study, Mr Brad, is that okay?" Carla politely inquired.

"Certainly, thank you very much, Carla," he dryly responded.

"Also, I have cooked one of your favourite meals, Mr Brad, New England seafood casserole in a sweet bread pastry shell." Carla smiled, knowing that this was a weekly favourite of Mr Brad's ever since he was a small boy. She hoped that enjoying some of his beloved meals would help lift Mr Brad's spirits.

Brad smiled and appreciated the concerted trouble that Carla had obviously made to prepare one of his favourite dinners. "Oh yes and it smells terrific too! Thank you very much, Carla, it's nice to know that you remember some of my special meals and that you went through all the trouble of preparing this for me, it's a lot of effort to prepare!" he replied to Carla as he bent over and then softly kissed her on the forehead in a motherly manner. Brad had never formerly shown such direct affection to Carla, aside from an occasional kiss on the cheek at Christmas or on her birthday, yet now he felt the need to do so. Carla had become the closest thing to his mom than anyone else alive. If he couldn't show Carla some affection at this point in his life, then he was indeed a dead fish of a soul. Instead of being taken aback, Carla blushed with the proudness of a natural mother.

"Carla, I'm going upstairs to shower and relax a little before dinner," Brad proclaimed almost in a tone of childish permission rather than adult emancipation.

"Oh, that's very good, Mr Brad, everything should be ready in about 90 minutes or so, I will call you when everything is ready!" she gleefully replied.

"That will be fine with me," Brad responded as he smiled and walked to the study to dutifully review his mail.

The Greystone manor was a massive and ornate architectural beast. Its exterior and interior design was based on a grand 19th century English manor house, to include the grey stone exterior and an ornate grand halls and staircases within the interior, from the exterior stonework. Fine exotic woods and ornately carved stone works were in abundance, no expense was not spared, and the Hamiltons had the cash to spend. The colour of the stonework thus bestowed the name of the Greystone mansion, to include the English spelling of the name. The great reception hall and English Edwardian styled study were two of the more expensively attired suites of the mansion, but these rooms were used mostly by his parents than by Brad or his siblings, as the Hamilton children preferred more the sedate comforts of their individual bedrooms, which were generously spacious for their individual needs.

Whereas once Juan and Carla had initially resided above the massive Greystone garage, throughout the past 10 years, they now resided on one of the several cottage guesthouses which dotted about the Greystone manor. With their children now adults, the Lopezes wanted their own separate space and the ease of single-storey living. The English tudor-styled 3,400 square foot cottage provided a quaint and comfortable relief from the imposing, lifeless, cold Greystone manor. Both Carla and Juan felt sorry for Mr Brad living all alone in the massive, empty manor house. They dreamed that he would marry Miss Katherine and again fill the manor with the welcoming voices of playful little children.

Quickly scanning the pile of mail, he was once again reminded of the life and death of his family, this by the continuous flow of letters of sympathy cards that still had arrived several months after their deaths. 'It was a strange thing – this thing called death,' that Brad pondered to himself. "It proved to be both a sinkhole of emptiness and also a well of fond remembrances." After more than over 30 years of living in Boston's High Society, he knew the names of every prominent American family and many foreign ones as well, to include those of royalty. Without having to open a single envelope, he knew that the preponderance of the correspondences were of polite and requisite sympathy which upper-class courtesy so demanded. He simply left these envelopes unopened for the time being. Yet, just as was the case in the Hamilton & MacAlister office, he also spied a generous pile of envelopes from unknown people as well.

Opening and reading one such letter, Brad immediately knew what all the other letters were going to relate. Additionally, there were letters and notes from the many benefactors of Arthur and Gloria Hamilton's generosity and charity. Again, these correspondences brought a smile and comfort to Brad. He could not bear to open any more letters this evening, but he vowed in time to reply to each sympathy card or letter that was sent to him. He would get Margie to assist him in ensuring that a formal and courteous reply was sent to each sender. Concerning those particular notes and letters that were received from his parents' charitable efforts, Brad was going to personally answer these correspondences. This was the least he could do to honour his deceased parents and it was also the proper thing to do. He resolved to have a good long hot shower and a sip of richly aged Cognac XO before dinner.

Turning off the den lights, he loosened his silk red tie and removed his crumpled and soiled cashmere pinstripe, double-breasted suit jacket, carelessly throwing it onto an empty, silk tufted winged chair. He made his slow way along the long and winding grand manor staircase. The destination was his singular sanctuary of security, his boyhood bedroom suite. Strangely, he instantly remembered the voice of his mother scolding him about running up and down the main mansion staircase and ordering him to use the secondary pantry stairway instead. He smiled faintly at this warm childhood antic recollection, which had emerged from the cobweb of his mind.

It was a mentally long and tiring day, he felt exhausted, even though his work tasks were not laborious in any sense of the word. His depression had a strange way of slowing his body down and robbing it of the essence to live. 'There was more to life than mere breathing and subsistence,' he reasoned. He needed to find the means to rejuvenate his spirit, lest he was going to continue to waste away in both body and soul. Brad was looking forward to a long and relaxing hot shower to help loosen up his tense body and spirit.

Strolling up the cavernous and now empty grand staircase, he was transported back in time to those magnificent grand parties that his mother so proudly orchestrated. He fondly remembered peeping out, along with his little brother and his sister, from the 2nd storey grand staircase balcony to secretly gaze at the soft candlelight and crystal chandelier lighting that dazzled the magnificent dresses and jewellery of the beautifully adorned ladies, who were all attired in full length exquisite evening gowns, exotic perfumes, glittering diamonds, and long white evening gloves; while the men were equally richly adorned in formal white-tie & tails, and an assortment of solid gold cuff links and watches. The clinking of champagne glasses, the smell of beautiful fragrances, and the soft tunes of a string quartet- could all be imbued amidst the mild chatter of feminine and masculine laughter and muffled discussions. The woman conversed of the latest scandals and of the sexual escapades of other couples, while the men spoke of business, wealth, and politics. It was a social ritual not far removed from those social gatherings from the past, which had beset all other generations and which would go probably on through time immemorial. This was the secret and unknown world of adult society, a world, which children could only speculate and imagine, yet each Hamilton child knew that they would be participating in similar fare upon their transition into adulthood. Discretely, Juan and Carla allowed the Hamilton children to spy from atop the grand stairway onto these rich adult events, knowing that the children needed some exposure to the Ultra-rich social world that they each would inhabit one day.

Despite their comparatively low social standing and modest backgrounds when compared to the Ultra-rich, even Carla and Juan marvelled at the display of magnificence, refinement, and high social manners displayed by America's most elite society. Like many immigrants to the USA, their dreams were not fostered by petty jealousy of their wealthy employers, rather it was their aspiration that through hard work and a little luck, maybe one day their descendants too could be part of this American Dream of 'rags-to-riches'. It was quite the thing of American culture for one to benignly envy and desire another's trappings of luxury and wealth, yet not to harbour hatred for those who possessed it.

Wearily he trudged into his bedroom, ritually turning on the light switch as he had done countless times throughout his life. His room was both a showroom and evolution of his life, with articles of his childhood intermixed with elements and materials from his adulthood. Brad wearily discarded his clothes and entered into his sultan-sized bathroom chamber. The bathroom was a massive 25 by 30-foot room, which contained a most ornate multi-faceted shower, a huge bathtub and whirlpool bath, a bidet, and a mirrored dressing area. He stripped off his rumpled garments, turned the shower faucets on full power, and enjoyed a long 20-minute steaming shower. Like many males, Brad preferred showers to a soaking bath and he liked his showering to be sinfully long and hot. The simmering water seemed to erase the bad feelings of the morning; it made him feel thankful to be alive. After 20 minutes of this water-fest hedonism, Brad finally left his shower; he felt and looked like a fine Boston lobster, of which he was an avid connoisseur. He towelled himself off, combed his chocolate brown hair, and attired himself in a thick white terry cloth robe, embroidered with the initials BWH arrayed in a fancy gold metal embroidery thread. Carla was always mindful that each Hamilton family member have a fresh and ready robe available each day. Brad still cherished this luxury and he prayed that this attention would not leave his life any time soon. He quickly gazed at his massive platinum diamond Rolex watch and noticed that he still had at least 30 minutes before dinner, so he elected to relax and perhaps enjoy a short drink.

Brad maintained a small liquor cart in his room, it contained three different types of scotch, bourbon, Canadian whiskey, vodka, gin, Cognac XO, and a bottle of aged Port. He poured a two-ounce serving of fine Cognac XO brandy from a heavy lead crystal decanter into a classic crystal snifter glass and relaxed into a huge reading chair. He placed his feet up on a footrest and slowly sipped the velvety, yet slightly burning tasting spirit. He closed his eyes and thought of the day's affairs and his future.

He pondered warm thoughts of marrying Kate and he knew that the MacAlisters were like second family to him, but still he wondered, 'was getting married and simply working at Hamilton & MacAlister – all that awaited him or was there something greater to life?' His middle-age years were upon him, so the question greatly haunted him.

He took another sip of Cognac XO, cherishing its warm, soothing, and sensory dulling effects. The soothing warm liquor was inviting enough to justify another small sip, so again, he closed his eyes, and once more, he thought deep and long. Again, he thought back on the day's events. 'The morning at St. Giles was a complete waste of time – it was self-pity, nothing more!' Brad surmised objectively. Kate's suggestion of taking a vacation seemed callous and uncouth, yet her implication of 'taking a break and getting away from it all' – was not a bad idea, as new venues offered new insights and much needed relaxation.

'Getting away from Boston and the firm was a positive and soul enhancing idea indeed!' Brad just had his eureka moment! Brad next turned his thoughts to the item that intrigued him the most – the active participation in the Hamilton Trust. This could be the legacy upon which to build for his family. In time, he could establish separate, dedicated trust funds in the names of his beloved brother and sister, perhaps the Robert & Melissa Hamilton Foundation for disadvantaged bright young people. The possibilities of the Hamilton Trust intrigued Brad, yet he was disturbed by his utter lack of understanding and maturity to administer the Trust. He compared himself to his parents and found himself totally inadequate. His life experiences were too sparse.

He didn't want to be the distant and wealthy administrator of a charity that merely dispersed money like a Santa Claus; instead, he wanted to administer the Trust exactly as his mother and father had done, that is, doing the charity directly and this meant being a hands-on Governor Trustee! However, there was one problem, his parents were not alive to show him the 'Hamilton way' for personal charitable giving, they had provided no roadmap or instructions to him. The Trust charity administrators like Mrs Peet could only provide him with administrative guidance. 'People, yes everyday people and their specific needs were the key to both administering and awarding the Trust monies,' Brad surmised in smug, self-satisfaction.

Unexpectedly, a loud knock upon the bedroom door suddenly punctuated Brad's early evening sojourn. "Dinner is now served, Mr Hamilton!" Carla politely announced through the massive oak door. She patiently waited a few minutes and heard nothing. "Mr Hamilton, Mr Brad are you awake? Dinner is served!" Carla eagerly repeated. Brad awoken from his twilight-like trance, opened his eyes, and slowly put the heavy lead crystal glass onto an adjacent nightstand.

"Yes, yes, of course, Carla. Thank you, I'll be down in ten minutes," Brad wearily responded. Carla was glad to hear the voice of Mr Brad, as she was always frightened that he might despair of his plight and perhaps do some foolish harm to himself. This act would have destroyed Carla and sent her into serious therapy or worse.

"Yes, thank you, Mr Brad, we'll dine in ten minutes then!" Carla replied as she smiled to herself and walked back down to the kitchen to prepare the table setting. Although it was de-regular in high society for the owner of the manor to eat in the pantry kitchen area, Brad insisted on this form of dining whenever the circumstances so permitted – he always liked talking to Carla and Juan when his parents were away from Greystone. It was not a privilege to eat by oneself every night, Brad thought. Unfortunately, this was now the permanent situation of his life, he could not stand to dine in the large, empty dining room, and he desperately wanted the companionship of Juan and Carla, even if they didn't eat meals with him.

* * * * * * * * * * * * * * * * * *

"So, how's your day going, my most beautiful wife?" Juan inquired of Carla, as he affectionately wrapped his arms around his wife's waist.

Carla couldn't help but contently smile, as many happy wives often do when their lifelong companions pay them a loving compliment. For many wives, these words came seldom, if ever at all. "Oh, very good, my dearest husband," Carla replied in a complimentary fashion. "Mr Brad said that he will be down for dinner in 10 minutes, Juan, and I have a feeling that his mood is very much better this day," Carla replied to her devoted husband.

"He's been drinking a lot lately, my wife, but the whiskey never solves anything and I hope that he recovers without becoming an alcoholic," Juan factually remarked.

Carla became angry and defensive of Brad. "Now don't you go saying or thinking anything bad about Mr Brad! He's in a bad way for sure, he's lost his family, and both of us are going to help him recover, Juan. I raised Mr Brad like he was our own boy, and, in a way, he is part of us," Carla cried as she turned and rushed into Juan's arms for comfort.

Juan held Carla tight and then whispered gently into her ear, "Not to worry, my wife, we'll take proper care of Mr Brad and help get him through this." Carla looked into Juan's eyes and they both smiled to one another with mutual affection.

"Greetings, folks, what's going on here, this isn't a lover's lane. Let's keep it respectable around Greystone Manor!" Brad jovially proclaimed as he strolled into the Greystone kitchen-pantry, briskly rubbing his hands in hungry anticipation. "I smell something very yummy! Well, so when do we eat?" Brad uttered in eager anticipation.

Both Carla and Juan were amazed at Mr Brad's seemingly positive attitude and extroverted utterances concerning the dinner meal, as he had traditionally shunned any such fare ever since his family's death some six weeks earlier.

"Well, what's the matter? Did I say something wrong? Did I come down too early?" Brad uttered jokingly.

"Why no, not at all, Mr Brad, of course everything is ready for dinner, it's just that we didn't expect to see you so hungry," Carla responded.

"Yes, Mr Brad, forgive my words, but for the past several weeks, your appetite was not so large, so this is a pleasant surprise for both of us," Juan added, as if to deflect any hint of a personal judgment. Faux pas remarks needed to be sheathed and avoided by a manor servant.

"No problem, Juan and Carla, I've been thinking over some things and I have made some decisions, so I want to share these with both of you! A man after a tragedy must get on with his life, don't you both think so?" Brad declared quite bluntly. A worried look enveloped over both Juan's and Carla's face that was quite obvious and disturbing to Brad.

"Oh no, it's not bad news, I think you will both be pleased, it's nothing for either of you to personally fear concerning your place at Greystone, if that's what you're thinking!" Brad comforted to Juan and Carla.

Both Juan and Carla were somewhat relieved by Brad's words, yet they were curious as to what exactly had transformed his previous sullen attitude and what major news he was going to announce? 'Perhaps it was the new marriage date to Miss Katherine?' the couple silently speculated. The decorum of upper-class tradition mandated that they meekly await any further revelation as to this great new mystery.

The rich and flavourful aroma of a traditional New England seafood dinner slowly filled the lower rooms of Greystone Mansion. Deftly, Carla carefully removed the seafood casserole from the Viking stainless steel high temperature oven and placed the heavy, cast-iron cooking pot onto the kitchen-serving table. Next, she presented the double baked potatoes and honey glazed carrots, followed by the baked cheese-flavoured breads. As a last serving act, Carla filled Mr Brad's glass with his favourite raspberry ice tea drink. As so befitted the master of the manor, the dining table was attired only a single setting for one platter and this disturbed Brad. After all, the last thing he needed was to eat alone and not share his conversation with those closest to him, which now meant the company of Carla and Juan. With the greatest of respect, Brad slowly and sincerely explained his personal plight in the most human of terms to his pseudo-parents.

"Juan and Carla, I know that you respect and adhere to the strict traditions upon which you were raised and practised, but I need your company and companionship now more than ever. You both helped to raise me, you are like family to me, despite what my social peers may say. I understand and respect the traditional manner courtesy that you still extend to me after all these years and I thank you sincerely. Yet I think under the strained circumstances of the past few months, that perhaps, we can relax some of our formalities to one another and right now in my life, I need friends so much more than I do that of mere servants," Brad explained slowly as tears began to fill his eyes, as he nervously glanced down at the floor. "If it disturbs you to sit here at the table with me, then please merely stay here in the kitchen, you can eat at the food service island and let's talk about the future!" Brad pleaded like an innocent lost boy.

The older couple wearily moved toward each other and embraced their arms around one another's shoulders. After a moment of silence, Juan and Carla again looked at each other ever so briefly and then Juan spoke out, 'Whatever you want us to do, Mr Brad, we are here for you!" All three of them embraced in a warm family style hug, crying and smiling at each other with child-like affection. A short, silent prayer was invoked by all. Carla smiled as she dished out a hearty portion of the seafood entree dinner – while also taking a small portion for both herself and her husband. They both uneasily sat facing Brad at the kitchen food serving island area located directly across from Brad. Both Juan and Carla were greatly heartened that Mr Brad had finally come out of his self-imposed exile and that he was enjoying eating again with a cosy family style meal in the manor's kitchen nook area.

Brad easily settled down to enjoy his first real full course meal since the demise of his family many weeks ago. He relished the fabulous feast laid out correctly before him; it all reminded him of his happy childhood. The food was not that of stuffy European haute cuisine, rather it was simple, rich and hearty New England fare that filled the stomach and placed meat on the bones. The kitchen aromas, colours, and noise were childhood memory true. During his eager consumption of a second bountiful serving of seafood casserole, double roasted potatoes, honey glazed carrots and baked cheese biscuits, Brad had decided to let Juan and Carla into his private confidence concerning his plans. "Well, family, I have been thinking about my future, that is, about life and things, and I think that I have good news for everyone," he explained as he placed his fork into the golden-brown seafood casserole crust and began to munch on a piece of shrimp and crabmeat. Both Juan and Carla looked at each other nervously, then back again to Brad.

"I want to perform and accomplish some of the fine things that my parents did, I mean through the Hamilton Trust Governorship," Brad snapped out loudly as he took a bite of Carla's homemade biscuits and dunked a piece of it into the rich seafood bisque gravy that amply filled the inner filling of the seafood casserole. Brad then continued to speak with an increased excitement, "I want to help downtrodden people and continue to administer the Hamilton Trust in the manner my parents did! I want to make a difference in this world and in this very short thing we call life. I want for my life to count for something good when I one day cash in my earthly chips!"

Carla and Juan eyed each other again and they both smiled to one another. Yet Brad had more to confess, so much more in fact, as he continued to verbally detail his plan in extemporaneous fashion.

"But I also need to get away from Boston and clear my brain out a bit!" Brad added as he placed a piece of tender lobster into his mouth.

This statement startled both Juan and Carla, as they eyed each other in amazement. Carla spoke first and with the greatest of nervousness. "Then you are leaving us for good, Mr Brad?" she inquired in a frightened tone. Brad noticed Carla's concern and he immediately allayed these by smiling and patting her gently on the hands.

"Oh, no, no...of course not, Carla!" Brad immediately responded, then quickly adding, "Greystone, Boston, the Firm, and both of you – are all a big part of me and I will never leave any of these things permanently," he explained with the utmost sincerity in his voice.

Still puzzled at Brad's explanation, Juan then asked the second question, "Then you are going on a vacation, Mr Brad? Perhaps you are going away with Miss MacAlister?" he added nervously and in fear that he was perhaps asking Mr Brad too personal of a question.

From Juan and Carla's questions, Brad knew that his statements were insufficient in detail, so he pushed his finished platter aside and gave a more complete description of his plan. "I'm sorry, but I guess that I need to be more precise about my intentions. So here it is, folks, I intend to take some time off and venture forth to see America slowly, up-close and personal. I'm not taking a vacation to sit out on a beach and relax, instead I'm going out alone and traveling to see a bit of this big fine country and its everyday people. I may be gone a month or I may be gone a year, but I am coming back to Greystone and when I return back, I am going to concentrate my activities between the Firm and the Hamilton Trust," Brad exclaimed in a determined definitiveness which awed both Carla and Juan.

Immediately, he realized that this was the first time he had defined his exact strategies for his immediate future and his own impromptu words sounded both sane and true, much to his own astonishment. His words continued to pour forth, "I want to get out of Boston and to do unorthodox things; I'm disgusted of living the same old planned and predictable life, I want to see and examine life for myself, I want to be a participant in life, not a mere observer...I don't want to have any regrets when my time is called. I can't continue to live in some remote East Coast office signing letters and cheques without ever knowing what people were actually going through in their lives. Well that's the crux of it, now what do you both think?" Brad inquired of his de facto parents.

The awkward silence hung heavy about the kitchen area. Both Carla and Juan quickly looked at each other with inquisitive stares. They each turned back to Brad to give their opinions, a situation which befuddled them both, but which they felt obligated to render. Again, Carla spoke-up first, "Well, Mr Brad, this sounds good to me, but isn't this a little premature, I mean, have you really thought the plan through?"

Juan immediately added his concerns, "Yes – I too think it is good for you to get away and see other things, but, Mr Brad, it does not seem as if you have everything planned out fully, exactly where are you going and what do you expect to see?"

Brad thought for a few seconds in concentrated determination, he smiled, then he responded, "I thank you both, very good comments, indeed… my quest is not exact, nor are my destinations known, nor do I have specific goals and that is the beauty of it! I just want to go forth across America with no strings, no agenda, no time schedule… I will be travelling free and light. I always did and acted as to that which was expected of me and in the manner prescribed to me by my parents, friends, teachers, peers…so this is my first chance to discover and be myself, Brad Wayne Hamilton. I hardly know myself apart from my indoctrinated and programmed persona! For the first time in my life, I am alone, and I need to discover through my independence exactly who I am, what I like, and what my priorities in life need to be!"

In utter shock, Juan and Carla sat in stoic bewilderment and thought to themselves that this was mere mid-adulthood rebellion.

Carla couldn't bear to keep her supportive feelings about this boyish trek to herself. "In whatever you do, Mr Brad, we are there for you…we just want to ensure that you are safe and well in whatever you decide; we would hate to lose you too," she cried as she hugged Brad like a mother saying goodbye to her own sons.

Instinctively, Juan stood up and placed his arm around Brad in a fatherly form of support. Brad keenly appreciated the affections and feelings that Carla and Juan expressed to him and he reciprocated these in kind. All three souls stood embracing one another for several precious seconds.

"Well, that's enough bonding for one-night, folks, I'll be needing to make some travel preparations, as I want to leave in the morning," Brad declared with great emotion and a tearful smile.

Carla and Juan stared at each other in utter amazement at the suddenness of Brad's proclamation. "So soon to be leaving us, Mr Brad?" Carla sighed.

Brad smiled a broad grin. "Now don't worry, I'll be in touch and I am going to be calling Katherine as well and letting her know the good news too."

Brad suddenly realized that when he left Greystone and Boston, he would be unleashed from every vestige of friend and family which tied him to this earth. The prospect of cutting these ties, even if only temporarily, made him shudder for a moment and his face now wore a more sombre mask.

"All right, Mr Brad, good luck then. We will be seeing you then in the morning?" Juan rhetorically injected.

"Why yes, of course, I would not dare to leave before having one of Carla's full breakfasts and I won't be leaving until about noon time anyway, I'll also probably drop by the office and visit everyone there before hitting the road," Brad exclaimed as he started to head up to his room.

"I sure hope that Mr Brad knows what he is doing, my dear wife, but I suppose in every man's life, this same type of decision of leaving home arises," Juan counselled softly to his beloved spouse. "Remember that we both had to leave the Philippines all those years ago and we were also filled with fear and anxiousness," Juan concluded.

Clearly distraught, Carla merely nodded in silent affirmation to her husband's sage words, yet she carried a very worried motherly look on her face and her body language clearly expressed her concerns; she could only hug Juan closely and squeezed his hand tightly. "It's like we are losing the last of our dear children, Juan and now we will be all alone also," Carla sobbed gently.

* * * * * * * * * * * * * * * * * *

Proceeding back to his bedroom and subsequently pouring a generous, three-finger malt scotch on the rocks, he comfortably reclined in his desk chair to examine the finer points of his quest planning. His confession to Juan and Carla was the right thing to do, they were his de facto parents now. He realized from their expressions, tone, and questions – that they each had second thoughts about his quest and to be truthful Brad had these same concerns, but he was resolved that his safe, sedate, and secure life needed to be challenged if he were to lead the life that he wanted to live.

'No second thoughts or regrets!' His mind was committed to discover himself, the land, and its people. He smiled to himself as he envisioned the stunned reaction that Kate would give him; she would probably think that he had finally flipped his wig on this crazy stunt. He resolved to set forth the task of performing some serious reflection and succinct decision-making choices. He was energized with a fire and zeal that made him one of the foremost investment bankers on the East Coast.

He carefully crafted his mental checklist. Concerning his legal obligations, he arranged for a Limited Power of Attorney for both Juan and Carla to administer for the maintenance and upkeep services for the Greystone estate, with funds for such being provided by his personal checking account within a generous preset limit. Lionel MacAlister had given him legal authority to administer the Hamilton Trust and the Hamilton estate was not to be fully probated for six months, at which time he planned to be back in Boston. For his finances, Brad ensured that he had unfettered access to all of his private, commercial banking and brokerage accounts, to include the access to the Hamilton Trust accounts, this to include having Points of Contacts for all relevant personnel, phone numbers, and e-mail addresses, all this information was readily available on Brad's smartphone and he had a back-up of these files and access to them through his remote computer access capability.

From his bedroom safe, Brad extracted $25,000 in cash and another $50,000 in old fashioned, but dependable Traveller's Cheques, this along with his credit card and bank access to a $20 million quick line of credit would suffice for any need that he might encounter over the next six months. Additionally, Brad had liquid access through his private brokerage and banking accounts, which contained ready access to over a hundred million dollars in liquid assets. This was more than enough capital for any contingency that he may encounter. Finally, he possessed Mrs Peet's speed-ready contact information, should he need to exercise a grant from the Hamilton Trust Fund.

For communications, Brad possessed his Apple iPhone and a Google e-mail account, so that he could access his private Hamilton & MacAlister e-mail account. For clothing Brad decided to travel light, taking no more than two portable travel bags – he would buy garments as he needed these and he stocked up on packing undergarments, such as undershirts, briefs, and socks. Concerning his mode of transportation, Brad continued to defy his past and embrace risk-taking; he opted to use his old favourite BMW motorcycle. It was a late Model BMW Sports Tourer, type K1200GT. The motorcycle was a beautiful and sleek beast that was painted a bright, two-toned Mandarin Yellow/Titanium-ice colour. This model of BMW was designed for serious, long haul travelling; it possessed a twin cylinder, 1130cc displacement, ABS integrated disk braking, electronic fuel injection, electronic ignition, Telelever suspension, and a huge 6.6-gallon gasoline tank, and heated seat and handlebars for added rider comfort in cold environments. The massive bike weighed in at 615 lbs without the rider, it possessed a top speed of 124 mph, and it had a range of several hundred miles between refuelling.

The idea to use his BMW was bold, imaginative, and risky. Yet this is exactly what he desired and needed at this point in his life! Riding a motorbike was dangerous, yet so too was the real risk of being T-boned on the urban streets of Boston, a fate that had befallen one of his friends. The Aspen plane crash keenly instructed Brad that safety and conformity were mere illusions of life. "As his family had died in a safe, private chartered jet, then there was no real totally benign means of travel, life itself was a dangerous process and no one gets out of it alive," he thought in Zen-like rationalization.

Travelling long cross-country distances with minimal comfort and support on a motorcycle was going to be a trying and interesting experience for a young eastern billionaire investment banker. He was never one who had ever needed to 'rough it' during his life, but now he wanted the opportunity to explore a drift-less, vagabond life of the man that he never had been or had the independence to be. He was sure of one thing, however; that he would come back a changed and more experienced man. He finished packing his personal items, toilet kit, and personal contact information. Next, he rummaged through his closet to find his old leather-riding outfit, riding boots, gloves, safety vest, and helmet. Although Brad had not regularly ridden his BMW motorcycle in over two years, he had maintained a maintenance service with various local mechanics and auto dealers, who had kept all of the estate's vehicles in tiptop operating condition. The BMW would be ready to start in the morning, but Brad's motorcycling skills were far less certain. He would have to be careful not to drive too aggressively at first and begin to re-learn his long-perished motorcycling skills, yet he was confident that he could pick up his expertise again in just a short while.

After three hours of organizing, planning, and gathering up of his assets for the extensive trek, he sat back into his easy chair and enjoyed the last few sips of his drink, which was now totally devoid of any form of ice. Brad's cell phone suddenly rang, the hour was 10:00 PM and he usually did not receive calls this late at night. He quickly spotted the number and name of Katherine".

"Brad, honey, this is Kate, how are you doing, darling?" his slightly distressed fiancée inquired in a disguised pleasant tone.

"Hello Kate, I was just thinking about you too," Brad replied.

"I hope that these were fine thoughts, Brad, maybe even passionate, sexy ones. Speaking of which, do you want to come over this evening and spend the night?" Kate rather eagerly and hopefully inquired!

Thinking quickly, he decided that it was best that he delay informing Kate of his travel decision, as he didn't want anyone to talk him out of his plans and he knew that Katherine might not approve of his new spontaneous scheme. She could be very persuasive when she became determined about something.

"Gee, Kate, I'm really tired and I'm going to get an early rest tonight, especially given the fact that I have had a tough couple of nights trying to get a good night's rest, this morning really knocked the wind out of me, Kate," Brad replied almost apologetically. Yet Kate felt only slightly dejected, she realized that Brad was having a tough time sleeping, let alone making passionate love to her all night long. Kate, however, did detect a positive tone in Brad's voice and she was hopeful that he was recovering his spirits, she remembered the positive conversation with her father earlier in the day concerning Brad's mood.

"Forgive me, but you can't blame a girl for trying, Brad. I understand, we'll get together soon, you owe me another rain check, which are quickly adding up to a week's worth," Kate laughingly toyed.

Suddenly, Brad changed his mind and reasoned that this was as good a time as any in the conversation to inform Kate about his intentions regarding the Hamilton Trust, as well as his general intentions of taking a break from Boston, the horrific haunting memories, and the firm.

"Understand, Kate, I have some good news, at least I think that it is good news, for you and for us!" Brad deliberately exclaimed in a monotone voice. Kate was caught off guard and she was temporally stunned by Brad's announcement. With hesitation and a little fear in her voice she dared to make inquiry of this sudden news, "okay just what is it all about Brad, what precisely are you going to do my dear?"

"So now, Kate, I'm going to take active control of the Hamilton Trust as its Governor Trustee," Brad positively exclaimed.

"Hey I am so glad for you and us!" Kate genuinely cheered into the phone. Kate knew that Brad sounded more upbeat from his tone and phone demeanour, this was a good sign as it indicated that Brad was perhaps on his road to recovery and back into her life again.

"Well, hold on a second, I have another thing to tell you, Kate," Brad chided carefully.

"Another good surprise for me, Brad? Well do tell me more!" Katherine purred in an almost mocking tone.

"Ah, I think it's something that will be good for both of us, Kate," he mysteriously hinted.

Katherine was intrigued and a little frightened by Brad's evasion, she wanted a direct answer, not evasiveness.

"Stop teasing me, I hate when you do that! Now what's the big secret, Brad? Please tell me now!" Katherine gently pleaded.

"Well, I was thinking about taking a break...getting away from it all, Kate. I think that I want to simply get away from Boston for a while, I want to discover myself and this country and its people," Brad calmly explained. There was an eerie long silence on the other end of the phone, as Katherine was stunned by Brad's proclamation. In short, Katherine was dumbfounded for one of the few times in her life. Not having heard an immediate response from Katherine, he inquired from her again, "Kate, did you hear what I just said? What do you think?" Brad anxiously pleaded.

Stunned by his announcement, Katherine thought carefully and calculated her words with caution before answering.

"Okay, Brad darling, I'm simply shocked, but I'm also delighted too! I mean, what can I say! Remember, I had personally suggested a vacation to you this morning!" Katherine declared rhetorically in a subdued tone. In reality, however, Katherine was startled by Brad's unexpected plan, yet she was very relieved that he was not mired in his usual deep depression or despondent mood. His interest in a journey or trip was a diversion against any prolonged depression and that was the most important thing to consider. Katherine, always the control freak, was desperate for details and she ached for more information.

"Now can't you tell me anything more, other than the fact that you are leaving to go to places unknown, for an unspecified duration and without an established goal? Are you going to Hawaii, Bora Bora, London, France or 'Bum Fuck' Egypt?" Katherine inquired in a concerned, yet humorous manner, slightly spiced with a dose of sarcasm.

Brad's response was business-like and declarative: "Actually, Kate, I do have a plan, I know my general direction, and I know my objective."

"Let's have out with it then! When will I know about these things or is it some great mystery? Am I even a part of your plans, Brad?" Katherine replied in an inquisitive mocking tone.

"Please let me explain, Kate, you are part of my life and you always will be, but in this instance, I will need to do this journey alone, so I'll be coming into the office tomorrow morning and I'll explain everything then, so don't worry!" Brad pleaded to starve off any further inquiry and possible dissuasions.

Despising the obvious verbal ambiguity, Katherine made one last attempt for specific information. "Are you sure that you don't want me to come over this evening, Brad? I could give you a nice Bon Voyage present!" Katherine toyed in a sexy, inviting voice. He devilishly smiled to himself and imagined the vampish things that Kate loved to do to him.

"Oh, you're much too generous for me, Kate. No, thank you, I have too much to do tonight and I am physically exhausted, but we'll talk more in the morning and then everything will become clear, Kate, I love you so very much!" Brad concluded in a hushed voice.

Katherine possessed the shrewdness to know that it was both pointless and perhaps dangerous, to push Brad for details, especially when he just seemed to be getting a little better and more positive in his mental outlook. "It was perhaps more dangerous in the long run not to let Brad go forth and finally get rid of his depression once and for all, than to keep it bottled-up within himself," Katherine summarized to herself cautiously. Always the rational one, Katherine was going to defer to her better judgment on this matter. She walked slowly and smartly over to a small salmon coloured silk loveseat.

"Have it your way, it's your passionate loss, Brad, you just gave up a great love-making opportunity again, but I'm a girl that keeps on trying. I'll see you tomorrow then?" Kate inquired again.

"Yes, yes, of course," Brad assured her. She didn't want the conversation to end on such a note, her emotions gained control of her and she leaped as quickly as a leopard to her feet, shouting into her phone. "I love you, Brad," Kate softly sighed with tearful emotions.

Brad was full of emotions and he was eager to reciprocate.

"Kate, I love you too and I always will... you're the only woman in the world for me, thanks for putting up with my wimpy problems. I love you and I'll be seeing you in the morning at the office, alright, Kate?" he stated reassuringly. Katherine was over-joyed to see that her Brad was finally making an emotional feeling toward her after these many weeks and it was a great feeling. She had to be certain that Brad continued making an emotional and psychological recovery from his depression and she was not going to do anything to jeopardize Brad's mental recovery.

"Yes, in the morning, my handsome boy, so good night, my love," Katherine softly replied as she hung up the phone. She was disturbed by Brad's evasive and mysterious travel plans. It was obvious from Brad's words and tone, that she was not to be part of this plan and it was not at all like Brad to be mysterious, brash, or deceitful.

* * * * * * * * * * * * * * * * *

Tomorrow came all too quickly for Brad. Like a shrieking suffering animal, a loud irreverent whine hailed from across the bedroom. The irritating tone from the alarm had sounded suddenly, its obnoxious shrill tone continued to reverberate across the darkened room and its shrill outburst would only be silenced by a weary arm that slowly surrounded and smothered the mechanical beast until finally the correct button was depressed. The old-fashioned contraption had performed its task perfectly. No matter, the sunrise slowly beckoned and Brad was eager to meet the new day. His bedroom was silent, dark warm and very comforting, yet the remnants of the previous night's shrouded black mantle were slowly surrendering its celestial soul to the new bright dawn, as the dull red orange colours were but mere harbingers of the warm, orange-yellow orb that would soon become the new morning's sunrise.

Like a newly-minted butterfly emerging from its metamorphic cocoon, Brad slowly emerged from his bedcovers, stretching his limbs and rubbing the night's sleep from his half-opened eyes, as he slowly made his way to the bathroom. He gathered his running clothes together, placed these on his well-toned body, then he began to stretch out his tense and tired muscles against the massive oak bed frame.

Methodically, he proceeded downstairs to take a short jog around the estate. Up until the time of his family's death, he had maintained a regular and rigorous health regimen at one of the local upscale Boston gyms, located just a few blocks from Hamilton & MacAlister. The firm actually gave its employees a 40% fitness membership discount as an incentive to stay healthy, get in shape, and help to reduce sickness at the firm. It also wanted to have lean and physically attractive employees – Hamilton & MacAlister was not a workplace for the flabby, lazy or over-weight employee. The clients were paying handsomely for the firm's professional and profitable services and they naturally expected the decorum of well-dressed, well-toned, and attractive employees. This was called premium marketing.

Attired in his nondescript grey running suit onto which the words 'Harvard' were boldly embossed, Brad ran slowly, then more briskly around the perimeter of the Greystone estate. The cool air and the exercise slowly awakened all of the senses. After 45 minutes, he looked at his custom Rolex watch and decided that he had done approximately three miles and this was a good time to finish his run. He victoriously walked into the manor's kitchen and he could immediately smell Carla cooking some country-smoked bacon. It was amazing how the sense of smell could instantly bring back childhood memories of the old family hearty breakfasts. The memories were as delightful as the aroma of the bacon.

"Greetings, Carla and Juan! Hello everybody and a very Good Morning too," Brad sounded-off as he cheerfully entered the kitchen and spotted Carla and Juan preparing the morning feast.

"Good morning, Mr Brad," Juan replied as he got up from his kitchen counter stool in a sign of respect.

"Hello Juan, how are you doing this fine day?" Brad sighed.

"Very well, can I get you some coffee, Mr Brad?" Juan offered warmly and politely.

"Sure, that would be just great after my morning constitutional," Brad cheerfully replied, as Juan poured Brad a huge mug of strong black coffee that was slightly spiced with a tad of vanilla and cinnamon.

Carla warmly smiled, as she momentarily watched this scene from the distant gas-fired range pavilion located at the far side of the kitchen. With coffee cup in hand Brad glanced over to Carla, he closely moved over to her and quickly planted a slight kiss on her cheek, just like he had always done to her since he was a child.

"Carla, I just couldn't resist the smell of that delicious aroma, how did you know that I wanted my favourite maple-bacon this morning?" Brad inquired childishly.

"I try my best and make the same meals for you and Juan that I have been preparing ever since I came to live and work at Greystone so many years ago, Mr Brad. Your appetite has not been huge lately, but I still prepare the same meals which I have always cooked," Carla replied in an expressive warm tone.

"Great and thank you kindly, after my run I am sure hungry, do you mind if I eat now before I get showered and ready for my trip?" Brad inquired of both Juan and Carla once more in a manner that was that of a son rather than that of the wealthy estate owner.

"That's fine, Mr Brad, this is after all, your home and you may do here as you please" Carla replied in a polite tone. Brad smiled and remembered that Juan and Carla still thought of themselves as both employees and semi-family members to Brad. The Old World discipline of estate servants was virtually impossible to break, diminish or dislodge – it was much akin to the particular socialization of lifelong military or police careers.

"I just didn't want to offend either of you and you know that my parents never approved of dining without us children being properly dressed or cleaned-up, yet here I stand in my musty running attire and perspired body!" Brad explained in an almost apologist tone.

"Today is your special day, Mr Brad, you do as you like," Juan exclaimed with a huge smile.

"Well then, what will my two men have this morning, omelettes, pancakes, or French Toast?" Carla pleasantly inquired. Brad and Juan just looked at each other and shrugged their shoulders to one another and Carla. Without any displayed emotion, Brad exclaimed, "You decide, Carla, whatever you make is always superb as far as I'm concerned." Juan smiled approvingly then added, "That goes for me too!"

"Fine then, my two favourite men, but no complaints if you do not like what I prepare," Carla replied defensively and knowing that both Juan and Brad enjoyed all of her breakfast entrees. Brad indulged himself in another strong steaming cup of coffee as he poured all three of them a fresh serving.

Carla prepared and served a breakfast composed of smoked maple-bacon, scrambled eggs, and French toast topped with white powdery sugar and Vermont maple syrup. After a short breakfast prayer, all three of them sat at the informal pantry table and cheered each another in a toast of hot coffee.

"Here's to Carla!" Brad declared as they all raised their coffee mugs and toasted the maiden of the meal. They all enjoyed the delicious, hearty breakfast and the reminiscence of bygone good times.

"Mr Brad, I don't mean to be too forward, but I hope that someday I'll be able to prepare such meals for your children too!" Carla exclaimed with some embarrassment. Brad smiled and blushed a little too.

"Well yes, of course, Carla, I would be very honoured by this kind act as well, perhaps in the very near future too," Brad replied, as an indication of his future marriage and family plans, which he had discussed with Katherine shortly after their engagement. "Right now, however, I need to get ready for my journey, so if you'll both excuse me, I need to get cleaned up and packed up. I hope that all the vehicles are ready?" Brad nervously exclaimed.

"Oh yes, Mr Brad, every vehicle in the garage from the Rolls Phantom V to your sister's and brother's Mercedes is ready to go, I have arranged for the maintenance of every Hamilton estate vehicle that is registered with the state of Massachusetts."

"Fantastic, I can always rely on you, Juan," Brad replied in jovial acknowledgement of Juan's efficiency.

"May I inquire which vehicle you are taking Mr Brad?" Juan asked.

"Well, I'm going to let that be a surprise, Juan," Brad replied as he strutted up the discreet pantry staircase that led to the manor's second story rooms.

"Forgive me, but I'm a little worried about Mr Brad," Carla confided to her husband.

"Yes, well, my dear wife, one thing is clear, it's that Mr Brad is in a better mood than any time in the past six weeks… he seems energized, but still unhappy I think," Juan replied to Carla.

Carla's eyes betrayed her acknowledgement of the words uttered by her husband. Juan caressingly placed his arms around his wife, as she placed her weary head on his chest. It was as if they were seeing one of their own children off to school again. The couple was once again acting like worried parents seeing off their child to an uncertain future.

Brad took a long, hot shower and then he carefully checked his listed items. Everything was there and ready to go. Brad anointed himself with some common Old Spice aftershave lotion, next he dressed carefully into his jet black and luminescent yellow striped motorcycle suit. He resembled more of a giant yellow jack insect than a feared road warrior. Yet his clothes were practical, as well as being very distinctive and in vogue. The full body leathers served as dual protection against nature's elements and these served as physical protection between the rider and the road. The bright yellow luminescent yellow strips served to notify and warn other drivers of the presence of the motorcycle in day, night, and limited visibility conditions. Finally, an inflatable riding vest provided upper body and neck protection should he ever fall off his BMW in any type of road accident. Grabbing his helmet, Nomex gloves, and baggage, he vigorously proceeded down the stairs to announce a sad farewell to Juan and Carla.

"Oh, Holy Mother of God!" Carla screamed as she covered her face with both of her hands upon seeing Brad enter the manor kitchen area. Juan came running to see what had so disturbed his wife.

"What the hell...oh my Lord!" Juan exclaimed in amazement as he stared in disbelief at Mr Brad, Juan's eyes blinking rapidly as his mind tried to comprehend that sight to which his eyes and brain could not fully comprehend.

"Now come on, Juan and Carla, it's only me! What's the matter with both of you? You have both seen me dressed like this before!" he exclaimed in bewilderment and frustration.

"Oh no, please Mr Brad, say that you are not going to travel across America on that crazy contraption, you will kill yourself!" Carla cried out as she hid her face in her hands and looked away from Brad. Juan tried to comfort Carla, but she would not be consoled. "I don't want to see any more death come into this house and my life," Carla sobbed uncontrollably, as Juan tried his best to comfort her.

"Carla and Juan, I want you both to know that I have no death wish and that I will be very careful. I'm going away for a couple of months, but I am coming back to both of you alive and well. Katherine and I will be getting married and you are both going to dance at our wedding, so please stop all of this needless worrying!" Brad explained in a reassuring tone that seemed to comfort both Carla and Juan.

"Excuse me, Mr Brad, and pardon me for asking, but don't you think that travelling on a motorcycle a great distance is not only unwise, but most uncomfortable?" Juan politely interjected.

"You are absolutely 100% correct and that's precisely why I am doing this travel and in such a manner, Juan and Carla! I want to be a bit uncomfortable too! My family's death has taught me one thing – that life is both uncertain and short…I plan to live life for all that it's worth and I want to take calculated chances in life, there's no such thing as a safe life!" Brad retorted back in a stubborn, defensive tone. Brad thought a few moments about what he just said and the tone in which he had said it. For a short moment, he felt a bit guilty too.

"Please, listen, Juan and Carla, I love you both and I'm sure you feel the same, but I need to get out and get away…to experience real people and places……to live my life with no regrets…I'll be careful, but I can no longer be safe, dormant, and secure!" Brad explained in a subtle, caring tone. "Besides the faster the road and the motorcycle beat me up, the shorter will be my trip and the sooner I will be back home at Greystone," he added in the hope of providing some emotional consolation to Juan and Carla.

Slowly Carla gained her composure upon hearing Brad's logic, besides she was helpless to stop her employer from doing anything that he wanted to do. She wiped the remaining tears from her eyes before speaking, then uttered, "You are a grown man and you must do as you see fit."

"Yes, you be careful my son, we want you back alive… yes, we both want to dance at your wedding to Miss Katherine!" Juan added as he continued to comfort his wife.

"I love you both for who you are and for what you have done for me and my family, I won't forget either of you and yes, I'm coming back, so no good-byes from me!" Brad commanded in both a sincere and half-joking tone.

"I request that you both continue to care for Greystone in the same manner that you have all these past decades. You have access to the household account and Mr Lionel MacAlister can approve additional household funds if a major problem or disaster happens, is that clear?" Brad stated in a factual manner.

Both Juan and Carla just nodded their heads in agreement, both of them knowing that further argument and discussion were futile.

"So – that's it! Thanks, folks, and now let's hug one another and get everything squared away…I have to sell this crazy act to Katherine!" Brad proclaimed, he hugged both Juan and Carla like the departing prodigal son.

"Great, let's all go outside now and get my Iron Horse ready for the journey," Brad remarked as he led a reluctant Juan and Carla out to the

Hamilton manor garage.

The garage was a magnificent structure also constructed in a like-manner and of the same rugged construction materials as that of the manor house. It was comparable in size to a scaled-down barn. The bottom floor was a literal automobile garage that could easily hold over fifteen full-size vehicles, although the Hamiltons kept only about twelve vehicles to include a vintage Royal Blue Rolls Royce Phantom V touring limousine, a silver-coloured Rolls Royce Silver Cloud III four door sedan, four different classes of Mercedes Benz sedans, a Chevy Suburban, a HMMUV, and an assortment of lesser vehicles, to include a small tractor equipped with a snowplough attachment.

As Juan had earlier attested, all of the vehicles were immaculately maintained, registered, inspected, insured and ready to go. Except for the BMW motorcycle, Juan took care to ensure that every Greystone estate vehicle was taken for a 30-minute drive at least every two weeks. Juan usually tried to take every vehicle out around the estate and sometimes the surrounding country roads, this to ensure that the motor vehicle seals were adequately lubricated and to give each vehicle a short work out. Those vehicles that Juan could not physically operate, he merely 'fired up' the engines and allowed the motors to get a good thirty-minute operating time. In a far south corner of the Greystone garage there silently stood Brad's bright yellow-titanium coloured BMW motorcycle. This was the perfect discovery machine for Brad.

"Okay, Juan, shall we move the beast out of this darkened cavern and out into the lightness of day?" Brad asked almost rhetorically of Juan.

"Yes, Mr Brad, it would be my pleasure to assist you," Juan replied as he secretly concealed a little pride and envy at Mr Brad's journey. To be young, adventuresome and without responsibility – this was every man's secret dream. Carla kept far away from the motorcycle, as she tried to avoid the contraption that would rob her of Mr Brad's everyday presence and perhaps his very life. Brad carefully checked the tyre pressure, oil level and gas tank. Careful attention was paid to the proper tyre inflation pressure, clutch and brake lines, as well as to the passing and brake light signals. The horn, headlights and heated seat worked as required. Everything was mechanically operational and in good working order.

He carefully stowed his gear onto the BMW by utilizing the bike's integral saddlebags and exterior mounting racks. When fully loaded with Brad's gear, the bike appeared as an overburdened camel or other beast of burden. He fired up the ignition and the twin cylinder, 1130cc displacement, electronic fuel injection engine roared to life with a smooth monotonous hum. It was a very refined, Teutonic engineered machine, most unlike the deliberately noisy American made Harley Davidson motorcycles.

Final farewells and hugs were made to Juan and Carla, certain to ensure that they all had each other's contact information. Brad promised both of them that he would call, text or e-mail them weekly and inform them of his status. A final hug and kiss to Carla, then a hug and a firm handshake to Juan, finally he was on his way down the Hamilton main driveway and then out the estate's main front gate. Juan looked like he had lost his only son, while Carla ran back into the house and cried for the next three hours. Brad's next stop was at Hamilton & MacAlister and that of Miss Katherine MacAlister in the flesh.

★ ★ ★ ★ ★ ★ ★ ★ ★ ★ ★ ★ ★ ★ ★ ★ ★ ★

Brad cautiously manoeuvred the sleek and nimble BMW along the exclusive secondary roads that led him onto the main Interstate 93 South into the Boston metropolis. The automobile drivers were as bad as ever – a biker had to possess a keen 360-degree situation awareness of the 'travel bubble' surrounding the motorcycle. He was fastidious in re-learning the characteristics and handling dynamics of his motorcycle, not having ridden excessively over the past two years, a time over which most of his fellow riding buddies either got married or tired of the sport, so he had placed the hobby aside in anticipation of future times when he would return back to the sport. The future for him in this regard, came earlier than he had expected.

He soon found himself in the financial district at a time that was well past the morning rush hour, so traffic was lighter than expected. Entering 45 Bromfield Street, Brad quickly took his reserved parking space in the front of the Hamilton & MacAlister building, where he carefully guided his BMW back tyre up against the kerb for stability purposes.

Possessed of self-confidence and enthusiasm, he secured the BMW, quickly dismounted his Teutonic engineered iron steed, removed his helmet, and headed smartly into the foyer of the Hamilton & MacAlister building. He rapidly scaled the main staircase and past the Hamilton & MacAlister executive receptionist, Gail Myers.

"Hello, good morning, Gail!" Brad announced as he strolled boldly and quickly past the receptionist desk.

Gail looked up quickly and noticed that Bradford Hamilton was attired like a sleek motorcycle rider and the sight was so unlike the usually conservatively pin-striped dressed CEO that she had come to expect of this man. Regaining her composure, Gail quickly got up from her desk, peeked down the main corridor hall and loudly yelled out a distinctively audible 'Good Morning, Mr Hamilton' to Brad as he speedily made his way to Katherine's office.

Margie DeTagelio's back was turned away from the front of her desk, as she carefully held a small compact mirror up to her face as she calmly tried to remove an eyelash from her eye. "Good morning, Margie!" Brad suddenly exclaimed to his personal assistant.

Nervously, Margie's hand jumped up in a nervous twitch and she smudged her mascara. "Oh shit, look what you made me do, I didn't need this grief this time of the morning!" Margie exclaimed in a brash and sarcastic tone and not realizing that she was addressing her boss. She slowly turned around to eye the person who had so rudely interrupted her personal care moment.

"Holy shit!" Margie exclaimed in a tone that flattened as she realized her office faux pas. Margie quickly clasped her hands over her mouth, after she had realized her rude remark. She was obviously embarrassed by her vocabulary and unprofessional exclamation.

Brad noticed the embarrassment in Margie's body language. "It's quite all right, Margie, I didn't mean to startle you so early in the day," Brad replied apologetically.

"Oh Mr Brad, is that you? I mean to say, you're dressed like a motorcycle rider!" Margie exclaimed in sheer amazement.

"Well yes, Margie, this is the attire for someone who is riding a motorcycle just like the one that I have ridden to the office today," Brad exclaimed. "Is Kate available?" he added anxiously.

"Why yes, of course, Brad. Let me ring her for you," Margie replied.

"No please don't, Margie, I want this to be a surprise," Brad exclaimed as he headed toward Kate's office door.

"Yes, Brad, you're really going to knock Kate's panties off for sure this morning," Margie mumbled to herself and thinking of the look that would shortly befall Miss Katherine. With this thought in mind, Margie just smiled and giggled in silence to herself.

He knocked quickly on Kate's door and waited for a reply of permission to enter. "Come on in," replied Katherine in a very business-like and definitive tone. Katherine was perturbed that once more,

Margie had not alerted her as to an unannounced visitor. Brad slowly turned the ornate highly polished brass doorknob and then he quickly entered Kate's office. Brad and Katherine's eyes met immediately, and Kate's eyes dilated rapidly, and her jaw dropped wide open at the sight that beheld her.

"Brad, what in the hell…is this some sort of joke? Are you for real?" Katherine exclaimed in amazement and shock, as her beau entered her office attired in a flashy black and bright yellow leather motorcycle outfit. Katherine sat behind her desk stunned and gazing at Brad's attire from head-to-toe. He remained silent to her exasperation, allowing his outfit and appearance to do all the talking for him. Several seconds of dead silence elapsed, as Katherine stared in amazement at Brad's wardrobe and his changed mood from that of previous weeks. Her initial shock slowly turned into mocking levity.

"Well, just look at you, Mr Brad Hamilton, the scone of Boston's financial district or is it now Mr Bad–to-the- Bone?" Katherine exclaimed with a wide smile, as she anxiously arose from behind her desk and approached Brad up close and personal. She wanted to ensure that the man before her was not just a figment of her imagination.

"So please, tell me, Brad, that this is some sort of a prank? Do you have a costume event to attend? Are you feeling okay this morning?" Katherine giggled as she slowly walked around Brad and admired his form and his smart looking leather attired motorcycle riding outfit. Katherine's long, slender manicured fingers gently traced their way across Brad's bright yellow and black-checkered leather riding jacket, as she toyed with the various flaps and pockets that abundantly adorned the jacket.

"It certainly appears like someone is hitting the road or more appropriately, may himself be hit while on the road!" Katherine mockingly added. "You look like a giant yellow jacket bee, Brad," Katherine remarked. "Well, you sure have regained your sense of humour. This is a great joke, Brad, I really love it, now please tell me the real trip that you are taking?" Katherine sighed and expecting Brad to reveal his true intentions as to his mysterious planned trip.

Upon hearing Katherine's taunting words, Brad's mood was instantly transformed from open optimism and cheerfulness to that of downright guarded defensiveness. "This is no joke, Kate! I'm no joke either, Kate! This is the real deal here, this is it! No kidding Kate!" Brad voiced in a sombre tone of seriousness. Brad continued his monologue to Kate. "I'm taking a trip on my BMW and I'm not sure where I am going or for what duration," he stated dryly.

Feeling the earnest explanation that Brad was vocalizing, Katherine suddenly stopped her kidding, as she became more serious in both her tone and discussion. Katherine's physical posture changed from that of a casual slouch to that of an erect and tall stance, this betraying a superior and challenging posture.

Thus, beginning to realize that Brad was serious about this childish, almost rebellious proposition, she was determined to change his brash boyish and dangerous idea of adventure. "Sure, Brad, you want to talk about seriousness, so let's discuss this matter as mature adults and in a calm manner," Katherine replied before continuing her dialogue with Brad. She nervously paced back and forth across a small patch of her office space that was adorned by a rich red and yellow Persian silk carpet.

"Look here, Brad, taking a trip is a great thing for you to do, in fact, I encourage it. A trip will help you reflect on your life, your family, and our future, but this is not the smart way to go about it, darling! Just think rationally here, Brad. You are not in the correct physical or mental condition to ride your motorcycle any great distance, you haven't ridden in some years, you are travelling alone, and finally it's a dangerous, reckless, and impulsive thing to do and I strongly recommend that you reconsider this romantic, but very childish decision. Why don't you try something a little safer and get a Winnebago or something else bigger in size and comfort?" she pleaded in a most logical manner.

He looked straight ahead into empty space, but he had clearly heard every word that Kate was speaking. There was a pregnant pause before Brad commented. "Do you know what, Kate? You're absolutely right! You are right on each and every point on which you have elucidated," Brad exclaimed as Katherine momentarily delighted in Brad's reply and she was thinking that she had deposed him of this crazy idea. Yet Brad continued to defend his decision to Katherine.

"You probably think that I am psycho or mentally impaired, but I assure you, Kate, that I am quite sane in this proposition. I have thought it through in my mind many times over the past evening and I am going whether or not you concur or not. I love you dearly, Kate, but I have to do this, or the hurting and emptiness will never be over for me. That's not a good way for a couple to start off their marriage, now, is it, Kate?" Brad exclaimed in a dry and subtle tone.

Kate listened in utter polite silence as Brad opened up his soul to her for the first time in weeks. "I need to leave Boston and I mean to leave today!" he boldly proclaimed. Kate was not relieved that Brad agreed with her argument and its soundness and she was angered by his illogical defiance, yet she knew that Brad could be very bull-headed and single minded once his mind was resolved upon an issue. He was an apex Alpha male and she admired him for being so. She also knew that Brad was telling her the truth, when he explained his reasons for making this trip on a motorcycle. Katherine was a smart lady, she knew that sometimes it was better to let a man do that which he wants, even those foolish things, and let him get it 'out of his system', rather than trying to discourage him from doing it. Brad moved forward and gently put his arms on Katherine's shoulders and looked deeply into her emerald-green piercing eyes. "But Kate, your reasons are exactly the ones for why I want to do this trip on my motorcycle," Brad remarked earnestly. Katherine was stunned into both silence and astonishment at his logic.

Undeterred, he continued his rationale, "Kate, I have been like the walking dead for the past six weeks and then yesterday I discovered all the great things that my mom and dad did for all those people over the years and I want to continue and be part of that… to be part of their legacy; but before I can do anything, I need to explore and find out what life is really about and how things work for everyday working people. All of my life, things have always been decided for me and I meekly went along with whatever my parents had directed for me. I went to all the prescribed schools, played all the suggested sports, wore all the correct clothes, joined all the proper clubs – oh yes, I was a real credit to my peers and class, right, Kate? Now everything is different. My parents are dead, my brother and sister are dead, and I want, no, I need to find out what the hell goes on in life besides the fancy parties, the summer retreats, and the social galas. I am going to do this, Kate. I am going to experience life as a Joe Average American and what better way than on a motorcycle, travelling with minimum possessions and looking forward to each new day as a new start that is full of new and strange possibilities."

Kate politely listened in silence and acute attention during Brad's discord, and before making her concluding argument. "That's a nice little speech, Brad, this really sounds like a great idea that is for someone just out of high school or someone who just retired from the middle-class grind, but this crazy idea is not for a mature, successful rich man like you. If you must do this crazy thing, then at least reconsider the mode of transportation. As for real work, Brad, you haven't done a stitch of manual work in your life, and besides, I need you here to work with me! I am up to my ass in alligators around here! Investment banking is real work, Brad!" Katherine justifiably remarked.

Brad was momentarily hurt by Kate's remarks, but he stayed focused on his own objective.

"No, Kate, I want to start taking chances in my life, not avoiding them! Besides, when your time is up, it's up and there's nothing that you can do about it! Life has a certain fatalism and course to it… my family's death has proved this to me. I used to live my life by the rules and by that which everyone expected of me I'm going to live and die with no regrets, Kate. I'll do this with or without your support," Brad sighed.

Katherine was shrewd; she knew that Brad was just over-reacting to a latent response concerning his family's death. Mentally, she was relieved that he was less despondent than in previous days, but his current serendipity behaviour was just as dangerous as his severe depression. From his eyes and firm voice, Katherine realized that Brad was determined in this and that further discussion involving dissuasion of this crazy quest was futile and probably counter-productive. She even reasoned that this little excursion would get the grief out of Brad's system and maybe bring him back to the world he had known prior to his family's death.

"Will you be coming back to me or do you no longer love me?" Katherine tersely inquired.

Brad smiled and put his arms around Kate and softly whispered to her, "Now stop it, Kate, you are talking nonsense, of course I love you, but this is something that I need to do for me… just for myself, Kate. I still and always will love you, Kate. The MacAlisters and Lopezes are now the only family that I have left," Brad replied.

Katherine knew Brad loved her; she just needed to hear some verbal assurance from the man she loved.

"All right then, Brad, you win on this one, so when does my billionaire Easy Rider take to the road?" Katherine muttered with a resigned sigh as she folded her long arms around Brad's neck and taunting him with a bedazzling warm smile.

Brad returned the smile and gave Kate a huge impassioned hug.

"That's great, Kate, I knew that you would understand eventually, I start my journey today. I have everything packed and ready to go. I have left instructions with Carla and Juan for handling all Greystone matters and your dad is finalizing the Hamilton estate and I still have the love of the best fiery Blue Blood woman in all of Boston."

Kate's eyes wallowed in tears as she spontaneously tightened her arms around Brad and gave him a long passionate kiss.

"Now don't you get yourself killed on that damn fool motorcycle of yours, Mr Bradford Wayne Hamilton, I need to have a healthy man to marry me," Kate sobbed as she tried to make light of the situation. "So how am I going to keep track of my fiancé?" Katherine sobbed.

Brad simply smiled and warmly responded, "At every one of my stops, Kate. I will communicate to you by cell phone, letter, post card, or e-mail concerning my latest exploits and you can hang a map in your office and post it with my progress. My general direction of travel is westward and don't worry! I will forward all my correspondence and communication through Margie to you," he reassured to Kate.

"Well, if you rely on DeTagelio to keep your affairs in order, Brad, then I' m afraid that you are in some real trouble, that girl is not competent to be your personal assistant, she lacks maturity, social decorum, breeding and sound judgment – she's just so low-class and common. Why don't you let me get you someone better, Brad?" Katherine sighed with a veiled contempt about Margie DeTagelio.

Brad simply shrugged off Kate's suggestion, knowing that there was some invisible dislike between the two women, but Brad personally liked Margie and he was the one who had hired her in the first place simply because he had liked Margie's street-wise spunk, honesty, and normalcy. "No, Kate, I hired Margie and I'm keeping her for now as my assistant, so she stays! Well then, I'm off then, Kate, I'll contact you this evening when I get my lodging for the night," Brad replied. Both he and Katherine embraced and kissed one last time.

"Remember, I'll never forgive you, Brad Hamilton, if you break your neck on that damn fool motorcycle, I want you back here healthy, in one piece, and ready for our wedding this Autumn, we will be having a wedding in late October. Now do you understand me, Mr Hamilton?" Katherine half-jokingly smirked as she saw the love of her life leave out of her office door.

Margie sat silently at her desk, keeping her eyes down and her ears wide open, as she tried to discern the conversations of the man that she secretly coveted and the woman who she obstinately despised. Margie was glad that Brad was getting away from the pit-viper Katherine and she secretly toyed with the prospect that Brad would never come back to Hamilton & MacAlister and leave Kit-Kat Katherine standing alone at the altar. Quickly, however, Margie realized that Brad was too respectable and well-bred to abandon his obligations and this aspect of Brad's character further enticed Margie's attraction to her boss.

Brad looked back quickly and smiled to Kate. She hated the thought that Brad was leaving her, but she knew that Brad needed this for his own good and that of their future marriage. She smiled and blew Brad a kiss from her hands. The faster Brad got this trip done, the quicker she would have Brad back in her arms and walking down the church aisle for their wedding, Katherine reasoned smartly.

He slowly walked by Margie's desk, then stopped to bid her a farewell. Still deliberately looking down at the papers, Margie felt the presence of Brad. The scent of Brad's favourite after-shave alerted Margie to Brad's immediate presence and this excited her immensely.

"Hey Margie, it's time for me to say goodbye, for at least a little while anyway," Brad resounded in a cheerful and confident voice that Margie had not heard for the past few weeks.

She unfolded her hands that had eclipsed her eyes from the outside world and slowly looked up into Brad's face. She almost wept with joy, as the smiling and anxious face of an energized Brad Hamilton greeted her. "Brad, you will be safe and return to us here at Hamilton & MacAlister, won't you now?" she pleaded softly.

Margie sobbed as she rose from her chair and without thinking, embraced Brad, giving him a huge affectionate hug as she carelessly threw both of her arms around her employer's neck.

"Now...now Margie, this is something I must do, and I will be back – I promise," Brad exclaimed as Katherine continued to spy scornfully upon the inappropriate degree of affection between employer and employee. "You have all of my contact information, correct?" Brad inquired, as she just nodded her head in an emotional affirmation of his inquiry. "Well then, you can continue to take care of my affairs and contact me if there is anything serious that requires my attention," he declared softly. He drew Margie closely to himself and he softly kissed her on the forehead. Briskly he strode through the main corridor, down the main ornate staircase, then out of the building. His departure was confirmed by the activation of his BMW motorcycle and the thunder of the exhaust pipes. The diminishing sound confirmed the fact that Brad Hamilton was now on his magic quest for a search of self.

Katherine quickly regained her composure after the emotional scene that she had just experienced with her fiancé. "DeTagelio, until my secretary Joan Peters returns back next week from vacation, you will work for both myself and Mr Hamilton. I trust that we will have no further problems or misunderstandings?" Katherine inquired of Margie and still cognitive of their previous conversations regarding proper office procedures.

"There will not be any problems, Miss MacAlister, and I will endeavour to fulfil all of your expectations of me," Margie uttered in an almost mechanical, unemotional response. Katherine still had no fondness for DeTagelio, but she only needed to interface with her for another couple of days.

"Good then, so we understand one another," Katherine declared tersely as she turned and started toward her office door before abruptly stopping suddenly.

Katherine paused with her back toward Margie. She seemed to be in a momentary trance. After a few seconds, Katherine turned and faced Margie DeTagelio. "DeTagelio, get me a map of the United States," Katherine announced sternly and with obvious authority of purpose.

"A map, Miss Katherine?" Margie remarked inquisitively and in slight amazement.

"You heard me correctly! I want a wall map of the United States, one that provides sufficient detail and illustrates the states and major highways. Get that map ASAP, have it posted in my office by tomorrow morning and make sure the map is arrayed onto a cork backdrop and that it is smartly framed and in good taste. I don't want my office looking like an auto garage or AAA office. Oh, and another thing, DeTagelio, tone down your make-up, we don't want to advertise a 'common' or cheap appearance around here at Hamilton & MacAlister... we must all keep up our best appearances and at all times," Katherine smiled and smugly commanded obstinately and loudly to Margie, as she entered her office and closed the door firmly behind her.

"Yes, of course, Miss MacAlister," Margie responded politely, yet unemotionally. Margie thought to herself and muttered under her breath that this was going to be a long couple of days until Joan Peters returned from vacation to rescue her from this period of personal purgatory. Margie knew that Katherine's remarks about her make-up and 'common looks' were an indirect attack against both her social class and female attractiveness. Margie angrily and silently thought to herself of all the times that Katherine adorned herself with enough eye make-up to look like a Boston streetwalker, but life was often a series of one-way streets. Her only redemption was Brad's future return and in this, the sooner the better she thought.

★ ★ ★ ★ ★ ★ ★ ★ ★ ★ ★ ★ ★ ★ ★ ★ ★ ★ ★

CHAPTER 3

Un-Easy Rider: The Moto-cross

*"I can teach you to do 'wheelies', 'hanging', 'The
Stripper', 'The Deadman', and many more stunts"*

Deftly he swung the sleek and agile BMW motorcycle onto
Interstate 80, an Interstate highway which dissected the
northern states from the east to the west coasts. Glancing
occasionally from his side view mirror, Brad noted the gradual
disappearance of the modern Boston skyline and perhaps with it, also
the demonic memories of the past six weeks. Ahead of him lay miles of
endless road and ambiguous possibilities. Suddenly self-doubts crept into
his mind about this seemingly crazy journey yet he quickly counselled
to himself that it was not the past that he was running from, instead he
was running to something – a new unchartered future. His parents had
always instructed him never to run from his troubles, but to face these
head-on and with determination and resolution. He was untethered
from all his past and present conventions. The whole thing was all so
exciting, dangerous, and out of character for the formerly reserved
Boston investment banker – that he giggled and laughed to himself as
he gently turned the accelerator throttle and set the BMW motorcycle
racing along at 75 mph down the highway. The rush of the speed and
wind in his face, suddenly made him feel childlike again – free of adult
responsibility and filled with simple idyllic joy.

It was only a few short hours before Brad found himself traversing
along the lush green Pennsylvania countryside and being buffeted by
a cool April breeze. The heavy insulated leather body gear provided

maximum warmth to his body. Additionally, the heated underwear suit, heated seat, and the heated handlebars – all served to guarantee that Brad's entire body was warm and crispy at the end of the day's ride; his only cold body parts were the exposed parts of his neck and feet. Still no amount of clothing could preserve one from nature's wind buffeting effects. Quickly he realized that a 65-degree temperature coupled with a wind stream of 60 mph meant an applied wind chill temperature of about 10 degrees and this temperature eventually took its exhausting physical toll on even a heat-suited motorcycle rider. The constant cold temperatures meant frequent rest stops for rehydrating and warming-up at the local diners and restaurants, while also providing an opportunity to stretch the legs and take those badly needed bladder 'health breaks'.

As with so many adults, the cold weather induced Brad to urinate more than in warm temperatures; this was especially true since he had reached his mid-thirties. 'Just a reality of getting older,' he thought amusingly to himself. He stopped at the next rest stop area to empty his bladder, exercise his legs, and top-off the BMW's gas tank.

He stopped at a Sunoco filling station along an Interstate rest stop and mini-mart just west of Pennsylvania State University. The seven hours of riding was more strenuous and exhausting than originally anticipated. The weather and riding had taken a toll on his nerves and attention, both of which also served to drain his energy levels. After filling his tank and emptying his bladder, he bought himself a cup of hot coffee, even though he knew it was dryadic and it would dehydrate him. While casually exercising his legs in the lobby of the rest area, Brad studied his map of the northern US. Anxiously looking for the next major exit, he decided that it was wise to get a warm hotel room for the night, perhaps a hot shower, then a good night's rest. 'Well now there's a Hilton Hotel at the next Exit #20 a couple of miles up west on I-80, I'll stop there and get a room for the night' he astutely calculated.

Retrieving his cell phone from beneath his heavy black and yellow-checked leather riding jacket, he engaged the voice-command application and spoke into the phone for the Hilton Hotel phone number. Automatically a synethic-generated voice responded back with the requisite phone number and offered Brad the option for a direct connection with a specified Hilton hotel, which he immediately selected.

"Hello and Good Day, this is the Hilton University City hotel, my name is Jessica, may I help you?" a cheerful female voice sounded into Brad's ear. It was great, Brad thought, to hear the sound of a positive, friendly, and feminine voice in a remote and strange place."

"Well yes, Miss, my name is Brad Hamilton and I would like a room for the night please if one is available?" Brad politely inquired.

"Let me check sir, one moment please! "Oh yes sir, we have several rooms, may I ask your preference sir?" Jessica cheerfully replied.

"Yes, let me have a non-smoking, King bed, deluxe suite, 3rd floor, and non-facing the busy highway," Brad replied definitively.

"Very good, I see that we have a room that has everything you requested, except that it's a double bed, is that acceptable to you, sir?" Jessica politely inquired. He thought for a brief second and decided that he had travelled far enough for one day and he just wanted to get settled and relax a bit.

"Yes, Jessica, that will be fine," Brad politely replied. He surrendered his credit card data to Jessica and this would hold the room for him until he arrived on site. An easy confidence came over Brad, now that he had both determined his next destination point and his nightly lodging. Years of corporate trips had instructed Brad to be ever mindful of security and safety planning and for these considerations, his hotel room should not face a major highway, nor should it be located too high up in the event of a fire or evacuation; finally, it also should not be located on the ground floor to which unfettered access by any criminal element was easily possible and inviting.

He re-mounted his mechanical steed and carefully attached the tether line to his inflatable safety vest. The huge BMW burst to life with a powerful, but muffled roar, as Brad engaged the ignition switch and throttle control. Still a novice to the motorcycle riding game and doing everything 'by the book', he fastidiously secured his helmet and gloves for what would prove to be a short 15-minute journey to the next exit and a relaxing night's rest. The Hilton Hotel was located a mere 200 yards off of I-80 and there was a series of customary chain and fast-food restaurants. From north-to-south, east-to-west, America was amalgamated with the same layout of non-descript hotel chains, gas stations and the fast-food eating establishments. The highway scene could be that of anywhere USA. Modernity had eventually transformed America into uniformity and mediocrity.

Brad deftly manoeuvred his now slightly road-soiled BMW into the moderately lighted parking lot of the Hilton University Park Motel. He wisely secured the motorcycle in a space beneath a high intensity sodium yellow coloured light, to which he deftly affixed a high tensile strength wire cable and lock. He was mindful to loop the cable through the bike's front wheel and engine frame components; this would not make stealing the bike impossible, just more of a challenge. He then engaged the bike's remote-control anti-theft alarm, the concern was not about the material loss of the bike, but rather the obvious associated social embarrassment of having his friends discover that his magic steed was stolen from him in the depth of the night and on the first day of his journey. Being a sensitive soul, he detested the idea or process of being teased unnecessarily.

Wearily he unwound the ties of the bungee cords which secured his personal gear, the elastic ties were affixed at strategic mounting points on the BMW frame. Next, he released the removable luggage bags and wearily walked toward the front office to register for his room. The evening fading sun was being eclipsed by some high cirrus clouds, the fading rays presented the clouds and surrounding sky in a soft pink salmon colour, like something from a stereotypical brash Las Vegas lounge room. It was the first time in many years that Brad had looked up into the evening sky and truly appreciated the beauty of nature. He cherished the colourful scene, perhaps because he was now closer to nature when riding his motorcycle or maybe because he was now alone to explore life without any of Boston's urban distractions. The beauty of nature was presenting a novel blessing to him and he was both humbled and most appreciative. A kind stranger held the hotel lobby door open for him, as his arms being filled with assorted travel bags and gear. "Thanks, Mister," Brad replied and nodded as the strange man held the door and Brad entered the lobby and made his way to the front-desk.

Behind the Hilton hotel reservation counter stood two young women attired in navy blue pants, white ruffled cuff shirts, and bright red button-down vests; both ladies greeted Brad with warm smiles.

"Hello Miss, I called about reserving a room for this evening, my name is Mr Hamilton?" Brad stated in a manner that was more of a polite inquiry rather than a mere cold statement of fact. Despite the motorcycle and accompanying leather riding attire, Brad's high-class Boston breeding and accent had followed him westward. The hotel clerk nearest to Brad spoke first. "Oh yes, sir, I was the one who took your reservation, my name is Jessica. How are you doing this evening, sir?" the young lady perkily replied with a beaming smile. Brad presented the ladies with his handsome facial features and tall figure; he was indeed quite the eye-candy to the fairer sex.

Jessica was slim, about twenty-five years old, she possessed warm hazel-coloured eyes that complemented her flawless porcelain complexion and perfect white teeth. "I have your name as Bradford W. Hamilton, Credit Card American Express Premium Platinum issued by First Boston with a reservation for one-night, deluxe suite, double-bed, the suite is on the 3rd floor and facing into the courtyard – correct, sir?" Jessica affirmed with a sweet, broad smile.

He could only delightfully grin as Jessica's smile warmed the cold of his icy disposition. "Yes, Jessica that sounds great, I've been travelling for over seven long hours on my bike and I need a good warm shower and a hot meal." Brad sighed as he smiled and continued to fill out his hotel registration form. He froze for a split second when the registration asked for emergency contact information. Previously he had always listed his father or mother, but having no immediate family living, he hesitated and thought for a moment. Brad listed the name Katherine MacAlister – she was the closest thing he had to family now and he was going to marry her soon anyway. Still, the registration form brought back bad memories for Brad and he felt a slight ting of pain and remorse for his lost family. Brad's eyes moistened with tears for just a scant few seconds – he was now virtually alone in the world. 'How lonely it was to be left as an orphaned adult!' he thought to himself with some generous degree of self-pity. It did not dawn on him that so many other people had lost their parents and siblings so much younger in life than he.

"Is everything all right, Mr Hamilton?" Jessica inquired as she noticed the tears welling in Brad's eyes. He immediately brushed his eyes and quickly regained his composure.

"Yes, that damn cold weather, it really makes my eyes moist and my nose run!" Brad jokingly lied as he camouflaged his emotions.

Jessica checked the personal data, as well as Brad's credit card, everything was in perfect order. "Here you go, Mr Hamilton, here is your coded key and your room number is inscribed in pencil on the reverse side of the key envelope holder. There is also a voucher for a complimentary drink in our lounge this evening. Your suite room is number 344, which also has its own stocked bar, refrigerator, microwave, and coffee brewing machine. A full buffet complimentary breakfast is served 6:30 AM through 10:00 AM in the restaurant area. Now is there anything else that I can assist you with, sir?" Jessica politely inquired.

Brad thought for a second, then he inquired in a monotone and tired voice, "Why yes there is, Jessica, are there any good local restaurants to catch a bite to eat?"

She immediately smiled back. "Of course sir, you have our famous Hilton restaurant named the 'Native Pennsylvanian' and if you elect other eating establishments there are numerous chain restaurants and fast-food outlets just outside the hotel's parking lot."

"Thank you," Brad softly remarked as he made his way to the elevator; it was a very short ride to the third floor. Exiting the elevator, Brad gathered his meagre baggage and inserted the perforated plastic key into the brass door receptacle and awaited the green entry signal. Opening the door and dropping one of his bags against it, he awkwardly searched for the light switch.

He immediately threw the bags onto the massive bed, and in quick succession he quickly gazed around the room and turned on more of the room lights. The room was typical of the middle-class accommodations that greeted millions of travelling Americans every day: it was cheap, it was clean, and it was very functional. Although Brad had never stayed in accommodations less than a four-star hotel, aside from his camping trips, he found the room to be well suited to his new Spartan travelling lifestyle. "First things first," Brad mumbled to himself as he began to strip his clothing away faster than a cabaret feather dancer. Upon disrobing completely, Brad took a nature break by immediately relieving himself; thereafter he turned the bathroom faucet on its highest water pressure. "God this hot water has never felt so good to me before this," Brad muttered as he generously lathered himself in hot soap and water for a long twenty-minute shower.

To further indulge in this warm bliss and to help ease his sore bones and tired butt, Brad did a most unusual thing by placing the stopper in the drain, whereby he enjoyed another thirty minutes of warm tub bathing. No ancient Roman citizen could have enjoyed a bathing experience any more than Brad did during this chilly and dark evening. 'Life was good and perhaps it was best when enjoyed by its simplest pleasures,' he mused with a complacent smile

Yet the warm, soothing indulgence was only temporal and besides, his pale white skin was withering from the prolonged exposure to the hot water. He vigorously towel-dried his hair and body, now feeling like a new man again and ready for the journey of the next morning. Suddenly it struck him! A surge of enormous hunger filled his senses. Aside from the morning breakfast which Carla had prepared for him and a hot cup of coffee at a rest-stop, he had neglected to take a regular mid-day meal. He was so concentrated on riding his motorcycle and noticing the scenic beauty of the countryside, that his hunger was abated until this very moment. Quickly he dressed into a pair of beige wool pants, a chamois button-down blue cotton shirt, and Timberline calf-level boots. The BMW's storage compartments allowed only a modicum of clothing and Brad had only two other complete outfits and some extra socks and underwear to accompany him on his journey. His modest wardrobe would make do for the present time. 'Less was more' when riding by motorcycle.

Walking out from the elevator, he spotted the warm and friendly Jessica greeting another weary client, this time it was a family of four, with the two children resting peacefully in the arms of each parent. Glancing up from her computer monitor, Jessica spotted Brad and beamed a huge and genuine smile. "Going out for the evening Mr Hamilton?" Jessica warmly inquired.

He smiled back in a friendly fashion. "Yes, Jessica, I'm going to get something to eat and I'm really hungry," he remarked.

Ever the model employee, Jessica responded back without almost thinking, "Sir, why not dine in the Hilton Dining Room, the food is better than the local fast-food variety and you can sit back and relax and enjoy your complimentary drink?" Jessica suggested in a wise, logical manner. Pondering for a second about all the future fast-food establishments that he was going to be visiting during this journey, a fine dinner with a drink sounded the perfect complement to the long, arduous day. "Good suggestion, a very good suggestion indeed, Jessica," Brad answered as he smiled back and made his way to the Hilton Dining Room.

"Sir, may I help you?" the aging, thin African American waiter inquired of Brad.

"Why yes – a table for one please," Brad responded politely and in good cheer.

"Of course, follow me, sir," politely responded the gravel-voiced waiter.

Brad was seated comfortably against a window, a view that betrayed the flicker of nightlife that existed around the surrounding quiet suburbs of Pennsylvania State University.

"My name is Bill, will you be having a beverage or drink this evening, sir?" inquired the waiter.

"Yes, Bill, do you have any malt scotch?" Brad replied eagerly.

"Yes, sir, here is our listing," responded the waiter, as he handed Brad the premium wine and spirit menu.

"I shall have a double Highland Park 12-year old whisky on the rocks," Brad replied as he placed down his complimentary free drink card in front of the waiter.

"Excuse me, sir, this card will cover one drink only, do you still want the double malt scotch?" the waiter dutifully noted to his guest. Brad was as thirsty as he was hungry, and he dearly wanted a generous sized drink.

"Yes, Bill – you bet I do! I will gladly cover the cost of the extra drink," Brad announced with a curt smile. He looked around the dining area and it was very sparsely filled with patrons – 'either the food was too expensive or else it didn't suit the palate of the hotel patrons,' Brad concluded, as he sipped some iced water from his crystal water goblet. A few minutes later Bill arrived back to the table with Brad's double malt scotch. Brad imbibed a generous snip, swooshed the peat-laden distillation in his mouth, and then slowly swallowed the heavenly smooth brew. "Ah, Bill, now that's a fine drink and one worth waiting for until the end of the day," Brad proclaimed with a broad smile and obvious heart-filled enjoyment.

The waiter smiled, as he enjoyed seeing a patron obviously relishing the finer things in life and he reciprocated the smile back to Brad. "Please tell me, Bill, what's on the menu for tonight?" Brad inquired of his loyal evening attendant.

"Here is the normal dinner menu, sir, and if I may, please let me point out that our Chef's Specials for the evening is Poached Pacific Coast Salmon in a light Dijon dill sauce, the roasted duck with orange sauce, and the Kansas City Filet Mignon 6 oz or 10 oz portions." Brad placed down the menu as he attentively listened to the waiter's flawless and mouthwatering descriptions of the evening's available bounty.

"Okay, Bill, I think that I will have the 10 oz filet mignon medium-well, with a baked potato, and asparagus, please," Brad replied with certainty.

The waiter smiled, as he furiously annotated Brad's dinner items onto a seemingly hideously small red-coloured booklet. "Very good choice, sir, your meal will be ready shortly, please avail yourself to our complimentary salad bar," the waiter announced politely and with a broad smile. The fragrant bouquet of the peat scotch had dulled Brad's ambitions of the salad bar and that which Brad now craved was a high calorie diet of meat and potatoes. The cool outdoor weather had burnt off more of his body calories than his normal office activities and his body craved bulk nutrition.

Savouring the meal like a condemned man on death row, he even ordered another double malt scotch, which he was resolved to take back to his room – this despite the unconventional nature and protocol that one was never to take a restaurant drink out of the dining room. He thanked Bill by giving him an overly generous $35 tip on a $65 meal. Stopping at the front desk, he requested a wakeup call for the next morning from Jessica.

Seated lazily back in his hotel armchair, he remembered that he needed to call Katherine. Kate's phone rung three times with no immediate answer, however, on the fourth ring, a polite and very feminine voice answered in a monotone voice, "Hello this is Katherine." Brad was harkened more than he thought at the tone of Katherine's warm, familiar voice, it almost sounded and tasted like candy to him.

"Hello Kate, this is your bad biker boy calling!" Brad announced in a toying tone.

Katherine was lounging around in her massive and comfortable bedroom suite at her parents' estate, affectionately known as 'Arisaig' a name taken from the western region of Scotland from whence her family originated; she was ecstatic when she heard Brad's voice. "Brad, my darling, how are you? Where are you? How have you been? When are you coming back, my darling?" Katherine inquired in a rapid machine gun-like fashion.

"Woo slow down, I am doing just fine, Kate. It wasn't a bad day at all, aside from some middle-age muscle pains gained from relearning my rusty motorcycle riding skills. I am at the Hilton University Park in the middle of Pennsylvania and I should be in Ohio tomorrow evening," Brad exclaimed with some sense of accomplishment and self-assurance. Katherine was not at all pleased by Brad's implication that this trek of his was more than just a one-day lark – she had half expected Brad to still be in the state of Massachusetts holed up in a cheap motel and moping about coming back home.

"Tell me, you are safe and sound, huh, Brad?" Katherine inquired rather mockingly and with a tone of disappointment.

"Yes indeed, Kate, I'm more than fine, the scenery in Pennsylvania is beautiful – it's awash in emerald green, you should see the beautiful pastures of the Amish farmers in Lancaster County and I hear that Ohio is more of the same beautiful landscape...I love being in the open wind and both seeing and smelling this great country!" Brad exclaimed in a boyish manner.

However, Katherine was not equally enthused by Brad's great adventure. "Brad, honey, I love and miss you greatly, I want you to be happy and safe, but are you really sure that you are doing well?" Katherine pleaded softly over the phone, as she paced nervously back and forth across the swath of a rich oriental carpet. She was so nervous about Brad's predicament that she would have lit up a cigarette if she was a cigarette smoker.

Brad pondered for a moment, he wanted to both assure Katherine, yet still keep true to himself. He chose his words carefully. "Kate, I'm fine and thanks for asking, I really appreciate it, you know it's funny in that the farther I get from Boston, the more I think of you, Kate. When I'm riding the BMW, it creates a great tranquillity and peaceful feeling in me. It's only been one day, but I love seeing this country up close," he confessed with unbridled enthusiasm.

Katherine detected the sincerity in Brad's voice and she knew that further arguments would be futile, perhaps even damaging.

"Of course, Brad darling, that's fine, I guess I'll just have to live with this. I am glad that you are eating well and enjoying yourself, but are you sure that there is nothing that I can do or send to you?" she anxiously inquired.

Brad smiled to himself; he was reassured by Katherine's genuine concern for his well- being.

"Thanks, Kate, I just ate a delicious steak dinner, had two scotches, and I don't need anything right now and thank you for inquiring," Brad responded with self-satisfaction.

"I love you, Brad, and I wish that you were back here with me," Katherine sobbed ever so softly.

Suddenly he felt a little guilty about leaving Katherine.

"I love and miss you too, Kate, but I'll be back soon, I just can't say when that will be at the present time! I'll be fine, don't worry about me. Is there anything happening back at the office that needs my attention?" Brad inquired with honest concern.

Katherine's response was most abbreviated and mean-spirited: "No, nothing that I can't handle, aside from that common DeTagelio working-girl."

Immediately Brad came to his personal assistant's defence. "Look, Kate, I like Margie, and besides, you get Joan Peters back next week and Margie will be out of your hair. Margie will be left to only handle my mail, correspondences, and telephone calls. So, Margie stays, Kate, okay, pussy-cat?" Brad declared in a playful, yet definitive tone.

"Yes, Brad, just promise me that you will be careful and call me, please," Katherine pleaded once again.

"Sure, Kate, but it's getting late and I'm off again early tomorrow, so let me say good night and I love you dearly, don't forget that!" he concluded.

"I love you too, Brad darling, and please promise to be careful, do you hear me? Goodnight, Brad," Katherine declared once more.

"Sure thing, Kate, and pleasant dreams," Brad whispered as he gently hung up the phone.

She stood motionless in her bedroom, happy that Brad was safe and that he thought enough of her to give her a call, yet she was also haunted by the fact that Brad had no intention of quickly coming back to Boston. He was serious about this cross-country trip, yet she was uncertain as to how this would affect her future plans, especially her unspecified wedding date and if there was anything that disturbed Katherine, it was uncertainty and not being in control of events.

There was a sudden velvet knock upon the bedroom door and before she had a chance to verbally respond, the door opened ever so slowly and gently. It was Katherine's mother, Faye. She was attired in a pale blue evening robe and white silk slippers; her hair was arrayed up into a petite bun, which only served to accent the attractiveness of her Anglophile features, her emerald-green eyes and blonde-grey hair being complemented by equally brilliant light green emerald earrings. "Kate, my baby, how are you doing, my dearest?" Faye declared with a pleasant, warm smile to her beloved daughter.

Kate's eyes were slightly filled with tears, as she turned away from the nightstand table and rushed into the arms of her mother, as they shared a heart-filled mother-daughter embrace. Katherine looked tearfully into her mother's eyes. "That was Brad on the phone, Mother. He called to say that he is staying overnight in some crummy hotel in Pennsylvania and that by tomorrow, he'll be somewhere in Ohio. He's not coming back to me, Mother, at least not as soon as I had expected… this craziness might go on indefinitely!" Katherine cried to her mother, seeking some parental consolation.

Faye gazed sympathetically into her daughter's eyes; both mother and daughter sat down in a comfortable love seat couch. "I think that we need to talk and to have ourselves a drink," Faye commanded in a stern, but mothering way. Faye poured two small glasses of amber-coloured aged sherry from a lead crystal nautical decanter. She took the two drinks and handed one to her daughter. "Now start sipping some of this fine sherry and tell me your problems, dear," Faye commanded to her daughter.

"Well, Mother it's like this, he's really serious about this journey. I have fears about him and about us...I mean our future together!" Katherine confessed as she eagerly sipped the smooth sherry.

Faye's reaction was muted, as was her reaction. "Please go on and tell me more, my dear," Faye MacAlister coolly encouraged to her daughter.

"I'm afraid of the uncertainties that this trip will have on Brad and myself. I fear for his safety driving that damn motorcycle, I'm afraid for our future together, and just plain afraid for myself too, Mother!" Katherine confessed as she took another generous sip of sherry.

"Kate, my dearest, thank you for being truthful with me, it's one of your better traits and one that a parent always appreciates, but I think you're stuck with this situation. Brad could be coming back next week or next year. Are you sure that you want to commit to this possibility?" Faye inquired earnestly of her daughter.

"Oh, Mother please – just be realistic for one minute, Brad is my future, he's the only man for me, and in case you haven't looked around the Boston social circuit, there is not exactly a plethora of eligible men in my category; every other man out there just wants to simply get into my panties for a quickie or get into my pocketbook. I've loved Brad since we were little children, we're simply perfect for one another!" Katherine replied defensively and with an obvious degree of class snobbery.

Faye sipped the final remnants of liquor from the diminutive sherry snifter, as she slowly arose from the couch. "Kate, my dear child, I guess from what you have told me, you're just going to have to wait for him to come back; perhaps you can even coax him back with your charms." Faye devilishly smiled as she placed her hands-on Katherine's shoulders.

However, Katherine was not in the least consoled by the sage advice of her mother.

"So, what happens if he meets someone else or he becomes disinterested in me?" Katherine sobbed.

Faye looked deeply into her daughter's eyes and smiled. "My dearest Kate, there are no guarantees in this life, either for the Hamiltons, nor the MacAlisters... you face what life offers and you deal with it, sometimes if you're lucky, you even get what you want. Yet I seriously doubt if any road diversion can detract Brad from your beauty for very long."

Katherine smiled upon hearing the complimentary remarks from her mother, or perhaps it was the numbing effects of the soothing sherry.

"I suppose, Mother, that I'll just have to deal with the problems as they come along, so good night and thanks for looking in on me, Mother," Kate smiled as she softly kissed her mum on the cheek.

"I'll see you tomorrow and sleep tight, dear. Also remember that Brad has had a crush on you as well, ever since your childhood and I know that he loves you," Faye replied as she closed the door to Katherine's bedroom.

★ ★ ★ ★ ★ ★ ★ ★ ★ ★ ★ ★ ★ ★ ★ ★ ★

Morning came quickly, as he slowly raised himself out of the hotel bed and shockingly discovered new aches and pains within his middle-age body. A long, warm shower helped to ease the torso pains and to restore a sense of rejuvenated spirit to his sore body.

Freshly showered and dressed, Brad was ready for his check-out and a hearty breakfast before hitting the road again. He headed to the hotel dining area, where he gorged himself on fat laden bacon and protein filled scrambled eggs. Tall goblets of orange juice and a huge pot of coffee complemented the hearty, if not unhealthy, meal. Fully satiated from his breakfast fodder, he returned back to his room, packed his bags and discreetly checked out of the hotel.

Attaching the luggage bags onto the bike, he unlocked the security devices, and fired up the ignition switch. The magnificent beast breathed into life immediately with a healthy roar. He decided to let the engine warm up a few minutes before hitting the road again. He looked about the various doings of the surrounding area, he spied the various delivery and service personnel go about their daily routines. Like organized insects, every person seemed engrossed and absorbed in his or her respective tasks and business. This was for the plight of working men and women across the country, each making their way the best that they could in order to make a living.

Glancing at the raw scenes of human movement, he wondered for a moment what the working man's lot in life was as opposed to that of his investment banking trade. He thought to himself, that aside from the money and socially contrived prestige factors inherent to various labour categories, that one person's work was not really different from that of another's, each job having its own satisfactions and limitations. His own personal advantage was that he was insanely rich, and he could do and act as he pleased, while everyone else had no such options, they were stuck in their daily drudgery.

The BMW was now warm and the scent of pure, non-combusted high-octane gasoline fuel, served to bring back Brad's mind to the immediate presence of his rumbling motorcycle. Mounting the iron beast and taking instant delight in the heated riding seat and handlebars, he aimed the BMW onto Interstate 80 and out into the west. After a few hours, the rich green countryside of Pennsylvania merged seamlessly into that of its cousin neighbour state of Ohio. The BMW's heated handlebars were a most welcome relief from the cool blowing Spring air. The emerging green Spring scenery filled the entire countryside and it verified nature's eternal resurrection rite after the long hibernation of the cold, white Winter. Throughout the morning hours, Brad played 'cat and mouse' games with both the passenger vehicles and lumbering commercial trucking leviathans that abundantly populated the Interstate. The more he traveled, the greater his motorcycle skills became. He knew that he was not a racing-League competitor, but neither was he a total novice biker either.

By noontime, the urge arose to necessitate a mid-day 'pit stop'. It was probably more accurate to state that it was Brad's bodily functions that required the temporary respite from the cold winds, vibrating engine, and a taxing crouched riding position. A gas station mart conveniently presented itself several hundred yards ahead and he wasn't prepared to wait for an alternative. Determinably, he pulled the BMW quickly into the nearest filling pump stall and turned off the ignition switch. Slowly stretching his back and whirling his arms in slow giant propeller-like swirls, he sought to loosen up his contorted muscles. Once again, Brad felt great relief upon dismounting the BMW motorcycle. His stiffened feet and leg muscles appreciated the short walk to the indoor food mart. Wearily he approached the counter kiosk, holding his helmet and gloves firmly under his arm.

"Yes, sir, how can we help you today?" greeted the salt and pepper bearded middle aged male clerk from across the service counter.

Instantly Brad pulled his wallet from inside his leather jacket pocket. "Please give me $20 premium on pump #5 please and a large cup of coffee."

"Yes sir, so how is the riding today?" inquired the clerk with some degree of vocal vicarious envy.

"It's great, not too cold and there's a lot of freedom out there on the road, still I must stay alert for the errant asshole," Brad replied as he sipped a mouth full of strong black coffee.

He began pumping his fuel and glanced about to admire the scenery and to stretch his neck a bit. The surrounding countryside was a scenic mosaic of rolling green hills and heavy forested planes. Nature and the last Ice Age had indeed been generous to the rich Ohio River valley, he thought. However, Brad's sight of the majestic natural attractions was interrupted by a sole billboard advertisement. The advertisement was bold, colourful, and punctuated by big, bold, letters "MOTO CROSS RACE & STUNT EXHIBITION – COME SEE DARING RACERS INCLUDING THE COPEN FAMILY – Ohio Fair Grounds."

The billboard initially attracted and then seduced his attention. He smiled to himself and he thought, "Why not spend a day or so and mingle with the common motorcycle gypsies?" Right then and there, he serendipitously decided to attend the event, he relished his newfound nature of being spontaneous, something he had never done back in his stuffy Boston elite circle of friends and something that his parents had always discouraged. Being free on the road was like being a reckless child again, alone in the fun and play of the moment, enjoyment being the singular and only necessary reward. Topping off the fuel tank, he placed on his helmet and aimed the massive BMW down I-80 toward the Ohio Fair Grounds some fifty miles down the road. Brad's face was grinning with a wide boyish smile all the way down the highway.

The uneventful ride to the Ohio Fair Grounds took but a few minutes with the BMW running on full open throttle. As with many popular events, however, he soon found himself snarled in a mini traffic jam, which soon tried his patience as an endless stream of cars, pick-up trucks, and mini-vans piled into the long traffic-feeder troughs. A huge, lumbering motorcycle was not the most pleasant thing to be stuck in bumper-to-bumper traffic and his nerves and body temperature started to fray at the seemingly endless delay. Brad picked the line that he thought was least congested and unhesitatingly moved the BMW into this lane of traffic. After another half-hour of stressful waiting, Brad bolted his BMW up the far-right median curb.

While darting across nearly a half mile of crawling vehicles, he was suddenly confronted by four burly and stern looking armed guards employed by the Ohio State Fair Grounds Commission. The guards were hired off-duty police officers and Ohio State troopers, who earned some nice pocket money during their off-duty hours, and each guard was hired for their intimidating looks, as well as their many years of police experience.

"Hey buddy! Yeah, I mean you over there – come over here right now!" yelled one of the security guards as he pointed menacingly in Brad's direction. All of a sudden, Brad felt like a little boy who had gotten caught with his hand in Mommy's cookie jar and not that of a toughened biker. Upon his motorcycle he sat in stunned motionlessness just starring at the guard. "Maybe this guard was talking to a different person," Brad hopefully thought.

"Yes, I mean you, buddy! Come over here, or didn't you hear what I just said?" shouted the officer as he pointed his finger directly at Brad. Quickly looking about, he saw no means of escape or evasion, so all that could be done was to face the guard with confidence and bravado. Brad toyed his BMW over to the location of the guard and raised his riding glasses very slowly.

"Yes, officer, what can I do for you, sir?" Brad responded slowly, strongly, and assuredly to the stern looking guard. "Hey, buddy, who the hell do you think that you are? You jumped the queuing line to get ahead of all these other folks who have been waiting in line just as long as you have been, so what's the deal here?" the guard inquired with impatience and obvious anger. Brad thought quickly for an answer, not wanting to be turned around and wait at the end of the ever-larger queue.

Confidently removing his helmet and squarely looking into the eyes of the guard, he spoke without hesitation and supreme confidence, "Officer, I am a sponsor of one of the highlighters of this event! I am here to personally see that my sponsorship is proceeding without any problems!" The officer was temporarily taken about by this answer, as he had expected this to be a normal line jumper with the usual stupid lying excuse.

Ever inquisitive, the officer pressed for more information. "Okay, buddy, and just who in the hell are you supposed to be sponsoring?" the officer snapped with an interrogating tone.

Another lightning thought entered his mind, as he retrieved the only other piece of credible information at his disposal. "Why of course, officer... I am sponsoring the famous Copen Family of motorcycle riders," Brad announced in a most self-evident tone.

The boast was profound and direct, yet it was made so boldly that the doubtful officer was starting to believe the information that this brash, self-confident man was selling to him.

The officer continued to seek satisfaction of his endless curiosity. "So, pal, do you have any proof or ID of who you say you are, Mister Big Shot?"

"Yes, officer – the name is Mr Hamilton of Boston!" Brad interjected boldly with air of eastern elite confidence. Brad deftly pulled open his fine Italian leather wallet with its embroidered Hamilton crest and presented both his Hamilton & MacAlister ID card and his richly embossed business card to the officer. The officer looked carefully at the identification documents... he was impressed by the sophistication and professionalism of the identification card. Brad's ID was not a simple, cheap ID card, rather it was laser embossed with a holographic picture similar to US currency and high-end debit cards. Also, the ID contained an embedded, visible computer chip that contained the latest personal and corporate data of the bearer; finally, the ID contained a holographic visible right thumb print etched on the lower right side. The title of the Hamilton & MacAlister ID card was annotated, 'Mr Bradford W. Hamilton, Hamilton & MacAlister Investment Banker, Chairman & Chief Executive Officer, Broomwall Street, Boston, Mass.' This ID was on par with those he had seen for FBI and Secret Service agents; this guy had to be the Real McCoy for sure.

"There's no flipping way this guy was bluffing!" the officer concluded, considering the biker's correct use and pronunciation of the English language, his elegant chowder Boston accent, his confident gestures, direct eye contact, confident attitude, expensive motorcycle, and finally the $100,000 + platinum and diamond watch on Brad's wrist – these all added up to a very rich, important citizen. "For sure this was no biker bum line jumper," the officer concluded. Wealth and a positive bearing could fool many people indeed.

"Okay, everything seems to check out here, Mr Hamilton, I'm sorry for the delay, but we just have to be sure that trashy, low-life, trouble-makers and fans stay away from the event riders, we don't want anyone disturbing our event here. I did not expect to see a CEO on a motorcycle or at a racing event like this!" the officer conveyed in an almost apologetic tone.

"No problem, officer, you have to watch out for shady people these days pretending to be something they are not. I rode my BMW from back east because I never seem to be able to get the time to ride in anything other than an expensive sedan or limousine," Brad injected with a devilish smile and knowing full well that he was pulling a fast-one on the police officer.

"Go right ahead and stay to the right, Mr Hamilton, this will take you into the restricted pit area, sir. Please say hello to the Copens for me, they are a local family and we fully support them." The officer nodded as he waved Brad and his BMW into the restricted private entry line.

The bold boast had paid-off and now he was going to get the best seat in the house with which to view the Moto-Cross motorcycle show, the details of which he had no idea what exactly to expect, save for some hot dog motorcyclists riding around an oval track at breakneck speeds. He confidently rode his BMW down a twisting road that led into a cavernous indoor arena, where in the centre lay huge mounds of freshly laid dirt, hay bales in strategically placed corners, and an abundance of orange mesh crash webbing. Around the perimeter of the auditorium forum was arrayed a circular racing circuit for speed racing; while the centre field was occupied by man-made dirt hills, water filled troughs, and speed ramps. Brad spotted the several white and blue coloured vans and trailers emblazed with the name "COPENS FAMILY MOTO-CROSS CYCLISTS", so he figured this was a proper place to park his bike and see the show. He might even get to see what all the hoopla was about the Copen family and what exactly they did to deserve such billing and recognition.

He neatly nudged his BMW into the reserved parking area that was located astride the Copens' reserved set of mobile trailers and accompanying array of at least a dozen well used motor-cross racing motorcycles of various makes and brands, to include Yamaha and Kawasaki. He was now a captive guest in this secluded and restricted arena area and he knew that if he was caught by the authorities, the best he could hope for was an outright dismissal from the area; at worst, it could mean a sleepless night in the local jail on some minor trespassing charges trumped up by some local-yokel Deputy Barney Fife-type.

Each trailer was painted in a motif of Americana red, white, and blue nationalistic colour scheme. Also painted on the side of the van trailer were the figures of five motor-cross racers depicted riding along a painted racetrack. Brad put the BMW on its jiffy stand, removed his helmet, and un-buckled his heavy leather jacket and finally his air safety vest. Although the second day's ride was good, so also was the feeling to have one's feet on terra firma and the ability to stretch out just a bit. Yet his relaxation was suddenly interrupted.

"Hey you, fella, what the hell are you doing here? What's your business? This isn't a place for the public," cried a middle-aged man attired in a faded, but colourful pale blue mechanic jump suit.

Brad merely stood there stunned for a moment, hoping that his appearance near the motorcycle pits would not gander any notice amidst the other people and activities. He had judged wrongly.

"Hey you! I said what the hell are you doing here, young fella?" confronted the middle-aged man once again in an angry tone.

Caught in the act of trespassing, Brad had no ready response this time and he stood there silently perplexed with his mouth aghast. Receiving no reply, the stranger quickly looked across to the far side of the arena, locked his eyes with those of a gazing security guard and placing two fingers in his mouth to blow a shrill finger-whistle which could be clearly heard across the wide arena. The stranger waved his arms for the security guard to come over to his area. The security officer nodded in acknowledgment and walked a slow pace across the motocross arena.

Possessed with juvenile-like nervousness, Brad immediately knew there was pending trouble with the law. He had only several minutes before the security guard would confront him and possibly place him under arrest. Once again, he thought fast and acted even faster. He approached the strange middle-aged man in the oily blue mechanic jumpsuit and tried to explain his embarrassed plight.

"Look, sir, it's like this, my name is Brad Hamilton, I am the CEO of the Boston investment banking firm of Hamilton & MacAlister and I got in here on a fib by claiming that I was here to help finance the Copens' racing team!" Brad explained earnestly as he withdrew his bank credentials and business card from his wallet and tried to present these to the disgruntled stranger.

The middle-aged stranger looked at Brad with utter disbelief and some degree of contempt, as he gazed at the security officer walking ever nearer to him.

"Please, sir, just look at my credentials. I'm really an investment banker and I can make this worth your while – will you please vouch for me? My ass in in a real vice here!" Brad pleaded nervously as he shoved his ID into the stranger's hand.

"Are you trying to bribe me, sonny?" the older man replied in a gruff and unemotional tone.

The security officer was now a mere 40 feet away from them and Brad made a last frantic plea. "No, Mister please, I am no trouble maker and I am no Moto-cross groupie either, I just don't want to get arrested for telling a minor white-lie by over-jumping the entrance line!" Brad pleaded in an earnest and anxious tone. The man deeply gazed into Brad's eyes then turned away toward the approaching security officer.

"Hey, Mr Copen, what is going on here? Is there any trouble here, Mr Copen? Who is this guy? Is he causing you any problems, Mr Copen?" the security guard professionally inquired in rapid succession, his right hand poised on his leather pistol pouch. Brad stood there with guilty and stunned eyes, shocked at the news that he had been speaking to the patriarch of the racing Copen family. Mr Copen dutifully handed the ID and business card of Brad over to the security officer, who looked at the credentials quite carefully before speaking once again. "So, Mr Copen what is the issue here with Mr Brad Hamilton of 'Hamilton & MacAlister Investment Banking?" the officer inquired and looking carefully at the faces of Mr Copen and Brad.

Mr Copen looked at Brad with a stone-cold face and then turned to speak with the officer, "It seems that Mr Brad Hamilton here has done something here that needs to be cleared up, in fact, it's something illegal, and you should be made aware of it right now, officer!"

As his heart and pulse raced, Brad was sweating bullets, he was sure to be arrested and taken away in hand-cuffs. His next phone call to Katherine might be from a jail cell. "I can explain everything, officer," Brad tried to plea anxiously.

"Hey, fella, you just shut your mouth and keep your hands where I can see them! I was asking Mr Copen here a question and not from you, now is that clear?" the officer sternly shouted as Brad meekly nodded in silent affirmation and dutiful compliance.

The officer placed one of his hands on his holster hand-cuffs and made a further inquiry. "Well, what exactly has this man done that is illegal, Mr Copen?" the officer inquired with an inquisitive, jaunted grin.

Brad momentarily hung his head in despair and held his breath, expecting to be momentarily hand-cuffed by the police.

Mr Copen drew a long, exhausted sigh and then spoke to the officer again, "Everything is fine; however, it seems that Mr Hamilton here has not gotten an official police-pass for his visit to the Copen Family riding team pit area, Officer; can you please issue this young man a special access pass for the duration of the show here? I don't want him getting into any trouble with the law!"

Quickly, Brad raised his head and smiled in astonishment at not being betrayed by Mr Copen.

"Why sure-thing, just give me your vehicle registration, driver's licence, and insurance papers, Mr Hamilton, and I will fix you right up," replied the officer in a jovial tone, all the while chewing on a generous wad of tobacco.

"Yes sir," Brad replied as he handed the officer his vehicle information and giving a short wink to Mr Copen.

"Mr Hamilton, here is your pass, which is good for the duration of the event, please contact me if you need anything," the officer replied as he handed Brad back his pit-pass and ID.

"Mr Copen, many thanks for not turning me in to the law and may I ask, why didn't you?" Brad asked in a puzzled tone.

Mr Copen stood silent for a second before speaking. "Well, son, you looked like an honest, but scared rabbit and you looked genuine enough, so let's just say that this is my good deed for the day, alright?"

Brad smiled and extended his hand in friendship. "That sure sounds good to me, Mr Copen and if I can ever repay the favour, well, just ask for it," Brad replied as the two strode around the Copen pit area.

"Just call me Paul, as I'm not that much older than you are and being called Mister makes me feel older than my years," the Copen patriarch dryly added.

Brad sighed in agreement. "Alright, Paul it is, and you can call me 'Wayne', it's my middle name and I never seemed to use my middle name enough, so 'Wayne' is my name!" Brad sighed laughingly.

The two took a slow stroll around the Copen trailers and Paul pointed out the figures of his three racing children. "That one there flying through the air is my Patricia, she's my daughter and 20 years old – a real Calamity Jane on the stunt work and a half-way decent dirt track racer. Now those two race track figures there are my two twins – Johnny and Ernst are two of the top 100 Moto-Cross racers in the USA and that's

not bad for being only 24 years old. Those other young riding figures in
the maintenance pits are of other family and friends; Mike Kozak is my
brother-in-law's son, while Billy Jordan has been their childhood friend
for the past 15 years," Copen proudly explained.

'Wayne' looked on in amazement on a vocation that drew its
young members from across the stable of American youth. It was wild,
high energy, irresponsible, and even juvenile, but 'Wayne' was clearly
mesmerized by the energy and excitement of the Motor-cross sport.
Paul Copen noticed the wonder and intrigue in the stranger's face and
eyes. 'Wayne', as Brad was now calling himself, was just starting to get
enthused by the motorcycle leisure hobby, but this professional motor-
cross cycling was many pegs above his riding or experience level. It
greatly intrigued him too!

Wayne inquired a little bit more into this side of life of which he
never dreamed had existed. "Well, Paul, if you don't mind me asking,
isn't this type of life a little bit rough on the family? What does Mrs
Copen say to all this?" Wayne inquired innocently.

A sudden sadness eclipsed the prevailing smile of Paul Copen.

"It's not a pretty story, Wayne, it's like this... the Mrs, that is my
Becky that is, she took ill with cancer a few years ago. It was a silent
killer that took her, Wayne. She had colon cancer Stage IV and none of us
saw it coming until it was too late. She died peacefully in my arms, she
weighed a mere 98 pounds at the time of her passing, a living skeleton,"
Paul meekly confessed, as he wiped the tears from his eyes.

Wayne's eyes moistened too, as he put his arm around Paul's
shoulder and silently remembering the death of his own family.

"The kids were almost fully grown and after Becky's death, the
family all figured that we should honour Becky and live life by doing
what the family enjoyed most and that was motor-cross racing and
motorcycle acrobatics. I sold my auto mechanic repair business and took
some of Becky's life insurance money and the family started the Copen's
motor-cross racing team. We win some/lose some races, but none of us
wants to do anything else and it does keep the Copen family together,"
Paul Copen sighed.

"So now, Wayne, what is your story? You're a young restless rich
city fellow from Boston – now everyone has a life story. We don't get
to see fancy rich Boston investment bankers at this type of fare, are
you slumming or something?" Paul interrogated jeeringly of his new-
found friend.

It was now Wayne's turn to relieve the pain of the past, as he slowly began to recount his own personal tragedy.

"So, if you want to hear a story, I'll tell you mine, Paul, it hasn't been all champagne and caviar for me, at least not recently. You see, my entire family died this past winter in a plane crash out West. My parents, sister, and brother, they are all gone – wiped out in the blink of an eye. My world sure came to a sudden change that black day…I'm uncertain if it is better for death to come suddenly or in a long, drawn-out fashion. Both stink to high heavens!" Wayne tearfully sobbed as moisture filled the sockets of his eyes, yet he continued to explain his situation to the honest stranger, who was respectful enough to take the time and listen. Wayne looked away from Mr Copen as he struggled to explain his grief. After a few silent seconds, Wayne regained his emotional composure and continued his tale of woe. With each passing sentence, he was confessing a great emotional burden off of his shoulders and even his heart felt lighter.

"My story isn't all self-pity though, I haven't lost everything, Mr Copen, you see I have a wonderful fiancée back East who loves me and is waiting for me to come back and marry her. I felt in all good faith that until I settled my loss, that I could not marry her… I couldn't contemplate marriage or anything else at a time when I mourn for my family, I just can't do it now," Wayne emotionally replied as tears welled up in his eyes and his voice cracked ever so slightly. "I just couldn't pick up the pieces of my life and begin where I left off, I needed to get away from Boston, my career, my smugness, my fiancée, and the entire rat race," Wayne confessed in a sobbing voice. "You know, it's funny how you think you have life all planned, then bang, you get thrown a curve ball," Wayne added in disgust, as he pounded his fist on one of the Copens' trailers and placed his head against the side trailer panel.

Paul Copen was clearly moved by Wayne's revelation, as much as he was surprised by his bluntness in revealing his own tragedy to a perfect, yet attentive stranger. It seemed to Paul that sometimes in life you just click with the right person and feel free to open up to them. Confession was perfect therapy for one's soul.

"You know, Wayne, I felt exactly like you did when my wife was stricken with that damn cancer. I thought that my whole world had ended, the only woman that I had loved was dead and I thought that I would go mad! After a week of drowning myself in Jack Daniel's whiskey, I realized that I wasn't alone, that I had my family to raise and with the help of my family and close friends, we made it through the tough times. Sure, it was rough at first, there were many fights and a lot of screaming – most of that being done by me! The family came to an understanding of our loss and what we wanted to do with the rest of our lives too. As a family, we came to realize how short and fragile our lives were and that we were going to stick together and live our dreams – no matter how small or ridiculous these ideas may have seemed to outsiders," Paul concluded, as he laid a fatherly hand on Wayne's shoulder. This was the exact feeling and resolve that Wayne now possessed.

Wayne appreciated Paul's fatherly touch and it fondly reminded him of the comfort that his own father had bestowed on him many times in his past. It was a good feeling to have someone reach out and warmly touch him. Wayne slowly picked his head up from against the trailer only to see five very loud motorcycles approaching him. "Ah, must be the young'ings, the Copen Clan that is!" Paul stated with a fatherly smile to Wayne. Both men smiled at one another, their self-revelations were broken by the reality that this was a race circuit, with a racing family, all of whom had motocross races and contests to win.

The sounds of the five racing motorcycles were almost deafening and the action of the riders turning on the handlebar gas throttles made the thundering sounds even more obnoxious, but very masculine. All the bikers appeared to be lean and energetic, this being only natural as motocross racing was truly a young person's sport with not many riders surviving past their early thirties. The riders in unison placed their machines in neutral, turned off the ignition switches, and slowly dismounted their bikes. Removing their helmets, they slowly moved toward Paul Copen. All of the riders were in their late teens and early twenties and three of the riders resembled one another, while the fourth rider was a lanky built white American kid with an easy-going smile. The fifth rider was a young African American with a short, stocky build frame and a friendly face that was complemented with a rugged moustache.

"Hey kids, come over here, I want you to meet a new-found friend of mine," Paul Copen exclaimed with some satisfaction. "This here is Mr Wayne Hamilton from Boston, he's a banker and biker too," Paul remarked. Paul Copen introduced Wayne to each member of the riding troop, "These are the riders of the Copen Racing Motocross Family, the twins here are Johnny and Ernst – the two oldest of the Copen Clan and they are both on the race track circuit, where speed is the name of the game. Next over here is Patricia, she is my youngest and she specializes in aerobatic and trick riding. Last, but not least, over here we have Mike Connors, my nephew, and Billy Jordan, a childhood friend of the family." Except for Billy Jordan, who was a lean and lanky African American, all of the other riders were white; fair-skinned and shared a family resemblance in terms of their flaxen hair, pale blue eyes, and medium frame build.

"Hello, nice to meet you all!" Wayne exclaimed as he held out his hand in friendship to all five riders and he shook their hands in due order.

"A banker, huh, well we could all use some cash around here, that's for sure!" shouted Billy Jordan as he shook Wayne's hand.

"Yeah, Wayne, we could really use a bank loan to get some new motorcycles for the team," Patricia grinned anxiously.

"So, Mister, what brings you to Ohio and this little piece of God's green earth?" Johnny Copens inquired in an inquisitive, almost sarcastic tone.

Wayne answered quickly and truthfully. "Well, Johnny, I just needed to get away from those rich, obnoxious assholes up in Boston during my summer vacation!" Wayne exclaimed in a serious tone before injecting his devilish frown. With that comment, everyone laughed and the ice among them was immediately broken.

"In all honesty, I am doing a little cross-country trip here and I just happened to see the Motocross billboard, so here I am," Wayne exclaimed.

"So how long do you expect to be staying here, Wayne?" young Johnny Copens inquired.

Wayne thought for a bit then honestly responded, "I blow with the wind, whenever the mood strikes me. I jump on my BMW and travel onward to places unknown, I'm a biker-bum this summer of my life; maybe I can stay here and learn some bike tricks and techniques from the team?"

Everyone was silent for a few seconds on hearing Wayne's request.

Johnny thought for a split second before answering with a devilish grim, "I think that we can teach an older guy a trick or two. So where are you staying, Wayne?"

He had no answer, as his plans for the evening were not finalized in any way.

"Is there a place to stay around here for the night?" Wayne inquired of Paul Copen.

"There's a Motel 6 and a Best Western just outside the Fair Grounds and while these may not be the fanciest digs around, the places are clean and within walking distance of the Fair Grounds, so what more can you ask for?" Paul inquired innocently.

Wayne returned the smile. "Yeah, what more indeed do I need?" Wayne thought for a quick second then offered a suggestion to everyone. "How about I buy everyone dinner at the Cracker Barrel Family Restaurant?" The Cracker Barrel was located just outside the Ohio Fair Grounds and it served wholesome, substantial servings of home style American food.

"The only stipulation I have is that everyone has to show this old man some of your fancy riding tricks, agreed?" Wayne pleaded jokingly.

"Sure thing, old man Wayne! We all have some real killer moves that may save your life on that highway of death out there!" Billy Jordan nodded as he swung his arms around Wayne's shoulder.

"Hey, I can teach you to do 'wheelies', 'Hanging', 'The Stripper', 'The Deadman', and many more stunts," Patricia exclaimed with eager excitement. Wayne just smiled at his new-found friends and the anticipation of learning the dangerous and exhilarating skill associated with motocross racing and cycle acrobatics. "This is great, folks! I'll have to invest in some bags of ice that my old bones are going to require after this instruction is done," Wayne remarked as they all headed off to a hearty dinner and light-hearted conversations. Wayne's future for the next two weeks or so was now locked in. He would watch, learn, live, and make some new friends.

* * * * * * * * * * * * * * * * *

Katherine lazily slouched upon her ornate antique French mahogany desk and boringly toyed the index finger of her hand around the end of her long straight black hair. A pile of routine and mundane financial correspondence generously covered the desk, none of which induced or motivated her attention. A mere week had passed since Brad had left on his quest of self-discovery or some other such nondescript nonsense. Initially he called her nightly, yet even now this ritual was becoming increasingly infrequent. How quickly Brad had forgotten his promise to call her each evening. 'What could be so diverting to make him break his promise to me?' she imaginatively mused with increasing worry.

The longer days of early spring generously presented golden ruby evening sunsets and flowering aromatic blossomings, the fragrances of which were easily sniffed on a soft breezy late April evening. For Katherine, none of these spring delights could help to pleasantly entertain the new season, as her only thoughts were of her Brad and her life's absence without him.

Out of both desperation and boredom, she quickly picked up her telephone receiver and called Brad's secretary. "DeTagelio, did any phone calls or e-mails come in this past hour from Mr Hamilton?" Katherine scornfully demanded of Margie DeTagelio.

Margie was taken aback by the impulsive and rudeness of both the tone and manner of the call, but Miss McAlister was an owner of the firm and this was suck-it-up time again for Margie the poor, working girl.

"Why no, of course not, Miss MacAlister, if you can remember back to a few weeks ago, you had instructed me to bring all correspondence and communication from Mr Hamilton directly to you and without delay, don't you remember?" Margie replied in an almost impertinent salutation.

Katherine really didn't care about Margie's explanation or her cheekiness either; she merely wanted a simple answer to her question and without any middle-class attitudes.

"Oh, just shut the hell up, DeTagelio! Don't mouth-off to me! My memory is perfect too! I also remember that you are the one with the poor memory issue! I do not need any correcting of my memory from the likes of you! Just make sure that you do exactly as I tell you to do from now on and without any smart-ass attitude, now do you remember that, DeTagelio?" Katherine replied as she forcefully slammed down the phone in a most rude manner without waiting for a response.

It was Katherine's frustration, lack of control, and dislike of Margie that made her behave so uncivilly around Margie. Katherine needed a break from the office, but with only a few token, social friends and no office mates, work life was a solidary affair. Most of her social peers had long ago settled down, married, and started families. Even her divorced friends had remarried and started families of their own. Katherine's few social acquaintances at the office were mostly male and were her social inferiors at that, thus these males were definitely 'off-limits' and her only family consisted of her aging mother and father. Middle age reality was

staring Katherine clearly in the face and she despised it! Her life was
stalled and she was resolved to solve that issue. She was not going to be
one of those women who 'hit the wall'!

In previous happier times, the Hamilton children had served as her
second family and they were a source of both fun and counsel. Katherine
especially loved talking with Melissa Hamilton, Brad's younger sister.
Melissa was the perfect friend for Kate, she was of the same social class
and she was of no threat or competition for Brad's romantic affections.
Melissa even informed Katherine of Brad's little pet peeves and habits.
To Kate it seemed as if both she and Brad had now become as orphans
in this world, yet presently neither of them had the properly formed
acumen, as to provide comfort to one another.

An unexpected knock shattered the silence and introspective
thoughts of Katherine's meandering and brooding little world.
"Come in," Katherine announced sweetly as she stumbled out of her
daydreaming haze. As the door opened, there appeared the smiling face
of Jim Stroud, a senior account executive at Hamilton & MacAlister.

"Hello Kate, you look a little unsettled these days, is there anything
wrong?' he innocently inquired.

Kate nervously brushed her hand through her dark hair, stood
smartly up, straightened her dress, and generated a soft, forced, fake,
smile at Jim.

"Wrong? Now what on earth could be wrong, Jim? I have the 'world
by the balls', don't you know! I am the definitive Boston professional lady
– I have everything! Everything, except any friends, siblings, a husband,
or children! I am not even sure if I still have my fiancé Brad," Katherine
joked pathetically.

Jim was dumbfounded, as it was definitely not a question that he
could hope to answer correctly, and he was a subordinate in the firm.
Katherine noted the puzzled and worried look upon Jim's face and she
decided to spare him any torment or uneasiness.

"Hey Jim, I didn't expect an answer from you. Now what makes you
pay a visit to the Spider's den this fine afternoon?" Kate playfully retorted.

Jim was relieved of the tension and so he set forth his bold invitation.
"So, Kate, it's near closing time, the office has been working very hard,
and that includes you! It's a pleasant Friday night in Boston, a few of the
executives and some of the guys and gals wanted to go to Olde Bailey's
and unwind to have a few drinks and laughs...come and join us, Kate...
please! It will do you some good to get out a little and get your mind off

the office!" Jim pleaded nervously and knowing full well that Kate had an aversion to Olde Bailey's and socializing with the common office staff. Still, Jim was a very loyal and competent Hamilton & MacAlister team player, and he wanted to politely invite the boss out for a few drinks with her staff.

Kate stared almost catatonically for a few seconds, looking blankly into the empty space in front of her face. She was in a day dream trance. Jim became nervous by her odd behavior, so he asked the question once again, "Kate, do you want to come and join us for a few drinks?"

Her trance was broken by Jim's question. A light smile quickly came over Kate's face, then she slowly turned toward Jim and spoke quite softly, "Sure, why not? Yes, I do want to attend, Jim. I need to get the hell out of this glass and concrete prison."

Jim Stroud was unexpectedly surprised by Kate's ready acceptance of his offer to go to Olde Bailey's, but he didn't want to question her motives either. He gave her a big genuine smile and a cordial pat on the arm. "Fantastic, Kate, glad to hear it, we're all meeting there around 5:30 at the bar area, okay?" Jim declared exuberantly. Kate smiled and returned a smart wink of acknowledgment, as Jim headed out of her office.

She returned back to her office correspondence and finished up the signature endorsements. Through her peripheral vision, she noted the blood orange glow of the sun slowly setting into the Spring night. She gazed at her custom-made Rolex platinum, diamond encrusted wristwatch; the time read 5:00 PM and she knew that it was time to put her tedious, but necessary work away for another day and to get ready for the office night out at Olde Bailey's. By nature, she didn't really relish the thought of mingling with her 'office mates' and other co-workers, it was enough that she worked and saw her employees five days a week as it was – yet to socialize with them merely made the work interactions more difficult for her. Save for Brad, none were her social peers, none shared her common interests, and none of them were interesting people to her. Still, she thought, she needed the break from the office routine and the Hamilton & MacAlister office crew were not a terribly bad or obnoxious lot, aside from that most common, lower middle-class DeTagelio girl.

Despite her personal reservations, Katherine prepared herself for the impending social ritual. She was determined to look her best as both the President of the firm and more importantly, as a MacAlister. Quickly, yet fastidiously, she filed her financial papers neatly to the side of her desk, she smartly arose and headed toward a recessed fancy maple office side door. This door led to a spacious and opulent private bathroom. Katherine's private privy contained a bathtub/shower, toilet, bidet, wash sink, and an overly elaborate French provincial make-up table. It was all quite girly-girl feminine. Katherine was all woman underneath that tough veneer of cold business decorum. All four of the executive suites at Hamilton & MacAlister had these private bathrooms, just in case the executives needed to freshen up or get showered before a big formal corporate meeting or high social event in downtown Boston. In this case, Katherine's private bathroom was decorated in the grand feminine manner that befitted her wealth and personal tastes. Colourful pastoral light pink silk wallpaper adorned the bathroom walls, while the bathroom floor consisted of a light cream and alabaster onyx. All the bathroom fixtures were finished in 18 carat gold. The piece de resistance was an ornate light rose-finished, sunken porcelain bathtub that was encased within a pink marble fixture. The entire boudoir, while modest in size, cost over $250,000. Ornate luxury had its price.

Katherine elected not to take a full bath or shower, deciding instead to merely rejuvenate her make-up, affix and style her hair, and refresh her perfume. She brushed her teeth and then partook a vigorous gargle. Her keen and piercing green eyes stared vainly into the mirror. Turning on the bright lights to her vanity mirror, she skillfully applied mascara and eyeliner, which only served to accent her radiant green eyes. She then gently applied some light reddish rouge to her prominent high cheekbones. A few quick atomized sprays of Chanel #5 perfume completed the personal touch-up. Finally, Katherine turned her attention to the jewellery that she would wear, always mindful that a lady was never properly dressed unless she was adored with some visible token of class and elegance. From a secured small vanity safe, she retrieved a regally adorned jewellery chest, whereupon Katherine withdrew a string of double strand white cultured pearls, which were periodically adorned with 18 carat gold oak leak clasps. Acutely gazing into the mirror, she was quite satisfied with the radiant flawless face which gazed back to her in the mirror. Now there was but one minor detail to further attend.

She dutifully turned her final attention to her enamel gold earrings, which she had worn elegantly throughout the course of the day. These earrings she had inherited from her great grandmother many years ago. The double strand of gold enamel spherical earrings was constructed for fashionable young ladies, who travelled in horse-drawn carriages in the early part of the 20th century, over time these baubles became known as 'coach & carriage' earrings. In addition to the seemingly simple and plain elegance, the carriage earrings were in reality a very fine disguise of sophistication and hidden wealth. Each earring was actually a clever design of two earrings in one piece of jewellery. In its normal daytime appearance, the coach earring had a simple decorative ornamental pretty external cover composed of a rich enamel material, which appeared as an oval sphere. However, each of these jewelled 18 carat golden enamelled spheres cleverly hid a pair of immaculate, flawless 6 carat rare canary yellow diamonds. A small spring pinch clip was used to mount and remove the 18K gold enamel spheres. The tandem pair of yellow diamonds hung above one another in perfect unison, by a small, sturdy 18 carat gold chain link connecting one diamond to the other. There was a dual purpose of design for these coach earrings: security and modesty. For security purposes, that which was unobserved was relatively safe from theft. As for modesty, the intent and the Old World tradition was that ladies of refinement did not adorn themselves with diamond jewellery before 6:00 PM, as only prostitutes and showgirls wore diamonds before the proper evening hours.

Katherine carefully observed her clan's stodgy social protocols and rituals, even if some of her peers did not - these social observations made Katherine appear even more refined and dignified from the others in her social circles. Katherine was mindful of her mother's saying that 'breeding could never be bought, it was something that one was either born or raised with'; however, in some rare circumstances breeding and manners could be learned from acute observation, self-determination and strict practice. The coach earrings dangled radiantly from Katherine's earlobes, as she smiled and admired herself in the mirror. She looked beautiful and refined and she knew it! Katherine was indeed the type of woman that every other woman loved to hate. Externally, she was flawless! However, internally, she was mortally flawed like every other human being.

Satisfied that her personal appearance was now up to her usual high standards, Katherine calmly exited the bathroom, activated the security lock, turned out the lights and exited out of her office. The only persons left in the office area were the nightly cleaning crew, most of whom consisted of immigrants from either the Caribbean or Latin America. Katherine cared little if these immigrant workers were legal or illegal; all that mattered to her was that they worked efficiently and that they didn't steal anything. The cleaning crew spoke a myriad of strange sounding dialects and tones amidst a confluence of alternating male and female voices. They sought to maintain their anonymity and turned their heads, looking downward and stopped talking when Katherine passed by, as they all feared drawing needless attention of their presence to any potential authority figure. They were 'out-of-sight and out-of-mind' to Katherine and many other American employers as well. They formed America's 'shadow economy'.

Although Olde Bailey's was only several city blocks from the front door of Hamilton & MacAlister, Katherine never gave it a second thought about not driving her stately Bentley convertible to the Olde Bailey's Tavern & Pub. Katherine carefully parked her Bentley in a conveniently VIP reserved parking space some 30 feet from the front of the tavern. With some degree of trepidation, Katherine entered the Olde Bailey's Tavern and looked around for her co-workers. After just a few seconds, Katherine keenly spotted Neal McGuire, a senior account executive at Hamilton & MacAlister. Neal smiled and waved his hand prominently in the air, visually motioning for Katherine to join him around the bar in a private enclave that the senior executives had sequestered for their private foray.

The massive Olde Bailey's bar was of an ornate dark green granite and accented brass railed fixture, arrayed with the executives of Hamilton & MacAlister sitting on one side, while the middle managers, clerks, secretaries, and mail sorters sitting on the opposite side, a classic stratification of 'separate & unequal'. In this latter group, Margie DeTagelio and Leona Jones comfortably sat in muted semi-sober silence and observed with jealous emotions the codified mingling of the upper-class employees.

Katherine broadly smiled and gave Neal a light social hug, while Jim Stroud and Nancy O'Donnell, the two other executives from Hamilton & MacAlister, gave Katherine a friendly pat on the shoulder. Mrs Peet, the firm's Trust officer, was also standing next to the executives.

"Oh Kate, so glad you could make it, we're glad that you got out of the office for once," Neil exclaimed. Katherine politely smiled, while sitting herself down on a reserved barstool.

"Thanks, everyone, with Brad being away, I didn't feel like socializing very much and the job of covering for both Brad and my own tasks keeps me plenty busy, and pretty exhausted," Kate cheerfully responded.

"No excuses or explanations are required! Okay, what are you drinking tonight, boss?" Nancy O'Donnell inquired cheerfully, yet ever so politely.

Katherine thought for a second before answering before replying, "I'll have a vodka blueberry martini with two olives please."

Dutifully, Nancy smiled, as she took Katherine's drink order to the bartender.

"Kate, I took the liberty of ordering drinks for the night for all the Hamilton & MacAlister employees, I hope that you don't mind?" Jim Stroud casually mentioned to Katherine during their passing conversations.

"That's fine Jim, expense it off of your corporate credit card, I'll approve it! The firm is cash loaded, and besides money is no good when we are all decrepit or dead!" Katherine added dryly as she spotted Margie and Leona, both of them raising their drink glasses in a casual salute of obligatory deference to Katherine.

Katherine grudgingly acknowledged their gesture and presented a forced smile in a visible mocking manner. "I hope that DeTagelio girl doesn't get drunk and embarrass the firm here tonight, that girl has such a common reputation!" Kate mocked sarcastically in a subtle voice.

"Ah, she's not that bad, Kate, maybe she's just a little rough around the edges, but she's an okay gal and she means well," Jim stated defensively.

Katherine could only issue a very visible frown when she heard Jim defending the reputation of Margie DeTagelio.

"By the way, Kate, how is Brad these days? Have you heard anything from him?" Jim delicately inquired.

Kate's facial expression immediately saddened upon hearing the inflexion of Brad's name.

"Yes, Jim, I heard from Brad a few days ago, he's in Ohio and he's spending some time at some sort of motorcycle racing event or something," Katherine added in saddened resignation. Nancy arrived back with Katherine's drink, with which Katherine took a long sip, then smiled. "Yummy - the perfect Vodka blueberry martini, I think I'll need another shortly," Katherine rejoiced, as the entire executive crew broke out in thunderous approving laughter.

"Just look at Miss Ice Princess over there, strutting her stuff and thinking that she is better than the workers over here! That means us!" Leona remarked wearily to Margie.

"No – Leona, she's not better than us, she's richer and that's all that matters in this world baby, and don't you forget it either," Margie responded dryly, while playing with the ice in her half-filled screwdriver cocktail.

"Look at those beautiful huge flipping fancy earrings, my God those diamond rocks swinging from her pretty little ears! Those babies must cost over $350,000 per earlobe – you know that's the cost of a very nice house!" Leona remarked in envy and admiration.

"Yeah sure, life must be hard when you are young, wealthy, and beautiful like Little Miss Proper over there, that bitch thinks her butt doesn't stink, that's for sure!" Margie remarked with both envy and obvious disgust.

"Yes indeed, sister, you sure are speaking the truth there and I think that Miss Katherine has the axe out for you girlfriend, so you just watch your step around her, understand, girlfriend?" Leona prudently counselled to Margie. Both women giggled as they both continued to criticize the Hamilton & MacAlister executives as the drinks continued to flow freely.

From their respective positions, the employees of the Hamilton & MacAlister Investment Banking firm were arrayed into two distinct physical and sociological camps, the 'haves' and the 'have nots'. The only redeeming feature for Hamilton & MacAlister rank and file employees were that the drinks for the evening were paid out gratis by the officers of the firm, usually Brad, Katherine, Neil, Nancy or Jim.

The firm consisted of approximately 75 personnel in total, thus it was the founder's intent always to keep the corporate affairs a small family business, yet be large enough to be able to handle some significant large Boston and Middle Atlantic corporate banking business. Large businesses also had the negative tendency to attract ambitious upstarts wanting to make a name for themselves at the expense of the firm and largeness also brought about unneeded attention from the Security and Exchange Commission (SEC) and other regulatory government bodies; it was much better to be small, successful, and quaint. Instead, social contacts and society standing were much more important than business school credentials and aptitude in the investment banking business, where a few chosen words over golf, a bridge game or society event meant the beginning or consummation of a substantial underwriting agreement.

The unspoken, but well known social clique also meant that even ambitious and smart 'outsiders' from the middle and lower classes were instantly and silently ostracized from the senior executive positions. Still, the employees didn't complain as the salaries for middle and lower-class workers were very generous by anyone's standards, plus the retirement and bonus packages allowed most Hamilton & MacAlister employees to live a very comfortable, middle-class life without getting their hands dirty.

"Oh boy, I sure wish that Mr Brad was back here, he sure used to make all of the firm's employees feel happy like a family! He mingled with everyone!" Leona sadly remarked, as she playfully toyed with her drink and motioned with her finger for the bartender to order her another round.

"You're sure as hell right about that, Leona! Brad was the only democratizing force at Hamilton & MacAlister, he sure was a happy-go-lucky type of guy, he made you feel like you were his equal at work and here at Olde Bailey's...I sure hope he gets his ass back here soon before Kit Kat finds a reason to fire me, I desperately need this job, it's the only thing that is keeping me and my mum from leaving Boston, this is not exactly an inexpensive place to live and work!" Margie dryly confessed in frustration and resignation.

"Hey, girlfriend, how about us having a little fun tonight, what do you say? I am feeling a little bit sneaky," Margie inquired, as she softly nudged Leona with her elbow. Leona's large brown eyes widened, and her mouth dropped in exacerbation.

"Now tell me, Margie, what type of delicious wickedness do you have in mind that is probably going to get us both into trouble? More importantly, what do you have in mind that will keep this little trick of yours a secret from anyone finding out it was one of us that did it?" Leona exclaimed with a guilty laughter. Margie whispered her secret devious trick into Leona's ear, after which Leona burst out in a wild giggle that forced her to hide her face away from the others at the bar rail.

Like a wild cheetah out for the prey, Margie turned her back and slyly looked around the main room of Olde Bailey's Tavern. Her huntress eyes quickly spotted the helpless prey. Margie's target was that of a tall, muscular-built, brown haired man in his early thirties. The stranger was attired in well-worn pants, a slightly soiled tie and a wrinkled jacket, he was definitely not the mark of either a professional or upper-class male, but that suited Margie just fine. Although a bit gruff, the tall stranger had the warm friendly demeanour of being the Joe-Average working stiff, who appeared to have had one drink too many for the evening. All the visual signs indicated that this guy was a real party animal and full of testosterone. He was perfect for the task.

The stranger was accompanied by two of his friends, who also wore the 'working-class hero' wardrobe of soiled clothing and exhibiting the social decorum of boisterous remarks and crude language. Their working occupation was clearly indicated as that of the construction trade, since they all had the telltale dust and grime from what looked like either dry wall or plaster flakes on their pants and shirts. Margie acutely eyed the tall stranger in anticipation that sooner or later he would look her way.

Sure enough, after about a minute Margie's hungry staring eyes met those of the stranger. Margie raised her glass and then produced a wicked enchanting smile and a soft flutter of come-on wink, as she seductively threw her hair back with a quick nod of her head. In an instant, the feminine seductive signals had worked their magic charm, as the tall dark-haired stranger left the company of his male companions and slowly strutted over to the bar stools where Margie and Leona had strategically perched themselves.

"Well, hello there, beautiful, I couldn't help but notice your feminine charms from the other side of the room...would you like another drink? My name is Bill, Bill Tiscone," the extroverted stranger announced with an obvious and overpowering beer-hops infused breath.

Margie smiled politely as she extended her hand in friendship and introduction. "Well hello Bill, my name is Margie and this is my friend Leona and yes, a refill is most appreciated!" Margie declared as she shook Bill's hand.

"So, your name is Bill Tiscone, huh!" Margie smiled as she shook the burly man's hand. Leona looked on with sinful fascination, as she knew that Margie had no interest in the barfly Romeos that inhabited Olde Bailey's and every other pickup joint in the city of Boston and Cambridge. Margie looked deeply into Bill's eyes, as she smiled and lightly grabbed his muscular arm in a semi-affectionate manner.

"Now, Bill, how would you like some hot action with a very beautiful and sexy lady?" Margie teasingly inquired.

Both Bill's and Leona's eyes widened in obvious disbelief at the words that Margie's proposition obviously implied. Encouraged by his obvious good luck, Bill affectionately placed his muscular arm around

Margie's shoulder and rubbed her left arm and back in a most crude sexual manner. Margie's facial and body language indicated an obvious displeasure with Bill's very forward and non-invited masculine affections toward her.

"Ah, now just wait a minute, Bill baby, before you get all worked up with some sort of great expectations or anything else about us for this evening, let me inform you that you are a little mistaken here, I mean that you must have misunderstood my words and actions just too literally, Bill," Margie defensively replied as she gently removed Bill's uninvited arm from around her shoulder.

Both Bill and Leona wore puzzled expressions upon their faces.

"Now just what in the hell is going on here, Missy, I mean you give me the come-hither look and you start to chat me up, then you say that I have the wrong idea...just what the fuck is your game, lady? You're nothing but a fucking bar-tease!" Bill angrily shouted at Margie.

Margie quickly gained her composure and tried to put Bill at ease.

"Look Bill, my invitation for tonight was true, but I wasn't speaking about myself, I was speaking about my very beautiful friend," Margie smiled as she sipped a mouthful of alcohol.

In obvious self-defence Leona butted in angrily, "You certainly aren't speaking for me about who my dates or pick-ups are going to be, Margie, now where do you get-off making passes for me, girlfriend?"

Margie looked pathetically at Leona and her boisterous outburst. "No, I wasn't talking about my friend here, Bill, I was talking about my other special friend," Margie replied apologetically.

Both Bill and Leona looked at each other and at Margie, neither seeing nor acknowledging another party at their immediate bar area.

"Look, what I mean is that my other girlfriend on the opposite side of the bar, the attractive one over there with the long black hair and big yellow diamond earrings," Margie subtly indicated as she pointed to the figure of Katherine, who was standing directly across the bar from the trio.

Leona's jaw just about dropped when she heard Margie's explanation to Bill. It was now clear to Leona, but still unknown to Bill, that a classic bar room setup was being staged by none other than Margie the bar fly herself. This was pay-back for all of the shit-sandwiches that Katherine the Ice Princess, had made her eat recently. Payback was indeed a cold bitch.

"Now, Bill, over there is my uptown girlfriend! Her name is Katherine, she is a very lonely lady tonight, her boyfriend has left her and all she has these days to hang out with are those stoogey suit dicks over there – a real pathetic lot they are too! Not one of those office 'pencil-dick' Beta guys over there with her will make a move on my lonely friend Katherine tonight and I was thinking that perhaps you would be the guy to light her fire and give her a break. My girlfriend has not been with a real man in weeks and she's really itching for some bedroom action!" Margie slyly lied with a most endearing doe-eyed, innocent expression.

Bill's eyes began to sparkle with the possibilities of getting lucky with a very beautiful brunette this evening, but he was still a little reluctant. The situation appeared too good to be true.

"This is no gag here! Hey, look Bill, I'll even pay for the first drink, I can send it over to Katherine and I'll tell the bartender that it was from an anonymous admirer, now how about it, Big Guy? Are you game tonight or are you just all bark and no bite?" Margie coyly verbally challenged and baited, as she lightly jabbed Bill in the shoulder.

"Yeah, our friend Katherine is real lonely and she really would appreciate having some big, handsome guy buy her a drink and show her a good time; she's been down in the dumps for weeks and really needs herself a man for the night, she's really hard up, if you get my drift, Bill!" Leona exclaimed with a big broad smile, as she too verbally stoked Margie's wicked plan.

"I still don't know about this pick-up thing," Bill muttered hesitantly to the two ladies.

Margie looked nervously at Bill, hoping that her devilish plan was not slipping away. Margie thought quick and calculatingly. "Look, Bill, honey, I'll make this really worth your while. Here is $50 for your initiative and the cost of the drinks for both of you! What do you say about going over there and being a little sociable to her? Hell, if you strike out, you are fifty bucks richer with nothing lost!" Margie playfully remarked with her big blue eyes and a stunning feminine smile.

Bill looked away and down at his drink glass, still somewhat reluctant to take Margie's offer.

"Now come on, big boy, don't let me see that you are that much of a shrinking violet and that you are just a big bag of Boston wind," Margie toyed encouragingly to Bill, as she gently tugged his strong masculine arm. Being partially embarrassed by Margie's remarks, Bill's masculine defensive ego rebelled against Margie's provocative antagonistic remarks, just as she had vilely planned.

"Ah, what the hell, I'll do it Margie, what's your friend's name again?"

Margie was ecstatic as she smiled devilishly at Leona. "Her name is Katherine, and please remember to be persistent with her, she really likes to play hard-to-get; and she likes an aggressive manly type guy too!" Margie cunningly lied.

Quickly, Bill took the $50 bill from Margie, as he left to try and conquer the world of Katherine MacAlister. Leona looked shockingly at Margie with her jaw hanging wide open like a garage door.

"Girlfriend, are you crazy or what? You are sending that poor guy up for trouble, don't you know that if Kit Kat ever finds out about this little charade, both you and I are dead meat!" Leona pleaded at Margie, as their eyes intensely followed Bill as he made his way across to the other side of the bar to where Katherine was standing.

Bill was about 15 feet away from Katherine and he now could clearly see what a beautiful and attractive woman that she truly was. Bill was highly attracted to Katherine's fine slim and tall figure and her raven black shining hair. Her green eyes were terribly seductive. Her laughing feminine voice bespoke of refinement, confidence and camaraderie. All in all, this strange feminine creature was very attractive in both form and substance, she was definitely worth the time of his efforts and he had even been marginally paid for his extemporaneous compunction.

Bill thought that life was too short for second chances or second thoughts, thus he proceeded toward his potential prize. He knew that many high society ladies sought out the company of a real working man like himself. He began his deliberate stare technique; this was Bill's personal pick-up manoeuvre in which he combined both charm and flattery to conquer the ladies of the lounge. It had worked dozens of times for Bill in the past and it promised to do so again this evening also.

Bill initiated his smiling stare into the direction of Katherine, knowing full well that sooner or later, she would feel his provocative vibrations, then he would make his move. Katherine began to develop the strange and unpleasant feeling that someone was staring at her and she tried to ignore it at first. Katherine continued to mingle and joke with Nancy O'Donnell, Jim Stroud, Neal McGuire, and Mrs Peet.

After a few uneasy minutes, Katherine continued to feel uneasy and as she looked about the bar area, she quickly eyed up the male stranger in her immediate vicinity. While her eyes journeyed around the room, she spotted that DeTagelio girl and Leona at the far end of the bar, both of them slogging down the free drinks like there was no tomorrow. As Katherine's eyes drew nearer to her own immediate area, her eyes met those of a smiling, handsome, rugged, tall guy with wavy black hair. Her eyes momentarily locked with his and she gently and politely returned his smile with one of her own, if only in a fleeting fashion. Although only mildly attracted to the stranger, Katherine entertained no serious second thoughts of anything more, her attention being focused on that of her friends and perhaps Brad. Bill mistakenly took Katherine's smile as a great big 'green light' to proceed with his famous pick-up strategy.

As Bill moved up toward Katherine, the free drinks which Margie had ordered arrived and were placed onto the bar. "Miss, this is from the tall dark-haired gentleman just over there," the bartender voiced as he served Katherine a new Vodka martini. Bill made his way up to and past Nancy, Jim, Neal, and Mrs Peet. He was now only an arm's length away from Katherine and well past the comfort point for a proper social introduction of any kind, even that of an upscale Tavern. It was 'hit or miss' time!

"Excuse me, Miss, my name is Bill Tiscone and I just wanted to introduce myself and buy you a drink; you are the most intriguing lady in this entire establishment," Bill stated bluntly, if not somewhat awkwardly.

Katherine knew a classic, poorly-delivered, pickup line if ever there was one and she wanted no part of Bill either this evening or any other; however, she was ever determined to act like a lady.

"Well thank you, Bill, but I am with my friends this evening and I do want to share my time with them and thanks for the drink anyway," Katherine responded smartly, as she turned and gave her attention back to the Hamilton & MacAlister partners.

Bill felt only slightly dejected and he remembered that Margie had said that Katherine would be a little cold in her attitude and that persistence was the key to romantic success.

Bill was of the badly mistaken belief that in the game of rejection, that one bad move merely merited another bad move. He pushed up even closer to Katherine and gently put his large hands on her shoulder, an obvious uninvited rude gesture for any social encounter.

"Hey beautiful, I understand that you are maybe feeling a little down and lonely tonight and I just want to be your friend!" Bill proclaimed arrogantly and quite loudly to Katherine.

Being the ever the true blue loyal employees, the Hamilton &
MacAlister crew immediately came to Katherine's immediate rescue.
"Hey buddy, you heard the lady, she thanked you for the drink, but she
doesn't want to be bothered – do you understand?" Jim Stroud protested
assuredly.

"It's okay, Jim and thanks, but I'll personally handle this matter
please," Katherine voiced calmly. "Listen, Bill, you seem like a nice guy,
but I'm just not interested, so why don't you just go and find yourself
someone else, like that cute little red-headed girl located across the bar
over there, she seems like your type of gal!" Katherine explained calmly
and earnestly.

Rather than being calmed, Bill felt very rejected and hurt and he was
not going to take this rejection very easily. This was no longer a mere
challenge to Bill, he felt that he was being pandered down by this rich
snooty bitch and he wanted some satisfaction from her at this point.

"Now you look here, Miss Beacon Hill rich bitch, who in the hell
do you think that you fucking are? Do you think that just because you
have money, that you are better than me or anyone else here in this bar?
What do these guys have that I don't?" Bill screamed out in a boisterous
verbal outrage as he tugged on Katherine's wrist.

Katherine's defences kicked in as she heard the stranger's rude
accusations and felt his hand invading her intimate personage.

"You crude low-life, jerk! I'll tell you who I am, buddy, I am
Katherine MacAlister, the President of Hamilton & MacAlister, and I
will not tolerate your common, rude behaviour to me or any of my
friends here, now beat it, buster!" Katherine sternly demanded.

Bill just stood there in momentary shock. Katherine decided to break
the tension, as she raised her right hand and slapped Bill across the face
with a loud 'whack' sound. Next Katherine looked around at the bar and
picked up the drink that Bill had bought for her. She tossed the Vodka in
Bill's face and the liquor also hit some innocent bystanders as well. Bill
wiped his face with his hands and he was about to pounce on Katherine,
when suddenly two husky bouncers intervened and forcefully escorted
Bill out of the Olde Bailey's Tavern.

"Katherine are you all-right?" Jim and Nancy earnestly
nervously enquired.

"I am perfectly fine, they taught us at Vassar how to handle jerks
like that! I'm sure that we will never see him at Hamilton & MacAlister
seeking any underwriting assistance," Katherine joked as the entire

entourage laughed the incident off as just a minor bad experience.

"Holy shit, Margie! Did you see what Kit Kat just did to that poor bastard Bill? She ate him up and spat him out!" Leona exclaimed excitedly and in disbelief. Margie could hardly believe her own eyes either! Margie had planned the perfect ambush on Katherine MacAlister and it had backfired in a grand way. It seemed that 'Kit Kat' MacAlister had all the luck in the world, 'she could even fend off rude drunk guys in a bar and get the better of them too,' she bitterly thought.

"Ah well, Leona, let's face it, Kit Kat was born with a platinum spoon in her mouth; she steps in shit and it turns to gold, she farts, and they call it perfume. Meanwhile, we can't win for losing with that Ice Bitch, I flipping give up!" Margie exclaimed bitterly, but with a quick resounding smile.

"Don't worry, girlfriend, we did get some free drinks this evening and some good entertainment too!" Leona exclaimed with some laughter to Margie.

"Yeah, poor Bill, he sure got more than his $50 worth tonight," Margie whispered.

Leona looked and smiled at Margie and raised her glass – 'This is to poor old Bill!' Both ladies laughed and ordered two more rounds of drinks before calling this an evening. They would each fondly remember this incident for years to come.

★ ★ ★ ★ ★ ★ ★ ★ ★ ★ ★ ★ ★ ★ ★ ★ ★

The cool, rainy weeks of April had metamorphosed into the light breezy and sunny mild days of May. Wayne had come to intimately know the Copen family. He came to appreciate the spontaneity and zest of the motorcycle circuit course, which most closely resembled a circus or carnival in terms of its entertainment and nomadic lifestyle. Over the past few weeks, Wayne had re-learned the bonds of family and friends, as the Copen family had in a way become his surrogate family. He bonded most easily with Paul Copen, who he took to like an older, wise brother. It was many a night that Wayne and Paul shared mutual sad stories of their past loved ones and the search to re-kindle the love of life that temporarily left each man when tragedy came knocking on their respective doors. For Paul, the tragic loss of his dear wife was made easier through the love and devotion that he shared for his family, and over time, Paul was able to re-start his life anew. As wacky as it seemed, the entire Copen family reacted to their mom's death by living their dreams and relying on calculated hunches – the result became the roaming Copen Motor Cross travelling circus. For Wayne, the situation was a little more complex, with his entire family dead, all anchors of stability were erased.

This short gig with the Copen Motor Cross show was as good of an excuse for living and getting away from the investment banking world as anything else, besides Wayne enjoyed the honest ways of the Copen family – they always told you the truth even if you didn't want to hear it. During his few hectic weeks with this vagabond troupe, Wayne worked the motorcycle maintenance pits with Billy Jordan and Mike Stroud, while the Copen children all raced the dirt bike circuit or performed the various stunt tricks. Patricia continued to enthral the crowds with her wild acrobatic stunts and fancy riding positions; her dirty-blonde ponytail was incessantly blowing in the air, as she performed her awe-inspiring act. With constant coaching from the entire Copen family, Wayne became very adept at performing numerous motorcycle road and track riding tricks and manoeuvres, to include rear wheel wheelies and freestyle stunts like the 'Stripper', 'Dead man', 'Superman', and the 'Heart Attack'.

Once while Wayne was attempting to do a daring jump on one of the Kawasaki dirt bikes, he flew ten feet in the air and landed soundly on his seat, causing him to incur a very painful groin impact. This little stunt caused Wayne a few painful days convalescencing in bed with 15 pounds of ice continually piled upon his private male crotch area, but he certainly did learn how to manoeuvre a motorcycle. Although Wayne was not a competitive rider, he was now a very competent road rider, able to hold his own against most other motorcycle road warrior want-a-bee's. As Spring progressed, he knew also that it was time to be moving onward and to say goodbye to his newly found friends. Once again, the road was calling for Wayne.

He was beset with some slight depression, as this was the day that he was going to say goodbye to his surrogate family. The parting would not be pleasant, but Wayne knew that he was outliving his stay with the Copens and the open highway was calling for him once more. He knew that he needed to continue to travel westward and today was as good as any other to say goodbye as the riding weather was projected to be excellent. 'It was always the best of form and manners to leave either a party or visit on a high note and not to stay past one's welcome,' Wayne figured to himself.

"Hey Paul and the rest of the Copen Family, could you all come over here please," Wayne shouted as he strutted from the trailer and proceeded out into the breakfast serving area of the stadium arena. All the Copen Team members were seated as per normal in one single table; all were sitting down and enjoying the American staple hearty breakfast of bacon, eggs, pancakes, and hash browns. Huge stainless-steel pots of coffee were appointed strategically at each table. The Copen entourage waved for Wayne to come over to their table, but Wayne remained aloof from their presence. His riding ensemble and face told the story that he was leaving their company that very morning. The Copen entourage arose to meet Wayne and perhaps try to change his mind too.

"Hello Wayne, my boy, good morning! How about some breakfast, we have a busy day ahead of us at the track, we are doing some qualifying runs today," Paul Copen explained as he greeted Wayne with a warm morning handshake. Wayne was reluctant to be the bearer of disappointing news, but he and everyone else knew that his stay with the Copens travelling circus was just a short summer stint anyway. Still just as the welcome had been sweet, so would the departure be bitter.

"Hello everyone, I have something to tell you all," Wayne muttered slowly and sadly. He gazed briefly at the dirt track and tried to find some easy words to say that he was leaving the troupe.

"We all know, Wayne, that you are leaving us today and that is what you wanted to tell us, correct?" Patricia Copen gleefully remarked, breaking Wayne's long silence.

"Yeah, Wayne, it's no big worry you know, we all kinda knew that you'd be leaving us someday and soon," Johnny Copen added with a friendly smile and hoping to deflate Wayne's obvious guilt.

Wayne looked at each of the smiling faces of the Copen entourage and he knew that he was truly among friends.

"Thanks, guys, my time with each and every one of you has been memorable and it's not an exaggeration to say that the last few weeks that I have spent with you all have, in a real sense, brought my spirit back to life. I feel the road west is calling me again and today is about as good of a time to leave as any other, so I'm leaving you all this morning," he announced sadly and with some emotion in his throat and some misty tears in his eyes too.

"Hey, Wayne, what are we going to do for a pit monkey to help us maintain the race bikes?" Ernst jokingly remarked. Mike Stroud looked at Ernst with a wily grin and then remarked to him, "With Wayne gone, our medical insurance premiums will definitely go down or at least our use of ice compacts will decrease." Everyone laughed, including Wayne, as he remembered all the falls and bruises that he had suffered while the entire Copen family patiently taught him the tricks of the riding profession.

"Yeah well, I'm going to miss Wayne the most around here, he's the only one that appreciated my acrobatic riding stunts and besides I think that he is cute!" Patricia teased in a mocking tone, as the male members of the family playfully jabbed and teased Patricia that she was sweet on Wayne.

Wayne merely laughed and smiled too, he knew that in Patricia's mild pun, she had just confessed to having a slight crush on him as well. Wayne made his way over to Patricia and planted a short kiss on her cheek and forehead. Instantly Patricia face turned red with girlish embarrassment.

Brad had one final surprise in store for the Copen clan. Like an old sea captain gazing in anticipation at his watch, Wayne waited in eager anticipation of an imminent event to occur.

"What's going on here, Wayne, why are you nervously looking at your watch? Are you expecting something?" Paul Copen inquired.

Just then a large tractor-trailer approached the racetrack area and stopped some 50 feet from the Copen trailer court area. The driver of the eighteen-wheeler rig dismounted his cab and headed promptly over to the Copen family gathering.

"Howdy folks and excuse me, but is there anyone here named B.W. Hamilton?" Everyone briefly looked at one another and then at Wayne, not knowing why on earth a cross-country eighteen-wheeler driver would ever want to be talking to the like of Wayne Hamilton. The Copen Clan was defensive at the innocent inquiry.

"Well, sir, that depends on what business you have with Mr Hamilton and if he might be in any trouble!" Paul Copen announced in a most patriarch manner, as all the Copen male members instinctively and defensively folded their arms across their chests.

The eighteen-wheeler driver gently lifted the brim of his straw hat and wiped his sweaty brow with a soiled red handkerchief that was most lazily stuffed into his shirt pocket. "Now look here, folks, I just want to get Mr Hamilton's signature on this manifest of ten, new Kawasaki dirt race bikes and then I'll be on my way. I got a lot of other deliveries to make today and I want to get this first load of freight unloaded so that I can be on my way," the driver explained. Everyone's eyes focused on Wayne for an answer to the Kawasaki bike delivery.

"What are you planning, Wayne, thinking of starting up your own race team?" Billy Jordan queried.

Wayne began to look and feel embarrassed and the driver was waiting for an answer, so Wayne decided that now was the time to spill his little secret.

"Paul and everyone else here, these bikes are yours to keep, these are a token of my gratitude for letting me into your family for the past few weeks and you will never know how much it has meant to me to have been part of the Copen Racing Team, if only for a short time. Besides I am tired of working on these ancient, broken-down machines that you good folks call motorcycles!" Wayne exclaimed with an embarrassed red face.

There was mass silence among all the Copen Racing Team members. Then all of a sudden, smiles appeared on the faces of the entire family. In unison they all jumped up, yelled, and headed to the back of the eighteen-wheeler and began to eagerly open up the rear of the truck to unload its precious cargo.

The driver again pleaded that Mr Hamilton sign for the motorcycle freight items, "Hey there, Mr Hamilton, could you please sign for this merchandise and I'll happily be on my way. I'll need to see some ID too as proof of delivery," the driver wearily moaned.

"Sure, here is my 'John Henry' signature and here is my driver's licence," Wayne exclaimed as he signed the delivery manifest for the Kawasaki racing bikes. Among the group, only Paul Copen seemed disturbed and did not immediately share in the enthusiasm of his youthful team members and family.

"Wayne, why on earth did you do this? This must have cost a God-awful bundle of money and we didn't really need the new bikes!" Paul growled defensively to Wayne.

Immediately, Wayne realized that he had unintentionally slighted Paul's manhood by making it seem that he could not provide for his family and team members. Suddenly Wayne knew that his gift had offended Paul.

"No offence, Paul, but I'm a spoiled rich guy from Boston, who is used to buying things like an excited little boy in a candy store and sometimes I buy things without thinking of the outcome for everyone concerned. I didn't mean to offend you and if I did, then I apologize, but I wanted to show my appreciation in the most meaningful way possible. Money is only good if it is used to help others or allow them to enjoy life a bit more, don't you think?" Wayne remarked solemnly.

Paul Copen continued to look down at the ground, he knew that Wayne meant well and that his words were true to form.

Wayne decided that he needed to break the tension with a small joke: "Well Paul, just be glad that I didn't order eight bass fishing boats for the family!"

On hearing this comic relief, Paul looked up at Wayne and burst into laughter. Paul and Wayne patted each other on the shoulders, as they laughed and helped to unload the motorcycles from the tractor-trailer. Each motorcycle was painted with the Copens' Racing Logo and the bikes were uniformly painted in the red, white, and blue colours of the nation's patriotic symbols.

After an hour's passing, all the motorcycles had been unloaded and Wayne was prepared to get onto Interstate 80 before the morning traffic got any worse. "Wayne, on behalf of myself and the entire Copen Racing Team, it's been great having you live and work with us these past few weeks, you're like family to us now," Paul Copen explained with regret and sadness in his voice. Wayne was getting sentimental too, but he decided to leave on a positive cheerful note.

"Well, Paul and family, it's been fun and just remember that while I am journeying out West, I will be returning back East as well, so if luck prevails, I might catch you all on my trip back across the states," Wayne exclaimed. He saw that Patricia was distraught at seeing him leave and that she was on the verge of tears. "Besides, I will need to come back and see the Copen clan again, since I want to someday come and see Patricia get married when she finally meets Mr Right one of these fine days," Wayne added, as he smiled kindly at Patricia. She turned her head aside and cried.

"Paul, you have my personal business card, cell phone, and e-mail address, so contact me if you need anything or even if you just want to stay in touch, okay?" Wayne exclaimed with a demurred voice.

As Wayne was about to mount his BMW, Patricia came running from her trailer with a cell phone and shouted, "Stop, everyone, let's all get a picture with Wayne! Come on, everyone, quickly now!"

Paul Copen shouted a command at the eighteen-wheeler driver, "Hey, pal, how about taking a few photos for us here?" The driver was most anxious to get on the road, so he was willing to do anything to get out of the racing arena and off on the Interstate and onto his next delivery.

"Look here, just show me what damn buttons to push and I'll take the frigging pictures, anything to get my ass back on the road!" the driver growled.

Patricia handed the driver her cell phone camera and then corralled Wayne and the entire Copen Racing Team for a close photo line-up. The driver lined everyone up in the camera's viewfinder and readied the group, "Let's go, everyone, on the count of three say cheese and smile." The camera flashed several times, as the driver made sure that he had gotten enough pictures to satisfy everyone. He saluted with his hat to everyone and in a wink, he was off on the road again.

"Thanks, Patricia, I'll have to e-mail this off to Katherine my fiancée along with a note telling her how great you all were to me," Wayne replied as he returned a kiss on her cheek.

It was time for some last-minute goodbyes. Wayne shook everyone's hands and there were multiple bear hugs from every one of the guys, to include Paul Copen. When he came to Patricia, he kissed her on the cheek and whispered to her that he was serious about attending her wedding. Patricia cried again as Wayne strapped on his helmet and rode away from the Fair Grounds and off onto Interstate 80 westward bound. Patricia later posted the group photo onto her social Webpage and onto to her bedroom wall. The picture fondly hung adjacent to the picture of her departed mother. Wayne would always remain a sweet dream in Patricia's heart and memory. 'Who knows, maybe Wayne would really someday return and dance with her at her wedding,' she mused to herself.

He had planted and harvested some good memories from his first roadside encounter. His abbreviated and occasionally absent nightly calls to Katherine would be rectified too. He was hopeful that his other future stops would be as productive and meaningful. The spring was ending and the entire summer was ahead of him. He smiled as the purr of the BMW rumbled under his legs and the cool wind blew across his leather clad torso. Some tall tales were to be told to Katherine when he returned to Boston, whenever that specific date might occur! His life on the road was a good thing thus far, he could only hope that his future experiences could be as fruitful as the preceding month had been.

* *

CHAPTER 4

'Chasing the Fire Dragon'

*"...hey - they're VC, get the fuck down!... Watch
out for the Papa Son, he's got an AK"*

"Keep a watchful eye out on that weather front approaching from the North...and I also want you to keep an eye out for any barometric anomalies that could occur in the next 24 – 48 hour period concerning that cold front emerging down from the Canadian Rockies" the stern and nerdy looking, middle-aged, white male commanded to the distracted, young weather centre worker, who was mesmerized in watching a high resolution computer weather monitor terminal.

"Gee-whiz, Mr Ciellerie... I mean Dr Ciellerie, I was going to do exactly that, I mean that I was going to keep a keen eye out for the Canadian Cold Front...you don't have to treat me like a child all the time," the young intern replied in a most bold, defensive tone.

"Now simmer down there, Billy...I just wanted to make sure that you concentrate on the little mundane developments, as well as those sexy hurricanes, tropical storms, and tornadoes...in meteorology it is from the small natural disturbances that the major storm systems develop-always remember that fact!" Dr Ciellerie explained in a more calm, explanatory manner, as he patted his young student on the shoulder in a comforting father-like way.

"Billy, I need to make sure that as a future meteorologist, you keenly appreciate the small, almost imperceptible chaotic details that compose the ingredients of our major weather patterns and this is why meteorology is still such an inexact science!" Dr. Ciellerie further explained patiently to Billy Coffler, who was a young PhD grad student at the University of Colorado.

"Thank you, Dr Ciellerie, I do understand what you are saying, and I'll try and remember it too," the budding meteorologist replied in a compliant fashion.

"Oh... by the way Billy, may I ask you a question? In all honesty, it's actually an offer that I want to propose to you?" Dr Ciellerie stated almost embarrassingly to Billy. The young student was aghast and flattered that such a senior scientist would ask either a question, much less a favour, from a PhD summer intern. Billy was naturally intrigued by the question.

"Why sure, Dr Ciellerie, go ahead and ask away, all I can say is no," Billy jokingly replied in a flippant, irreverent-like tone.

The doctor was relieved by his student's wit and lightheartedness. "Fine, Billy, I have an opportunity for you to apply for a permanent research assistant with me here at the National Weather Service after your graduation next year... would you be interested in such an opportunity?" Dr Ciellerie inquired hopefully.

Billy thought for a second, stunned by the prospect of working with such an esteemed member of such a dynamic team and he was just 26 years old to boot. Jobs were not easy to obtain in this field.

"Boy, oh boy, are you kidding me? Sure, you bet I do, professor, this is the opportunity of a lifetime!" Billy replied eagerly.

"I'll give you the details next week, but I warn you... the hours will be long and the tension high. Between the job and your PhD course work, you will not have much of a social life," Dr Ciellerie counselled in a most fatherly manner.

Dr Ciellerie was a brilliant, if not sometimes eccentric, meteorologist, who had been working for the National Weather Service (NWS) for the past 30 years. He had gotten hooked on the science of meteorology in the US Air Force, where as a young man he had been a staff weather specialist at Davis-Monthan AFB in Tucson, Arizona. After the service, Peter Ciellerie attended Northwestern University, where he majored in mathematics. Peter performed his post graduate and doctoral work at MIT, where he met his wife Peggy McBride. Peggy was attending Boston University, where she was studying for her nursing degree.

Peter and Peggy were the proud parents of two energetic children, a boy and a girl, both of whom were attending post-graduate schools in Boston and Philadelphia. Since Peggy was a native of the state of Maryland and given the fact that Peter Ciellerie was going to be employed by the National Oceanographic and Atmospheric Administration and its subcomponent the National Weather Service, the couple decided to put down roots in the rapidly growing suburb of Silver Springs, Maryland, which was just about 20 miles north of Washington DC.

The suburban life in Silver Springs was very comfortable, if not predictable, but like most regions of the country, the Cielleries were finding their quaint suburban home being encroached by ever increasing roads, traffic congestion, high property taxes, and the non-descript, uniformly-constructed, strip malls. In their hearts, Peter and Peggy longed for the simple and quiet home of their early marriage; however, reality dictated that they settle for the realities of the suburbs with all its modern comforts and detractions, after all, they and most Americans were living better than 90% of the population of this ever-shrinking world.

Over the course of his career in meteorology, it had been Peter Ciellerie's privilege to have predicted some of the major storms in the past 20 years, a feat which had saved many thousands of lives and billions of dollars in property damage. Dr Ciellerie's Artificial Intelligence research into weather emergence patterns was giving meteorologists the ability to predict severe weather several days before the systems had a chance to climax. His work along with that of many other less notorious mathematicians and meteorologists was paying handsome dividends in the areas of severe weather prediction. Future progress in this field would mean that evacuations could be done much earlier, and disaster response services could be more succinctly pinpointed for specific disaster areas that needed the assistance the most. Although the mathematical models for transcontinental storms were becoming more refined, the predictive pattern area for forest fire prediction remained elusive at best.

Until quite recently, funding for forest fire predictive research had been largely ignored, the research efforts mainly directed instead into tropical storms and hurricane predictions. However, with the recent advent of many Americans migrating into the wilderness of the great American West and with the increase of the loss of property and lives becoming more endangered, the NWS and other institutions were starting to devote more research into the nature of western forest fires. Political funding was finely attuned to the 'squeaky wheel phenomena', where the most publicly visible weather culprit received the most funding. In America the ranking was hurricanes, tornadoes, forest fires and then flooding.

Over the past 100 years, the loss of human life from wildfires had fallen almost miraculously. In contrast, during the early part of the past century, there were wildfire incidents where hundreds of people were killed. Wisely, Native Americans had merely let the fires burn themselves out, as did many of the frontier settlers. However, with the advent of modern technologies, it was rare for more than a score of people to die annually from wildfires. The goal of everyone in the wildfire business, of course, was for the total elimination of all human causalities and the minimal destruction to real property, especially high-value residential homes. Most of the causalities of the fire wars befell upon those whose business it was to fight the fire demon; they were the men and women who went into Harm's Way to save the life and property of others. They were nameless faces in both life and death, the performance of service and sacrifice for which many Americans merely took for granted.

"Hey there, Billy, could you do some research for me on the National Weather Service's IBM mainframe and get data on the humidity and precipitation for the states of Idaho, California, Wyoming, New Mexico, and Colorado for the past 20 summers and have it presented in a bar graph, pie-diagram and numeric spreadsheet formats!" Dr Ciellerie voiced dryly.

Billy looked up from his computer terminal in astonishment, his mouth wide open at Dr Ciellerie's request.

"Dr Ciellerie, sir, that's a voluminous amount of data and it will take me a few days and a request for additional off-line disk storage to store and manipulate all that data!" Billy exclaimed in a wild and innocent youthful tone.

Dr Ciellerie was passively amused at the innocent, if not naïve, pronouncement of his young and inexperienced summer intern. "Yes, Billy, I expect that this request will take that minimum stated amount of resources that you have just estimated, maybe even a little more, I suspect. Unless you start work on this project now, I imagine that it might take even more time and resources than you have projected, so get cracking on it!" Dr Ciellerie replied matter-of-factly, as he peered into Billy's eyes from above his gold framed wire rim glasses.

"Yes, sir, I mean, yes, Dr Ciellerie, I'll get right on it!" Billy replied as he hurried up from the computer terminal and raced down the hallway to the information management resource office to request the appropriate computer resources.

Dr Ciellerie smiled as he envied the innocence and vigour of his youthful summer aid. He sent Billy on this data quest because he had a hunch that there was a correlation of factors that were contributing to the severity and magnitude of forest fires which were occurring with increasing frequency and ferocity over the past few years. He needed to determine what common factors were contributing to these increases and then he could make some predictions for the upcoming summer fire season. Without this data and trend line analysis, the Bureau of Land Management (BLM) and National Forest Service (NFS), the two main US agencies responsible for fighting the nation's forest fires, could only guess as to where to devote their resources and they would be relegated to merely fighting fires as these popped up. If Dr Ciellerie could provide a reliable estimation of forest fire predictability, the finite resources of the NFS and BLM could be strategically balanced and finely tuned before the fires occurred and so more efficiently defeat the fires in quick order once these had started.

* * * * * * * * * * * * * * * * * * *

If the NWS represented the brain trust and long-term research arm for fighting the wildfires, then the National Interagency Fire Center (NIFC) was its heart and the executor of the brain's information. As wildfires most often occur mainly in America's vast western wilderness, stretching across many states and government interests, it was decided that a centralized and consolidated body was needed to seamlessly coordinate, plan, and execute the assets necessary to fight the numerous wildfires that erupted in the American wilderness each year – the result was the NIIFC.

The NIFC is located in Boise, Idaho and it is the geographic home for seven federal agencies that work in cooperation to support combating the wildfires. The agency ensures for the time- sensitive coordination and provisioning of the country's firefighting resources and that these assets reach the most dangerous fires immediately. The NIFC provides every resource from shovels and personnel to airplanes and helicopters. During the fire season, which generally lasts from spring until fall, the NIFC operates on a working schedule of 24 hours x 7 days a week basis. Although the NIFC does not directly fight the wildfires itself, the agency does coordinate and direct the necessary resources and information is made available to the front-line fire fighters, these being the personnel who physically combat the blazes.

Providing key information and the latest weather forecasts to the fire fighters was a primary task of the NIFC. The successful coordination between the National Weather Service and Bureau of Land Management along with the NIFC – was vital in successfully fighting wildfires; the lack of cooperation could prove disastrous for all parties concerned, especially to the fire fighters and wildlife environment. The seven agencies within the NIFC consisted of: The Bureau of Land Management, National Park Service, Fish and Wildlife Service, Bureau of Indian Affairs, the Department of the Interior; the National Forest Service, and the Department of Agriculture. Of all these seven agencies, it was the BLM and NFS that performed most of the direct firefighting tactical operations, and these two agencies contained the vast amount of professional staff that were going to fight the wildfires each summer.

Lori Clarkson was one of the young, bright, and devoted NIFC professionals who fought the thankless fire wars on a full-time basis. At five foot seven inches tall and with attractive honey blonde hair and bright blue eyes, Lori was a real looker in this land of rough-country men. She was a 35 year-old Federal employee GS-14 NIFC employee, who lived year-round in Boise, Idaho. She was a divorced single-mother of a cute-as-a-button, nine-year-old girl, named Bridget. Lori had divorced her former high school sweetheart only two years after her daughter Bridget was born. Lori was left to pick up the pieces of her life and by luck, hard work and personality she landed a coveted, but lowly GS job at the NIFC. She started as a GS-7 entry level grade, which barely kept mother and daughter going through the cold Idaho winters. Yet steady jobs of any consequence were scarce in the Boise area and yet with stubborn determination, Lori went from administrative assistant, all the way to the position of fire shift supervisor.

She was as ambitious, as she was pretty; prudently, she figured that lacking a formal higher level of education, she would use the 'talents' that nature had bestowed on her. If was not Lori's fault that society treated pretty women and handsome men better than normal or ugly people, and there was little that she could do about this fact of life even if she had the inclination to do so. Like many a government service worker, Lori knew that time, perseverance, hard work, a good attitude, and a big smile would serve her well in the long run.

Lori's main problem, and her single major character deficiency, was that she leveraged too heavily upon her beauty and extroverted charm to get various jobs and positions. This was not an evil thing in and of itself, yet she never went the 'extra mile' to really learn the specific job dynamics for each of her higher-level positions. She performed her various jobs competently, but never with a full level of functional and judgmental expertise. She never served as a fire fighter for even a single season and this instantly led to her lack of work credential credibility among her co-workers. She was a bureaucratic pencil-pusher! The trials and dynamics of having to physically fight raging wildfires were hopelessly lost on her intellect. This shortcoming could not be easily overcome, yet she tried to over compensate for it through the virtue of her high GS rating and lofty titled position.

She shrewdly used the talents of her subordinates to coverup for any lack of expertise or knowledge. It was a strange thing indeed for the world condemns superficial beauty, only to artificially embrace the prejudice of intellectualism. Both were given from providence and both deserved the same level of attention or inattention. To date, this strategy had served her well and she saw no need to either abandon or modify her behaviour. Such career 'shortcuts' worked well when times were smooth, but in a crisis this personality deficiency could spell disaster. In fact, Lori was looking forward to her next promotion to GS-15 and that of becoming a district fire coordinator, in charge of managing the fires for several states and thousands of personnel. She had never known defeat or failure on the job; consequently, she never learned from her mistakes and it was only by making little mistakes that one learned big lessons in the wildfire business. Like so many others in this life, Lori progressed steadily up the career ladder to the highest level of her incompetence commonly referred to as, 'the Peter-Principle.'

For any shift supervisor working at the NIFC upper echelons, the most difficult task was that of deciding when to commit resources: one could either commit resources at the outbreak of a fire threat or wait until later – when there was greater clarity of data and facts. This was a crucial decision process, which depended as much on mature judgment, as it did on factual data. Fire resources, once committed, were usually very difficult, if not impossible, to recover and re-divert in a timely manner. As firefighting resources were finite, the commitment to the wrong fire, or of an insufficient quantity of needed fire-fighting resources – could well prove deadly to both the landscape and the fire fighters.

Finally, the changing climate was making fires both more intensive and numerous, so resources were always limited.

The NIFC supervisor was often in a Catch-22 situation, one where the supervisor was caught in a 'no win' event: commit fire resources in an area where there was minimal destruction or threat of a growing fire and it was viewed as a waste of resources; or instead send insufficient fire assets to a large fire and you were viewed as having poor management skills. It was a truly perfect occasion where you were a hero by providing just the right amount of resources, at the precise correct time, and at the optimal place. Last but not least, was the rogue factor of being lucky in the job. As in most organizations good decisions are based upon the combination of sound judgment and luck, but in many cases, there isn't enough of either to suffice. Yet even the best technical staff personnel could not hope to compensate for the deficiency of poor judgment or the lack of sound decision-making skills. No education could instruct on such a critical, mature life skill, only experience and character could do that!

"Hey, Good Morning there, Lori! How's my favourite boss and the most delightful sight in Boise this morning!" growled Reggie Flowers in a playful tone, as he slowly passed Lori's desk. He slowly placed two large black coffee cups down upon her desk. Reggie was a Federal GS-12 NIFC employee, who had worked at the agency in Boise for the past 15 years. Reggie was a tall and slender African-American male in his late thirties. After a three-year tour in the US Coast Guard, Reggie decided to keep both feet on dry land and only visit the sea on one of his rare vacations to the Pacific Ocean. It seemed that Reggie had one-too-many bad experiences of fishing-out too many drunks and idiots to further risk his life in the open seas, but he still enjoyed the great outdoor life. Upon completion of his Coast Guard tour, Reggie decided to take advantage of his GI Bill benefits and enroll in the University of Idaho School of Game and Forestry Science. This career field led to a job with the NIFC, a GS-7 assigned to the field occupation of forest ranger, then as a NIFC dispatcher, and now as an Assistant Fire Coordination Manager at the Boise Headquarters.

To his credit, Reggie also performed several summers as a fire fighter augmentee and this provided him with both invaluable firefighting experience and instant credibility within the community of fire fighters. He had learned his craft slowly, thoroughly and in the correct manner of progression – that is, from the trenches up through the management levels. Lori was lucky to have such a dedicated fire-fighting manager working with her and to act as her #1 back-up expert.

While at Idaho State, Reggie met his wife Gale, an architecture student. Shortly after Reggie made his GS-11 grade and received his relatively safe and stable position as a coordinator dispatcher, they were married. For the past five years, they had been the proud parents of two bubbling little girls. Although Boise was quite lonely and far from the sophistication of the big urban lights, the quaint city was a very safe place in which to raise a young family. Although both Reggie and Gale were pillars of the Boise community and they loved their neighbours, they both sometimes missed and yearned for greater ties to their previous urban African-American roots and Boise was not exactly a hub of African-American urban activity. They both thought that in time, as Reggie increased through the GS-grade system and responsibilities, that the opportunity would arise for them to move to the more urban right or left coasts of America. At least this was the dream that they had planned and they often said, 'that without a dream and plan, you are stuck in a dead-end situation.'

Lori gently twirled her hair with her left hand and smiled as she looked up at Reggie. From its mere aroma, Lori knew that the coffee was strong and rich in taste; she loved a good strong cup of coffee the first thing in the morning and Reggie always knew how to make a good brew from his special blend of African and Middle East coffee blends.

"Ah Reggie, my dear, you sure know what a lady needs the first thing in the morning, besides her lipstick and make-up that is!" Lori replied in her girlish manner, as she eagerly took her coffee cup and sipped a generous mouthful of delicious strong black coffee.

"Now, what's the big news for today, Reggie? It's too early in the season for any critical mass fires brewing, correct?" Lori inquired in an almost lax tone. Reggie knew that Lori had risen quickly on her looks, not her innate technical or managerial talents. He was slightly annoyed that his career stood still, while hers progressed almost exponentially. This was the nature of most things in this world, that the beautiful and handsome people get the majority of life's breaks. Reggie was just sorry that he was not one of the select beautiful people. Besides he thought, in the US Government service, the work was steady and secure, 'so why not just go along with the flow'. Finally, both he and Lori were social friends and she was a decent, supportive boss who took care of him and gave him good evaluation ratings annually. "Only a fool rocks a steady boat!" he reasoned pragmatically.

"No, boss, nothing major is happening. We just have to attend a Video Teleconference (VTC) tomorrow with all the components of the NIFC and the NWS concerning the upcoming fire season and our status of operations and resources...also to articulate our strategy and mission planning methodology," Reggie replied matter-of-factly as he sipped a large gulp of coffee.

"Exactly what time is the VTC and what is the speaking agenda? Do I need a speaking script or 'talking points' Reggie?" Lori inquired as she finished off another swig of strong coffee.

Reggie pulled a folder from under his arm and handed it to Lori; it was the NIFC VTC agenda and the list of participants. The list of attendees read like the credits at the end of a movie credit scroll.

"Oh shit, this damn VTC is going to be going on for two full frigging hours, what the hell is going to be discussed that will take two full hours? After all, we've been through this same pre-season management drill, year after year and it never changes substantially, Reggie!" Lori exclaimed in a wining tone.

Reggie knew that Lori was right on this point and that she was merely venting her frustrations. Lori realized with subdued resignation that it was useless to try and change the format or duration of the VTC.

"Hey Reggie, be a pal and e-mail me all your thoughts on the topic of fire resources allocation, interagency communication chart topology, budget resource summary and information sharing venues. I have some ideas on these topics and please add your own notes to mine and we will be fine for the conference...I also want you with me during this damn VTC, do you hear me, Reggie?" Lori stated in a professional command tone. Lori knew how to speak the bureaucratic walk-around techno-lingo, but when pressed for specific technical details, she was frequently lost for an answer. Reggie merely nodded, knowing that he had to play the 'second banana', while Lori merely had to look pretty and bask in the limelight.

* * * * * * * * * * * * * * * * * *

A soft, cool spring breeze blew across the waters of Puget Sound and a rainy early mist formed over a new fog-soaked morning in Seattle. In just a few hours, a new dawn would be breaking and many a resident slept the final hours of an all too short night's sleep. However, not all souls were as fortunate as to lay slumbered in a blissful night's repose; some worked night shifts, while others were tormented by the nightly ghosts of insomnia and past guilt. One such unfortunate soul was even now exorcising his nightly demons from over forty years ago, as he tossed restlessly among his blanket and bed sheets, he flung his arms and contorted his body as if he were in an actual physical wrestling match with another person. This ordeal went on incessantly year after year and it was only his liberal daily use of alcohol that made his pain seem less acute, yet tonight alcohol no longer helped Hank Ransome to either rest peacefully or forget his nightmares. His screams pierced the quiet solitude of the darkness from which no verbal confession was uttered and for which no absolution was to be granted. His sins remained within the recesses of his memory and that of his sub-conscience.

"Get away... get the fuck down quick!... Oh no, no, not that...duck brother...get the fuck down buddy! The VC, they're coming over this way, they are going to overrun us... get down... get fucking down quick!" Hank cried out, as he tossed and sweated profusely onto his bed sheets. Instantly, Hank awoke from this same frequent night haunting. His heart was pounding, sweat poured profusely from his forehead and chest. The pyjamas that he wore were sloppily arrayed and his shirt was torn wide open. His eyes were opened wide and his pupils were completely dilated. Suddenly, he uncontrollably sat up in his bed screaming "get down, get down brother – 'Charlie' has us targeted!". Yet in just a few seconds, the climax of the most familiar nightmare was completed, and Hank was now fully cognitive that he had lost another nightly battle with his past demons.

Wearily, he glazed over at the alarm clock and it was 4:30 AM and he knew that it was fruitless to try and get back to sleep again. He slowly got up from his ruffled bed and proceeded into the kitchen of his small condominium. He opened the refrigerator and looked for something to eat or drink. It was too early for the strong spirits and besides, he had enough of the whiskey from the previous night. Nothing in the refrigerator interested Hank and he closed the door in impatient frustration. This ritual was becoming intolerable and he thought that he was slowly going insane.

Wearily he journeyed back into bed and he tried to get some twilight rest before he had to awake in several hours and report to work, yet sleep was to be a fleeting phantom. He sunk his head in the crumpled sweaty pillows and hoped to catch some light sleep without the return of the demons of Vietnam. In the solitary darkness, he cuddled in his blanket and mourned for those comrades that never came back to the states with him. Advancing age had a mysterious way of resurrecting bad youthful memories of the seemingly long forgotten past. A young warrior's actions are often robbed and eclipsed by the older man's laments.

Two childhood friends named Hank and Lee Roy grew up together in foster homes in the inner-city slums of Chicago. They were both estranged from their foster parents, often being beaten and abused nightly by uncaring adults who were more interested in the flesh of their own blood children than that of mere strangers. The two boys sought and found refuge in the companionship of one another and so a lifelong friendship was forged. They both wandered throughout their youth and adolescence and their lives were on the road to nowhere, when out of nowhere the intervention of a kind stranger changed their lives forever.

Seemingly from out of nowhere, she came into their lives like a guardian angel, a youthful, free-spirited and socially enlightened woman from one of the newly formed social welfare agencies that were becoming quite popular during the 1960s' Great Society programs. Tall, attractive and white – she was like a mirage in the black and Hispanic slums of Chicago. The mysterious and kind-hearted young woman saw something in these two youths, so she made the extra effort to get to know the two personally and she tried to give them more help than the standard social client. Through the efforts of this kind- hearted social worker, both Hank and Lee Roy's lives were starting to look up, when she encouraged both of the youths to enroll in a local community college. Both young men were excited, neither of them had any aspirations beyond the next paycheck. Now they were both enrolled in some courses at the local community college with the future possibility of escaping the Chicago ghetto that had unceremoniously enslaved many of his brothers and sisters.

While formally uneducated, Hank was a naturally gifted bright young man. He could learn quickly and remember facts at the drop of a hat. Lee Roy was more intellectually gifted and had a higher-than-average intellect – his educational preferences were for literature, history, music and the classics.

Then one day – bad luck struck! Both young men received letters from the local Selective Service Board, stating that they were being drafted. Unlike many of the social elite, neither Lee Roy or Hank possessed the connections or opportunities to get excluded from the draft – they were neither rich nor did they have an enrolment at a four-year degree granting institution of higher education. Their community college courses did not qualify them for any type of deferment. This was just like Hank and Lee Roy's luck, always getting the shaft just when things were starting to look bright in their lives. Serving in Vietnam was a very probable draft outcome. The odds were all in their favour, they were young, healthy, unconnected and black. Yep, there was no doubt about it, they were going to Vietnam and all they could hope for was that it was not in the military designated code of an 11B- straight leg infantryman or 'grunt' as it was called by its military slang name.

While living in the turbulent 1960s of Chicago's burning ghettos – the prospect of dying in the city were much higher than those encountered in the jungles of Vietnam. Neither young man, however, thought of death or dying. Off to Southeast Asia, both Lee Roy and Hank went, as Air Assault infantry troops with a 365 day in-country tour. "It would be a cakewalk," they both foolishly thought. "Flying to the battle action was much more preferable to walking through all the booby-trapped rice fields and jungle," both men carelessly reckoned to themselves. Besides neither man had a family unit to leave behind or fret about them being in danger. Upon reaching majority age, each man was self-emancipated and on their own as adults in society.

To Hank and Lee Roy being in the Army, even in miserable Vietnam, was preferable to the urban-strife environment which both men had just left. They saw a lot of death in their first year tour of duty, but both men were strong, and they got used to seeing the dead and the wounded, or at least they made a good effort at hiding their emotions in booze, sex and sometimes light drugs. Re-enlistment presented even better opportunities! The Vietnam War was going very badly for the American military, casualties were rising, the war was not being won and more and more young men were refusing to register for the draft. One of the Army incentives being offered was for an enlisted soldier to re-classify into another military specialty in return for another year or two of military duty obligation. Each man thought how great it would be to get to learn to operate the marvellous helicopter flying machines which daringly dashed like frenzied hornets across the skies of Vietnam.

The helicopters were the newfangled fighting aerial beasts in the Vietnam War and each man knew that this was both an exciting career choice and perhaps a valuable skill for their future. Anything was better than being a 'straight-leg' 11B infantryman trudging through the countryside inflected that was rampant with booby-traps, snakes, and the infamous VC. Besides, being a helicopter pilot meant more prestige, the rank as a Warrant Officer and monthly tax-free flying pay- it was a total win-win choice or so both men thought. Yet the year was 1967 and US Army helicopter losses were great, with thousands of the complex and fragile flying machines being shot down every year. To these two desperate men with an unplanned and dubious future, statistics mattered little; it was always the 'other guy' who was going to get shot down, not them! They were both accepted by a despairing Army that needed helicopter pilots desperately and in great quantity. Few, if any, questions were being asked of new trainee helicopter pilot volunteers.

Like newborn babies, both men emerged nine months later from helicopter flying school as certified UH-1Huey helicopter Warrant Officers. Naturally, their first duty station was Vietnam, of course. By hook and crook, Hank and Lee Roy managed to eventually serve together side by side, with Hank being the senior helicopter pilot and Lee Roy serving as his co-pilot. The men thought it better to live or die together, rather than to soldier on separately in different units. Both men were comfortable with one another; they each knew the others' weaknesses and strengths. So well did they know one another that they could almost finish off each other's sentences.

Hank and Lee Roy served as pilot and co-pilot for two years and during that time they became seasoned Army helicopter veterans, earning numerous military decorations as well as a few undesired Purple Hearts to boot. The war was going from bad-to-worse and so was the quality and attitude of the US Army soldiers. Drugs and alcohol abuses were rampant, racial tensions were high, and there was the direct disobedience of the orders by enlisted troops to the orders issued to them by their green, newly-minted junior officers, who were unofficially called '90-day Wonders' as per the duration of their training period to become newly minted officers. The incidents of enlisted AWOLS and officer fragging was rising as the public and political support for the war declined. President Nixon started to draw-down the US military presence, trying to instead to get the South Vietnamese Army to do more of their own fighting. At this stage of the war, it was a hopeless plan, but one that needed to be tried, less all the other countries in South East Asia should fall to the Communist domino theory or so many in Washington truly, but wrongly, thought.

In the year 1970, Hank and Lee Roy were supporting flying missions of US Special Forces and that of their fellow South Vietnamese soldiers. The President had just launched and declared military operations against the Communist military forces that were being staged in the neighbouring country of Cambodia. Since Cambodia was being used by the North Vietnamese Communist forces as a logistical and assembly area for the conduct of military operations into South Vietnam, it was the goal of the US military and South Vietnamese forces to attempt a lightning thrust invasion in an attempt to deny and eliminate these sanctuary areas to the enemy or so the top-brass Pentagon and White House pundits vainly believed!

It was during a Vietnam-Cambodian border incursion mission, commonly known as a 'deep insertion' mission in the area known as the 'Parrot's Beak', that both Lee Roy and Hank met their cumulative military destinies. The conduct of a search & destroy raid was fraught with anxiety, fear, and danger. While the US Special Forces were cool and professional, their South Vietnamese military counterparts were visibly nervous and quite frightened, many of them chain smoking American made cigarettes and drinking Cokes. As was so often the case with counter-insurgency operations, the Viet Cong or VC or simply 'Charlie' for short, were often alerted as to the time and place of the raids, a direct result of superior intelligence information and indigent local countryside peasant spotters. Actual contact with youthful, fighting-age VC males was sporadic, since the vanguard of the VC and regular North Vietnamese forces prolifically were aggressively using both male and female insurgents of every age to directly confront and fight against the US and South Vietnamese forces.

The enemy was very cunning and saved his best forces for a time and place of his own choosing to engage high-value US or South Vietnamese military targets. As a consequence, most villages consisted of young children, adolescent girls, mothers, and old people. Most of the prime age males were already serving with the VC, South or North Vietnamese forces, or else they had already been killed during the previous decade of fighting and bombings.

The flying missions were never routine and each flight could have been their last one, both men had a keen appreciation of the risks, yet each man had a fatalism about it all, 'if your time was up, your time was up' and there was nothing that you could do about it, so needless worrying was not part of their attitude, both men developed the popular phrase – 'it don't mean nothing' as their personal philosophy. For their current tour of duty, both men had already served over 600 days continually in country, which meant that Hank and Lee Roy were the senior two short-timer soldiers, meaning that they would get priority on leave or R&R (Rest & Relaxation) as the veterans called it.

They were eagerly counting down the days when they could leave the miserable rice paddies of Vietnam and get 30 days' R&R to Australia or Hawaii. Being seasoned veterans, they knew full well the ways of the enemy and their tricks. Neither Hank nor Lee Roy was going to press their luck this day and each was very careful, as well as being on utmost alert. Their mission was to insert a 12-soldier team into Cambodia on a Special Forces operation about which they were told nothing.

The UH-1 or Huey troop transport helicopter swiftly flew at 120 mph and very low, just above the triple canopy of bright emerald green jungle. "If the Communists ever won this war, they wouldn't be getting that great of a deal," Lee Roy half-joked to Hank. He was nervous, as were most soldiers who had performed long tour combat missions. A man was born with only a given amount of luck and both Lee Roy and Hank were close to using up their fair share and then some.

Hank laughed too and replied, "Yeah Lee Roy, this real estate here ain't worth nothing, man, it's a damn third-world cesspool that is crying out fucking loud for development, no way these sorry-assed folks here are ready for democracy as we know it! Damn, they got no flush toilets, clean running water, refrigerators, automobiles – they got Jack Shit here man! Trying to bring those type of things to this arm pit of the world is pure bullshit, man. I'd like to have some of those politicians back in Washington DC do a 365-day tour here! What a bunch of sorry-assed mother fuckers!"

Lee Roy only smiled and nodded his head in affirmation. "So, brother, what you going to do when you get back into the real world?" Lee Roy inquired from his soul brother.

Hank thought carefully before answering. "Well, Lee Roy, maybe settle down and start a family like everyone else in the US, I'm getting too old to be bumming around without any roots, a man needs a dream and a future. I could always try to find a job flying these crates or maybe use the GI Bill to go to college or get a trade skill of some sort, maybe I'll get into auto repair, electrician, plumbing or some other thing...some trade that everyone always needs!" Hank replied as he eyed the green scenery and looking for any telltale signs of Charlie below.

"How about you, Lee Roy, what you goanna do, bro, when you get back to the world?" Hank queried back to his lifelong buddy.

Lee Roy thought for a few seconds before answering back into his helmet microphone, "Oh I don't know, maybe go to the university and study law, engineering or something... that social worker has me thinking of all sorts of possibilities and I like her, Hank, I think I really like her...you know what I mean, bro?" Lee Roy confided.

Hank merely looked over at Lee Roy and rendered a glancing wink of approval to Lee Roy's dreams of post war life. "Yo, bro, I can't see either of us two ass-kicking brothers settling down in middle class civilian life, going to college and getting married; I used to think those things were only for other people and not guys like us, maybe we owe ourselves a second chance in life!" Lee Roy roared in laughter.

"Yeah, bro, another month here and afterwards I'm going to take me the longest, hottest bath in the world!" Lee Roy added in wild anticipation of getting back to the world and secretly realizing that after this tour in Vietnam, he could never go back to being the same youthful, street hanging guy that he was before the war. As in all wars, both men were changed forever by the war experiences and yet neither of them wanted to confront this reality at the moment either. They hated the war, yet they had become addicted to its high emotional energy and rhythm – it was predictable, while civilian life out in the world was so very strange, unpredictable and frightening. Ironically, the war had more defined rules than those crouched within the civilized world of peaceful society.

In the larger scheme of the war, Hank and Lee Roy were part of the 101st Airmobile Division, the division of World War II fame and whose nickname the Screaming Eagles, was a testimony to the ferocity of the unit's fighting zeal and the nobility of the American eagle whose mobility the division emulated through the extensive use of helicopter tactics in the jungles of South East Asia. The Pentagon sought to make democratic and equal, the service of those serving in Vietnam, so a grand military management game plan was established that gave each service member assigned into Vietnam an in-country exposure of 365 days per combat tour. This minimal exposure to presence in country ensured that no soldier, marine, sailor, or airman served more time than his peers and it ensured that troops did not get worn down and were replaced with a like-replacement in a predictable order. This individual part replacement system meant that individual soldiers, not whole units, came and went at various times throughout the war. Although this system may have worked well in other commercial organizations, it was a disaster for the military, where it destroyed unit cohesion, morale, and esprit de corps. Old soldiers and new green recruits all served together, and the military units were constantly re-learning battle lessons, tactics, and techniques, as senior soldiers, NCOs and officers all rotated through the units at varying times. There were few resident experts in the units as a consequence. New battles were being fought with new, inexperienced troops and with frequent repeated mistakes and soaring causalities

The US military personnel turn-over rate and drawdown of US troops in Vietnam was so drastic and fluid, that few fellow unit soldiers knew either Hank or Lee Roy personally. Being senior flying members, Hank and Lee Roy were picked for unique and special missions, which each man eagerly sought – as these missions took them away from the normal military unit bull-shit jobs. Their constant flying of Special Operations missions also took Hank and Lee Roy away from their fellow flying officers, thus increasing their anonymity within their unit organization. There were rampant signs of racial discrimination within the US Army and within their own unit, especially in the early 1970s. Each man coped with this the best they could; trying to avoid senseless fighting that would not prove anything or change anyone's mind.

Hank and Lee Roy preferred to fight racial discrimination by example, that is, by setting the highest degree of military and flying professionalism. Each man was determined to be the best helicopter officer possible. Even growing up black, poor, and disadvantaged, the USA now seemed like heaven compared to the hell that each man had been living for the past several years. Yet they had extended their military tours and they were volunteers for these Special Operations (Spec Opns) missions. They chose this life, so they had limited reasons to complain. Still, they envied the comforts of home in the USA, the flush toilets, big automobiles, and big juicy steaks – that were soon to be theirs to enjoy in bounty once again.

During mid-May 1970, they were returning back from across the recent Cambodian Parrot's Beak border operation, when they were suddenly given a new task from higher headquarters. Their new secret mission was to clandestinely take a small group of Spec Opns troops for insertion into a remote and highly contested parcel of VC territory. After flying fast and low for over an hour at high cruising speed, both Hank and Lee Roy keenly spotted their Landing Zone or LZ as it was commonly referred to by military jargon. The mission was to simply drop-off the dozen Special Forces and South Vietnamese troops to perform counter-insurgency operations, yet there were no simple operations in this war, especially for these 'spook' missions.

A single helicopter flying alone was just too tempting of a target for the enemy to ignore. Just as the helicopter was hovering several feet off the ground and getting ready to unload the elite Special Forces and South Vietnamese troops, the entire area became engulfed with 122 mm rockets, mortars and enemy small arms fire. Bullets were cutting into the UH-1 thin metal skin like wild hornets. Hank quickly radioed in his situation to the Squadron Command Post, while Lee Roy tried to make a quick exit from the hot LZ.

Just as the UH-1 was getting enough thrust to make a rapid lift-off, the turbine engine was hit by enemy machine gun fire. The engine made a horrific rumbling sound and black smoke quickly emerged from the engine. The mighty, expensive aerial leviathan was fatally wounded by a few pieces of cheap ballistic steel. Almost immediately the UH-1 lost all of its power and it crashed to earth with a decidedly loud 'thug' sound. The aircraft had only fallen several feet, yet all aboard were physically and mentally jarred by the sudden ground impact. Mercifully, no one died from the crash! No one could be certain if military reinforcements were on the way or if they were in this ambush alone.

Hank and Lee Roy yelled for everyone to rapidly exit the targeted, mortally wounded aircraft, yet by both instinct and training, no one needed to be told to exit the aircraft. Everyone tried to scramble from the burning helicopter, as mortar shells and machine-gun fire ripped into the smoking helicopter. Instantly grabbing their gear, Hank and Lee Roy dashed from the UH-1, when suddenly there was a huge explosion. Both men were toppled to the ground by the blast; a mortar shell had ripped directly into the helicopter and blew it apart with a tremendous roar. Random pieces of metal and human body parts were blown irreverently into all directions and the acrid smell of burning human flesh and JP4 aviation fuel could be readily discerned.

Those soldiers who survived the helicopter attack, instantly scattered rapidly away in all directions and made a mad dash across the open rice paddy and into the village located 150 yards off into the distance. Fear took second place after that of their combat experiences, as each soldier sought to distance themselves from the open field target area and into the more secure, but still dangerous, confines of the village. The enemy's ambush tactic was to 'shoot & scoot' that is to hit 'unexpectedly, hard and fast' then to simply melt away into the village and jungle to fight another day. These guerrilla tactics were a far cry from the classic European Clausewitz set-battle doctrine, yet the battlefield results were remarkably successful.

Everyone and everything in the village was suspect. This had to be so, since the mortar rounds and automatic small arms fire had originated from this village, the enemy's rifle muzzle flashes told no lies. The remaining soldiers, along with Hank and Lee Roy, moved cautiously through the village, eyeing each grass hut with ultimate suspicion. Danger lurked in every unfamiliar hut and peasant face. An emergency radio dispatch for assistance by a Special Forces Sergeant was radioed back to the Battalion HQ on the FM PRC-77 or 'Prick-77' portable field back-pack radio. It was good news! More helicopter support was coming in about 30 minutes, maybe less. The survivors were nervous that they would soon be dead before any promised help arrived. The fears were real, since the VC enemy was still active and in the area. Utmost caution was their watchword. The enemy would pounce on any perceived weakness or target of opportunity.

The rancid smells of chickens, animal faeces and other livestock odours permeated the soldiers' nostrils, even the peasant people smelled strange and alien to them. Every new and unexpected sensory sensation raised the soldier's anxiety level, but still no enemy soldiers, weapons, or contraband was to be found. Yet that was to be expected too, for this was a shadow war with an unseen enemy and sudden ambushes. As they neared the end of the village, the thick jungle foliage began to uncomfortably enclose and terrifyingly embrace every soldier.

The soldiers were ordered by Standard Operating Procedures or SOPs to fan out and search and secure the village and the immediate surrounding area. It was not uncommon for the VC to place tunnels and weapons caches immediately outside of a village perimeter. The VC needed the support of the local villagers to both survive and conduct their deadly military ambushes. Any attempt at village resistance or passivity, resulted in immediate and cruel reprisals in which elders, mothers and children were equally subjected with torture or death. Over time, resistance became impossible! The poor and non-combatants always bore the brunt of any war!

Lee Roy and Hank teamed up together to secure an area to the southeast part of the village. They each carried their compact Carbine-15

(CAR-15) weapons and a Colt .45 automatic pistol. Their standard ammo load issuance was very limited too, this consisting of one rifle bandolier of 140 rounds and 21 rounds of .45 pistol ammo and a several hand grenades apiece. This was not enough ammunition for a prolonged firefight with a superior enemy force. As the two soldiers approached the end of their perimeter search area, they spotted a small clearing in which two old Vietnamese men were gathered.

The two old peasant men were dressed in the iconic triangular straw rice farm hat, dark baggy pyjama bottoms and black rubber sandals. They were crouched over with their backs toward the approaching soldiers. Both peasant men appeared to be talking excitedly about something and each man was holding something in their hands, most probably a farm implement like a hoe or shovel. Neither Lee Roy nor Hank spoke or understood Vietnamese aside for a few curse words and some GI slang. The surviving South Vietnamese soldiers were not present either; they were posted at the far end of the village along with several Special Forces advisors.

Suddenly the two old Vietnamese peasant men stood erect and turned fully around to face Lee Roy and Hank. Immediately Hank and Lee Roy eyed to their horror that both men were armed with deadly AK-47 automatic rifles, which were now pointed directly at them! Lee Roy saw the threat first, "Hey – they're VC, get the fuck down!" he shouted instantly to Hank.

"Watch out for the Papa Sons, they both got AKs!" Hank yelled out as he spotted the old man raising-up his rifle. Everything happened as if in slow-motion fashion, neither man could believe that these two old village peasant men were going to kill them. Suddenly the war had become most personal and deadly. Hank ran a few feet to where Lee Roy was standing, he tried to push Lee Roy out of harm's way, but the rattling of the two AK-47 automatic rifles had already begun to sing their deadly tune.

A burst of automatic rifle fire struck both Hank and Lee Roy in the chest with several rounds of 7.62 Russian calibre ammunition. The distinct 'clank' of metal hitting metal was easily heard and both men experienced an immediate hot painful burning in their chests. The audio metallic jingle was that of the AK-47 bullets piercing and shattering their identification dog tags, while other bullets benignly grazed their steel helmets, canteens and other metal pieces of their field gear.

The crimson colour of blood immediately splattered from their wounds, as their injured bodies spurted blood two feet into the air. Hank gave out a loud yell and immediately his body slumped onto the ground next to that of Lee Roy.

Lee Roy looked over at his friend's bloodied face and he saw the unmistakable blank look of shock trauma' in Hank's eyes. Yet despite their grievous wounds, the enemy threat still persisted, and it meant to kill them both. Lee Roy grabbed his CAR-15 rifle, quickly popping-up from the tall jungle grass, and fired a generous burst of automatic rifle fire at both of the enemy, wildly emptying the entire 30-round magazine in the process. One old VC man dropped in an instant with blood rushing from his torso. One enemy was dead, yet still another remained as the hunter.

Lee Roy looked down quickly and saw blood squirting like a spray from his chest. His breath was shallow and with each passing breath, he felt the warm blood trickle down onto his chest, he felt lightheaded and on the brink of passing out. He quickly grabbed his first aid bandage and pressed it strongly against the spurting wound, it hurt like hell, but at least the blood flow was easing somewhat.

Both men were now grievously wounded and were going to die unless immediate medical care was rendered. Survival rates were greater than 90 percent, if a medical aerial evacuation was performed in time; yet time was something that was very scarce in Vietnam. Minutes seemed like hours when one was wounded on the battlefield waiting for either death or medical aid to mercifully arrive and claim the soul. In the distance, he glimpsed an old Vietnamese bearded, grey haired man approaching his location. Lee Roy was damned if he was going to let this SOB of a VC live longer than himself and his buddy Hank. "That old mother fucking Papa Son was going to be breathing his last breath on earth," Lee Roy vowed and cursed bitterly to himself.

Lee Roy had been shot in the side and upper chest areas with AK-47 bullets. Despite the pain and blood loss, no major organs were damaged, but a small upper chest secondary artery was ruptured. Hank, on the other hand, had experienced multiple 'sucking chest wounds' in the upper -torso region. This was a military medical term used to describe an instance whereby a bullet pierces the lung and allows blood to enter the lung instead of vital air. As the air exited the lung and blood enters into the lung, the victim slowly suffocates by drowning in his own blood. It was a potentially fatal wound, unless immediate first aid was rendered quickly.

Hank was no longer a combat functional soldier. Bordering between the state of conscious and unconsciousness, Hank knew he was hit bad and possibly even dying, yet he was still breathing even under great effort and pain. Hank felt Lee Roy compress several first aid bandages onto his chest area and this immediate action stopped the air-blood mixture from further entering into his lungs.

"Lee Roy – you get that mother fucker, you hear me! You get that fucking old bastard for me!" Hank whispered out desperately to his dearest friend. Hank's voice mercifully went silent as he quickly fainted from the pain and loss of blood.

With all of his remaining strength, Lee Roy painfully squatted up from the obscurity of the tall elephant grass and spotted the second VC combatant cautiously approaching his position about thirty-five feet in the distance. The old VC man was still pointing and firing his AK-47 rifle into the tall elephant grass that had safely camouflaged Lee Roy and Hank. Even while being wounded, all of Lee Roy's senses were on a full alert status – the adrenaline was pumping through his body, making every nerve alert and every cell alive with excitement. The human body when faced with fear and the will for survival was a sensory marvel to behold – every sense was alive and heightened to its maximum reception capability. He could smell every scent, hear every sound, and feel every vibration of the earth around him. Like a wounded Cobra snake, Lee Roy was ever deadly, ready to pounce on his approaching prey. He thought quickly and developed his ambush strategy.

He would have just one chance to kill this old VC bastard or else he and Hank would be dead. His CAR-15 weapon was loaded and ready to fire and he checked to make sure the weapon's selector was on full-automatic fire, as he knew that he would have no chance of a second shot. He needed this VC dead in one quick burst of automatic rifle fire. For insurance purposes, he also readied a hand grenade, just in case his weapon failed to fire.

The adrenaline was fully pouring throughout Lee Roy's body and for now, he was almost oblivious to his wounds. He looked over at Hank, who was now pale and unconscious, but lying safely hidden in the tall green elephant grass. "Now was the time to pounce!" Lee Roy acutely judged. His military training and human instinct for survival were his main benefactors. Lee Roy rose quickly and sharply from the tall, wind-swept elephant grass, as he quickly spotted the old man crouching forward with his AK-47 in hand, now a scant 20 feet from his position. From the stunned look in his eyes, the old VC never expected the sudden emergence of Lee Roy from the elephant grass.

With all his remaining strength and determination, Lee Roy pulled the trigger of his CAR-15 rifle. His weapon rattled and spat forth a burst of bullets that ripped into the second VC man, killing him instantly as the bullets exploded into the old man's skull. A huge momentary aura of bright red blood and grey brain matter mist filled the air and splattered a generous crimson red stain across the surrounding elephant grass. The man's entire skull had exploded from the high velocity bullets violently impacting into his skull. The VC old man was dead before he had even fallen onto the ground.

Lee Roy knew that he had killed the old VC and that the immediate enemy threat was abated, thereby saving himself and avenging his boyhood pal Hank. Yet there was little time for rejoicing, as both men had been critically wounded by the VC ambush. With his last remaining strength, Lee Roy took a few steps over to where Hank lay gravely wounded and unconscious. He vainly tried to revive his boyhood friend, yet his efforts were to no avail as he huddled his friend in his arms, his strength was weakening as he loosened the grasp on Hank's limp body. He slowly took Hank's bullet-shattered dog tags and placed these into his fatigue shirt pocket. As tears filled Lee Roy's eyes, he became light-headed and on the verge of un-consciousness from his great loss of blood.

Each man now lay near death's door crumpled-up like two small lumps of lifeless flesh amid the tall blowing green grass. The two men lay huddled together; both were near death's door. The remnants of the Special Forces and South Vietnamese troops from the destroyed helicopter had successfully secured the entire village area and had rounded up all of the villagers for interrogation. They also continued radio communications with the soon to arrive MEDIVAC helicopter.

The all too familiar whipping sound of an approaching trio of helicopters was faintly heard in the far distance. Help was on the way, but maybe it was too late for both of the grievously wounded soldiers. A US Special Forces Lieutenant pulled a red smoke grenade from his flak jacket and tossed it onto a cleared spot of dry ground just a few feet from where the valiant wounded warriors lay unconscious. The red smoke grenade was used as an emergency signalling device to convey to air crews that an emergency situation existed on the ground and that fellow American soldiers were in grave danger or needed immediate

MEDIVAC assistance.

The remaining US Special Forces and South Vietnamese (ARVN) troops quickly saw the vibrant red smoke and a few of them cautiously made their way over toward their fellow soldiers' aid. The US troops in Vietnam knew that the VC insurgency forces had also used the red signal smoke technique to lure un-suspecting US soldiers into ambushes, so the US and ARVN team proceeded swiftly, yet cautiously to their injured comrades, less they too became ambushed by the VC. Two UH-1 helicopters landed with a medical and security detail team, while the third helicopter, the Attack Helicopter or AH-1 Cobra gunship, flew cautiously overhead and provided continuous and deadly overhead security support to the ground forces.

The two wounded heroes were evacuated to an Army forward field medical unit, an updated type of MASH medical unit just inside the border of South Vietnam, except that this medical facility was larger and much more modern. Only Lee Roy was semi-conscious, while Hank was totally oblivious to the world. Lee Roy's senses were dulled by the apparent pain and from the morphine medication that he had been administered. Through his dulled senses, he could still discern the screams of the other soldiers around him, as well as his own dulled pain. He could also feel the cold, sharp insertion of various needles and probes being placed into his limp body. He slumbered off into a deep sleep and was wheeled off into the confines of the emergency operating room.

"Hey there soldier...can you hear me? Wakee-up...good morning soldier, how are you feeling?" inquired a soft, gentle, soothing feminine voice. "Hello there, brave soldier, how are you doing today?" the soft, pleasant voice echoed again, this time with the soft warmth of her hand being placed onto his forehead. His eyes opened ever so slowly, he could barely tolerate the harsh light. Every muscle in his body seemed to be on fire. He was sure that he was on some heavy medication as well.

"You're alive, soldier! You're going to be all right, young man! Do you hear me? Can you speak?" the nurse inquired anxiously.

In vain he tried to move his arm, yet it would not respond to his mental command. He tried to speak, and it was only with great difficulty that any words emerged from his dried-out mouth and seemingly wooden tongue. "Where the hell am I Miss?" he muttered with an obvious strain from his throat.

Gently the nurse held his hand and tried to comfort him. I'm Nurse Lt Debbie van Dorn and you're in an Army Hospital just outside Saigon.

You are going to be fine soldier, I have just a few questions to ask you before I let you rest some more, alright?" He merely nodded in tacit acknowledgment. "Hey, there soldier, your ID tags and those of your buddy were pretty much mangled up with rifle fire damage and we found two sets of dog tags on you, but none on your friend...so can you tell me your name and that of your friend please? Where are you from? Who are your family contacts?" Nurse Van Dorn politely inquired in rapid succession.

"Where's my buddy, my bro?" he inquired of Nurse van Dorn.

She was silent, and he knew that something was not right. "I'm very sorry, soldier, your friend didn't make it! He lost too much blood and his injuries were too severe, I'm so sorry!" Nurse van Dorn sincerely replied as she softly patted his hand.

There was a dead silence for a few seconds, as he thought carefully to himself. "Sure, Ma'am, I got a name, it's Hank...Chief Hank Ransome and my Army pal, my dear and now dead co-pilot, is WO1 Lee Roy Jenks; we're both from Chicago and we got no family except for each other!" was the blunt, yet utterly false, camouflaged response.

Lt Nurse van Dorn was relieved for receiving this vital information, but she felt deep compassion for the wounded young soldier who had tragically lost his best friend. "Oh, Chief Hank Ransome, if you like, I can leave with you the remnants of both sets of shattered dog tags and the rifle bullets that were taken from you! It seems strange, but a lot of wounded fellas like to keep these things as trinkets of their wounds and war experiences. Would you like that?" Nurse van Dorn meekly inquired.

"Yeah, sure, Miss, I would like that! It will be my constant reminder of this fucking experience, as if I could ever forget this damn thing! Oh, one more thing please, nurse, please have my buddy buried with full military honours at Arlington National Cemetery – he deserves that dignity and to lie with the other fallen heroes!" he muttered back in bitterness and remorse.

Having received the requisite identification information and burial deposition, Nurse Lt van Dorn quickly left his side and he was left to weep silently for his dead boyhood friend.

"This fucking war ain't good for nothing and nobody except for the undertaker!" he cried as he lay in subdued torment. In a hastily ill-conceived plot, Lee Roy had exchanged his identity with that of his dead friend Hank. Being an imposter could solve a lot of his problems.

Lee Roy had just become Hank Ransome. It was the chance for a new identity and a whole new life under the auspices of his old boyhood friend's identity. He wanted no one from his past to know that he was alive, 'better to let everyone think that I am dead, what's in a name anyway?' he conjured to himself in a twisted form of urban logic. 'A new start and new name might be better than his own one!' he figured with a very flawed convoluted logic. Still the evil deed was done!

In time, the resurrected 'new Hank' had fully recovered from his physical wounds, but not the mental ones! The ghosts of Vietnam lived in his memories daily. Immediately after his wounding, he became hooked on pain drugs and then illegal drugs, but after a few rough years, a caring minister helped to save Hank's soul and get him off the heroin. Hank was still not fully recovered, if such a word could be used for Post-Traumatic Stress syndrome. Hank was off the heroin, but he still used alcohol as a crutch and his insomnia was forever with him. Another infirmity for Hank was his past and the recurring dreams, which often took the form of nightmares. He knew that he could never go back to his girlfriend, get married, and start a family. He fled Chicago, never to return to it. He had a new name and identity, and he also had a new start in life. Yet it was all one big lie and it haunted him daily!

Hank elected to start a new life without any painful reminders of the past, so he chose to settle in Seattle, Washington and begin life anew. Seattle was peaceful, quiet, and green – all a stark contrast from the Chicago inner city ghetto of his youth. A man could make a new life for himself in Seattle and this is exactly what he did. After getting off drugs, Hank got a job in one of the local Boeing plants as first a semi-skilled labourer, then as a journeyman machinist. The Boeing 747 assembly line had started up and the work was steady and profitable. Having his Army aviation experience under his belt, Hank applied for aerial maintenance mechanic school and after a few years of hard work and study, he received his certificate as an aviation engine maintenance specialist under the GI Education Bill. He also received his civil fixed-wing and helicopter rotary licences, as well as his Bachelor's Degree with a concentration in history. He filled up his spare time by taking part-time auxiliary flying work with both the Civil Air Patrol and the various Seattle hospitals as an emergency medical helicopter pilot. The pay was very good, and the work kept his mind and body busy. He avoided socializing with his work peers, instead he lived a life of quiet solitude. He developed insomnia and had nightmares from fearing the discovery of his identity masquerade.

About 20 years ago through a series of friends and introductions, Hank was afforded the opportunity to become a part-time NIFC Helitrack pilot. Sensing some excitement and an opportunity to do something different, Hank applied for and was granted status as a part-time pilot for the NIFC firefighting helicopter team; these helicopter pilots and crews were known as Helitrack crews. Hank was in his 60's, but he still retained his lean tall masculine figure, his warm brown eyes still glittered with the hue of friendliness and compassion.

Every summer, Hank was able to negotiate with his civilian employers for a summer leave of absence to support the NIFC and its firefighting tasks. Hank enjoyed the work, the excitement, and the fine people that he had the opportunity to meet. Yet past ghosts remained with him. Sometimes during periods of quiet solitude, he thought of the girlfriend and street pals that he had left behind, wondering how their lives had turned out. He never returned back to Chicago; it was part of his past, not his present or his future.

During the long and isolated nights, he took to the bottle and started to have the nightmares from Vietnam. He could barely wait for June to arrive, at which time he would begin his annual NIFC Helitrack position and his time would be filled with long tiring 18 hour days of wildfire work. For Hank at least, the summer fires took the loneliness away from a shattered, guilt-ridden man. This wasn't the life that he wanted, but it was the one that he had forged for himself through his mistakes and bad decisions, yet he was doing his best to cope with it every day of his life.

As he poured himself a generous glass of Tennessee sour mash whiskey, he wondered to himself about the strange path that his life had taken and what the purpose of it all had been. Little was to be shown for his life aside from his increasingly greying hair and beard. It seemed that his experiences in Vietnam had claimed more than the life of his buddy, the war had also claimed Hank's spirit and his ability to form lasting friendships and relationships with others. Consequently, he never allowed himself the luxury of ever becoming close to another human being again, the cost of losing friends became a price too dear for him. The annual NIFC summer tour gave him a chance to stay in the action of doing the closest thing to war combat – the fighting of forest fires from the air! Still, old age was upon him and soon only his social security and pension benefits were going to be his life's legacy. This was real loneliness for certain.

Hank sipped another mouthful of whiskey, it went down smooth and warm. He just smiled to himself and thought that in just a few weeks, he would be leading an alternate life as a NIFC Helitrack pilot. He could almost smell the scent of burning ash in his nostrils and the acidity of smoke in his eyes. In a strange way fighting fires made Hank feel more alive than almost anything he had done, except for his combat experience in Vietnam. Perhaps this chance to escape one's present life and circumstances, coupled with the camaraderie of fellow fire fighters, was the secret reason why so many normal men and women wildly abandoned their normal lives every summer and went out West to fight the wildfires.

* * * * * * * * * * * * * ** * * *

CHAPTER 5

Soul Sisters: Sammy & Robin

"...if I see one more dirty old man that wants me to give him an alcohol bath or rub his back, I'm going to just scream"

"**O**uch you sadist witch, you're not the gentle angel of mercy or the Florence Nightingale-type, now are you honey? Ohhhh, please stop it! Aaaah, you flipping bitch, where did you learn patient care... at the Dr Mengele School of Medicine?" cried the grumpy old man, who was dressed in urine-soiled pyjamas and complaining in exaggerated boisterous agony for everyone to hear. Yet out of the noisy hysteria came a voice of calm, reason, and uncompromising authority.

"Hush now, you old curmudgeon, just be still now and please be a little more relaxed and civil, Mr Gottlieb; besides, I'm almost through here, just a few more pieces of glass and you will be out of here!" the pretty nurse exclaimed with a smiling frown. Gently and methodically, Emergency Care Nurse Samantha Evans removed the tiny shards of broken glass from the bottom of Mr Gottlieb's bleeding, wrinkled, old white foot.

"There now, I've just removed the last bit of foreign object material and now I'm going to have to apply some antiseptic ointment on the open cuts and we'll be done, but just a warning that this may hurt a little bit, Mr Gottlieb," Samantha explained quite methodically.

"Go ahead and finish me off, honey, I doubt that I'll ever walk again! I should sue you and this hospital for malpractice for providing excessive pain to an invalid senior citizen!" the old man grumbled in gross exaggeration and in hope of receiving some sympathy and attention that he now lacked in his later cloistered years.

"Oh, my fucking foot…you're killing me, nurse!" he screamed as the antiseptic was applied to the slight, yet painful open skin wounds located on the bottom of his right foot.

"You hush-up now, Mr Gottlieb and be a big brave boy for me!" Samantha teased as she gently applied the disinfectant.

"I have very good news, Mr Gottlieb, no stitches are required, and it looks like no serious harm is done, you'll have your foot bandaged for a few days and you'll have to stay off your feet as much as possible, but that's it, you're fine!" Samantha cheerfully exclaimed to the old wailing man.

"Now that's easy for you to say, honey, I'm the one who's hurting," Mr Gottlieb uttered in frustration and with some mild chauvinistic, resentful annoyance.

Samantha merely smiled away at the old man's frustration and anger, fully knowing that this patient was more bark than bite and he was just doing some venting at her expense. In reality, the old man wanted sympathy and attention; he was broken-down, retired and very lonely. It was no big deal for Samantha. In the last 12 years, she had witnessed numerous gunshot wounds, cranial fractures from falls, and impalements of varying body parts with all sorts of shaped instruments, household poisoning, massive 3rd degree burns, drug overdoses, and now Mr Gottlieb's bleeding foot. It was all in a day's or night's work, this depending on what shift she was assigned, and it never seemed to matter what shift she worked, it was always a hectic pace in the hospital emergency room.

"So how do you feel, Mr Gottlieb?" Samantha inquired as the crabby old man tried to place some weight on his sore right foot. "Ouch, son of a bitch, it hurts like the devil, nurse! Are you sure that you got all the glass out?" Mr Gottlieb scornfully inquired. Sam merely rolled her eyes in abject resignation to the complaints of this old and lonely patient. 'Perhaps his medical complaints were the only form of solace that this old man had left in his life,' Sam pondered silently to herself.

"Yes of course, sir! I removed all the glass, but remember the wound is still fresh and the flesh on the bottom of your feet is some of the most tender portions of the body," Samantha carefully explained to her patient. Old Man Gottlieb thought and smiled at Samantha's statement.

"Not as sensitive as some other parts of my body that I can think of, cutie," Mr Gottlieb devilishly implied about his other tender, unmentionable male body parts.

Samantha ignored his rude comments and she just continued to smile and ignored the old man's attempt to chat-up and embarrass her.

"Never mind about that, you just remember to keep off your feet, especially your sore right foot – come back here next week to see me again. I have ordered up some antiseptic ointment too, you can pick it up at the hospital pharmacy. You will come back sooner if there is prolonged blood or other wound discharge after 48 hours and remember to keep the sterile gauze dry and clean!" Samantha authoritatively ordered to the dirty old man.

The grumpy old man mulled Samantha's words for a moment before being assisted with the kind aid of a burly orderly, into a waiting wheelchair. Mr Gottlieb was relentless in his pointless quest to bother Samantha. "Can I still have my beer? Can I still use the toilet like a big boy? Can I have a little kiss?" Mr Gottlieb shamelessly cried out in a shrill plea to Samantha.

She paused just a moment before firing back her verbal broadside. "Yes, yes, and not tonight. I don't want to instigate a heart attack in you, Mr Gottlieb!" Sammy smartly responded. The old man was finally dejected and frustrated.

"Oh shit, that's the same answer that my dear wife gives me too!" Mr Gottlieb replied with an expected tone of self-indignation. Samantha gave Mr Gottlieb a faint smile, a parting gift for a cranky old man.

"Here now, let me help you get your robe on, position yourself in this wheelchair, and you'll be all set and ready to go on your merry way," Samantha cheerfully replied as she readied her grouchy patient for discharge from the ER.

"The only thing that's ready to go tonight, darling, are my bowels, I feel a good crap coming on!" Mr Gottlieb crudely grumbled to Samantha. Yet she was neither deterred nor shocked by Mr Gottlieb's continuing complaints. He was merely venting and hoping for some attention again. This time, she was having none of his crude remarks.

"Well, if you need to go, there's the bathroom and I can call a male orderly assistant, otherwise you'll be taken to the discharge desk and then to the visitors' room; your family is already waiting to take you home and I have already spoken to them," Samantha added firmly. The old man thought about Nurse Samantha's proposition and he elected to take the safe option.

"No, no, no... on second thought, I can take a dump when I get home, I don't like male hospital workers and I prefer my own throne!" Mr Gottlieb bitterly and coarsely confessed as a hospital attendant slowly wheeled him out of the ER and down the corridor to the discharge station. The cantankerous old man Gottlieb felt the need to get in one last departing remark. "Maybe I'll be back next week so that you can take a look at some of my other body parts, honey," Mr Gottlieb shouted to Samantha.

Undeterred, Samantha managed to get the last word on the subject. "Of course, Mr Gottlieb, and perhaps I'll have a nice barium enema or chloric examination waiting for you too!" Samantha forcefully, but jokingly replied.

The dirty minded, foul-mouthed, grouchy old man was suddenly dumbed into submissive silence by Samantha's keen wit and sarcastic comebacks. "Oh, I almost forgot, Mr Gottlieb, here's your walking cane, keep off that right foot now!" Samantha exclaimed as she ran down and handed Mr Gottlieb his new aluminium walking cane. He grudgingly grasped the cane and thanked Samantha in a bitter tone that befitted his cranky wrinkled old face.

"Boy, some of these old men are sure dirtier in their thoughts and verbal expressions than the younger guys, it must be a last hurrah for them or maybe it's' all they have left at this stage of their lives," Samantha bitterly muttered to herself.

Quickly, she glanced at her watch and noticed that her shift was about to end. "Another exciting Friday night in the ER over with and nobody to go home to again," she sighed to herself. Both her attention and thoughts were diverted to her next immediate summer endeavour – her annual 12-week sojourn as a volunteer western firefighter. Like many others employed in the national firefighting business, Samantha was a part-time, seasonal fire fighter, known as a 'Hot Shot'.

A 'Hot Shot' was a fire fighter who had on-the-ground field experience with fighting wildfires. It was front line, in-your-face combat with the beast of fire itself. The hospital was not happy about losing one of its valued employees for 12 weeks, but it was one of the terms of her employment with Chicago General and with the shortage of nurses being what it was in America, the Hospital Administrative staff was glad that Samantha hadn't left them for another hospital or private practice.

Samantha Evans or simply 'Sammy' to her friends and co-workers was a bright, attractive, and single woman of mixed White Afro-American parents. She had made a successful life for herself. She was a light-skinned woman, and this did not bode well for one raised in the hardscrabble existence of the Chicago slums. America was (and still remains), a multi-segregated community in those days, this prejudice extended to both white and black communities. Her white mother was named Nancy Evans, who was a single Mom, forced to raise her daughter alone, when her boyfriend was tragically killed years ago in Vietnam. Nancy's family had disowned her because of her relationship with an Afro-American man and that she bore a child of mixed blood, which sealed her social and family ostracization. Not being married, Nancy Evans was left with no survivor benefits, although her boyfriend did bequest to her a GI life insurance policy and this helped to raise little Sammy.

Nancy was a tough lady and she got through life the hard way, by working her butt off. There was no support system for herself and her fatherless little girl. Nancy Evans had a degree in sociology and worked as a social worker in Chicago and she was always busy with the myriad of inner-city social problems. The work was long and hard, the pay was barely adequate, but at least she was able to provide food and housing for her little girl. The best gift of all was that of being an actively involved parent in her little girl's life.

Wearily, Sammy got into her car and drove to her comfortable middle -class condominium located in the lush green suburbs of Chicago. She dreamed of buying a single house, but then she figured that it was more of a maintenance upkeep burden than was justified by the advantages of a green front lawn and a nice sidewalk. Her pets were none and her friends were few. Samantha had wisely figured out that her work would keep her busy most of the time and that this would be unfair to any pet, except maybe a goldfish. Ditto also for raising any child by herself, again for the same reasons that she had no pets. Her childhood had taught her that there was no substitute for a two-parent household and although her mom had done a great job in raising her, she always felt a void, she lacked something major in her childhood – a loving father! Maybe that was the secret of why she made no lasting relationships with a man. Feeling cheated, she carried a grudge around within her, in her dreams she created the perfect father figure to which no actual person could match, thus she found imperfections in every man that she happened to meet.

Putting aside her work clothes, Samantha took a casual hot shower, after which she prepared herself a nondescript microwave meal, accompanied by a brew of hot cinnamon spiced tea. Samantha turned on the TV and looked for some old re-runs to view. Taking up her cup of hot aromatic cinnamon spiced tea, she began to have sweet dreams of her future 12 weeks as a Hot Shot and emergency medical care nurse. She was to be posted somewhere out West. This had been her summer routine for the past several years and she got hooked on the firefighting gig when she spotted an article on this subject in a local news magazine article. She liked the idea of doing something totally new, exciting, and dangerous.

Initially, Sammy attended the 'Hot Shot' training, but now she performed this task only as a secondary skill, since personnel with medical skills were far too precious to be employed as 'Hot Shots', except in dire circumstances. The Emergency Medical Care (EMC) and Hot Shot jobs were not easy, but Samantha knew that she could easily handle it, and besides, it got her out of the noisy, urban Chicago summer. Additionally, it provided her the opportunity to meet old friends outside the medical field and to perhaps make a few new friends as well. Hyped by the anticipation, she decided to call up her fellow Hot Shot girlfriend and soul sister, Robin.

Several states away, Robin Wolf's phone rang out. "Hello," Robin answered in a voice which reeked with exhausted breathing. Samantha smiled as she pondered the possibilities of her friend's exhausted state.

"Hello to you, girlfriend, now is that the breathing of an exercise work-out or the exhilaration of being caught in a sensual moment with one of your hunk boyfriends?" Samantha joked into the phone. Robin was ecstatic to hear from her summer Hot Shot pal.

"Yeah sure, sister, my love life is about as active as yours, here we are two bright, attractive, educated, and independent women and neither of us can get a serious-minded man into our lives!" Robin only half jokily remarked, as she secretly hid her pain of being lonely too. Neither Samantha nor Robin had been married and both ladies were in their early thirties. Each of them secretly dreamed of 'Mr Right', but with each passing year they realized that their odds at finding an ideal husband were getting slimmer and slimmer. Neither woman financially needed a man, but each of them secretly yearned for a soul-mate, someone to come home to every night instead of the normal empty apartment or house. As with most desires in life, the quest was not for necessities, but that of heartfelt desires – companionship and love. Independence possessed its own brand of quicksand, that of a solitary life of a few good friends, a nondescript love life and the prospect of living forever alone in small rooms.

"Seriously, girlfriend, how have the past few months been treating you? I haven't received a phone call from you since Christmas and all I get from my Hot Shot soul sister are some short, stinking e-mails!" Samantha accused Robin in a very friendly manner. Yet Robin had been a very active woman indeed, having just completed her Master's degree in Special Education from the University of Wyoming.

"Yeah well, Sammy, I've been busy with my teaching position and working for my advanced degree!" Robin replied in a defensive tone and being a bit embarrassed by the lack of contact with one of her best friends.

"No worries, Robin, I totally understand your hectic schedule and congratulations again on getting your Master's degree, you go, girlfriend!" Samantha applauded eagerly over the phone.

"Thanks, so, Sammy, how is work going these days?" Robin inquired as she tried to drum up the conversation.

"Well, Robin, if I see one more dirty old man that wants me to give him an alcohol bath or rub his back, I'm going to just scream! I need a break urgently!" Samantha cried out over the receiver. Robin could only laugh at Sammy's humour and over-exaggeration of the hospital working conditions.

"What's that you are saying, girlfriend? No engagement to any of those rich doctors, honey?" Robin teased half-jokily in a soul-sister sounding metropolitan accent.

Samantha didn't even have to think twice to prepare her reply. "You are dreaming, girlfriend – there are not as many eligible male doctors as you may think and those that are here – well, they're already married or else they merely want some closet room action on the side, if you know what I mean, girlfriend?"

Robin tried to reply without providing an immediate cute reply this time, but Sammy's answer had hit too close to home to let her take any additional satisfaction. Hearing a pregnant pause from Robin, Samantha decided to short stop the conversation. "So, Robin, what about you and that hunk of an unmarried man, you know that sexy Smoke Jumper Rick Conroy? I think that he has the hots for you, Robin; he is available and without any major baggage or hang-ups," Samantha noted in an encouraging tone.

Robin was caught off-guard by Sammy's directness, but Sammy was her close friend and she was not offended by her friendly prodding, yet Robin didn't want to address the topic at this time, so she merely diplomatically deflected the question, "Well now, Sammy it sounds like you have the hots for Rick yourself, girlfriend!"

Samantha wanted to move on from this conversation and flipped Robin a quick kiss-off response. "No way, Robin, he's not my type and anyway, I think that this portion of the conversation is now history, girlfriend."

"Hey, look, Robin, the reason that I called was to touch base with you for this summer's Hot Shot schedule – are you still attending?" Samantha inquired eagerly.

Robin didn't even pause before answering, "Hell yes, girlfriend, this is the one activity that I look forward to every summer, it's my sanity break and pressure relief valve for the rest of the year...I mean I love teaching those kids, but the school routine after nine long months really gets to a girl?" Robin replied as she grabbed a bottle of water from her refrigerator and took a healthy swallow.

"Did you get any reporting instructions from the US Forest Service and BLM?" Samantha inquired. impatiently.

"Funny that you should ask, yes, I did. The assignment papers came in the mail just the other day, I got assigned to Camp Haller, Wyoming!" Robin replied as she took another sip of water and relaxed to sit down on her living room sofa.

"That's flipping great, girlfriend, I just loved that place," Sammy replied in a girlish scream. "I sure hope that I get that assignment too, Robin," Sammy voiced in an anxious manner.

"Let me see if I can pull some strings, Sammy... I have some clout now with the US Forest Service and BLM staff and I think that I can get you assigned to Camp Haller too!" Robin countered in a confident manner.

"Are you really sure, Robin?" Sammy inquired anxiously. "Yeah, sure enough, girlfriend, let me make some phone calls, you should be getting something in the mail in a week or so confirming your summer appointment and I can be your ride from the airport to the camp. I also have a few surprises to show you too!" Robin toyed in a devilish tone.

"Wow, girlfriend! Well, you know how I just love surprises, Robin, and thanks for all your help, hopefully I'll see you in a few weeks and I'll call you once I get my summer work posting confirmation," Sammy replied. Concluding their joyful conversation, the two friends promised to stay in close contact over the next few weeks. Theirs was a true friendship built on trust, loyalty and mutual circumstances.

For Robin, the summer firefighting job was a welcome respite from her gruelling duty as a Special Education teacher of grade school students. She wanted her independence from her parents, but she also desired to stay close to home. Her parents were advancing in age and they would someday need her help in growing old. Robin's Special Education work was demanding, and it required a special person with the gift of compassion and patience. Robin possessed ample quantities of both, which was a credit to both her childhood rearing and her natural personality disposition. She was a young woman of 32 years old. She was a mixture of Native American, Irish, Italian, and German stock. She was strikingly attractive, being possessed with shoulder length, flaxen golden-brown hair. Robin's eyes were hazel coloured, which seemed to change with her mood and the weather. She stood 5 foot 6 inches tall and she was of a slender, but athletic build. The crowning glory of Robin's natural beauty was her personality, which was almost always friendly and warm. This kindness was not to be confused with passivity and being introverted, as Robin could really wipe out a tongue lashing when the situation clearly threatened her family, friends, or beliefs.

****

"Hey, you guys, get that fucking lumber unloaded and set it out neatly for the work crew for the next pick-up by tonight. I don't give a rat's ass if you guys miss dinner and have to work till midnight, I need that 15,000 sq. feet of lumber unloaded off those trailers," barked the tall, crude and muscular man from across the muddy field. The tall man with thick black hair turned his back to the work crew and walked slowly in disgust back to his late model Ford pick-up truck. He unlocked the cab door and wearily reached into the centre arm rest area and grabbed a half-filled thermos bottle. It was going to be another late night again, but this was not particularly unusual in the construction trade, where long hours, tight schedules, late material deliveries and money – all seem to converge at one place in time. It all made the construction business crazy, exciting and fun loving for a man of ambition and energy. Instantly, he spit out the strong bitter black coffee in utter disgust, as he winced at the acid flavour that had developed in this last brew. 'This shit must have perked too long,' he thought to himself" as he threw the remaining cup of coffee onto the ground in anger.

"Hey, Boss, how much longer are we going to be working tonight, the men are all tired?" Burt Paxley the construction on-site foreman wearily inquired.

"Well now, that just fucking depends on how fast these dick-heads want to get home tonight! Now you listen here, Burt, we are on a tight schedule and the rest of these 34 homes need to be completed in the next five weeks, with all the framing and major fixtures installed. That's the contract and that is the commitment that we will meet! Do I make myself flipping clear? After that, we can all get paid along with a complete on-time bonus, then we can all rest easy, Burt! With this shitty housing market and economic down-turn going on, the men should be happy to get this construction work! Is that clear enough for you?" the boss man replied impatiently.

Burt merely grunted with a despaired face and headed back to the unloading crew, barking orders as he approached the men. The agitated and bad-tempered boss on this home sub-division construction going up just outside Fort Worth, Texas was that of Rick Conroy.

Rick was the part owner of a struggling Dallas-based, small, third generation, family-owned construction firm, Conroy Construction. Rick operated the family business along with his two older brothers, Roy and Jeff. Their grandfather, Ken 'Red' Conroy founded the business shortly after his service in World War II and the family business just took off steadily as millions of GI's bought single family homes of their own after the war, followed in succession by their children, who also desired their own homes as well. The family patriarch and father of the three Conroy sons – Owen, was in semi-retirement and more or less had left the day-to-day operations of the firm in the hands of his sons, while he and his wife Sue enjoyed their semi-retirement along the Galveston coast for the better part of the year.

Being the youngest and most brazen of the three Conroy brothers, he was quick to anger and slow to forgive, yet he was a man of quiet determination and he possessed a streak of anger and jealousy for issues involving those he loved. Still well-built and handsome for a man of 36 years old, Rick had married his childhood sweetheart Mary

Beth McFadden, only to divorce her on amiable terms that were best described in the court records as mutual irreconcilable differences. He was only thankful that there were no children involved in the divorce.

Rick assumed that he was the 'bad guy' in their break-up and he was right, too. He married Mary Beth because everyone including his parents thought it was the right thing to do and they had known one another since they were both children and they truly liked one another and got along well. The problem for Rick was that after the first year of marriage, there was no more fire in their love, if there ever was any at all to begin with. He steadily lost interest in Mary Beth, yet he sought no professional counsel. Escape was to be found in a whisky bottle and the bed of one-night stands. He only wished that he had been man enough not to have married Mary Beth in the first place and spare her the embarrassment and pain of a sham marriage. Their divorce was final three years ago this spring and both of them had moved on with their lives.

Rick became interested in the family business as a result of a tour of duty that he performed in the U.S. Army, where he served out his ROTC scholarship obligation as a junior officer in the Army Corps of Engineers with the infamous 82nd Airborne Division stationed at Fort Bragg North Carolina.

Initially, Rick wanted to just jump out of airplanes and play the 'John Wayne infantry role' which most boys of a certain age all dreamed of one day doing. Yet when he was assigned the branch specialty of Engineer, he was dumbfounded since he had chosen Infantry as his first selection. As with many things in the Army, Rick quickly discovered that his desires were quite different from those of the needs of the U.S. Army. As Rick was a civil engineering student and he worked in this area as a civilian, the Army tapped him for the requirement that also fitted his background – being a Combat Engineer. At first Rick balked at this assignment, but then he warmed to it once he discovered that when he was assigned to the 82nd Airborne Division, he could do the John Wayne duties like go Airborne and also get to perform military construction duties that leveraged his civilian and educational background. Rick served his obligatory Reserve Officer Training Corps (ROTC) scholarship commitment of six years, which also paid for his education at the University of Texas, Austin as well.

Along the way, Rick served in Southwest Asia, to include duty in Afghanistan, where he was awarded a Bronze Star for bravery during an ambush attack by insurgents. The Army taught Rick organizational skills, engineering/demolition techniques and leadership skills, this in addition to airborne training. After his Army commitment, Rick decided to join the family business and carve out a name for himself in the very profitable home construction business. Rick was successful in this endeavour and his lifestyle was quite comfortable and getting better each year. The love of a good woman and a family were the main two items missing from his life, but Rick was determined to remedy this deficit whenever Cupid's arrow presented its opportunity to him.

Yet good business timing was not on Rick's side. After Rick's separation from Mary Beth, the Great Recession occurred, and the family construction business was affected severely. He became personally restless and he needed money badly. One day he saw an advertisement for Smokejumpers with the National Forest Service and the Bureau of Land Management, so right then and there he decided to become a 'Smokie.'

Rick was Army airborne qualified and young, naturally he figured, 'what the hell, go for it!' Rick's tall and lean 6-foot-tall frame and muscular build were indicative of his fine physical shape and he easily conquered the physical fitness test for Smokejumper and his airborne background gave him an extra leg up over the other candidates. The break from the construction business and the excitement of working 12 weeks for the National Fire Service and jumping to put out fires was a great way to leave the stress and memories of his civilian life.

For the past four years, Rick had been a Smokejumper for the NFS and BLM organizations. He loved the excitement and chance to get away from his construction business; besides, his business minded brothers welcomed the fact that their extroverted Neanderthal younger brother was away from them for a few months. Rick was the mercurial member of the family and he was a real handful whenever he felt that he was in the right, this had caused many business conflicts with his brothers, but the family had always managed to allay Rick's volatile temper flare-ups. Rick was always the 'bull in the China shop' and inevitably he took the China shop with him wherever he ventured.

Rick had another main reason to look forward to the firefighting season – romance! For the past two years, he had worked with Robin Wolf and she was the object of his romantic attention. He had been one of her instructors when she was just a novice 'smoke chaser', this jargon being an informal and irreverent vernacular for a ground-based fire fighter. A seasoned fire fighter was called a 'Hot Shot' and it was these ground crews that performed the stevedore heavy burden jobs of the wildfire trade.

Rick, being a 'Smoke Jumper', was a more exalted, higher-paid, and trained fire fighter, as he had to have previous experience as 'a Hot Shot' and he had added skills as a parachutist. The 'Smoke Jumpers' were also glamorized because they parachuted into dangerous fires as a small unit, which formed the vanguard to help arrest, divert and defeat dangerous fires before these became too large. The 'Hot Shots' also helped to shape the fire and steer the fire into the direction where the fire strategists wanted it to go.

There was a natural and inevitable rivalry between the Smokejumper and Hot Shot community, yet it seldom resulted in any serious or lasting friction between the two elite groups. Each fire-fighting specialty possessed their own respective strengths and weaknesses, yet neither group could succeed or exist without the other one. It was a friendly rivalry that played itself out each fire-fighting season to see which group could obtain the greatest achievement and glory.

★ ★ ★ ★ ★ ★ ★ ★ ★ ★ ★ ★ ★ ★ ★ ★ ★

CHAPTER 6

Swinging Hash

"This kitchen is your life and so is your daughter or have you forgotten?"

The apprenticeship of working for the Copen family was a real eye opener about how some people made a living and yet still flourished amidst similar family misfortunes. Wayne began to appreciate the fact that most working Americans were breaking their butts to raise their families, just putting food on the table and a roof over their heads was about all of the good life that many a family could expect out of the tarnished American dream. For the first time in his life, Wayne had worked for his keep in a real manual job, it was tough, it was dirty, it was sometimes even degrading, and yes, it was at certain times very satisfying for him too. Seldom the fool, he realized that he was no mere Joe Average and he never would be either. He keenly realized that one day his road adventure was going to end and that he was going to go back to be a New England billionaire. In contrast, the working-class stiffs were stuck with their lot in life until they either retired or died. Life was indeed unfair, unforgiving and tough!

The difference, of course, was that the working men and women did their back-breaking work for 50 weeks out of the year, whereas he would always be free to go back to the silver spoon life that he had always known, and which would someday be his certain future. When that day of stability and predictability came, he would never again have the luxury of totally being his own person or having the opportunity to do whatever he wanted to do. It dawned on him that even the wealthy had life style obligations, which needed to be met. He realized that he had only one opportunity left before marriage, family, and Boston society- painted him into the corner of snobbishness and social class conformity. Yet during his short adventure on the road, he had started to lean the valuable lessons of friendship and common goodness. Having tasted the freedom of the road and the life of the working man, he was ready for each and every opportunity that would help expand his limited and cloistered world. Thus, the journey continued westward across the American landscape.

The bright rays of the early May morning quickly defeated the remnants of the previous nights' tar-pitch blackened sky, as the last traces of evening disappeared, along with the vestiges of a light, grey-coloured mist. The temperature was still cool, but soon the pale orange sunrise was transformed into a buttery-yellow globe. After a pleasant, but totally forgettable night at a Sheridan Hotel, Wayne consumed a breakfast of scrambled eggs, bacon and hot black coffee. With both his gas tank and belly full, he departed the hotel and headed out onto the now familiar Interstate highway 70.

He noticed that most of America seemed to look and feel all the same; at least this was the view that he gleaned from riding his BMW along the concrete ribbon of road that composed the Interstate highway system in America. All the billboards advertised the same fast food and lodging arrangements and it was a rare sight to see a billboard advertisement that was unusual or unique to a certain part of the country. 'Corporate America excelled at producing modern, non-descript amalgamated living and consumerism,' he mused with a smile as he steered his BMW carelessly along the highway.

He continually marvelled at the exquisite detail and realism that he experienced while travelling on his motorcycle. It was an open-air dynamic which no traveller in an encased automobile could ever really appreciate. His experience was akin to those of the cowboys who had trekked across this same country 150 years ago! Not only did he smell the countryside odours in primitive rawness, he actually appreciated a bike rider's closeness to the land. It even seemed as if he actually absorbed more of the countryside, perhaps this was because as a biker, he had to maintain total control of his senses and his riding environment. A person in an automobile could remain distant from the land and become engrossed with the distractions of an FM radio, cell phone, TV, or cruise control. It was at times like this that Wayne simply smiled and let the steady grip on the throttle move him gently down the highway. He had indeed chosen the correct mode of travel!

He became affixed by the vastness of the land and the Spring transformation from the rich green cornfields of Pennsylvania and Ohio to the lush golden fields of the great mid-West and its almost endless stretch of rich farmland. As the miles of highway disappeared rapidly behind the odometer and wheels of his smooth-running BMW Tourer, Wayne eagerly consumed the warming fresh air and incessant bugs of the late spring and soon to be arriving warm summer winds. Maps could not do this scenery any form of justice or accurate descriptions.

After a few hours, he stopped the BMW at a western Ohio Exon gas station. Going through his ritual conduct of 'fluid exchanges', he topped off the gas tank, emptied his bladder, and then consumed a burger and large hot coffee. Riding in the cool spring air seemed to only add to his consumption of high protein calories, yet his body seemed none the worse for wear, since he was not gaining any additional weight. Before mounting his noble mechanized steed, Wayne took out his Rand McNally map of the continental United States from one of the saddle bags. It was a bit old-fashioned to be using the paper map, but it gave him a feeling of nostalgia and the map possessed a romance seemingly lacking on the modern electronic navigation systems.

His eyes smiled with delight, as he imagined the possible opportunities that awaited him. As his eyes continued to examine the map, he reasoned that he had essentially three major options at this junction of his journey. His first option was to take the northern route across the country, a path that would take him along Interstate I-80 across the Dakotas, through to Idaho, and then onto the Northwest and then the west coast. This route was intriguing, as he could travel to Mount Rushmore and the Badlands. He next eyed the middle route, which was illustrated by Interstate I-70 and this route dissected the great American mid-West and western states and the Rocky Mountains. The third option was the southern route and it offered travelling along Interstate 40, 20 or Interstate 10.

The numbering conventions of the US Interstate highway system had the Interstate arteries arrayed in a logical and sequential manner, an amazing feat for any modern Federal bureaucracy. The Interstate highway system was numbered with even numbered highways traversing in an east-west direction, with the higher numbered routes being arrayed at the uppermost part of the country and descending down in numeric order into the southern part of the country. Conversely, the odd numbered Interstate highways were labelled with odd numbers and these traversed the country in a north-south direction.

Suddenly both his eyes and fingers stopped to focus on a single blue strand of Inter-State highway. He had made his decision! He was going to choose to stay on the I-70 route, which meant that he intended to take the way of the middle America heartland route. He reasoned that while this meant that he would have to travel through the beautiful, but monotonous mid-west section of the country, it also meant that later in his journey, he could get to choose to traverse either the scenic Rocky Mountains or travel into the southwest basin to Las Vegas, Flagstaff, and Tucson. These travel destination points were a decision that he could make after he crossed America's great grain breadbasket and it conversely presented him with a versatile option. He also reasoned that he could select either the northern or southern routes upon his return journey back to Boston. "Yes, I'll continue to take the middle route and split the difference this time" he mumbled to himself.

He aimlessly journeyed across the lush blossoming green corn fields of Iowa. This was rich farmland as was that of the entire mid-west of the USA, it had been formed as a result of the last retreating ice sheets some 15,000 years ago. The resulting lush, thick, black topsoil from this ancient glacier retreat, allowed America's farmers to feed the entire world. After several hours, the initial quaint visions of rolling green fields of corn became redundantly routine and eventually boring, especially to a seat-of-the -pants biker. There was little scenic diversity to divert one's gaze from the seemingly endless straight interstate highway and monotonous farmland. Instead, he concentrated his attention away from the country side and onto the next destination state. After several more hours of riding, Wayne had enough saddle time and he decided to call it a day and book into the nearest hotel or motel. The day's travelling placed Wayne in the state of Iowa.

A roadside billboard appeared in Wayne's field of view and it advertised that the Exit #43 was only five miles ahead. He quickly spotted names of available hotels: Holiday Inn, Motel 6, and Radisson Hotel. He knew about the Radisson Hotel reputation and so decided to take a chance there for the evenings' respite. In accordance with his nightly ritual of hotel squatting, Wayne moored his BMW into the Radisson parking lot. Again, not having made any reservations, he remained at the mercy of there being a vacancy status. Wearily he trudged into the Radisson Hotel Lobby. Once again, he approached the receptionists with a tired look that soon broke into a broad friendly smile unto the awaiting eyes of the evening Radisson desk staff. Both breeding and personality instigated Wayne to smile automatically upon his contact with strangers and he had discovered that these social traits usually disarmed any impending hostility, anger, or fear. Good manners incurred no cost and usually returned positive dividends.

"Good evening, Miss, do you have a room available? Please I'll take anything that you have!" Wayne exclaimed wearily.

The clerk whose nametag was imprinted with the name Kim, smiled warmly. "Let me see what I have, sir," she replied politely. The clerk asked another question, as she clicked away at the computer keyboard, "For how many nights, sir?" One night should be sufficient!" was his weary reply.

After a few seconds, Kim looked up from the computer screen and smiled politely at Wayne. "You are in luck, sir! I have rooms on several different floors and with varying options, to include smoking/non-smoking and various size of beds and finally the executive suite?" she sounded off quickly and in an almost rehearsed manner.

Wayne, ever thinking himself deserving the very best from birth didn't blink twice, when he sounded his response. "Miss Kim, I'll take the Executive suite," as he confidently exhumed his alligator leather wallet from his jacket breast pocket. He smartly withdrew his credit card and handed it to the smiling hotel clerk. In ritual procedure, he signed the hotel registration card, giving his personal data and contact information. The entire hotel registration took less than ten minutes.

"Do you have any luggage, sir?" Kim politely inquired.

Wayne did not need anyone to carry his two small BMW overnight bags and he had become used to taking care of his own luggage, a strange twist from his former days where porters and Bell Captains were at his beck and call at every five-star hotel in which he had stayed. "No, but thank you, Ma'am, I'll do it myself," Wayne confidently replied.

"Have a pleasant night, sir and thank you for staying with the Radisson Hotel, Mr Hamilton" Kim replied in a cheerful voice. Wayne politely acknowledged her comment with a reflective nod, as he slipped his room card key and credit card back into his leather jacket pocket.

He slogged back outside to the BMW motorcycle to retrieve his hard case luggage. Every muscle and bone ached from the long hours' sedentary seating and from being bent over the handlebars of his bike, this despite the fact that the BMW motorcycle was one of the best touring bikes around, yet the eight hours of saddle time weighed heavy on his middle-aged body. It would have been even worse he thought had the weather been 15 degrees colder. Walking back into the lobby, he noticed a small gift shop that was getting ready to close for the evening. As was his normal custom, he wanted to obtain a post card and mail it off to Katherine in the morning.

"Please, Miss, can you wait just one-minute?" he pleaded as a woman in her early sixties was beginning to close out her cash register for the evening.

The woman glanced up ever so quickly before turning her attention once again to her task at hand. "Oh, I'm so sorry, sir, I am closing the shop for the evening, you'll have to come back again tomorrow morning at 9:00 AM, sir!" the older lady exclaimed in a raspy cigarette throated voice.

For Wayne, this answer was unacceptable, so he persisted in his pursuit. "Look, Miss, I know it's late and you're in a hurry to get home after a long day here, but I won't be here tomorrow morning at 9:00 AM! I'll be back on the road!" Wayne exclaimed emphatically, but to seemingly no avail.

The older woman slowly raised her eyes above her silver framed granny glasses, her cold, grey eyes betraying only her cold emotions as she looked un-sympathetically at Wayne for a few seconds, before dropping her eyes again to the cash register drawer.

Wayne tried one last emotional appeal. "All I want is a post card of this town to mail to my fiancée!" Wayne pleaded emotionally.

This time the woman smiled ever so slightly. The older woman seemed almost oblivious to Wayne's presence, as she finished counting the money and shut off the lights of the small shop. Before closing the skeleton gate, she grasped a postcard from the postcard carrousel and handed it to an astonished Wayne.

"Here's my wedding gift to you! I hope you have a great marriage and it's so sweet that you think of your fiancée while you are travelling," the older woman stated as she smiled and handed the postcard to Wayne. Wayne tried to give the woman some money, but she would have none of it.

"Thank you so very much, Ma'am," Wayne remarked as the woman walked away and waved to Wayne as she walked out to her car. Wayne smiled to himself, as he thought how great it was to see normal people be so nice to him without even knowing that he was a Boston billionaire.

His smug and pretentious perceptions concerning human nature and the American middle-class were steadily being challenged and eroded throughout this road trip. Most people were actually better than he had stereo-typed them to be. There were some jerks around for sure, but people were mostly kind and understanding, they were merely concerned with existence living and going about life without looking for or creating any unwanted chaos or trouble.

As he carelessly strolled into the Radisson Lobby elevator, all Wayne could think about was a prolonged hot shower, a relaxing meal, and a good drink of malt scotch whiskey. Initially, his mind dwelt on the more plebian aspects of his circumstance. His mind quickly drifted to thoughts of Kate. He was determined to call her later this evening, despite his fatigue. Wayne reached his suite on the sixth floor. Upon entering the hotel room, he was amazed at how well laid out and spacious this room was for a non-five-star hotel. The entire room was attired in salmon coloured wallpaper and topped off with rich mahogany furniture. To his pleasant surprise, there was a wet bar, sitting room, extra-large bathroom, and an ornate king-sized bed. There was even a simulated crystal chandelier.

Getting tired of sitting alone in the dining room every night, Wayne decided to forgo that venture and instead opted for room service. He looked at the menu, eyed a fine 12-ounce steak filet, potatoes au gratin, and white asparagus in hollandaise sauce – all topped off by a pot of hot black coffee. 'Boy that sounds like a feast for a king' he relished as he smiled and smartly called in his order to the hotel kitchen desk. The long exposure to the chilly open-air had served to increase the body's appetite.

The arrival of early stages of middle-age had not yet extorted its vengeance upon his body; he still had the lean and lanky body of his youth. The kitchen staff asked for a delivery time and Wayne informed them that he desired his meal to be delivered in 90 minutes, thereby affording him a chance to take a shower, relax, and give Kate a call. He opened up his BMW cruiser hard-case luggage, which amply contained his underwear and associated sundry items. He took a quick stock of his clothing, murmured an unintelligible sentence to himself then called up the front desk.

"Hello this is the Front Desk, my name is Alex, how may I assist you, Mr Hamilton?" a pleasant voice was heard to say over the phone.

Wayne was reassured by the professional tone and manner of the clerk. "Yes, I seem to have an unusual request," Wayne stated almost embarrassingly to the clerk.

"Not at all, sir, difficult requests are our specialty here at the Radisson," Alex replied with a cheerful tone.

"Okay, Alex, here's the deal, I've been riding light on the road and I seem to be running out of clean undergarments and there have not been any launder facilities on the road and I was wondering if..."

Wayne was quickly interrupted and interjected in mid-sentence by the young and anticipative hotel clerk. "Yes, sir, you were wondering if the Radisson could send your laundry out for cleaning and to have it ready for you by tomorrow morning!" Alex replied quite confidently.

"Why yes, exactly! How did you know?" Wayne replied in wonder.

"Mr Hamilton, after working this job for three years, I have learned to anticipate a guest's needs," Alex replied immediately. "We can absolutely meet your request, however, it's a bit expensive, Mr Hamilton, about fifty dollars for a small bag of clothes."

Wayne was not to quibble about the cost, he was just glad that he could get all his underwear cleaned by tomorrow.

"That's fine, Alex, should I bring the clothes down to the lobby?" Wayne inquired?

Alex was non-discreet in his reply: "Not necessary, sir, just go into your closet, grab the laundry clothes bag, place your items in it, fill out the item checklist, then place it on the outside of your hotel doorknob and we'll pick it up within the hour."

Wayne was very relieved as he thanked Alex and quickly packed all his dirty underwear into the hotel laundry bag and then placed the bag onto the outside of the hotel door handle knob.

He looked into the mirror and noticed a face that was red with windburn and dirt. Quickly washing his face, he took a quick shave and brushed his teeth; the road grime seemed to have impregnated his entire body. Next the shower faucets were turned on for maximum flow, the hot water quickly formed a mountain of steam which encapsulated the entire shower room. For what seemed like a serene eternity, Wayne once again indulged for over 30 long minutes in the hot and soothing water spray. Like a baptism that washed away the sins of a lifetime, all the crud of the day's riding had vanished down the drain.

Conveniently hanging on the back of the bathroom door was a hotel furnished terry cloth light grey robe. He quickly grabbed it and strolled into the suite's sitting room area. Strolling over to the suite's amply stocked dry bar, he and poured a half-full glass of Glenfiddich malt scotch. From the small refrigerator, he withdrew a handful of ice cubes and carelessly dropped these into the awaiting crystal cocktail glass. He sipped the peat-flavoured brew and he was warmed by the flow of the alcohol down his throat and then into his upper stomach. He gleefully thought of his home estate, in the lush green suburbs of Boston, of his past, and of his lovely fiancée, Katherine. He plopped himself into a comfortable high back reading chair, took another sip of his scotch, and turned on his phone. He pressed the speed dial button and eagerly awaited the voice of his fiancée.

Katherine was sitting in her cavernous and ornately Louis XV style decorated bedroom; she was just finishing up some light reading from the initial chapters of an early 20th Century Edwardian Romantic mystery novel. Yet her thoughts were on Brad. She was most concerned about his safety – after all, driving around in an automobile was dangerous enough with the number of bad drivers on the road, yet doing so on a motorcycle was even more treacherous. She figured that if she kept her mind busy, she would worry about him less. This was a false premise. Katherine had received almost daily phone calls from her Brad and this provided her some comfort, yet she was still ill at ease with this juvenile motorcycle journey of his. Katherine still lived in the estate home of her parents despite the fact that she was a financially emancipated woman in her early thirties, yet she had come to see her parents and her childhood home as a safe haven from the uncertainties of life. Being an only child, Katherine found comfort, stability, and safety in the abode of her loving and dotting parents.

With a sudden and almost unwelcome outburst, Katherine's bedroom phone erupted in a flurry of melodic classical music tones. In momentary astonishment, Katherine broke away from her novel and hurried over to her phone. Without bothering to look at the incoming phone call number being displayed on her phone, Katherine moved smartly to answer the incoming call. "Hello, this is Katherine," she inflexed in a plain, nondescript manner.

"Why are we being so formal and straight-laced this evening, did your mummy send you to bed with no dinner again for being such a bad girl?" Wayne teased in a cheery and almost playful voice. Katherine immediately recognized the voice of her lover and fiancée, at which she immediately became enamoured and enchanted.

"My dearest Brad, how are you doing? Where are you now? Is there anything I can do for you, darling?" Katherine fired off in rapid machinegun-like succession.

"Now hold on one minute, Kate! I can only answer one question at a time!" Wayne exclaimed in a jovial voice. "First, I apologize that I have not called you over the past few nights, but it was late when I finally got settled in my room and I thought it best not to disturb you. Am I forgiven?" Wayne playfully inquired. Katherine wasn't a bit concerned about Brad's excuses, all that mattered to her now was that she was talking to the man she loved.

"Brad, you don't have to ask for forgiveness, just come back to me soon....so where are you now, Brad darling?" Katherine softly pleaded, as tears started to fill her eyes.

"Northing exciting is happening, Kate, I'm currently in the mid-West, I passed through western Ohio and I am now in the far western part of Iowa tonight. By tomorrow I will be God knows where, as I have no definite destination or timeline. I'm just relaxing, enjoying the great scenery, and trying to make peace with my life as it exists now, Kate," Wayne slowly exclaimed.

Such summary information were not the words that Katherine wanted to hear. Ever the pragmatist, she came straight to the point. "Brad darling, when are you coming home? Maybe I can help you get better! Maybe if we have some time together, we can work things out and then get married!" Katherine pleaded tearfully.

Wayne knew that Katherine was missing him and that she wanted him back desperately, yet he knew that there was still something unsettled in his grieving soul, and he needed to find it out there on the road, not in the splendour and confines of Boston.

"Kate, I love you dearly, but I'm still not right with myself. I feel such an emptiness in my gut that you can't believe it!" Wayne slowly sobbed into his cell phone receiver. "I just can't come back to Boston and you, not now, not the way I am, Kate; you deserve a full-time man and husband and not some mental crack-up case like me, Kate," he continued.

With these haunting yet truthful words, both Katherine and Wayne were now sobbing into their phones. Katherine knew that her Brad needed psychological help to assist him in dealing with the sudden death of his family, but she was sceptical of his self-diagnosis and the method of therapy that he was prescribing for himself. She pondered 'What if,' he didn't get any better and all this road therapy was for naught?'

"Look, Brad, honey, I think it best that you come back here to Boston and we'll get you some professional help; we can beat this thing together, dearest!" Katherine cried heartily. Brad was not entertaining any diversion or persuasion to his self-discovery adventure.

"Kate... Kate, listen! Just stop crying for one moment and listen to me please! When I come back, we're going to have ourselves a beautiful New England wedding that will be the talk of all of Boston! We'll honeymoon in the Southern France, Tahiti or even Bora Bora! Wouldn't that be worth the wait, Kate?" Wayne pleaded ruefully.

Katherine was calmed down by Wayne's assurances. She wanted to believe him and more importantly she needed to believe his words, for these served as the foundation of the myth that was to be her future. A storybook idyllic childhood, the finest schools, the correct type of friends, the executive position, a perfect husband, and children – these were the veneer that became the identity, super-ego and persona of Katherine MacAlister. Her life was that of materialism and the elite of the Boston social milieu.

"Do you really mean it, Brad... I mean about coming back to Boston and getting married?" Katherine questioned in an almost innocent tone of disbelief. Wayne knew that the words just spoken to Kate were the truth, he believed it and more importantly, Kate believed it too.

The pregnant pause between the two lovers was suddenly interjected by a sudden loud knock on the door. Wayne had correctly surmised the untimely originator.

"Yes, I do, Kate, but please excuse me, this must be my dinner knocking at my door, it's room service for me tonight...look, darling, I have to go now, Kate, I'll give you a call in a night or two, I promise! Now don't worry about me or our future, it's all going to work out... I promise it will!" Wayne earnestly promised.

Katherine was consoled by Wayne's sincerity and reassurances, yet unspoken doubts still remained. Katherine had to accept reality – that her Brad was in Iowa and she was in Boston and only time was going to bring Brad back to her.

"You're right, Brad, get your head together and get your ass back to me as soon as possible... please call me often and especially if you need anything, okay darling?" Katherine asked almost rhetorically.

Wayne knew that it was best to leave this conversation at its positive high point.

"You bet, I'll be talking to you soon, I love you more than anything else in this world," Wayne proclaimed earnestly.

"I love you too, Brad," Katherine exclaimed emotionally.

Once again, there was again an urgent, loud knocking at the door. "Look, Kate, I have to go, my dinner is calling! I love you! Goodbye!" Wayne exclaimed in a hurried voice as he rushed to the door.

"I love you, too darling," Kate exclaimed as she set down the receiver of her phone.

* * * * * * * * * * * * * * * * * *

The annoying ringing of the early morning wake-up call was about as charming and inviting as a visit by a hospital proctologist. It was most lazily unwelcoming to exit from the warm blanket and wearily venture into the bathroom, yet he needed to get a start on his day. The now perfected regimen of performing the daily three Ss (Shower, Shave and Shit) were quickly and dutifully performed before making an eager retreat of a fine, hot mist of water shower spray.

Unexpectedly, a loud pronounced knock on the door interrupted the morning hygiene rituals. After a brief several seconds, the distinctive obtrusive knocks on the door were repeated in similar tone and sequence. "Oh hello, Mr Hamilton, good morning," voiced an unknown party at the door. Rushing to put on the hotel furnished white terry cloth robe and dark blue slippers, he moved smartly toward the door. Delightfully presented before him, there stood a serving cart arrayed with shining silver-coloured covered dishes that contained the servings of his morning meal.

The inviting smell of an awaiting hearty breakfast engulfed the air. A smiling male bell hop in a maroon-coloured blazer extended a morning salutation, "Good morning, Mr Hamilton, here is your breakfast and I also have your clean laundry ready for you too!" announced the room attendant in a cheerful tone.

"Sure, that's fine, please come on in and just move the serving cart over to the table," Wayne exclaimed as he pointed toward the oak vanity located near the window of his room.

"I'll just hang this laundry in your closet, sir. Is that okay with you?" inquired the attendant.

Wayne merely waved the waiter onward and he reached into his leather jacket to withdraw his wallet and then a hundred-dollar bill to the attendant. "This is for the breakfast service and the laundry delivery, have a great day," Wayne exclaimed earnestly with a smile.

"Wow, thanks, Mr Hamilton! This is a very generous tip, sir! My name is Mike and if you need anything else, please do not hesitate to contact me at the front desk" – the young man exclaimed in an excited voice as he left the room and closed the door discreetly behind him.

Comfortably seating himself upon a small chair that faced the highway, he wondered briefly what journeys and destinations that the other travellers were having this fine mid-western bright day. He carefully tasted the eggs benedict and he was surprised that the preparation was on par with the exclusive restaurants in which he had dined in Boston and the eastern United States. He poured himself a full cup of coffee and added a spoon of honey and a small splash of cream. He sipped the golden coloured brew and gave a warm sigh of satisfaction. "There was nothing to rival a hearty breakfast and a good strong brew of coffee to start off the morning," he concluded. If he were back in Boston, he would be starting off his day with a two-mile run and eating only cereal and coffee, but this road regimen required far more hearty calories than sitting on one's ass as an investment banker. Riding the roads in the open cool spring air required serious eating and this is exactly what he intended to do.

Finishing the meal, he promptly dressed and packed his clean gear back into the BMW portable motorcycle bags. He made sure to leave a $75 tip for the maid; he realized that he could well afford this generosity and that service workers drew much of their compensation through the de facto practice of tipping. "Hello, how was your stay with us at the Radisson?" a young and attractive female desk clerk inquired as he approached the hotel registration desk.

"It was great, just great. I really appreciated the fine clothing cleaning service that was afforded to me; it was a life saver, as I was running out of clean underwear. It was either get the dirty clothes clean or go out and continue to wear the old ones!" Wayne exclaimed with a crackling humorous tone. The female attendant was about 23 years old with big blue eyes and sandy brown hair. Her name- tag read 'Emily' and she quickly presented Wayne with the lodging bill.

"Mr Hamilton, will that be cash or charge?" Emily inquired politely with a smile.

"I'll pay by credit card, thank you," Wayne replied as he reached into his wallet and produced a Platinum American Express Corporate Credit

Card. Emily quickly ran off a bill and presented it to Wayne to endorse.

"Thank you, sir, here's a copy of your receipt. May I make any additional reservations at any other Radisson hotel for you, Mr Hamilton?" she gleefully inquired.

Wayne paused a second before responding and then asking the question "are there any interesting sites or landmarks between here and the state border along Interstate I-70?"

Emily thought for a split second and then definitely stated to Wayne, "Sir, I am afraid that there are no natural or historic sites along I-70 in the State of Iowa and probably not much more until you hit the Rocky Mountains," Emily responded in an almost apologetic tone.

"That's fine and thank you, Emily," Wayne replied as he tucked the hotel receipt into his pocket.

Stopping in the hotel lobby, he was delighted to hear that the weather was projected to be mostly dry and with a slight 8-10 mile per hour wind. The summer of the mid-western United States presented the real daily possibility of a slight isolated shower throughout the remainder of the week. Riding a motorcycle through wet weather was ever more challenging and dangerous, in addition to making life physically more uncomfortable for a rider with rain and mist in one's face and water getting into every possible clothing opening.

Rumbling serendipitously across the broad green corn fields of the Interstate-70 highway was becoming drudgery to Wayne. He effortlessly breezed through Kansas City and continued westward. He possessed 'no particular destination, nor was time a critical factor either,' he concluded. His mind was made up, he was going to take the next Interstate exit and travel along the secondary roads.

Quickly he spotted a sign indicating an Interstate highway #40 and with an unhesitating right push on his motorcycle handlebar, he deftly angled the BMW into the right lane, dropped down into third gear and preceeded off the Interstate and onto the secondary Highway #40. He came to a T-intersection. As with most highway intersection signs, there was an option to take either direction A or B; the A would lead to the north to Topeka, while B would lead him south into Lawrence Kansas. He had a scant few seconds to decide and it really made no difference to him to take one direction over another. As the light changed, he made his decision, he would follow the direction of the 18-wheeler semi-truck vehicle located immediately to his front. The huge mechanical behemoth bellowed crept slowly forward, while churning a light-grey puff of diesel. Slowly the truck veered to the right lane and headed toward Lawrence Kansas, home to the infamous U.S. Civil War raid incident in which several hundred 'Free Staters' were killed by raiders loyal to the South. Oblivious to the history of the region, Wayne gently poured on the right throttle and rapidly passed the 18-wheeler truck.

Spotting a small Gulf Oil petroleum station in the distance, he figured this was as a good a place as any to make a pit-stop. He pulled into the small four-pump filling station, dismounted the BMW, then quickly removing his helmet and heavy leather gloves and jacket. Without hesitation, he opened up his travel sack and vigorously stuffed his heavy leather jacket into the sack. He would not need this until at least this evening, if even at that. As always, it felt very liberating to dismount the motorcycle and stretch his legs; this was one reason for his frequent number of hygiene 'rest stops' throughout the travel day. He spied the modest kiosk, where he used the latrine and handed over to the gas attendant $25 for his gasoline.

Slowly and carefully, he started to fill the tank and he eyed the small town and countryside. Lawrence was a beautiful and modest-sized town, which gave every appearance of being 'Anywhere USA' and it was probably a good place to live and raise a family. Suddenly the gasoline nozzle made an audible click sound, which clearly indicated that Wayne had reached his tank filling capacity and he had three dollars left coming to him in change from his $20 bill payment. Wayne marched back into the kiosk and indicated to the clerk to collect his change.

"Hey, this is a nice town that you have here, is there a good little place to get a decent burger around here?" Wayne casually inquired of the attendant.

"Sure, pal, just go down the highway about five miles and on your left, you'll see a small place called the Calico Diner. It has some pretty good food for a family type diner, it's clean and very reasonably priced too!" the attendant cheerfully replied dryly.

"That sounds good to me. Thank you, sir," Wayne announced as he shoved the three dollars quickly into his left pants pocket. It was still early noon and the weather was perfect and sunny. He was hungry and in need of an hour of eating and relaxation before heading back onto the road again. If nothing else, this vagabond trip had taught him the importance and luxury of eating and relaxing.

Pushing on the ignition switch, he rolled the BMW slowly down the road toward the Calico Diner. He was very comfortable and much cooler now that he had stowed-away his heavy leather jacket. The warm summer breeze rolled up and down his ruffling light blue denim shirt and it quickly evaporated all vestiges of sweat that had previously drenched his back, underarms, and chest. It felt God-awful-good to be mounted on that thundering BMW in the warm Kansas summer wind. After just about eight minutes travel, he spotted a small, aluminium and red coloured encased emporium sign which was adorned with a bright bold red lettering that read, "Calico Cafe and Diner: Home of the Best Country Fixings in Kansas".

He precisely maneouvered the massive BMW into the parking space and quickly eyed-up the eatery. The shining silver and red coloured building was positioned 20 yards back from from the main roadway and toward the upper outskirts of the city of Lawrence.

The parking lot was filled with about 35 cars and this he assumed was some sort of a local positive testament to the popularity of this establishment. "This place had to have something going for it!" he accurately concluded, yet he only hoped that it was not that of offering cheap, greasy food!

Wayne slowly eased down the kickstand and angled the BMW onto its left side stand. Once again, he disrobed himself of his safety vest tether, leather riding gauntlet gloves, eyewear, and helmet. He gathered up his riding belongings and strode slowly into the restaurant. Immediately upon entering the foyer of the Calico Inn, he was rushed by a sudden and welcome blast of cold, arctic-like air, a worthy testament to the generous over-cooling air conditioner that protected this establishment and its occupants from the relentless hot sun.

Upon opening the sturdy glass and chrome cafe door, he was suddenly transfixed backward in time to the 1950s era. The decor of the Calico Cafe bespoke of all things from the 1950's America to include the classic chrome bar counter decor, an old-fashioned stainless-steel milk shake mixer, and brilliant red coloured Classic Coca Cola soda dispensing machines – all of which adorned the front serving counter area, that could sit about 15 patrons, but which was now vacant. The colour design was a vivid red and white motif and the tables and booths both had alternating red and while vinyl colour patterns. The floor was even tiled in bright red and white ceramic tiles, as were the table cloths and draperies that adorned the retro-decorated establishment. All along the walls were classic 50s pictures of legendary and infamous Americans to include President Eisenhower, Senator Joseph McCarthy, Albert

Einstein, Montgomery Clift, Elizabeth Taylor, Frank Sinatra, James Dean, Elvis Presley, Walt Disney, Paul Newman, Richard Widmark and of course, Marilyn Monroe. The pas de resistance was a vintage looking chrome and glass jukebox that was playing tunes from the 1950s era.

One could clearly discern the classic song of the Platters singing 'Only You' playing in the background, mixed with the chattered sounds of family conversations and the thrashing of silverware from the counter and kitchen area. The tables and booths were about 30% filled with families, couples, and groups, all gathering to eat and relax on a typical hot, careless Saturday afternoon.

"Sir, may I help you?" a pleasant voice suddenly interjected.

Wayne turned about to ascertain the source of this feminine voice. There standing before him was a petite, pretty woman in her mid-forties wearing a broad red and white candy stripe style 1950s style blouse, skirt, and a small white cardboard peaked hat. She possessed a generous mange of shoulder-length fire engine red hair, generous light freckles, and sparkling bright blue eyes. This woman radiated a naturally pleasant composure and a broad smile which engulfed her entire face. "Hello sir, my name is Mary Ellen and welcome to the Calico Cafe and Diner! Now what sort of seating do you desire?" the waitress announced in a most welcoming tone.

Dumbfounded by this sudden interruption, Wayne verbally paused, as he looked around at the seating; he really didn't want to occupy a complete table or booth. Besides, after several weeks of dining alone at a table for one, he didn't need to be reminded of his solitary eating status. Looking over his shoulder, he noticed that the bar serving counter area was almost completely empty of customers.

"Excuse me, Mary Ellen, how about one of those stools over there by the bar counter?" Wayne inquired casually.

Mary Ellen looked over at the near-empty area, smiled smartly, and directed Wayne over to the bar counter seating area. "Seating is at your discretion, sir, so sit anywhere you like, the waitress that services the bar counter and booth areas will be taking your order shortly," Mary Ellen interjected, as she waved Wayne over to the diners' counter area. He seated himself smartly in front of the kitchen doors, which was located immediately behind the serving counter. The view afforded Wayne an occasional view of the kitchen, to include its activities and those of its occupants – every single time that the swinging kitchen doors opened and closed. Since this dining area was virtually devoid of patrons, he placed his helmet and other riding accessories immediately onto the adjacent stool.

The restaurant was clean and the food appeared to be the type of meals consumed by the normal American family, nothing fancy, just plain old-fashioned meals served in a nostalgic atmosphere. As nature was always calling a weary motorcyclist, he decided to go to the lavatory. Thankfully, the bathroom was quite clean in both appearance and overall attire. During his short time as being a road warrior, he had come to know that a sure sign of a well-run restaurant establishment was the cleanliness of its bathrooms; if these were clean, the odds were that the kitchen and other areas were clean and efficient too. In Investment Banking this was known as summing up the small balance sheet details.

Upon his return, no counter waitress was evident. After a few more awkward minutes of waiting without having had the slightest degree of customer acknowledgement, he started to become a bit anxious and disturbed, playing nervously with the set form napkin and eating utensils that lay before him. Mary Ellen glanced back toward Wayne, as she was making one of her normal table rounds. "Hey, handsome, hasn't anyone waited on you yet, darling?" Mary Ellen inquired in a folksy and playful waitress manner, as she gently slapped her open palm on Wayne's cotton twill blue shirt.

Never one to take a well-meaning gesture the wrong way, Wayne merely smiled as he took Mary Ellen's blue-collar salutations in good stead. "Why no, Mary Ellen, I'm afraid that no one has waited on me since you seated me and I'm getting a bit hungry!" Wayne remarked almost defensively.

Ever so playfully, Mary Ellen patted Wayne gently on the shoulder and served him a glass of water and handed him a menu to look over. "Here, sweetie, you just look the menu over, we're a little short-handed today, one of the waitresses is having some personal problems and she is running late, you know how hectic modern living is, don't you, dear? Well anyway, if she doesn't show up, I'll be back in five minutes and take your order, honey! In the meantime, a new pot of coffee is brewing and this one's on the house, it will also be ready in about five minutes, my dear!" Mary Ellen yelled flamboyantly, as she walked away to greet another set of customers who had just entered the Cafe foyer.

"Come this way, folks, and welcome to the Calico Cafe and Diner," Mary Ellen trumpeted warmly as she greeted and seated a family of five at the other side of the cafe. Wayne smiled to himself and thought that Mary Ellen epitomized his stereotype of the American waitress – an extroverted person who was always cheerful and full of zeal despite the unpleasantness and tediousness of the job. With a sudden spirit, the front door of the Calico Cafe opened and from it whirled an attractive woman in her early thirties. She was rushing frantically to get behind the counter and then into the bowels of the kitchen area.

Thunderously barking out from behind the kitchen doors, there burst forth a litany of vulgar yelling and screaming. "I don't give a good fucking damn what is going on with your snotty-nosed, brat kid... I'm running a flipping restaurant here and not some charity ward sister!" echoed the growling masculine roar. Still more words volleyed forth: "Hey Joyce, this is the third fucking time this week that this crap has been going on, now when in the hell is this shit going to stop?"

Feeling somewhat embarrassed, Wayne could not help but to hear the ruckus between an angry man and a defensive, apologetic woman. The shouting and threats were all one-sided, originating from the still anonymous bellicose angry man. The proper conclusion was that this was the missing waitress of whom Mary Ellen had alluded, the waitress who had been responsible for the delay of his order, yet he decided to take the matter in simple stride. This poor waitress was having far more difficulties in her deadpan life than he was having with a mere intolerant growling stomach.

Suddenly there emerged from the kitchen's red coloured flapping doors, a dishevelled waitress, hurrying to tie the back of her red and white Calico serving blouse and matching apron attire. From all appearances she was a handsome woman in her early to mid-thirties with light shoulder length chestnut brown hair. The woman's pale grey eyes were almost lifeless, the redness of a lost evenings' sleep and the despair of the moment, foretold the story of a life of hard times. The agitated waitress looked tired, disgusted, and angry. Her physical condition and slow, disjointed body movements, indicated she was not suffering from one night without sleep, but rather several sleepless nights in succession. While still struggling to blouse-up her waitress attire, she instinctively grabbed a freshly brewed urn of coffee, along with a white ceramic cup and saucer, while then proceeding to deftly pour Wayne a cup of piping hot black coffee.

For a few lonely moments she didn't even glance up to meet her customer's face. All of her serving movements had been so routine and memorized so as to become automated. As the coffee cup was being filled, she suddenly realized her waitress manners and her good-hearted nature kicked-in. "Oh sir, I do hope that you wanted coffee otherwise I can bring you something else, but most people do desire coffee in the morning!" the waitress explained in an almost apologetic tone that was caressed with a genuine soft smile. Wayne was glad to see the woman recover somewhat from her personal problems, but he was even happier to see her warm mid-west smile. Her eyes seemed to transform themselves into sparkling silver disks when she smiled. Wayne politely smiled back to her, as he pondered with pity this poor woman's plight of having a very difficult job that was coupled with an overbearing, verbally abusive boss.

The waitress struggled with her self- dignity, this being made all the more difficult by her tearful red eyes, which she tried to camouflage from the patrons for as long as it was practical. Keeping her back to the counter, the waitress continued to tie up her apron and placed her iconic red and white petite waitress hat on her head, while affixing bobby-pins in between her hair and the cardboard hat. Wayne smiled just a bit at the waitresses' circumstances, before he suddenly realized that the working reality of this woman was no laughing matter. Her plight and millions of others like her across America, was nothing to laugh at, especially considering the bawling out that she had just received in the kitchen from her supervisor. No one at work or in life had ever laughed at him or had given Bradford W. Hamilton his comeuppances. Privilege acted as a dual-purpose fence which served to artificially keep bad things out, while imprisoning one in an ivy tower of ignorance and conformity.

In a sudden gush of self-realization, Wayne felt ashamed about himself and his own privileged status, if even just for a few self-reflective moments. When he spoke back to the waitress, it was with a soft and humbled tone. "No ma'am, fresh brewed coffee served by a fine waitress is the best that there is for me," Wayne replied politely, as he tried to place the waitress at ease. Her pale grey eyes glazed back to Wayne as if to say 'thank you' for the small politeness.

The waitress couldn't help but notice the physical attractiveness of her customer: he was tall, lean, well groomed, and well spoken. Their eyes betrayed an immediate mutual attraction. In an almost defensive tone for a waitress, Joyce introduced herself to her morning patron. "Hello, my name is Joyce and I will be your waitress today, sir, here is a menu and I'll be back in a few minutes to take your order. The lunch specials for today are the double-baked meatloaf with two sides and a salad or the turkey roast with two sides and soup," the waitress exclaimed as she softly smiled at Wayne, she turned around to see Mary Ellen coming her way with a concerned frown upon her face.

"Hey, girlfriend, that bastard Johnnie is in an awfully sour mood with you being late again the third day this week! I tried to cover for you again, but it was of no use this time, girlfriend," Mary Ellen explained in a hush tone that Wayne could barely hear.

"You're too late, Mary Ellen, Johnnie bawled me out real good this time and he told me that if I'm out one more time, I'm going to get fired! Thanks for trying to cover for me, Mary Ellen, my little Heather was sick again, she's been up for two nights now with a fever and she has been unable to attend school. I have her grandmother minding her now, but I can't get a decent night's rest!" Joyce replied with tears in her eyes. "Besides, I have minimal medical coverage and I cannot afford to be out of work anymore than I have been especially with that SOB Johnnie threatening me again," Joyce sobbed in desperation to Mary Ellen.

"Yeah well, that Johnnie is one cold hearted bastard; has he been trying to get you to sleep with him again or threaten you in any way?" Mary Ellen demanded.

Joyce only looked up with teary eyes at Mary Ellen before speaking. "No, at least not this time, but I know if I did give in to Johnnie that I would have one less thing to worry about around here!"

Mary Ellen was a motherly figure to Joyce and while she loved her job at the Calico Cafe, it was not a financial necessity for her; instead, she used her waitressing money to supplement her husband's salary. However, Joyce was a single mother, who had divorced her husband three years earlier due to his infidelity and hard drinking. For Joyce, the waitress job was a necessity, not an option.

"No, honey, don't you do anything like that! You keep any ideas about sleeping with Johnnie out of your mind, he's just a user and he's no flipping good! He will use you like an ass rag and then throw you away and then where will you be? You'll be without your self-dignity, that's where you'll be!" Mary Ellen sternly lectured to Joyce.

"I guess you are right, Mary Ellen, I just don't see any light at the end of this dark tunnel. I'm getting tired of fighting this daily grind and for minimal pay to boot!" Joyce sobbed tearfully.

Mary Ellen patted her gently on the shoulder then straightened out Joyce's hair and dried her eyes of their tears.

"Come now, honey, you get back over there and put on a sunshine face and take that good-looking young man's food order over there! We'll talk later after work, now go on, honey!" Mary Ellen commanded with a smile and a quick wink. Reinforced by the motherly advice, Joyce returned back to the counter.

"Okay, what will you have today, sir? Have you made up your mind yet?" Joyce professionally inquired.

Wayne looked up and decided to engage the waitress in a bit of small talk. "No, Miss I have not decided.... I was hoping that perhaps you could provide me some suggestions," Wayne stated with a friendly smile.

Joyce couldn't help but smile back at this handsome heartbreaking guy. "You know, sir, all items on the breakfast menu are outstanding, except for the creamed chip beef. For lunch, I would advise the Blue Plate Special, which consists of double-baked meat loaf, mashed potatoes, and a vegetable. If you so prefer, the burgers are great and so is the chilli. Would you like a few more minutes, sir?" Joyce politely inquired.

He thought for a few seconds and smiled as he placed his order with Joyce. "No, Miss, I know exactly what I want!" Wayne coyly toyed, as his eyes flirted with those of Joyce's. "I'll have the Blue Plate Special with southern greens, gravy over the meatloaf and mashed potatoes," he replied as he smiled and handed her back the menu.

Joyce could not help but hide her physical attraction to Wayne, as she smiled and blushed a bit before placing Wayne's order onto the kitchen metal turnstile and pushing the kitchen order bell. A silver-haired short-order cook slowly and routinely picked the paper chit from the turnstile and started to prepare the order. Mary Ellen also happened to be placing her customer's meal order onto the kitchen turnstile and she couldn't help but notice the changed disposition in Joyce, who was now all smiles and charm for her new handsome customer.

"Hey now, you just watch it, there girlfriend, he's just a passing fancy, an illusion, so put it away, girl, and get back to reality! This kitchen is your life and so is your needy daughter or have you forgotten?" Mary Ellen scorned in a heated, almost motherly tone.

"I don't know what you're talking about?" Joyce replied defensively.

Mary Ellen knew an outright lie when she heard one. "Now you look here, Joyce, I know he's great eye candy, but he's not for you! You're a single mom, working for almost minimum wage! You survive off of customers' tips! You can't be wasting your time on guys who won't be around in the morning...sure we all dream of the guy who's going to ride in here one day and take us away from all of this crap, but that's a Cinderella dream, honey, now let it go, darling!" Mary Ellen pleaded. Joyce's pleasant demeanour was suddenly shattered by the cold truth of Mary Ellen's words.

Joyce hesitated a few seconds before speaking. "All I have left in my life is my little girl and my dreams. I know that no decent guy in his right mind is going to stroll in here and place his future happiness with a single mom working in a backwater diner. I guess I just wanted to escape a little, Mary Ellen, you know – do a little daydreaming!" Joyce sobbed as she sadly confessed the limited realities of her life to her co-worker.

Mary Ellen affectionally patted Joyce's shoulder and a gave her a quick, understanding wink.

"Now, now.... everything is going to be fine, Heather is doing better, and Johnnie has settled down, so let's get back to work and we'll talk more later, okay?" Mary Ellen suggested as both women smiled and resumed their mundane waitressing duties.

The chattering conversations of the diner's boisterous patrons were suddenly interrupted by the caustic harsh tone of the kitchen order bell chime, its metallic high-pitched tone being unmistakable for anything other than getting the attention of its intended recipient. All of the waitresses' attention was instantly drawn by the ringing bell followed by the rustic voice of an aging male voice, who heralded a number commensurate with each waitress's order. By the number being called out, Joyce knew that her customer's order was ready for pick-up and delivery. The food servings were placed by the kitchen staff onto a long, shoulder high counter, which was constructed of burnished stainless steel and being ten feet in length. This huge area afforded for a huge array of orders to be placed under the infra-red warming lights, which were conveniently located immediately above the entire length of the kitchen's counter.

"Here's your order, sir, I apologize for the delays, but it's been a crazy morning," Joyce announced apologetically, as she served Wayne his food. Wayne smiled softly at the waitress. He vicariously sympathized with the waitress's personal problems, having heard the heated dialogue between the waitress and her intemperate loud-mouthed boss.

"Oh, it's no problem, Miss, I'm not in a big hurry today anyway," Wayne replied.

Joyce appreciated his mildly thoughtful remark. She walked over to the coffee brewing station and retrieved a pot of freshly brewed elixir.

"More coffee, sir?" she inquired.

"Yes, ma'am, that would be great, I really needed the first cup this morning," Wayne exclaimed as he finished a sip of coffee before placing the ceramic cup down for another re-fill. Joyce Miller noticed Wayne's riding gear and the BMW motorcycle parked in a prominent spot outside the Calico Diner. "So, you're a motorcyclist, where are you heading fella?" Joyce inquired innocently, in passing the time with the quite attractive stranger.

"Nowhere, ma'am! I am not heading anywhere in particular, just heading out across the country, taking the summer off from work and the world you might say!" Wayne nonchalantly answered. The waitress smiled and thought that she would engage in a bit of harmless flirtation with the young man, after all it wasn't like her life was full of romance, she hadn't even been on a date in the last eight months and flirting with a handsome young man was innocent and sometimes even better than the trouble of sleeping with one.

"Most of the motorcycle guys that come through here are riding those horribly loud mean-sounding Harley Davidson's. I'm not a motorcycle enthusiast or anything, but I do know that the fancy bike you are riding is no Harley, so what kind of machine is that?" Joyce inquired with a flirtatious wink. Wayne fancied the waitress, the same as she did of him. He too thought that a harmless bit of flirtation was good for his ego.

"No, ma'am, it's not a Harley. I think Harleys are for those with an over-active ego or libido problems. My bike is a BMW cruiser and it rides like a sailor's dream. Would you care for a ride?" Wayne asked half-heartedly.

Joyce merely smiled at Wayne's schoolboy suggestion as she turned her back and walked over to the kitchen counter and placed the coffee urn back onto the stove warmer. Her mind was instantly transported back to a time some 12 years earlier when she was but a kid fresh out of high school. Back then another handsome young man offered her a ride on his motorcycle too. After a torrid courtship period lasting all of several months, she eloped with that young man, only to soon discover that an unplanned pregnancy and an abusive, drug-addicted husband, didn't make for a happy marriage. Eventually the marriage ended in divorce; however, she left the marriage with a beautiful little girl and a very uncertain future. The schoolgirl dreams of a young knight on an iron steed were almost forgotten until she spotted Wayne and his BMW.

For even just a few seconds, she was that same young girl of so many years ago. Such was the thing of fond memories.

"Nah, you have to be kidding me, Mister, I'm too old to get on one of those crazy things; and besides, I'm in enough hot water with my boss that I really don't need any more trouble entering my life," Joyce sparked in a obvious defensive tone. Wayne felt a bit dejected at his innocent offer, now he felt like a rude jerk. Immediately noticing the dejection in Wayne's eyes, she decided to make things right. "Hey, fella, don't fret, I didn't mean anything by that wise-crack remark! I just had some passing nostalgic memories from my innocent youth, that's all!" Joyce inquired as she warmly smiled and gently squeezed Wayne's strong left forearm.

Wayne simply patted her hand and smiled. He quietly finished up his double roasted meat loaf. He was ready to get back on the road and head off west and the great unknown. "Excuse me, Miss, may I have my check please?" Wayne politely inquired as Joyce was about to offer him another cup of coffee.

"Wow – you sure do eat fast, sir – is there anything else I can get you, perhaps another cup of coffee for the road?" Joyce eagerly suggested in hopes that the handsome young stranger would linger a few more minutes in her otherwise drab life.

"No, thank you, Miss, one more cup of coffee and I will never make the next rest stop down the highway," Wayne exclaimed as he reached into his leather jacket for his wallet.

Joyce smiled as she presented the bill to Wayne; the amount came to $18.25. He looked at the bill and at that moment Wayne decided to be very generous with the waitress, given her difficult circumstances and her sick daughter. He took a twenty-dollar bill from his wallet and then he placed a crisp, new one-hundred-dollar bill directly below it and folded it neatly in half. The waitress would merely notice the twenty-dollar bill and only think that she was getting the remaining change from it as a tip and then she would also discover the one-hundred-dollar bill too.

He placed both bills discreetly down onto the Calico Diner counter. Under the coffee cup, she saw the face amount of twenty dollars which barely covered the cost of the meal. In her mind, this was a very cheap tip and she had thought that a customer riding a fancy BMW motorcycle and possessing cultured manners could afford a more generous tip.

"Oh well, there goes another big spender in my life," Joyce scornfully thought as she gazed at the twenty-dollar bill on the counter. She also thought that this was to be the bane of her life as well, a ceaseless string of five, ten, and twenty-dollar bills on the counter for the next 30 years. Joyce's youth and dreams were slowly disappearing with the daily ring of the cash register. She thought that if she were even ten years younger, she would become one of those topless bar dancers and at least make some decent money for her little girl's future.

"The best of luck to you and your little girl! I left the bill, money and a tip for you, Miss," Wayne boldly exclaimed, as he took up his motorcycle gear and headed out the front door of the diner. Getting into his leather jacket, gloves, and helmet, he was looking forward to another day on the seemingly endless ribbon of roads that crisscrossed America. Turning the BMW key into the ignition socket and invoking the electronic ignition switch, he expected the fine-tuned turnover of the Teutonic engineered engine. Instead, nothing happened! There was only silence and the display of a red and an amber light on the BMW's instrument panel. Maybe he had done something wrong this time, so he tried the electronic ignition sequence again. There was another dead silence and the display of the same ignition lights. Wearily he dismounted the BMW and tried in vain to trouble-shoot the malfunction, but he could find nothing readily amiss. He couldn't believe that this expensive and reliable BMW motorcycle refused to start. "These things do not happen to the world-famous BMW motorcycle!" Wayne bitterly cussed as he frantically tried to wiggle every dangling part that protruded from the engine. Nothing he tried worked.

Meanwhile, Joyce wearily walked over and picked up the money that Wayne had left. Walking over to the cash register, she placed the food receipt into a separate container area where the food receipts were compiled. She then typed into the cash register the amount of the food bill and then the amount of the funds received, from which she would extract her meagre tip that Wayne had left her. She quickly calculated a whopping tip of $1.75 from Wayne and this fact again began to depress her. Suddenly, Joyce's fingers felt the obvious presence of another bill directly beneath that of the twenty-dollar bill. To Joyce's amazement, it was a very crisp bill, so new in fact, that it clung to the twenty-dollar bill. It took a second or two, but Joyce finally separated the two bills and she was astounded to discover a brand new $100 bill.

"This was crazy, it must be some stupid mistake!" Joyce thought. "No one ever gets a lunch tab for $18.25 and then leaves a $100 tip! The stranger must have made a terrible mistake, he must have retrieved the wrong denomination from his wallet." Her initial financial delight suddenly turned into confusion, then a mild panic.

"Maybe I should run out into the front parking area to see if the handsome young man was still there!" she anxiously mused to herself nervously. If anything, Joyce Miller was honest and being honest meant having a conscience, and having a conscience meant feeling guilty when things did not seem right. She struggled for a moment, being tempted at having an extra $100 for her little girl's medical bills or instead returning the money to some stranger who had mistakenly left her the wrong bill denomination.

Wayne again turned the ignition switch on the BMW – it simply refused to start. Several more attempts and still no engine turnover. "Damn it must be the ignition system," he muttered. Wayne decided that the only thing to do was to call a local motorcycle repair shop, even better would be to locate the local BMW dealer, even a mid-sized city like Lawrence was bound to have one. Although he had his cell phone, his Wi-Fi connection was weak. He decided it was just as easy to go back into the Calico Diner and get a stronger signal off of the Calico Diner WiFi router.

Slowly and with a disgusted frown on his face, Wayne opened the glass diner door and peered into the lobby. "Excuse me, Miss, but I need to come back inside and get onto your WiFi Internet, my damn motorcycle just died out there in the parking lot and the signal out there is too weak. I can't turn the engine over, it just won't spark," Wayne exclaimed as he looked desperately into Joyce's pale grey eyes.

"Hey there, fella, I was going to come out running after you!" Joyce exclaimed in an almost guilty tone. Wayne looked at her with some puzzlement upon hearing her remark.

"Did I leave something behind or anything like that, Miss?" Wayne questioned in a bewildered tone.

"Oh no no…it's not that, it's just that you made a mistake with the bill. I mean, you left me too much money. You must have pulled the wrong bill from your wallet!" Joyce replied as she slowly held out the $100 bill in front of Wayne's eyes.

He didn't want to take the money, he had wished to leave the excessive tip as a pleasant surprise for a struggling waitress; however, he didn't want to be seen as some rich 'do-gooder'. He had thought it best to discreetly handle the situation by just taking back the bill and just leave a generous regular guy type of tip. So much for his attempt to play the Robin Hood fella this time he figured.

"Thank you, Miss, please give me some change from the $100 bill please, you are a very honest person too!" Wayne replied as he withdrew his leather motorcycle wallet.

She counted out and handed the assorted change back to Wayne and then exclaimed with a faint smile, "Are these denominations fine with you, sir?"

Smiling, Wayne took the wad of bills from Joyce without counting it, and he immediately handed her back a $5 bill.

"Oh, here's the tip that I meant to give you, Miss, I am sorry for any misunderstanding. Again, I thank you for your honesty, it's becoming a rare commodity these days!" he remarked with a deep regret with his broad smile of immaculate professionally maintained teeth; still he had wished that she could have kept the $100 tip since she needed the money badly. Joyce was glad to receive the smaller tip anyway; she was smitten by the young vibrant motorcycle rider. Temporarily, Joyce was relieved in knowing that she had just done the right thing, but it was awfully hard in giving up that $100 bill. Yet it had always been so all of her life- being honest and poor!

"So, Mister, your motorcycle is broken huh? That's a real pity!" Joyce sighed earnestly. "It's really a gorgeous bike and it would have been a beautiful day to ride too," she added in a sad tone.

Wayne merely shrugged his shoulders. "Oh shit, it must be an electrical ignition problem or something similar, this stuff happens!" he exclaimed. Taking out his Apple iPhone, he quickly typed in the words 'BMW Dealer' and instantly a listing of BMW links appeared. He spotted the name, 'Taylor Brothers BMW Motorcycle sales and repair.' His heart jumped with joy as he instantly clicked on the BMW dealer phone number icon. Eagerly, he imagined that a quick service call would relieve his problems and that he would soon be on his way.

"Hello, is this Taylor Brothers BMW and how may I assist you?" echoed forth a friendly feminine voice from the other end of the telephone connection.

"Well, yes, ma'am, I have a BMW cruiser and it's not working, it's an electrical ignition problem I think," Wayne replied back definitively.

"Okay, yes sir, can you bring it in and we'll have our service department look it over for you?" the BMW service operator sounded in an almost scripted reply.

Wayne thought silently for a minute and then he lost his patience. His temper suddenly flared.

"Look here lady, if I could get the motorcycle operating, I wouldn't be making this call to begin with! My motorcycle is broken, which means that it cannot operate or be moved to your shop! Now can you send a service pick-up vehicle over to the Calico Diner at the intersection of 12th and Main Street and have the BMW cycle picked-up?" Wayne impatiently and loudly voiced into his phone.

Joyce could clearly hear the anger and frustration in his voice. There was a pregnant pause on the line. The BMW service desk operator again sparked her polite sounding voice into the phone. "Sir, we'll have a service vehicle there in about an hour or so, is there a phone number where we can reach you?" she politely inquired.

Wayne quickly rattled off his cell phone number before tersely terminating the conversation. He was a man in obvious frustration and it physically showed in his tense posture and despondent expression. He was an anxious and privileged man used to having his own way on everything and unexpected delays greatly frustrated his usually calm demeanour.

"Hey, big tipper, how about a cup of coffee while you cool-down your temper?" Joyce joyfully shouted with a smile and a wink, as she motioned for him to come over to the serving counter. Initially, Wayne's reaction was one of rejection, but he broke into a broad smile and his mood changed when he saw the inviting smile on the pretty waitress's face.

"Why the hell not... that's an offer that I can't reject!" Wayne replied as he swaggered over to the serving counter at which he had moments before enjoyed a late morning lunch.

"Excuse my temper, Miss, but I hate incompetence!" he remarked with an air of superiority. Joyce noticed that that her modern knight was not infallible after all. Wayne quickly decided to change the subject, "Thanks, Miss, that extra cup of coffee is what I really need right now, by the way, what's your name?" he inquired as he laid down his helmet and jacket onto an empty seat immediately next to his counter stool.

The waitress smiled as she placed a coffee setting before Wayne. "My name is Joyce, and what is your name kind sir?" Joyce smirked in a pleasant toying tone.

Wayne emptied a small capsule of cream into his fresh cup of coffee and stirred in a spoon of sugar before answering. "It's Wayne, I mean it is Brad Wayne Hamilton. I'm travelling through from Boston," he answered briskly.

"Now that's a fine sounding name, I like it, Mr Hamilton, it sounds so refined and traditional. Where are you headed, Mr Hamilton?" Joyce inquired with increasing interest.

"I had a little bit of time off this summer, so I had thought that I would do some continental sightseeing and perhaps a little soul searching too, to see a bit of America and discover it for myself," Wayne confessed as he slipped off his leather jacket and threw it casually onto the top of his helmet. "Yeah, I took a break from the rat race to see what it's all about, I guess I am a summer motorcycle bum!" Wayne commented almost arrogantly.

Joyce was neither moved or romanticized by Wayne's apparent rich boy comments – 'here was some spoiled guy who got bored from his daily drudge and escaped for a summer jaunt on his fancy motorcycle, must be nice!' she scornfully thought.

"Yeah well, welcome to my little rat race! I'm stuck here in middle America with my sick daughter, working for almost minimum wage, and for a cold blooded, hard-assed, Neanderthal manager'!" Joyce retorted snottily, as she wiped up the counter top with a damp cloth.

Wayne was slightly shocked by the woman's frankness and he felt a bit embarrassed by his previous insensitive proclamation. In a flash, the waitress was suddenly gripped with a feeling of guilt for her sudden outburst and jealousness at a virtual stranger.

"Heck, Wayne, I'm sorry to have said that! I am out of line! I have no right to judge you or your actions, but it's hard living here for me. I guess I have always envied some of those rich customers coming in here in their fancy cars and going on their fancy vacations and here I am trying to make ends meet from week to week. I guess it's a lot easier in life to look up at others who are better off than yourself than it is to look-down at those who are less fortunate than yourself," she meekly confessed in far greater detail to a stranger than she prudently had a right to do so.

"Ah, that's fine, Joyce, I guess I am still a bit of a child and a spoiled one at that, I didn't mean to flaunt my trip or demean your situation. I apologize for anything I said that may have offended you," Wayne replied with concern. It was now Joyce's turn to be impressed by this young man's sincerity and obvious superior breeding; his manners were definitely cultured, as was his earnest delivery and tone.

"Okay, Wayne, let's call it Even-Stevens, how about a top-off of that coffee and something to read while you wait for that BMW truck to arrive?" Joyce tactfully offered.

"Sure, why not!" Wayne replied in a jovial voice.

Joyce dutifully topped-off Wayne's coffee mug, then walked swiftly over to the Calico Diner lobby area, where a stack of magazines and newspapers sat awaiting eventual disposal. She took up a fresh copy of the USA Today newspaper and a People magazine for Wayne to look over. "Here you go, Wayne, if you don't like these, there are other selections as well," Joyce remarked as she handed Wayne the newsprint items.

In 30 minutes, a white and blue coloured Chevy long-bed pick-up truck with the adorned stencilled name of 'Taylor Brothers BMW' drove up beside Wayne's motorcycle in the diner front parking area. A tall and pudgy man in his mid-forties and sporting a full-beard emerged from the Chevy cab and slowly approached Wayne's BMW. Upon seeing the Taylor Brothers tow truck, Wayne unceremoniously hurried out from the diner and ran up to the bearded man.

"Hello, I am sure glad to see you, my bike just died on me...I think it's the ignition switch!" Wayne exclaimed in a semi-expert tone.

The gruff, bearded employee from Taylor Brothers looked at Wayne in a slow up and down manner, clearly unimpressed by his appearance and appraisal. A huge wad of a chewing tobacco prominently protruded from the bearded man's cheek.

"Hey there buddy, what the hell do you know about motorcycles? I bet you never got your hands dirty doing any maintenance on this beautiful little baby here!" the bearded man spoke with a dry disgust. Yet Wayne was clearly not impressed or insulted by the flagrant boisterous remarks.

"Well, pal, all I know is that this motorcycle was working great for the past 1,200 miles and I had it fully checked out about six weeks ago!" Wayne retorted in an authoritative voice.

The bearded BMW man rolled his tongue, opened his mouth and forcefully spat out a huge brown wad of tobacco spit juice prominently onto the kerb. Wayne thought this a most vulgar and nasty gesture, designed both to intimidate others and make a crass statement. "Did you try the ignition switch several times? Is the fuel tank filled up? You know these BMW machines are a bit tricky," the bearded man bellowed dryly. Wayne was getting more disgusted with each succeeding elementary remark which the rude man made.

"Of course, I tried the ignition, about half a dozen times, that's why I called you!" Wayne exploded in arrogant frustration.

"Well now, let me try starting it, I have had several years' experience with these foreign bikes," the BMW man stated tersely with a smug air of confidence. After the hit of the ignition switch and several pulls on the throttle, there was no response from the engine. "Mummm, well I just can't understand it! Everything looks fine, there's no outside mechanical problem, yeah looks like the bike will definitely have to go back to the shop", the bearded man declared in a final tone of resignation.

Wayne simply shook his head in disgust and muttered some obscenity under his breath. "Okay, whatever the hell that I have to do to get my baby back on the road – I'll have to do it," Wayne huffed in an irritable voice.

"Hey, Mister, let me drop the ramp down and we'll roll this baby onto the truck bed, tie her down, and be on our way back to the shop! Hey, can you help me out here?" the bearded man smiled inquisitively.

Initially, Wayne brandished a scornful frown, which then blossomed into a gentle smile, "Sure, pal… let's roll it aboard the bed of your truck, the sooner it gets to the shop, the sooner it will be fixed, and I'll be on my way," Wayne replied. Soon the BMW was loaded, and the two men took an uneasy and very quiet 20-minute ride to the Taylor Brothers BMW Motorcycle shop.

Wayne glanced over at the bearded man's coveralls, and through the grease and stains, he could barely made out a name, 'Bill'. The drive to the Taylor Brothers shop was a long and lonely one. Both men sensed their mutual differences; they were quite obviously worlds apart in both background and interests. Both men had clearly sensed the tensions between them and each had wisely concluded that silence was the best form of conversation. Every now and then, the bearded man commented on the traffic or the weather, topics on which Wayne merely parroted the man's sentiments, if not his exact words. Wayne let his eyes and mind wander over the monolithic semi-urban scenery. The dotted landscape adorned with picturesque small cottage houses and farms in the distance, was devoid of any unique or majestic vistas.

"Okay, here we are, Mister," the dirty and frustrated BMW man exclaimed with some evident satisfaction.

Immediately, Wayne's attention shifted away from the mundane landscape. He was immediately relieved to see the tall silver and red BMW lettering atop the two-storey building, as this meant that he was that much closer to getting back on the road and out of small-town USA!

"Boy, that's a sight for sore eyes, I thought that we would never get here with all that slow traffic we ran into," Wayne exclaimed excitedly. The bearded man stopped the truck and both men got out of the truck cabin. Wayne walked to the back of the truck, as the bearded man followed. The bearded man looked around the garage and spotted a mechanic, he blew out a loud, shrill whistle. "Hey Bobby, get your ass over here and lend me a hand why don't you," he yelled in a loud and common tone. Wayne smiled at this display of blue class salutation, as he slowly withdrew a wallet from his jacket.

"Hey there, Bill, this is for you and your buddy Bobby and thank you," Wayne shouted to the driver. The bearded man turned to Wayne in shocked amazement. Wayne handed the man two crisp $20 bills and a broad smile. The bearded man was speechless as he gazed for a few seconds at the bills and the generosity that it was intended to convey.

"Geez, sir, thank you, but there's no need for this, I am only doing my job," the bearded man sighed defensively.

"Yeah, and a hard and thankless job that it is too! Please, I insist, you were more than helpful, and it makes up for my lack of social conversation on the ride down here!" Wayne smiled.

The man almost blushed with embarrassment. "Well thanks a heap, Mister, I really appreciate it and I'll tell my friend Bobby to give your bike a good look over! Just go over to the Service Department and they'll take care of you, buddy," the bearded man exclaimed as he and his partner unloaded Wayne's BMW down the ramp of the low-boy flat-bed truck.

"Boy, I hope this wait is a short one," Wayne muttered to himself, as he walked into the Service Department, where he gave his BMW data to a friendly reception clerk. He was told to go sit in the waiting room and that a mechanical diagnosis on his BMW was due back in thirty minutes. He felt like he was awaiting the medical diagnosis of a loved one. The BMW shop was well kept, clean and modern. The typical waiting room availed itself to its singular guest. There were the normal amenities of a coffee station, national magazines with mundane cover and stories, and the ever-prevalent TV. After about 45 minutes, a skinny, middle-aged man with thinning brown hair emerged from the service department and came into the customer waiting area.

"Hello Mister Hamilton, my name is Mike Johnston and I am the Service Manager, I have some information on your BMW and I'm afraid it's not good news. The electronic fuel control ignition module is broken, and it looks like you'll need a new one, the price is about $850, not including the price of labour of course."

Wayne was only slightly disturbed at this minor monetary annoyance.

"Okay that's not too bad, go ahead and put on the part! How long until it's installed and I'm back on the road?" he inquired nonchalantly.

This time the service man's body posture grew defensive, as he folded his hands across his chest and looked off into blankless oblivion.

"Okay, you see, sir, now that's the problem we have here, your bike is a few years old and we do not keep stock of every part for every model and year of BMW motorcycle, do you understand?" the man started to explain. Wayne immediately cut the man off in mid-sentence, "Look, I asked you how long before I get on the road again?"

There was a pause of a few seconds before the now nervous skinny service man replied, "So sorry, sir, it may be only a few days or as long as a week. It just depends on how fast the part is packed-up and delivered!"

"That really frigging stinks! What the hell am I supposed to do in Lawrence Kansas for a week?" Wayne retorted back in obvious disgust.

"Mister Hamilton, sir, can you please come with me and sign some papers for your rental motorcycle?" Wayne annoyingly walked up to the service counter, he and the BMW clerk exchanged personal information and some papers were signed. "Will you be staying locally, Mister Hamilton? You know that you are not supposed to be taking the loaner vehicle out-of-state, correct?" Mike explained in a bureaucratic tone.

"Yes, of course, I know that, besides the farther I drive, the more distance I will have to backtrack to get back here, and my aim is to see new places, not revisit old ones!" Wayne impetuously replied.

"By the way, Mike, where are some good hotels around here where I can cool my heels?" Wayne casually inquired.

Mike thought a few seconds then replied, "There are many corporate-chain hotels and motels right off the main highway where Bill the mechanic picked you up, or you can go further in the middle of the city, where there are some swankier places!"

"Thanks, I'll get my personal belongings and be on my way then," Wayne exclaimed with a sigh of relief.

"That's not necessary sir. Bill grabbed all your items and he placed them onto the loaner BMW for you."

Wayne smiled and was relieved in a way; it saved him the chore of retrieving his belongings. 'It really did pay to be nice and generous to people,' he thought to himself.

Wayne was handed the keys to his loaner BMW; it was a silver and black beast that looked like it could outrace the devil himself. Bill was standing next to the bike and he was smiling as Wayne approached. "It's a beauty, sir, fast and almost brand new to boot, you'll have a real blast playing with this little baby until your own bike is fixed," the bearded, gruff mechanic replied. He handed Wayne his helmet and jacket. Wayne nodded in silent appreciation at the friendly gesture.

"Thank you, Bill, try and make sure my baby gets its part soon," Wayne exclaimed as he mounted the BMW and turned the ignition switch. 'Varoom' sparked the roar of the engine. Wayne gave a thumbs-up sign to Bill, as he released the kickstand and rode out of the garage and off down the route from which he had just travelled some hours ago.

Once again Wayne was in view of the Calico Diner and he eyed a non-descript string of modest chain hotels. He had made up his mind to take his temporary lodging in this area; one of the reasons was that he was slightly familiar with the area. Next to the typical chain motels, Wayne spotted a local lodging establishment, the 'Willow Inn'. The name sounded a bit comforting and the two-storey stucco light brown building looked as if it had been well maintained. His mind was set, as he smoothly steered the silver and black BMW into the shaded motel vestibule area. He parked the bike and proceeded directly into the lobby and smartly walked up to the desk clerk. The motel lobby appeared clean and well kept. A grey-haired lady of about 65 years old smiled and greeted Wayne as he approached the counter. "Good day, sir, may I assist you?" the silver-haired lady inquired pleasantly. Wayne knew from the tone of this employee that he had picked the right lodging. 'Good manners and cleanliness bespoke a good, clean hotel,' he concluded silently.

"You look a wee bit tired and worn-out, I suspect that you will need a room, huh, young fella?" the grey-haired matron voiced in a superior tone. Wayne tucked his helmet up under his arm as he leaned casually up against the black Formica and wood trimmed front counter.

"Yes, Ma'am, that is correct, my bike broke down and I have to wait in Lawrence until it gets repaired," Wayne noted wearily. The old lady noted the Wayne's biker clothes and the sheer mention of it made her a little suspicious of this otherwise clean-looking young man.

"Then I'll be needing some identification, can I see two forms of ID and a credit card?" the old woman demanded in a more serious tone. The old woman was being careful, as she had been burnt by some bikers in the past, who had either trashed their rooms or took off without paying their bills.

Wayne sensed the old lady's defensive nature, and he did not like being at the apex of her prejudice. He was starting to feel the discrimination against those who looked and dressed outside the mainstream. He drew his wallet and handed the old lady his driver's licence and two platinum credit cards. The old woman ran the credit cards and in a few seconds the results revealed that Wayne was good for a $350,000 limit on his credit card, this limit being placed by Wayne himself to limit abuses should his card ever be stolen. On seeing the results, the old lady's eyes' sparkled and her entire demeanour changed from guarded inquisitiveness to one of outright politeness. She was brimming with a smile now that she knew that this boarder was as good as his platinum credit line and oh what a credit line it was!

"Yes, sir, Mr Hamilton, now what sort of a room would you like and for how long do you wish to stay with us?" the motel matron inquired with a contrived soft voice and a faint smile. Wayne also smiled to himself, for he had erroneously and foolishly thought that he was liked throughout his life for the person who he was and not what he had in the way of money, yet now it suddenly hit home how naïve and sheltered his entire life had been. Perceptions and prejudices ruled the world.

"I'll have one of your 'nicer rooms', king size bed preferred, and bill me on a weekly basis and renew it from there as necessary," Wayne muttered in a soft and unemotional tone.

"Anything you say, honey, I can bill you for the entire summer if you so prefer!" echoed the hotel matron. Wayne merely smiled as he signed the motel registration and took the key for his room. "Oh, my name is Barbara, if you happen to need anything," the old inn keeper announced as Wayne nodded in silent acknowledgement as he slowly walked toward the hotel stairs.

The second-floor room was away from the main street, it promised to be quiet and away from any road traffic. Upon entering, he found the room to be spartan yet clean. The room was adorned with the typical bed, non-descript bureaus, and TV vanity. It seemed that the further west he journeyed, the more mundane became the lodgings. No matter, he was settled in for the next week, so why not make the most of it. He anxiously peeled off his leather jacket, shirt, and boots. The sweat made a musty smelly aroma and his damp undershirt clung uncomfortably to his trim body. Instantly off to the warm relaxing shower, the soothing warm water washed all the grime and toll of the day's frustrations.

After his shower, Wayne plopped himself in an easy chair and turned on the TV. Only old TV reruns were playing; in frustration he turned off the boob tube and decided to make a phone call to Kate. It was turning early evening, yet back east Wayne correctly deducted that Katherine was still at work. He decided to give a quick call as he grabbed the hotel room telephone and dialled the number to the firm.

"Hello Kate, how are you doing?" he voiced pleasantly.

"Brad darling, are you all right?... is anything wrong?... where are you honey?" Katherine sparked quickly in a quick inquisitive fashion. Katherine's voice lent an inviting charm to the austere room setting.

"Hey, I'm fine, there's no worry, Kate," he assured in a reaffirming tone. "I'm in Lawrence Kansas, a very charming but non-descript part of the great Middle America," he continued.

"Kansas! Brad, what the hell are you doing in Kansas of all places? Did you just stop there for the night?" Katherine inquired with some degree of bewilderment.

"Well not exactly, Kate, you see the BMW is broken down – it just would not start-up this morning and it's in the shop for repair, it may be down for a week or so until the electronic ignition part comes in," he fully explained.

"Oh shit, do you mean that you are stuck in Kansas for a week or more? I'd go stir crazy myself! What are you going to do there – look for Dorothy and the Wizard of Oz? It's not like there's any cultural or social events happening there, at most you'll be limited to watching some second run movies and eating at some greasy fast-food places!" Katherine snobbishly sounded in an obvious and superior mocking tone.

"You're probably right, but the people here seem very nice, besides I'll just have to make the best of it, I guess. I'll find something to keep me busy and it will relax me from riding the BMW for a spell," Brad replied dryly.

Katherine decided to change the tempo of the conversation to the matter of utmost interest to her. "Brad honey, you know that you can just leave that damn BMW and boring Kansas all behind you by just hopping on the next plane back to Boston! You know the early summers here are really beautiful, there's plenty of indoor and outdoor activities to delight in," Katherine suggested seductively.

He knew that this was no solution to his problem and he was starting to fully enjoy himself too, yet he didn't want to hurt Kate either. "Kate, honey, I can't return to Boston right now, but give me a few more months and I'll be back to you forever," Brad promised solemnly. This was not the answer that she wanted to hear, but she accepted it, she really had no other choice or leverage in the matter at this point.

"Well, have it your way, Brad, my darling, you just continue to call me and know that I love you dearly," Kate replied, as tears formed once again in her eyes and in her voice reflections. This emotional roller coaster happened every time she spoke with Brad and she was frantic for its final cessation.

"I love you too, Kate and don't be too concerned, I'll find something to do around here and besides what can happen to a Boston banker in Lawrence Kansas?" Brad verbally toyed as he tried to calm Katherine's anxiety and concern. "Look, I will call or text you every evening this week to let you know about the progress on the BMW motor part?" he pronounced in an assured tone.

"I love you, Brad, be safe and hurry back to me soon" Katherine pleaded.

"You bet, Kate, and remember you'll always be my girl. Please say hello to everyone at the firm and tell Margie to keep me posted on any emergency mail or correspondences that come into my office that require my immediate attention?" Brad calmly requested. The quick conversation ended with mutual terms of affection. Not wishing to dwell on her feminine instincts, Katherine diverted her attention to more worldly matters.

She deftly picked up her office phone and rang for her personal assistant, Joan Peters. The phone rang three times before it was answered by Margie DeTagelio. "Good afternoon, Miss MacAlister, may I assist you please?" Margie politely replied as she answered her co-worker's private line.

While waiting for a reply, Margie was suddenly interrupted by a harsh and demanding female voice, "What are you doing answering my phone, DeTagelio? Where the hell is my private secretary, DeTagelio?" demanded a most perturbed Katherine MacAlister.

"Oh, I'm so sorry, but Mrs Peters just went down to the mail room and then off to make some photocopies for the Landers Account. Is there anything that I can do, Miss MacAlister?" Margie inquired in a still polite, scripted monotone voice.

There was a pregnant pause for about three long seconds before the phone line crackled again. "Yes, come in here, I want to see you!" Once again, Margie expected to be bitched-out by the Queen Bitch of the Financial District in all of Boston. Since Brad was away and with Mrs Peters back from her vacation, Margie was enjoying her job of merely maintaining Brad Hamilton's office mail and diverting business contracts to either Miss MacAlister or her father Lionel MacAlister, who was once again working part-time with the firm until Brad's expected return later in the year.

Upon every summons, Margie dreaded the no-win confrontation with the dragon lady. Politely and with a forced smile she entered the dragon's lair, otherwise known as Katherine MacAlister's office. "Yes, Miss MacAlister, how may I assist you?" Margie subserviently inquired.

Katherine looked up and slowly pushed back the elegant royal maroon coloured, tufted leather chair from her desk. She loosely dangled a fine blue lacquered Mont Blanc pen between her slender fingers in an almost toy-full fashion.

"Have you been getting all of Mr Hamilton's mail while he has been away?" Katherine inquired directly.

Margie looked puzzled, but answered straight away, "Yes, of course, Miss MacAlister, those were Mr Hamilton's instructions to me before he left. He has also been forwarding his personal mail to you, which Mrs Peters has been tracking."

Katherine sat there motionless. Her eyes transfixed into space. Suddenly another question flew from Katherine's lips, "Were there any strange or unusual correspondence or messages?"

Margie looked perplexed but answered the question: "Well none that I could see, Miss MacAlister. In fact, the only items from Mr Hamilton are those postcards that he has been sending to both you and the staff, and of course there are his personal bills and expenses – which are all paid automatically from his checking account.

"Now about those financial transactions, have you seen those too?" Katherine interrogated further.

Once again Margie answered in kind: "Well yes, Miss MacAlister, I have seen these and Mr Hamilton has authorized me to see and audit all his correspondence that have been sent to him at the address of Hamilton & MacAlister."

Katherine was now getting to her main inquiry. "Have any of these bills seemed a little strange or inconsistent to you Miss DeTagelio? I mean, have you seen any items being billed that run outside Mr Hamilton's normal spending profile?"

Margie thought for a few seconds carefully before answering, as Katherine keenly looked for any sign of deceit or evasion on Margie's face, but there was no guilt to be betrayed. Margie was a faithful and honest person who was totally devoted to Brad Hamilton. Then suddenly, a thought was perked by Katherine's inquest and suddenly Margie remembered that she had also kept the unopened personal bank account statements from Mr Hamilton, these she never opened since these were personal finances as opposed to Hamilton & MacAlister business expenses.

"As part of my job, Miss MacAlister, I do remember receiving Mr Hamilton's personal banking statements, but I never open these personal type of financial correspondence – I wait to hand these to Mr Hamilton for his personal review," Margie quibbled. Katherine was now excited that her hunch might be paying off.

"So, as I explained to you previously DeTagelio, I am Mr Hamilton's remaining family and his future wife, so why don't you run along and get those personal financial statements for me now like a nice little office girl," Katherine condescendingly ordered with a devilish smile. Margie rushed outside to the pile of private mail that she had set aside for Brad's opening when he returned. She thought it a bit presumptuous for Katherine to be going through Brad's private financial mail, but she had a valid point in being his closest confidante and she was to be his future wife too.

"Here it is, Miss MacAlister," Margie announced as she handed Katherine a large manila envelope with a seal from the First Bank of Boston boldly embossed on the upper right-hand side of the envelope.

Katherine deftly used an elegant, gold-plated letter opener to neatly dissect the long firm envelope. A large letter-sized sheet portrayed the activity and account balances of Brad's personal account. His total personal checking account was $25 million dollars, a hefty balance for even a Boston financial billionaire. Brad wanted to have a hefty balance to ensure that he could write sizable cheques without undue concern. Katherine noticed a debit amount to the Copen Family for $175,000 – it was dated at the end of last month. Katherine's eyes widened, but she was not concerned about the size of the cheque, rather she was more concerned with its payee.

Margie eyed Katherine's silent interest in the bank statement. "Is there a problem, Miss MacAlister?" Yet Katherine said nothing for a few seconds, before looking sternly at Margie.

"I am going to be sending a memo to both you and Mrs Peters. This memo will state that you have my direct orders to bring to me all of Mr Hamilton's personal financial correspondence that come into my office without exception! Is that clear, Miss DeTagelio?" Katherine softly demanded.

Margie was startled by this demand, yet she knew that nothing could be done to avoid it either.

"Yes, Miss MacAlister, I will do exactly as you order. Is there anything else for today before I leave?" Margie inquired.

"No, have a nice night, DeTagelio" Katherine replied as she slid the ornate Parker pen slowly across her red lips. Katherine had discovered that her Brad was playing the Sugar Daddy to some hay seeds or white-trash motorcycle folks while he was out on the road, a gesture that could prove to be worth careful watching. "Brad was changing and getting better, but it was best to keep a watchful eye out for his activities, for Brad was like a small vulnerable child open to the wicked ways of those less well-bred than himself," Katherine smartly calculated as she carefully examined the bank statement records. From now on, all of Brad's personal issues were Katherine's personal issues as well. The unfortunate fact of the matter was that Brad had no knowledge or veto in Kate's secret decision.

* * * * * * * * * * * * * * * * *

As the sun closed its eyes on a warm mid-west summer evening, Wayne walked impatiently around his smallish hotel room. He had quickly grown tired with the mundane local news and all of the 63 cable channels were filled with nonsense programmes and talking-head chatter. He quickly discovered that his hunger was growing and that it was time for dinner. He got up off the motel bed and attired himself in a loose-fitting set of blue jeans and tan cotton knitted polo shirt. Wisely he decided not to wear his heavy, hot knee-high BMW riding boots, electing instead to wear a pair of cordovan low quarter chukka boots, these being more comfortable and practicable for the hot and humid mid-western summer nights. Sitting in this dreary motel room and watching second-run TV programmes was driving Wayne almost stir crazy.

In a sudden dash, Wayne Hamilton left the Willow Inn and strutted down the main street. He walked about a quarter mile distance and discovered nothing but fast-food establishments and chain restaurants, of which he already had his ample fill during the past six weeks on the road. About 100 yards ahead he gazed to where he had enjoyed lunch earlier in the day- the Calico Diner. The atmosphere was cosy and family style, additionally there was the possibility of flirting with that pretty waitress, although by now she was most likely off-shift. 'What the hell, it's worth a try and the dinner there is probably as good as the lunch,' he logically figured as he drifted slowly down the street in the comfortably warm night.

Opening the massive door, he noticed that everything was as he had left it earlier that day. There were just a handful of diners scattered among the mostly vacant tables, he quickly noticed that the near empty serving counter. He took up the same front counter seat, which he had occupied earlier in the day. A passing waitress of Mexican heritage passed Wayne and greeted him with a pleasant smile and soft Spanish accent, "Would you like a menu, sir? Perhaps some coffee and a glass of water too while you read over the menu, sir?" she politely inquired. He politely smiled and nodded while looking over the menu dinner fares. All of the selections looked even better than the lunch entrees.

Wayne's mouth started to water as his appetite was teased by the hearty homemade-sounding country-style entrée dishes. He sipped some strong hot coffee and thought of Boston and home. Suddenly there were the sounds of an increasingly angry and vocal commotion from the kitchen area, which was eerily reminiscent of his lunchtime fare. The strong exchange of emotion-laden words between a man and a woman could clearly be discerned, despite the loud kitchen sounds of ceramic dishes clanking about, pots being banged, and the sound of food frying on an open grill. Wayne could clearly smell the aroma of fried onions and the cooking of meats. Abruptly, the kitchen aromas and sounds were interrupted by an agitated feminine voice. "This is really unfair of you... you're a real bastard of a man, Johnnie! You're a selfish jerk with manners of a pig and the understanding of a jackass!" the woman yelled in an angry, but clearly audible tone. The female voice was a familiar one too!

The kitchen door flew open with a sudden fury and through it immediately barged forth a visibly disturbed waitress, whose eyes and tears betrayed her agitation and anger. "You wait one fucking moment, girlie, you walk out on me and you walk out of this fucking job too, do you hear me?" shouted an angry middle-aged man, who followed Joyce Miller down the opposite end of the serving counter from where Wayne had quietly seated himself. The arguing adults had positioned themselves outside of the main diner traffic area, yet still their angry words could be heard for anyone interested in perking up their ears to listen. Wayne's ears were in complete reception mode.

"You fucking think that you can come and go around here anytime you like, just because you have a sick brat kid and you bat those baby blue eyes at me every now and then hoping for sympathy; well, sister, it don't work like that with me! No way, baby! You want me to do you a favour, then you have to do Johnnie a favour, you get me kid?" the boisterous, foul-mouthed man roared in a threatening tone. A few seconds passed before Joyce had dried her eyes and gained her composure; she was sick and tired of Johnnie's rude remarks and sexual advances toward her, and she was fed up with his threats as well.

"Screw you, Johnnie! You don't have any right to demand anything from me, that includes my body and the welfare of my little girl! You're every woman's worst nightmare of a boss and I'd rather starve on the street than to sleep with you!" Joyce sobbingly responded with a tone of sarcasm and spitefulness.

Johnnie paused for a second and then he approached close to Joyce's face. His angry eyes locked with hers and they stared down one another as gunslingers in the Old West. Unlike past confrontations with Johnnie, this day Joyce stood firm her ground, she was tired of turning her back on her sexually frustrated boss. She was unsure if she was going to get fired or bitch-slapped across the face.

Johnnie got an uncomfortable six inches from Joyce's face, his disgustingly stale and acrid smoke-laden breath was all that Joyce could perceive as her universe closed to within the short distance immediately in front of her face. As he got closer, Johnnie suddenly grabbed her chin with his left hand, then he quietly smiled and whispered, "Honey, this summer has just begun and I bet that you'll be eating those brave words before the first frost comes!" With that crude threatening remark, Johnnie slowly past by Wayne, his faced framed with a wicked shit-eating grin smile. The self-satisfied tyrant triumphantly tread back into the sanctuary of the busy kitchen. Joyce was stunned by his words, as she knew that she had burnt her last bridge with her manager and boss, Johnnie Porter.

Clearly Wayne discerned that Joyce was being abused by a very rough, ill-mannered overseer. The fact that he also fancied Joyce at some primal male level, made the embarrassment even more intolerable to his personage. Without thinking the situation logically through, Wayne reacted with guttural fortitude. As Johnnie was starting to walk back toward the swinging kitchen doors, a loud male voice rocked the air. "Hey Mack, what's the deal with the lady?" Wayne challenged in a voice toned with subtle inquisitive authority. Johnnie turned quickly and aggressively eyed-down Wayne, who was clearly the only patron at the counter.

"Hey, what the fuck did you ask me, fella?" Johnnie exclaimed in utter amazement as he walked slowly over toward the lunch counter where Wayne boldly and defiantly sat.

Wayne slowly put down his coffee cup and eyed Johnnie with a cold menacing stare. "I said, what's the deal with the lady? That's not a proper way to treat anyone! I don't like to see people treated that way, especially a lady!" Wayne exclaimed with some degree of anger and noble Don Quixote ideals.

Johnnie walked up closely to the lunch counter, his physical distance was a mere12 inches away from Wayne's face and he was clearly inside Wayne's comfort zone. Johnnie tried to face-down this customer upstart, who had just interrupted his cloistered domain of the Calico Diner.

"What the fuck does it matter to you, pal? This is a private matter and it's my private restaurant to run as any damn way I please! Now what the hell have you got to say about that, Mister?" Johnnie proclaimed in a menacing arrogant tone. Johnnie was master of the Calico Diner domain and he was not going to be intimidated by some wayward, transient customer. Determination, however, went both ways and Wayne was not about to be intimidated or talked-down by some mean mannered, morally corrupt, greasy grill-joint bully.

Wayne had managed many multi-million dollar and billion dollar underwriting offerings, he was not about to be eyed-down by some ill-mannered local yokel. Slowly he arose from the bar counter stool and faced down Johnnie across the narrow countertop. He towered over Johnnie by over six inches and his physical frame was lean and well-toned, as opposed to Johnnie's slumping shoulders and bulging waistline. Johnnie could not compete with Wayne's physical prowess and he didn't think it worth his dignity to further antagonize a customer. "Well, I 'm saying, ah…I'm only saying…" Wayne spoke before being cut off by the crass diner owner.

"No…you ain't saying nothing, Mister, just finish your damn meal and be on your way, in fact, consider your meal is on me, Pal! Just get the hell out of here…fast!" Johnnie stuttered with some degree of hesitation.

Wayne felt only half-vindicated in his valiant words, but he also wanted to do something more substantive and compulsive. Emotionally, he acted on his basic instincts. "Hey, you Mister Boss Man, how about a job instead!" Wayne snapped back extemporaneously.

Hearing Wayne's words, Johnnie was stopped suddenly in his tracks as was Joyce, who was spying the scene from a safe distance, was visibly shocked too with her eyes popping wide open and her mouth open wide in exasperation. Johnnie turned around and looked directly into Wayne's eyes.

"What the hell did you say there, Mister?" Johnnie repeated in a guttural, scratchy-voiced, bewildered tone. Wayne repeated his offer.

"I said that I wanted a job here, as a short-order grill operator, the sign says that you need help right, so I am applying for a job!" Wayne replied as he pointed to the Calico Diner 'Help Wanted' sign posted in a dark corner located above the cash registers.

Johnnie was dumbfounded by this stranger's challenge and he did his best to discourage any outside trouble- maker from coming into his pathetic little controlled world.

"That sign is wrong, buddy! I don't need anyone in my flipping kitchen, especially from the likes of you! The sign is wrong, so be on your way! You've done your good deed for the day fella," Johnnie replied in hope that this pain-in-the-ass stranger would quietly leave. Wayne loved a challenge and although this was not his normal multi-million-dollar challenge, he desperately wanted to win this battle with the little mean man Johnnie.

The vulgar, crass-mannered, ego-centric man who had viciously spat the angry words at Joyce was none other than the diner's manager and partial owner, Mr Johnnie Porter. He was the perfect example of a 'man acting badly stereotype' in both form and function. He was middle-aged, in his late thirties, with receding greasy black hair and possessing a visibly evident middle-age bulge around his waist, this resulting from a lack of physical inactivity and grossly consuming too much fat-laden diner free food. Standing at a portly, almost Rubenesque five foot five inches tall, Johnnie appeared a lot shorter than his actual height, this due to his poor posture and extra weight. The product of a solid middle-class family, Johnnie and his older brother and sister all inherited the Calico Diner upon the death of their father some years earlier, but it was only Johnnie who had any daily actual management with the diner. In this capacity, Johnnie was the newly-minted epitome of 'King John' and he used his authority with utter obnoxiousness, rather than finesse and kindness.

To compound Johnnie's negative demeanour, he was a frustrated married man, entrapped in a stale marriage in which he had lost romantic and sexual interest and for which he saw no future. Frustrated and meek at home, he sought power and ego at his workplace.

Johnnie sought to relieve his personal and sexual frustrations onto the most available and vulnerable women that he could find, and this naturally spelled doom for the waitresses at the Calico Diner. The older waitresses were not on his 'target list' for amorous adventures; however, the younger girls who were either too innocent or too vulnerable to reject's Johnnie's advances, were like fresh meat to a hungry dog. It was Joyce's unfortunate fate to fall into this latter vulnerable category. Her options were few, so she put up with Johnnie's guff, ass-grabbing and rude advances, since the Calico Diner was one of those few remaining small business establishments which offered its full-time employees fully subsidized medical care; Joyce and her young daughter desperately needed this support net. It was a daily battle royal between each of them and Joyce knew that sooner or later she would have to either find a new job or surrender to Johnnie's animal lust.

Just as Johnnie was about to walk back into the kitchen, Wayne shouted out one last dare, knowing that he had an attractive piece of bait that would entice Johnnie. "Hey there, Boss Man, let me sweeten the offer for you then, how about I work for you at minimum wage with no benefits or days off, plus…I'll work under the table, off the books, no records or withholding for the employer…you can't beat an offer like that, now can you, Mr Boss Man?" Wayne exclaimed in a challenging and almost confrontational tone.

Johnnie was stopped in the middle of his tracks! He seldom had an offer like this from an ordinary white male, especially from an eastern yuppie snob male to boot! Still, the opportunity of busting the chops of this East Coast yuppie interloper was enough to give Johnnie serious thought to consider the offer.

Johnnie slowly turned to face his challenger. "Did I just frigging hear you right, chum? You want to come and work here and for minimum wage, no bennies, and under the table – is that what I heard you say, Mister?"

Wayne knew that he had Johnnie's greedy interest and he was not going to let it slip away.

"Yes precisely, you did hear me correctly," Wayne smirked with a wide grin. Becoming quite intrigued, Johnnie had more questions of this impetuous stranger, as he walked back up to the serving counter.

"Hold on there now, fella, I don't think that a candy-ass guy like you will last a week here, but I can take a joke too! Okay, buddy – now why would someone like you want to work at my place of business? Do you have any experience of working in a diner?" Johnnie snorted back in an antagonistic, bullying tone.

Wayne was up for the reply and his logic was flawless. "Look it's simple, my bike is broken down here and I have nothing to do until it gets the necessary parts to get repaired... I'm bored, and I want something to do with myself...you win too because you don't have to pay me expensive wages or benefits and you do need the help, right? I have swung some hash in my days too!" Wayne lied quite believably.

Instantly, Johnnie became defensive. "I don't trust you, nor do I like you, buddy, I'm not sure about this offer...you don't talk, look or act like my regular workers and I don't want any trouble-makers around here – do you understand me?" Johnnie demurred in a low voice, as his eyes moved away from Wayne and off into empty space.

Wayne uttered a final appeal. "You're supposed to be a savvy businessman! Come on, this is a win-win proposition for both of us, so let's give this a try? I can start at 7:00 AM tomorrow morning," Wayne rationalized to Johnnie.

Feeling himself challenged by the insane offer, Johnnie replied in an almost obtuse manner. "No, buddy, around my place the hired help reports for duty at 5:00 AM for the morning breakfast preparation, and don't be late either!" Johnnie remarked as he immediately turned around and thundered off into the kitchen, then up to the 2nd floor office areas.

Wayne was very proud of his small victory and he couldn't wait to show this rude, loud-mouthed little man that he could swing hash with the best of grill cooks and he couldn't have been happier if he had underwritten a multi-million-dollar stock IPO issuance. All of those who witnessed this verbal duel stood silently aghast – they had never seen anyone argue Johnnie down before and to get the better of him.

"Now what the hell was that all about? Of all the stupid things that a person could do, I think that was one of the dumbest things that I have ever seen anyone do in my life and that includes a biker guy too! I don't need some White Knight on his fancy BMW motorcycle saving me from distress!" Joyce thundered in an almost demeaning tone. Wayne was caught off-guard by this sudden expression of anger and what he took to be ingratitude.

"Hey there, lady, you think too highly of yourself! I did this for myself, not for you, not for anyone else either," Wayne responded proudly. "I'll see you tomorrow bright and early," Wayne barked as he slapped down a $20 bill on the diner counter, as he walked angrily out of the Calico Diner and down the street toward the Willow Inn. It was a warmish evening and he was in no great hurry to head back to his empty hotel room. In retrospect, he pondered what a foolish scene he had just made at the diner. "Was it because of his machismo, anger, or the desire to impress a totally unknown pretty waitress which had possessed him to challenge Johnnie Porter?" he wondered with some degree of angst. Suddenly he grew unsure of his motives or his intention to even fulfil this very silly wager. Before he knew it, he was at the entrance to the Willow Inn. Swiftly he realized that his hotel refuge offered him little in the way of mental condolences, since his BMW was broken for a week or longer and he didn't want to return to Boston with his tail between his legs nor to sit aimlessly around his hotel room. He had to do something to employ his idleness.

Resolved in his decision, Wayne was going to work at that greasy diner, he was going to be the best short-order hash swinger at the Calico Diner, and finally he was determined to enjoy himself; after all, this was but a temporary road bump in his journey into the greater West. He shrugged his shoulders and headed up to his room and a good night's long sleep.

* * * * * * * * * * * * * * * * * *

Once again, the shrill alarm sounded and the low moan of a barely awakened man filled the hotel bedroom. After about 10 long seconds, a weary masculine arm slowly reached over to the night stand and smothered the annoying pre-dawn salutation that announced the beginning of the work morning. While reaching for the alarm clock button, an empty pint bottle of Pinch scotch was felled onto the floor, its impact and integrity cushioned by the cheap rustic beige motel carpeting. He looked over at the alarm clock, he saw that it was 4:15 AM; he needed to be awake this early to get to the diner at 5:00 AM for the breakfast shift. He thought to himself how crazy it was to take this job in the heat of anger, he could just as easily have stayed in the

Willow Inn and watched re-runs of 'I Love Lucy', the 'Price is Right', or just an old movie, but instead he foolishly had to play the part of the shiny rescuing White Knight. He vowed to himself that he would try and ignore this of extemporaneous-type of action in the future. Sudden dares were most emotionally satisfying, but often very childish and even potentially dangerous.

He slowly pulled his naked body from beneath the warm bed blanket. Prior to entering the bathroom, he made sure to turn on the complimentary coffee pot that was located on a small vanity table, the machine soon hissed with subtle sounds, which indicated its active state of brewing. The previous night of consuming off the remainder of the scotch had the negative effects of slowing his reactions; it also dehydrated him and made him crave water. Taking a glass from the bathroom vanity cabinet, he filled it with cold refreshing water. The cold tap water relieved his parched throat. In quick succession, he consumed a second glass. He completed his hygiene tasks in quick routine fashion, then partook a lengthy hot, soothing shower. As he stepped into the hot effervescent mist, all weary morning concerns were soon surrendered to the warm, relieving waters.

A full ten minutes of this regimen was all that he needed, Wayne was now a new man and ready for the day's work activity. Modestly attired in a white cotton towel draped around his waist, he exited the bathroom and headed directly toward the vanity table. The modest coffee maker had adequately performed its mission of preparing a small pot of strong black coffee. Grabbing a white plastic cup from atop the vanity table, he poured a full cup of black coffee and added some sweetener in it.

"Ah this is one proof that there is a God," he remarked in a most satisfied manner. He quickly consumed the cup's contents and then quickly refilled it. He took another large sip and then threw the towel aside and started to get dressed. Out of the four sets of pants that he had packed, he selected the beige cotton twill pants along with a light blue cotton polo shirt. His low quarter chukka boots completed his informal attire. He gulped up the cup of coffee, took up his wallet and keys, and then proceeded down the stairs and out of the Willow Inn parking lot. "This was going to be an interesting day," he thought to himself and he wondered if he was even going to put up with a complete day of bullshit that Johnnie was sure to throw at him.

While the morning sun awaited to blink forth its welcoming presence to the still darkened morning mantle, he leisurely walked without the intrusion of either auto congestion or industrial noise; it was a pleasant sensation for him to behold. The walk took only 15 minutes. Wayne tapped vigorously and forcefully upon the front door of the diner. He waited and there was no reply, in fact, the entire dining room gallery was dark and empty. He knocked again, this time louder and more persistent than the last. The figure of a dishevelled looking man appeared in the darkened doorway. A stout, black-haired man slowly peaked his head through the blinds; it was Johnnie Porter. 'He looked even nastier and grumpier in the darkness of the early morning hours,' he scornfully thought. With a most annoyed look, Johnnie jerked his right thumb in a quick horizontal jerking motion several times and grumbled in a harsh tone, "Hey, Pal, the kitchen workers report to work in the rear entrance, the front door is for paying customers buddy, now get your ass moving."

"Well, that was a fine welcomed greeting on my first day on the job!" Wayne muttered, as he trudged around the back of the diner and located an employee entrance door. Outside the diner's loading dock were several trucks unloading fresh produce and food for the day's menu.

Slowly he opened the door and there before him was a bevy of activity and semi-controlled confusion; there must have been half a dozen workers each going about their respective pre-dawn rituals. He saw some men hauling crates of food, some preparing the ovens and grills, while still others were storing items in the freezer. Each of them had their tasks to do and they performed their work without direct supervision, an indication of both their work ethic and experience.

"Yo, buddy, this ain't no spectator sport going on here, we all work here and none of us don't watch others work, we get busy doing our jobs!" the ill-tempered Johnnie growled in a most low-class tone in obvious imperfect English grammar. Wayne was startled a bit, as he turned around and saw Johnnie's beady eyes staring him down. The contempt that each man felt for the other was palpable.

"I almost made a bet with the head cook that you were not goanna show up this morning! I thought maybe you just wanted to sleep-off your soft, lazy ass this morning," Johnnie coarsely barked. "No matter, your sorry candy-ass is here now, but you're going to work hard for me, Pal! Before you start, we had better get some things straight. First, I want you to understand some of Johnnie's simple rules. 'No lateness, no drinking, no fighting, no drugs, no hanky-panky with the skirts, and no lip to the boss- and that's means me by the way, buddy! You got any questions

Mister?" Johnnie snapped out in a cocky and almost challenging manner.

Totally aghast, Wayne stood in stunned amazement at a figure whose persona he had only seen characterized in old movies and TV shows. This guy was like someone out of Hollywood central casting, a real blue-collar union man of the 1940s. He was sloppy, rude, self-centred, ill-mannered and cocky. He thought himself lucky that he had to only work for this clown for a week or so, while the other poor slobs at the Calico Diner had to work for this Neanderthal for years. Slowly Wayne was appreciating the trials of the American working man.

"I have no questions or issues with you, 'Boss Man'," Wayne replied smartly as he directly and confidently stared into Johnnie's bitter beady eyes. Johnnie knew that he did not scare or intimidate this new guy from the east, but he really didn't care either; after all, this guy was just like a piece of dust or tumbleweed rolling across the planes of Kansas, here today and gone tomorrow.

"Hey there, 'Boss Man', aren't you forgetting something?" Wayne smartly inquired.

Johnnie looked puzzled for the first time this morning. "Now what's that you say that I am forgetting, fella?" he snorted defensively.

Wayne walked up-close to Johnnie, almost too close for comfort. He looked down on Johnnie and sparked a devilish smile, "You forgot to ask me my name, boss man!" Johnnie turned in disgust and walked away, shouting, "I forgot nothing, pal…when Johnnie needs anything from you, buddy, you will definitely know it," as the agitated little tyrant stormed up the stairs and into the restaurant's private offices, all the while muttering some non-audible caustic remarks.

"Boy that was some kind of talking that you had with Senor Johnnie," a heavy built male proclaimed with a hearty Mexican accent. "My name is Hector Rodriguez and I am the head cook here for the past eight years. What is your name, Senor?" the cook inquired with a genuine tone.

"Hello there, I am very pleased to meet you, Hector," Wayne replied as he pondered Johnnie's rude 'Meet & Greet' session.

"Come along, son, I will help you learn the ways around here, that Senor Johnnie is a lot like a barking junk yard dog, all growl and teeth, but not much else! Before you start work here, you have to silence your cell phone for the entire work day, Senor Johnny forbids the annoying use and interruptions from these cell phones," Hector laughingly proclaimed as he took his young apprentice by the arm and started him on a work detail. "At first you start by helping unload the trucks and storing the food supplies, next you'll set-up and help close the restaurant, then in a day or two, I start you on the grill, so what's your name, Senor?" Hector explained and enquired in a cheerful tone.

"Please excuse my poor manners this morning, my name is Wayne, Wayne Hamilton and it's a pleasure to meet you, Hector. Okay, let's get started then!" Wayne exclaimed as he presented and extended hand in friendship to Hector.

He brashly threw off his jacket into the corner, rolled up his sleeves and proceeded with the work at hand. Throughout the morning hours, Wayne worked like a stevedore; his muscles ached from the toil and not having exercised certain of his muscle groups in the past several weeks. He now appreciated why the miners, farmers, and deck hands never needed to have to worry about staying in shape – their hard, manual labour ensured the development of strong muscles and also that any excess fat was worked off from their bodies. Throughout the daily grind, Wayne hoped to spot the pretty waitress named Joyce, who he had met the previous day, but she did not show up for either the breakfast or lunch shifts. After busing a few tables, Wayne thought that he would make an informal inquiry about this mysterious waitress.

"Hey, Hector, have you seen the waitress Joyce today, I sort of know her," Wayne inquired, hoping to show some degree of discretion.

"Why no Wayne, I think that she called in sick again, it's her little girl, she has been sick lately and Joyce stays home to look after her. Senor Johnnie hates when she does this, he docks her pay and yells at her all the time…. that man has no idea how to treat people, especially those with family issues," Hector explained while shaking his head with despaired resignation.

Wayne was disappointed, but this feeling was soon replaced by more manual labour, to include preparing the grill surfaces and pre-heating the ovens. Next, he was dicing-up vegetables for the day's meals. The restaurant toil never stopped and soon Wayne had done all of the manual chores that were demanded of him and he longed to start work on the grill, which would probably be the very next day according to Hector.

The hours clicked away without notice, before he knew it, his first day was finished. Being tired and frustrated, he wondered if taking this job was such a smart thing to do. Oh well, he always had the option of quitting, but right now he didn't want to give any sort of satisfaction to some greasy-haired, overbearing idiot. After a difficult 14-hour day, two greasy hamburgers, and countless cups of coffee, it was finally time to

get off of work. He pondered his ironic work circumstances and his self
-imposed plight. 'Boy if only Katherine could see me now – working as
a hash-swinging, short-order cook working in a mid-west greasy spoon
restaurant and all of this at minimum wage to boot,' he humorously
thought. In this reality, neither Katherine's world nor that of the average
Joe or Jane would ever intersect.

★ ★ ★ ★ ★ ★ ★ ★ ★ ★ ★ ★ ★ ★ ★ ★ ★ ★

"Hey Kate, how's my favourite investment banker doing?" Wayne chided
cheerfully, as he propped his feet up on the motel's ottoman, while he
nipped on a short sip of scotch on the rocks.

"Brad, darling, how are you doing? Where are you at?" Katherine
queried in rapid succession and remembering not to inquire about his
possible return.

"I'm great, Kate; I'm still in the middle of flat, dry, hot Kansas. The
liquor laws here are something out of the Prohibition Era, you can't get
a drink around here when you want one and finding a bar is practically
impossible; they think that by regulating alcohol that they get people to
drink less," he responded in an almost spiteful tone.

"How much longer will you be in frigging Lawrence?" Kate
directly inquired.

"I'm not quite sure, that darn motorcycle part will still take another
couple of days or so, besides, I'm in no great hurry to leave just now,
it's may be a dull town, but the people here are nice and polite," Wayne
responded in a casual tone.

"Well at least you're off that dangerous motorcycle for a while
anyway, so let's be thankful for that!" Katherine retorted back in
personal delight and relief.

Katherine decided to chide Wayne about his prolonged absence from
the firm. "Dad and Mom are fine, and the business is doing fantastic too,
although I could use some assistance around here, I need you back here,
Brad!" Katherine softly sobbed into her phone receiver.

He felt guilty and compelled to console Katherine's feelings. "I'll
be home shortly, Kate; it's only been several weeks since I departed
Boston and I want to come back to you without any regrets or unfinished
business. When I come back to you, I want it to be for keeps with no
looking back." These weren't the words that Katherine wanted to hear,
but at least Brad's answer gave some simmer of light at the end of this

dark tunnel. " I love you, Kate, and you keep safe now, alright?" he implored Katherine.

"You got yourself a deal, Brad, just keep yourself safe, my dear. Goodnight, darling!" Katherine purred softly as she bid farewell to Brad.

The phone call was short and sweet, yet it fulfilled his fidelity obligation to Kate. He took another sip of scotch and he relished its malt flavour and warm mellow feeling. 'Boy, manual labour was a lot harder than I had expected, I really got to hand it to Mr and Ms America in doing this grind every day – thank God it's not me!' he smugly concluded.

He decided to retire early, as tomorrow was promising to be another ball-busting day. At least, Johnnie did not get the better of him and his immediate supervisor, Hector, was a great guy. From discussions during their coffee break, Wayne discovered that Hector was a naturalized US citizen, who had jumped a border fence some twenty-five years earlier. When he met his wife, also an illegal immigrant, he decided that it was time for him to learn the language and make himself a legal US citizen. After many years of hard work and study, both he and his wife became bona fide US citizens, and this was going to make their new life in America easier and legitimate, as well as for the lives of their four children.

The next morning came without any usual fanfare and par normal, as Wayne put on his old outfit and made his way to the diner. The second day on the job brought the expected and burdensome duty of unloading food supplies, yet it also offered some glimmer of excitement, as Hector was going to let Wayne work the grill and perhaps do some short order breakfast cooking.

"Good morning, Hector, how are you doing today?" Wayne rejoiced with a smile and a pat on Hector's back. Hector was already supervising the movement of the first delivery vans, he was sipping a huge mug of hot black coffee. He liked Wayne and thought him to be a hard-working young man.

"You worked good and very hard yesterday, how do you like working here?" Hector inquired while offering Wayne a sip of his coffee.

"Ah, no thanks, Hector, but maybe later I'll get a cup. Yes, sir, this is hard work, but I'm not sure that I could do it all my life or when I get to be your age," Wayne confessed in an embarrassed tone.

Hector took the compliment all in his stride. "When it's all you got in life, you have to do what you have to do, that's all there is to it."

Wayne thought again about his fortunate fate in this life and Hector's comments counselled his soul.

After only 45 minutes, the cumbersome cartons of produce were finally unloaded, and the contents stored away. The two men shook hands on a job well done; they had both built up a healthy appetite. "Let me buy you a cup of coffee, your first of the morning Wayne," Hector proclaimed with gusto. Just as both men turned to enter the kitchen area, a dark figure appeared from the alleyway. The clothing betrayed a feminine figure, as the figure approached the loading dock lights, a face appeared. It was Joyce the waitress, looking pale and tired once again.

"Hello Miss Joyce, how are you doing this morning?" Wayne inquired cheerfully. She managed only the barest of acknowledgement and a faint forced smile before heading quickly into the kitchen changing area. "Don't worry about that, Wayne, she must have had another sleepless night with her daughter," Hector whispered, as he noted the obvious interest that Wayne had in the young waitress. Wayne decided to take Hector up on his offer of that cup of coffee. The two men walked slowly into the kitchen area and poured themselves generous cups of invigorating black coffee.

Hector patiently instructed the fundamentals of starting up the gas fired grills and the two industrial sized ovens. Wayne was a fast learner and he picked up all the nuances of the kitchen appliances. He thought back cheerfully to his childhood and the times that he spent in Greystone's massive kitchen, ignorant to its inner workings and only aware of the delicious wonders that Carla and other cooks had brought forth magically from its depths. As opposed to the buttery aromas of the Greystone mansion, the Calico Diner's grills gave off the distinct odour of metal being heated with perhaps a slight residue of old grease or cooking oils. The heat from the pre-heated appliances quickly encompassed the room. It was going to be a long, hot day in this kitchen. Having gotten the major kitchen appliances on-line, Wayne and Hector proceeded to change into their kitchen white uniforms, which consisted of white overalls, aprons, and head covers. The other members of the kitchen crew were incrementally checking into the kitchen, where the clatter of their time cards was being recorded into the ancient employee punch card machine.

A short lull ensued between the kitchen set-up time and the opening of the restaurant; Wayne took this opportunity to take a quick break. He poured his second cup of coffee, as he grabbed a disposable paper hair cover, which was required by all kitchen and food preparation staff. Dressed in a long white apron and white paper head cover, Wayne appeared as an over-aged kid working at an after-school job at a fast-food joint. Just then Joyce walked back into the kitchen, also in search of a caffeine fix. While Wayne was checking the large surface flat grill's heat level, Joyce took a determined path to the huge coffee brewing urn. She turned the tap and filled her ceramic cup with simmering coffee. As she turned, she stared at the young man at the grill – 'he looked new, yet somehow familiar', she thought. Satisfied with the grill temperature, Wayne turned slowly around, his coffee cup raised up to his lips. His eyes instantly met those of Joyce and she fully recognized this young man.

"You stupid jerk! What the hell are you doing here? You must be crazy or foolish – maybe both!" Joyce muttered loudly.

Wayne was shocked, he'd expected something more civil. "Well good morning to you too, Joyce," Wayne exclaimed in a calm tone.

She took her cup of coffee and walked within two feet of Wayne, she looked at him from head to toe and a grin appeared on her face. "Boy, when you make up your mind to do something, you really carry through, don't you buster... I bet you don't make it through day one at this dump!" Joyce purred as she slowly sipped her coffee.

It was now Wayne's turn to be sardonic. "Well, Joyce it's actually my second day here and I'm working under Hector here in the kitchen today...and by the way, the name is Wayne."

He extended his hand forward in friendship to Joyce, she burst into a smile and shook Wayne's hand firmly. "It's nice to meet you again, Wayne, and welcome to Hell's Kitchen, don't say that I didn't warn you about this joint!" Joyce was glad to see a new friendly face at the Calico Diner, especially a young handsome guy like Wayne.

"So how long are you here for, Wayne?" Joyce inquired, as she sipped her coffee.

"I'm here until my BMW gets a badly needed part, a few days, a few weeks – I really don't care, I am not on a fixed schedule, like I said, I'm bumming the summer away," Wayne nonchalantly replied as he finished off his second cup of coffee.

In an all too short of a period of time, the coffee was finished, and Hector looked at his watch. "Okay everyone, let's get ready for business, the doors open in 20 minutes," Hector shouted in a loud but friendly voice. "Wayne, you stay here at the grill beside me, we'll work the orders together for a while, then I'll let you do the orders by yourself. So, you say that you know how to cook, huh?" Hector inquired of Wayne in a doubtful, yet fatherly manner.

"Terrific, Hector – anything you say, boss and yes, I had some experience cooking; besides what I don't know, you'll teach me right, Hector?" Wayne replied with a devilish grin.

Hector smiled back and explained the routine of the kitchen process. He explained how the waitresses placed the customer's abbreviated orders on a stainless-steel carousel that was placed immediately atop the kitchen counter, which separated the kitchen from the front sitting counter area where Wayne had first eaten and saw Joyce. It all seemed pretty simple. "Scrambled – side bacon," shouted a waitress, as she placed an order chit on the carousel; "French toast – sausage," shouted another waitress; "three #4 breakfast specials," still yet another yelled. Soon the order carousel was full of orders twirling from the breeze produced by the powerful kitchen fan.

"Wayne, get me 10 lbs of bacon, 5 lbs of sausage and some corned beef hash from the fridge and throw it on the grill! Go, fast boy!" Hector shouted as heat, fumes, and grease filled the air. Wayne grabbed the meats and started to throw these onto the grill for frying, while Hector tended a huge serving of scrambled eggs onto the grill. The hectic pace continued unabated throughout the morning, then lunch came and the only things that changed were the grill items – hot dogs, burgers, greasy French fries, grilled sandwiches the list went on and on. Finally, at about 2:30 PM the lunch rush ended, and things settled down. Now the kitchen crew and the waitresses got to eat their food – not that any of them were very hungry after the hectic day thus far.

After nearly eight hours of standing on his feet in front of a greasy 400-degree Fahrenheit cooking grill, Wayne was glad to finally get his belated lunch break. "Hey Wayne, go take your lunch break, be back in 45 minutes to relieve me," Hector shouted over the clatter of dishes that the bus boys were loading into the industrial sized dish washing machines."

"Okay, boss," Wayne shouted with a smile, as he wiped his brow and threw off his white kitchen overalls. He chose a platter of country fried steak, home fries, and sweet peas. Taking his fare and walking into the now mostly empty dining area, he spotted a small corner where Joyce was seated with her friend Mary Ellen. With a wide smile, he made a bee line to their table.

"Greetings, ladies, do you mind if this humble 'grill monkey' takes his lunch with you very lovely ladies?" he announced politely with a charming Boston accent. Joyce seemed unimpressed, but Mary Ellen was cheerful and happy of the offer of the newest of Calico's employees.

"Sure, handsome, you just make yourself comfy and sit on down here and keep us gals' company, I am Mary Ellen, and this is Joyce and I believe that your name is Wayne, is that correct, handsome?" Mary Ellen exclaimed, as Wayne took a seat across from Joyce.

"Thank you, Mary Ellen and yes, my name is Wayne and I already know Joyce from a previous encounter. Yikes, my feet are killing me, I usually spend my days sitting behind a desk or operating my PC, this kitchen work takes the wind out of a man," Wayne exclaimed.

Joyce had just finished taking a sip of her ice tea, and then she shot Wayne a zinger. "Yeah sure, you ought to try doing this work year after year and then you'd see how hard the work really is on a person! None of us here have our summers off, nor do we wear expensive Rolex watches." The deliberate insult created a vulgar silence.

Mary Ellen was clearly embarrassed by her friend's rude, frustrating remark, she saw Wayne's discomfort by it, so she quickly changed the subject. "Okay, Wayne, what brings you out to Kansas and how long are you here for?"

"Well, my BMW cycle broke and I am here until it is repaired and I am travelling across the USA this summer from Boston," he replied smartly as he consciously fiddled with his custom Rolex watch, attempting to turn it around in order to somehow diminish its richly vulgar appearance. He looked intensely into Joyce's eyes. She meekly turned away, not wanting to confront him. Wayne had never before been made to feel guilty about his wealth and he disliked the social indictment of his birth and success.

"I underestimated the work at the Calico was harder than I had expected when I challenged Johnnie for this short-order job!" Wayne exclaimed as the two ladies frowned at one another at this interloper's seemingly casual remark about his expensive motorcycle and idyllic amount of leisure time. Undeterred by their feminine silence, Wayne continued to chat up the waitresses, especially Joyce.

"If I am not being too bold to ask, but what does a pretty lady like you do for excitement on her time-off?" Wayne quibbled, hoping that his question might lead to a better relationship with Joyce or maybe even a possible date.

Joyce paused for a brief second, as she finished swallowing a bite of hamburger, before answering him back. "For those of us who work on our feet all day and having children to raise, usually stay at home and dutifully mind our responsibilities Wayne, we don't have much time for anything else or the money to do it."

Knowing that the remark was directed at his advances, Wayne naturally felt dejected, as he tried to shrug off the remark by simply trying to eat his country fried steak in silence, even though his appetite had vanished with the insults.

"Well, that's it for me, I'm done with this same old greasy food, time for me to make a phone call," Joyce proclaimed as she slowly got up from the corner table. She sensed Wayne's dejection that was caused by her rude remark, so she decided to throw him a graceful bone.

"Hey, Wayne – this is a great burger that you prepared…I think you have real career potential as a grill jerk!" Joyce remarked with a quick one-eyed wink and a scant smile. He was dumbfounded by Joyce's initial rejection, then her quite unexpected personal compliment; he couldn't quite figure this lady out, she was both fire and ice.

"She's a great gal, she just has a lot on her mind now and the last thing that she thinks she needs is another man passing through her life," Mary Ellen casually remarked, as she noticed Wayne's interest in her girlfriend.

"Well, she's a pretty lady that's for sure, I just wanted to chat her up a bit, that's all," Wayne replied.

Mary Ellen gently smiled and put her hand gently on Wayne's forearm. "She's young and pretty, but in this job, and with all of her personal problems, these charms won't last very long. Just give it some time, she'll come around to you," Mary Ellen remarked as she got up and left the table. He felt somewhat consoled by Mary Ellen's remarks.

"How about relieving me in the kitchen, young buddy?" Hector snapped, as he strolled into the corner of the Calico Diner, carrying a full tray consisting of Yankee pot roast, carrots and mashed potatoes with gravy. Wayne looked up and smiled smartly. "Sure, boss, sit right on down and take a break, I'll be happy to cover the kitchen, this is a slow period anyway," Wayne remarked as he patted Hector on the shoulder and made his way to the kitchen.

He passed Joyce at the counter area. "Wait a minute, Wayne, I didn't mean to shut you out back there, I know you're a nice guy, but you are just passing through and I really don't want any complications in my life right now, no hard feelings, right?" Joyce announced in a definitive and almost apologetic tone.

Wayne recalled his conversation with Mary Ellen and he appreciated the frankness of Joyce's explanation, he really couldn't blame a single working mom for keeping her distance from a temporary passer-by.

"No worries, Joyce, I understand your situation, I'm a stranger here, but perhaps we can be friends for the time that I'm here...by the way, it's payday tomorrow night and I was wondering if you'd like to hit the movies and dinner afterwards?" Wayne inquired.

Joyce hesitated for along moment and before she had an opportunity to reject his offer, Wayne decided to sweeten the proposition, "I'd be pleased to take both you and your daughter out tomorrow night...how about it?" With his seductive smile, he awaited Joyce's reply.

She was initially going to reject his offer, but 'any guy who was willing to take both herself and her daughter on a date, couldn't be that big of a jerk,' she modestly concluded.

"Okay, but the film must be family-oriented, and it will have to be an early night, my daughter Heather has school the next day," Joyce replied with some reluctance in her voice. Wayne was thrilled by Joyce's acceptance; however, he noted one additional caveat to the date.

"Joyce I'm afraid that you'll have to drive, as my only means of transportation is in the repair shop and besides, it could only accommodate one passenger. I have a loaner BMW, but it cannot safely accommodate three people."

"Lucky me! Okay, no problem, big spender, let's meet at 7:00 PM tomorrow night and I'll pick you up at your hotel, just give me the address and I'll be waiting in the parking lot for you," Joyce smiled back. He provided Joyce his hotel location, which she was happy to learn was just a few blocks down from the Calico Diner. Embarrassingly, he suddenly felt like a high school kid on his first date, it had been a few years since he had been with a woman besides Katherine and this date seemed almost novel to him. Joyce moved off to the dining room floor as new customers entered the diner and Wayne marched off to the bowels of the cooking grill; it was going to be another long day for both of them.

After several more hours of cooking dozens of meals over a hot and greasy grill, another day of unskilled labour was finished! His muscles ached from the long hours of standing on his feet, a routine for which his body was not accustomed. Johnnie Porter worked his staff over and above the normal eight-hour day and the overtime that was paid as compensation, did not equal to the hours of leisure time lost. Wayne was determined to stick out the work routine and not give this ogre any satisfaction in seeing him quit or complain; besides everyone else was working hard and not complaining, so neither would Wayne Hamilton. A newfound appreciation was made for all of those who made their living by standing on their feet for long hours throughout the day; he had no idea until now the luxury that sitting on one's ass afforded an office worker like himself. Anyway, the work day was finally finished, and he was eager to retire to the humble comforts of the Willow Inn.

Upon entering his room, he quickly stripped off his clothing, brushed his teeth, and set his alarm for the morning wake-up. He was too bushed to even have a drink of scotch or to call his fiancée Katherine. He stripped naked and immediately ploughed into the warm, sinfully inviting and snuggly-soft bed. Immediately he was fast asleep, his body earned and yearned, a full night of badly needed rest.

* * * * * * * * * * * * * * * * *

All too quickly, the new morning dawn beckoned as the alarm clock rudely rattled him to awaken. It seemed as if he had never gone to sleep. Wayne had slowly grown to despise this routine, but he was determined to prove to himself that he possessed the right stuff of a working man just like that of millions of other diligent Americans. Besides there were two good things happening today, he was getting paid for the past several days of labour and he was going out with Joyce on a date, even if he was to be chaperoned by Joyce's little daughter. A fringe benefit was the satisfaction of seeing that low-class Johnnie fork-over his under-the-counter wages. He showered and dressed quickly, he wanted to remain the model employee at the Calico Diner, thus making Johnnie even more jealous of his work ethic. Being embarrassed by a mere motorcycle bum was sweet revenge! Wayne chuckled to himself of how much Johnnie would resent him if he had known that Wayne originated from one of the wealthiest families in America. This fact would remain Wayne's little secret.

This day at the Calico started like any other day of the past week. The bulk items were fastidiously unloaded in the dark of the morning, the grill was fired-up, coffee urns were percolating, other supplies were stored, and the restaurant was made ready for the general public. Hector and Wayne shared their ritual early morning coffee and they were joined an hour later by Mary Ellen. They chatted about the past week's events and their plans for the upcoming weekend as well. Joyce was absent from these discussions, as she was on a schedule that allowed her to drop-off her daughter at school and make up the hours on the back-side of her shift. The cool air of the Calico central air-conditioning system was a welcome relief against the scorching growing heat and humidity of this early Kansas summer morning.

"So, Wayne, I understand that you are taking Joyce and Heather out tonight, what are your plans?" Mary Ellen asked directly, as she sipped on a cup of coffee in the back of the Calico serving counter.

"Oh, I think that Joyce spotted some Disney feature at the theatre on Main Street and then afterwards I thought that we would get a bite to eat somewhere," Wayne eagerly replied.

"Just don't bring that nice lady and little girl back here to eat at the Calico, I know the cooks that work there!" Hector humorously interjected. They all laughed at Hector's comments about the Calico, they had all eaten their fill of food here and none of them was overly fond of the fare anymore.

"Heck no, Hector, I'll find someplace else to dine tonight," Wayne reassured his newfound friends. "In all seriousness, Wayne, you be nice to Joyce, she likes you and you should not start something that you cannot finish, she has had one too many men in her life break her heart and she does not need any more hurting, do you understand me buster?" Mary Ellen warned in a very protective and motherly tone.

Wayne was silent for a second before he responded to Mary Ellen. He respected Mary Ellen and Joyce.

"Rest assured, Mary Ellen, that I will never hurt or mislead Joyce, she's a real friend to me and I only want the best for her. I'll be on my best mannered behaviour, you have my word on that!" Wayne replied. Mary Ellen trusted Wayne and she knew that he meant what he said to her. The three refilled their cups and toasted one another to the hard day's work that lay ahead of them.

As Wayne began his pre-emptive breakfast preparation of cooking up several pounds of bacon, sausage, and corned beef hash, he had the uncomfortable feeling of someone staring at him. He looked up from the grill and looked around. About six feet behind him was Johnnie Porter looking at him with a contemptuous stare. Johnnie walked up to the right side of Wayne. The smell of the stale bourbon from the previous night was evident on Johnnie's breath.

"How is Mr Easy Rider getting along these days? I noticed that the hard work around here hasn't gotten you to quit yet, buddy! How much longer are you going to be working here, College Boy?" Johnnie inquired in a rather impulsive and challenging voice.

Unresponsive to rude and unwelcome verbal indictment, Wayne ignored Johnny and continued to look onto the grill and flipped the hash, bacon and sausages that were precariously close to the danger stage of burning.

"Hey, fella, I'm fucking talking to you! You fucking stop whatever you're doing when I'm talking to you!" Johnnie shouted in a tone that was heard throughout the kitchen. Wayne continued to work the grill and rotated the cooked breakfast meats onto a large empty stainless-steel vat that was heated by infra-red warming lamps. Once the meats had been dutifully stored under the heating receptacles, Wayne turned slowly to Johnnie and took off his paper head gear. The entire kitchen staff area became silent.

"Now you listen to me, Mister Porter, I work for you in this hot, greasy, miserable kitchen for less than minimum wage and I work an honest day's wage, I also ensure that my work is professional and that it is performed efficiently, on-time, and with minimal food wastage – now if you want to speak with me about my work performance, you do so when I am not up to my ass in frying eggs, sausage, burgers and anything else that is cooking on the grill. This professionalism will better serve you, me, the kitchen staff, and the paying customers. Now, what the hell is so damn important that you have to burst in here and scream like you were hawking in an outdoor vegetable market?" Wayne exclaimed in a loud and articulate voice that resounded throughout the Calico kitchen.

There was an unnatural pause among the entire kitchen staff, as no one before had had the audacity to publicly challenge the boisterous ravings of Johnnie Porter. The kitchen staff merely toyed at their menial tasks, hoping to catch every aspect of this hostile encounter and the ushering of its ultimate conclusion. Even Johnnie himself was astonished by the direct logical challenge from this temporary kitchen hire. Wayne framed himself in an upright stance and he was not backing down from this little dictator's challenge. Johnnie knew that he was both physically and intellectually inferior to Wayne, so he decided it was best to diffuse the situation with light humour.

"Okay, Pal, no worries here! There ain't nothing to get excited about here, buddy! I just wanted to see how you were getting along that's all! There's no need to get defensive or hostile around here, we're all like frigging family!" Johnnie irreverently sparked in a half-hearted attempt to laugh off the incident. He knew he had lost yet another confrontation with this biker bum and he was resolved that it was to be his last humiliation too! The kitchen staff were meekly silent and tried to hide their eyes from Johnnie's menacing glare and his rude attempt to intimidate Wayne. Johnnie became infuriated at his kitchen staff's silent demeanour, as his bad temper and shallow ego once again got the best of him.

"Hey, everybody, let's get the fuck back to work around here! If you want your pay cheques today, let's get busy!" Johnnie shouted in a lame attempt to deflect any embarrassing attention away from himself and to distance himself from his confrontation with Wayne. He quickly departed up to his upstairs office, muttering profanities all along the way. Wayne pitied everyone who had to work for such a tyrant, especially Joyce.

Upon Johnnie's cowardly retreat, everyone in the kitchen staff breathed a sigh of relief, as they each patted Wayne on the shoulder or in the case of some of the ladies, patted him playfully on the ass. The tributes continued throughout the day and Wayne was proud of himself for standing up to Johnnie the bully, then again, but he slowly came to realize that he had little to lose in this confrontation, he was, after all, only a temporary worker and he was wealthy. "How brave would I have been if there had been true personal stakes on the line in my confrontation with Johnnie?" Wayne soberly mused.

"Well, hello hero, how is the David of the Calico Diner this wonderful day! I just heard that you slew a little giant this morning?" Joyce pouted to Wayne as he took a short break away from the grill in an empty corner of the kitchen. By now Wayne was kind of embarrassed by the whole affair and he preferred to put it all behind him.

"Ah, it was nothing serious, Johnnie and I had a lover's spat, that's about the size of it, it's all over and forgotten by now!" Wayne replied as he sipped a cup of hot coffee.

"Yeah well, nothing is ever over and forgotten as far as Johnnie is concerned, he's a small man with a short temper and a long memory," Joyce scoffed in a condescending tone.

Wayne merely frowned at Joyce's remark and then softly remarked, "Let's forget about Johnnie and let's talk about tonight, okay?"

Joyce admired the independence of Wayne's defiance and she secretly wished that she possessed such an attitude and independent resources to do the same thing. "Yeah, sure, Wayne, well most of us here at the Calico are beholden to Johnnie and we'll be working under his thumb a long time after you are gone and forgotten around here!" Joyce replied in a rather blunt, but true statement.

Wayne knew the naked truth when he heard it. Joyce was right; it was easy to be brave when you had nothing at stake. It was now Wayne's turn to deflect the conversation. "Being a stranger in town, I have to ask you as to where do you want to dine this evening, Joyce?" he inquired with playful inquiry.

Joyce was not used to her dates asking her for her opinion, instead she was used to being taken out on a predetermined and usually cheap night, topped off with her date trying to get into her blouse and panties. Wayne seemed different and she hoped that it would be so this evening. "Well after the movies, let's go to a nice quiet Italian restaurant that Heather and I have been dying to try, please?" Joyce announced hopefully.

Wayne smiled and simply added, "That sounds great to me too!" Before he had even realized it, his shift had ended and it was 5:30 PM. The work day had raced by and it was quitting time for Wayne. He eagerly awaited his pay from that tyrant Johnnie.

Throughout the day, the 'regular employees' were handed their pay cheque envelopes by Mrs Hendel, the Calico Diner secretary and bookkeeper. The grey-haired lady handed each employee their pay envelopes throughout the early afternoon hours. Wayne had not received any pay envelope, this he wisely guessed was because he was being paid in cash and under the table to boot. He was approached by Mrs Hendel and told to report to Mr Porter before he left for the day. That was fine by Wayne, as his previous encounter with Johnnie had not endeared him any closer to the boss man. Wayne walked sprightly up to Mrs Hendel's office on the second floor and he spotted the kind faced old lady sitting by her computer terminal. She gazed up and smiled at him.

"Well, hello there, your name is Mr Hamilton, correct?" she inquired softly.

"Why yes ma'am, I am here to see Mister Porter for my pay," Wayne replied.

"Why yes, of course, Mister Porter is expecting you. Please tap on the door, then enter his office," Mrs Hendel replied in a motherly tone.

Wayne proceeded to knock forcefully on Johnnie Porter's office door. He heard a grumpy and gravel-throated voice that seemed to mutter the words 'come in' at which time, Wayne had entered the bastion of power at the Calico Diner. The office was dark and grim, as befitted the character of its owner. There were papers and kitchen supply catalogues scattered atop the desk and even upon the sitting chair and sofa. There was so much clutter in the small dark abode, that it could have hidden a small army of rats or mice. A dim, old fashioned banker's desk lamp revealed the recessed figure of a man smoking a stinky cheap cigar. He was hunched over a cluttered desk and reviewing a sordid stack of papers. He glanced up at Wayne and howled forth an order much like a shipyard stevedore.

"Come on in here, Hamilton… Mister Easy Rider of the Calico Diner," a male voice bitterly echoed out. Wayne approached the desk slowly and stood there with some awkwardness, there being no empty seat available. Johnnie puffed almost nervously on his half-consumed cigar. "Boy, that was some discussion that we had down there in the kitchen today, Hamilton…you made me look bad and I don't like that sort of thing in my establishment, but you have guts – not many people have that today!" Johnnie proclaimed in a voice filled with sarcasm and modest praise.

"Let's just forget about today's events, it's history and forgotten as far as I am concerned," Wayne replied dryly. Johnnie did not care to pursue this line of discussion any further and he deftly moved on to other business.

"So, Pal, I guess you are here for your 'pay-out', right Mr Big Shot?" Johnnie probed wryly. Wayne merely nodded his head in silent affirmation to the impudent inquiry.

"Remember that you agreed to cash-only, no benefits, and minimum wages – right?" Johnnie inquired. Again, Wayne nodded in silent agreement. "Well, it ain't much money you know, only several days' worth of work, not enough to pay even your hotel room or your date with Joyce tonight," Johnnie quibbled with a wistful, mocking tone.

Wayne was taken aback by Johnnie's condescending monologue and especially his interference in his personal relations with Joyce. "I can get by on the money that I have and who I date is of my own affair, now can I have my pay, Johnnie?" Wayne inquired in an indignant tone. Johnnie pulled open his top desk drawer and withdrew a standard sealed white bond envelope. Not wishing to extend any degree of courtesy to Wayne, Johnnie sat in mighty repose behind his desk, as he carelessly tossed a small opaque envelope across the desktop.

"Here's your just rewards, Hamilton," Johnnie exclaimed in an emotionless dry voice. Wayne took the sealed envelope and thrust it into the breast pocket of his jacket, as he turned and proceeded out of Johnnie's dark, dingy office. "Not gonna count it, huh? You are a trusting type guy! Well, you go ahead and have yourself a nice little date with Joyce...oh by the way, that cold bitch don't put out, buddy!" Johnnie proclaimed with a hideous vulgar laugh.

Wayne turned around and gave Johnnie a dirty look of contempt and for a quick moment he was tempted to slug that piece of shit who called himself a man, yet he thought better of the situation and he turned about. Johnnie was the stereotype bad boss who gave all men a bad image. Before leaving Johnnie's office, Wayne threw up his right hand, blew a loud whistle, and raised his third finger and threw Johnnie 'the bird'. "That's for you Johnnie, have a nice night yourself!" Wayne boldly cheered and laughed loudly as he exited Johnnie's office.

Johnnie clearly saw Wayne's finger silhouette and he also heard his proclamation too, at which time Johnnie's laughter quickly died down into utter silence. "That fucking smart ass, eastern motorcycle riding punk!" Johnnie grumbled to himself. "Well, you just enjoy your date with Joyce, Johnnie Porter will be the one who laughs last around here, Pal," he growled in a low voice to himself. Johnnie opened a drawer in his desk and withdrew a bottle of Jack Daniels sour mash whiskey and a tumbler whiskey glass. He poured himself a half-glass of whisky straight-up, took a generous mouthful of whiskey. "Yes sir, I'll teach that yuppie bastard not to fuck with Johnnie Porter!" he sighed as he relaxed back into his huge leather chair and gulped another generous mouthful of the powerful intoxicant.

Wayne was now off work and Johnnie was out of his thoughts as well. He was headed back to his room to take a shower and to prepare for his date with Joyce and Heather. Ordinarily he would not have entertained the possibility of a mother and daughter date affair, as the chance for romance with the mom was almost certainly precluded by the drabbling attention to be afforded unto the child, but at this particular circumstance in his life, Wayne was just glad to be out of the diner and off doing something with a pretty lady to whom he was attracted.

He strutted eagerly into his hotel room and emptied his pockets of his belongings. He casually threw Johnnie's sealed pay envelope onto the room desk table, since this payday was only a lark, being a billionaire had obvious perks.

He quickly stripped down and took a leisurely shave and shower. As always, the warm waters re-energized his tired body and he was quickly refreshed. He exited the shower, dried himself off and dressed into all new under garments and a new shirt and pants. His hotel key, wallet, and a handkerchief were the only personal items that he needed. He patiently awaited the arrival of his dates.

Lackadaisically, he watched the local news until the appointed hour approached. Anxiously, he gazed at his custom Platinum Rolex wrist watch, it was 7:00 PM sharp. Several minutes passed before Wayne heard the murmur of a car horn blowing in short three burst intervals. "That must be them!" Wayne muttered in excited anticipation. He popped off the main bedroom lights, leaving lit only a dim corner 40-watt table lamp that served as a silent sentinel for his return. He closed and locked his room and proceeded down into the Willow Inn courtyard. He felt like a high school kid out on a first date.

There in the Willow Inn courtyard was an old white Jeep Wrangler. The vehicle had some external dings and it was an understatement to say that the vehicle had seen better days, with its white paint being faded to a dull lacklustre tone and the lower part of the body frame was matted with the telltale signs of light rust body corrosion. He knew that both the car and its owner had seen better days, both the owner and vehicle had struggled through tough times. He tried his best not to let his appraisal of the vehicle affect his feelings for his night out with Joyce. He put on a broad heart-felt smile as he walked toward the car. Joyce opened the door to greet him. She was neatly dressed in beige casual slacks, a white blouse and cordovan loafers. A cute girl of about eight years old, dressed in blue jeans and blue jumper top was seated quietly, but anxiously in the back seat. She was a seemingly delightful girl, who had long sandy blonde hair, large hazel eyes and a cute button smile.

"Good evening, Wayne, are you ready for a wild night out with two crazy Kansas ladies?" Joyce announced as she greeted Wayne with a polite handshake, to which Wayne reciprocated with a friendly hug and a warm smile. "There's someone special that I want you to meet," Joyce announced as she gestured to her young daughter. Without missing a beat, Wayne immediately dotted his attention from Joyce to the young girl seated in the back seat of the car. "Well, this must be the beautiful Heather, of whom I have heard so much about!" he exclaimed in genuine adulation. He extended his hand and greeted her as a miniature adult. Heather was positively taken aback by his mature and polite greeting, she instinctively realized the good nature of this man.

"Hello Miss Heather, my name is Wayne and it's my honour to take both of you fine ladies out for a date on the town," Wayne announced in an almost corny salutation.

"Gee, that's great, can we get some pizza later on?" Heather innocently inquired with childish enthusiasm.

Wayne and Joyce just smiled at one another in their adult surrender to the child's eager request. "Sure, honey that will be our treat," Joyce warmly announced as she and Wayne entered into the car.

"Where shall we start, Wayne?" Joyce announced with careless abandonment.

Wayne looked at Joyce then he turned around and eyed Heather. He knew the perfect evening out for everyone. "So how about a movie and then some dinner?" he announced with glee.

"Great, Mom – let's go see Harry Potter! Please Mom, please Mr Wayne?" Heather innocently pleaded.

The adults knew when they were licked. "Okay, sounds good to me… Joyce, do you know a local theatre nearby?" Wayne inquired.

"Yeah sure, I know a great little theatre where Heather and I always go to the movies!" Joyce announced with enthusiasm. In short order, they were off to the movies.

Wayne chatted up the pre-adolescent girl, hoping to make a positive impression on both mom and daughter. Along the short 20-minute journey to the theatre, Wayne learned that Heather liked 'Johnny Depp', 'Lady GaGa', hamburgers & French fries and 'modern music'. Both Wayne and Joyce were befuddled with the vast list of rock bands that Heather mentioned and which neither adult possessed the foggiest knowledge. Despite her tender age, Heather also demonstrated a degree of maturity, she had a keen appreciation for her future and she talked almost endlessly about becoming a physician when she grew older. Joyce tried not to discourage such dreams, but this would be a difficult journey for Heather to achieve.

"Finally, here we are, folks, and it looks like the lines will be short tonight. We'll have our pick of seats!" Joyce proclaimed in amazement. The three quickly exited the vehicle; Wayne strolled up to the ticket booth, where he purchased three tickets. A purchase of cokes and a tub of buttered popcorn completed the American movie night ritual. The three perched themselves in the middle of the theatre and soon the light dimmed and the movie began.

Heather sat enthralled as she gazed at the movie and munched popcorn in utter oblivion to her mom and Wayne's presence. The two adults sat quietly and detached from the surreal aspect of the movie and its child alluring plot. Halfway through the movie, Wayne took his left arm and reached out to touch Joyce's shoulder. She looked over and smiled encouragingly at Wayne's masculine attention being paid toward her; it had been many months since she had let a man get close to her and his warm masculine hand felt sensuous against her body. After a seemingly endless duration, the movie completed its run. Heather was raving about the movie's plot, but both Joyce and Wayne were less enthused. "Okay, so how'd you two like the movie? I thought it was great and I can't wait for the next one," Heather voiced in utter childish enthusiasm.

"Where are we going to eat, Mom? Can we go to the Italian restaurant?" Heather asked excitedly and with the innocence of a child.

"Well honey, if Mr Wayne is willing, I do know of a nice little Northern Italian restaurant that we can go to," Joyce replied as she spied a short smile of acknowledgement from Wayne. "Can I get pizza, Mom, can I please?" Heather pleaded incessantly.

"Sure, darling, just as long as you can eat what you order, I don't want you wasting any food, remember what I told you about that?" Joyce lectured Heather in a typical motherly tone.

"Sure thing, Mom and what I don't eat, we can take home and I can eat it for lunch," Heather announced in almost childlike insolence. Wayne was enchanted by the youthful innocence of his young date, as well as her practical thoughts about not wasting food.

"That settles the issue for me. I'm hungry too, ladies, I take it that you have a favourite Italian haunt?" Wayne jested exuberantly.

"Yes, we know just the place," Joyce replied, as she eye-winked Heather. In short order, the well-weathered Jeep had made its way to a sedate, but non-descript strip mall. Joyce stopped the car outside a storefront that was attired in the white, red and green colours of the Italian flag. 'Tastes of Venice' read the restaurant sign, their obvious dinner destination. The aroma of freshly baked bread, roasted garlic, and rich tomato sauce lightly fainted across the warm summer breeze and it smelled delicious. They all smiled instantly at each other and Wayne proceeded to open the door in gentlemanly fashion for Heather and Joyce. The aroma inside the restaurant was even more delectable and inviting. Romantic candles complemented the light salmon coloured wallpaper and replicas of Italian frescos completed the visual dining allure. The rich, soothing Italian atmospheric promised to seduce those of all ages.

"Ah Miss Joyce and the lovely Heather! What a pleasure to see you again after so long of an absence! I was thinking that you didn't like my cooking anymore!" proclaimed a very friendly dark haired and slender middle-aged man. He looked at Wayne, smiled and shook his hand. "Hello sir, my name is Angelio, I own this restaurant along with my wife Lucia." The restaurant owner's accent was of northern Italy, but from its inflection and pronunciation, Wayne had correctly surmised that the man had lived in America for at least the past 20 years or more.

"Hello, I am Wayne and I am taking these fine ladies out for a date tonight," Wayne proudly advertised.

"Ah Signore, you are a man doubly blessed by two such beautiful ladies," Angelio sighed with a smile. "Well then, I will place you at my most secluded and romantic table, this way, sir and ladies," Angelio declared as he led the party off to a small corner table that was adorned with two candles and a place setting for four. Angelio quickly took away the fourth setting and filled the three glasses with ice water. He also politely handed them three menus and indicated his return to take their orders in approximately ten minutes' time. All of their eyes quickly scanned the menu, everything on it was inviting.

"This is a great place, Joyce, it is very deceiving from the outside and it is actually quite charming, also it appears to be very well operated," Wayne announced in complimentary amazement.

"Yes, well, it's not all meat and potatoes out here in the mid-west, Wayne, you know that Kansas does have its charms!" Joyce announced with a witching smile and a devilish wink. Before Wayne had a chance to react to these feminine charms, a voice erupted the private moment.

"Ah, Miss Joyce, it is so good to see you and the lovely Heather tonight…and your new boyfriend?" sounded a polite, boisterous middle-aged man sporting a slim black-greyish moustache and receding hairline.

"Good evening, Roberto, it's good to see you again and this is my co-worker Wayne," Joyce announced with some satisfaction.

"Good evening, I'm Roberto your waiter, it's very good to meet you Wayne – is everyone ready to order or do you need more time?" Roberto inquired.

Everyone eyed one another in silent agreement, they were indeed both ready and hungry.

"Yes, Roberto, I think everyone is quite ready, so why don't we start with Heather" Wayne announced. The pre-adolescent's eyes beamed with delight, as she became the centre of attention.

"Roberto, I'll have minestrone soup, an appetizer of beef ravioli, and a medium pizza with sausage, extra sauce and extra crispy thin crust… oh and a large coke too!" the hungry young girl announced matter-of-factly as she smartly folded her menu and smartly handed it back to Roberto.

Joyce and Wayne smiled and laughed in delight at the voracious appetite of the young girl and her maturity. Roberto smiled at the child's healthy appetite and then he turned to Joyce and Wayne.

"Geez, everything looks so good," Joyce exclaimed as she traversed the menu, when suddenly her eyes affixed onto a house specialty. "I think I'll have the Osso Buco with roasted mushrooms in the white truffle wine sauce."

The entree sounded great to Wayne as well, as he wisely decided to defer to Joyce's selection. "I'll have the same as well, Roberto, and could you please bring some bread, extra virgin olive oil and a bottle of red wine," Wayne requested politely but definitively.

Joyce was beaming, as she and Heather enjoyed some tales that Wayne had experienced back in Boston. He fondly spoke of his youth and the fun which he had enjoyed with his siblings, especially their winter adventures building snow men, sledding, and ice skating in the frigid winters of Boston. They were all having a fabulous time, almost like those of a typical American family. Briefly, Wayne could comfortably picture himself as a family man.

"What are you smiling about, Joyce?" Wayne demanded in a playful tone. "Ah nothing Wayne, I was just thinking about something that was funny from my childhood," Joyce lied with an innocent reply. Secretly, Joyce silently admired the demeanour and refined manners of her date. Wayne was young, handsome, charming and very confident in himself. It was not so much a flashy display of power, but rather a subtle confidence and refinement in the way he used his words with certainty and authority. It was also nice to be out with an attractive and refined man for once, a divorced, single-mom did not exactly draw out the most eligible bachelors in town; those few dates which she did have were with men with as many problems and baggage as her own. Over time, she abandoned dating all together and instead devoted herself to her daughter and the dead-end job at the Calico Diner.

Appetizers consisting of artisan cheese and fruit were served first. The hearty soup course came second. Finally, their dinner entrée was served, and it was a feast. Last, but not least, came the huge dessert cart which paraded a rich variety of sinfully rich chocolate and crème-filled Italian desserts, of which all three of them heartedly consumed. Finally, a pair of rich Italian creamy cappuccinos coffee finished off the meal. Wayne motioned politely for the waiter. He opened his wallet and pulled out a platinum American Express Card, which he placed onto the bill tray. The waiter returned back with the final bill tally, which Wayne duly signed, along with a discrete, but generous $100 tip.

"Boy, that was a terrific dinner, Mr Wayne, I really loved the tiramisu dessert," Heather exclaimed wildly.

"Yeah, that was a great dinner, Wayne, a lot better than the fare from the Calico Diner, don't you think?" Joyce voiced in agreement with her daughter.

"Not at all, ladies, you both got me out of that boring, stuffy hotel room," Wayne echoed.

After a few minutes Heather was fast asleep in the back seat of the car. "Wayne, that really was a great dinner that you treated Heather and I to this evening, we'll remember it for a long time," Joyce confided.

"It was my pleasure, Joyce, to tell you the truth, it's been months since I had some good old-fashioned family fun myself," Wayne confessed as he thought back about the outings that he so fondly enjoyed with his own family. He thought again of how often he had taken his family and good times for granted. He vowed to correct such transgressions starting with this evening.

An eerie silence suddenly filled the car, as both Joyce and Wayne pondered the next topic of conversation. Joyce decided to make the next move. "Hey, why don't we have a night cap of some coffee back at my place?"

This was just the invitation that Wayne secretly desired, but was afraid to initiate. "That's fine with me, I could use another delicious cup of coffee," Wayne confessed with a smile.

A few minutes later, they pulled up to a small, darkly lit, well-weathered Cape Cod style house. "Okay, Wayne, we're here, home sweet home! I know, it's not much to look at, but it is mine and after the divorce, it's about all that my ex-husband left to me, along with all the house payments as well!" Joyce sadly exclaimed.

Wayne smiled approvingly at Joyce, then he turned around to see that Heather was still asleep.

"Hey, it looks like we have a sleeping beauty on our hands, Joyce, do you want me to carry her inside?" Wayne quietly inquired.

"Oh, yes please, that would be great if you can do that for me, I just hope that she's not too heavy for you." Joyce sighed.

Wayne gently lifted Heather from the back seat and carried her up to the front door, while Joyce fumbled with her keys, finally opening up the front door. She quickly switched on the lights and held the door open for Wayne.

"Please just put her in the back room and I'll get Heather ready for bed," Joyce instructed softly. Wayne laid Heather atop of the bed and let Joyce get her daughter undressed and tucked in for the night. Deftly, he withdrew from the bedroom and retreated into the confines of the living room.

He carefully viewed the modest living room, which contained aging, but well-maintained furniture. Liberally scattered among the tables and bookcase were pictures of Heather and Joyce in staged playful moments. One picture was taken when Heather was only a toddler who was accompanied by a man, whom Wayne correctly surmised was Heather's father. He was a handsome man with full dark hair and blue eyes. Family pictures were the unspoken history of a person's life.

"Oh, dear Lord, he sure was a great looker, now wasn't he, but unfortunately not a great dad, I hate to admit," Joyce announced as she saw Wayne staring at the photo.

He was startled by Joyce's sudden interdiction. "I'm sorry, I didn't mean to interject into your private life," he replied in a genuine embarrassed voice.

Joyce smiled and made her way slowly over to Wayne's side and took into her hand the picture that Wayne had been gazing and admiring. "We were too young, too passionate and too stubborn, but at least Heather was the one good thing to come from our marriage," Joyce snickered as she laid the picture back onto the table.

"Okay, enough of the past, how about a nightcap?" Joyce announced with an almost wistful tone.

"Of course, Joyce, let's drink to the future," Wayne replied as he pondered his recent wanderlust of the past several weeks.

"Is scotch okay with you?" Joyce inquired.

"Sure thing, make it a short one please, I have to get up early tomorrow, and so do you!" Wayne stated remorsefully.

Joyce poured the two drinks and brought these over to the living room couch area. She handed Wayne his drink and they both sat down onto the couch. "Here's to the future," Wayne toasted as he raised his glass slightly in the air. Joyce soon joined him, as her glass gently clicked with his.

"May I inquire, what are your future plans, Wayne? What do you really do for a living? Where are you headed?" she asked in rapid succession.

He settled back into the sofa and there was a pregnant moment of silence as his mind retrieved the memories of his dead family and fiancée. He took a long sip of the cheap blended scotch before tactfully answering.

"Here it goes, Joyce...my family suddenly died recently, I'm unmarried, and I am on a sabbatical from a mundane banking position back on the east coast; you might say that I'm taking a break from the rat race, and my future goal is to tool around on my BMW and see the USA before middle-age settles in on me! I know that it is a sinful indulgence, but I desperately needed a change," he sighed in a weary voice, as his eyes glazed off into the distance. Joyce knew that his sorrowful words spoke true.

She was moved by his genuine sincerity and felt sorry for him. She gently placed her hand on his shoulder and gave a gentle reassuring hug. Wayne gently clasped Joyce's hand in appreciation. "So, Joyce, what are your future plans?" he inquired genuinely, then thinking the question most foolish.

Suddenly throwing her head back in an act of emotional resignation and nervously running a hand through her hair, she bellowed forth a long sigh. "Yeah sure thing, now that's a good one, Wayne, You have to have a future, to have future plans! I'm just working hand-to-mouth, I don't have any dreams anymore, just a harsh reality of raising a young needy daughter as a single mother, so welcome to my shitty little, suck-it-up world." Wayne was most embarrassed by the arrogance of his question and Joyce noticed his unease.

"Oh, I'm sorry, I didn't mean to sound so bitter, I once had dreams of being a nurse, but I gave that up for my husband and when we got divorced, well that dream vanished. Now all my energies are directed toward my daughter, Heather," she confessed in a sombre, resigned tone as she took a mouthful of cheap scotch.

"Yeah, she's a great little girl that any man would be proud to call his daughter," Wayne announced as he gently stroked Joyce's hand.

She smiled gently at Wayne's sincerity. "Yes, she wants to be a doctor when she gets older and she's bright enough too, but getting her a good education is expensive. Life is an ironic thing, Wayne: I wanted to be a nurse and now Mommy's little girl dreams of being a doctor – there's a zero chance for either of these things happening, I just hope that Heather does not end up like her old lady," Joyce half-joked as she finished off her bitter scotch.

Only a brief second had passed before Wayne moved intimately close to Joyce, he softly brushed her hair and gave her a tender kiss, first on her forehead and then passionately on her mouth. She gently pushed him away if only to gleam the look in his eyes – she saw a mirror reflection of her own pale eyes that were filled with longing and tears. She gently took Wayne's hand and led him into the master bedroom. They were soon both partially undressed atop the master bed and each responded to the other's passions. Both Wayne and Joyce were possessed of youthful, lean bodies and each had been without sexual relations for many months. They each enjoyed each other's flesh, as their unbridled passion made them seem as two snakes intertwined in an animalistic mating ritual.

The night wore on like a slow ticking clock and time seemed to stand still for each of them, as the young lovers explored the most intimate aspects of each other's sexuality. Their sexual consummation was complete, they lay naked and exhausted in each other's arms, vulnerable and exposed to each other's most intimate, whispered secrets. There they lay motionless and naked for the next few hours with only the company of hushed giggles, moaning, whispers and the soft heartbeats of the other. They both enjoyed the roles of being lovers again after such a long hiatus and each felt themselves privileged to be alive for the first time in uncountable months. Yet time was their thief.

"Joyce, darling, I have to go!" he whispered softly into her ear. There was only the low soft moan of an inaudible feminine tone. The velvety soft and warm allure of Joyce's body was almost too tempting for a grown man to vacate, but he knew that it was going to be an early day too. He looked at his Rolex watch and noticed that it was 2:30 AM. Wayne gave Joyce a quick peck on her cheek, as he slowly untwined himself from her twisted arms and long slender legs. Even as he quietly dressed into his underwear and outer garments, Wayne was feeling a little guilty for acting impetuously and sleeping with a co-worker. This affair was neither love from the blue, nor was its unbridled passion; it was more one of desperation of the heart. He was pretty sure that Joyce felt the same way too. His motel was only about a mile from Joyce's modest little house, so he would have no trouble in walking back to the Willow Inn. He almost felt like a cheap, one-night stand character, but he had to leave.

Softly he walked over to where Joyce lay, and he softly kissed her on the lips. "Joyce, I'll see you tomorrow, I love you and thank you so very much," he whispered gently in her ear. She only moaned mildly with a soft smile, as Wayne looked back to the beautiful naked woman lying on the bed. He smiled too, as he realized that this beautiful lady had restored a degree of humanity that he thought was lost in his soul. He gently closed the front door and departed for the Willow Inn.

Returning to his motel room, he quickly threw off his jacket onto the corner desk chair. Suddenly, for some unknown reason, his left eye caught a glimpse of the red light blinking on the desk telephone. Tired and exhausted the last thing that Wayne wanted to do was to answer this hotel phone. It was most probably a trivial message from the hotel front desk anyway, yet discretion was an infallible trait in Wayne's character. He decided that it was better to answer that damn phone than it was to let it blink unceasingly throughout the night. He dialled in the answering code and waited impatiently for the message to be read aloud.

"Hello Mr Hamilton, this is Mike from the Taylor Brothers BMW Motorcycle dealership. I have some good news for you, the part is in for your BMW and I think that I can have it installed by tonight, so your BMW will be ready to go early tomorrow morning." The voice message tape ended, as Wayne disappointingly hung up the phone.

This seemingly good news was a shocker for Wayne. Instead of being happy, he was dejected and sad. He had just had a marvellous night with a fine lady, with whom he was just starting to know, yet he was far from ready to commit himself to a relationship. He had also cheated on Kate, the lady he was planning to spend the rest of his life with. For the first time in his life, Wayne felt like a heel. He had never taken advantage of a woman's heart and he despised one-night stands. Yet, his original reason for staying in Lawrence was now irrelevant. Wayne was riding a roller coaster rise of emotional highs and lows within the span of a few hours. It was like being a manic depressive, he imagined. The passionate heart once awoken, was impossible to place back into silent, obedient hibernation.

What he had thought was the conclusion of a very good night was turning out to be something else entirely different. What he needed was a drink to steady his nerves and perhaps something to dull his emotions, so he poured himself a short two-finger scotch from his stainless-steel hip flask. While taking another sip of his drink, his eyes wandered over back over to the desk, where he noticed the envelope that Johnnie had handed him earlier in the evening. Curiosity got the best of Wayne, so he decided to open his pay envelope. The letter contained a short, typed paragraph, which pragmatically read:

Dear Mr Hamilton:

Please be advised that that your temporary services as a kitchen staff employee at the Calico Diner have been terminated immediately upon receipt of this letter. The management has determined that your services are no longer required. Although there is no formal obligation to provide you any financial compensation for your termination, the cash amount of $120.00 is enclosed to cover both your wages to date and to provide you some transition expenses. Good luck in your future endeavors.

Respectfully,

Mrs Jo Ann Hendel
Calico Diner Administrative Staff

"That cheap, fucking cowardly bastard, he didn't even have the guts to fire me in-person, man-to-man! This wage is less than that earned by a fast-food employee! That Johnnie isn't fit to be a bus boy in his own restaurant. I guess that being an entrepreneur can make a man either a bastard or an angel. I don't ever want to abuse my position of power and authority the way that little dictator Johnnie does around his diner," Wayne mumbled to himself as he scornfully threw down the letter upon the desk.

He sat down and took another jolt of scotch and began to think very carefully to himself. One thing immediately came to his mind, there were now two good reasons to move on, his BMW was finished, and his temporary job was over too. Karma was speaking to him. There were two good reasons to leave and only one to stay. He was torn between the desires to move on against the guilt of having to stay. The raw animal behaviour of some men to 'fuck and run' was never a trait that Wayne practised, but the last few hours with Joyce were just that, two lonely people who were attracted to one another and needed each other, if only for a few hours. In his soul he knew that he would not be staying, yet he felt a profound gratitude to a woman who had shared so much of herself and her family in just the short time that he had spent with them. For this, he was eternally grateful. 'Best to get a good night's rest', he concluded as he slipped down the last mouthful of scotch; it was going to be a busy morning. This time, Wayne didn't bother to set the alarm clock, he was tired, and the night was short, he wanted to sleep long and late into the next morning.

The warm Kansas sun rose all too soon and its warmth and radiance soon became an unwelcome nuisance to the lonely cavalier from Boston. It was 9:00 AM before he finally arose. Even in his half-awake state he was wondering exactly what Joyce was thinking about his lateness in coming to work? He again felt like a heel for not calling Joyce, especially after their intimate evening together. Surely a woman like Joyce deserved an explanation and this needed to be done in person, Wayne figured to himself. He thought some more about what he needed to do; he slowly got up from the bed and went to the bathroom. The long hot shower gave Wayne the time to think about his future actions. His path soon became clear and honourable.

Upon exiting the shower Wayne made a series of phone calls, the first one was to the BMW dealership, this to arrange for his motorcycle pick-up time, the other call was back to Boston. He gathered his belongings and soon he was ready to leave the room that had become his modest, temporary abode. A feeling of melancholy soon overtook him. He quickly checked over the room one last time, turned out the lights and without a glance back, he quickly jaunted down to the front desk for check out.

"Good morning, Mr Hamilton, are you sleeping in late today?" the old inn keeper Barbara announced in a pleasant tone.

Wayne gently placed his bags and jacket onto the floor and smiled. "Good morning, Barbara, no, in fact, I'm checking out now, it seems that my BMW is fixed and I'm ready to be on my way," he announced in a mild tone.

"The Willow Inn and I are both going to miss you, Mr Hamilton. You have been a wonderful guest and we hope that you will come back and join us again soon in the future," Barbara stated in a memorized tone.

He smiled earnestly as Barbara handed him the hotel bill. He signed the bill and took the copy of the receipt and before long he was at the Taylor Brothers BMW motorcycle dealership.

"Yes, sir, may I assist you?" inquired the BMW Taylor Brothers Service desk clerk.

"Yes, the name is Mr Hamilton, I'm here to pick up my BMW – it had a defective ignition control valve, Mike the Service Tech called last evening and informed me that it was ready to go," Wayne exclaimed softly.

"Oh yes, I got the invoice right here, Mr Hamilton. I see that you also got a rental bike from us too, just let me add up the repair and the rental sir," explained the young clerk. Wayne gazed nervously around the office, not being totally sure that his leaving Lawrence was the honourable thing to do.

"Mister Hamilton, I have the bill, it comes to a total of $3,595.34, including tax," the service clerk exclaimed.

Wayne was not astonished by the hefty amount, as the rental bike cost about $175 per day; even so, he knew that the price was high.

"Wow, that's a lot of money for such a small part, I always knew that BMWs were expensive to buy, it seems like these are even more expensive to get repaired!" Wayne quibbled in a nasty tone.

"Yes, sir, I agree, but you know, it's the labour costs that really add up, after all, this was a tricky job and it was difficult to get into the repair part placement cramped area," the clerk explained.

Wayne withdrew his credit card for the second time this morning and handed it to the clerk. He was soon handed the bill, which he promptly signed in an almost annoyed manner.

"At these rates, I should think about becoming a BMW mechanic or better yet, invest some of my spare money into the BMW Corporation," Wayne sneered.

The clerk simply handed Wayne back his credit card and a copy of the signed receipt. "Have a great day, Mr Hamilton and here are your keys," the clerk announced, as he handed Wayne the keys to his repaired bike. He placed his luggage and belongings back onto the bike.

The BMW thundered up to a gentle rumble as Wayne turned the ignition key. It was a good feeling to once again have his own bike, it felt like an old familiar rocking chair. He exited the Taylor Brothers parking lot; the bike fired on all cylinders in perfect harmony. He rode only a few miles before he came once again to the Calico Diner; however, this time he dreaded his entry with trepidation. In familiar ritual he removed his helmet, sunglasses and gloves. He didn't know how to gently break the news to Joyce that he was leaving and not staying with her.

A man with a conscience was always torn between doing the things that he wanted versus doing the morally right thing to do. There was never an easy way to say farewell to a woman with whom you had just slept with and even now, Wayne had regretted his midnight affair. Joyce was too nice a lady to hurt, but to stay with her would be an even bigger deception. He walked slowly into the familiar diner front door and sat himself at the front counter, the place where he had first laid eyes on Joyce just over a week earlier. She was not immediately in sight, but Mary Ellen had already spotted Wayne, as he walked up to the counter. Mary Ellen made a bee line break to the kitchen's unofficial break area, where Joyce was standing despondent, sipping on a cup of coffee.

"Hey, Joyce, he's back, he's sitting at the front counter," Mary Ellen cried out to her friend in excitement.

Joyce's eyes lit up with excitement, she had heard from the kitchen staff that Johnnie had fired Wayne and she thought for a minute that she would never see him again. Joyce quickly dumped her coffee in the sink, put on her apron and headed directly to the kitchen counter area. As she burst through the swinging kitchen doors, their eyes immediately met. Wayne gave a faint smile, yet his clothing betrayed his actual intentions. Wayne rose to greet Joyce; they locked in a tender embrace and a tender kiss. Yes, Wayne was leaving her, his entire facial expression, eyes, and even his kisses were those of a lover coming to say goodbye, yet she longed to hear his explanation.

"You look beautiful in the morning, Joyce. I wanted to call you, but I thought it was better to come by and to see you in person!" Wayne exclaimed in a hesitant tone.

"I heard that bastard Johnnie had fired you, Wayne, it was lousy of him, he hated you and he hated the idea of you dating me even more!" she confessed into Wayne's ear softly.

"My BMW is fixed, Joyce and I'm leaving Lawrence today," Wayne exclaimed in regret.

Joyce drew back from Wayne's embrace. She looked at Wayne with a cold stare, a stare of betrayal, that of a new lover's abandonment.

"Joyce, I know what you're thinking and it's not true! Last night was a beautiful thing for me, you made me feel human and alive again," Wayne confessed. Joyce felt a deep loneliness in her heart and soul. "It was not a one-night stand for me, Joyce, and I know that it wasn't for you either," Wayne continued.

No words could help explain the hurt that Joyce was feeling now. She had opened her heart to a beautiful young man and now the door was being slammed into her face.

"This is a cruel joke on your part, Wayne, I trusted you and let you into my life, and into my daughter's life too. You gave me a reason to hope again, Wayne, and now you say that you are leaving me, so your damn bike is fixed, and you'd had your summer fling until the next town comes along, I suppose. Great, that's flipping great, where the hell does that leave me damn it?" Joyce cried out loudly.

Wayne tried to put his arms around Joyce, but she rejected all his advances. "You got what you wanted from me, Wayne, now why don't you just get the hell out of my life right now! I never want to see you again and I wish that you had never stepped into this damn diner either. Now get out please, I never want to see you again!" Joyce voiced tearfully.

Further talk was useless on his part. He felt like an utter cad. With tears in his eyes, Wayne slowly walked out of the diner, mounted the BMW and slowly departed down the road and out of town. Before long he was on I-70 once again and Lawrence Kansas began to disappear in his handlebar mirrors, save for that of its memories.

Mary Ellen tried to console Joyce the best that she could. "Hey now, honey, it will all be fine. If it didn't hurt so much, it wouldn't be called love darling! Sometimes love throws you a curve ball in life, but it's better to be up at the plate and take a swing at the ball than it is to sit it out on the bench, right?" Mary Ellen aptly explained in an American baseball game metaphor.

"I was lonely! I just wanted him to stay a little longer, Mary Ellen, he was a great guy and now he's gone, just like a puff of smoke. People are not meant to live a lonely life. Life is simply not fair! My life will never change and yet here I sit in this shit hole, I'm in the best years of my life and I'm condemned to spend it in this greasy spoon diner!" Joyce sobbed as Mary Ellen softly hugged and comforted her.

The morning wore on into midday, which then morphed into the early evening. Joyce tried to console herself in her work, but her mind remained firmly entrenched on Wayne. "Boy, it was great to be around a genuine gentleman like Wayne. He was tender, educated, honest and a hard worker to boot," she lamented. Throughout the day, she reflected on Wayne's short presence in her life. She slowly came to the realization that her relationship with Wayne was more of an illusion than a reality. He had made no promises to her, so she had no right to expect anything from him. It was the shattering of the dream that was most painful.

On further reflection, Joyce realized that she had childish dreams for a man who was merely passing through her life. Before long, her work day was over. She hadn't seen Johnnie the rat fink, all day long; he was probably too embarrassed to look her in the eyes. She knew that it was only a matter of days before her daily feuding with Johnnie would begin anew. Still depressed, Joyce made the short journey home. Her residence already had the kitchen and bedroom lights on, this indicating that Heather was at home and had the doors securely locked from the inside. Joyce had wisely taught her daughter to beware of strangers and to never answer the door when she was home alone.

"Hello, honey, I'm home!" Joyce prominently announced as she unlocked the front door.

Heather came running from the living room and noticed that her mommy was sad. "What's wrong, Mom? Did you get fired or something?" Heather definitively inquired.

"Ah no, it's nothing really, my dear, it's been a long day and I'm awfully tired," Joyce sadly responded. "How was your day baby?" Joyce asked in a usual manner just as she had inquired of Heather each day.

"It was fine, Mommy, nothing out of the usual," Heather replied in a most mature response.

Just then the doorbell rang, and Joyce wondered who could be at the door at the dinner hour. Joyce peeked through the peephole and noticed that a FedEx man was at the door. It must have been his last stop considering the hour of the day, it was nearly 6:00 PM. Joyce opened the door slowly and with a curious look on her face.

"Good day, are you Mrs Joyce Miller?" the FedEx man inquired politely.

"Well, yes, I am Joyce Miller," she replied matter-of-factly."

"Ma'am, I have an Express package for you, but you have to sign for it," the man replied dryly.

"Certainly, I'll sign for it," Joyce replied and not knowing what item she had ordered recently to warrant this delivery.

"Thanks, Ma'am," the FedEx man replied as he retrieved the electronic signature receipt board and handed Joyce a modestly sized FedEx folder. So, whatever it was, it sure was not a piece of merchandise, and it was more of a document-style, flat FedEx packet. Joyce closed and locked the front door and took the folder into the living room, followed closely by eager Heather.

"I wonder what it is, Mommy?" Heather inquired.

Joyce was hoping that it was not bad news and this envelope had the potential to be just that, as it looked like an official document folder of some sort. Joyce put on a strong reading light and sat herself on the living room sofa with Heather in attentive repose.

No good news ever arrived by mail! Especially a special delivery mail; she feared that it was another bad omen of a financial foreclosure or related type of item. Joyce deftly opened up the FedEx mailer envelope, inside of which was a very elegant and formal manila envelope. Joyce removed the envelope most carefully. The sender of the envelope was from the Arthur & Gloria Hamilton Foundation, 136 Beacon Hill Street, Boston Massachusetts. Joyce was puzzled for a moment, and then she recalled that Wayne's last name was that of 'Hamilton'. The envelope was definitely addressed to Joyce Miller. Nothing on the envelope indicated its possible contents. There was no use delaying the large envelope's opening. Joyce carefully opened one end of the envelope and withdrew a fancy blue coloured folder.

Within the blue folder were contained several letter-sized documents on the right side, while the left side contained a simple white oblique envelope and a small folded sheet of paper. Joyce's eyes widened in bewilderment as she read the letter.

Miss Joyce Miller:

It is with great pleasure to inform you that you and your daughter are being afforded the opportunity to be a recipient of the Arthur

& Gloria Hamilton Charity Trust Foundation. This trust award is for an all expenses paid financial charitable scholarship(s) designed to assist the recipient (s) in attending select educational programs and institutions without matriculation limits, of their choosing and in any field of their selection.

All and any educational expense vouchers and matriculation information are to be send directly to the Arthur & Gloria Hamilton Charity Trust Foundation in care of my personage. Additional stipend funds have also been allocated to assist the candidates in meeting living expenses and associated incidental educational costs. This is a non-revocable, non-obligatory educational award from the Arthur & Gloria Hamilton Foundation extended unto the personages of Joyce and Heather Miller. Should you have any issues associated with this trust award, please contact me immediately. Once again, congratulations on your selection as a Hamilton Trust recipient.

Respectfully,

Mrs Patricia Peet
Administrative Head of the Arthur & Gloria Hamilton
Charity Trust Foundation

Joyce could not believe her eyes! "Surely, this must be a joke!" she thought. Wayne didn't seem like he had this level of wealth. She thought that he might be well-off, but not this level of wealthiness. This couldn't be happening to her! Joyce quickly took out the small note and saw that it was a note that had been copied and scanned from an original hand-written note. The note was from Wayne Hamilton. She read the words to herself silently and carefully.

Dearest Joyce:

"You won my heart and deepest respect that day that you returned that $100 tip that I had tried to give to you that first day that we had met. I came to admire your honesty and sincerity, later I came to love the woman herself and her charming little girl. You will always be one of the tender moments in my life. I hope that I have not hurt you greatly by my leaving, but staying would have been much too difficult for each of us. I guess that I still have a wandering spirit in my heart and my staying with you would only be cheating the two of us. I thank you for your honesty and sincerity, but most of all I thank you for your tenderness and love. Let me present this opportunity to make a better life for you and your daughter. Just consider this a farewell tip to you. This is one tip that I hope that you will not return to me. Remember: Never give up hope!

P.S. I have some more surprises in the process for the other Calico employees too!

Love & Affections Always,

Wayne

Tears started forming in Joyce's eyes. She folded Wayne's note and she placed it carefully back into a pocket of the blue folder. She then proceeded to open the 8 ½ X 11-inch white envelope. She removed two separate certified cheque. One cheque was for $750,000 paid to the order of Joyce Miller and it was annotated for general expenses and it was also drawn against the Arthur & Gloria Hamilton Foundation. The second cheque was a personal certified cheque in the amount of $275,000 payable to the order of Joyce Miller and it was to be used as desired for unrestricted living and associated personal expenses. This gratuity was in addition to the education scholarship awards and stipends for herself and her daughter. She could live anywhere and buy herself whatever she needed. Her head grew light and she felt the need to sit down on the living room couch.

"What's the matter, Mommy? Is it bad news? Are you alright?" Heather pleaded in nervous inquiry.

Joyce could hardly believe her good fortune. This was an opportunity for herself and her daughter to fulfil their educational pursuits in the medical career fields and it also extended to her the flexibility to immediately quit the Calico Diner and that rat of a man, Johnnie Porter.

Joyce started to cry and grabbed Heather to her bosom. "Honey, a White Knight on a motorcycle just delivered a miracle into our lives," Joyce exclaimed and wept happily at her good fortune. This was her last day at the Calico Diner, tomorrow she was quitting her job, look around for a new house, buy a new automobile, and loudly and publicly denounce Johnnie for being a lousy bastard of a human being that he was. She was also going to immediately re-enrol back into nursing school. She would now spend all her energies in improving herself and shepherding her daughter for medical school. "They were both going to make it this time!" she joyfully thought. Joyce hoped that one day; she would have the opportunity to thank Wayne in person.

The additional 'surprise' that Wayne had hinted about to Joyce, concerned the Calico Diner proper. He hated working for that little bastard dictator Johnnie and he pitied all of the employees working there and each of whom he had abused in one way or another. Thus, Wayne had also instructed his Boston real estate agent to perform discreet inquiries into the Calico Diner and to ascertain the fair market value of the business and to propose a buy-out offer of the establishment to its three owners for a very generous sum. If this transaction was successful, Wayne empowered his real estate broker agent to purchase the Calico Diner and to have the property legally transferred to Hector and Mary Ellen.

★ ★ ★ ★ ★ ★ ★ ★ ★ ★ ★ ★ ★ ★ ★ ★ ★

CHAPTER 7

Road Rage

"I'll get that Harley, knuckle dragging Neanderthal bastard if it's the last thing I do today" Wayne swore angrily to himself.

"Ladies & Gentlemen, this is your Captain, my final weather report as we approach Cheyenne Airport is the following: it's a warm 85 degrees, 45 percentage humidity, with clear, sunny skies. It was our pleasure having you on our flight today and thank you for flying Western Airlines today. Crewmembers, prepare the cabin for landing, please ensure that all trays are stowed, all passengers fasten their seat belts, turn off your electronic devices and take your seats in preparation for our final approach and landing. Once again, thank you for flying Western Airlines, connecting flight information will be available at the debarkation gate," an almost monotone, emotionless sounding male pilot voice announced, as he skillfully guided the agile aircraft into a gentle descent and then a successive quick smooth landing.

Within a few short minutes, the dual-turboprop Twin Otter aircraft landed on a warm, sunny day in southern Wyoming. The 'puddle jumper' aircraft's wheels touched the landing strip just a single time, attesting to both the aviation skills of the pilot, as well as that of the extremely calm, dry weather condition. Soon after landing, an old-fashioned, mobile stairway was quickly rolled into place and the cabin staff opened the airplane's doors. Quickly, the passengers began their debarkation from the aircraft.

"Hello Sammy! Hey over here, Sammy!" the boisterous young feminine voice yelled out to the slender, beautiful African-American female, who immediately reciprocated back with a broad smile, while vigorously waving back to her old friend. Samantha Evans never did like plane flights and this one was no exception – initially, the air was choppy, and the plane was packed to the gills with human cargo. Yet despite it all, Sammy was energized by the sight of her friend and she hurried down the stairway, stopping only briefly enough to blow a kiss with her hand before heading off to get her travel gear from the airport luggage carousel.

Robin rushed from the tarmac gate into the airport luggage area to meet her anxious friend. "Hey there, girlfriend!" Sammy joyfully screamed at the sight of her friend.

Robin ran to embrace her old fire-fighting mate from Chicago. "It's hard to believe that it's been a year since we last saw each other! You look wonderful, Sammy," Robin exclaimed with wild enthusiasm.

"Naturally, it must be all of that good clean living, boring single lifestyle and the hanging about with all those sick patients of mine, which is giving me this special glow," Sammy replied and smiled back, as she verbally alluded to her nursing duties back in Chicago.

"Well, Sammy, you should exchange places with me, all of those screaming and feisty seven-year-old children are a real handful," Robin remarked as she blatantly referred to her teaching of Special Education students in Cheyenne. Both women continued laughing and hugging one another in a sorority-type embrace. Each appreciated the precious gift of friendship, which was made even more so delightful with the passing of time.

"By the way, Sammy, I forgot to tell you – there's a new love in my life!" Robin sighed nonchalantly. Sammy's eyes widened in amazement, since the two women never kept secrets from one another. In fact, they spoke or e-mailed one another at least every two weeks.

"You have got to be flipping kidding me, Robin! When did this happen and why didn't you tell me anything about it?" Sammy shouted accursedly.

Robin made a devilish frown and announced, "Well, girlfriend, I wanted to surprise you with the news, a girl has to have some secrets, right?"

A bit dejected, Sammy thought that no secrets existed between them!

"Now you have really piqued my interest, so what does he look like? What does he do? Where did you meet him?" Sammy inquired in a rapid succession of questions.

Robin merely smiled and added a terse remark, "You'll get to see my new love shortly, he's waiting out in the parking lot."

Sammy was now really perturbed – 'this was a really dumb way to introduce her to somebody special and it was out of character for Robin to be so cagey with her best friend,' Sammy scornfully thought.

"All that I will tell you, Sammy girl, is that my new masculine companion is very sexy, dependable, strong, powerful and a little bit dangerous too! To tell you the truth, I'm not sure if I can handle him, he's so powerfully wild!" Robin smiled with a wicked wink of her right eye.

Totally mesmerised, Sammy couldn't wait to get outside of the airport terminal and see this new love of Robin's. Sammy retrieved her two large travel bags from the luggage carousel, one of which Robin eagerly helped to carry. Being a strong and athletic woman, Robin easily threw the bag over her shoulder and the two strolled out into the warm sunshine and out into the airport parking lot.

"Well, here is my new love, Sammy, isn't he a beauty! A real hunk, huh?" Robin exclaimed with proud enthusiasm.

Sammy's jaw dropped in girlish disbelief and screamed, "Now that's real bitchin, Robin! It's quite a bit butch too – so very masculine. I love the colour too!" The object of their admiration was not a man, but a vibrant blood-red, Dodge Magnum 3500 series diesel pick-up dual cab truck with an extra-long bed.

"Holy Smokes, Robin! When did you get this bad boy of a monster truck?" Sammy inquired.

"It's a gift 'from myself to me!'; I acquired it a few months ago; after all, I'm single with no kids and no steady man, so why shouldn't I treat myself to a little luxury?" Robin replied rather smugly.

"Oh wait, girlfriend – this is not the entire surprise either, there's another item that I have to show you too," Robin exclaimed, as she grabbed Sammy's hand and led her to the rear of the imposing monster truck. As they faced the back of the vehicle, there appeared a heavy blue weather resistant tarp, which draped a huge four-foot-high object that consumed the entire rear -length of the massive truck bed. Sammy merely stood there motionless, her eyes were transfixed with awe and eagerness in nervous anticipation for the next big surprise, as Robin jumped up into the truck bed and unloosened several tie-down knots. With a single energetic motion, she threw off the plastic blue tarp, suddenly revealing before the stunned Sammy - a massive chrome encrusted Harley-Davidson touring motorcycle.

Sammy's mouth dropped open with wonder and her eyes opened up wide in both amazement and admiration.

"Isn't it a beauty, Sammy? I saw it at the Cheyenne Harley dealer and I just had to have it! Besides, I think that the Harley complements the Dodge Magnum quite well, don't you think so, girlfriend?" Robin rhetorically commented as she smiled like an adoring mother to a new-born baby.

"I'm completely speechless, Robin…I would never have thought of you as a Harley girl, that's for damn sure!" Sammy pronounced in utter bewilderment.

Robin speedily jumped down from the truck bed and she placed her hand gently on Sammy's shoulder. "Well, like I said, Sammy, I am not waiting for Mr Right and I'm old enough to start enjoying myself and begin living life to its fullest and having some real fun before I get too damn old, right?" Robin declared smartly. With a determined motion, Robin unlatched the tail gate of the Dodge Ram, thereby letting it fall into its full downward position. Next, she proceeded to pull out a lightweight alloy ramp that was nestled beneath the bed of the Ram's truck bed. Robin then expertly disengaged the tie-down straps and gently slid the massive Harley down the Ram's truck ramp.

Robin's Solo Custom Harley was an 825 lb chrome and steel monster that beamed with brilliance in the late morning Cheyenne sunlight. The model was a Road King Classic with custom modifications. The engine was 114 cubic inches; the sequential fuel injection provided precise computer calculated fuel-air mixtures as both the environment and rider controls so demanded. This made the Harley very responsive to throttle demands at all elevations and in an almost instantaneous manner. The featherweight set of ear-shattering Super Trap stainless steel exhausts - provided for a burley ear-grabbing sound that was loud even for a Harley Davidson motorcycle. The steel steed's colour was a stunning combination of bright yellow, red, blue, and turquoise with streaked flaming colours painted across the fender and gas tank. The decal of a Native American Plains Indian War Chief in full feathered attire adorned the gas tank. Finally, both the seat and saddlebags were made of a custom light brown buckskin colour, speckled with an adornment of Indian bead piping and design inlays in colours of vibrant white, blue, red, and Indian turquoise. Both the bike's saddlebags and seat contained six-inch buckskin fringes, the saddlebags were detachable for use as overnight bags just like those used by the cowboys of the old

West days. The entire bike had a distinct adornment and accent of the Native American Indians and that of the old West.

Like all Harley owners, Robin had made this Harley her own through individual customization and there was not another one like it in all of North America. The bike exclaimed both individual and sexual overtones immediately on first sight. The bike spoke of trappings of power and freedom, while its customized accents bespoke individualism and old West Americana. Robin had done a great job in researching and customizing her Harley from both an operational and visual perspective. The bike was both fast and distinctive. There were two additional hidden custom features that this Harley Road King possessed, anti-lock integrated front and rear brakes and a selectable air-adjustable suspension system. The integrated anti-lock brakes were an added safety feature that prevented rear brake lock-up and allowed the Harley to stop in a straight line, while the on-demand, air adjustable suspension allowed the rider at the flip of a switch to control the suspension height from that of a comfortable boulevard cruising low-rider mode up to a higher suspension, which afforded very manoeuvrable high ground clearance mode required for fast performance riding. All these custom features and additions made Robin's Harley second to none. It cost in excess of $28,000.

"Wow, girl! That is one bitching Harley!" Sammy exclaimed, as her acute eyes examined the intricate detail of chrome and buckskin.

Robin felt like a proud mother. "Yeah – it's powerful, fast, reliable, ever-ready, and best of all – it won't leave me in the middle of the night like many of the jerk guys that I have known," Robin firmly voiced as both she and Sammy laughed in obvious comparison of the reliable Harley to that of the more fallible male of the species.

"Well now, Sammy, I want you to drive the Dodge Magnum off to Camp Jeffrey Haller and I'll grab some road time by riding several miles in front of you on my new Harley Davidson," Robin decidedly declared.

Sammy didn't mind driving the Magnum by herself, but she had wished that Robin had made the polite gesture of asking her first, yet that was the nature of Robin's strong personality, she was ever the dominant partner in their friendship.

"Sure thing, Robin, go and blow the stink off your tail for a few hours… I'll drive a couple of miles behind you and enjoy the new huge truck that you have just bought!" Sammy replied in a joking tone.

Robin grabbed her helmet, gloves, and riding jacket from the Magnum's crew cab rear seat area. Robin's custom jacket also mimicked that of the Old American West. Her honey-toned buckskin jacket was arrayed with colourful Native American intricate beadwork, and a generous six-inch long fringes along the length of the jacket's arms and back yoke area- it perfectly matched her Harley seat and saddlebags. In classic Western fashion, the jacket was fastened with old fashioned buckhorn cut buttons and buffalo hair rope cords. A richly detailed Indian inlay of silver threading designs and hand-crafted blue, white, yellow and red beaded artwork adorned the entire jacket. A small prominent red-beaded Robin bird adorned the upper right chest portion of the jacket – this visually and artfully served to uniquely identity its proud owner.

After performing a quick 360-degree visual safety check, she smartly mounted the iron and chrome plated beast. The sound of a loud, low exhaust thundered through the stillness of the parking lot, as Robin fired up the ignition of her Harley. She tied back her long blonde hair and fitted on her full-faced helmet complete with a tinted visor. She gave a quick 'thumbs up' to Sammy, kicked up the jiffy stand and sped slowly away out of the airport parking lot. She blasted her horn several times as a way to announce her happy departure.

* * * * * * * * * * * * * * * * * * *

Travelling aimlessly along Interstate highway 80 was unremarkable and boring in terms of scenery. It was a homogenized pattern of one exit marker after another, each with its own typical pattern of gas stations and motels. He made a change to proceed onto the secondary roads that were less traveled. Heading north into Wyoming's secondary roads afforded Wayne of both challenging road conditions and beautiful scenery.

Now he was riding along a scenic two-lane nameless back road, which was characterized by scenic Rocky Mountain vistas, lush pine tree laden mountains and numerous switch-back two-lane roads that seemed to go on forever. The early June weather in the Rockies furnished warm summer rays and the precipitation was dampening his heavy leather riding garments. It was now almost mid-day and any vestige of the cool summer morning was all but vanquished. He needed to abandon his heavy clothing and try to get comfortable; still, he still had many hours of pleasurable riding ahead of him and doing so in sweat-soaked clothing was no fun.

To his welcome relief, he soon spotted an emergency truck run-off area, which was a safety clearing of some thirty yards of gravel area to be used by large trucks in the event that their brakes failed on the downward slope of a mountain descent. He parked the BMW onto the escarpment, and then diligently packed away his heavy protective leather jacket onto the back of the bike with some bungee cord, although he wisely decided to keep wearing his Bates leather riding trousers. Relieved of his heavy leather jacket, Wayne now sported a lightly coloured black and red checkered nylon windbreaker that was quite appropriate for safety and visibility purposes, but not so good for any road abrasions. Still, the breathability of the garment and its lightness was a most welcome attire. Finally, to compensate for any potential road accidents, Wayne sported a high-tech riding-vest, which contained an instant-on, inflatable air bladder vest, should he ever become unintentionally disconnected from his BMW.

Pleasantly back on the road again, the light summer breeze felt like heaven as the welcoming cool air poured into the crevices of his liberally loose-fitting windbreaker. His mind was carefree and his destination was indeterminate. He was feeling cocky and the vacant road was free of all traffic in either direction on the small two-lane mountain road. His biggest threat was that of a deer darting out of the woods or some old road kill that some previous motorist had tagged earlier in the morning. To the majestic American Bald Eagles soaring high overhead, Wayne appeared as a large dashing beast, whose thunderous echoes bounded across the majestic hills and canyons of the western frontier.

The early summer dry winds were a delight to feel against one's skin, as these quickly evaporated the perspiration and sweat from the confinement produced by the constricting riding gear. Like a cowboy of the Old West, Wayne pushed his modern-day mechanical horse to the height of its capabilities, as he confidently manoeuvred the BMW along the grey and beige coloured canyon walls of the Wyoming Rockies. This being a secondary, scenic route on which he had elected to travel, Wayne was alone along this long stretch of winding asphalt and he savored the moment.

He was feeling quite good about himself and the people he had thus met along his travels; in fact, he felt smug and cocky in his self-assurance. For the first time in many months, he actually felt good about himself, his actions, and his philanthropy. His feelings of family despair and mourning were at last being transfigured into feelings of acceptance and accomplishment. He realized that he couldn't change the past, but he could make a difference in the present and future lives of those with whom he was meeting. He had no set plans and he merely was going to meet challenges and make a difference to those people's lives with whom he was meeting. "Life is a crapshoot anyway, so why not live one's life in a serendipitous manner," he confidently concluded to himself.

"There's not another swinging dick on this road, so why don't I have some fun today," Wayne self-justified to himself, as he spied his horizon and both side mirrors. He was correct, there wasn't as much as road kill on this lonely, winding stretch of road. In a flash, Wayne abandoned any and all pretences of a disciplined, professionally trained motorcycle enthusiast. Like a child at schoolyard recess, Wayne started running the BMW in all manner of erotic riding contortions. He started to swerve the massive bike into close leaning turns, almost touching his knees on the sun-baked asphalt. He then rode his bike in a series of S-turn manoeuvres, generating exhilarating excitement that comes from the energy pulse of pushing the bike from side-to-side in a very rapid order. The centrifugal force felt enchanting.

Long gone were the days of the nervous, neophyte motorcycle rider! The Copens' riding experience had made Wayne a very confident, competent and extroverted motorcycle rider. Having tired of these centrifugal force riding games, he decided to try some real hot-dogging feats – the one he enjoyed the most was the one-wheelie trick; this involved getting enough RPMs and torque to the rear wheel and thereby allow the front wheel to stand up in the air. Done by the properly trained person and under the correct conditions, this stunt was safe to perform, but it was never to be done on a commercial roadway. Seeing no other road traffic, he decided to take the chance. He grabbed a fistful of right-hand throttle and sternly pulled back on his handlebars, the BMW's engine responded and roared out the higher RPMs and the bike rapidly sped down the winding road on only its rear wheel.

"Wow that felt really great!" Wayne chuckled to himself, while broadly smiling beneath his visor helmet. At this moment in time, nothing felt better than doing one-wheelers on a warm summer day under the clear blue Wyoming sky. Fondly, he recalled for a moment the playful enjoyment of childhood, which was simple, pure, and sometimes a bit naughty. He liked it and he wanted more of it; at least, he wanted the feeling to last longer than just a few fleeting seconds. For the next 15 minutes, Wayne continued to perfect the style and longevity of his one-wheelie stunts, eventually being able to keep the bike upright for periods exceeding a several minutes at a time.

The road trick was only discontinued when one of the numerous mountainous switch-back turns were encountered, this forced him to slow-down and momentarily keep both front and rear wheels onto the ground, as he negotiated the blind turn, after which he felt free to return to his one-man road show. Having just completed one of these dangerous turns, he was once again up on his rear wheel doing his perfected, and very foolish, one-wheelie tricks.

Whoosh! There was a sudden sound, the rush of warm air and that of a blurred image rapidly passing by him! All his fantasies and self-delusions were suddenly shattered and he was aghast at the uninvited phenomena which had just interrupted his afternoon juvenile delight. His balance was shaken, as was his confidence and pride in himself, if even for just a passing moment. As the BMW quickly grounded itself onto the asphalt on both of its wheels, Wayne was able to spot a fleeting glance of another motorcycle in the near distance, passing quickly around a very pronounced hair-pin turn.

His emotions immediately transformed into primal anger. "Who the hell was that ass-hole riding at such a breakneck speed? Why hadn't that bastard slowed down or even beeped his horn at me?" Wayne muttered in both anger and frustration, not bothering to contemplate the stupidity of his own road antics. It did not dawn on him that his own foolishness was equalled by that of another daring rider. Still, there was no time for logical analysis, only the notions of anger and revenge mattered now. He had been instantly transformed into the modern 21st century phenomena known as 'road rage'.

The innocent object of Wayne's anger was none other than Robin's Solo Custom Road King, which had come so dangerously close to having clipped Wayne's bike. She had been riding rapidly, but safely, along the serpentine canyon lined road and she hadn't expected to see some idiot doing 'one-wheel wheelies' in her right-of-way travel. Robin was startled and angry too, but she had calmly let the incident pass as just another careless event in the dangerous life of a biker. She had hoped to dismiss the incident entirely, when she suddenly eyed Wayne's BMW approaching her rapidly in her right view mirror.

"What an arrogant bastard! That asshole probably wants to show-off his testosterone or some other macho bullshit," Robin contemptuously thought to herself. She had been riding many years and was used to assholes in both automobiles and motorcycles giving her a hard time on the road. Thus far, she had managed to vanquish all these ill-tempered idiots, by simply doing nothing to further antagonize them and simply allowing them to vent their anger at her. These road jerks usually honked their horns or gave her the middle-finger and that was the end of the outrage. Like spoiled children, they would pass her quickly and she would continue safely on her way. She expected this hot-tempered jerk to be of the same genre, but this time Robin was to be utterly wrong!

Wayne's anger and adrenaline allowed him to quickly catch up with Robin in just the span of a few minutes. He was only about 50 yards behind her now and he could make out the bike's details quite well. "I'll get that Harley, knuckle-dragging Neanderthal bastard if it's the last thing I do today!" Wayne bitterly swore to himself in self-righteous indignation. For a moment he was like a crazed dog chasing a vehicle, unsure of what to expect or do should he ever catch up with his intended target. He delighted to himself that he could outride this slow-moving Milwaukee behemoth in short order.

Flawed logic soon came to dominate his reptilian-rendered, angered and revengeful brain; he would use some of his Copen riding experience to put a little scare into the Harley rider. "Just some good, clean teasing and perhaps a slight scare, that's all I want for my payback," Wayne arrogantly thought. He braced his body and mind for some serious bike manoeuvring, as he took up a low- profile, forward position on the BMW seat. He flipped down the helmet visor, making sure that it was secure against any possible movement. Finally, he pushed himself down into the seat, took a firm grip of the handlebars and took a full fist-full of right-hand acceleration on the throttle. The BMW jumped like an excited cheetah into a rapid acceleration. With the eyes of a hungry predator, Wayne spotted exactly where he would make his attack move against the Harley rider.

Upon a straight patch of road, Wayne intersected the Harley, forcing Robin to make a sudden left turn into the oncoming traffic lane and almost forcing her to lose control of her bike. "That fucking, idiot BMW bastard! He almost killed me! He must be fucking crazy. I might have a real psycho on my hands!" Robin thought to herself and she started to nervously sweat with fear. Like little children sparring in the schoolyard,

Robin and Wayne took their revenge against one another on the winding narrow back roads of Wyoming.

Wayne made an obnoxious middle finger 'fuck you' gesture, as he passed the Harley and then proceeded to execute a sleek 60 degree leaning turn immediately in front of Robin, rapidly leaving her in his rear-view mirrors. "That will teach that Harley bastard a thing or two!" Wayne delighted with gleeful revengeful, as he had gotten some superficial satisfaction by trouncing that bastard Harley rider.

Wayne had never really liked Harley riders anyway, he always thought of them as 'afternoon or Sunday' novices, not actual serious riders. It was now Robin's turn to get pissed off. Initially, she was sorry that she had cut-off that BMW ass-hole, even if he was a jerk for doing rear-wheelies on a highway, but now she was angry at him and at all those other inconsiderate and macho bastards that had insulted and almost killed her over the past ten years of riding. Anger and revenge were indeed equal opportunity traits and now it was Robin's turn to go primal.

"I'm not going to let that BMW Frankfurter SOB get away with his rudeness this time! I am not taking any bullshit from anyone anymore!" Robin vowed angrily. "I'm going to get myself some BMW revenge this time!" she silently vowed to herself. In a dramatic reversal of roles, it was Robin's turn to spot the BMW as her target and pursue a similar line of attack. Exactly as Wayne had done previously, she took up an aggressive riding position, spotted her target in the distance, and then made her interception attack.

Whoosh again! Twice in the span of the past ten minutes, Wayne had just experienced the high-speed, passing rush of the Harley into his immediate direction of travel and this time, it was he who had almost lost control of his machine. "This is going to be a long fucking morning and that Harley bastard is not going to ever get the better of me!" Wayne cursed to himself as the BMW and Harley motorcycles exchanged an endless repetitive series of cut-off tactics. The desired goal of each rider was to either get the other one to back-off and retreat or to get the other rider to fall off their machine.

Neither Wayne nor Robin had it in their aggressive and independent character to quit a fight and each rider was competent enough to control their bikes to ensure that neither one of them was going to lose control of their machines either. So, it went on for countless minutes, each rider taking high speed outside turns, hoping to cut the other one off. It was like a dance of two deadly snakes, each manoeuvring along a long winding serpentine road with endless switchback and hair-pin curves. While each rider was competent in the control of their bikes, the same was not true of their emotions.

Sammy had taken the Dodge Ram on the same route as Robin and Wayne, but she had stopped at an elevated scenic rest stop overview site in order to take a slow gaze at the beauty of the Rocky Mountains with its majestic vistas and rugged beauty. The memorizing azure blue sky was periodically punctuated by some high puffy cumulonimbus clouds that passed slowly across the endless horizon. The invitingly warm, constant breeze made for a very pleasant feeling. Everything felt right with the world, if even for just a few passing moments. "Ah, if this feeling could only last forever," Sammy sighed to herself, as she was suddenly distracted by an internal craze. Sammy felt the urge to take nature's call and was going to slip behind the back of a gravel pile for a quick pee. Yet some rapid road motion below suddenly caught her attention instead.

"What the fuck is that shit going on down there?" Sammy shouted, as she looked down in horror from high above the scenic rest stop area. Sammy looked on in horror on the duelling scene of Wayne and Robin trying to cut-off one another on the narrow and dangerous curving roads below. She was not certain what exactly was afoot, but she was certain that Robin was in mortal danger.

"Oh, holy shit, I gotta get the fuck down there, they're going to kill each another!" Sammy shouted, as if there was someone there to hear her cries of desperation. She frantically hopped into the Ram and made a mad dash down the winding mountain road, hoping to find Robin safe when she finally had caught up with her at the bottom of the canyon.

The hair-raising motorized jousting continued unabated, as both Wayne and Robin each became frustrated with every succeeding white-knuckle manoeuvre trick. Sammy was driving as fast as the winding roads would afford her, but the huge Dodge Ram was not a nimble beast on these rapidly descending and narrow roads. All the worst forms of fear entered her mind, Robin being as close to her as those in her extended family. She wasn't sure what she would do when she finally caught up with the duelling duo, but she was certain that she would do anything to see that it Robin was safe and uninjured. The minutes passed like hours, as she prudently descended down the dangerously winding road. She had lost any possible glimpses of Robin and that of the other rider. Sammy was at least a generous twenty-minute distance from Robin and Wayne. Drops of sweat profusely flowed down from her brow, as she both cursed and prayed silently to herself, hoping that she could get more speed out of the Ram truck without becoming an accident herself.

Upon entering a precarious hairpin turn, Robin was forced to drop down into a lower gear, her body and the bike leaned into a tight forty-five-degree angle. She was now clear for a distance of one hundred yards of straight, open road before coming into another set of switch back turns. Sensing a fleeting opportunity to outrun the BMW, she grabbed a fistful of the Harley's throttle and got an immediate jolt of acceleration from the massive 114 cubic inch engine. Quickly, she left Wayne in the dust, which afforded her a slight revengeful smile and a slight degree of vain satisfaction. However, Robin was most mindful that this BMW rider was very skilled and also very vengeful. She knew that he would not give up easy.

Wayne was not to be distracted from this simple, yet skillfully executed manoeuvre. He also downshifted into a lower gear and also applied a fistful of the BMW throttle and quickly sped around the turn and caught Robin in his view one hundred yards off in the distance. "I'll fix that fucking Harley rider," Wayne swore to himself, as he set up his target and performed another wide turn to the immediate front of Robin.

In a few seconds, the BMW was aimed with deliberate skill like a fighter pilot in a dog-fight interception, Wayne quickly and deafly cut in front of Robin. The BMW accidently clipped a small piece of her front fender, this causing Robin to lose some balance on her Harley; she panicked for a mere second and applied the front and rear brakes with excessive force. Like many riders who had not ridden over the winter season, Robin's riding skills were somewhat rusty, and it was natural that a rider's instincts would over-compensate for their dormant riding training. The Harley's advanced ABS, (known as Anti-Braking System) prevented any dangerous skidding wheel problems, but it could not prevent her from experiencing what is known as a 'low-end crash', an accident where the rider falls off the bike and slides behind the travel of the falling motorcycle. This accident was far preferable to the life threatening high-side crash.

Although she did not realize it at that moment, fate was on her side and today Robin was a lucky lady. Her bike had temporarily lost its centre of balance and she was so startled that she could not take correctives measures to control the bike. The massive Harley front end

wobbled and then the rest of the bike came off its centre of gravity –
without rider control, it was one big massive 825 lb. piece of moving
metal and rubber.

In a mere instant, she was thrown off her seat and the massive Harley
started to tumble and roll on its side immediately in front of her. Yet it
was far better to have an 825 lb. metal mass traveling in front of you than
behind you. The laws of Newton had both bike and Robin travelling at
an equal speed across the road. Both Robin and her Harley journeyed
down the black asphalt road separated only a few feet apart from one
another and both skidded and rolled along the road for another 35 feet.
The road friction acted as a perfect braking media, yet it was a painful
way to quickly reduce momentum. After the span of just a few short
seconds that dilated out to a seeming infinity, both Robin and the Harley
stopped their momentum in the middle of an open piece of curving road.
Both woman and machine were lifeless. However, her antagonist in the
road rage episode would not fare as well.

In utter horror, Wayne saw the Harley's destruction in his side view
mirrors and he was engrossed with utter personal revulsion and fear. He
had never wanted to hurt anyone, especially a fellow biker. His childish
taunting had hurt, and possibly killed, a fellow biker; someone who had
done nothing wrong to him other than to deflate his male ego. At this
moment, he hated himself and his ambitious traits that had made him
such a success in the Boston financial circles and Wall Street.

There was no other choice to morally make! He had to get back and
assist the other fallen biker – that was a primary and unwritten code
of the biker community. Wayne quickly swerved his bike into the oncoming traffic lane, as he had designed to make a wide turn around and
follow-back to the scene of the accident where the Harley rider now lay
motionless. Before he could complete his U-turn, however, a massive
Kenworth truck semi-rig suddenly pulled around the hair-bend turn in
front of him. Wayne was seconds from crashing head-first into a massive
three-ton semi-truck and he knew that the truck's size and momentum
would not afford the truck driver to take any evasive action.

At all costs, Wayne and all other motorcycle riders wanted to
avoid the dreaded head-on crash with an oncoming vehicle, so he tried
instinctively to influence another alternative, in this case it was the
dreaded and very dangerous 'high-side crash', an accident event where
the rider is thrown over the handlebars of the bike with the possibility
that the falling bike will also roll into or over the top of the rider.

Thinking back to the Copen training, he knew that in rare instances when one was faced with a head-on collision, the best thing to do was 'ditch' the bike and take the direct punishment of the road abrasions.

He instinctively leaned the BMW into a steep unrecoverable lean angle away from the oncoming semi-truck, the front and rear wheels became unsynchronized and the bike began to flutter and turn erratically. He quickly jumped off the bike. The screeching sound of the Kenworth's grinding brakes and the skidding sound of the BMW metal frame across the road asphalt were some of the last things that Wayne remembered before falling from his BMW. Instantly, his air vest puffed-up and inflated within a millisecond, his chest, spine, and neck were immediately encased in a personal air bag, he looked like the Michelin Tyre Man rolling helplessly across the warm black asphalt.

Like a giant inflated toy, Wayne's body rolled and skirted along the same stretch of road only several feet's distance from behind his tumbling BMW. The BMW went sliding across the path of travel of the Kenworth semi-rig, as it tumbled head- over-tail in the air across the narrow two-lane mountainous asphalt road. The BMW continued its unaccompanied skidding and tumbling across the asphalt surface and then down over the side of the mountain and landing about fifty feet from the top of the road. Lying mortally wounded at the bottom of the mountain gully, the BMW's wheels were freely spinning like a child's toy top.

His outer garments quickly heated-up from the rapid friction with the rough road, as the outer veneer of his jacket and pants were tearing into shreds. Everything was very vivid, yet it seemed that time had stretched out unto many minutes, when in fact, only mere seconds had elapsed. Life-threatening situations were always like that – slow moving and dream-like. There was an unmistakable mechanical friction sound, there was screeching of metal against the hard asphalt, the screaming sound of massive truck brakes, and the burning of both brake pads and the outer shell of his vest jacket. The semi's wheels had locked up and the semi was headed in a perfect straight line off of the highway and into the roadside gravel shoulder. A small pillar of burnt rubber trailed for some fifteen yards behind the semi cab, illustrating massive and sudden braking of the big truck rig.

Wayne felt the heat of road friction as it wore away his outer garments and slowly warmed his body. Yet there was nothing he could do, he was at the mercy of God and maybe this would be his chance to be united with the rest of his family, whose collective death he felt that he had somehow cheated by not being on that plane with them that fateful day. Wayne's rolling body motion had its intended consequences, as his friction with the road had managed to dramatically slow down his body travel speed. As he rolled, the world twirled round and round fast at first, then slower and slower. A horror gradually filled his face-visor as the last item that he remembered seeing was the advancing approach of a massive grey highway road guard, the impact of which would surely decapitate various parts of his body and the avoidance of which would send him tumbling down the mountainside and to a sure, quick death.

Neither of the two possibilities enthralled him, but the outcome was out of his hands. He uttered a quick plea to God and prayed for the best outcome. In a few seconds he would either be sliced apart by the highway metal guard or he would experience a drop down the cliff, just like the one experienced by his BMW a few seconds earlier.

Suddenly, he blacked-out and his world became a dark, quiet realm of the near-dead. The last thing that he remembered was the sound of a high-pitched tone, similar to that of a medical vital sign monitor; it was the high pitch tone of a flat line. All was suddenly quiet. Everything in his vision had gone deep-black. Everything was over, and it seemed good. Yet, there was no expected 'tunnel of light', no angels, no images of deceased loved ones – only silence, darkness and peace; 'so this was death,' he contemplated to himself.'

The over-weight and highly agitated semi-truck driver stopped his big rig dead along the side of the road and he raced out from its cabin – huffing and puffing like an agonizing dragon. The man was having an anxiety attack and he was also suffering from asthma, high blood pressure, and a shortness of breath. Despite his physical challenges, the worried trucker ran like a Good Samaritan over to assist the clearly injured biker lying helplessly on the deserted roadway. His eyes bugged out like a frightened frog.

"Hey there! Hey Buddy! Fella, fella! Are you alive? Are you alive? Oh, my dear God! Are you even breathing, my Lord, I hope you are not dead!" cried the obviously frantic voice of a hyper-ventilating male. He knelt down by the lifeless body and nervously shook Wayne and listened for a heartbeat. Ever so slowly, the soft glow of the radiant, warming sun began to diminish the dark sphere of his vision and soon Wayne's eyes became focused on the frightened ruby-red face of a distraught white bearded middle- aged man, who was almost hysterical with high anxiety.

Wayne's eyes slowly began to focus more clearly, but he could still hear only the high-pitched sound of a hum in his ears. He could feel the man shake his body and every part of it hurt. The trucker retreated back to his parked truck and tried to climb back into the truck cabin, when suddenly he was caught grasping for his breath – the man was suffering an acute anxiety attack aggravated by the accident, the high altitude and his asthma. The stranger's presence suddenly left as quickly as it had arrived. Wayne now felt a distinct feeling of being alone again.

The higher levels of his reasoning and intellect had begun to return to his consciousness. Wayne realized that he was alive, now it was the time to make the terrifying test to determine if all his vital body parts worked or if he were to be consigned the fate of a lifelong invalid – the life of which he could barely contemplate. Always being the logical creature that he was, Wayne first tried to move his head. "Great – it still works!" he marvelled with great satisfaction, as he silently and humbly thanked God beneath his breath. He moved his head up and down, right and left – all very slowly. He was greatly relieved that at least his head and neck were feeling and moving correctly, albeit with some soreness and pain. Yet soreness and pain were good things, for these aliments signaled that he had possession of his nervous system.

He proceeded to test his courage and extremities by slowly flexing his arms, legs, fingers, and toes. With each exertion came the joyful feedback of feeling, movement, and soreness. He was alive, and all his appendages seemed to have feelings. This was indeed his lucky day. Wayne slowly tried to move his entire body. He rolled his torso over very slowly and sat himself up on his ass. Nothing seemed broken and he looked for any signs of blood, but he saw none and again he thanked God for not being seriously hurt. As he sat on his buttocks, he began to slowly stretch his arms and neck. Everything worked, but everything also hurt like hell. Like any person who quickly anticipates an imminent collision, Wayne had tensed up his body for the impending impact and this had caused his body and muscles to tense up during the accident and fall. His helmet and inflatable air-vest had been a true lifesaver.

After what seemed like an eternity, which was actually only a few minutes, he possessed enough physical recovery abilities to be able to stand up and test his legs, feet, and general body movement capabilities. Upon his first attempt to stand-up, he lost his balance and fell down on one knee. He got up and tried again, this time he was more stable and did not fall down. His arms ached as he lifted his hands and slowly unstrapped the helmet that had served him well as his portable 'brain bucket'- the helmet had literally saved his life and preserved his mental facilities. His helmet was most visibly scarred from its impact and friction with the road surface.

He dropped the helmet to the ground and it made a dull thud onto the black asphalt. The eerie constant flat line noise was now gone from his ears and he could hear the frantic voice of a distraught man holding a cell phone in one hand and a CB radio handset in his other hand, speaking frantically into both devices. The bearded stranger stood outside a Kenworth semi cab and Wayne aptly concluded that this was the same guy who he had just barely managed to avoid hitting and thus becoming a truck hood ornament. Somehow, the courageous trucker had gotten the stamina to retrieve the CB handset from his semi-rig cab and he was calling for 911 emergency assistance, for both himself and the other injured biker.

Wayne was momentarily tempted to go over to the trucker and to help avail his immediate concerns; however, just at that moment it dawned on Wayne that there was another injured party to be considered. "What had become of that poor Harley rider?" he thought in an almost panicked frenzy. He realized that he was the primary cause of both his own accident and that of the Harley rider. He could never forgive himself if he had killed or maimed another motorcycle rider, especially when this accident was due solely to his own pride and need for revenge.

He was guilty of the first biker rule of 'doing no harm unto a fellow biker.' The second unwritten biker rule was 'to never leave a fellow biker who needed any sort of medical aid or assistance' and he was certain that the Harley rider was in a very bad way, if not dead.

Slowly, Wayne began to walk away from his immediate accident area and down toward the road location just behind where the narrow road curved into a sharp bend, this was the area location where the Harley rider had spun out of control. His walk was slow and uneven, he moved as a man awoken from a long, uneven sleep. A lifeless body laid upon the warm asphalt. He approached the fallen Harley rider with the greatest of trepidation.

Yet, Robin was none for the worse from her fall. She had had the wind knocked out of her lungs and she was sore with aches and pains, but otherwise she was physically uninjured. She was very lucky; many other motorcycle riders had perished from similar such road accidents. Lying spread-eagled on the asphalt, she spied through her tinted, scratched face visor that a strange man was standing over her; he appeared to be young, handsome, and full of contrite concern for her welfare. "Are you all right? Oh God, I hope that you're still breathing!" the man's voiced echoed with grieving emotion. Robin was still in mild shock and said nothing.

Despite his present foolish actions concerning his own wounded body, Wayne knew better from his first-aid classes that he had received as a Boy Scout to never move or unnecessarily touch an injured person. He remembered in his life-saver training that the first things one checked on were the 'A, B, and Cs' (Air Way cleared; Breathing; Circulation) for an injured person. He saw that the Harley rider was breathing, there were no visual blood wounds that needed to be bandaged, and he quickly checked the Harley rider's neck for blood circulation; the circulation was fine with a regular and strong pulse rate. Robin tried to speak, but the fall had knocked the wind out of her like a stomach punch from a prize-fighter. All she could do was relax, breathe normally and wait for her lungs and body to recover from the sudden trauma.

Vastly relieved that the Harley rider was now alive and without any visible trauma wounds, Wayne quickly got up and painfully walked as fast as he could back to where the semi-rig and driver were located. He needed to get first aid medical staff on the scene as quickly as possible. Suddenly, he spotted the distraught Kenworth semi-rig driver still nervously pleading for assistance into his CB and cell phone.

"Hey, you over there, come quickly over here, I need your help! There's an injured person just down the road, come quick and bring along a first-aid kit if you have one!" Wayne shouted with unquestioned authority in his voice. He sounded like an anxious commodity floor trader on the Chicago Commodity Trading Exchange, a position that he once held briefly before entering the 'family business' back in Boston. Wayne turned and headed back toward the downed Harley rider, as the truck cab driver followed some twenty or so paces behind him. Several minutes had passed since Wayne had left Robin, but she was duly recovered enough to be able to sit up and she tried to stand, but she fell back down as her equilibrium was still off balance.

Robin was up on her knees again when Wayne and the semi-driver approached her; she saw both men clearly. Instinctively, she saw that Wayne was wearing the attire of a motorcycle rider; she saw also that his outfit was amiss from road trauma and that he too was physically dishevelled. "So, this must be the bastard BMW guy that ran me off the road! That fucking idiot bastard!" Robin quickly thought to herself. She knelt there on the road on all four of her appendages like a hurt dog as Wayne approached her.

"Hey Buddy, are you okay? You shouldn't be moving around in your condition! Are you hurt?" Wayne asked earnestly as Robin tried again to stand-up, but she wobbled once again and went down to her knees once again. From the lean and slim figure of the Harley rider, Wayne quickly and wrongly judged that this was either some young kid in his early twenties or some middle–aged small framed man trying to compensate for his inadequate physical size and testosterone levels through the possession of a big manly Harley Davidson motorcycle. "It was probably some middle aged inadequate-type of a guy, who was trying to relive his youth," Wayne quickly surmised to himself.

Nevertheless, Wayne was genuinely concerned for the health and safety of this rider, despite his smallish physical stature. Wayne knew that he had done the Harley rider wrong and now he wanted to make sure that this rider was safe. The Harley rider was probably going to sue Wayne's ass off, especially when he found out how much money Wayne was worth, but lawsuits were nothing new to Wayne and he smugly figured that at worst, the accident may cost him a few million dollars, to a multi-billionaire this was chump change anyway.

Wayne walked very slowly over to the Harley rider to lend out his arm for support and leverage. The semi-rig driver stood back about eight feet, also hoping that the rider was unhurt. Wayne was the first to speak as he lifted the Harley rider slowly up onto both legs. Wayne in all sincerity and concern fired off a rapid series of questions to Robin: "Can you stand up?", "How do you feel?", "Does anything hurt on you?", "Do you know where you are?". "I really didn't mean to cut you off like that, buddy! Is anything hurting you, I am so sorry this happened, it's my fault!"

Wayne tried to get some feedback from his questions, but the Harley rider only pushed away from him when he gently placed his arm on the Harley rider's shoulder. He looked in vain into the rider's heavily grey tinted face shield. Wayne still could not see the Harley rider's eyes or face. Robin while physically hurting was also equally mad, she was fit to be tied!

While Wayne was making his own prejudiced conclusions, Robin was making her own conclusions as well! "So, this is the fucking reckless, arrogant bastard that struck me and my Harley! I can't believe how many fucking dumb questions he is asking me! Yeah, I'm fucking hurting and you're an ass-hole, buddy! I'd like to take that that condescending arm of yours and stick it right up your fucking ass," Robin angrily thought to herself as she slowly stood upright on her own and gained her sense of balance. She moved very slowly and took a few steps. 'Everything worked! Thank God! What a miracle it was to survive such a spill! How lucky she had been in this accident! Every movement was stiff, but this was good too,' Robin thought to herself.

She took a few more paces, this time toward that BMW bastard who had run her off the road by his hot-dogging antics; she was really going to rip into this guy. "He's probably got minimal bike and accident protection," she silently scoffed to herself and imagining the worst possible situation. Every fucking bone and joint in her body hurt. She felt like she had just gone into the boxing ring with a heavy-weight prize fighter.

Slowly and stiffly, Robin slowly walked over the short distance to where Wayne and the semi-truck driver were standing. Carefully, Robin removed her helmet. Her shoulder length sandy blonde hair fell down from its pinned position, as she finally removed her tinted full-face helmet. She held her helmet by its chin strap and let it loosely hang dangling in her right hand. She moved forward, now standing only a foot or two away from Wayne, never letting her angry hazel-eyed gaze leave Wayne's astonished stare. This woman was red-hot angry, there was no doubt of that to any neutral observer. Wayne and the semi-driver were dumb-struck; neither had expected this Harley rider to be a woman, especially a beautiful, young woman to boot.

"It's a girl, she's just a girl! I can't believe it!" Wayne chauvinistically exclaimed in amazement as Robin looked on in utter disbelief at Wayne and his continued stupid, prejudiced mutterings. Robin didn't expect any smart words from this arrogant BMW guy anyway, but his sexist exclamation just continued to reinforce her angry feelings. Wayne's eyes were wide open, as was his mouth in amazement at seeing the sight of this pretty young Harley rider. Robin's physical appearance had broken Wayne's stereotype image of the 'typical Harley rider' and this was one of the few times in his life that he was caught speechless.

It was now time for Robin to speak. "Yeah, buddy, it's a fucking girl, so what about it? Welcome to the 21st century, asshole! Women are doing all sorts of things today or have you been living in a fucking cave – you asshole!" Robin screamed as she swung her helmet by its chin strap and awkwardly hitting Wayne in the right side of his head and upper shoulder. Wayne was caught off-guard. He didn't expect to be attacked by an injured biker, especially a pretty female one. The impact of Robin's helmet on his bruised body hurt all the more as Wayne tried to deflect and move away from his attacker. Robin continued her rage and swung her helmet again at Wayne; this time he moved away and her contact on his body was only partially successful as her helmet hit Wayne in the upper chest area. He instantly recoiled from the pain and the attack.

"You fucking, ignorant, arrogant bastard! What the hell were you thinking about out there on the road doing stunt wheelies?" Robin angrily shouted. Robin tried to strike Wayne for a third time, but she lost the grip on her helmet strap and her helmet went flying off onto the asphalt. Robin kept on her attack by slapping Wayne in the face and body with her open gloved hands. These impacts hurt far less than the blows of the helmet on Wayne's body, but he was still in a defensive mode, not wanting to do more injury to the Harley rider, especially a female Harley rider. The middle-aged, semi-driver looked on dumb-founded, he was afraid of getting in the middle of a fight between two youthful angry adults. "If these two are in good enough physical condition to fight, then they can't be hurting too bad," the frustrated trucker accurately grumbled to himself.

Suddenly, a cloud of tyre smoke appeared along with an accompanying screech of a truck's vehicle tyres. The smell of burning rubber and brake pads only added to the acridity of the scene that was taking place between Wayne and Robin. It was Sammy in the massive Dodge Ram truck – the cavalry had arrived just in the nick of time too!

Sammy could barely believe her eyes. There before her was her best friend Robin attacking and slapping some other biker guy; the two were fighting like cats & dogs, with Robin doing the slapping, while the other rider was playing defence and trying to push off her slapping attacks. Some over-weight, middle aged guy clutching a cell phone and a medical kit, was standing a short distance away in a trance-like state, just looking at the two parties fighting one another. Something had to be done and Sammy was the woman to do it! She had the street smarts and experience of working in the ER of an inner-city hospital, so getting two angry, fighting people apart was not a novel situation for her.

"Hey, cut that crap out!" Sammy screamed, but neither Robin nor Wayne could hear her, so intense was their primal interaction. Sammy repeated her order this time and physically moving up between the two parties and forcefully shoving both Robin and Wayne apart.

"I said cut this fighting crap out and I mean now!" Sammy yelled. Both Robin and Wayne's hearts were filled with the rush of adrenaline, both of them were clawing away at one another full bore, so much so, that neither of them had noticed their previous cuts, contusions, and bruises. Robin and Wayne stood there in the middle of the late morning sun, separated only by Sammy's adult refereeing presence.

"Oh, that's good… now you kids just cut that shit out, do you hear me, right now! Wasn't that accident enough excitement for the both of you two?" Sammy angrily demanded, as she looked incredulously at both Wayne and Robin. Robin and Wayne's mutual looks of anger had suddenly melted into child-like guilt, as they both responded to the chastising by Sammy. Both of them slowly and painfully walked away from the presence of one another.

"Now is anyone here critically hurt?" Sammy mockingly inquired as an almost rhetorical question, as she approached the two warring parties. In ER nurse fashion, Sammy immediately took Robin aside, quickly took her pulse, felt her body for broken bones, and examined her eyes and motor reflexes. It was only a one-minute evaluation, but this was enough. Robin was fine from at least any acute, visible traumatic injuries.

"Well, Robin, you seem to be okay, except for some minor bruises and superficial cuts, thank God. Now go over there and walk off some of that anger while I see if that other guy is okay," Sammy stated smartly to Robin. "Now you come over here, Mister," Sammy barked almost rudely at Wayne.

Not used to being ordered about, especially by black women of whom he knew absolutely nothing, Wayne hesitated and stood motionless; he looked at her with an astonished, defying glare. This 'uppity white-guy attitude' infuriated Sammy and she had almost wished that she had let Robin continue to beat on the hapless BMW rider for few seconds longer.

"Hey Mister, maybe you didn't hear me correctly; maybe you don't respect women; maybe the accident did something to your hearing or something! Do you understand English? I am a trained ER nurse and I want to see if your sorry white-ass and other body parts are not injured, so come over here…and I mean now, Mister!" Sammy ordered in a firmer tone. It annoyed her that many people questioned her authority, yet disrespect had been her constant companion throughout her life. First it had been the disrespect in her neighbourhood, then in the schoolyard, then college, and finally at her job – and now it was this white guy giving her an indignant, superior attitude. She was having none of it today!

Wayne started to think better of the young black lady for some non-logical reason; maybe it was the authoritative way she spoke when she was serious. He wisely decided that a quick examination and medical check-over was prudent. Wearily, he trekked a few short steps over to where Sammy was standing, limping along as he walked. Sammy performed the same quick coordination tests on Wayne and he too was in a healthy condition. "Sit down on the road here, tough guy!" Sammy commanded to Wayne. This he did with some evident discomfort as some body pains accented his face.

"Does this hurt? How about this? Do you feel this? Let your eyes follow my finger direction!" Sammy medically interrogated Wayne in quick succession, as she pressed firmly on various parts of his body and examined his eye coordination.

"Hey lady, I'm all right, just a few scratches, that's all, and who the hell are you anyway?" Wayne responded rudely.

Sammy said nothing, she merely grinned and concluded that nothing was broken and that no immediate medical action was required. Sammy went over and started to talk with the dazzled semi-truck driver and determine the chain of events. Both Wayne and Robin continued to eerily eye one another, Wayne still wanting to explain himself and to apologize, while Robin wanted to vent her anger and frustration.

Sammy returned back to where Wayne and Robin were located. "You both seem to be healthy, but you'll both have to be checked out at a medical facility and have X-rays and perhaps even an MRI performed in addition to other tests to confirm that there are no internal injuries. I'd say that you were both very lucky to be alive or at least not to have been seriously hurt, so say your prayers tonight, if you believe in a God that is," Sammy sternly lectured loudly to both of them.

Wayne and Robin looked slightly embarrassed at their conduct if even for a fleeting moment, each looked away from the other and gazed out into empty space. The sounds of an approaching array of ambulance and police vehicles could be heard approaching off in the distance and these vehicles would be at the scene in a few minutes. It seems like the semi-truck driver's CB and phone calls had finally paid off.

"I'm too old for this frigging shit, my wife was fucking right about big rig driving at my age! I don't need any more of this shit in my life" the old trucker sobbed, as he leaned wearily against his big truck rig.

In all the excitement, Sammy had all but forgotten about this Good Samaritan trucker. This man was clearly emotionally distraught, and Sam needed to check on his physical condition as well. The last thing that this incident needed was for a sickly old man to have a heart attack and die.

"Please come over here, Mister and sit down, try to stay calm, there's an emergency vehicle on its way here in just a few minutes! I'm a trained Emergency Care nurse, do you understand?" Sammy explained with the coolness of a trained trauma professional. "Let me hear you repeat your name, age and address to me very slowly please," Sammy calmly instructed to the old trucker as he sat sweating profusely on the foot ledge of the Kenworth truck cabin. The man's pulse was elevated, as was his breathing, but not dangerously so. The trucker confessed his personal medical information to Sammy, his medications being taken, along with the fact that he was asthmatic.

The trucker informed Sammy that his medicine and breathing in-hailer device was in the truck's cabin. Quickly, Sammy retrieved these items, but only allowed the trucker to use his inhaler in limited amounts, she knew from her medical training and experience that medication given under physical and emotional duress was sometimes more dangerous than not giving any medication at all.

A true health care professional, Sammy deferred to caution, especially hearing the shrill sounds of an emergency vehicle approaching their position. Emergency assistance would soon be on the scene; she instructed the truck driver to perform slow, deep-breathing exercises to calm-down his anxiety, then she left the trucker in a more calmed state of emotion and instructed him to remain in-place until the ambulance crew had arrived. The trucker noted her instructions and thanked her. Sam walked back to the two more seriously shaken victims of the accident. None of the accident parties should have been walking around, but Sam was powerless to stop them!

"My bike, my fucking beautiful custom Harley bike – it's fucking ruined!" Robin screamed as she gazed down the road at her wrecked custom Harley Road King. Her voice was hysterical, as she painfully walked down the road and peered in amazement at her mangled motorcycle.

"It's wrecked! It's wrecked for good!" she cried out as she drew up close and kneeled by the side of her broken machine just as an old cowboy would kneel down next to his maimed horse. She was disgusted with the sight of her previously prized metal steed; it was her baby and one of a kind.

"You fucking, stupid bastard, you wrecked my beautiful custom bike!" she screamed again, as she turned and looked angrily into Wayne's face.

Wayne sensed genuine hatred by this young pretty lady, an emotion of which he was not familiar, having grown up in the sheltered and refined Brahmin Boston society. For the first time in his life, he felt personal guilt and he was uncomfortable. Wayne struggled to make a defence and an apology, "I have insurance, and it will cover your bike and any damages." Yet making the monetary offer further compounded the situation.

"Oh, that's flipping great! The insurance company will make everything better, huh! Well now, how about an apology, buddy, or is that something that the insurance company will do as well?" Robin bitterly shouted in disgust.

"Hey there, Mister, you'd better stop talking before she kills you… sometimes saying nothing is saying more than words!" Sammy wisely counselled to Wayne as she walked over and placed a comforting arm around Robin's sore shoulder. Wayne kept his counsel and his mouth shut – for the time being!

The string of sirens from the screaming fire engines, emergency ambulances, and police cars from the nearby city of Casper, Wyoming arrived on the accident scene and the road was quickly secured from oncoming traffic. Sammy quickly approached the police officers and medical crews, she showed them her nurse credentials and explained both her account of the accident, as well as the medical conditions of the two accident parties and that of the poor, old trucker. The police and medical crews proceeded to take accident report information and medical information from Wayne, Robin and the truck driver.

As it was standard emergency response policy, both of them were taken to Casper County Medical Center for further examination, blood tests and medical testing. The Cheyenne Medical facilities were farther away to quickly offer assistance and there was no need of a Level 1 Trauma Care Centre. The police called in the necessary wreckage removal contract vendors, both the BMW and Harley would undergo the typical insurance evaluations, settlements, or repairs as was so deemed prudent.

Sammy looked around the road and picked up the various pieces of personal gear and other loose items that had fallen off both of the motorcycles, like the BMW saddle bags and the motorcycle helmets. Most of these items would be given over to the police for eventual return to their respective owners. She knew the locations of the regional medical treatment facilities, where she would meet up with her friend in due time. "This was one hell a start of the fire season for her and the real forest fires had not even begun yet!" Sammy mused with an ironic grin.

* * * * * * * * * * * * * * * * * *

Escorted by the shrill sounds of screaming ambulance sirens, Wayne and Robin were separately whisked off to the nearest medical facility. Casper was well over a forty-five minute drive to the south and given the nature and condition of the patients, the Emergency Medical System (EMS) staff were given authorization to take Wayne and Robin to a regional branch of the Casper Health Care Network, to a facility right off I-25 and adjacent to the Wind River Indian Reservation. The facility was moderate in size and it possessed the latest in medical technologies, except for having a large operating room and numerous overnight patient care facilities. The emergency room was top-notch and well-staffed, both Wayne and Robin were brought immediately into examination rooms where senior residents took their vital signs and performed preliminary examinations.

The medical attendants were efficient, thorough, and professional. As Sammy had earlier diagnosed, the EMS crews quickly confirmed the health and stability of their respective patients. Cuts, bruises, and muscle strains were the only apparent trauma, however, as was the standard EMS routine – medical diagnosis screening for broken bones and organ injury needed to be conducted and this meant medical scans, X-rays, blood tests, and a complete body physical by an attending physician.

A full medical report was also required by the Wyoming Highway Patrol, who needed to ensure that no drugs or alcohol had played a role in the accident. Both parties had the requisite health care insurance, which made first class medical care possible and therefore resulted in less waiting time and paperwork for the patient and the medical staff. Robin was released first, her road trauma being less than that of Wayne's, and both she and Sammy trotted off to get sleeping accommodations, a dinner, and perhaps a well-deserved drink or two. It was a hectic and traumatic day for everyone. Funny, the day had started like any other, full of sunshine, hope, and careless enjoyment – all to be concluded in vehicle destruction, angered emotions, and bruised bodies. No one had come out the better for this incident.

Wayne was finishing up his array of medical examinations; the doctors confirmed his good health and his extraordinary luck as well. The normal pain medications were prescribed, as well the direction for a follow-up examination in a few weeks with either the resident medical staff or his own physicians. He slowly and indignantly walked out of the dressing room, attiring himself back into his tattered clothes. He looked a mess, but he was grateful to be both alive and uninjured, he was grateful too that the Harley girl seemed to be healthy too. She was, after all, healthy and fit enough to wallop him thoroughly after the accident.

A knock came onto the door and a middle-aged nurse entered the room, "Excuse me, sir, please sign this release form and the other forms attached where the "Xs" are indicated. Your bags and personal effects from the motorcycle were picked up by the Highway Patrol and the bags will be available for you at the front desk." Wayne nodded his understanding and compliance, signing the forms carefully after scanning the contents.

"Excuse me, nurse, can you please tell me the condition and name of that girl that was brought in with me? You know, the girl that was in the accident with me!" Wayne passingly inquired. The nurse looked at Wayne in a rather nonchalant manner. "Sir, both privacy and hospital regulations forbid the discussion or issuance of private patient information, I'm sorry, sir, but it's the law!"

"Yeah sure, more government bullshit, well thanks anyway, ma'am," he cynically remarked as he got off the examination table and handed the metal clip board back to the nurse. "It doesn't matter, I'll probably see that little gold-digger bitch and her lawyers soon anyway, they'll probably want a minimum of several million dollars after they find out what I do and who I am" he muttered in an egotistical, self-inflated resigned tone. Suddenly he noticed that a valuable item was missing- it was his diamond platinum Rolex wristwatch. At first, he did not notice it to be absent from his wrist until this very moment and he challenged the nurse regarding its whereabouts.

"Excuse me, nurse, my valuable watch is missing, it was a present from my fiancée and it is an item dear to me," Wayne stated in a stern, almost accursedly manner.

The nurse was understanding and also defensive – no one liked being accused of stealing and she considered herself an honest woman.

"Sir, these are all the items that the police brought in from the accident area, here's the Highway Patrol Police Accident Report too... maybe someone else picked up the watch?" the nurse stated defensively.

Wayne quickly realized that a $175,000 custom Rolex watch was a highly pilferable item, especially in working class areas like this part of the country. He quickly became disgusted and he was sadly resigned to the fact that his valuable watch was now gone, and he only hoped that the person that took it, really needed the money.

"I'll contact the State Police for you, sir, and have them keep an eye out for it," the nurse replied. Wayne just nodded his head and gave a faint smile, resigned to the fact that his prized Rolex was gone.

His thoughts next turned from anger and despair, to that of fatigue and body pain. "This was the end of a very bad day, I lost my custom Rolex watch, trashed my BMW motorcycle, almost killed a girl and I'm probably going to get sued – boy what a hell of a day!" Wayne cussed to himself.

His body and muscles were still sore from the tensing up that had happened during the accident; he really needed a comfortable bed, a couple of drinks and most of all – a long hot soothing shower or bath. Immediately it dawned on him that he was out of wheels. At the front desk he picked up his bags and made an inquiry of the young nurse on duty. "Ma'am, can you tell me where I can get a decent room, a place to eat, and a place to get a drink – but not necessarily in that order!" Wayne grinned, while putting on the famous Hamilton flair.

The young nurse was flattered at the way Wayne flirted innocently with her. She smiled almost embarrassingly for a moment before answering. "Well yes, sir, there is a quaint western style restaurant and small motel right off I-25 on the Wind River Indian Reservation; it's not fancy, but the food is good, the beds are clean, and the beer is icy cold... it's about a twenty or thirty- minute drive from here," she concluded with a smile. Thanking the nurse, he grabbed his iPhone, retrieved his BMW Luggage, and ordered up a taxi ride. About a short cat nap and a half hour cab drive later, he found himself in front of the Wind River Valley Inn, as the late noon sun drenched its rays onto the lush green foliage. He quickly paid the taxi driver, grabbed his gear and proceeded directly into the old western décor styled motel.

"Hello Miss, do you happen to have a vacant room? One that comes with a bath tub!" Wayne inquired of the petite young Native American receptionist at the front desk of the Wind River Valley Inn.

The young lady smiled, her dark eyes sparkling with genuine hospitality. "Oh yes, sir, we have a standard room with a double wide bed at a very modest $75 per night! Will that do, sir?" the hotel clerk responded with authentic cheer.

"That's fantastic, Miss, this is the best news I have heard all day! Here's my credit card," Wayne gestured as he handed the card to the receptionist.

"Oh, how many nights, sir?" she immediately inquired. Wayne thought for a few seconds, then added, "A few nights at most, Miss, you may feel free to transmit the bill at your convenience to my credit card company."

The young lady nodded with polite understanding and processed the bill, after which she handed to Wayne his room key. He took a short set of stairs to the second floor; the room was in the back of the motel – it was remote and quiet. This was perfect for him. Upon opening the room, Wayne found it to be small, neat, and very well air-conditioned. He threw his now very well-worn BMW luggage on the bed and prepared himself for a well-deserved hot soothing bath, a short rest, and then dinner. Before any of this, however, he decided to make a call back home to Boston. It had been one hell of a day and now all he wanted to do was strip off his worn riding clothing and sit down in his underwear on a comfortable couch. His body ached all over.

In the city of Boston, Katherine was concluding her hectic workday. The time was 4:30 PM Eastern Standard Time and the working tempo at Hamilton & MacAlister was concluding without fanfare. The eastern market exchanges had closed and it was now time to wrap-up the business day before heading for the suburbs of the Boston Brahmans. A skeleton night crew would come in later in the evening and perform trading and monitoring of the global trading markets in the Far East, as well as preparing a morning market report and trade summary for Katherine and the other executives. The phone rang in a series of rings before a slender feminine hand deliberately picked up the handset. "Hello this is Katherine," a very polite, definitive, and feminine voice resounded into the receiver in a rather formal, reserved, almost unemotional tone.

"Hello Kate, it's me, it's Brad! How are you doing?" he bemoaned in an almost tired and painful tone.

Katherine immediately threw down the daily trade transactions which she had dutifully performed every day since Brad's unofficially diagnosed nervous breakdown and recent road adventure, but all this animosity was forgotten with Brad's call.

"Brad darling, how have you been, I've been worried sick not having heard from you in the last few days, are you all right? Is there anything wrong?" Katherine questioned almost passionately into the phone receiver.

He was happy to hear a familiar voice which sung of both love and compassion; he was starting to realize how much he had missed Kate and those emotional strings that tie one to their roots. "Kate, I love and miss you too and yes, thank you for the concern, I am well," Brad announced only half truthfully.

"Brad honey, where are you and when are you coming back home?" Katherine inquired tenderly.

"Kate, you were right, that damn motorcycle did get me into a slight jam, I have a minor fender bender here in Wyoming, but I am fine, absolutely fine, although the BMW is in bad shape – I think it's safe to say that I am grounded here!" he exclaimed in a nonchalant manner, carefully trying not to upset Katherine.

"What! What the hell! Are you in the hospital? I'm coming out to see you on the next flipping plane, that damn motorcycle!" Katherine sobbed hysterically into the phone.

He tried his best to calm down Katherine, knowing that her coming to Wyoming was useless, since he was perfectly fit and only had some minor scratches and bruises according to the medical staff.

"Not to worry, Kate, as I said – I'm fine, look here's a picture of me from my cell phone," Brad noted as he activated a Facetime video feed of himself smiling from his Apple iPhone. Upon seeing the video, Katherine was somewhat relieved, but still very concerned about her fiancée.

"Just what in the hell happened, darling?" Katherine demanded tearfully. Brad didn't want to tell Katherine what a jerk he had been on his BMW, so he stretched the truth a bit. "Ah, I was not paying attention to the road and I swerved to avoid some road kill and the bike fell over," he calmly lied.

"I knew that you should never have ridden that death machine, especially all alone!" Katherine shouted, her grief now verbalized into condemnation, anger and mockery.

"Please simmer down, Kate, as you can clearly see I'm fine, I'm feeling fine and still have all my wits, plus my bike is gone, so everything is okay, so please don't be so upset," Brad pleaded in a calm and logical tone.

"Just tell me, when are you coming back to Boston, Brad?" Katherine inquired anxiously. Cautiously, he paused a few seconds before answering.

"It's like this, Kate, I had planned to come back in mid-fall, but with the BMW busted up, it may be sooner. Let me give you a call in a few days and be assured, my riding days on the BMW are over, so don't worry, Kate," as he calmly tried to calm her.

Kate suspected that Brad was starting to make excuses for not returning back to Boston and this trepidation disturbed her. 'The broken BMW was merely an excuse to hide a more sombre underlying reason,' she accurately concluded.

The conversation ended in words and assurances of tender endearments and abiding love, yet each party was left with mutual anxiety. Brad still yearned to fill out the summer with serendipitous abandon, while Katherine deeply desired the intimate closeness of her fiancé and assurance of having her fall New England wedding. Katherine was glad of one thing; that her Brad was not seriously injured and equally consoled by the fact that the dangerous motorcycle was damaged and no longer an attractive nuisance. She would await his call and see what exactly that would reveal. Katherine's day was now shot, and she didn't bother to pick up the daily trading papers. She simply made a quick exit for the door.

"Mrs Peters, I'm gone for the day, don't call me unless the building catches on fire!" she proclaimed half-jokingly as she closed her office door and headed out toward her Bentley. It was going to be another long night at the MacAlister mansion with the conversation centering on Brad's boyish and dangerous behaviour.

* * * * * * * * * * * * * * * * *

Never before in his cloistered life had a clean austere room, a firm bed, and a hot bath all seemed so primitively inviting. The Wind River Valley Inn room was a very modest and home-like abode, that he immediately admired and to which he felt very comfortable. The lack of having a lunch was lost on him, as was his usual desire for a cocktail. He quickly threw his exhausted body onto the inviting warm bed. His thoughts wandered back to the morning's tragic events. It was good to know that neither he nor that Harley girl had suffered any serious injury. He knew that he needed to get refreshed with a lot of hot , soothing water. Although he normally took a long hot shower, this day's event and his sore body demanded a long emersion in a deep hot bath tub! The water felt amazing and soothing! Alone and relaxed, he pondered the encounter with the cute honey-blonde Harley rider.

"That little bitch was as lively as a wild mustang and just as pretty too, she'd be a handful to manage," he sinfully thought to himself. He again reckoned that it was just a matter of time before the buzzards of the legal profession descended onto him and the inevitable personal lawsuit that was sure to result. It would be another white trash person trying to get rich off the wealthy. No matter, Wayne was prepared for the eventuality and he had also made a call back to his attorney to be on the lookout for any lawsuit or litigation letters. The hot bath had loosened his sore muscles and aching bones, but now he needed a nap. He set his alarm for a few hours of badly needed rest, placed the 'DO NOT DISTURB' sign onto the hotel outer doorknob, stripped down into his underwear, and then fell deliciously asleep. Exhausted, he was dead to the world.

The hours passed as mere minutes. The annoying alarm clock rattled forth like a termagant wife! Wayne snapped out abruptly to quickly silence the shrill alarm. A groggy glance at the clock on the table betrayed the time of 6:00 PM, he had slept long and well. The traumatic events of the day had obviously taken more of a toll on his physiology than he had expected, his body and mind needed sleep and that is exactly what he had received.

He awoke slowly out of the comfort of his warm bed blanket and out into a cold air-conditioned room. His torso, shoulders and legs still ached from the muscle tension and trauma from the day's early morning motorcycle accident. He glanced at the alarm clock and wondered how quickly the day had evaporated; ironically it had begun with such great positive promise and yet it had ended in the tragedy of a broken bike, a bruised body and a second-rate hotel on a small Indian reservation somewhere in the forgotten vast expanses of Wyoming.

His stomach loudly resounded its emptiness with strange sounding noises – he had not eaten all day given the hectic events that had tragically transpired. Now he was most hungry. In amazement and disgust, he looked upon the tattered and worn motorcycle clothing which were draped in a hapless mass across the desk chair. His outer garments and especially the instant-inflatable air vest had truly saved his life this day. He smiled in muted reverence to both the clothing's testimony of ruggedness, as well as to the earlier day's disastrous events. Sometimes in hindsight, even tragedy became comedic. "The clothing would one day make for great memories and story-telling," he mused.

Digging into his now badly beaten, scratched BMW hard case travel bags, he withdrew a smart, if somewhat wrinkled, blue button-down cotton shirt, khaki trousers, and a pair of burgundy-coloured casual shoes. A dash of after shave and he was set for the nearest eatery. He hadn't thought much about transportation, but at this hour and place, a rental vehicle was probably not a viable option, this was fortunate in an ironic way, for he had had enough of vehicle riding for the day, be that for either two or four wheels. A good walk would do wonders for his mental facilities and bruised body.

"Hello Miss," Wayne smiled wearily and wearing a newly placed band-aid on his upper temple area, "is there a good restaurant that is close by, a place where I can get something simple to eat and maybe a beer?"

This time a new motel clerk, also of attractive Native Indian extraction, was on duty, her name tag was engraved with the name 'Rebecca'. She warmly smiled as she saw the handsome, if somewhat bruised man and admired both his looks and polite manners.

"Certainly, sir, take a left outside the motel entrance and walk about 250 yards down the road, you'll see a massive old looking log and stone building called Indian Joe's Tavern, it's a popular place for the locals and especially the fire crews who frequent the tavern this time of year. You'll like the food and the beer is cold and locally produced."

Wayne's taste buds were watering already, and he could almost taste a big, frosty mug of beer. "Thanks, Miss," he replied as he walked slowly out the door and down the road.

The evening sun now appeared as a dull red coloured tomato in the western sky. Again, he pondered how lucky everyone had been this day, especially himself! A high-end crash was something that not too many people walked away from without a hospital type injury, the air vest and the grace of God had saved his life. His mind wandered back again to that Harley girl and what she was possibly doing now. He quickly imagined that his curiosity would soon be answered by the serving of lawsuit papers in a few days or weeks at the most and that he would be seeing that young lady in a court of law – all bandaged-up, walking with a cane and an exaggerated limp. Still, he couldn't stay mad at this prospect, it was all his stupid fault and he could afford to spare a few million bucks to some middle-class working stiff, he figured with some upper-class, arrogant resignation.

It was a casual, warm 15-minute walk to the local watering hole. The early evening sun was transforming its golden dominant halo to that of a dimmer blood-red disk, the rays of Helios the sun god, were ever slowly retreating. There before him stood a medium-sized rustic timber and stone structure, which outwardly resembled an old frontier trading post with its weathered wooden post beams, large crystal glass panes etched in fading gold leafed lettering, and a prominent wooden plank boardwalk. In fading gold leaf lettering a sign boldly declared above the doorway entrance, "Indian Joe's – Tavern & Lounge". The establishment even had the old swinging bat-wing doors reminiscent of a classic western saloon.

Wayne instantly sniffed the telltale operation of a kitchen grill, there was a very familiar and distinct smell close about, indeed it was that of hot vegetable oils and cooking meats being barbecued and seared atop a very hot metal surface grill. His time as a short-order Calico Diner cook had taught him at least that much about the restaurant business. He smiled to himself at the feast that would soon advertise itself to him from the tavern's menu. He couldn't resist the urge to burst through the bat-wing doors 'Old West style' and see throngs of rough, hungry people, getting their fill of greasy cholesterol laden ribs, chicken, beef brisket, baked beans and all other things barbecued and grilled. 'A man could well afford to nudge himself in such epicurean sinfulness every now and then,' he rationally assured himself. The sturdy bat-wing doors were significantly heavier than one imagined, these opened less forgivingly than those which were casually depicted in the movies and TV shows. Some upper body strength was needed to open these doors and deftness was required to keep from getting hit in one's ass from these spring-loaded contraptions. Immediately upon entering the tavern, he felt the distinct application of sawdust generously sprinkled upon the rustic wood floor planking; this served to the atmospherics of the old saloon décor and it aided in the absorption of spilt drinks and food made by the careless and rowdy customers.

Instead of the convergence of noisy crowds, thirsty whiskey-drinking timber loggers and fork wielding rough-necks, Wayne had found an empty western-styled cavern populated by a few lone bar personnel. In the background there was a time-warp melody, lazily cascading from a classic-styled jukebox from the 1950s, playing equally antiquated 1950-style songs by long forgotten crooners. Arrays of empty antique wood tables, chairs, and a deserted dance floor and stage - only served to betray the future possibility of boisterous good times and dancing, but this now seemed for naught. Wayne suspected that his yearning for a hearty, if not all together unhealthy dinner, were dashed for this evening. Yet he was here and he was hungry too. An inquiry to the bar staff was in order.

He confidently swaggered slowly up to the ornate, long, wooden bar, where he had spotted a pretty young bar maid and a much older bartender, both of whom were engaged in an apparent process of pre-opening activities. The primal urge of hunger manifested itself again, so he decided to find out if or when dinner was being served, slowly. He strutted over to the bar area.

"Excuse me, sir, may I inquire as to when or if you are serving dinner tonight...I don't mean to be rude, but I'm really hungry?" Wayne politely grinned as he inquired of the older bartender.

Behind the long, old mahogany bar, there stood a tall and robust man of Native American descent; his hair was ebony black, generously punctuated with vivid streaks of steel coloured strands that visually attested to the journey of a long life. Numerous amounts of character lines were deeply etched across his face, which attested to a rugged and hard lived life. The eyes were large, almost overwhelmingly so, and yet it seemed that the virtue of kindness lurked just beneath these deep pools of mysterious onyx. A handsome bronze complexion framed and completed the masculine facial ensemble. The bartender appeared to be in his late- sixties or early seventies and his black-grey hair was gracefully long and neatly tied back into a pony-tail. The old man extruded the rich details of a Native American male. He was puffing on a strong, aromatic smelling cigar, a Churchill or magnum of an unknown brand, Wayne accurately calculated from his own personal experiences with fine, aged cigars.

"Well son, the bar's open now, the kitchen will be serving in about ten minutes; however, would you like a drink while you wait?" the older man's voice heralded in a rich chocolate-toned, authoritative-throated, baritone voice.

With instant acknowledgement, Wayne winked and head-nodded in silent affirmation.

"Yes, sir, you bet I would! I'll take a local brewed beer if you have one and I'll just wait for the kitchen to open, I'll eat at the bar if you don't object, sir?" Wayne interjected as the older gentlemen professionally drew a pint-sized frosty mug of ice-cold beer from the tap; its foam was a picture perfect one, crowned with an inch of white ferment gracefully seated atop of a amber-red body. He proudly raised the mug in a half-salute to the old bartender and to the small, but conspicuous American flag that stood on the bar wall. The beer was so cold that it was almost to the point of freezing, or so it appeared, its coldness almost seemed to paralyse the throat tissues as it quenched the eager thirst of the drinker. It was frequently remarked that 'the first beer was the best beer and the first sip was the most satisfying'; if so, Wayne's facial expression proved the point. At this place and time, the brew rivaled that of the finest and most expensive champagne. He smiled from ear-to-ear, as he grasped his breath and put the heavy glass mug down smartly and loudly onto the bar top.

The barkeep looked almost catatonically at Wayne, a smoking cigar was still anchored in the corner of a non-emotionless face. Wayne looked back at him and smiled with satisfaction. "Now, sir, that's one of the best beers that I have ever consumed, not that it's my normal drinking spirit, but on a hot day like this and after what I have been through, it's just what the doctor ordered!" The old bartender said nothing, but his face did break into a slight grin as he presented Wayne a quick, small wink of appreciation. "Excuse me, sir, don't you think that you should put out that fine stogie before the owner or some patron complains? Not that I mind, I love cigars myself from time-to-time," Wayne noted almost apologetically.

The older man was disturbed by the remark, he drew up-close, almost uncomfortably so, to Wayne's face. The old bartender stared coldly into Wayne's eyes. "No one will object to my smoking a cigar in my own establishment, I'm Indian Joe, some people refer to me as Chief Joseph Hawk, and another thing, young fella, this establishment is on Native American Indian Reservation land and we can do things that the white man cannot... they can take those silly laws and worthless treaties that they made with us and shove these up their political asses! I am sick and tired of the government telling me what I can and cannot do – so screw them!"

Wayne was embarrassed into an uncomfortable silence. He didn't know the specific status of the bartender, nor the fact that the tavern was located on Indian Reservation land... He tried to make honest amends, "I'm quite sorry, sir, I meant no offence of course, I offer my apologies please! The government gets under my skin too!"

Realizing that the young man's words were true, the bartender's chiseled stone-cold face instantly broke out into a wide smile, as he firmly patted Wayne's arm in a fatherly manner, "I have to vent my frustration every now and then, you can just call me Indian Joe from now on, young fella. "I'll go and get the waitress, she will take your order ... your food will be ready in about twenty minutes," the owner replied as he withdrew a cigar from the top pocket of his shirt and tossed it to Wayne. "Here's a sign of peace between the Indian and the White Man, my young friend!" Indian Joe cheerfully announced as he trudged off to the kitchen to fetch the waitress.

'It is always a pleasure to make a new friend,' Wayne mused to himself.

"Boy that beer was really great, I could sure go for another tall cold one, along with some food too," Wayne thought to himself.

A petite and very young sandy-blonde haired girl in her mid-teens appeared. "Hello, sir, Joe said that there was a hungry customer out here, now what can I get for you?" inquired the attractive barmaid with an almost perky inquisition.

Wayne unconsciously flashed his trademark Boston smile. "Yes, Miss, another cold one and how about something to eat, I will have a big bison burger neat-up and some fries too!" he chuckled back to the waitress."

"Sure thing... medium-cooked on the burger. sir?" she asked politely, taking a mental note of the order.

"Yes, that would be fine. That funny old Indian guy is quite a character, does he always dress-up like that or is it an act for the tourists?" Wayne noted half-jokingly to the waitress.

Quickly she turned about with an utterly stern gaze on her face. With an obvious look of disapproval, she walked away in an unexplained huff.

"Oh boy! Never piss-off the waitress, she'll spit in your food or something worse!" Wayne thought to himself and wondering what he had said to upset the young lady. He began to think that he possessed an innate ability for pissing-off strangers, this indiscretion was continually occurring throughout his summer sojourn thus far.

The food order was taking longer than he had expected, so Wayne examined the stogie that Indian Joe had given him. He sniffed the cigar and appreciated the fine aroma of the tobacco filler and wrapper. It smelled grand, he looked for the cigar band, it merely read 'Indian Joe's'. He bit-off the end of the cigar and was about to light it up, when the pretty blonde waitress reappeared with his order, a huge plate of golden steak fries and a huge barbecue-fired hamburger which appeared to be a half-pound of lean and healthy buffalo meat. Wayne's eyes almost exploded with disbelief at the sight of the meal.

"Here's you order, sir. Now is there anything else that I can get for you?" the waitress inquired dryly, absent her previous smile and cheerful mood.

"No, thank you, Miss, but if I might so inquire, just what did I do to unintentionally upset you?" Wayne asked quite earnestly.

The waitress took a step back with a look of astonishment before answering, "Okay, sir, since you asked, I think that you are insensitive and prejudiced, Mister!" she stated accusingly.

Wayne was flabbergasted at the charge for which he was being publicly accused.

"What's that you say, Miss? Are you crazy, young lady? I said nothing prejudiced to anybody and you don't know me well enough to judge me of that blantant offence!" Wayne responded defensively and with some firm degree of indignation. He was at a loss to explain the waitress's attitude, he was still hungry, but now suspicious of the great smelling hamburger, as he carefully lifted open the top bun to see if there was any mischief placed onto his burger.

Gazing up from the hamburger, he again spied the pretty young waitress, pouring a tall mug of cold lager. A small gold name tag on her blouse read, 'Jennifer-Louise' – 'a nice name for a pretty young lass', he thought. Jennifer-Louise headed his way and then placed the heavy cold mug directly astride the dinner plate. "I'm sorry, sir, I forgot your beer," announced the waitress in a continued cold, impersonal tone.

"Oh, thank you, Miss," Wayne exclaimed before mockingly stating, "I didn't think that the law allowed a mere teenager to serve alcoholic beverages?"

The waitress half-turned her head, as she walked away from Wayne. "We're on a Native American reservation, I'm a Native American, and my Great Uncle Joe owns this establishment – oh Mister, I am also of legal age too – now any more wise-ass comments, sir?" Jennifer-Louise Hawk snorted out in a voice that sparked of obvious defiance and disapproval.

"Wow! She's a little hot under the collar, she must be on the rag!" Wayne chauvinistically muttered to himself. Immediately, he realized that he had unintentionally insulted the young lady, her uncle, her gender and her ethnic background. He had stereotyped the young lady, just like he had type-cast the Copen family and Joyce Miller. He was wrong again! He felt morally guilty, but he hadn't meant anything malicious in his remarks or thoughts. It was ironic in a sense, but he previously never had any second-thoughts about any of his coarse remarks or conclusions.

Hunger now dominated both his anxieties and guilt, as he consumed the burger and steak fries with animal abandon. He didn't realize how good middle-class fare tasted when one was really hungry. The second beer went down as good as the first one. Life was good once again; he had survived an almost fatal motorcycle accident, irked a hot female Harley rider and now he had antagonized a young Native American barmaid – all in one day! He was tossing about the idea of either getting a brand-new BMW or returning back to Boston. He was unsure if he was pushing the luck of the road or if the wanderlust was still in his bones.

"Hey, now, young man, did you enjoy the burger and food that my grandniece served you?" a rough male voice echoed from behind his bar stool. It was Indian Joe puffing away on a large magnum-sized cigar.

"Oh yes, Indian Joe, I sure did, the proportions were quite hearty too. I'm afraid that I unintentionally insulted your grand-niece, I'm sorry for anything that I said to offend her," Wayne explained in an earnest tone.

"You probably meant nothing by it, young fella, you are a stranger to this place and our ways are strange to you, but maybe if you lived here or stayed here a spell, you would understand the feelings of injustice done to the Native American or 'Indians' as you commonly refer to us. It takes time to appreciate our injured past and our present reservation problems," Indian Joe calmly explained as he patted his hand gently on Wayne's shoulder.

"Can we arrange a peace here? An unbroken truce between your tribe and mine and simply have a smoke together?" Wayne pleaded.

Indian Joe smiled as he took a match from his pocket and struck it vigorously along a grain of the bar stool, immediately igniting the friction match. "Sure enough, here's to a new treaty between us, we don't have the Peace Pipe, but we do have peace cigars to smoke!" Chief Joe proclaimed as Wayne took the cigar in his mouth and puffed away on the initial cigar lighting. The Indian Reservation stogie smoked as smooth and rich as an old pre-revolutionary Havana or even that of a modern deluxe Jamaican or Dominican Republic import.

"I get these from another tribe in the far western part of the state," Joe exclaimed proudly. "Oh please, Miss – two more beers for myself and for Chief Joe and I apologize to you again for any unwelcome remarks," Wayne noted to the pretty blonde-haired waitress, who this time smiled back at him, sensing his genuine apology and the obvious good time that her uncle was having with this strange handsome patron.

"So, young fella, what the hell are you doing here, if you don't mind me asking? You do not look like one of us Natives, you are not a local by the looks and sounds of you, and you are not one of the seasonal workers either!" Indian Joe inquired politely of his new-found friend.

Wayne picked up one of the beers and handed it to Indian Joe, then he took the other mug in his right hand, he raised his glass in the air and toasted Joe, while lightly clinking the two beer mugs together. "Here's to friendship, Indian Joe, my name is Wayne Hamilton of Boston, I'm on holiday from the Rat Race!" Wayne exclaimed gleefully as the two men saluted one another and took a healthy sip of beer.

Wayne felt relaxed enough to confide some personal facts to his new-found friend. "No, Joe, I'm certainly not from around here and as you may have guessed from hearing me speak, I have a definitive Boston accent. I came traveling from the East…I'm trying to clear my head of some family issues…to exorcise some ghosts from my past. My private little world was unravelling, nothing seemed to matter anymore, I just needed to get away before I did something bad to either myself or others who I cared about," Wayne finally confessed to his new friend. The confession felt relaxing.

"Have you ever spoken to a friend or a professional about any of this stuff?" Indian Joe directly inquired. Wayne took another swig before answering.

"No, Joe, I'm a private person and I don't believe in head-doctors either, I think that a man should be tough enough to solve his own problems," Wayne noted dryly as he stared off into oblivion for a few seconds.

Indian Joe knew that it was best not to push the matter any further with this young man. "Okay, Wayne, but any time that you want to talk though …I'll listen, but never judge!" Joe stated in a fatherly fashion, as Wayne nodded in sincere appreciation of this new friend's offer of support.

The two men were finishing off their stogies and beer mugs, when suddenly a thunderous commotion erupted into the sedate tavern from seemingly nowhere. A crowd of about 60 boisterous men and women seemed to suddenly descend and enter Indian Joe's tavern in a matter of minutes. They all seemed to be in their twenties and early thirties, with only a handful being in their forties. The men outnumbered the women by a margin of 4-to-1.

"What's this all about? Who the hell are all these rowdy people?" Wayne anxiously inquired to Indian Joe.

Indian Joe didn't seem to be surprised in the least, in fact, he seemed resigned and full of regret that this party of people had appeared. "Well, to paraphrase the Queen of England, this is the 'Annus Horribillis' my annual summer time of dread, but it's also my financial salvation," Indian Joe profoundly muttered in the most erudite manner and coupled with a heavy resigned voice.

Puzzled by the poignant, distressing remark, Wayne looked to Indian Joe for a further clarification, the sign of bewilderment was visibly evident in Wayne's facial expression. "These folks are the firefighters, the denizens of summer – they fight the annual wildfires throughout the west – they're a bunch of summer trouble, but they bring hoards of badly needed cash to the reservation and my tavern, they are my unwelcome guests. Without them, the reservation would be a basket case," Chief Joe explained with slight contempt in his voice. Wayne merely nodded his understanding, but still remained a little bit confused as to the troubling nature of these folks – they seemed like decent people upon first glance.

"Ah come-on now, they can't be all that bad, Joe! They look like a decent lot to me," Wayne quibbled, hoping to dispel any truth in the older man's statement. "Surely you're exaggerating?" Wayne sparked jokingly.

The old man chomped nervously on the cigar hanging from the corner of his mouth and looked at the young easterner with some disdain. "You'll see, my friend, you stay here the summer and you'll see that what I say is the truth."

Wayne, however, had no intention of staying the summer in this backwater of the Rockies – as soon as he figured out his next move, he was out of this place.

"Well, let me start to welcome these 'pain in the ass' good-paying customers," Indian Joe remarked as he headed back behind the bar and worked his position as lead bartender.

"All hands on deck! Waitresses, front and centre, we have hungry, thirsty and good-paying customers here!" Indian Joe shouted back into the kitchen area, as the hordes of noisy patrons mustered up to the long bar.

He was clearly outnumbered, as the patrons rudely started yelling for service. "Hey Chief, how about some fire water? Where can we get some eats around this dump? Hey where are you keeping the squaws? Come on! Let's have some fucking service around this stinking joint!" the firefighters arrogantly yelled their demands from the lone barkeep.

Despite the obnoxious tones and ethnic slurs, Indian Joe maintained his calm decorum and took it all in good stride. The young people didn't say their words in meanness, but in boastful ignorance based on Joe's appearance and the stereotypes that they had grown up with about how Native Americans were grossly depicted in old movies and TV series. In his youth, Indian Joe fought many a fight for the very words now being carelessly uttered, but time and maturity had taught him that a man's fists only took an argument so far in life, he was getting old now and he thought that his positive, cheerful actions and deeds of both himself and the tribe, would serve as the best, longest lasting tools in fighting Native American stereotypes and prejudices. He knew that hatred never really died, it merely metamorphosized into different forms with each passing generation.

The image of the Native Americans was slowly changing in America, especially in the East, where the lucrative gambling business was bringing great wealth and thereby respectability to many eastern tribes, but the West was far less populated and cosmopolitan than the east and many like Chief Joe thought that there were other alternatives to selling-out the tribal rights to the big corporate gambling concerns. 'Far better to keep local conservative control of the reservation assets for sole tribal than to bring in an excess of outsiders, money, booze, prostitutes, drugs, and other corrupt things,' Indian Joe thought to himself. Most of the other tribe members agreed with this sentiment, but the financial temptations were growing ever-stronger with each passing year, as the tribe struggled to make ends meet on Federal subsidies, Internet tobacco sales, a marginal tourists trade, and the lucrative, but seasonal firefighting business. The Tribe's reservation was located off the beaten-path of most travelling Americans and tourists, this deprived it of sorely-needed revenues.

The Great Recession had richly manifested its negative social and economic impacts upon the Wind River tribe, with unemployment reaching nearly 60% of the working age men and women. Alcoholism was high and few of the youth remained on the reservation past their teenage years. No one was buying any of their crafts or goods, only tribe tobacco sales and the Tavern were making any money, and both lines of business were barely profitable. The fire crews with all their vices were very welcome for the cash that they brought into the tribe's coffers. Most fire crews worked for either the BLM or National Fire Service, the distinction in the two US Government organizations mainly being those of bureaucratic organization and stationery letterheads.

In short order, a flurry of waiters and waitresses emerged from the back room and relieved Joe Hawk from his front-line duty of dealing with the new age savages. Wayne was perched at the far, lonely part of the bar, as he looked on in fascination at watching a mob slowly get itself fed and drunk. Indian Joe slithered slowly down to Wayne's bar stool. "See what I told you about these folks and the bad days of summer? It's early June and the season has barely begun, just wait until August when they get their fill of firefighting!" the older man sounded-off bitterly and with disgusted resignation.

"I think that my grandson is going to play up the music in a little bit, music is supposed to make the savage animal civilized," Joe cracked softly to Wayne, as he pointed to a wooden-planked band stage that was darkened out but had the clear silhouette image of a drum kit set-up and along with some microphones. "He calls himself and his band, the 'Tom-A-Hawks' a funny Indian parity of his first and last names coupled with those of the noble war instrument," Joe announced, as Wayne chuckled at the cleverness of the name.

"Well, it sounds like clever marketing to me! Is he any good, Joe?" Wayne asked. "Good? What the heck is good about that crazy music that they play these days? You can't understand the words, not one damn word I'm telling you! Like the great Frank Sinatra used to say, 'If I could only understand the words that they were singing, I could tell you if I like the music!' So that's why I have that old jukebox over there, it's filled with golden oldies from the 40s, 50s, and 60s – I have full control over its volume and I get to play the old tunes when I want for these young whipper-snappers to simmer down or even to leave my place of business!" Indian Joe announced with adult authority and proprietor indignation in his voice. Wayne merely nodded his head in positive understanding and agreement.

Into the massive commotion of people eating food, drinking cold mugs of lager, and laughing boisterously at dirty jokes, a trio of three figures walked unnoticed through the bat wing doors, one tall white male and two attractive females, one woman was white-skinned, while the other was a light-skinned African-American. Both of the young women's beauty drew instant attraction and turned the heads of the men. The trio was quite familiar with one another, their arms hung loosely across the shoulders and waists of one another, all three laughed and giggled in self-absorbed oblivion to the unruly hordes in the room. They smartly marched up in unison to the long inviting wooden bar and began to bark-out strange sounding words.

"Hey give me a 'Wild Coyote!' Make mine a 'Snakebite!' Give me a one of those ass-kicking 'Jackhammers!'" the trio shouted-out to the bartenders in quick succession and referring to the concoction of flavourful drinks that were all made with the Canadian liquor known as 'Yukon Jack' – this a potent, yet seductively sweet golden Canadian liquor that slammed a drinker out cold after only several drinks. The 'Snakebite' was Yukon Jack over shaved ice with a sliver of lime juice, the 'Jackhammer' consisted of Yukon Jack, a dash of peppermint schnapps over ice, and the 'Wild Coyote' was Yukon Jack with ginger ale with a dash of lemon juice over ice.

The giddy trio boldly seized an empty area located at the far- right end of the bar. With drinks in hand, they raised their glasses and made a loud vocal salute in unison, "all for one and one for all, now here's to a great fire season!" They all sipped the sweet nectar with glee, the warmth of distilled liquor gently burned down to their stomachs. Rick Conroy decided to complement the sweet Yukon Jack liquor with a bitter rival, so he took out a six-inch long Rocky Patel cigar from his breast pocket, while his free arm was strung loosely around Robin's shoulder in a rather friendly fashion. The three chatted in a warm and friendly fashion, a clear indication of their years of comradeship. "Hey, barkeep, bring me another Yukon Wild Coyote," Rick yelled loudly as he quickly downed the sweet intoxicating cocktail.

Deeply immersed in their camaraderie, the three old friends joked of the upcoming fire-fighting season, and then drifted into discussions about Robin's motorcycle accident earlier in the day. "I sure wish that I had the chance to see that yuppie SOB who knocked me off my Harley! Can you imagine doing a wheelie down a two-lane mountain pass road? That jerk was a real asshole!" Robin angrily exalted as she slipped the ice-cold drink that barkeep Jennifer-Louise had just placed before her.

"Yuppie is an under-statement, he was wearing a platinum-diamond encrusted Rolex watch – it must have cost at least six figures, girlfriend!" Sammy rapped smartly to Robin.

"A jerk is a jerk, money or not! That was my brand-new bike, I saved up for it for three years and he walks away from it like it was nothing! I want to get his fucking name too!" Robin snapped quickly and in obvious disgust. She was still madder than a roaring blast furnace over the road accident and justifiably so.

"Well, honey, just wait until the police accident report is available, you'll get all the information that you want!" Sammy chuckled with a devilish smile before adding a pun, "Are you going to sue him?" Unemotionally, Robin looked straight ahead with a blank look upon her face.

"I don't know, but I'll do everything to make sure that my custom Harley is restored to its original flipping condition and without even the slightest of a minor defect," Robin scorned solemnly. Sammy and Rick both looked at each other, then uttered out in almost a unison outburst, "Yeah we know a good Indian Tribal shyster lawyer" – an obvious insider-joke in which they all shared a common understanding. They all burst into ruckus laughter.

The merry trio all raised their glasses in a mocking salute, "Here's to Jay Blackhawk, Esq. attorney to the sleazes" – an obvious insult to a mutually known and disliked local corrupt attorney. As she rolled her eyes to the left, Sammy almost coughed on her drink. She had spotted in a quick glance, the face of a very familiar figure, it was that of Brad 'Wayne' Hamilton, the man who had been in the accident with her best friend and whom she had administered some first aid at the accident scene. "Holy Shit, guys, look who I see over there on the far-left side of the bar, isn't that the same BMW bastard who knocked Robin off of her Harley?" Sammy gasped in a hushed tone.

Both Robin and Rick looked down to the far end of the opposite side of the bar with keen observation. Sure enough, the handsome white guy joking with Chief Joseph was the same BMW rider who had the altercation with Robin. If stares could kill, Wayne would have been dead on the spot. "Yeah, that's real good spotting, Sammy... you always were good at seeing trouble early, and it looks like he's having such a wonderful and carefree time too. I'd like to stroll down there and knock him on his yuppie rich ass," Robin added bitterly.

"How in the hell did that yuppie bastard end up here? What's he doing in our joint? Just look at him over there drinking merrily and chatting away with the Chief, he didn't even have the courtesy to inquire about my well-being with anyone; boy, he is one cocky asshole of a guy," Robin angrily sparked. Never one to over think a problem, she acted with her feelings and she was about to get ready and act with her anger and frustrations.

As Robin was about to get up to make her move, Sammy quickly interceded and instantly put her arm out and blocked her path; softly touching Robin's forearm, she whispered, "No, I have a better idea! Let's have some fun with this asshole, give me about ten minutes, then you and Rick can come on down." Sammy smiled, as did Robin, while Rick looked on with a bewildered expression. "I'll be back in a bit, otherwise you all come to the rescue," Sammy remarked as she winked at her two pals, then trotted up off her stool and headed forcefully through the crowded bar toward Wayne and Chief Joseph.

The bar was loud, smoky and becoming very humid from the throng of tightly packed bodies. Old songs from the 1950s were playing on the old-fashioned juke box – this was an inalienable right that Chief Joseph insisted on exercising, except when the live band played. The song 'Young at Heart' by Frank Sinatra played softly in the background against the grumbled sound of loud men and women. Now only a hair's breadth away from Wayne's back, Sammy quickly executed her devilish monologue. "Hey Chief, how's it going? What's a woman got to do to get a drink around here? You're getting too slow, Joe!" Sammy's voice barked out loudly to Chief Joseph.

Wayne turned abruptly around on his stool and discovered a beautifully smiling, attractive African American lady. She appeared to be in her early thirties and somehow eerily familiar to his sight. The two stared and smiled at each other for a few seconds.

"Hey Chief, it looks like you're getting some good-looking beefcake around here, so how about another round here for my handsome friend and get me a Yukon Jack Snakebite," Sammy remarked as an obvious and crude compliment on Wayne's handsome face and lean body. Both Wayne and the Chief stood looking at Sammy silently, not knowing exactly what to make of this beautiful lady's sudden appearance and boisterous remarks. Sammy continued her almost permanent radiant smile, as she notched-up the conversation. Yet this was Sammy's game to play.

"Well now, my handsome BMW bad boy, how are your sore bones feeling after that bike crash earlier this morning? From where I stand, it looks like you've fared pretty darn well, at least you're alive, you look better than earlier this day when I last saw you!" Sammy remarked smartly and hoping for some reaction from the almost animated young man.

"Hey I know you! You're the young lady that tried to help me today at the scene of the accident! You're a nurse or something, correct?" Wayne exclaimed in sudden amazement.

"Oh yeah, we got a bright boy here, Chief," Sammy purred in a sarcastic tone.

"I'm sorry Miss, I didn't recognize you on first sight...I thank you for your humanity and for the drink," Wayne replied quite politely and with a slight kiss of an upper-class Bostonian accent.

"Okay, handsome... my name is Samantha Evans, but you can call me Sammy and yes, I'm an Emergency Nurse out of Chicago...I'm just here for the summer," Sammy announced proudly. Sammy was disarmingly charmed by this man's manners and polished speaking. "Maybe the handsome stranger was not as big a jerk as she had initially suspected," Sammy speculated as she sipped her Yukon Jack. The stranger had disarmed Sammy's initial anger and hostile mood. Her feminine curiosity was being perked, if not stroked by this handsome stranger.

"Please excuse my manners, Miss, but would you care to have a seat? I've been polishing this stool with Indian Joe for far too long this evening, please take my seat, you're far too pretty to be standing around," Wayne sounded off to Sammy as he got up off his bar stool and extended his bar stool to the young enchanting lady. Sammy hadn't been treated like a real lady in a long time and it felt good. 'This handsome man has obvious breeding,' she thought and smiled back to Wayne. Wayne was intrigued by this pretty young lady too.

"Why thank you, sir, do you have a name, Mr Tall, Dark and Handsome?" Sammy coyly inquired in a flirtatious manner as she flashed her long eyelashes and bright smile. Chief Joseph chewed on his cigar and wondered to what end Sammy was up to with this young stranger, something did not seem quite right from his long years of studying human behaviour in the highly interactive bar environment.

"My friends call me Wayne, I'm from back east, Boston actually," Wayne stated almost apologetically, after which he took a sip of ice-cold beer.

Nodding her head vertically, Sammy smiled as she acknowledged the handsome man's response. She took the cocktail shaker glass and raised it in a traditional toast salutation to Wayne's beer mug. "Here's to Boston, BMW motorcycles and new friends." They both raised their glasses and made the traditional glass clink salute.

Sammy wanted to perk up more than small talk from Wayne. She deftly withdrew a small item from her denim jacket pocket. "Ah Wayne, while we are getting to know one another, I thought that you might like to have a valuable item that you had unintentionally deposited onto that switch-back this morning as you rolled across the asphalt," Sammy remarked as she placed her hand into Wayne's hand and slipped him the bezel-scratched, platinum and diamond encrusted Rolex watch. "I was going to surrender your Rolex to the police department tomorrow, but now that you are here tonight, it's all yours, handsome," Sammy casually explained.

"Wow, Sammy, I had thought some hospital attendant or police officer had stolen my Rolex. My fiancée Kate gave this to me for my birthday last year! Thank you very much, Sam," Wayne emotionally announced with glee.

Suddenly, Sammy felt rebuffed by his remarks, 'why would he think that everyone was dishonest or trying to steal things from him?' Sammy reckoned with immediate revulsion.

"Well Wayne, not everyone who is less fortunate than you are, should be considered as a thief! I work in the emergency room and I am not a thief! That pretty bauble must have cost a small fortune!" Sammy replied in a mocking voice.

Although Wayne had not been concerned with the actual cost of the Rolex, he was attached to its sentimental value and he was also aware of Sam's inference to his character and he did not like it. He decided that it was best not to belabour the point with a stranger that he would never see again; besides she had been merciful to him during the accident. "Better to let sleeping dogs lie" he best thought.

"Tell me, Wayne of Boston, what do you do for a living? What brings a rich eastern boy like you from Boston to the sticks of Wyoming? I can see that you are not a biker drifter, not with that fancy watch and your high-class manners!" Sammy inquired as she took another sip of the Yukon Jack sweet liquorice flavoured liquor. His past was the last thing which he wanted to discuss or remember, especially with a total stranger, no matter how cute she might be. He only smiled in silence to Sammy's question and this disturbed Sammy. She decided to probe deeper.

"Now what's the matter, handsome... cat's got your tongue? You know what I think? I bet you don't work at all, Mr Wayne big shot from Boston.... you're probably just some rich kid or a well-educated drug dealer or something...maybe even a Mommies Boy coupon clipper!" Sammy indicted in a suddenly intense confrontational tone that could not be misunderstood. Immediately, Wayne grew defensive and he decided not to take any guff from anyone, especially this pretty stranger.

"Now you look here, I barely know you, lady! Don't try getting into my life's history or family with the cheap purchase price of some flirting and chatting-up, it's not for sale," Wayne defensively snapped. He had keenly discovered Sammy's game, the gig was up. Sammy was on the defensive and she shamefully turned her head away in obvious guilt at the young man's remarks. She looked up straight ahead at the bar, avoiding Wayne's stare. Quickly, she slammed back the remaining amount of Yukon Jack liquor. Its warmth momentarily numbed the verbal wound. The victory for Wayne was fleeting, he saw the hurt look on Sammy's face and he felt like an arrogant jerk. Once again, he had handled himself badly with strangers of a different background and class. A few tense moments emerged during which neither Sammy or Wayne acknowledged each other's presence, he finally decided that the silence and child-like drama had gone on long enough. "The moral high ground was the most prudent one to initiate," he wisely calculated.

"Look here, I'm sorry, Sammy, but if you must know, I'm in the banking business back in Boston," Wayne spouted out matter-of-factly.

This declaration sparked Sammy's attention and it also opened up an opportunity for her to explore more details on the handsome young man. "Oh, you mean like being a teller or loan officer at the local bank?" Sammy replied in a manner that sounded rather innocent and common, but instead it was slyly intended to generate the surrender of more personal information and information to be used to attack Wayne. It was an ego-trap and Wayne easily fell into it.

He was about to fall for the verbal bait that Sammy had just espoused. As intended, he was insulted by being compared to a journeyman bank teller or low-level banking officer; after all, he was an Ivy League business school graduate and partner of a long established and highly lucrative investment bank. In an almost boastful tone, he generously elaborated further, "That's not quite correct Sammy, I'm an investment banker and our clients are large corporations, other financial institutions, private equity underwriting and hedge funds…I do not deal with ordinary customers, passbook savings accounts, checking accounts or home mortgages." His reply was smug, elitist and most condescending to Sammy.

She had merely expected this guy to inflate his ego by calling himself a junior executive at some local branch bank, but not to be that of a high-level private investment banker. Sammy had heard many unfavourable TV reports about these 'investment bankers and hedge fund managers' – the rich guys that made more money in one year than movie stars and entertainers made during their entire careers. By his highly cultured manners, rich Boston accent and expensive Rolex watch, Sammy surmised that this guy was the genuine article – he was an eastern rich banker boy, who had probably never done a lick of real work in his life. His daddy probably even groomed him at every stage of his childhood and career. Sammy hated people who were born with platinum spoons in their mouths and had no idea how the other 99 percent of Americans lived. Her thoughts turned from resentment to anger, she hated this guy's profession, his ultra-wealthy class and the fact that he had the arrogance to cause the injury to her best friend Robin. She despised both who this man was and all that he represented – the bloated fatness of the American super-rich, as well as his personal cockiness, gross stereotyping and smug self-assurance.

Sam sat there silently fuming for what seemed to be an eternity, her anger boiled to the point where she couldn't hold it in any longer, she blew up like Mount Saint Helens, "Investment banker huh!…hell, Mister that's just another flipping fancy name for an uppity, rich shit, who never did a spank of real work!"

Wayne was stopped dead in the middle of sipping his beer, he stood motionless, stunned at Sammy's sudden verbal attack. It was an indictment on his life, career, and class!

To Wayne's surprise, instead of a pause. Sammy's verbal assault escalated unabated. "You know that investment bankers have screwed up the economy; the Wall Street'ers always do and then they try to get the little guy or the government to bail-out their losses…your fancy Ivy Leagued inventions like junk bonds, sub-prime mortgage bonds, loan bundling, private equity deals, oil speculation and hedge funds – you throw billions around like it's nothing, you drive-up the price of real estate, gasoline, every fucking thing! Yeah, sure – this little old city girl from Chicago knows a thing or two about high finance, I know lots of people who have lost all of their savings and homes because of investment banker jerks like you, Wayne baby. Don't you talk to me about welfare moms, when some uppity rich shit is on high-end welfare; I bet that I contribute a greater portion of my pay in taxes than you do, Mr Boston Investment Banker!" Sammy snorted in an angry self-righteous tone. She stopped her raging tome, now being utterly breathless and exhausted, she turned away and finished her Yukon Jack, then quickly shouted to Indian Joe and ordered a double. Sammy was still red-hot mad, not with Wayne personally, but everything that he and his class represented and did, she was fit to be tied.

Wayne looked at Sammy in disbelief and horror. This nice girl had suddenly turned rabid over his seemingly innocent conversation. With malice, she spoke out against economic injustices that she had witnessed throughout her life. Never in his life had Wayne been spoken to so bluntly or crudely, the words stung not so much because they were uttered, but because there was some degree of truth that he sensed was contained in Sam's scorning sermon.

Sammy turned to Wayne and she saw that he was silently holding back, now she wanted to hear what the rich Boston banker man thought. "Why don't you just tell me what you really think, Mr Rich white boy, the son of rich, white parents who never did anything good for anybody!" Sammy uttered in defiance to Wayne.

If honesty was good for Sammy, then it was good for Wayne too. He decided to let his stereotype prejudiced venom out too. "You're nothing but a fucking, low-class, black bitch from the Chicago ghetto... you are probably fatherless as well! A pure street-trash slut. Your people sell drugs, give birth to gang-bangers, possess a victim complex, and live off multi-generational Welfare Queens!" Wayne angrily snorted out with a stereotypical racial slur, yet the fact that Sammy's childhood was riddled with the guilt of being a fatherless daughter and a white mother - cut her to the bone. Stereotypes were the vocabulary for prejudices and the fuel for raw enraged emotions.

Yet mere acrid words were not enough for Sammy this time; she took the Yukon Jack whiskey and threw it straight into Wayne's face. He was stunned, as was everyone else who was close to the bar area. Chief Joseph threw the cigar from his hand and loudly scorned, "Hey, you over there, there's no throwing of good whiskey in my bar, lady! Do you understand me?" Immediately, the entire side area of the bar became hush with utter silence.

Robin Wolf and Rick Conroy had keenly eyed the entire scene from start to finish. They scurried their way over to be at Sammy's side. Chief Joseph sensed trouble and muttered quietly under his breath, "not another flipping bar fight so early in the fire season, my Dear Lord!" as he rolled his eyes slowly up into his brow and shook his head from side to side in disgust at such nice mature people behaving so badly. "It seemed that it was not only the Native American who had trouble handling the fire water," he rightfully thought.

"Hey there, buddy, why are you hassling our friend Sammy?" Robin suddenly interjected to an astonished Wayne, as she pushed his torso briskly aside, in order to be next to her best girlfriend. The pain of the day's injury had yet to fully abate, his face clearly attested to the discomfort from the tender rib jab. Wayne was sick of taking rudeness from strangers, so he briskly shoved Robin's hands away from his personal comfort zone.

"Yo, pal, don't manhandle my girlfriend, are you one of those guys that gets off rough handling women?" Rick Conroy mockingly yelled in a threatening tone.

"Oh no, he only likes to knock other riders off their bikes and act like a road pig, doing idiotic wheelies on a two-lane road," Robin quickly added scornfully and in an obvious pointed, accusing manner. Robin and Wayne's eyes locked onto each other, like wild animals studying one another.

Like Sammy, Rick's eyes were filled with rage and disgust. 'Oh yeah, fella, I heard a lot about you from my pal Sammy here, you're the hot-dog jerkoff riding that BMW motorcycle! You almost killed my girlfriend, you idiot son of a bitch! I have a good mind to deck you right here and now!"

Wayne tried to take a quick analysis of the situation – it was not a good one. The scene was becoming ugly, three antagonist locals against a stranger and the argument was personal, which made the situation even more tense and dangerous. No help could be expected from any of the other people at the bar; they were all firefighting crew members and acquaintances of these three people. Wayne tried to diffuse the argument before it came to physical blows.

"Look here, folks, I'm sorry for what just happened, we all said some stupid things! How about I buy everyone a drink and we'll forget about the whole thing – okay?" Wayne pleaded calmly and in a logical fashion, as he nodded to Chief Joseph to re-fill the glasses. Joseph blinked in approving acknowledgement and quickly filled four whiskey tumblers with double shots of Yukon Jack whisky, liquor would either fuel or subdue this personal feud.

An uneasy silence brewed. The three antagonists eyed-down Wayne with a unified, contemptuous stare. Wayne quickly took up the first glass and raised it in an uneasy salute cheer to the other three: "here's to tomorrow and better times, folks." Awkwardly and with hesitation, the three took up their glasses from the bar counter in preparation to respond to Wayne's somewhat shallow-hearted toast.

Suddenly Sammy uttered a toast in mocking challenge to that of Wayne's: "and here's a toast to the Mister Boston investment banker, Mr Wayne Hamilton...may he continue to support the elite, corrupt establishment of sub-prime mortgages, mysterious private equity financing, unregulated hedge funds and leveraged corporate buy-outs." Everyone in the bar heard and understood that this was a deliberate and public humiliation and rejection of Wayne's gesture to make nice.

"What the hell! A fucking Boston investment banker! You and all of your kind get me sick," Robin cried out in an obnoxiously loud voice. She spit on Wayne's clothes, missing her intended target of his face.

Rick added to the caustic firmament: "You guys dressed-up in clean white shirts and striped silk ties are nothing more than white collar pimps, who suck the marrow from the working man and small business owner, my family almost lost their construction business to you jackals, yet you loan billions to corrupt foreign leaders and big businesses!"

Robin was still mad, so like Sammy, she also threw her whisky into Wayne's face. Rick followed with his drink a second later.

Things were getting way out of hand! Chief Joseph had had enough of this nonsense. "Hey, no more wasting of good whiskey in my saloon, it's for drinking, not throwing! You either drink it down or you don't drink at all, now it is that clear, everybody? This bar is for good times and relaxation, not personal grudges, politics or fighting!" Yet this party of four was still seething with anger and none of them was going to back-down. Chief Joseph aptly read the tenor of the situation and decided to up the ante.

"Okay – that's enough! Now, everyone, listen up now! This bar is closed for the rest of the evening. Everyone finish-up their drinks and get the hell out of here, you can thank your friends here for spoiling your good time tonight!" the Chief shouted as he slowly restored order to the establishment, while also losing a thousand dollars in lost business for the night. A collective grumbled moan erupted from all the disgruntled heavy drinkers. A man of integrity and mature judgment, Chief Joseph knew that it was better to establish order early in the fire season than to let the patrons think that he was running a loose saloon where any behaviour was tolerated. He would make up the lost business in short order when the fires began, and the crews came back hungry, thirsty and generously paid. They had no other available social outlet that was located so close to the proximity of the Camp Holler fire-fighting base.

Wayne stood at the bar embarrassed and dripping wet with liquor. The whiskey burnt his eyes as he wiped the sting with his shirt sleeves before reaching into his pants to withdraw a white handkerchief. As he was vulnerably wiping his soaked face, Rick grabbed Wayne by his shirt collar, leaving Wayne in an almost helpless situation where he could not defend himself with his fists. He threw Wayne down onto the wooden plank floor and was ready to either kick or stomp on Wayne as he lay there helpless.

"Now you stop that shit right now, Rick, and I mean it!!" Chief Joseph yelled as he suddenly pulled a pump-shotgun that was hidden, but within easy reach, from beneath the bar. The action of Chief Joseph yielding and audibly chambering a loaded 12-gauge shotgun got everyone's attention real fast – including Rick. The entire bar was in utter silence as they watched Wayne get slowly up off the floor.

"I think that it's best that you leave and not come back here, young fella," Chief Joseph announced loudly as both a suggestion and warning to Wayne. Be it fair or not, Wayne was now an item of contention in his bar and the Chief had an obligation to not only stop trouble, but get rid of it as well. Wayne's leaving would be good for everyone, especially for Wayne. "You go and get safely out of here now, young fella, I'll cover your back," Indian Joe announced loudly so that everyone could hear and be forewarned.

For a Boston billionaire, this was the most humiliating experience in his life. Wayne was shocked to have seen the dark and dirty side of a middle-class society of which he had never been a part or even heard about. The breeding of its men & women was akin to that of swine, as far as Wayne had observed this evening. He was livid at the crassness of both their words and actions. "He was a better man for never having gotten to know or mingle with these middle-class, trailer-trash, low-lifes," he silently reassured himself with a certain degree of

self-assurance and personal élan. He really took an instant dislike to
Rick Conroy; for the first time in his adult life, he had wanted to punch
another man across the face. Revenge was stupid and primitive, but
sometimes it sure did feel pleasurable.

He wearily stood up and approached Rick with an angry look, he
was primal-ready to pounce on this Neanderthal jerk. Suddenly, Indian
Joe with shotgun at the ready, jumped between the two angry men.
All of the bar patrons held their tongues and their silence; you could
hear a pin drop. The tension was palpable. The two angry young men
merely gazed at each other and everyone's eyes were gazed on them.
Their hearts pounded in their chests and the seconds slowly ticked away.
Slowly coming to his senses, Wayne concluded that it was best just to
simply leave the bar and to dissipate the anger, but he would not walk
quietly into the dark summer night either, yet he had nothing to say
except some raw animal emotions and he was determined to not stoop
to this level. As he slowly trotted toward the bat wing bar doors, Sammy
yelled out to him, "Hey, Mister Boston, don't forget your jacket…to keep
your candy ass warm!" she snickered and carelessly threw the garment at
Wayne's head. Wayne turned smartly and caught it, almost as if on cue.

He contempously looked at his three tormentors, who all stood
together smiling like jackals at a prized kill. Instantly, he had found
inspiration for his parting diatribe. He spoke the truth as he knew it!
"You people think that you are so noble and righteous only because you
go out and work a certain job every day for a living, well I work too…I
can't help my social or birth circumstances - no one can, but at least, I
can control my anger and behaviour. You all beat your chests claiming
how great you are as the down-trodden working-class heroes, well from
what I can see you're no better than any of the high-income people that
you hate, and if it were not for them, many of you would not have jobs or
businesses. You're all a bunch of followers – mere sheep who need to be
led by others! From what I have seen tonight, you're just a trio of working-
class cretins, barely out of the Dark Ages. I hope that none of you ever
breed and contribute your stinking offspring onto humanity! I'm glad I
won't have the 'pleasure' of seeing any of you working-class heroes again,
while you're working and sweating your fannies off here for a few bucks,
I'll be clean and comfortable in my cushy, plush Boston office!" Wayne
loudly and clearly articulated as he pointed his finger at Robin, Sammy
and Rick. There was an eerie silence as he turned once again to leave this
nest of beer drinking slobs and ill-mannered smelly patrons.

Quickly, Robin gathered Sammy and Rick into a football-style huddle. Although no one could hear their words, their heads were bobbing in a slight North-South direction, indicating an agreement or consensus of some sort. Only a few seconds had elapsed, but all three of them had emerged from the huddle, prominently showing off their tooth filled smiles. Clearly, something of mischief was afoot.

"Hey there, wait a minute, Mr Boston, what about my Harley?" Robin shouted in an offensive, castigating tone. Wayne was just about to push open the bat wing door, his left hand was on the top of the door, when he was stopped again in his tracks by the sudden loud verbal inquiry from Robin.

"What was this crazy lady talking about?" Wayne wondered. Her inquiry was worthy of a polite response he thought, but nothing more. He slowly turned around, by as much for curiosity as anything else. He had an obvious puzzled look on his face.

"I said, what about my Harley? My broken Harley, which is now in pieces in the repair shop and for which your personal destructive behaviour was directly responsible," Robin yelled out in no uncertain tone, as she defiantly stood erect with her hands braced on her hips. Wayne was filled with hatred and disgust at the entire night's escapades, especially at Sammy and her blonde-haired female companion. He correctly suspected that the two were in cahoots concerning the entire evening's events.

"Hey lady, you'll get a copy of the State Police's accident report and my lawyers will be in contact with you when you sue me. That's the way it works with you noble middle-class working types, now, isn't it? Don't worry, we rich, eastern, investment bankers have generous insurance if that fact comforts your greedy souls and pockets," Wayne replied with a contemptuous and bitter growl.

Robin didn't like this guy any more than Sammy, in fact, she probably hated him more because he had physically caused her, and that of her prized property, a lot of harm and she was not going to let him off the hook that easy either.

"No way, 'Boston'! That's not good enough, it's not half good enough and it's not what I'm after, Mr Boston," Robin loudly heckled.

Like déjà vu: Wayne again had a perplexed frown on his face. "Hey lady, I said that you could contact my insurance agent and personal attorney if you want your accident money!" he snorted back angrily.

Robin and her cohorts were still wearing their cunning, shit-eating-grin smiles, as if they knew something sneaky and nasty about this entire discourse. "Hey now 'Boston', it's not a lawsuit I'm after, I want some honest payback satisfaction…are you man enough to pay me back?... so how about a little hard work instead of a lawsuit?...how about a little middle-class bet with a working-class woman?...Well, how about it, Mr Boston?" Robin sang out loudly and walking a few paces forward toward Wayne as if to enhance her physical challenge. There was a continued eerie, uncomfortable silence throughout the tavern. Wayne didn't know what to make of this crazy lady's remarks, was she serious or only publicly kidding him? He was more confused than ever. 'This woman said that she did not want any lawsuit money, then what was her game?' he wondered.

Now utterly confused, he did not say 'yes' nor did he reply 'no' – he just stood there motionless and confused in a room full of intrigued people. As he turned to face the bat-wing door, Robin quickly added another personal confrontation remark, "What's the matter, Mister Boston Investment Banker, are you scared to take an honest bet with an honest working woman?" She scowled with a slight mocking laugh.

"I bet that he's chicken," Rick interjected in a loud reply, then he made the childish chicken perking sound, the one that was a child's school recess favourite in any child-to-child schoolyard challenge.

A comforting and fatherly voice echoed out some sombre baritone flavoured words: "Be the bigger man here, son, just walk away, it's the smart thing to do!" Chief Joseph growled as he stood as the armed shotgun toting sentry between Wayne and his taunting nemesis. Wayne looked into the Chief's wise, warm, deep brown eyes and he knew that the words were true and smart. He wearily looked back at the front, bat-wing door again; safety was just one simple step away, along with a farewell to this entire road house ruckus. Rick continued to make the chicken sound, so too did Sammy and Robin, soon all 60 half-drunk and whipped-up patrons were also making the mocking chicken sound. It was like a scene from a bad high school nightmare. It was so childish that it was really stupid to the rational person, but raw emotions often ruled over the logical part of the mind.

Logic counselled Wayne to immediately vacate the tavern; after all, he would never see any of these middle-class losers again in his life; yet a basic instinct or ego mechanism in him couldn't be subdued. Even though they were strangers, Wayne had suddenly developed an instant hatred for Rick, Sammy, Robin and all the other bar patrons, except

for Indian Joe and the bar staff. His hatred also fed another instinct –
revenge! He wanted revenge on these middle-class strangers who had
merely mocked him in a childish bar scene. He knew, or at least thought
that he knew, that he was superior in every way to these three idiots,
still he was foolishly curious too.

"So, what did you three geniuses have in mind, as if I'm even mildly
interested in your offer?" Wayne bellowed loudly to the three instigators
of this ruse.

Robin walked slowly and gracefully to within six-feet of Wayne, with
Chief Joseph still acting as the honest broker and potential mediator
between Wayne and any other third party antagonist.

"I want for you to start and finish the fire season with the fire crew
here in this tavern until the late August Labor Day weekend," Robin
calmly and loudly proclaimed for everyone to hear. She smiled defiantly
into Wayne's face as she awaited her antagonist's meek reply.

Wayne was caught aghast, off-guard. He half-understood Robin's
challenge, yet he needed to make sure that he was understanding her
correctly; he inquired for an explanation. "What did you say? What's
this fire crew business about?" he asked earnestly.

Rick came up to Robin's side and put his arm affectionately around
her shoulder, they smugly embraced, then Rick announced arrogantly,
"It means you work your ass off helping fight the wildfires until the end
of the summer or you walk out that door with your tail between your
investment banker legs and you get a hefty lawsuit and as much bad
publicity as we can dig up and throw at you, 'Boston'."

Wayne thought for a few seconds, then replied, "I think I can defend
myself against any lawsuit or minor publicity that your little minds
can contrive, and the people in my circles don't give a crap about the
goings-on in this bear-shitting, neck of the woods joint," he muttered
in a defensive and an almost egalitarian manner.

This time Sammy responded to Wayne's arrogance, "Just like I
thought, spoiled rich White boy buying his way out of trouble again!...
Why don't you just go back to Boston, to your rich Mommy and Daddy."

Like quicksilver, a primal anger ignited within Wayne and a fierce
appearance of rage came across his face, immediately Sammy became
scared of this man. A verbal indictment about his dead family and their
good name could and would not be tolerated, especially from the gutter-
trash plebeians who were accusing him now. No working-class trash was
going to defame his personal integrity, family or pride.

"Listen up, you three damn, low-class fools, you're on! I'll consider your childish bet, but it's not nearly rich enough to tempt me! I want higher stakes than your puny offer! I'm putting out all of the sweat and effort and I think that you all need to share more of the risks here. I'm not getting anything from your wager…I am not getting any personal satisfaction from your challenge! So, here's my counter-proposal, if I win and stick it out through the fire season, you each owe me 30% of your summer net earnings; if I lose, I pay you that same 30% net pay to each of you. Now do you want to take my counter-bet?" Wayne responded confidently and knowing that he had turned his business negotiation skills onto the backs of his enemies. It was Wayne who was now smiling mockingly as his three tormentors' smiles had turned to ashen, sombre, worried frowns. If he was thinking clearer, he would have bet 100% of their salaries in this wager.

This joke had turned into some really serious business! Robin, Rick and Sammy had never expected this eastern shave-tail to have turned the tables on their little wager, which was only supposed to be a gag-bet, soon to be forgotten in a day or so. Wayne's quite public counter-offer now promised to out-trump and raise the stakes of this gag bet to serious money for all of them. A third of one's net pay meant up to twelve thousand net dollars for Rick and about eight thousand dollars for both Sam and Robin. The stakes were raised considerably since everyone was dependent on this extra money for car payments, vacations and home mortgages. The three once again huddled together, but this time not one of them was giggling or bobbing their heads.

"Damn, that is a lot of money to wager on a gag bet!" Sammy cried out.

"Yeah, that's a lot of money for me to lose too," Robin announced in unison.

"That Boston guy is a lot smarter than I gave him credit, he knows that wages are our weakness and he is leveraging that asset against us," Rick echoed.

Not one of the three had a single adamant position on Wayne's counter-offer. It was they who were now being placed on the spot in front of all of their friends and co-workers.

"Well, what's it going to be, folks? Is the bet too rich for you working class people…or are you guys now the chickens?" Wayne announced loudly as he now was the one making the childish chicken sound. The gesture was childish, but it felt so good to Wayne. It was now he who was wearing the broad, cocky smile and confident straight upright posture.

"That Boston bastard is not going to get the best of me!" Rick quibbled in a bitter outburst. Before Sammy or Robin could say or contribute anything to the decision, Rick yelled out defiantly, "We accept, all three of us accept your bet, Boston...and I can't wait to see your candy-ass washed out before the first week of training is over," he spitefully added in a sarcastic yell. "I'll see you at 0630 hours sharp at the fire camp reception centre...you had better be there, Boston!" Rick challengingly added.

The entire bar crowd erupted in a jubilant outburst, as the masses had had their full of reality entertainment.

Both Sammy and Robin looked on with trepidation; after all, neither of them had voted with Rick's position and he did not even bother to take their views into consideration. "Rick was a real jerk at times," Robin thought to herself about her casual summer boyfriend. Sammy was angry too! Once again, Rick had done only the thing that Rick wanted to do without considering others. For better or worse, the decision was made, and they had to live with it. Their jolliness of a few moments ago had faded to a gloomy acceptance of the reality that they might be losing a third of their summer net pay over a stupid, ego-based bet.

The trio turned and headed back to their original place at the far opposite end of the bar. They all spoke about the audacity of the eastern stranger, who they irreverently and mockingly named as 'Boston' for his city of origin, as well as to make him something less familiar than a real, named person. Wayne also returned to the old bar stool at which he had earlier taken dinner and a few beers with Indian Joe. The conversation sounded the same, yet nothing was the same either.

"Son, that's one of the boldest and dumbest things that I have seen a grown man do! What are you trying to prove? Those strangers are like dust to you, they are nothing, invisible people after tonight! You could just do the smart thing, boy and just walk away from the whole thing... you'll never see them again," Indian Joe muttered with the wisdom of an ancient oracle. Yet Chief Joseph's counsel befell deaf, prideful ears.

"Yeah, Joe, you're logically correct, but I just wanted for once in my life to take action head-on based on 'what I feel' and not 'what I think'," Wayne explained in a low, almost regrettable tone. He downed a chaser of the Yukon Jack that someone had forgotten to drink, he kicked it back full and fast. The Canadian liquor was sweet and candy-like in its taste, yet potent and richly warm. It wasn't like the smooth extra rich malt scotch that he usually drank, but it was not a bad drink either, an acquired taste to be sure he suspected.

"Well, Chief, that's the last drink for me this evening until I complete this fire training thing, I'll see you after I get fully situated," Wayne explained as he liberally threw down a hundred dollars to cover his costs for the evening. It was over-generous by many folds and the Chief appreciated the tip and Wayne's gentlemen character. He liked this young man for some unknown reason and he wished him well. He secretly hoped that Wayne would win this bet, as he too disliked Rick's arrogance and boasting nature, it would be good to see Rick get his comeuppance busted up good for once.

Bidding his ado, Wayne this time was successful in walking out the front bat-wing doors, as he began the short walk down the pitch-dark street and back to his hotel. The warmth of the summer air was a welcome respite from the overly-chilled tavern. As he walked back, he wondered if he had made a serious mistake. Naturally, he could just as easily be off, like a thief in the night back to Boston and Katherine, with no one being the wiser. It was a lonely walk home to his room. He was plagued over and over again in his mind the events of staying or leaving. Yet running away was something he had really been doing ever since his family died in the terrible plane crash outside Aspen. He ran from work, he ran from Katherine, he ran from his wedding – no, this time he was not going to run from this challenge. Tired of running, this was his last stand, here in the sticks of Wyoming.

The hotel room now appeared to be even smaller and dingier than he originally remembered it to be, yet it was comforting in the mere fact that it offered some familiarity and security. All humans needed the assurance of the familiar, even if ever so slight. This small room was to be Wayne's safe cocoon of the familiar for the time being. Turning on the lights, he threw his clothes onto the chair in disgust and the resignation of the night's events. He boldly opened his flask of scotch and poured himself a full glass, then removed his boots and took a big gulp of the velvet liquid gold. The humming of the hotel air conditioning unit and his heartbeat were his only company. Comfortably lying down on the bed, he gazed at the empty white ceiling and wondered about his decision. The phone rang, odds were that it was Katherine for her nightly ritual call. The day had been a trying one, he ignored the cell phone call, Katherine would have to await a call back. He quickly stripped down, brushed his teeth, set the alarm, and quickly fell asleep.

* * * * * * * * * * * * * * * *

CHAPTER 8

Novice in Training: The Fire Chaser

*"Fire is a chemical reaction that occurs in nature- it thrives
in an environment that is hot, dry, and windy"*

O nce again, the alarm screamed out a most shrill, unwelcome
cry! It was 5:00 AM, the room was cold, and it was utterly dark
outside. Getting out of the warm bed was the hardest part
of the morning and having accomplished that simple feat, he thought
himself to be the rash fool for taking the stupid bet; he could have simply
rented a vehicle, bought a new BMW or else hopped onto the next plane
back to Boston. Anger and pride were not competent companions in the
process of sound logical decision-making and he should have realized
this. "I'll show their sorry working-class asses a thing or two!" he
muttered to himself as he slipped into his slacks and shirt. After placing
on his socks and boots, he grabbed a jacket and darted forth toward the
motel lobby.

In the hotel lobby, an older Native American woman was setting up
coffee urns and platters of pastry for the motel guests. The coffee aroma
was too seductive to resist. Without hesitation, he boldly partook a spoon
of honey and mixed it into the rich steaming ebony brew. It tasted as
good as it smelled – this was indeed the start to a good morning, that of
simply being alive, healthy and imbibing in the small joys of life. Feeling
hungry, he boldly partook of two pastries, a raspberry tart and a cheese
bear claw. He comfortably seated himself on a lobby sofa and enjoyed
the morning feast. He wondered if the motel staff had the schedule and
information for the transport to the fire centre.

"Excuse me, Miss, how do I get to the local Fire Service Camp?" he innocently inquired.

"Yes, sir, you go out the front door, turn-right, then walk down to the green bus station sign; a tribal reservation blue coloured bus will stop there, the bus should be arriving in 30 minutes' time and the bus makes round trips to the camp four times a day throughout the fire season" the motel clerk announced smartly. After leisurely finishing his coffee and pastry, he journeyed a short walk and seated himself comfortably down on a sturdy wooden bench to await his modern-day chariot ride to his destination.

The wait was not a lengthy one. No sooner had he arrived at the bus stop when suddenly a set of dim yellowish coloured headlights faintly appeared in the distance, the image of an old faded blue bus gradually appeared and slowly approached the bus stop. In the front of the bus were the faded yellow-coloured words 'Blue Bird' a standard letter embossment for bus transporters that were used by the US Air Force. The age and condition of this vehicle clearly betrayed the fact that this was a surplus vehicle procured through the US Government surplus program and transferred to the Native American Reservation tribe. A crude hand-written cardboard sign was emplaced onto the bus windshield, 'Camp Haller: Fire Camp'.

The bus came to a creaky stop. Slowly, he cautiously entered the bus stairwell. Always wanting to be certain of the facts of his circumstances, he made an unwarranted inquiry. "Excuse me Miss, is this the bus to the fire camp?" The bus driver was an old woman with a thick grey halo of hair. She merely smiled and pointed at the front window sign. "That's what the sign says, young man, and that's where I'm paid to drive during the season and the bus makes a shuttle run to Camp Haller every two hours day and night throughout the fire season. Now you just sit back and get some shut-eye, there's nothing to see at this hour and the trip takes 30–45 minutes."

During the sedate, 45-minute bus journey, the sun arose from its nightly slumber and it was now sunrise with only a few remaining clouds dotting the clear blue azure summer Wyoming sky. "Camp Jeffery Holler!" the older Native American bus driver loudly sang out in a shrill brash voice. Hastily grabbing his jacket, he departed the bus and spied the scene around him. Before him there stood a huge compound of over a dozen buildings surrounded by an eight-foot-high cyclone fence topped with three strand barbed wire for physical protection. A prominent white metal coloured sign stood atop and adjacent to the large sliding cyclone fence gate, "Fire Camp Jeffrey Haller". A small silver-coloured corrugated metal guard shack was positioned at the entrance to the compound and it is where he headed next.

"Sir, is this where new fire fighters report for training?" Wayne awkwardly inquired to a pair of men attired in beige colored uniforms manning the guard building.

"You're at the right place, buddy! You must be the new trainee that we are expecting, so welcome to the U.S. Fire Service and Bureau of Land Management National Fire Fighting Western Resource Center. Please show us some picture ID and sign in for a temporary visitor's pass and we'll call in your information to the Training Office. Take this clip board and attached forms, just fill these out over there on the table," the guard ordered as he took Wayne's driver's licence. There was a small pot of coffee brewing, which one of the guards was gracious enough to offer Wayne a cup of the inviting brew. To Wayne's surprise, the coffee smelled better than it tasted.

"Well, well, well, look'ee here, if it isn't the shave tail wantabee trainee, or should I say investment banker, Mr. Boston. I was wondering if you had the guts to show up here, 'Boston', you are either braver than you look or dumber than I expected…you've got some guts anyway, now we're going to see if you have enough man in you to be a forest fire fighter," Rick announced gleefully with a voice full of obvious personal disdain, arrogance and abundant taunting glee.

"Okay, Rick, you see me here! So, let's get this show on the road or perhaps you're the one who is having second thoughts about this wager, huh?" Wayne replied caustically in a most unfriendly and challenging tone.

Instantly, Rick's face transformed from mocking smug smile to that of a cold sombre frown. "Hey 'Boston' – you won't last the fire training session, let alone the first fire!" he bitterly replied with an almost certain spiteful conviction.

"You can still back-out of this bet, 'Boston'!" Rick quibbled with a tone of self-satisfaction.

Wayne did not answer; his only non-verbal reply was an utterly dirty look of contempt. "Hey 'Boston', come this way for your processing and indoctrination sessions," Rick commanded as the two men left the darkness of the guard shack and headed toward another set of inconspicuous corrugated grey metal buildings. The loathing between the two men was quite mutual and clearly manifested in both conversation and demeanor.

Not a further word was uttered between the two rivals, one could almost smell the tension between the two men as Rick led Wayne to the building called the 'Bunker' building. "Hey, 'Boston', this is where you'll be spending your next two weeks, pay close attention and learn or you'll be dead. Go into the large room and wait for further instructions," Rick warned as he quickly turned away and walked out toward another set of buildings.

Suddenly, a group of young men and women entered the conference room. They all seemed to be college age, most were in their early to mid-twenties, a few were in their thirties and none were older than forty years old. In a corner, Wayne noticed Robin and Sammy, part of the trio who had taunted and trapped him into this stupid stunt. They both eyed Wayne from afar and then turned their heads and giggled to one another in hushed girlish laughter upon seeing him sink meekly down into his seat at the back of the room. The entire scene was sheer adolescent foolishness. He played with the idea of simply getting up and leaving this ridiculous place.

Just as he was getting up out of his seat to leave, there was a sudden baritone voice thundering through the lecture room. "Now listen up, you Newbies! The following pearls of wisdom that I am going to tell you may well save your ass and those of your fellow firefighters as well. Three words, just three simple, flipping little lovely words, ladies and gentlemen: fuel, oxygen, and heat! Together these three simple words spell one terrific word and the bane of your existence and employment for the next three months – fire! Fire is a chemical reaction that occurs in nature – it thrives in an environment that is hot, dry, and windy. It also helps if nature provides a bit of a catalyst like lightning or static electricity, but humans also enormously assist in the form of careless camp fires, carelessly thrown cigarettes or matches, and sometimes downright deliberate arson itself! For you beginners here, most wildfires are caused by lightning, not surprisingly so, considering that the earth's surface is struck with several thousands of lightning strikes every day!"

That short oration commanded everyone's attention! The hall grew so quiet that you could hear a pin drop. "For any of you here that have an ounce of brains and wants to get the hell out of here and quit, now is the time to do it and I'll think none the worse for you having the brains and the courage to do this," Mr Sanchez growled. Not one soul moved an inch!

"Now that's good, no flipping quitters! I like that, but enjoy this day – it will be your last easy day of the season ladies and gentlemen," Peter Sanchez warned the group as he smiled and took a pile of forms from one of the front tables. He continued his un-rehearsed monologue without a gasp, as if he had said it a hundred times (which he had): "Neatly, fill out the forms being handed out, you'll be paid as temporary GS7-GS9s, depending on your background and education. For billeting, you can select to stay in the dorm building here or at a local billeting establishment at your own cost. Provide us with a copy of your address, phone number and email. Most importantly, ensure that you fill-out your life insurance forms, beneficiaries, and name of the notification of next-of-kin!" With these stark words, everyone in the room became quiet and most serious

"Let me have your undivided attention, folks, my name is Mr Peter Sanchez and I am your training supervisor for the next few weeks, during which time you are going to hate and curse the things that the US Fire Service and Bureau of Land Management staff are going to inflict upon you both physically and mentally, but if you don't give up, you listen and learn and you pass your Physical Training (PT) test – then you will become a certified and trained forest fire fighter, some of you may even safely survive the summer firefighting season. For any of you that have any sort of heroic or glamour-filled ideas about this job, leave those silly notions behind you right now! This job is dangerous, dirty, hard, long and non-forgiving on both the novice and the foolhardy; while you are all novices now, I pray that none of you are fools. Remember that fire is an equal opportunity enemy, it cares nothing of your race, gender, education or social background – it kills and destroys with perfect equality and dedication." Everyone's previous, easy-going manner was now vanquished by Sanchez's short sombre sermon.

After an hour of speaking, Sanchez finished-up his introduction lecture. "Great, folks – no questions or concerns at this point! So, your next stop is a quick physical and the issuance of fire gear, which you will store in your lockers here at the Camp Haller bunkhouses. This afternoon, you get four hours of fire theory, equipment and tactics. Tomorrow and every day thereafter, you will be doing PT as we refer to it, for at least one hour daily under supervisor instruction, this is going to help build-up your bodies into excellent condition, this to better cope with the rigors of firefighting, which involves intensive physical tasks. All genders and ages must perform to the same rigorous physical performance standards, the wildfires do not discriminate and neither can we afford to do so either! I sure hope that everyone came to camp physically prepared because one cannot get into shape in only two short weeks!" Mr Sanchez warned dryly in a business-like fashion. Everyone in the class looked and made nervous grins to one another.

"Now before we get started on the more 'technical' aspects of this lecture, here are some personal rules that I will enforce as your trainer and ground fire coordinator, some of these 'do's' and 'don'ts' are even official and legal, while others are strictly from my twenty-five years of personal experiences on fighting fires and staying alive, so if you're smart, I suggest you keep your eyes and ears open while I'm lecturing," Sanchez announced sternly to his attentive audience.

Suddenly, two burly men appeared through the classroom door carrying an enormous 10-gallon metal cylindrical vessel; they laid the giant container onto the sturdy wood table immediately adjacent to Peter Sanchez, along with a long stack of white cardboard cups. "Ah great, folks, we have coffee and as some of you might have guessed, the forest fighting organizations run on adrenaline and that means coffee – nasty strong, black, heaping cups of coffee, we'll try to get this nasty brew out to everyone in the field whenever we get supply drops to the ground based 'Hot Shot' crews – which means all of you! So come up here and grab some coffee, it will make the lecture go better for you, as I don't want any sleeping newbies in my class today or any other day, if you start to nod off, you will be standing for the rest of this class," Sanchez stated both encouragingly and with a tone of warning to boot.

The lights went low and video was played from a DVD projector located at the rear of the classroom. The films were a series of short 15-20-minute clips covering the phenomena of fires, the organization of both the National Fire Service and Bureau of Land Management organizations, field safety procedures, field personal hygiene, basic emergency first-aid procedures, the tactics of fighting fires by the Smoke Jumpers and Hot Shots and the specific equipment employed by the National Interagency Coordination Center. As a capstone lecture, it was noted that the entire fire tracking centre responsibilities were managed by the National Interagency Fire Center located in Boise, Idaho.

The entire series of film clips ran for almost two hours, yet the time went by quickly and the material was presented in a concise, informative, and interesting manner. No one went to sleep out of either the fear of retribution from Mr Sanchez or the enticing nature of the subject material. Wayne was impressed at the complexity of the forest fire organizations, as well as the abundance of the Federal, State and local support that was provided to fight against the summer wildfires, yet he also pondered the relentless nature of these wildfires which he had mundanely watched on TV. Each year seemed to be worse than the preceding one, this despite the proliferation of manpower and resources. Annually, the fires were fought to a draw, but never to a final victory.

The darkened room was suddenly bathed in the bright gleam of bright fluorescent lights accompanied by a seemingly mocking smile from Mr Sanchez. "Well, that's it for now ladies and gentlemen, I address you in politeness because none of you have the honour of being addressed as 'forest fire fighters' until you have passed the orientation training course and the initiation of your first wildfire encounter, it is only then that you can be called 'fire fighters' or as the outside world will refer to you as 'Hot Shots' or 'Fire Chasers'. Respect is always earned here, not merely verbally conferred."

After the films, Sanchez's authoritative monologue lectures continued unabated, as the facts and figures that he quoted from memory and experience filled the already bulging heads of his young attentive students. "Fire, and I mean all types of fires, are born out of three basic components: fuel, oxygen and heat. Forest fires are complemented by other natural phenomena like the weather and terrain. It is our job to deprive, starve and kill the forest fires by robbing it of its fuel, barring that tactic, we will try to influence a fire's direction of travel or its intensity. Your main tools and weapons in this fight are the unglamorous, simple and highly effective shovel, chainsaw, and the infamous Pulaskis, but your biggest and deadliest weapon is your brain! Through your training and experiences each of you will learn how to use it to defend against and defeat the wildfires! Remember, you are trained as individuals, but you work, act and fight as a team! A wildfire is too big and dangerous for any one person to tackle," Sanchez concluded with a note of finality in his tone. The films and lecture had now consumed the better part of several hours and Peter Sanchez was growing tired.

The USFS and BLM shared the assets of Camp Jeffrey Haller or simply 'Haller' for short; this was the name of a brave forest fighter who had died in the line of duty in this very county some twenty-five years ago, a time before most of these future 'Hot Shots' were born.

He decided to forgo lunch at the Camp Haller Mess Hall and instead simply stroll around Camp Haller for the 60 minutes that still belonged to him. Camp Haller, like most other US Fire Service and Bureau of Land Management camps, was a huge cyclone fenced-in area that contained over 30 buildings, helicopter pads, numerous depot staging areas, motor pools and cleared flat training areas on which there seemed to be no particular or special designated courses. The camp was devoid of trees; however, there existed numerous man-made tall wooden poles, atop of which were affixed simple loudspeakers, which he correctly guessed to be for announcements and fire alerts in a manner similar to the old TV series MASH.

The afternoon was occupied with physical examinations, lectures and equipment draw. The basic equipment issue consisted of: Hard hat w/light, two pairs of leather work gloves, two pairs of fire resistant Nomex gloves, one bright yellow coloured flame-resistant jacket, two quart-sized plastic canteens, one signal mirror, a metal whistle, three olive coloured over-shirts, two pairs of black coloured flame retardant pants, two sets of brown canvas timber boots, black wool socks, simple compass, stocking hat, flashlight, a medium sized backpack, bandage/ first aid packet, one shovel, one Pulaski, small personal gear bag, two padlocks, and finally two large Army green well-worn surplus duffel bags with which to load all of this gear. They all struggled to get all the gear into the two issued duffel bags, and everyone wondered how they would be able to carry all this gear to a fire – it must have weighed in excess of 65 lbs.

"Surprise, surprise, surprise, boys and girls! Get your shit together and head back to the billeting building. Get all your fire gear stowed away into your lockers and then change into that PT gear, to include a set of those boots that you were just issued," a voice yelled from the exit doorway. Your PT uniform consists of wool socks, boots, brown canvas pants, shirt, and yellow fire jacket and full canteens" – now is that flipping clear?" a deep male voice rocketed at the gaggle of new fire trainees. A uniform loud response of 'yes sir' was almost immediately echoed back by the newbies in cheerful unison. The bellowing voice belonged to Frank Stanton, another senior U.S. Fire Service superior, and for the next two weeks a trainer and sometimes tormentor to these young Newbies.

"I mean now, people! Double time it...I said on the double!" he yelled in a commanding manner akin to a well- seasoned Drill Sergeant, as the young men and women struggled with the two heavily laden duffel bags in the warm Wyoming sun. "If you think this is bad, people, just wait until August and the full heat of the wildfires are upon us," Frank added in almost a joyous tormenting tone to his young trainees. Everyone grumbled in low tones and dreaded the arrival of any further commands. This forest fire training was not going to be a cakewalk by any stretch for any of them, yet they were young and healthy, only a lack of individual resolve would terminate any one of them. As with military and police training, the greatest challenges were psychological.

Despite its perceived crudeness, Frank's bellicose orders presented a dual purpose: to get the Newbies to react to orders immediately without question and also as equally important – to get these soft-assed civilians into physically, ship-shape forest fighters. After some additional minutes of yelling, the stressed-out trainees emerged in front of Frank Stanton. Everyone appeared in visible disarray, there was a visual absence of uniformity and assembly. It was literally an unorganized gaggle.

"My name is Mr Frank Stanton, your master and trainer for the next two weeks, don't forget my name or my orders! If you have any personal issues, come to me first – this is called using the chain-of-command. I have found in my many years that whenever it is so possible, I try to explain why you are to do something, but there will be times when you will be told nothing – so just obey the command given to you. This is because in a wildfire, one needs to react instantly to commands by those in authority simply because there is no time for discussions, explanations, or arguments." The point was well understood, as everyone merely nodded their heads in silent acknowledgment.

Frank continued his lecture. "At the USFS and BLM Training Centers – there is minimal simulation, realism is the best teacher. We have discovered, like all realistic training, that there exists dangers and risks, just like during an actual fire environment...so pay attention and ask any questions that you may have of me or the training staff! Do you understand?" "Yes sir," was the collective response.

"Second, everyone needs to get used to wearing their fire-fighting gear from day one. You are wearing your new, uncomfortable boots and you will continue to wear your boots alternating from one pair to the other on alternate days because you need to break-in these boots and there is no way short of wearing these boots that will suffice for this task. Your feet are going to be hurting, so go out today to the Camp Shopette and buy ace bandages, insoles and any other cushioning materials that you need to maintain your feet. Take care of any blisters, since your feet are your transportation and the only inherent means of survival in this trade, so take care of them. I also want everyone to get a pair of good running shoes; these will be used for your running exercises and for taking your final qualifying PT test in two weeks," Frank succinctly directed.

"Okay, everyone, get the hell up! Left face – forward march!" Frank commanded in a roar reminiscent of an old Army drill sergeant. The long walk of the first day had begun. After two miles, many of the newbies were becoming fatigued and the formation lost all resemblance to any organized group, as many of the new trainees began to become exhausted and stagger, some began to lose their footing on the uneven road surface. Unabated by these distractions, Frank continued the fast pace without even a stumble. The rigid new boots were taking a heavy toll of the 'Newbies' – even those in great physical shape encountered minor foot injuries.

"Come on! Hurry up, people, this is only your first day and we are barely half-way done and it isn't even summer yet," Frank yelled out in an intimidating and challenging tone at his young recruits. Throughout the endless afternoon, they walked endlessly up and down the country hills and valleys of lush ponderosa pines and Douglas firs. Another two hours went by when suddenly the exhausted group turned around a bend atop the fire road and saw to their delight off into the distance the USFS/BLA Haller base camp. Everyone's morale was raised immediately by the sight.

"Newbies, line up in a file of two ranks just like before! That was a nice little workout that got the blood moving – right? Well, your first day of training is over, well almost! Now – Attention! Now get down everyone and give me twenty push-ups, on the double...right now!" Frank yelled as the sweaty, dirty lot of trainees gave out grunts of desperation and fatigue as each one of them did their best to knock out the push-ups as ordered.

Most of the Newbies only performed about fifteen push-ups before Frank barked out another command, "Okay, everyone stop and get up to the position of attention. Relax and stand easy folks, stretch it out now! That's the end of your day, I'll see everyone at 0600 hours, so look at your schedules for a reporting location. Tomorrow you will report in wearing your other pair of boots, work pants, shirt and yellow jacket. We start our PT running exercise tomorrow afternoon in sneakers, this so as to give your sore feet a day of recovery. Remember to buy those foot bandages, inserts, etc. Our next forced march will include hard hat, half pack, Pulaski and canteens. "Newbies Dismissed," Frank commended with a smile.

Every Newbie fell out of the formation half exhausted from the heat, stressful exercise, lack of hydration or a combination of all three. Everyone's feet were sore and blistered from the new boots and the long marching. Most of their canteens were empty. It was a slow, yet hurtful walk back to Camp Haller. Yet every PT exercise had an intended purpose, the walking and running to build up leg strength and endurance, while the push-ups were to build-up the necessary upper body strength required to work both manual and automated tools and equipment.

Being without personal transport, he waited, dirty and tired at the front gate for the next reservation sponsored Blue Bird bus, which was going to be his main transportation until further notice. He was exhausted, filthy, in pain and yet he felt accomplished. He was in great physical shape and he had maintained his health and fitness through participation in the best gym and physical fitness trainers back in Boston; still, this training was tough.

The weary passengers slowly trekked into the almost empty bus, each slumbering back into the hard vinyl seat that was to be their abode for the next half hour or so. Wayne's motel was the first stop, he had some time to shut his eyes and get some badly needed rest. Before he knew it, his destination point was announced. Drenched in perspiration and grime, Wayne quickly entered his room, began to strip off his clothes and quickly entered the shower. It was the end of a long day. As the hot water enveloped his body, the tub basin filled with the remnants of brown, discoloured debris, he became confident of his ability to not only finish the training, but to even win the bet from those blue-collar Neanderthals. "One day down, another 13 to go, not a problem, not a problem at all!" Wayne chuckled to himself.

* * * * * * * * * * * * * * * * * *

There was another ragged soul who was checking into the US Fire Service/BLM Fire Camp; his old, lanky and rugged physical appearance was adamant testimony that he would never be mistaken as a Hot Shot Newbie. Both his well-wrinkled skin and mature age attested that he was a seasoned veteran long accustomed to the annual summer ritual of in-processing into the US Fire Service and Bureau of Land Management menagerie of forms and examinations. From the slums of Chicago to the steaming elephant grassland of Southeast Asia and onto the landscape of a dozen metropolitan cities, he had fought the pains and pitfalls of every working man – to earn enough money to put shelter over his head, food on his table and have a little cash leftover for some few fleeting moments of enjoyment along the way. He was nearing retirement and he wanted to relish every summer that was left to him.

This thin, tall, well-aged, almost regal bearing mahogany-skinned man with greying hair was Hank Ransome and he, too, was mustering-in for his seasonal fire duty as a Fire Helipilot. The Helipilots were the timely disciples of the forest fire fighting profession; they arrived on critical fire scenes with the right equipment and personnel, often just in the nick of time. The Helipilots were a blend between the 'Hot Shots' and the 'Smoke Jumpers' thus being able to easily fit in with either fraternity, yet never being fully accepted by either group. Many of them were individualistic loners. As their name implied, the Helipilots flew the rotary aircraft or 'choppers' in support of both the 'Hot Shot' and 'Smoke Jumper' teams, their main duties were off-loading supplies, dropping huge buckets of water and fire retardant, embarking/debarking personnel, injury and deceased removal and also fire observation and reporting. Like everyone else, the contracted pilots were seasonal employees.

Being a Vet from the Vietnam War helped to aid Hank in his piloting duties. Forest fire conditions were very dangerous and akin to war combat missions in terms of danger, unpredictability and stress placed upon the pilots. Most of the newer Helipilots were in their late twenties and thirties, most had been in combat in either Iraq or Afghanistan and Hank was the only one this year who had served in Vietnam. He was being eclipsed by the younger generation and his departure was only a matter of time. His eyes, reflexes and stamina were all deteriorating and soon he would be forced by age to leave this chosen profession.

Like the other fire fighters, Hank Ransome had come to enjoy his seasonal sojourns with the US Fire Service and the BLM organizations, as it gave him a break from commercial flying, the jobs for which at his age were becoming fewer and fewer; the world belonged to the young and he knew it. His full-time helicopter job was that of being an auxiliary helicopter pilot for a local Seattle news station, the pay and hours were good. Yet time was not on his side.

Even now, he could sense the slightest pains and discomforts resulting from an early case of arthritis in his lower back and small left toe, in a few years who knew how bad his health would become? By that time, he would be ready for his social security and pension. "Then what?" he nervously thought to himself in disgust, as he lay on his cool bed staring at a TV programme that he couldn't even remember the title or characters.

Hank had arranged for a very modest local motel to be his residence this firefighting season. A man well into his sixties was not going to share his privacy and sleep time with an open bay barracks full of whipper snapping twenty-year old, testosterone laden, beer guzzling, loud mouthed Hot Shots. His age had earned him some badly needed respect and privacy.

The liquor bottle was now only half-full, and Hank was in no shape to get up and drive out for dinner, not that he had any appetite at this point anyway. In sheer disgust, he turned off the nonsensical reality TV programme and dimmed the lights. He took a light puff of the Padron cigar, of which he was an occasional smoker. As he watched the twirling ceiling fan, his eyes grew heavy and he was once again in Vietnam.

The twirling ceiling fan mimicked the visual rotation and the hum so reminiscent of the UH-1 Huey helicopter that he flew in Vietnam on so many sorties, as these military air missions were so named. A few big gulps of whisky and he was in twilight sleep and back to the rice fields of Vietnam. The war had been over for many decades, but not his nightmares that were born of it. It was a constant fight that was never won by either his angels or demons.

★★★★★★★★★★★★★★

Tuesday morning was starting out slow and mundane at Hamilton & MacAlister. As per their usual morning routine, Margie DeTagelio and Joan Peters were sorting through the early mail of the account executives. As per her normal timetable, Katherine MacAlister showed up to her office promptly on the hour and she was dressed in another gorgeous custom-made designer suit costing at least $10,000.

"A very good morning to you, Miss Katherine, I'll have your coffee ready in a few minutes, if that's fine with you?" Joan Peters announced in a very polite and cheerful tone as Katherine strode up in front of

Joan's desk.

"Yes, that would be fine Mrs Peters," Katherine replied in an almost aloof and resigned voice. She looked over to where Margie sat and gave a somewhat forced smile, which Margie returned in kind.

"Now that's a darling little outfit that you have on DeTagelio, it looks so charming on you too!" Katherine stated in a rather sincere manner.

For once, Margie was delightfully surprised by the compliment.

"Oh, thank you, Miss Katherine, it's nothing really," Margie replied in an almost defensive meek manner.

Katherine then turned back to Joan Peters and loudly quibbled in a tone for Margie to clearly hear, "Joan is it is amazing what stuff they sell at those outlets with the Blue Light Specials?" as she smiled and quickly walked into her ornate private office. Instantly, Margie's face fell from being relatively cheerful to that of downright dejection.

"Joan, that woman is a real Ice Bitch and I can't for the life of me imagine what Brad likes about that woman!" Margie snorted as she wiped her eyes and blew her nose.

Joan felt bad for Margie, but she worked directly for Katherine and she was in her early sixties, she was never going to get another job like the one she enjoyed at Hamilton & MacAlister, so she just kept quiet, like so many countless other working-class Americans. Independence was a right reserved for the wealthy or foolish.

The morning uneventfully wore on as both Joan and Margie went through their e-mails and processed the daily incoming mail, which was voluminous to say the least. Unexpectedly, Tommy the young office mail clerk appeared before Margie's desk. "Good morning, Margie, I have a piece of urgent mail that has just arrived special courier delivery for Mr Hamilton, can you please sign for it?"

"Sure, thing Tommy, no problem," she smiled in a half flirting, devilish manner, confidently knowing that Tommy had an almost adolescent crush on her.

"If I'm not being too inquisitive, Margie, what is that item all about?" Joan inquired as she too became intrigued by the special delivery item addressed to Brad. "I'll let you know in a minute," Margie cheerfully sighed as she took a sip of strong hazelnut coffee. Margie looked at the envelope; it was from the firm's insurance company. She deftly applied a careful and neat flick of the office letter opener and proceeded to read the contents of the medium sized manila envelope. Her eyes widened, and her mouth opened with a wide expanse.

"What's the matter?" Joan asked in an almost nervous demanding tone.

"Holy Shit, Joan, this is a medical insurance claim concerning Brad, he's been in some sort of an accident out in Wyoming! He's alive, thank God and it appears that he's not injured too badly!" Margie sighed in a tone of both relief and despair.

"Damn it, Joan, this means that I have to go and inform Miss Katherine, the Ice Princess herself, about this incident ASAP!" Margie confessed in a nervous tone. "Well, better now than later," Margie muttered in a low tone as she wearily knocked on Katherine's door.

"Come in," a strong demonstrative feminine voice echoed from behind the recess of the massive oak office door. Margie slowly entered with the insurance claim papers, she saw Katherine looking down and engrossed in the reading of some e-mails on her computer terminal. "Well, come on and be out with it, DeTagelio, do you have something to say or are you just going to stand there, and act dumbfounded as usual?" Katherine challenged quite coldly.

"Well, Miss Katherine I just received a special delivery mail item here on Mr Brad Hamilton, it's an insurance medical claim, he's been hurt," Margie slowly spouted forth in a slow, deliberate, and frightened voice.

"Oh my dear Lord! ...When?...How?...Where?" Katherine shouted out and almost on the verge of panic. "Brad had only told me that he was in some small fender-bender or fall," Katherine screamed out. Margie tried to verbalize the few facts that she had gleamed from the medical claim, but Katherine was in no state to hear words of logic at this point. "I need to see the flipping facts now!" she shouted hysterically at Margie, as she anxiously grabbed the insurance papers from Margie's hands, almost tearing the papers in the process. Katherine's eyes digested the details in a frantic, yet methodical manner, a trait of both her nature and the financial trading-pit days.

"These are medical examinations and reports... indications are that Brad is not seriously hurt, some slight lacerations and a few bad bruises, thank God!" Katherine rejoiced and almost in a state of tears.

"Good work for once, DeTagelio! Now your next task, and I don't give a crap how long it takes, is to track down the details of this incident and to get me personally in contact with Mr Hamilton, is that clear? I mean no out of office lunch breaks, water cooler chatter or anything else today! Is that clear, girlie?" Katherine ordered sternly while looking menacingly into Margie's eyes.

Once again, Margie was frightened and intimidated by Katherine's power and resolve. "Yes of course, Miss Katherine, I understand completely!" Margie replied obediently as she walked quietly and docilely out of Katherine's office, closing the door behind her as she exited. Until Brad's disposition was clarified fully to the satisfaction of Katherine, there was going to be hell to pay around the office and a lot of the shit was going to befall on Margie – who was Katherine's favourite whipping girl.

★ ★ ★ ★ ★ ★ ★ ★ ★ ★ ★ ★ ★ ★ ★ ★ ★

Back at Camp Haller, Wayne had finished up his second week of basic firefighting training as a newbie. The class were finishing up the last of their basic qualification course training and examinations. This day culminated in the final Physical Training (PT) test, a 2.5 mile run in boots, push-ups and sit-ups, complemented by a written examination in which each student needed a passing grade of 80 out of 100 questions and finally a written appraisal by Frank Stanton. Wayne and his entire class were both lucky and worked hard, because of their grit and determination each and every man and woman in the class had passed their physical, written examination, and individual evaluations.

A short informal ceremony with the presentation of a certificate and a picture was the final event of the training programme, after that each Newbie would be assigned to a fire crew on the following Monday. Each Newbie was now a valid Fire Fighter, yet the name of 'Hot Shot' was only to be bestowed by the 'regular' fire fighters once each of them had proven themselves in the actual 'baptism of fire' in which they fought a real forest fire and not some mocked-up version of one on the sanitized grounds of the fire training ranges.

Instead of any wild class party or drunken celebrations, Wayne decided to take his tired carcass back to his 'tried and true' hotel room, which had become something of a semi-permanent home for the past few weeks. Upon entering the room, he noticed that his hotel phone red coloured message light was blinking, indicating that a call was awaiting his review. Wayne took out his cell phone, which he was required to deactivate during the training day and upon activation, it also revealed that there was a message awaiting his response. It was an urgent call from Katherine earlier in the day, so too was the second message as was the third and fourth messages as well. He checked his cell phone messages, and these too were from a frantic Katherine expressing concern and an urgent reply to her phone calls. He also noted urgent calls from Margie DeTagelio.

"Hello Kate, it's Brad – now what's the matter, darling? I just received your call on my cell phone," Wayne exclaimed in an excited and quite inquisitive tone.

"What's the matter? Are you serious? You must be kidding me, right! I just received insurance papers stating that you were in an accident...a serious accident and not some fender-bender...you didn't tell me that you were admitted to the hospital, my God I am going half-crazy with worry about you." Katherine screamed out frantically.

"Okay, Kate, please simmer down, there's no problem...really, I am perfectly fine!" Brad replied as he generously stretched the truth. Yet Kate would have none of this deflection, she wanted answers and she wanted these now. "Well, it's that DeTagelio girl – she just brought to me your medical insurance claim to me this morning. The report clearly stated that you were in an accident with a motorcycle, now that sounds very serious to me Brad!" Kate sounded-off alarmingly.

"Well naturally, Kate, I didn't want you to get upset or anything, I guess I failed in that endeavor?" Brad replied in an embarrassed tone. Katherine was not satisfied with Brad's tepid response; he was being overly coy with her.

"I am very upset, give me your flipping address, I'm coming out to that God-forsaken place on the next flight," Kate avenged in a still angry and determined voice.

"Oh no, Kate, there's no need for that! You are over-reacting! I am completely fine! Remember I am no longer riding the BMW, it got beat up badly in the fender-bender and I am physically fine, just look at the accident report for yourself," Wayne rattled off in a short reassuring response.

Katherine remained silent and there was a pregnant pause at the other end of the line.

"Look here, Kate, I'm really fine and I have a safe job here for the summer, a liaison-type job with the U.S. Government as a temporary grounds keeper and forest warden for some government-owned wilderness land, it's on a Native American reservation. I am really getting back to mother nature!" Brad casually lied without any hesitation. This was the second time that he had deliberately lied to Katherine in less than two minutes.

Always the sceptic, Katherine was still not convinced. "Are you sure that you're no longer riding that killer BMW motorcycle?" she deftly inquired in a now half-sceptical voice.

"You bet I am, Kate, that bike is down for the rest of the summer, by which time I should be done this temporary position and then I'm back to Boston no later than October – we can get married then!" he added almost as an afterthought. The reminding sound of the word 'married' immediately perked Katherine's mood up.

"Well, all right, Brad, but I want to hear from you a few times a week, remember that as the future bride I have a lot of wedding plans that I need to talk with you about and the remaining four months until October are going to be crammed pack for my planning," Katherine reminded Brad in an almost condescending tone.

"You got it, Kate, I'll be a good boy and I'll chat with you a few times a week and I'll send you a postcard too, the outdoor scenery here is just beautiful and grand," Wayne replied earnestly.

"Well, okay... you've convinced me for the moment, Brad, but you better stay safe and if you need anything, you just let me know and if anything becomes a problem, I am personally going to fly out to wherever you are working and put you on my private jet, is that clear, Mister? I want to have no more of your monkey-business, do you understand me, darling?" Kate resounded in a joyful and playful tone. Yet this determined lady was fully serious about her demands. Kate hung up the receiver and was pleased as punch about her future wedding commitment from Brad. Yet by all reckoning it was going to be a very busy summer for all parties concerned, and, in more ways than anyone would have imagined possible.

* * * * * * * * * * * * * * * * * *

CHAPTER 9

Baptism in Fire

"All around him was a vision from Dante's Inferno of Hades. Yet he was not dead, and he had no intention of dying either"

I t was the Monday following the Newbies' graduation; by now Wayne could almost sleep-walk through his daily ritual of an early morning awakening, the bus ride to camp, class, PT, lunch, fire drills and instruction and then back to the motel again, so it had been for the past fourteen days. "I guess my years at Harvard really paid off," he dryly scoffed to himself about the ridiculously low weekly pay rate. It seemed that despite his training as a forest fire fighter, he was still deep-down a Boston snob. No matter, he had graduated from the grueling firefighting training and he actually appreciated the work and the associated physical and mental challenges that the fire fighters had to endure.

The past Saturday's graduation event, although a joyous time and one to be celebrated by each new fire fighter, had been an abstentious affair by any standard. The 'graduation' was conducted in a simple lecture hall with some urns of coffee, light refreshments and the traditional cake – which was adorned with small figurines of fire fighters, a simulated forest and a blaze of yellow icing. Absent were the traditional presence of family members, spouses or friends – this was by design a 'stag affair' with only the graduates themselves and other Camp Haller Fire staff being in attendance. In all fairness, no one really wanted to have their family and friends present, some like Wayne, never bothered to tell the outside world what exactly they were even doing over the summer, preferring to keep both their training and the new occupation a secret until the 'time was right'. Peter Sanchez was the graduation speaker and presenter of the graduation certificates.

Also in attendance, but well to the rear of the lecture hall, was Sammy, Robin and Rick – they were all were wearing long faces and none of them had thought that 'Boston' as they crudely referred to him, would have made it this far. Their negative attention paid unto him had increased since he was one step closer to fulfilling his end of the bet. Each of them stood to lose a piece of their pride in addition to a hefty percentage of their summer fire pay should Wayne eventually win the bet. They each chatted to one another in low rumbles of self-assurance about how this new shave-tail would not last past his first test of fire. Their hushed laughter only served to camouflage their silent, mounting fears that 'Boston' would somehow defiantly succeed.

The new fire fighters had a beautiful warm Wyoming Monday morning to begin their new summer careers. Peter Sanchez casually strolled into the well-lit lecture hall, while grasping a generously-sized coffee container. He smiled with a careless frown, unlike that of his previous stern classroom manner, which he had artificially adopted while being their fire teacher.

"Hello everyone, now listen-up for your fire team assignments! I'm a simple guy and I made this breakdown very easy, it's based according to the alphabetical breakdown of your last names. Your fire team leader assignments are as follows: those with names ending in A-G, see Mr Ben Ross; H-N go see Danny Birch, M-R go see Tom McGuire, and last but not least, S-V go see Donna Velasquez." Each fire team chief raised their hand up, as each of their names were called. The fire graduation group divided itself up accordingly to each fire team leader, who in turn took each group off into a separate location for private introductions and discussions.

Wayne and the others in his alphabetical grouping moved up toward a tall lean brown-haired man in his late thirties. "Greetings, new fire fighters, welcome to my team and my name is Danny Birch, but you can call me Dan for short. I've been fighting fires for the last ten years, so I guess that makes me a veteran of sorts and I hope that I can impart my enthusiasm and experiences to each of you and make your secondary chosen career an enjoyable one!" he announced in a confident and low-keyed manner. Wayne had an almost immediate confidence in Danny Birch – he possessed an ephemeral quality of a professional and a leader, a trait that he had witnessed on Wall Street and the financial business world; Danny was a rare commodity in this world, that of being a natural leader.

After a short introduction, Danny laid out the work schedule for the new members and informed them that they would be forming the part of a larger team consisting of 50-100 members and that his group was broken down in a military fashion of platoon and squads. Danny explained that he was their fire section or fire platoon leader and that he had four sub-section or squad leaders to assist him; the fire squad leaders would be met at a later date. He went on to explain that their formal two weeks of training was only the beginning, not the end, for becoming a seasoned fire fighter.

The real 'learning' was both constant and challenging. Unless there was a fire or fire support mission, the fire team members would be involved in continued firefighting training, physical conditioning and mock exercises. "Being in perfect physical shape was going to be a constant requirement, as well as that of possessing acute mental alertness – few of them would have the need of a gym this summer, since their training and calorie expenditures was to ensure that everyone would remain in optimal physical shape and many of them would even lose weight and continue to build muscle mass and tone throughout the season," Dan explained with some degree of satisfaction and proof. His physical frame was the evidence of his words. The work schedule for this day was half lecture in the morning on fire communications techniques, while the afternoon was a demonstration and practical exercise of properly using a chain saw, topped-off by some PT – a three mile run with some sit-ups and push-ups added in for 'shits and giggles'.

By the end of the day, most of the new fire fighters had blisters on their hands and their muscles were sore. The chain saw was a heavy beast weighing 20 lbs and the wielding of heavy firefighting gear bore a great strain upon even those who were in great shape; even the heavy canvas gloves did not prove adequate protection from the inevitable hand blistering and sore finger joints. While in training, hearing protection was mandatory; however, in the reality of an actual fire fight, hearing protection was often ignored or discarded entirely because it often proved to be a handicap to hearing the commands of the fire team chief and other co-workers; besides the loud roar of a wildfires often made hearing protection irrelevant.

The chainsaw, along with the humble Pulaski and shovel, were the true workhorse instruments of the modern forest fire fighter. After mastering the chain saw drills, Wayne and the other fire fighters were drilled in the field use of the shovel and Pulaski, both of these tools were physically demanding. In firefighting, like that of a battle, both teamwork and effective communications were vital in the victory over the wildfires.

The young men and women were getting 'broken-in' and using parts of their anatomy that had never been physically challenged before, the pain was tolerated, but it was also psychologically satisfying. With each day the various pains became dulled through repetitive physical exercises and exertions, while their proficiency in using firefighting instruments and procedures increased. While everyone was eager to 'test their mettle' against an actual fire, each one of them was also scared of the unknown dangers that would await each of them during a real fire. Like soldiers in battle, each untested fire fighter longed for the first battle and dreaded the fear of the first bullet fired at them and their possible failure in the deadly confrontation.

The next functional training module was communications, this consisting of the visual hand signals and FM communications between the fire team members and the fire base camp and other fire team groups. Like a military battle, successfully fighting the fire battles required effective teamwork and communications. Although not every fire fighter had a mobile FM radio, the fire platoon leaders and some select fire squad leaders did and in the event of an emergency, everyone had to be able to use the communication equipment and know the call signs of their group.

Wayne's fire platoon's call-sign was known as 'Sierra Bravo' (SB) so named for the indication of the name of Mr Sanchez as the fire group leader and Mr Birch as the fire platoon leader. The other platoon call sign designators followed the same naming convention protocols, these being name Sierra Romeo (SR), Sierra Mike (SM) and Sierra Victor (SV) respectively. Mr Sanchez's personal call-sign was Sierra Gulf' (SG), which used his Christian name and echelon ranking for Group. In addition to the FM radio call signs, each squad was named for tracking and management purposes by the designations Alpha, Bravo, Charlie and Delta. The day ended with the introduction by Mr Birch of the team's squad leaders. Each squad leader had between 8- 12 fire fighters reporting directly under them and the squad leader was directly responsible for the personal actions and job tasks assigned to and performed by each member of the squad.

As per military fashion, each platoon had four fire squads in it, this depending on the number of fire fighters that had signed up and were assigned to the camp for the season. Wayne spotted a familiar and most unwelcome sight, it was that of Robin Wolf standing off in the distance. He had not forgotten her rude manners that night at the bar; with only limited success, he tried to look away with an inconspicuous, stoic 'stare-ahead' posture.

Mr Birch barked into his bullhorn and ordered that each squad come to attention and perform the ordered drill movement on his command. Accordingly, the first squad performed a left face movement and trotted-off in route step march to an area some fifty yards away at which time Birch ordered a 'halt movement' command. At this time a tall, thin man appeared the squad leader, to take command of the new squad. Being in the second squad, Wayne's unit was called next, as they were ordered by Birch to perform a 'right face march' movement for a distance of about twenty yards at which time Birch yelled a 'halt' command into the bullhorn. The twelve-person squad stopped in unison upon hearing the halt command and anxiously awaited their next order.

A new, feminine voice was now heard. "At ease, relax folks! Good morning! I am your new squad leader, my name is Robin Wolf," she announced in a firm, yet very audible commanding voice. Wayne was flabbergasted – how ironic it was that one of those low-class assholes was to be his squad leader for the season! 'This must be a conflict of interest!' he thought as the squad broke down in an uneasy semi-circle around the petite pretty blonde streaked-haired woman. Yet the bet was personal and private, so unless Wayne made a direct objection to his superiors, nothing was to change.

Instantly Robin's eyes met Wayne's and one could almost cut the level of acrimony between them, yet Robin was if anything, a true professional and as such, she ignored any personal issues and addressed the concerns and welfare of her squad first before that of any personal issues. "Hello, people and welcome to the firefighting trade, you're all volunteered to be part of an elite group that fights Mother Nature each year and draws the same verdict each and every year – a tie! We will never be victorious over Mother Nature and we cannot afford to ever lose this fight either, the cost to both environment and property is too high, yet if the scientists at the National Interagency Fire Center in Boise Idaho are correct, global warming is going to make the forest fires even more severe and frequent. This means more work for us and more danger too! Let me point out that while this is an adventure or lark for some of you, it is deadly serious business and we lose fire fighters each year, sometimes its destiny, sometimes it's stupidity! I aim to make sure it's not my fault or your stupidity. I want everyone here to come to me with their issues or concerns, I put professionalism ahead of personal issues when it comes to firefighting," she lectured in a most business-like manner. Robin finished off her verbal introduction by stating her past eight years of firefighting experience as a Hot Shot, to include the scores of fires that she had fought. It was an impressive record and it was clear by her speech and command of the facts, that Robin was a seasoned, self-assured and worthy squad leader.

Strangely, Wayne became intrigued by Robin in spite of his initial dislike for this woman and her friends. He respected her words, attitude and accomplishments. She was no 'flash in the pan' or candy-ass leader; she had earned her stripes the hard way – by fighting forest fires for many years. Not knowing her personality or nature, he pondered if it would be wise to seek a transfer to another squad, but after hearing Robin's oratory, he decided to give her the benefit of the doubt. Wayne figured that he could always yell 'personal foul' and call off the bet if Robin started any personal animosity that negatively affected his firefighting performance.

For the remainder of the day, Robin led her squad in the dynamics of fire-fighting techniques, fire dynamics and PT. Although small in stature, Robin proved herself a worthy coach capable of drilling her squad to their physical limits. She was in top physical and mental condition. Wayne could only hope that Robin would maintain her personal demeanour throughout the fire season, 'the size of the bet was a healthy wager to a working woman.' He knew from his investment banking experiences the low-level actions that people stooped to where the issue of money and ego was concerned, and his wager confronted both of these demons. Only time would tell if Robin was a creature of professionalism or that of mere petty revenge.

★ ★ ★ ★ ★ ★ ★ ★ ★ ★ ★ ★ ★ ★ ★ ★ ★

Friday morning started out like any other work day at Camp Jeffrey Haller. As was the normal camp routine, Robin conducted a verbal and visual roll-call, having memorized the names and faces of each of her squad members. Although she promised herself to be fair with Wayne, she would not allow this eastern wealthy rich shit guy to get away with any behaviour that was outside the USFS norm or which was below that of the other squad members. To avoid any perception or accusation of prejudice, she never doted on Wayne or had a private conversation alone with him. 'Business was business' as far as Robin was concerned. Although fire fighters were always 'on-call' and worked six days a week, unless there was a fire or imminent chance of a fire, the typical Friday mornings were usually a dull affair, anticipated by the coming of a more leisurely weekend work schedule and late drinking parties at Indian Joe's pub.

There was a morning formation and roll call and as per usual, everyone was 'present and accounted for' as per the verbal report of that Robin would send up to her supervisor, Danny Birch. Suddenly from out of the camp loudspeaker came a short, but loud audio squawk from the camp's communication centre known as the Ready Shack: "Alert, Alert, this is not a drill! Red Flag warning for all camp resources: squad, platoon and group leaders please report immediately to the Ready Shack for a briefing and orders! I repeat, this is the Real McCoy...Red Flag alert... all leaders report to the Ready Shack for further orders, all other fire personnel are ordered to full ready status and standby, Out!" As the loudspeaker fell silent, there was a momentary silence as the shock of reality fell on everyone, especially to the new unseasoned fire fighters. The moment for which everyone had eagerly awaited and dreaded, had arrived! The Red Flag alert indicated an actual wild fire event.

"Squad Bravo, go get all of your personal fire gear and clothing from your lockers and report back at this exact location in 10 Mikes (the alpha numeric military designation for minutes)," Robin shouted in an unmistakable command voice. There was no need for any grumblings or questions, everyone was a mature adult and trained for the task at hand, both Robin and everyone in her squad was suddenly pumped with adrenaline. While Wayne and the squad quickly ran to their lockers and changed into their field clothing, Robin and the other squad and platoon leaders rushed to the Ready Shack to receive their briefings and mission task orders.

Robin and the other squad and platoon leaders were assembled into the Ready Shack small briefing room that was about the size of an average school classroom. "Listen-up! The National Inter-Agency Fire Center in Boise gave us a Red Flag alert to provide immediate fire-suppression to a Class D fire of about 750 acres of brush land about 20 miles south of Casper...source of the fire is suspected to be lightning from the recent passing thunderstorms. I need several sticks of jumpers, one Hot Shot platoon with a supporting 'six-pack' of trucks and a reserve fire platoon for a stand-by 'push package' with Emergency Medical Personnel (EMP) and helicopter services on-order...we are in the initial attack! Any questions?" Mr Sanchez inquired in a very businesslike tone, as he looked around the crowded room.

"Yeah, Pete, are you sure that only several 'sticks' of jumpers are enough? Personally, I think six or eight sticks are needed!" Rick Conroy loudly barked-out almost challengingly.

Pete Sanchez knew that Rick Conroy was trying to grandstand the Hot Shot ground operations and increase the role of his Smoke Jumpers – these were the parachutists who attacked the fires first and helped to stomp out the fiercest parts of a raging fire and redirect its path to a benign direction or into the direction of the ground Hot Shots. Robin had known Rick for several years and while she found him handsome, loyal and hardworking, she also knew that his ego for fame, prestige and greed – were his fatal personal character flaws.

"No, Rick, fire intelligence reports indicate that the resources that I have prescribed are sufficient...don't fret, Rick, you'll get your glory this season!" Pete Sanchez replied dryly. There was a low rumble of laughter as the veteran fire fighters knew that Rick the 'hot dog' had just been put in his place at the beginning of the fire season. Like most people, Rick hated to be embarrassed, but he especially did not appreciate Sanchez's public ridicule in front of his fellow Smoke Jumpers and his seasonal girlfriend. Rick was growing tired of the same summer ritual and he was also cognitive of his maturing age in a field that was mainly populated by people five or ten years younger than himself. Each year the physical pressure and exertions of performing a 3-mile PT test, daily physical conditioning and actual fire jumps – were becoming harder to endure. His efforts to revitalize both his professional and personal life had come to no avail. He needed a sudden and drastic positive change in his life! He didn't want to end up in his middle-age years as a failure or 'Average Joe' – yet his dreams of becoming a rich man were fading fast,

Sanchez tried to console Rick concerning the limited number of Smoke Jumpers for this mission by providing a more eloquent justification. "Look, Rick, since this is a medium-sized fire, I suggest a three stick drop because more sticks cannot be justified by the size of this fire; there's a cost-benefit to fighting fires and the fire season is only beginning." This answer did not placate Rick one iota.

"What about aerial photos or video on this fire? Do we have a Hunter or Predator Unmanned Aerial Vehicle available?" Rick inquired in an almost demanding tone from his superior.

Once again, Sanchez levelled a disparaging reply at the antagonist Smoke Jumper, "I'm sorry, Rick, the fire's too small and the Predator Unmanned Aerial Vehicles (UAVs) are not within range and by the time these get here, the fire will be out of control…we have to jump into this one right now based solely upon ground reports. We'll try and get a spotter plane or chopper up ASAP, then we can give you a report once you're in route in the air."

"Fuck me again!", Rick muttered, as he was clearly not satisfied with the response, especially from someone who was never a part of the elite Smoke Jumping fraternity.

"That's just flipping great, boss! You're not the guy that has to jump his ass into this fiery hell hole, but for me and my team, that's exactly what we will have to do, not you!" Rick shouted in an almost insubordinate disgustful reply.

"Now that's enough bitching, Rick! You Smoke Jumpers have your orders, you'll get the fire intelligence as soon as it's ready, that's all, now go get your gear, stick members and report to the flight line," Sanchez replied in a frustrated voice as he left the front of the room and walked toward the camp's Command & Control centre, which contained the latest communications and data reporting systems interlinked with the National Weather Service and National Fire Inter-Agency Center.

The Smoke Jumpers were an elite cadre of mostly male personnel, whose numbers totaled about 1,000 nationwide. They were all in their twenties or thirties and all possessed a 'hot-dogger' mentality similar to those invincible attitudes possessed by a jet fighter pilot, race car driver or down-hill Alpine skier. 'If anyone was going to get killed in a fire, it was going to be the other poor guy, not me!' thus was the arrogant thinking of each Smoke Jumper.

The BLM and US Forest Service both employed 'Smoke Jumpers or Smokies' along with the ground 'Hot Shots'. Each department was originally assigned to fight fires on their own respective US Fire Service and BLM territories; however, over the years the need for the conservation of resources and limited separate funding made the sharing of US Fire Service and BLM resources a priority. Small differences remained between the two services like the types of parachutes employed by each organization: the US Fire Service used the round canopy, military style parachute, which merely dropped the fire fighter using a static line that automatically opened the parachute and facilitated a straight-down, vertically, over the ground landing; while the BLM allowed the optional usage of a free-fall, rip-cord activated parachute deployment of a square, wing-like canopy that was more adept at being manoeuvrable like a glider or wing, but which was conversely more difficult and dangerous to use. Over time only the most experienced and daring Smoke Jumpers used the square wing-like parachute, this due to its complexity and potentially dangerous nature.

Most jumpers, whether they be from the US Fire Service or BLM, lacked sufficient training throughout the year to quickly re-master the rectangular parachute in the span of only a few short summer months, so most everyone now used the round canopy parachute – it was simple, reliable and relatively safe. Rick Conroy, however, was not a man to ever play life or fighting fires the safe or traditional way if he could help it. Now in his mid-thirties, Rick was the elder Smoke Jumper or Smoky, the diamond shaped jump wings sewed on his blue Nomex fire resistant jump suit, attesting to his seventy-five free-fall jumps.

All Smoke Jumpers carried approximately 65- 85 lbs. of gear and their main purpose was to try and put out the core of a wildfire or re-divert its path, so that the ground pounding Hot Shots could do the main job of putting out the bulk of the fire. The Smoke Jumpers were formed into jump teams known as 'sticks' each of which normally consisted of six or seven jumpers and there could be several 'sticks' to a fire, this depending on the fire's size, intensity and the danger to critical private and public property. The Smoke Jumpers were an elite and each of them knew it. They also knew that each jump and year of duty – could well be their last. Physical injuries were common, if not eventually inevitable. It was a dangerous profession and one best performed by the stamina and eagerness of youth and not that of the middle-aged.

* * * * * * * * * * * * * *

Whenever a raging wildfire erupted, the entire fire camp awakened to a frantic life, it was like an organized Army of ants had been alerted to move to a specific location, all the camp workers and fire fighters were ablast with energy and a dynamic set of organized actions took place as if on cue. As the small group of Smoke Jumpers arranged themselves on the camp's airfield, the frenzy of the ground Hot Shots was just as intense. An assorted caravan of about twenty pale yellow coloured fire trucks and transport vehicles were even now being staged a short distance away from the main gate. The vehicles for personnel were sometimes unofficially called 'six-packs' because this was the average number of fire fighters that these vehicles contained, along with all their fire gear and assorted equipment.

"Okay, Team Bravo over here…line up for an individual personal and equipment check," Robin yelled to her small crew that was assembled with all their fire clothing and basic individual fire gear at her team's staging area. Wayne and the other new fire fighters were pumping with adrenaline, this being their first fire and not knowing exactly what to expect. Robin's crew consumed two vehicles of space and she checked each fire fighter personally before each boarded their respective vehicle. She grinned with an almost devilish satisfaction at seeing Wayne approach her – 'it was great being able to be in charge of this Boston candy-ass,' she thought to herself with a degree of smugness and obvious superior satisfaction.

"You hold it right there 'Boston', let's see if all your equipment is squared away," she commanded with an obvious authoritative delight. She looked up and down his uniform and personal gear to ensure that every button and fastener was snapped tight. Even though she didn't like this Boston guy and she didn't want to lose her bet, he was still a Hot Shot asset under her charge and she wasn't going to lose any of her crew, especially this guy. "You scared, 'Boston'? If not, you sure as hell should be!" she inquired with a smiling grin.

Wayne wasn't going to give Robin the satisfaction of any weakness, thus he replied with a sarcastic response of his own, this being typical of his defensive nature. "Scared? Maybe excited a bit, but I've seen more nervous and imposing situations on the Wall Street and Chicago trading floors!" he arrogantly barked back smartly.

"I just love that ego of yours, 'Boston', you can't admit any weakness to anyone, , especially to a woman…now get your sorry ass on that vehicle!" Robin replied as she lifted her foot and pressed it against Wayne's backside in a thrusting motion, as she inspected the next new fire fighter. Wayne was only somewhat embarrassed by Robin's remarks and physical gesture, it only served to reinforce his perception that Robin was endowed with low-class breeding and manners, she was a woman obviously as coarse as 60-grade sandpaper. "I pity the poor bastard that has to hump that bitch, he must need a set of hearing protection and a full body condom," Wayne chauvinistically remarked to a fellow male fire fighter who was seated beside him.

"Hey, girlfriend squad leader, mind a little company on this trip?" Sammy yelled as she tapped Robin on the shoulder.

"So, you've been assigned as the Emergency Medical Tech (EMT) on this fire, huh, Sammy?...well it's great to have you aboard, girlfriend. I might need for you to remove some splinters out of 'Boston's' fragile, manicured hands!" Robin remarked in a frustrated tone.

Sammy was ready to reinforce Robin's prejudice of Wayne all too eagerly. "Yeah, I was shocked that he was assigned to your crew. Can you maintain a neutral position in this, Robin?" Sammy asked earnestly.

Robin's mouth quickly dropped at the mere suggestion of any sort of personal grudge. "Sammy, there is no way that I am going to allow my personal dislike for that Boston creep or any wager to colour my professional attitudes or work ethics...that Boston guy is going to be treated like every new fire fighter – tough and with discipline! I don't want any problems with him. If he doesn't toe the line with my squad, I'll have him transferred out, okay?" Robin sounded off to Sammy as she gently placed her hand on Sam's shoulder. Sammy knew that Robin had high personal integrity, as she nodded in silent affirmation as to Robin's professionalism regarding 'Boston'. Still, having a third of one's net pay riding on the bet, could dissuade even those of the most noble character. Money changed everyone's character, perceptions and ambitions.

The fire convoy moved out in rapid order, initially following gravel roads and then onto the paved highways. In about two hours, they would all be engaged in a real firefight. Everyone was charged with excitement, especially the new fire fighters. Robin, on the other hand, was preoccupied with nervousness and fear – as this was her first year as a squad supervisor and she was unsure of her abilities to lead the crew. Although a very accomplished fire fighter, it was one thing to do a job well as an individual, it was quite another to be supervising the actions of others; now she had more than just herself to worry about on this job. Her actions like those of every fire unit leader, involved life and death decisions and she could not afford to make any mistakes with the lives of her team members, even those who she personally disliked, like 'Boston'.

Robin preoccupied her fears with keeping busy, listening to the fire platoon leader's reports on the FM radio and studying the topographic maps of the fire area to which they were heading. It was much like taking troops into combat; however, this enemy was not human, it was a fundamental element of nature that was never really vanquished, it was merely temporarily suppressed and like a cancer it would reappear in another guise on a different future hot summer day.

At their present travel rate, it would take the Hot Shots another 90 minutes or longer to reach the area where the fire was raging and then another 30 minutes or longer to actually reach the fire itself – everyone had more than enough time to check their gear, counsel their fears, play some cards or if they were lucky, to get some badly needed rest. Firefighters needed all the rest that they could get, and this was especially true for the eager, uninitiated, new fire fighters. There were no sleep or rest breaks in firefighting! As long as the fire lived, the firefighters stayed awake to battle it.

For Rick Conroy and the rest of his Smoke Jumpers, there was no such thing as the luxury of playing cards, relaxing or sleeping. The Smoke Jumpers were akin to the military Special Forces – they got into the fight first, influenced the situation on the ground and laid the path for the conventional follow-up forces. The DeHavilland Twin Otter turboprop's passengers were traveling to the fire at over 200 miles an hour at 10,000 feet altitude and they would arrive at the fire at least one hour before the ground Hot Shots had even reached the visual fire zone and this was the standard USFS and BLM strategy – namely, to get the elite Smoke Jumpers quickly on the scene to appraise and influence the fire, follow it up with the ground Hot Shots and aerial fire retardant assets as necessary, then reinforce the ground and aerial forces until the fire was directed into a 'neutral path' or until it was extinguished.

Being a small, yet vital unit – the Smoke Jumpers had the critical task of quickly dampening the fire or the less favourable task of getting the fire to 'move' into a path or zone that would eventually hinder its growth through diversion onto rocky or barren areas. Sometimes they even set 'backfires' to get a moving fire to burn itself out by meeting another deliberately set fire. This required skill, daring and desperation – a solution of last resort to say the least. It was ironic that one of the tools of the fire fighter was that of setting a deliberate back-fire, but sometimes it proved to be very effective.

The other major task of the Smoke Jumpers was to clear an area for the helicopters to land, so that badly needed supplies could be brought in and for medical evacuations to be performed if so needed. As so befitted the Smoke Jumpers' dangerous trade, they tended to live and party hard, they also had the highest suicide rates among all the firefighting professions. Akin to PTSD, many couldn't stand the post-summer season let-down of going back to regular jobs and this was the time when most fire fighters took their lives- during the cold, grey, dreary days of winter.

The Twin Otter and its ugly big brother the C-23 Sherper were the two preferred Smoke Jumper firefighting planes because these were small, manoeuvrable, rugged, reliable and controllable in the worst of conditions and forest fires produced some of the worst low-level flying conditions possible, to include heat, unexpected wing updrafts, thick smoke and worst of all – heavy turbulence. In the 'old days,' Demerol was carried by jumpers to help reduce the air sickness caused by the rough and erratic turbulences caused by the forest fire updrafts, but the bureaucracy and possible lawsuits made the practice illegal and only prescription drugs could now be taken by the smokejumpers. The cabins were often filled with vomit, especially if the crews had to scramble after having just eaten a meal. The other aircraft which completed the air fleet stable included larger planes such as the 747, KC-97 and DC6/7 series. The larger aircraft were usually designated and configured to be the fire-retardant dropping planes.

This particular Twin Otter was named the 'Icarus' by the pilot and co-pilot, Bill and June Preston and as so befitted her name, the Twin Otter's nose was adorned with a wild and colourful nose painted picture of the mythical wax-winged creature who was foolishly trying to touch out to the sun. Bill and June also were co-owners of their beloved aircraft. This husband-and-wife team leased their aircraft and piloting services to the US Government during the fire season to the tune of up to $15,000 a day when actually fighting fires and a much lesser 'stand-by' daily amount rate when the plane was grounded. Their call sign was either 'Icarus' in clear spoken English and Lima-Juliet in the FM radio jargon.

In addition to doing summer firefighting support missions, Bill and June flew their plane to shuffle commuters back and forth among Canada's metropolitan areas. The work was steady, and it gave them a comfortable living. Accompanying them on their flights was Thomas Nickolas, the aircraft's Fire Spotter. Thomas's role was to select the drop zone for the Smoke Jumpers, to include their initial supplies and their re-supply of food and equipment. He controlled the time and place that the jumpers would make their descent from the skies to the ground; he also determined if the winds and conditions were safe for a jump. Located in the fuselage of the aircraft and physically removed from the immediate vicinity of both the pilot and co-pilot, Thomas was in constant cabin communications with the aircraft pilots via a communications headset and he would also be in receipt of radio communications with the base camp by another earpiece that was affixed to a portable radio which he had snugly affixed onto his waist belt.

Due to the nature of the firefighting mission and the fact that there had to exist multiple open-air vents within the plane, the Icarus was flown in a de-pressurized configuration – this made for both a cold and windy aircraft environment. The noise from the wind coming into the aircraft fuselage was all but deafening to the human ear. Thomas either sat or laid on the floor of the plane with Rick as they both visually eyed the fire for the best drop plan possible. Thomas would also drop lead-weighted coloured streamers periodically to determine wind speed and direction. It was an awesome responsibility and Thomas looked forward to it every season, he was like an umpire in a baseball game, getting to enjoy the action without any of the exertion.

"Levelling off to 5,000 feet, grey smoke direction 145 degrees off of the starboard (right) side of the plane, Over," June Preston reported into the aircraft's intercom, as her husband vertically-nodded in silent affirmation of her observations. Only Thomas, the pilots, and the Camp Haller Fire Control Center could hear the information, as the plane was being filled with the ample air flow and noise from the opened observation hatch which was vital for performing this specific aviation firefighting task. Thomas shouted into Rick's ear the information concerning the fire's direction.

Both men's attention was soon focused on the increasingly large mass of dark black smoke that was fast approaching the aircraft. The plane circled the large acrid smelling smoke clouds that soon engulfed the entire plane's exterior. "I can't see a damn thing, let's get a better look through this pea soup – take it down lower," Tom shouted into his microphone headset, as the pilots rapidly responded to the Spotter's command and took the Icarus down to 3,000 feet.

The 'Icarus' precariously arched up and down violently as if being played with like a child's toy yo-yo. All the members of the crew cabin held on to any fixed object for dear life, as the plane hit a particularly strong and unexpected pocket of clear turbulence. Several men in the rear cabin chucked-up their stomachs, some got nosebleeds, some pissed their pants, while others were on the verge of passing out. Just as suddenly as it appeared, the plane's yawning was gone – the turbulence was over as quickly as it began. After being rolled on the floor of the plane and rolling into a pool of vomit, Tom and Rick regained their belly positions at the plane's open hatch. Both men were relieved to breathe in the slightly smoky air instead of the stale, sour smell of human vomit and urine. The clouds had parted before them and they suddenly saw the extent of the actual fire on the ground. It was about several hundred acres and burning uphill and then spreading out in two perpendicular directions – almost like the letter 'T'. Both men took a long glance at the fire and memorized its details and position. Tom clicked on his GPS device and took an immediate reading along with an abbreviated description of the fire's size and location – this was called a Situation Report or SITREP for short, which he then forwarded off immediately to the Camp Haller Operations Centre.

This was a Class 'D' sized fire (now over 900 acres) and growing fast; such a size fire would be classified as the largest fire. The priority of placing so many fire resource assets against this type of fire so early in the fire season was obvious to see from the air. Located five miles away and nested among the thick Ponderosa pines, there were two dozen expensive multi-million-dollar homes, automatically making this a priority fire. Despite all official government discouragement, some people still wanted to live close to the great outdoors despite the cost and impracticality of this silly idea, yet since they had money and influence, the rich naturally expected Uncle Sam to come to their rescue. In many respects, fighting to save luxury homes built in forest fire areas was akin to welfare for the upper class.

Thomas dropped a series of lead-weighted, blue crepe, wind streamers as the plane slowly circled the fire. Each blue streamer drifted ever so slightly in a vertical drop, indicating a wind speed of 12 mph - safe enough for jumping. The wind was blowing from a south-to-northeast direction and the ground was elevated and populated with thick shrubs and heavy resin laden pines – the perfect fuel for wildfires. To complicate matters, the fire was proceeding up onto elevated land and this would make fighting the fire more difficult for the ground crews, who now had to fight a fire on steeper ground. The terrain also contributed to the dynamics of the fire, since wind travelling up a sloped piece of land would be amplified along with the fire dynamics. The only saving grace was that at the present time, the fire was in a moderate, steady-state of advance. Any winds speeds over 20 mph would cancel the Smoke

Jumpers from exiting the aircraft - it would simply be too dangerous.

Rick smiled as he gave Tom the 'thumbs up' sign, this indicating that he was satisfied with the wildfire fly-over and that he was going to jump his team. "Okay, let's get ready, we jump in five minutes – get your gear checked out and get ready to jump!" Rick screamed at the top of his lungs to his sticks of Smoke Jumpers. At his disposal, Rick had a total of eighteen jumpers, which he had divided into three jump sticks of six personnel each. Rick briefed his plan to his sticks and informed them that they would attack the 'head part' of the fire and thereby seek to change both its intensity and direction. The fire had a present nature of being bi-directional and the goal was to reduce it down to only one direction, while also robbing it of its tail-driven energy – its forest fuel.

Like a good leader, Rick checked the parachutes and equipment of all his personnel, which was a combination team consisting of both US Fire Service and BLM jumpers. Only Rick wore the rectangular wing style parachute, the other jumpers having either elected or been ordered to use the military style round parachutes. Most jumpers were fine with the old round canopy parachutes – these were simply, proven, and descended more slowly and possessed limited manoeuvrability. Simplicity was inherent virtue for both equipment and Smoke Jumpers alike, since complexity and deliberate cerebral thinking became the first attribute to disappear during an emotionally driven and dangerous filled fire jump zone.

Besides parachuting from a rumbling, tossing plane amiss a raging forest fire raging below them, the fire jumpers had to contend with other things throughout a fire jump. These included: avoiding large trees, raging flames, landing on boulders, uneven landing sites and even wild animals. No wonder that few had the time or inclination to think about how they would handle a rectangular manoeuvrable square parachute. Yet Rick was different, he was the leader and hotdogger of the Camp Haller jump fraternity and his ego could ill afford to be simply ordinary. He thought himself the supreme master of parachuting and besides, this may be his last year as a jumper, so he figured that the risk and excitement of the square chute merited his use throughout the fire season.

While Rick Conroy was the sole Smoke Jumper to make a free-fall jump, all of the other jumpers simply hooked up to a static line, which automatically pulled open the jumper's parachute upon exiting the aircraft; none of them had to think about pulling a rip-cord. The static line was also essential to letting the Icarus deliver supplies and equipment by dropping these from the plane and having the static line deploy the parachutes' automatic opening.

After witnessing the nature and spread of the fire, Rick made a drastic change to the fire strategy for his team. He wisely decided to deploy two of the three 'sticks' of jumpers to the tail or base of the fire, while the third 'stick' would deploy to the top of the 'T' – this tactic would divide his forces, yet it would also provide for a two-front attack on the fire and this was important if the fire suddenly shifted due to weather conditions, he would have some jumpers in a disbursed position. The lead jumper always had the unspoken privilege of naming-the-fire, this was something that Rick traditionally performed once he had his team safely assembled on the ground.

All of the jumpers liked Rick, but neither he nor his team were never more than seasonal buddies; Rick made many acquaintances, but few friends. Nevertheless, the jumpers as a seasonal group - all stuck together like glue throughout the summer fire season and an attack on one of them was an attack against the entire jumping fraternity – this applied to both professional and social settings.

"Get up, buckle-up and shuffle to the left door," Rick ordered at the top of his lungs in military fashion, as he made hand signals that also mimicked his verbal shouts. His actions made it obvious that Rick had prior parachute training in the military. Everyone was a seasoned jumper, and they all knew the jump preparation routines and signal commands by heart. Thomas Nickolas was still situated on the floor of the plane and on his command the aircraft descended to 2,500 feet and then it levelled off in a circling pattern just outside the outer perimeter of the fire. He reached to his side and threw a drift streamer out of the plane's hatch. Thomas observed the wind effect on the weighted streamer through a pair of compact wide-angle binoculars. The streamer drifted rapidly to the ground with a twenty-foot long blue crepe streamer that was steadied by a lead weight that was attached to the bottom of the streamer.

Tom repeated this process two more times, each time Tom yelled into his microphone and alerted the pilot and co-pilot. All three of them noted the results and verbally communicated the drift and descend speed to each other. They all agreed that there was an 8-mph wind on the ground and they noted this on their drop approach sheets. Tom knew where Rick wanted all three sticks deployed and this was also relayed to the air-crew. Rick selected the two Smoke teams which would be in the initial drop, then after the plane made its circle pattern, the third and final stick would jump last.

The side rear door of the Icarus was prepared and opened for exiting. The gust of wind and the air slip noise made all verbal communications now utterly impossible; hand signals and Standard Operating Procedures (SOPs) were now the order of the day for the Smoke Jumpers. Rick was positioned in the door first, with his eyes and head facing Tom, who throughout the jumping would remain flat on his belly, eyes affixed on the fire and ground dynamics; his ears focused on the commands from Bill and June Preston. Tom would give the visual command to jump by simply raising his left hand high above his head and then dramatically dropping it in a swift movement. His hand was slowly raised in such a fashion and every jumper felt the pucker factor of butterflies in their stomachs and the urge to bodily relieve themselves. It was too late for any second thoughts, as every jumper wanted to get the hell out of the bobbing aircraft and onto the ground to perform their real job – that of fighting the wildfire.

On the verbal cue from the cockpit, Tom suddenly lowered his left arm, shouting the word 'go' as he dropped his arm, fully realizing that no one save the wind could hear his voice above the gust of deafening wind slip that guided along the outer skin of the aircraft. Rick turned quickly, then threw himself as hard as he could forward from the rear door opening, clearing the airplane's wind slip air flow. His body suddenly stabilized in a free-flowing oblong type form, his legs held together by straps that would protect a Smoke Jumper should they ever have the misfortunate to land upon a tree. He could see the blue sky, now punctuated with increasing buffs of grey, brown and black smoke. The ground was a mixed mass of green timbers, brown earth and yellow burning embers.

Yet he had no time to appreciate the poetry of the scene which was a mixture of something between heaven and hell, all that he and the other jumpers had was a few precious seconds to prepare for their landing and deploy down to the ground as close to the fire site as was possible. Almost instinctively, Rick pulled his initial rip-cord handle and nervously waited for the canopy to deploy – it seemed like an eternity! "Whoosh" was the gusting aerial sound that Rick heard, and he welcomed, it! Above him was the welcome deployment of the three-foot diameter drag chute known as a drogue, the drogue in turn signalled to Rick that he needed to pull the main parachute rip cord, which he promptly performed in an almost instinctive manner. In about four seconds, the main parachute deployed and soon Rick's white and red coloured square plane-like parachute was deployed, and he began the arduous task of manoeuvring his parachute to the tail end of the fire. He gracefully swirled in a large circular pattern above the ground fire, making careful mental note of his horizontal speed, direction and rate of descent.

He calculated that if he slowed down his descent by prudent use of his parachute direction cords, he could be within fifty feet of the fire and on the ground in only a few seconds. Time was of the essence and he had mentally made his decision. He aimed the parachute to his desired landing location and adjusted the toggles on his chute. He hit the ground in a gentle glide and extremely low speed, so slow in fact that he landed standing up and only had to make a short trot to keep his upright position. This was another virtue of the horizontal square parachute, an extremely precision landing with low impact – both of which meant fewer injuries and a better, more precise ground landing. He had landed safely and that was all that mattered.

Rick had intentionally landed in the recently charred terrain that this fire had just consumed, this type of burnt terrain was called 'good black' because it was considered safe from further threats from the fire; burnt land was not a further source of fuel for a fire. Rick now drew his attention to his other stick members of his 'tail end' fire team, 12 in all to include himself. He looked up and he saw 11 round white-coloured parachutes drop about 200 yards from his position outside the tail fire position. Farther off in the distance, Rick spotted the third stick of Smoke Jumpers making their descent and who were landing near the head of the fire. A quick FM radio transmission confirmed that the fire head team had all landed successfully and were in quick operation against the fire's headward advance.

Within several minutes all the 'sticks' were safely on the ground, busily rounding up their personal chutes and moving toward Rick's position in rapid order. Everything seemed fine. "Those poor bastards are going to have to hump it over to me ASAP with all their gear," Rick muttered to himself as he basked in his personal prize landing. There was little time for self-congratulations, even for the seasoned Rick Conroy. He quickly threw off his parachute gear and placed it in a small bundle next to his personal gear (PG) bag, which was like a large military duffle bag, that was filled with critical firefighting gear. Rick quickly took one of the two FM radios from his trouser cargo pocket and contacted the circling Icarus.

"This is Smoke Jumper One to Icarus, Over," Rick shouted into the handset. There was a brief pause, then a quick reply: "This is the Icarus, read you Lima/Charlie (radio/military slang for 'Loud & Clear'), Over!" Rick's reply was rapid and with an urgency in his voice, "I read you the same, have landed safely, all the sticks have landed safely. I can confirm that this is a Class D fire that is on the verge of becoming a Class D plus if this wind keeps up. I need the Hot Shots here ASAP and I need an Initial Attack of retardant too!" Rick declared in a demanding, no nonsense tone. The air crew all heard the urgency in Rick's voice. "Roger Jumper One, we'll relay your info to base camp, anything else, Over?" June Preston asked politely, but in a non-descript monotone military style.

Rick thought to himself for a brief second before responding, "Yeah, I name the fire 'Hammerhead'.... I say again, I name this fire as 'Hammerhead', it's shaped just like a frigging Hammerhead shark! Tell Tom to drop the equipment chutes on my blue smoke signal, Over."

Tom, who had come up from the passenger compartment to sit with the pilots and await Rick's first transmission SITREP, took a free communications microphone in his hand and immediately responded with the verbal assurance of "Roger...Wilco" this to indicate that he understood the transmission and exactly the specific actions, which he had to perform.

"Great, Tom, I'll give a new SITREP in about 30-45 'Mikes', depending on how intense this fire fight becomes, out!" Rick voiced in a much-abbreviated phrase. Fighting fires left little time for social pleasantries and the key in critical communications was to always be succinct and clear. Tom attached a long stainless-steel container to the plane's static line and pushed out the heavy equipment containers, then another one and finally the last one. These containers fell away from the plane and quickly opened in a few seconds to reveal a bright red coloured round canopy. The container landed about 100 yards from Rick. All the 'sticks' had made their check-in's, as well as their fire employment locations.

"Hey, over here, jumpers! Head count, count off jumpers," Rick yelled as the Smokies surrounded him and sounded off a numeric number starting with the number '1' along with their last name. Everyone was present and accounted for, a great relief to Rick. Despite his failings in other respects, Rick's leadership and loyalty to his fellow

Smoke Jumpers was second to none.

"Okay, Jumpers, let's get to work, I need the area here established as our base of operations, so let's clear this area of all debris and make a GPS reference of this point! Also, I need jumpers one through five to go out and retrieve those equipment chutes and start to unload and prepare the bulk fire equipment and supplies – got it? I named this fire beast the 'Hammerhead' because from the air, it looks like a shark with one long body and a hammerhead with two emerging sides…we're presently located at the 'tail' end of the shark. Our goal is to attack the fire from its tail, dampen the fire's intensity and hopefully change the fire's position into the wind. The Hot Shots should be here in 60 minutes, and I have also requested that an aircraft with fire retardant to make an immediate Initial Attack on this fire! Any questions?" Rick announced as he looked around and saw only the grinning faces of his 'jumpers.' Everyone was eager and even excited to be on this job, Rick inspired confidence in all his team-mates and no one was overly worried about their safety with a professional like Rick in charge.

The stick #1 jumpers dug a fire line to the upper front left flank of the fire, this to limit the fire's travel by robbing it of its fuel, while sticks #2 and #3 came up the tail of the fire and started to dig up and cover up the fire and potential sources of the fire, these being the dry pine timber and shrubs, which acted like fuel material that fed the fire. The right side of the Hammerhead fire was left exposed and free to grow, there was simply not enough jumpers to put out a Class D fire that was morphing into a Class D-plus fire. Through his FM radio earpiece, Rick was able to discern the Camp Haller weather report that the winds were due to increase to 20 mph and that the low humidity was going to continue with little chance of precipitation. The jumpers had been fighting the fire for nearly 45 minutes and everyone was getting exhausted. Every jumper was required to be in both eyesight and earshot of another jumper, this was to ensure that safety could be reinforced, communications were passed on quickly and that the 'buddy system' was working. This same safety standard was also maintained for the ground crews as well.

"Where the fuck are those Hot Shots? I need those flipping ground pounders right here and now!" Rick cursed bitterly to himself. Just as he uttered these words, the Camp Haller dispatcher radioed that the Hot Shots crews had arrived approximately a mile away and were making their rapid progress to the jumpers' position. Rick was relieved by the news and he was always glad to see the 'grunt' Hot Shots arrive on the scene. As elite as the Smoke Jumpers were, they knew deep down that they were merely the glorified spearhead of the much-needed Hot Shots and their great numbers of staff and equipment that only ground support could provide. The jumpers continued their fever work of using chain saws, Pulaski and shovels to dig fire lines and rip up the wildfire's sources of fuel, their yellow fire-retardant suits and helmet mounted headlamps made for a bizarre sight as the beams from their helmet lights cut arches of surreal yellow-coloured beams of light through ashen grey and chocolate coloured smoke.

"Hey Rick, Rick Conroy…over here!" yelled Jeff Campbell, the Camp Haller appointed Field Fire Chief, who was responsible for coordinating all field fire activities for the Hammerhead fire. From the billowing haze, Rick turned around to see a figure clad in a yellow smock, helmet headlamp and carrying a Pulaski. As Jeff approached, Rick recognized one of the senior members of the Camp Haller fire suppression staff.

"I've got three platoons of Hot Shots and one held in reserve at Camp Haller on quick stand-by, along with portable water tanks," Jeff reported in an excited tone after having sprinted several hundred yards from the logging road that the Hot Shot convoy had made its way up until it had finally run out of road to go and everyone had to make the remaining distance on foot. This is one main reason for why the Hot Shots and Smoke Jumpers had to have high endurance and the importance of the PT tests and the daily conditioning. Hard training was going to pay big dividends this day.

"Okay, great Jeff, send two platoons up to the right flanks of the fire about 250 yards up the slope, keep the other team here to assist us jumpers in fighting the tail and possibly to move over to the left side of the Hammerhead; if that doesn't do it, we might need some reinforcements. I also requested an Initial Attack with fire retardant from the air…this is a D level fire on its way to becoming an all-out Level D-plus fire," Rick concluded with a sense of urgency.

Jeff took stock of the situation and he concurred with Rick's initial plan, even though Jeff was now the senior person on the scene. Fire Chiefs usually deferred to the initial judgment of the Smoke Jumpers, since the jumpers were there first and they usually had the best field information on the wildfires. Jeff was going to follow Rick's plan, it made tactical firefighting sense and he was placing fire resources against the right part of the Hammerhead fire which most endangered those multimillion- dollar homes.

"Let's get to it," Jeff shouted, as he ordered his three fire platoon leaders to gather around him and get briefed on the fire attack plan. The platoon leaders soon thereafter briefed their squad sections and in about five minutes all the Hot Shots were in the process of organized chaos known as firefighting.

"Everyone double time their butts and follow me," Robin yelled as she took control of her section of Hot Shots up the slope to fight the right side of the Hammerhead fire. She kept a watchful eye out for those in her charge, to especially include the rich guy 'Boston'. The smoke and heat became increasingly thick as the young, energetic Hot Shots made the difficult trek up the gentle sloping hill with their heavy ruck sacks and cumbersome fire-retardant clothing. To top off the strain, it was 90 degrees in temperature and getting hotter as they approached the fire.

"Okay, rule #1 is to stay in clear visible contact with your fellow squad member and if you don't see someone who should be working next to you, then you're wrong and so is that other sorry ass Hot Shot! Rule #2 is to tell the Hot Shot next to you your situation, to include taking a piss or crap break; if you need to go back to the assembly area for some supplies - simply tell your buddy! Rule #3 is to stay hydrated and to drink plenty of water. I want everyone here to have a head count of the person next to them, it's hot and smoky here, so visual accountability is critical....do I make myself clear, Hot Shots?" Robin shouted in no uncertain terms.

"Yes, Ma'am," was the loud reply of everyone to include Wayne. Even though he despised this young woman, he cottoned to her – she possessed a 'no bullshit attitude' and business-like ways.

"You guys start a fire line here and work steadily up the hill until I tell you to stop," Robin commanded as her squad formed a rough fire line that stretched up the smoke-filled hill and into the right side of the Hammerhead fire. Each Hot Shot had dropped his or her pack immediately behind them, not having time to drop off their gear at the assembly area. They drew out their Pulaskis and shovels and started digging up the underbrush and forest floor debris that would fuel the advancing fires. The forest debris floor was covered with energy-rich fuel such as old leaves, pine needles and old dried out tree bark. Old forests made for the best fires. They all drenched their neck scarves with water and wrapped these around their faces, this to filter out the thick smoke. Each Hot Shot was separated from the other by about 15 feet distance, sometimes more and sometimes less depending on the visibility conditions.

All along the length of the fire line, Robin walked and instructed her fire crews in the nuances of firefighting. Wayne furiously used his shovel to dig up burning debris and cover it back over with dirt. He then started to shovel out the earth and construct a slight earthen depression devoid of any fire fuel in order that a fire break could be established. Just as Wayne was making serious progress, he heard a sudden 'snap' sound. He looked down to discover to his disgust that his shovel handle had broken in half: it was a perfect, ultra-clean break too. "What sort of luck is this?" he scornfully thought to himself in disgust.

"Damn, what sort of crappy equipment is the fire service providing these days?" Wayne cursed in a hushed mutter, as he quickly threw aside his shovel and started to work the fire line anew with his Pulaski, a half-ax, half-adze sharpened hand tool that was a basic fire-fighting tool named after the man who had invented it. After half an hour he had managed to make a fire break about twenty yards in length; the perspiration was soaking through his shirt. He took a big gulp of water from his quart-sized canteen, letting the excess water soak onto his under-garments and thereby cool-off his body core temperature. The water was warm, but refreshing and an absolute necessity to staying hydrated in this hot, exhausting environment. Suddenly, there was a shrill human cry about fifteen feet away from Wayne's position.

"Aaah, my fucking leg," frantically yelled one of the new Hot Shots on Robin's crew.

Robin clearly heard the very audible scream too, as she instinctively rushed to investigate the problem. A Hot Shot named Tom Phillips had a fifteen foot tall burning tree fall onto his left leg. "I need Hot Shots over here now!" Robin yelled out. Wayne and another fire fighter were just yards away from the injured fire fighter, as they rushed immediately to Robin's position only a few short yards away.

"Help me get this trunk off Phillips' leg," Robin yelled in desperation, as the wounded Hot Shot painfully screamed out in agony. Together, the three of them used all their strength to lift the heavy burning timber off Phillips' leg – it was definitely broken, perhaps even fractured, no one could tell for sure, but he was in terrible pain and immediate medical treatment was a priority.

"Hey 'Boston' – you and the other Hot Shot take this man down to the assembly area, it's too dangerous for him to remain in an active fire area, I'll have to call this in to Jeff Campbell for immediate medical attention and possible medical evacuation...be careful to place no strain or pressures on the leg – I want a two-man shoulder-carry for this injured fire fighter!" Robin yelled over the noise of the fire. "Do you guys remember where the assembly area is and how to get there?" Robin inquired nervously.

"Yes, Ma'am, we sure do, I think we can carry Tim down without any problem and get back here ASAP," Wayne calmly replied. Robin merely nodded her head in a slight vertical movement to indicate her acknowledgment.

Wayne and another Hot Shot slowly lifted the wounded Tim Phillips into a vertical, upright position and buddy-carried Tim down the hill very slowly. Despite his pain, the wounded fire fighter was conscious, and he was able to provide some support from his good right leg. Each movement felt like a hundred needles were piercing his wounded left leg and lower body. Tom Phillips' 'baptism of fire' was going to keep him off front line fire duty for probably the rest of the season, the best he could hope for was to finish up the season as a base camp support staffer. Accidents were to be expected for both novice and veteran fire fighters alike, it was just a matter of luck as to who was injured or not.

"Robin radioed Jeff Campbell about her injured Hot Shot to include name, social security number, and injury type. Robin had done well and exercised excellent judgment. "Great call, Robin, it sounds like this guy needs an evacuation ASAP, I'll have Sammy give him a medical evaluation and first aid, I'm going to err on the side of safety and call in a MEDIVAC helicopter lift too," Jeff explained to give Robin the latest situation awareness of the actions being taken to ensure the health and welfare of her team member. She knew that she was going to lose this new Hot Shot for the rest of the season in all probability, yet this was the nature of fighting forest fires – people got injured and sometimes they even died.

"Roger that, Jeff, just keep me posted on my Hot Shot's condition as well as any other fire or weather changes," Robin requested in a professional and business-like tone.

"No problem, Robin, just worry about your squad, I'll keep everyone posted, keep your radio channel open and the audio on maximum sound, these fires get roaring loud, Out," Jeff replied in a definitive response.

Sammy established her emergency medical position in the 'good black' assembly area established by Rick Conroy's Smoke Jumper crew as per SOP. Out of the haze she noticed two men advancing her way, carrying a third evidently injured Hot Shot between their arms.

She rushed up to assist them in getting the injured Hot Shot onto the blackened ground of the assembly area. She was stunned to see that one of the two Hot Shots was her nemesis – 'Boston'.

"Hey you, over there, it's 'Boston' isn't it? What happened to this guy?" Sammy inquired in a startled voice.

"This Hot Shot had a burning tree fall onto his leg… my squad leader Robin Wolf sent us down here to get him some medical attention," Wayne exclaimed with obvious physical exertion and with an audible strain of his voice.

Sammy looked at the Hot Shot's leg and at his identification dog tags; his left leg was definitely broken, maybe even fractured and he was losing consciousness. She cut open his trousers and discovered that a leg bone was protruding from the skin. Jeff Campbell came over to get a firsthand report of the situation.

"What's his condition, Sammy?" Jeff inquired calmly.

"It's a bad leg wound, a protruding leg bone fracture, foreign object and infection exposure and potential arterial intrusions, but I think that he'll be okay as long as he remains sedate and keeps any pressure off that bad leg… I'm going to stabilize the leg with a field splint, but I require a helicopter evacuation ASAP, Jeff," Sam pleaded. Jeff needed no additional convincing after eyeing the seriousness of the actual wound.

"Alpha Romeo, this is Charlie Victor, I request immediate aerial medical evacuation ASAP at the Hammerhead assembly area!" Jeff voiced to the Camp Haller communication unit. The response took only 3 seconds.

"Good Copy, Charlie Victor this is Alpha Romeo, provide the details of the injured party, grid coordinates/GPS of the pick-up and any specific medical support required, Over," the Camp Haller communications operator replied in a monotone, un-emotional, yet very professional vocal tone.

"Injured party is one, named 'Tim Phillips', blood type-O, social security last four are 5068, require direct transport to medical-surgery facility with leg injury, protruding bone and fracture, trauma expertise needed…victim is partially awake and in great pain, no medications have been prescribed to date, no patient allergies or drug prohibitions noted…Good Copy, Over," Jeff voiced loudly as Sammy listened keenly to ensure that Jeff had provided all the correct medical data on her patient.

There was again a pregnant pause as the slight sound of static feedback filled the FM microphone. Suddenly, the silent mic burst into life: "Roger, Good Copy, expect MEDIVAC in about 20 Mikes, provide a blue smoke cluster for additional visual signal marking, litter and medical staff will be provided, Over," Sammy and Jeff nodded to one another in silent acknowledgment. "This is Charlie Victor, Roger, Out," Jeff replied with professional radio communications brevity. All they could do now was to await the arrival of the chopper, Sammy counselled the injured Hot Shot while Jeff went to get his personal gear bag to retrieve a blue smoke canister to signal the helicopter. All the requisite grid coordinates had already been given out by GPS signal from both Rick's and Jeff's team members.

Sammy wanted to commend 'Boston' and the other Hot Shot, yet when she turned around to thank them, both of them had disappeared, they had immediately returned back to the wildfire and smoke from whence they had emerged. Wayne and the other Hot Shots had been trained to use all their time and resources to fight the fires at hand and not to linger about on any other issue. Through the thick grey and black smoke Wayne and his Hot Shot companion got back to where the original fire line had been. It had only been 45 minutes since the two had left the fire line, but in that short time, both the fire and Hot Shot teams had moved onward to fight the rapidly moving fires.

The two men became separated in the smoky haze, confident that each knew where their firefighting companions were stationed. Yet the fire and smoke confused many a fire fighter's mind and physical senses. Robin had moved her fire squad 150 yards up the hillside and neither Hot Shot knew the present position of their team members. Both men soon lost sight with one another, each step taking them father apart from one another. In only a few seconds, Wayne lost visual sight with the other Hot Shot and before him were the raging yellow and red flames of the killer fire. He couldn't locate his previous fire line position and he saw no one around him either

He was lost in the wildfire and his heart throbbed quickly and his blood pressure climbed with his increasing anxiety. He yelled out for anyone to hear him, but there was only the noise of the fire destroying trees and brush with an ever-rapid appetite, a hungry fire was as noisy as a passing freight train. Along with the sounds of the consuming fire, there was another alien, low rumbling sound that he could not readily discern.

The ominous, mighty sound grew louder with each passing second. Suddenly out of the smoke-laden inferno, there appeared a large boulder barreling directly toward him. There was no time to think, only to react. Instinctively jockeying to his right, the table-sized boulder sped past his contorted body, continuing its irreverent advance and terminating with a great thunder at the bottom of the ravine. Smaller rocks soon followed in successive pursuit, as the fire robbed the upper hillside of its dry grasses and trees that had previously retained these mighty boulders. Gravity was now their only master.

He needed to escape from this bowling alley shaped natural depression in which he was caught and through which the fiery winds were greatly amplified. He turned to his right and unknowingly stumbled farther away from the fire line and his companions. He had neglected to make proper use of his compass to initiate an initial direction reading to which he could easily take a back azimuth to find his way back to his point of origin. The proper and valuable use of the compass in land navigation was now insultingly instilled upon him, yet it came too late to be of any immediate help.

He was utterly lost! With each step, he became more and more confused, his instincts as to direction were worthless and even dangerous in this smoke-filled environment. Any fire fighter, especially a newly-minted one, who had lost his way in the midst of a raging wildfire – was in a very dangerous situation and death was a very distinct possibility; this is why it was stressed that fire fighters stay within visual contact of one another at all times. All around him there was natural chaos, there were trees burning with columns and rings of fire moving near vertically up the exterior of the tree trunks. This phenomenon was the result of great reservoirs of resin burning within the tree and thus adding fuel to the fire. Precipitously, as he turned, he saw a terrifying swirling column of fire coming his way, it was like a small tornado composed of fire itself - it was aptly named as a 'fire devil'.

His heart was beating like a wild drum roll, he frantically ran from the fire devil's menacing path, only to find himself in a patch of even more intense burning ponderosa pines. He coughed violently and repeatedly to evacuate the poisonous fumes from his lungs. The smoke was so thick that he could barely see anything, as his eyes watered and rejected the caustic smoke. Every tree was afire and swirling in columns of ringed fire. Struggling over fallen timbers and uneven burning debris, he passed a huge burning tree with rings of fire dancing merrily up its bark. The sight was equally memorizing and fascinating. Without warning the tree burst into a thousand fractured pieces of burning embers that lit the surrounding area with bright pieces of glowing red and yellow embers. Like a giant firecracker, the tree had exploded from its over-generous, resin-fuelled diet.

Plagued with instant and horrific eye pain, Wayne fell to his knees, as he was temporarily blinded by the hot tree bark embers. The pain in his eyes was unbearable. The eyes were one of the most sensitive and vulnerable of the body's organs. He had suffered a temporary corneal abrasion from the ashes and tree bark debris. The natural body defence of tears to the injured eyes provided a watery blurred view of this blazing, hellish world. He lay helplessly crouched for several minutes on his knees in agonizing pain, as his tears washed away the carbon debris from his eyes. Gently he wiped his fingers across his still sensitive, teary-filled eyes, mercifully he could still see! All around him was a hellish vision drawn straight out from Dante's Inferno. Still, he was not dead and he had no intention of dying either.

Survival was his singular goal. He struggled onto his feet to try to compose himself. He had learned from his fire training that statistically fires do not tend to travel downhill in most circumstances. He weighed the odds and decided to try and make his way from the higher to a lower level elevation, yet his senses were impaired by the fire and smoke. His sense of both balance and direction were impaired by the fiery elements. Slowly he stumbled through the burning woods, ever mindful that an injured and lost fire fighter was to be a dead Hot Shot. Wayne vowed that he was not going to die this day. The will to live was now greater than either his previous personal remorse or desire to seek danger.

With caution and methodological movement, he made his way across a small batch of 'good black' soil that had just been consumed by fire. Unknown to Wayne, he was to the immediate east side of the Hammerhead fire and in the prime path of the wildfire should the fire turn toward an easterly direction. Ironically, this is exactly what occurred, as the winds turned to push the fires east toward Wayne's position with greater intensity. The wildfires were pursuing Wayne like a wild animal hunting its prey.

The fire-laden winds were upon him in an instant. As the fiery whirlwinds and fire devils descended upon him, Wayne looked to his surroundings. He noticed the panic travel of snakes, foxes and deer. Wayne correctly surmised that the wild animals possessed a sixth-sense or instinct concerning the dangers of nature. 'These wild animals knew a safe haven and a safe way out of a fire!' he correctly thought and the fleeing animals had given him an idea too. He fled as the animals fled. Suddenly, out of the blazing fires, there rushed at him a charging deer, its fur afire and smoking. The frightened and anguished creature was in full stride and as it passed Wayne, the deer's rear foot kicked him in the head and knocked him unconscious onto the ground. As in his recent motorcycle accident, there was a sudden pain before everything became black to his consciousness.

The Camp Haller Operations Center (Opns Center) during the management of a wildfire was anything but calm and orderly. People were busy delivering slips of paper to various experts and supervisors. An array of monitors displayed the latest computer weather updates and fire resource summaries. The main purpose of the Opns Center was to conduct the fire strategy and the coordination of vital fire resources to the field units. Mr Sanchez commanded the Camp Haller Opns Center and all critical command-level information came directly to him. A Private Line of dedicated T-1 phone lines connected all the elements of the national and regional fire centres into one fail-safe communications grid. With the T-1 Private Line, no phone numbers were needed to be known or dialled, the direct point-to-point circuit switch was already engineered into the configuration, the users merely had to pick up the telephone receiver and then merely await for the other party to pick up their phone receiver and speak. A generous row of phone banks illustrated the link-to-link circuits of this Private Line phone network, despite computers and the Internet, voice phone communications was still the best and most reliable means to communicate with one's fire coordination counterparts.

A phone line suddenly lit up on the incoming National Fire Inter-Agency Center (NFIC) private line phone which originated from Boise, Idaho. Sanchez took up the phone receiver. "This is Sanchez of Camp Haller," his voice gravelled in a dry tone. The voice originating from the NFCIC was most masculine in tone and vibrant.

"Mr Sanchez, this is Reggie Flowers from Boise, my boss Lori Clarkson wanted me to pass you the word that there is a wind shift in the weather and that the fire that you called the Hammerhead, is going to be shifting to the east, the speed will be increasing to 25 mph as well… warn and adjust your fire crews accordingly. Also, we're arranging a two plane Initial Air Attack with retardant in about 45 minutes, Good-Copy, Over?" Reggie stated and waited for a positive response to the understanding of his message.

"Yeah, Reggie, Good-Copy the info and tell Lori thanks for the air assault tankers on this one," Pete Sanchez replied smartly as he hung up the Private Line connection with the NFIC. Radio lingo even while using the telephone was common practice among the field fire-fighting brethren.

Pete lifted a microphone that was seated on his desk top and made a public announcement to all the Opns Center personnel. "Attention Opns Center staff, just got a call from Boise – the wind direction and speed for Hammerhead is shifting from south-north direction to that of west-to-east direction at 25 mph...also in 45 minutes two aerial retardant tankers will be hitting the Hammerhead. Alert all field firefighting units by every communications mode and post your data- bases accordingly. This data will be posted by the NFIC to our central computer maps in a few minutes," Pete announced with delight. The word soon went out to all the Hot Shots and Smoke Jumpers to re-position their crews and to be alert for incoming fire-retardant air drops from the forthcoming air assets.

Robin received the fire updates simultaneously with all the other Hammerhead fire crews via her portable radio. The squad leaders were the last echelon of fire fighters to have FM radios and even this was extremely rare – usually only the fire platoon leaders had FM radios. Giving the squad leaders portable communications this year was just a trial experiment to see if radios were worth the money at such a low level of distribution.

"Squad move 300 yards south – down the hill and assemble onto your squad leader...pass the word to the next Hot Shot," Robin shouted as loud as she could to the squad member next to her. The Hot Shot merely nodded his head in a vertical motion and gave the hand signal 'thumbs up' sign, thus indicating that he understood and would comply with her order. She positioned herself at the half-way point to more ably monitor her unit. As each of her squad's Hot Shots passed by her one-by-one, she counted both their number and last names until all of them had passed by her.

"That's it, Robin, I'm the last Hot Shot in your fire line," muttered a blackened faced fire fighter.

A curtain of concern suddenly imprinted itself upon Robin's face. "Someone was missing!" she muttered to herself nervously. She coughed as a whiff of smoke filled her lungs. She went down to the area where her squad was assembled. "Every Swinging Dick and Bloody Mary sound off loud, by last name ASAP!" she screamed like an irate drill sergeant to her squad. In turn all the Hot Shots had quickly rambled off their last names. The verdict was final – Robin was missing one of her Hot Shots. She knew that Tom Phillips had been evacuated to the Assembly Area for medical treatment, so that only left 'Boston' as being unaccounted for among her squad.

"Oh shit...anyone around here see Hamilton?" Robin anxiously yelled out. Everyone just shook their heads from side to side in a negative response. Everyone nervously looked at one another, not knowing what to do next.

"Okay crew, the winds have changed in both intensity and direction, its coming directly our way, Hot Shots. We are ordered to move and let it pass through, after which we attack it from behind once again.... everyone move down to the Assembly Area, report to fire platoon leader Birch, tell him I've gone to find my missing lamb named Hamilton," Robin remarked as she briefed and ordered her squad off their fire position and into safety. She now went forth into the den of fire to look for the one guy in her squad who she personally disliked. 'Shit, God must really hate me...I really don't need this shit today!' Robin scornfully thought to herself as she gathered up her Pulaski and small personal kit pack.

As the last images of her squad melted away into the smoke and haze, Robin journeyed into the opposite direction. 'Boston must have moved back into our original deployed position, lost his bearings and was now hopelessly lost,' Robin counselled silently to herself and she was correct. Robin trekked up to the original fire line position only to find a wall of yellow and red flames being fuelled by the changing winds. She recoiled defensively against the advancing flames. The barks of the resin-laden trees were again ablaze with the circling rings of fire bands and burning embers were as thick as fireflies on a summer's night. As the winds increased, so too did the intensity of the fires. She looked up and saw that the fires from the top of the burning trees was advancing to the tops of the other still un-burnt trees – a 'crown fire process' was occurring, a sure sign that this was becoming a deadly advancing fire.

Cautiously, she withdrew from this cauldron of hell and took to a new direction. To the northeast she spotted a slow burning area of timbers that had just been ravaged by fire, though it was not totally burnt out or 'good black' as some virgin trees remained un-burnt and it seemed as if the winds had suddenly shifted in this spot of forest. "Hey

'Boston', are you there...Hamilton...Hamilton?" she yelled out furiously, but was merely greeted with silence. For the first time, her heart sunk, and she began to think the unthinkable, that 'Boston' had been killed and was consumed by the wild fires.

Driven by the factors of devotion, professionalism or just plain old stubbornness, Robin refused to give up her supervisory responsibility and let one of her team members go missing in a wildfire, so she continued the dangerous quest for 'Boston' despite the increasing threat of being lost or even physically consumed by the fire. She continued to look for 'Boston' in desperation, yet she discovered nothing, everything was dark and smoky to her sight.

Immediately the hairs on the back of her neck rose up, a sure sign of an impending catastrophic or imminent personal danger. She was alone and in a very dangerous fire situation. No help was available. Fear and a sense of self-preservation had suddenly grasped her. Basic human survival instincts were slowly over-riding the more cerebral rational traits of her character. She took a moment to breathe deep and to close her eyes for a few seconds to compose and focus on her rescue mission and it worked. Discipline and logic overcame her primal fears.

Opening her eyes, she cautiously walked ever deeper into the partially burnt thickening maze of ponderosa pines. The sun's summer rays vainly struggled to penetrate through the thick dark smoke, which had produced a warm chocolate brown haze through the overhanging forested canopy. Her acute eyes, masked in clear protective goggles, tried to discern reality from conjecture, every object of potential hope brought nothing but dejection and despair. Awkwardly she stumbled over burnt tree trunks and hidden rocks. Her helmet and attached Pelican lamp had fallen into a pile of ash debris. Retrieving her gear, she looked about and observed an ever-evolving mass of charred forest remains. 'The fire had won! 'Boston' was hopelessly lost!', she anxiously feared. As the warm winds of the fire continued to increase, Robin decided to make quick her retreat and to exit this part of the forest where she had first entered it. As she tried to retrace her movements, Robin suddenly discovered the yellow coloured, slumped, curled-up remnants of a fire fighter – it was 'Boston'. Yet was he still alive or merely a corpse?

Robin's heart jumped a few hopeful beats upon seeing the dirty yellow coloured figure of a human being crumpled up on the forest floor. Wayne had fallen onto the 'good black' of the burnt-out portion of the forest floor, none of the wild fires had succeeded in vanquishing him, nor that of his fuel-poor surrounding area. Robin knew well that most fire fighters died of suffocation from the hot air and noxious smoke, which forest fires produce in generous amounts. She threw down her Pulaski and back-pack to afford herself more bodily freedom of movement. Gently kneeling down to his side, she turned him over, looking for breathing, a pulse - any sign of life!

She placed her head to his chest; there was breathing, it was shallow breathing, but breathing none the less! Her heart raced with excitement for finding her missing squad member, who was barely alive. Almost instinctively, she performed CPR to get 'Boston' more fresh air into his lungs.

"Breathe, 'Boston', breathe, damn you, I'm not losing one of my squad members today!" Robin defiantly commanded. She continued her CPR unabated for several more minutes. She crouched over him as she waited for signs of recovery. Suddenly, he coughed, then he coughed some more, then he started to cough a lot, his eyes opened slowly, and he desperately gasped for air.

Yes, he was alive! He saw above him the last sight that he ever expected to see this side of heaven, that of Robin Wolf beaming a wide smile over him. He fought to sputter out the words as he coughed some more. "The last thing I remember was a fiery deer charging in my direction, then total darkness," Wayne confessed slowly as a tincture of agony sparked in his face.

"Are you all right, 'Boston'? Do you know your name and place of birth?" Robin inquired to test his mental acuity and memory. She generously assisted Wayne to slowly sit up on a burnt tree trunk.

"Yeah, sure, Robin, I know all too well who I am and where I was born, that's why you call me 'Boston', is that correct?" Wayne uttered with an almost sarcastic and comical retort. Robin grinned knowing that this was the same sweet sarcastic 'Boston' fellow whom she had the pleasure of meeting in the bar some weeks back.

"That damn deer that was half on fire – it must have kicked me in the fucking head, it feels like it's on fire," Wayne remarked tersely. Robin felt his head; there was a good gash and some blood from the right rear side of his head and it was also swollen too.

"Yeah, 'Boston', something sure as hell did hit you on the head, you're going to need to see a Doc and get some rest after we get the hell out of here, just let me apply this pressure bandage around your head and we can get going…can you get to your feet, 'Boston'?" Robin inquired as she quickl wrapped a sterile field pressure bandage firmly around Wayne's injured head. The head pain was excruciating, but tolerable. Wayne nodded silently to Robin, affirming his ability to walk. He brandished a broad, bright smile at Robin. Wayne was most appreciative of the first aid and that of Robin's bravery and initiative to trek out and to rescue him.

"Why did you come looking for me? If I die, you don't have to pay off on the bet!" Wayne mockingly quibbled.

Robin merely took his remark as an affable, harmless retort, and not that of an ungrateful insult.

"Boy, someone sure as hell thinks a lot of himself! I don't collect on cheap or stacked bets either. It's not a question of money with me, 'Boston'… you're in my charge and I'm not going to allow any one of my squad members die or get fucked-up on my account, now is that clear, Mister?" Robin replied sternly.

Robin located Wayne's helmet from the burnt-out forest floor, its Pelican lamp was still softly glowing. She noted the generous dent on the side of the helmet. "Yeah, 'Boston', you were really lucky to be wearing this gear and you sure do have a hard head too!" Robin jokingly remarked.

"The fire is advancing on us, we gotta move out right now! Can you get up and walk, 'Boston'?" Robin urgently inquired. Seeing the fires in the distance advancing, neither of them were going to stay in this place one minute longer than necessary.

"That's a big affirmative, boss, I'm either going to get up and walk the hell out of here with your help or I'm going to die here!" Wayne proclaimed boldly. Robin smiled and placed the helmet gently back on Wayne's head, as she assisted him to his feet and the two walked 'arm-around-shoulder' through the forest and away from the advancing wildfire.

Quickly the winds began to shift to the east with ever greater intensity and in the same direction of travel as that of Robin and Wayne. The pair could feel the increasing heat and see the smoke that was heading in their direction. Unless they made better time, the advancing fires would shortly be upon them. Both of them knew that they were in a death field of potential fuel for the advancing fires. "Our only chance is to try to outrun or outflank the fire, and to tell you the truth I do not know where the hell I am anymore," Robin nervously confessed, as Wayne looked intensely into her eyes.

"Yeah, I was lost too, I tried to follow the path and direction of the fleeing animals, they have a sixth-sense for survival," Wayne replied to reassure Robin. She smiled and knew that there was some truth to this shave-tails' hypothesis.

"That's not a bad idea coming from a rich, city boy 'Boston', so let's go with it!" Robin replied as they watched for the retreat of nature's creatures from the wildfires. They spotted a rabbit, some deer and a fox frantically dash directly to their left and then run down into a gully.

"That must be the way to the stream, it will be safer there for us... the fires usually don't travel downhill toward a stream area," Robin remarked in a voice laden with experience and an abundance of hope.

"You don't have to tell me that a second time, Robin! Okay, let's do it quickly, any place is better than the one in which we are now standing!" Wayne yelled out, and the two rushed as best they could down the hill and toward the anticipated area of safety. Like every other animal in the burning forest, Robin and Wayne made for the safety of the river stream that lay downhill.

Although the two moved quickly, the fire moved even quicker. Fire Devils danced to their left and burning embers were flying at their backs and falling onto their Du Pont Nomex fire resistant clothing. It was like being inside the foundry of a blast furnace pouring huge volumes of molten steel, yet this natural furnace was much larger and unconfined to those of the industrial enterprise.

Their heavy fire garments did not make the moving any faster, yet these heavy Nomex garments were their life rafts in this sea of combustible materials. They trotted and sometimes stumbled down the ever-precipitous sloping decline, hoping to avoid any falls or injuries. Now fully exhausted, the two stopped to take their bearings of the situation. Behind them was a yellow and red monster, a wall of flames and smoke 100 feet in the air and it was advancing on them quickly. They were still far from the stream banks.

"Either we find a miracle or we're dead 'Boston'!" Robin cried out as she struggled to help Wayne limp forward, and the two struggled to make it down the ravine to safety. The two fell down onto the forest floor with both a thud and some seasoned cursing from both Robin and Wayne. The two had fallen on a well-camouflaged rock. They stumbled on all fours to find their footing. Miraculously before both their eyes lay a slight vertical fall off on the side of the hill. Possible salvation came in the form of a small rock ledge that had been sheered away untold thousands of years ago from a small bit of a glacier tongue that had carved this steep ravine. The two looked at one another with eyes aghast and mouths open; they had each read one another's thoughts perfectly.

"Quick, let's get down beneath this small ledge and hope that 'old man fire' rides right over us!" Wayne blurted out. Robin nodded in obvious agreement.

The rock ledge depression was a mere five feet in depth, but it did afford the only chance to thwart the rapidly advancing fire. They carefully dropped themselves down onto the barren ledge depression.

"Let's strip out of these Nomex jackets and try to form a field expedient fire shelter! Quick, take off your jacket and join it to mine using the fasteners, then throw it over us and place only one of your arms into the sleeve and I'll put my arm into the other opposite sleeve," Robin expertly commanded.

"Hey boss, have you ever tried this technique before?" Wayne nervously inquired.

Not desiring to either betray her lack of experience or to utter an outright lie, Robin quickly replied back, "Well, I've seen this type of thing done in some old Hollywood movie and it worked there, besides 'Boston' – there has to be a first time for everything... now hurry up!"

Wayne naturally deferred to Robin's survival skills and besides, she made good sense too. They quickly made an improvised 'body shelter' and then huddled close together as the fire approached. He threw his body tightly against Robin's and she complemented him in a similar fashion, since two closely intermingled and concentrated objects tended to resist the fire winds much better than any separate objects might.

Alone in their makeshift yellow coloured cocoon, the two frightened firefighters prayed silently to themselves and hoped that the wildfire that would soon over sweep them was not also going to consume all their oxygen and cause them death by affixation. As the hot breath of death neared ever closer, Wayne and Robin only concentrated on the several feet of Nomex that was to either be their lifeboat or their funeral tent. The roar of the fire was deafening, all that either of them could distinguish was the individual rapid beatings of their hearts.

The critical moment had arrived! The fire was upon them! With a thunderous roar, a wall of yellow fire swept over Wayne and Robin, like a roaring hot oven, the blast of hellish wind and fire rushed overhead, along with untold thousands of blazing small pieces of pine needles, leaves and burning embers – it was literally a fire storm. The heat was akin to that of a commercial grade convection oven, except this heat did not flow upward, it fell downward and all around them, even their boots were starting to smoke from the heat.

Robin and Wayne struggled with each painful breath; it was like breathing a hot toxic vapour, it was causing their throat and nasal passages to cook from the inside out. Every breath became more painful from the previous one; neither one of them wanted to take another breath of this hellish hot toxic air; still, death was not an option either. They took tiny, sniffling snorts of air through their nasal cavities and airways. They crouched directly into the ground, hoping to inhale some last remnants of clean, cool air. Neither of them imagined that breathing could be so painful. Their air passageways were becoming scorched.

The two cried out with pain as the heat penetrated their clothing, ears, nostrils and lungs. Breathing became too much to bear and they both instinctively gasped the final pockets of breathable air. They held their breaths for what seemed like an eternity. More forest ash, half burnt pine needles and fiery branches liberally sprayed upon the make- shift fire 'body shelter', this debris heavily littered over their pale yellow Nomex jacket canopy to the point where the colour of the yellow Nomex was totally obscured by the colour of pitch black and muted chocolate brown.

The relentless fire at last had consumed its fuel and continued its advance across the ravine. There was nothing but silence and the remnants of a hot sooty breeze. Physically, the fire- storm had literally fire-raped the entire swatch of hillside that had previously been a vibrant living forest. The wildfire had had its fill of consuming the fuel rich forest and it had merely proceeded onward to either consume more fuel or it would die out due to a topographic impediment. The terrain was now uniformly destroyed, nothing remained living, there was just a mass of blackened, charred rubble that had previously been a majestic lush green canvas. Not a single sound, living or inanimate, could be mustered from the ebony-coloured carnage. Yet was the human sacrifice to nature's fires forestalled?

Suddenly from the blackness of the forest floor there arose the stirring of life – a hollow cough, then another, then a flurry. They were alive, damn it! Robin and Wayne hacked out the filth, debris and pollutants that had filled their lungs in their final moments of consciousness, they both sounded like two candidates for the TB hospital ward, but with each breath, clean fresh air was being pushed into their oxygen starved bodies. They both thought that they were going to cough up a lung or some other vital organ, yet after about ten minutes they both managed to gain their physical composure. As their bodies unfolded from their cramped foetal-style positions, they threw back the now heavily black, ash-encrusted Nomex jackets that had well served them as their life preserver in the sea of fire. They both looked like two raggedy black sooty creatures from a Charles Dickens 19th century English chimney sweep tale.

Ever so slowly they pulled away from one another, their muscles aching from their un-natural contortions and huddled foetal position and also from the excessive bodily stresses upon which they had just been exposed; their soreness felt like the aching muscle trauma that one experienced after a concerted brace for a sudden vehicle impact. Yet it was also comforting for both of them to breathe again and realize that despite their aches and pains, they were both alive and relatively unharmed at that, a fate that few in the forest fire profession would have had the good fortune to survive. With blackened faces they looked child-like at each other and they both began to immediately laugh uncontrollably. This was literally a Baptism of Fire for both of them, for Robin it was as a fire team leader and for Wayne it was as a new Hot Shot. They had both magnificently passed the field initiation with flying colours.

In a few minutes, Wayne regained his composure enough to utter, "I can't fucking believe that I am alive, that both of us are alive!" he exclaimed wildly, as he shook Robin's shoulders in a very friendly and enthusiastic manner. Robin was flabbergasted too, "Yeah, by all accounts in the fire fighter's handbook, we should both be dead, but we're not, Wayne!" Robin blurted out in utter familiar exclamation.

"You know, that's the first time you called me by my first name, Robin... it feels great to have you treat me as a human being and not some inanimate object that was easy for you to stereotype and hate," Wayne exclaimed in a very sincere tone. The verbal indictment was spot-on! Robin was both embarrassed and sorry for her past behaviour toward Wayne, she realized that it was both childish and callous behaviour; it was not befitting that of a mature, responsible woman.

"Yeah, I was a real jerk...maybe we both learned some mutual respect today! Maybe be both made our own selfish prejudices and foolish stereotypes. I'm an emotional woman at times and I feel passionate about certain things that are dear to me. I'm sorry for that,

Wayne, myself and the others. We were wrong about you, I guess it's easier to hate and scorn something or someone who is different from you, a person who lives a world apart and away from anything you know or can ever hope to know, so my apologies, Wayne," Robin replied in a very sincere, soft voice.

He readily appreciated her sincerity and they both hugged one another in a very friendly fashion. "I was foolish, pig-headed, and prejudiced too, Robin, so let's call a truce then, what do you say, boss?" Wayne replied as he exchanged a smile of friendship unto Robin.

"I say that we get the hell out of here and back to the Hammerhead assembly area. Speaking of which I need to make radio contact and give a personnel SITREP to Jeff Campbell, he along with everyone else probably thinks that we are both dead," Robin smartly admitted, as her firefighting professionalism once again clicked into gear.

"Charlie Victor, this is Team Bravo, Over," Robin urgently voiced into the radio hand mic. There was a ghastly silence, she silently wondered if perhaps the Hammer head base camp was even still intact or did it succumb to a fate that she and Wayne had just escaped? Again, she tried the radio: "Charlie Victor this is Team Bravo, do you read me, Over?" She sighed with an inflected slight tone of distress in her voice.

"Holy Shit, is that you, Robin? You're flipping alive, Over?" queried an anxious voice of a very worried Jeff Campbell, who had quickly forgotten all pretence of the formal radio protocol responses. Robin smiled at Wayne – it was terrific to hear from their fellow firefighting comrades.

"Charlie Victor, that's a big affirmative, please be advised that two paxes, that is myself and fire Hot Shot Wayne Hamilton, are A-Okay and that we'll be walking back to the Hammerhead assembly area in about 30-45 Mikes, Over", Robin dryly replied to her supervisor.

"Roger and I 'Good Copy' that last transmission Team Bravo and congratulations for a job well-done and to also having survived that beast of a wildfire… see you upon arrival, Out," Campbell replied excitedly.

Robin and Wayne assisted one another to make the slow, dangerous trek out of the blackened field, embers were still aglow and there was still the ever-present danger of falling burnt trees and rolling boulders from the high slope of the hill located immediately above them. Their movement was slow, careful and tedious, especially considering the fact they were each wearing heavy perspiration, ash-laden clothing. The temperature was in the mid-90s and it made walking all the more difficult. A sudden dull roar emerged from above, it was the turboprop sounds of two low flying DC6 air tankers that were used during an 'air attack' of wildfires from the skies, these fire support aircraft were carrying a load of anti-fire retardant.

"Quick, get down – we're in the middle of an aerial fire attack, get down and cover your head," Robin shouted, as she pushed Wayne toward the ground, quickly following him as they both lay face-down in the dirty burnt forest debris. At that exact moment the two planes unleashed their internal cargo tanks containing thousands of gallons of liquid pinkish fire retardant on their immediate position. All of a sudden there was the sound of crackling in the air, as both Robin and Wayne were completely drenched with the thick pinkish liquid. Although not inherently toxic, the fire retardant if properly dropped on a land position, could quite easily injure a person standing directly beneath the path of the liquid retardant. Just as soon as it had started, it was over. They were both now unceremoniously covered in pinkish liquid and black ash, they appeared to be even more hideous than before and they both smiled childishly at each other's appearance.

"The only thing worse than not getting air attack support on time, is getting it late! Well at least it put all the remaining fires and burning embers out, welcome to your literal Baptism of Fire Hot Shot!" Robin joked as she got onto her feet.

Upon making their way back into the Hammerhead fire assembly area, Robin and Wayne were both met with fascination, disbelief and unrivalled celebration from all the Hot Shots and crew chiefs. They slowly stumbled out of the now charred remains that had once been a canopy of lush evergreen now transformed into an insulting blackened morass. They made their way slowly into the makeshift assembly area, the pair of dirty, exhausted, stinky fire fighters was a comical and rare sight, they were the rare survivors of a deadly wildfire Blow-Up. The reddish coloured fire retardant made them almost appear as zombies from a class B horror movie, the white sockets of their eyes evoked a stark contrast to that of their ash darkened skin.

Everyone, including Robin and Wayne, knew just how miraculous their feat of survival had been. Although some of the fire crew chiefs would argue that it was superior fire survival techniques that had saved their lives, both Robin and Wayne were humbler and more realistic in their belief that it was just sheer luck and the grace of God that had saved them and that they could just as easily been found as crispy critters in the forest.

The Hammerhead assembly area was secured and demobilized after the wildfire had burnt itself out by rushing down the mountain valley and into the river creek below, the fire had simply run out of wind and fuel, so it died a silent death. This fire had brought Robin the respect of being an experienced fire team leader and it made Wayne an official Hot Shot, this from both his wildfire encounter and that of being a Baptism of Fire survivor. It also made former enemies into friendly co-workers. The only thing left to do was to make out an official After-Action Report (AAR) by all the fire team leaders and fire chiefs, get evacuated and then get showered. Robin and Wayne would also undergo medical check-ups and body scans to ensure that there was no physical trauma or respiratory problems from the fire, inhaled smoke or fire retardant.

That night everyone who had fought the Hammerhead wild fire that day would sleep the repose of the dead and they all deserved it too. Boisterous celebrations at Indian Joe's would have to wait a wee bit. As for Robin and Wayne, several days of rest and recuperation were ordered by the medical staff and each of them gleefully obeyed. Robin would be honourably cited for her actions and she was going to be recommended for an official Lifesaver citation and merit-bonus award. She became an instant, de facto celebrity within the close-knit fire-fighting community. Her 'body shelter' survival technique was going to be taught in future fire fightinglectures and classes.

* * * * * * * * * * * * * * * *

An uneventful week had passed since the Hammerhead wildfire had occurred and the weekend once again beckoned for the fire fighters. As had become the weekend custom, all the fire fighters joined at Indian Joe's tavern to let off either personal inner angst or the tedium of the past week. For Wayne, Robin and all the others involved in the recent Hammerhead wildfire, it was for the former reason. The fire fighters who survived the ravages of the wildfire often suffered inner frustrations and tensions that needed to be exorcised and for many this meant one thing – strong liquor and plenty of it. In social attendance were husky logging roughnecks, as well as the seasoned fire fighters; both were rugged individual types quite capable of sudden physical violence. Everyone found a ready watering hole at Indian Joe's and both bar rumbles and spontaneous fights were not uncommon. These skirmishes seldom resulted in any sort of serious situations, but then again - there were exceptions to the rule. Each group respectfully mingled within their own social and drinking dens.

It was still early evening when Wayne travelled from his motel room and into Indian Joe's bar, looking to partake a hearty meal, have some drinks and generally to enjoy himself. He had survived his first 'wildfire, made a friend in Robin, and he was fully relaxed and ready to enjoy himself. Having lived through the Hammerhead wildfire, Wayne learned the truth of his desire to live and he intended to take advantage of every second that he had left in this very unpredictable thing called life. A long-standing tradition at Indian Joe's Tavern was the christening of the first season's forest fire with an appropriate tune, so there bellowed forth from the jukebox player, the 1950s song by The Platters of 'Smoke Gets in Your Eyes'.

"Hello Chief Joseph! How about a bowl of hearty buffalo stew, steak fries and an ice-cold pale ale?" Wayne echoed cheerfully as he sat down at the bar and greeted Chief Joseph.

The old Chief threw his bar towel over his shoulder, smiled warmly, and then extended his strong, bronze-toned arm out unto the young man. The two men shook hands heartedly. "Son, I'm very glad that you and that young lady, Robin, both made it out of the Hammerhead fire...you were both very lucky, my son, your first beer is on me along with your dinner. You're now a legitimate 'Hot Shot' and you have been baptized in a wildfire 'Blow-Up' and came out alive, now that's quite a feat! You and Robin are all of the talk around here and the survival tale is spreading throughout the entire fire-fighting community too!"

Being on the verge of blushing, Wayne humbly grinned and smiled in cheerful appreciation of the Chief's kind gesture. Wayne feasted on the lean buffalo stew; it was tender, hot, spicy and filling. He washed down the meal with an amber ale and was in the process of ordering another, when suddenly a loud, forceful feminine voice echoed from directly behind him, "That Hot Shot's beer is on me...in fact, rack up four 'tall ones', please Chief Joseph." In startled amazement, Wayne turned quickly around to locate the origin of the voice. There standing stoutly behind him stood Robin, Sammy and Hank – all smiling and gathering at his place at the bar.

"Hey there now, you didn't think that I wouldn't buy one of my new baptized Hot Shots a well-deserved drink! What the hell kind of Fire Team Leader would I be Mister Hamilton?" Robin exclaimed, as she patted Wayne on the back in a very friendly manner, her eyes beaming with excitement. Robin looked stunning, her flaxen coloured hair complemented her fair skin, she wore faded tight-fitting blue jeans, Tony Lama cowboy boots and the same fringed deerskin jacket that she had worn on the day of her Harley accident with Wayne's BMW.

"Please, Robin, let me buy the next drinks," Hank remarked with a broad smile. Not being married or having any children of his own, Hank instinctively likened his relationship with Wayne to that of a beloved old uncle to a young nephew. "Boy oh boy, both you and Robin were very lucky, I'm glad that you two young people were crouched down on recessed flat ledge and not exposed on an open, steep slope when that firestorm Blow-Up and passed over you."

Wayne wore a puzzled look upon his face upon hearing Hank's mysterious remark. "Hey, Hank – what do you mean when you say that we were 'lucky' to be on a flat, recessed ledge?" Wayne muttered with a respectful curiosity, as he sipped his beer.

Hank gazed at Wayne like a wise old teacher making a lasting impression upon his young student. Hank withdrew a long wooden match from his pocket and held it up before Wayne's inquisitive eyes. "Now I want you to carefully watch this match after I strike it and then you'll know what I'm talking about, young man," Hank explained in a mature knowledgeable tone. Both Sammy and Robin also gathered around to silently watch Hank's bar stool demonstration. Hank lit the wooden match, which burned straight up and slow. He then tilted the match at a 45 degree angle and the flame rushed quickly up the angle of the tilted match. Hank then softly and steadily blew on the slanted match flame and the fire quickly consumed the entire match length in an instant. The point was aptly and visually codified.

Immediately, Wayne realized that of which Hank had smartly demonstrated. Like a lighted match at a slanted angle, a fire moves rapidly up a hillside, more importantly a fire moves very rapidly up a slope or angle when wind whips up the flames. If he and Robin were trying to out run a fire coming at them from below on a hill, they would both be dead! "Wow, that's a bad thing to see, Hank and I hope that I only see it as a bar stool match demonstration too!" Wayne confessed in an uneasy voice. They all meekly and silently pondered the omnious demonstration that they had just witnessed and each of them knew that they were each at the mercy of nature and sheer luck.

As the four friends were talking at the bar, a group of fellow veteran fire fighters shook up bottles of beer and held their fingers over the bottle openings, producing a fine spray of beer mist. "Congratulations to our two heroes for making it out of the Hammerhead fire, you're the first celebrities of Camp Haller for the season," the veteran fire fighters cheered, as Wayne and Robin were spurted with beer mist. They both smiled at the child-like pranks and traditions of the fire fighters, but it was all in good humour. The cost was only some slightly stained clothing, which reeked of stale beer for the rest of the evening and for the following day. Robin and Wayne silently knew that neither of them were heroes, but merely lucky survivors.

Wayne devoted his attention rapidly back to Robin, who was looking especially attractive this evening, her blonde hair smelled of coconut shampoo and her eyes were sparking with girlish excitement. Her clothing really impressed Wayne. "Wow! That's a mighty impressive jacket, Robin, where can I get one like that?" Wayne exclaimed with a flattering jovial tone.

The jacket was indeed special. It was entirely hand crafted by Native American seamstresses, its golden honey colour was accented with vivid and finely detailed inlay of Indian beadwork in the varied colours of red, blue, white and yellow – all forming an alternating one-inch wide pattern, along the length of the sleeves was a generous six inch long set of hanging buckskin fringe, almost in a Davy Crockett-style mode. Aside from some slightly worn areas on the elbow, one could hardly tell that this jacket or the pretty young lady wearing it, was ever in a serious road fall, the deerskin hide was as tough as its owner. Across the back and up the lateral seams of the jacket was the embroidered pattern of a robin bird, which was made out of native hand-worked hammered-silver and various coloured beads. Somehow the jacket naturally befitted Robin and her character.

Robin took Wayne's admiration with light-hearted charm, "Well, Wayne, we're going to have to request that I contact my relatives, my aunts made this jacket up special for me for my birthday last year, I'm so glad that you like it!" Wayne sexily winked at Robin's suggestion, as he also smiled at both Sam and Hank, then offering up a round of drinks in the celebration.

"Hey, Sammy and Robin, I want to say something to you ladies, if I may?" Wayne proclaimed in a serious tone as Robin, Sammy and Hank each partook of their beer. It was evident that Wayne now had the young ladies' attention, so he continued to vocalize his thoughts. "Having just survived this Hammerhead wildfire with the help of my new-found friend, Robin, has made me realize how much of a spoiled child I was in participating in that wager that we foolishly made; so if you both agree, I am willing to forgo the bet and I will just try to finish up the season alive with the help of both of you. If you reject my offer I will naturally understand," Wayne finished speaking as he looked them all in the eye with a solemn glare.

Both Sammy and Robin nervously looked at each other. Robin made her reply first and she seemed to speak for Sammy as well. "Sure thing, Wayne, I think that perhaps we were guilty for having baited you into this revengeful bet thing, we wanted revenge on you for causing my Harley accident. Honestly, I never thought that you would go through with the training, let alone participate in the fighting of actual forest fires. So as far as I'm concerned, I accept your offer, the bet's off!" Robin proclaimed as Sammy nodded her head in immediate affirmation.

"A toast then to friendship and surviving until Labor Day," Hank toasted as they raised their glasses and laughed with delight. Chief Joseph arrived with more ice-cold mugs of beer and some complimentary appetizer steak fries and Hot Buffalo wings.

Conspicuously absent from the festivities, but most acutely observing from a darkened remote distance and with a very clear view, was the arimonious Rick Conroy. He was sipping liquor from an iced chilled glass that was filled with his favourite whiskey, Yukon Jack. The Canadian sweet honey-based whiskey went down smooth, but when it was drunk in quantity, its effects brought many a man to their knees. Yet Rick was not alone, he was being entertained by the companionship of a tall, raven-haired man named Jay Blackhawk.

Jay was very extroverted, a natural charmer, a man with big ideas and even bigger talk. Jay was a Native American lawyer and businessman. He was from the local tribal reservation, a local boy who had been educated at the tribe's expense, initially at Wyoming State College and later at Yale University Law School. Jay, however, had serious flaws in his character: self-centredness, greed and blind ambition! Jay's interests came before anyone and anything else. Yet, his higher education and exposure to urban society, only served to dysfunctionally sharpen his personality vices, thus making him more cunning and ambitious. Jay had mysteriously returned back from the East to act as the tribal lawyer for the reservation, yet he always placed his own financial interests above those of the tribe and his people.

Jay's legal connections led him into numerous business ventures, each one of which he was sure to get his 'cut' or percentage up-front. Jay never came out of a legal or business arrangement poorer than when he first entered the deal. Recently, Jay's business connections involved land speculation, land grant arbitration, and commercial development projects. He had made a small fortune back east in helping many eastern Native Indian tribes establish gambling operations on their reservation lands. Jay not only made up the legal arrangements, which in itself made him millions of dollars, but he also managed to weasel out a percentage of the construction contracts and a take of the gambling gross proceeds for a certain number of years. Now in his late-forties, Jay was looking to become the next Native American casino czar – a billionaire and perhaps maybe even a Congressman, Governor or Senator. The sky was the limit for Jay and he took advantage of every person and opportunity to make his ambitions pay-off.

Jay's personality was complemented by his large and well-built masculine frame, he stood at a solid 6'2" tall, and his hair was raven black with just a touch of greying at his temples. He wore his hair medium length, neat and with a slicked-back gel treatment. He hung around Indian Joe's bar for only one reason – he desperately wanted a piece of the Wind River Indian Reservation land for the development of a casino, hotel and entertainment park. The Reservation commercial properties and small businesses were barely making a profit and he knew that he could make untold millions from developing the reservation land 21st century style. He was going to get his hands on the reservation land no matter how long it took, or the amount of money needed to influence the right people. He would employ any degree of subterfuge or deceit to get control of the Tribal council and subsequently Indian Joe's tavern. Ever the keen observer, Jay Blackhawk looked for both vulnerabilities and strengths in both people and businesses alike.

"Hey there, lonely Rick, it looks like your gal pal Robin fancies that handsome young guy over there! You'd better watch yourself or you may lose her to that new Hot Shot, I understand that he's quite wealthy too!" Jay Blackhawk muttered in a deliberate antagonizing tone to Rick. As was his practice, Jay liked to turn a person's vices into his own advantage and self-interest.

Rick was clearly annoyed by Robin's new-found fascination and interest in 'Boston', and Rick didn't need much chiding from Jay to get his anger going about Wayne and Robin. Rick had always taken it for granted that he and Robin had a 'special friendship' yet Robin never expressed any romantic feelings toward Rick and their relationship had always been limited to the platonic summer encounters at the fire camp for the past few years.

"That guy 'Boston' is not going to make it through the fire season, I'll guarantee you that as a fact, Jay," Rick replied in a vehement tone. Jay wanted to have some fun with Rick, so he put a little more salt in Rick's emotional wound. Slyly, Jay wanted to play on Rick's emotions and vulnerabilities for his own nefarious, self-serving, reasons.

"Seriously now, you do know that a handsome, wealthy, young guy is a real chick-magnet, especially for a country-gal like Robin. The only way to compete with a guy like that is to have some serious money of your own, I mean real money, not this 'nickel & dime' salary crap that you have to work like a dog for either fighting fires or doing construction projects... a man like you needs some serious cash, say six or maybe even seven figure level cash my friend. What does the future hold for you, my friend? Honestly, you're getting too old to play fireman in the woods and construction is a hard-scrabble business these days, the recession and inflation have knocked the hell out of the residential construction market, my friend. If you want to get married to Robin or anyone else for that matter, with a nice house and some kids – you need serious, big money, fella. A woman like Robin is looking for a guy with some serious money in the bank, big dreams require big money my friend!" Jay delightfully teased as he took a sip of the smooth, ten-year aged single barrel bourbon.

Rick keenly heard Jay's taunting words and he knew that the only way he could compete for Robin's attention was to have a huge cash reserve, but his current jobs could never bring about such cash acquisition. Jay having planted his seed of discontent in Rick's ears now merely waited for his idea to sprout and he did not have to wait long either.

As he slowly sipped his Yukon Jack and uncomfortably swivelled on the bar stool, Rick knew that Jay's words were spot-on. "Well now Jay, just how the hell can I make or get any money like that in this shit-ass economy – those fucking bankers and Wall Street'ers like that 'Boston' guy and his friends, really screwed up the economy and the middle class! So, what's a regular guy like me supposed to do, go out and buy a lottery ticket, Jay?" Rick stated sarcastically.

"Well, my old friend, I just might have a proposition for you that could make you an independently wealthy man; that is, if you have the guts to be rich! Well do you, Rick?" Jay challenged in a rather inviting, yet cloistered manner. Jay continued to talk vaguely of his plans to Rick, the details which Jay explained to Rick were sparse, but the general tone was that concerning the exploitation of the Wind River reservation land for a future casino and land development deal. Rick listened to Jay's enticing words as he continued to angrily eye the affections being exchanged between Robin and Wayne. The more he spied Robin and Wayne together, the more Jay's plan made sense to him. Anger and jealousy were strong motivators and Jay knew just how to use these emotions which Rick amply possessed.

While Robin and Wayne enjoyed each other's company with discussions of family and backgrounds, Sammy decided to disengage herself from their conversation and seek out other social chit-chat. She turned to Hank, a man who seemed like he had lived an interesting life by the character lines of his mahogany wrinkled face and his distinguishing grey hair.

"Hey Hank, thanks a bunch for helping me fly that injured Hot Shot, Tom Phillip's, off of the mountain the last week, he was in very serious condition and your flying helped to save that young man's leg. You really handled the chopper through some pretty choppy fire turbulence. Where did you learn to fly that chopper?" Sammy inquired in hope of getting the quiet man to reveal some aspect of his past. Never one to speak too much, Hank only made some low rumble mutterings and smiled at the pretty young girl. Hank turned away from Sammy and tried to focus his attention on his golden ale and hoping that the pretty young girl would devote her attentions to some younger guy that was nearer to her own age. His life was a closed book.

Yet Sammy was not to be deterred, she was fascinated by older people who could teach her something about things and events, of which she had only read about in history books. Hank was especially interesting to Sammy, he had the aura of a vagabond, yet he had a worldly sophistication about him as well. The old crow was mysterious and worldly, unlike many of her youthful contemporaries, so she continued to pursue her inquiry.

"So, are you married? Any children? Have any hobbies? Where's your family from, Hank?", Sammy inquired in a series of rapid, if not totally impolite, quick succession.

Wearily Hank looked up from his half-empty mug of beer, the look of amazement was shown on his face, perhaps even some embarrassment, so he decided to 'entertain' Sammy's inquisition a bit.

"Not too much to tell really...you might say that I've loved some, killed some, saved some, and been around the world a bit you might say, young lady...I was in the Nam back in the sixties when I was just a youth. The Army was a way out of the slums, they taught me to fly and to kill, that sure as hell beat walking the bleak pavements of Chicago as a young, poor, uneducated black man," Hank vaguely confessed and hoping to diffuse any further inquiry into his past. Ironically, it produced just the opposite effect.

Sammy was almost knocked off her bar stool; she had just met a man who could be a stroke of good fortune. She looked carefully at Hank's chest and noted his dog tag chains and the items that were dangling from it, to include his mangled Service identification tags known as Dog Tags and several AK-47 bullet projectiles. Sammy's mom often referred to her dead dad as having served somewhere in Vietnam and also being from Chicago. Maybe it would be her good fortune if Hank, a fellow Chicago native and Vet, knew something about her father. 'It was worth a try to find out something!' Sammy figured to herself.

"Hey Hank, my dad was a Vietnam Vet, his first name was Lee or maybe Lee Roy, ever hear of someone with that name from Chicago who was over in Vietnam with you?" Sammy inquired with wide-eyed eagerness and hoping for any thread of information that would shed light on her mysterious father.

Suddenly, Hank's facial composure changed from jovial to sullen, there was an obvious expression of withdrawal in his body movements, as he awkwardly looked away from Sammy and blankly stared at the bottles neatly arrayed behind the bar. A cold chill ran up his spine. His contrived past and progeny was suddenly catching up with him.

"Hey there, Missy, that was a frigging long time ago, Chicago and Nam were places that I care to flush from my mind. I simply blot these things out of my life! Guys came and went every month in the Nam. No, Ma'am, I don't remember anyone by that name from either place, my mind blanked out those terrible years and I suggest that you leave it alone young lady! I put the past away and I suggest that you do the same Missy, let the dead lay in peace, they sure as hell deserve it!" Hank lied in an abrupt defensive tone.

Before Sammy or Hank had a chance to continue their conversation, both they and everyone else in the tavern was distracted and interrupted from their bar-fly celebrating by the obnoxiously loud, low rumbling of Harley-Davidson motorcycles equipped with enhanced illegal street pipes, the decibels emitted were sufficient to cause permanent ear damage to those constantly exposed to such hazards. Still the gang of cyclists was not too concerned about their hearing impairments; as middle or old age was not on their life's horizon. They numbered half a dozen in all. Suddenly, the thundering sounds came to a disturbing and abrupt cessation, everyone in the bar had hoped that the rumbling motorcyclists would merely pass them by, but no such luck was forthcoming. Bikers were usually trouble makers!

The mysterious riders had parked outside the tavern in a clearly yellow lined marked area normally reserved for fire or rescue vehicles. These fragments of the posted law were mere annoyances to the members of the gang, something to be ignored like the posted speed signs. The dead calm was interrupted by the menacing intonation of heavy footsteps being impressed by large men attired with heavy boots and chains rumbling their weight atop that of the old wooden boardwalk planks. The clang of metal-touching-metal was self-evident, almost like the staccato clanging of an old western cowboy or gunslinger's spurs. The wooden boardwalk accented and amplified the echoes of the heavy boots and the metal chains. All the eyes of the bar room intrigued patrons were singularly focused at the bar front entrance and no one's curiosity was disappointed by the emerging shadows that soon revealed the bodies of the men behind the foreboding sounds.

Slowly piercing through the old western wooden bat-wing doors, there emerged six 'road warrior' attired creatures. The scene would have been comical, if it were not actually happening in the flesh. Yet no one in the bar was laughing. Menacing before them stood these intimidating huge men, their faces betrayed a hard-weathered day of riding and their expressions were of a dead-pan somber expression. Every man sported tattoos and facial scars from past fights involving knives, chains, chairs or fists. They wore dark brown or black leather garments, to include chaps, vests, gloves and jackets. One gangster wore a sweaty red bandana around his head, everyone had facial hair of varying lengths, while their hair ranged from shaved skin-head to shoulder length locks.

From their motley appearance and acrid smelling sweat, it was evident that these were not the typical weekend middle class Harley rider; these boys lived on the road and this day they had ridden long and hard; they craved for some drinks and eats, maybe bust a few heads too if that's where the night's adventures took them. Yet these 'Iron Horse' gangsters were not your 'typical' biker gang types either, this troupe was a mixture of African-American, Caucasian and Hispanic – while most other gangers were of a predominant or dominant racial type. The bikers were un-patched and without any 'gang colours'. This indicated that this posse was an independent group that was based on its members joining out of a common goal, affiliation or friendship. By racial complexion, the group contained three African Americans, two Caucasians and one Hispanic. Each 'ganger' was as burly as a body builder with bulging muscle-laden arms and full-barreled chests. Obviously being a wimpy man excluded one from this unholy fraternity and one had to wonder what level of felony one needed to commit to become a pledge of this group.

As in nature, actions are the telltale sign of the leader. The large Afro-American male was the first one through the bat-wing doors and the other gangers stood subordinately behind or to either side of him. He was over 6' tall, bald shaved, and he wore a bushy moustache. Prominently brandished along his left cheek, was a long, nasty looking, 4 inch knife scar, probably earned in some now forgotten brawl. Finally, a well-groomed goatee completed his hideous facade. Distinct tones of anger and arrogance adorned his motley face, which instantly deterred others from rendering him a pleasant or casual greeting. This man's entire physical persona signified trouble and serious business; if you had neither for him, then you dared not approach him with a cavalier demeanour.

Everyone in the bar looked at the leader and his unsavoury pack of thugs and knew that these guys were looking for trouble tonight. Yet the 'regulars' who patronized Chief Joseph's tavern every night over the fire season were not exactly the skinny 'Barney Fife' or choir boy type either. The fire fighters were young, tough, rugged, and brave – each of them could easily take care of themselves in a fight if they had to do so. There were also numerous, huge 'Paul Bunion' lumberjack types too – these were the muscle-bound human monsters of the great western and northern frontier states. Lumberjacks were huge, tough men who could give a professional football linebacker a run for his money. Neither of these groups of men were going to be intimidated by these transient, dirty, loud bikers. The fire fighters and lumberjacks stood stoically guarding their recreational turf from these biker interlopers.

Following the guide of their leader, the motorcycle gangers slowly trudged up to an open spot at the bar just astride from where Robin, Wayne, Sammy and Hank were standing. No direct eye contact was exchanged with the motorcycle gang members. The feelings were mutual as the gangers wore their stoic iron mask faces that were chiselled with anger and determination. Bar patrons and gang members confronted one other with deliberate animosity, each were like two competing camps of wild animals.

"Hey there, barkeep, give me and my boys beers and some eats," demanded the tall intimidating African-American leader to Chief Joseph. There was a tense filled silence from everyone, including Chief Joseph, who looked at the angry young man with a distrustful glare. "What do you and your men really want here? Why don't you get on your bikes and go somewhere else, like some biker bar?" Chief Joseph replied with a suggestive fearless defiance.

The leader's eyes filled wide with defiance, the whites of his eyes almost bulging from his face in bug-eye fashion. "What the hell's the matter with this joint? Hey, Indian man, me and the boys, we like this place, it's the reason we stopped here and not some other place …besides, this is a free fucking country, you as an Indian should know this better than me, right, Indian man?" the gang leader rudely shouted out loudly for everyone to hear.

'This bastard biker had a legal point, even if he said the words so crudely and with prejudice,' Chief Joseph thought to himself. The Chief was still highly suspicious of these characters' true intentions.

"Okay, stranger, we're not prejudiced here, we just like our patrons to be friendly and respectful, that's all," Chief Joseph replied defensively. "Now what do you want to eat?" the old Native American inquired of the gang leader.

Upon hearing the old Indian's reply, the leader's face blossomed into a broad satisfied smile, as several gold teeth sparkled and accented his face, as the biker delighted in his cowing down of the old bartender. Once again, the leader rudely barked out his preference, "Okay, old Indian, how about some large burgers, fries, beer and chasers of rye whiskey for me and the boys here?"

Chief Joseph nodded silently, professionally taking the orders and never betraying any thoughts of anger or disgust. The years had taught Chief Joseph that it never paid to antagonize a rude patron, unless that person was physically abusive or plain out drunk.

Having scored one victory of intimidation, the gang leader was merely emboldened to make another attack on someone else, this being the trait of bullies. He drew up to the empty bar stool right next to Sammy, he picked up the glass of rye whiskey and shot back the drink in a single gulp. Boldly he then took up the full mug of golden lager that lay before him and he took a mighty gulp of the ice-cold refreshment. He slammed the beer mug firmly down atop the bar with a loud report, as he crudely wiped the excess beer foam from his lips and onto the sleeve of his black leather jacket. His manners were as foul and disgusting as was that which befitted his irreverent language.

"Now that's what a real man needs after a long day's ride, a warm powerful shot followed by a cold beer, like a man needs a woman on a cold winter night!" he growled vulgarly as he eyed-up Sammy like a wild animal expecting a huge meal. In disgust, Sammy turned her eyes away from this beast of a man. Yet the gang leader would not be deterred by such a conventional social rebuff.

"Hey there, young sexy stuff! How did some fine brown sugar like you get messed up with this bunch of refined, tight-assed, confectionary white folk? I bet you're sweeter than anything on the dessert menu! How about having a drink with me? My name is Vic; well, how about it, 'Miss Brown Sugar'?" the gang leader purred to Sammy as he uninvitingly planted his arm around her shoulder. In obvious disgust, she tried to release Vic's arm off her shoulder, but the gang leader was not deterred. "What's your name, sweet thing? Let's not be strangers, honey," Vic obnoxiously inquired again. This time, he tried aggressively pulling Sammy closer to him in hope of stealing a quick kiss or a hug.

"Her name is none of your frigging business, sonny, because she's never gone to mingle with the likes of a low-life loser like you ...now take your grubby hands off of her, you don't know her and she obviously doesn't want to know you!" Hank yelled back angrily, as he pushed Vic's arm off of Sammy's shoulder. Hank raced to place himself between Sammy and Vic the gang leader.

Vic was momentarily taken aback by the old black man's actions and words, very few had ever dared to challenge him publicly without getting themselves seriously hurt and this old man was no exception.

"Hey there, grandpa, this is between me and the lady here, but before I put a hurting on a senior citizen, I want to give you fair warning that I do not discriminate or take pity on people just because they are old!

Now just go back to your rocking chair, old man," the young hooligan warned Hank. Wayne and Rick quickly charged to Hank's defence, as both men quickly arose from their stools and rushed to Hank's side.

"Hey there, Vic, I think that you've outgrown your welcome here, now how about getting your sorry ass out of here!" Rick smartly demanded of the leather clad bully. Vic was both unimpressed and undaunted by Rick's bravado, he merely ignored Rick's warning and he again boldly made a direct advance to place his hands upon Sammy's shoulder. Immediately she tore away in obvious revulsion and fear.

"Hey, pal – the lady doesn't want to be bothered by a jerk like yourself," Wayne shouted, as he slapped Vic's hand away from Sammy's shoulder. With an automatic animal reflex, Vic quickly turned sharply and hooked Wayne with a direct punch to his right jaw.

Caught totally off balance, Wayne fell instantly to the floor, surprised at how sudden he had been sucker-punched by Vic. His jaw hurt like hell, but he tasted no blood, and nothing seemed immediately broken. Immediately, Rick pulled forcefully on Vic's leather jacket and made a forceful solid punch into his jaw, sending Vic reeling backward and stumbling onto his heels and into the surprised arms of his fellow gang members. It was an embarrassing and compromising position for a gang leader to be found. Vic needed to save face with his gang and he wanted pay-back now!

All six gang members were now ready to rumble, as Vic regained his upright position, along with his renewed anger. Without command or urging, the gang members automatically unleashed their knives, chains and cut-down axe handle clubs from beneath the sanctuary of their heavy leather clothing. As violence was about to erupt, the distinct, unmistakable metallic sound of Chief Joseph's pump shotgun cut through the air, Vic stopped dead in his tracks on distinctly hearing the shotgun round being chambered and seeing its blue metal finish shimmering in the muted bar room lighting. Vic and the others knew that knives and clubs were no match for a 12-gauge pump shotgun. It was a stand-off, neither side knew what was next to come and who would blink first. Neither side wanted to back-down. The swollen pregnancy of anxiety was dramatically broken, as several Paul Bunion lumberjack types positioned themselves behind several of the gang members. As if on cue, the hulking lumberjacks quickly grabbed a few gang members by the back collar of their leather clothing and slowly raised the gang members up off of the ground.

There they hung up in the air like hapless little children, their feet kicking in the air helplessly, their hands and arms useless, their weapons fell and lay harmlessly on the wood floor. Sheer fear and feebleness were worn as expressions on the dangling gang members' faces. Vic turned to see his men wailing and shouting as they hung in the air like powerless puppets. Vic knew that this was a dead-end play.

"Okay...okay – hey, Old Indian, you win...we're fixing to leave this dump, right now! Tell your Neanderthals to put my boys down!" Vic bawled out desperately, his voice breaking with obvious nervousness and fear. He was resigned to eating some crow this night, yet his nature was as defiant as ever. Chief Joseph nodded to the lumberjacks, each of them bobbed at one another and in unison they suddenly dropped the gang members onto the hard-wooden floor. Two muffled thuds were heard throughout the hushed tavern. The gang members slowly got up and brushed themselves off, being more embarrassed than injured. They slowly picked up and packed away their assortment of weapons.

"So, you fucking people think you're so tough because you're all together now...well let me tell you that someday you won't all be together and have one another to help you out...on that day me and my boys will be there, and you'll be the sorry suckers. Let's blow from this dump boys!" Vic screeched in defiance as he yelled a final threat to everyone in the bar and especially at Sammy, Hank, Wayne and Rick. Vic eyed the four with hatred and revenge in his eyes. Their egos bruised, Vic and his gang made a hasty exit from the bar, the low rumble of the vanishing sounds of the motorcycle's exhausts were audio proof of their hasty retreat.

"Next time, 'Boston', you stay the hell out of our business, we take care of our own here and you're just a passing summer interloper," Rick bitterly howled as Wayne brushed off the dirt from his shirt and pants. Wayne was angry too, he hated Rick for his insensitivity and possessive behaviour. The two men looked at each other angrily; their animosity was complete and evident.

"Hey, Rick, Wayne has dropped the bet with us, isn't that great?" Robin interjected cheerfully, hoping to diffuse the tensions between Wayne and Rick.

Rick merely looked with disdain at Robin and then looked with disgust at Wayne. "No thanks, if you and Sammy want out, you can do as you please, but my bet with 'Boston' still stands unless he wants to forfeit! It's a long way to Labor Day, he was just lucky the other day when he got lost in the woods and almost got both you and himself killed. If 'Boston' wants to quit, that's fine with me, but I'm no quitter and I'm going to win this bet, you hear me, 'Boston'!" Rick cowed angrily as he turned his back and returned to his stool next to Jay Blackhawk.

"Boy oh boy does that bitter man have a personality disorder or something, he's almost like a psychopath!" Wayne remarked to Sammy, Robin and Hank. Robin had a sad, pitiful look on her face. She saw Rick talking with Jay Blackhawk and that was not a good thing. She couldn't believe how much he had changed in the past year; his hatred of Wayne now eclipsed his former fondness for Robin.

"Yes, that's for certain, Wayne, Rick has changed a lot and it's not for the better either! His personal and family finances have been rocked by the building slowdown and credit crisis. I think that's one of the main reasons that he hates you...you are rich and successful, a banker in the trade that has led to the ruin of his builder profession and his family's construction business," Robin muttered softly and with some regret.

"Only one of the reasons, what else could he be mad about?" Wayne announced with child-like wonder.

Robin turned away from him, knowing that she was becoming a decisive factor in the conflict between the two men; she could sense it as a woman. Sammy and Hank eyed each other, and they too knew that Robin and Wayne had a natural attraction to one another and that they were becoming more than just pals, the way that they each looked at one another was evidence of their budding relationship. Chief Joseph could see it as well, everyone could see the attraction between the two, everyone that is...except for Robin and Wayne.

The night had been filled with ample melodrama, so the Chief got his nephew Thomas Hawk to strike up his rock band and get everyone into a jovial mood. "Hey Tom, can you and your rock group crank up some tunes and get this place rolling a bit?" Chief Joseph pleaded with his grandson. Even though the Chief didn't care much for the modern rock band sound – he was amenable to any type of live band music that was available. The music would relieve everyone's tensions, as well as sell some more drinks. Young Tom Hawk was a second-year college student at Wyoming State University, majoring in accounting. The rock band brought in some extra money, especially over the summer months and it provided a sorely needed outlet from the mundane accounting books.

"Okay, folks, we've had enough action this evening from some unruly patrons, but now me and my band, the 'Tom-A-Hawks' want to present you with some entertainment of a more traditional sort, so let's have a round of applause for the band as we liven up the night for everyone and get this bar hopping? We're going to get some active participation from the patrons here too, so let's start up a line dance with guys on one side, ladies on the other! Come on, you aren't doing anything better, so get up off the bar stools and get onto the dance floor, fire fighters and lumberjacks," Tom Hawks commanded in an encouraging tone over the microphone. Everyone applauded and rushed to the middle of the floor. On the count of three, Tom strummed six chords on his Fender electric guitar, the drummer performed a quick rhythmic drum beat and the bass and keyboard chimed in on cue.

The 'Tom-A-Hawks' had obviously performed this tune many times before, their execution was flawless and it seemed that the fire fighter 'regulars' knew the song too, it was a summer ritual dance. Men and women lined up in opposite formation, there were about 25 men and women equally paired, while a much larger group of men stood on the periphery of the dance lines, there not being not enough of a fair male-female ratio as things stood anyway. An even larger group of men never left the bar, preferring to be spectators of the entire event. Both Jay and Rick were those counted among the bar stool commandos.

The band played an upbeat tune that was a mix of Native American war-dance beat, coupled with rock-and-roll rhythm and interspaced with an Irish-jig melody, it made for an exhilarating mood and Tom Hawk provided the lead vocals, as well as being the lead director for the dance directions. According to the dance ritual directions, a male was supposed to partner himself with a female from the far-opposite side of the line, the two would join arm-in-arm and then they each tried to duck under and dance their way down the gauntlet of arms arrayed over their heads. After each couple had made their way down to the end of the gauntlet, both men and women would move back and forth to one another, exchange sides and repeat the process with another new couple. It was reminiscent of an old western barn revival dance that was intermixed with a modern line-dance. It was simple, great fun and very exhilarating.

By chance, Hank and Sam were at opposing ends of the line, so Hank ran down the line, grabbed Sammy and the two proceeded arm-in-arm down the gauntlet until they reached the end of the line. A joyous choir of yells and laughter sprung up as each succeeding couple proceeded their turn in the dance. After fifteen minutes, all males and females had gone through one complete dance routine, everyone was charged up and the drinks were flowing, men at the sidelines were yelling and encouraging the dance to continue, so the band played on; everyone had decided that it was too much fun to stop at this festive time and thus, so the merriment continued.

Once again, male and female dance partners lined up and faced one another and once again the couples ran the dance gauntlet. It was nearing the end of the second chorus when Wayne raced down the gauntlet and picked out his dance partner. It was Robin this time. The two smiled with delight, as Wayne embraced Robin and led her down the corridor of folded arms. They ducked as low as they could and made the most awkward dance steps, but they managed to make it to the end of the line. Their eyes locked, as they smiled at one another. The music suddenly stopped as Tom Hawks excused his band for a short intermission before resuming the bandstand. The men and women quickly filtered away to either the bar area or bathrooms for some sorely needed drinks or to relieve themselves of drinks previously consumed. Robin and Wayne now stood nervously alone in the middle of an emptying wood dance floor, their eyes affixed on one another, oblivious to the emptying emporium. Chief Joseph keenly spied on the two awkwardly standing pair; he slowly walked over to the old jukebox and inserted a coin.

Almost magically, soothing music filled the tavern. It was an old ballad sung by Tony Bennett, 'The Good Life' – a slow song that was meant for slow dancing and romantic embracing. All eyes were on the young, handsome couple as they stood momentarily staring at each other like two freshmen at a high school dance.

"It appears that everyone's gone away, but would you have this dance with me, Robin?" Wayne asked almost shyly. Robin was unexpectedly flattered by the question; she said nothing, only nodding in affirmation her acceptance of the gentlemanly offer. Wayne took Robin's hand and put his arms around her waist. He started a simple foxtrot dance that was abbreviated with a few gentle turns.

"Robin, thanks again for coming to find me in that firestorm, you saved my life you know!" Wayne confessed earnestly. Robin was embarrassed by the remark.

"You've already thanked me several times, you're welcome and it's also part of my job, it's nothing special really," Robin voiced softly, as she badly lied defensively.

"What was that? I thought that I was at least a little special to you Robin; after all, we were 'shaked & baked' together, not to mention splattered with gooey red fire retardant…now that's what I call special! So how many guys and gals go through that on their first outing together?" Wayne inquired in an obviously sarcastic manner.

Robin burst out in a sudden laugh; he had broken down her defences.

"Well maybe you're just a little special to me; after all, how many guys can I thank for knocking me off my prized Harley and onto my ass?", Robin fired back with equal sarcasm.

"Yeah, about that Harley, how much you going to sue me for?" Wayne exclaimed with a broad smile.

"So how about just getting my bike fixed back to normal and taking me out to dinner, Mr Big Spender!" Robin jokingly, but truthfully replied.

This time Wayne didn't or couldn't reply, he was singularly focused on Robin's slender body, the softness of her skin, the smell of her hair and the warmth of her breath as she hugged his body. Even through her clothing, he could feel her heart beating like a drum; it was pounding fast against his chest. He was physically and emotionally excited by Robin's sexual allure. Wayne wondered if Robin had similar feelings too. He made a short swirl turn, as Robin's eyes and his met again. Her eyes were locked onto his, everything else in the room diminished in appearance. The song ended suddenly and there was an uncomfortable silence. Neither of them could say anything, they were both in love and neither of them wanted to admit it.

"The music has ended, I think we can stop now! Thanks for the dance, Robin, you're a great partner," Wayne voiced tenderly.

In reply, Robin muttered an almost inaudible and soft 'thank you.' Wayne didn't know what else to say as he slowly let go of Robin's hands.

"Geez, Robin, do your hands always get so sweaty…it must be hotter in here than I had thought!" Wayne noted in a stumbling and awkward manner. Robin looked at her hands, they were generously perspiring with profuse sweat, an obvious true sign of her nervousness. She knew instantly that she loved Wayne, but she couldn't stand to be near him, not at this moment anyway, the emotional impact was too great for her to continue with any more social interaction. Robin's eyes swelled up with tears, she panicked with fear as she ran from Wayne's sight and out of the taverns bat wing doors. Sammy had been standing next to Hank and they both knew that Robin had fallen in love with Wayne. Quickly, Sammy grabbed her coat and ran out of the bar after her friend; after all, this was no time to leave a girlfriend who had fallen in love.

"What the hell's going on here, Hank? Two women come in with us and now two women run out without us? I don't get it!" Wayne lamented as he walked over to the bar and tried to finish off his beer.

"Oh, it's nothing, sonny, a beautiful woman has just realized that she has fallen in love with you, that's all!" Hank nonchalantly sighed as he finished off his beer. Chief Joseph chomped on his cigar and nodded in silent affirmation to Hank's candid remark. Most dumbfounded, Wayne awkwardly stood leaning up against the bar and pondered the words carefully. He knew that Hank was right, and he didn't know what to do about it either. He loved Katherine, but this new woman was different, she was active, adventurous, carefree, brave and genuinely very caring. Her nature was as seductive as was her beauty; there was nothing phony or false about Robin.

Wayne ordered up a double scotch, he needed to think about what his heart was feeling. 'Well I'll be damned! I neither said and did anything to encourage her or to lead her on! Maybe it was just a passing flirtation or summer fling?' he pondered to himself, as he sipped on the aged brew. "Experience and upbringing had trained Wayne to always temper emotions with cold calculating analysis and judgment. It had seemed that events of the summer had not yet fully changed the man.

A generous 45 minutes had passed since Robin ran out the tavern door, quickly followed by Sammy, and during the intervening time Wayne had consumed two double malt scotch drinks. He and Hank talked about women and love and Chief Joseph Hawk sometimes added a few wise thoughts of his own. Both of the older men provided their worldly counsel to the troubled young man, yet nothing they said seemed to console his soul.

"How the hell did this happen to me, I did nothing to provoke this thing – it just happened, zap! Just like that!" Wayne confided as he snapped his fingers in the air. Both Hank and Chief Joseph just laughed.

"Well now, sonny, that's the way love happens, it comes up and bites you in the ass when you're not looking," Hank explained with a slow drag in his voice.

"Okay, you smart old guys, what's next? What the hell do I do? I have to work with Robin every day and I'm not going to quit or request a fire team transfer either? To top things off, I'm engaged to a very beautiful lady back home," Wayne replied snappily. Both Hank and Chief Joseph looked at each other, yet now Chief Joseph was the one doing the talking.

"Look here, young man, I'd say that you should go and see Robin, talk it out and let her know your feelings and she'll tell you her feelings too, you're both adults and you'll work it out," Chief Joseph counselled as he patted Wayne on the hand in a fatherly way. It felt good to be talking to two older men with whom he deeply respected. There was a short silence as Wayne dwelled upon the advice.

"Damn it! You're right! You're both right! I'm going to go out and find Robin, I'll try to talk to her," Wayne exclaimed indignantly as he slammed down the whiskey glass loudly on the bar, almost causing it to shatter. "Thanks, gentlemen!" Wayne sighed as he turned away and made his way out of the tavern.

Wayne stopped at the bathroom at the rear of the bar, just to the right of the band stand area. Finishing up his personal hygiene business, Wayne decided to discreetly exit the tavern using the main side exit of the tavern instead of the more prominent, but more uniquely western bat–wing door entrance located at the front of the tavern. He wanted and needed to get some solitary fresh air and think matters out in private. He emerged into a darkened black alley way in which was located various refuge and trash containers. He took only a few steps, he sensed something was not quite right, but he foolishly ignored his instincts. He took a few more steps and heard some ruffling sounds ahead of him. There was an unknown, menacing presence there.

"Hey there, buddy, how'd you like to have a nice slow dance with me?" a rough male voice echoed from the darkness. Wayne thought this was just an off-coloured joke from some guy passing through the alley to take a quick piss on the wall, but before he could even reply or get a glimpse of the stranger, a hard fist clobbered him in the chin and left jaw, knocking him off his feet and down onto his knees. Dazzled, he felt two men pick him up by the shoulders, while a third man punched him in the stomach. The initial punch knocked the wind from his lungs, which left him gasping for air. Before he had a chance to react, two more forceful punches followed in quick succession. He dropped to the ground almost unconscious. 'This must be some God-awful nightmare, this can't be happening to me!' Wayne thought to himself in agony. He heard several voices laughing, then a heavy booted foot struck him in the stomach, then another one and yet another. He passed out in pain, as the three men quickly vanquished the scene of their cowardly crime.

Wayne lay there in the tavern's alleyway motionless. It was two o'clock in the morning, some two hours after he had been jumped in the dark alley, it was only upon closing up the building that anyone had a chance to discover Wayne's crippled, battered body. A voice cried out from the darkness, "Hey, there's someone hurt out here! Someone help me, quick!" Tom Hawk screamed out, as members of his band ran from the tavern to assist him. "Wayne, Wayne – are you all right, buddy? He's all beat-up, let's get him inside fast," Tom commanded in a clearly anxious tone.

"My God, he's beat up really bad, someone call an ambulance and emergency 911!" Chief Joseph yelled to one of his bartenders. The Chief and Tom took Wayne to a back-office room and laid him out on an old comfortable couch. Wayne had been beaten up pretty good with numerous facial cuts and forced blows to the stomach. He regained semi-consciousness after a swift dose of smelling salts were applied by the Chief.

"Wayne my boy, who did this to you? Did you see any of their faces? How bad are you hurt?" Chief Joseph pleaded in a fatherly tone. Wayne coughed up some blood and gasped in despair – with each passing breath, he was clearly in pain and it was not known if he had any internal injuries. "No, I saw nothing, it was too dark to see anyone, before I knew it, about three guys jumped me for no known reason," Wayne confessed in agony.

About 10 minutes after making the emergency 911 call, both the tribal medical ambulance and the reservation Sheriff Dave Carney, arrived and took Wayne to the tribal medical clinic. The clinic performed a thorough examination. Concurrently, Sheriff Dave Carney started an initial police investigation too. Being now more lucid, Wayne informed the sheriff of the same details that he had told to Chief Joseph.

"Did they take your wallet or any other personal valuables, Mr Hamilton?" Sheriff Carney inquired dryly.

"No, sheriff, they didn't ask for any money, I still have my wallet and all of my personal effects," Wayne replied in an agonizing voice.

"Well, I guess that we can rule out robbery as a motive, it might just be an act of random violence or maybe an act of revenge! Maybe it was those outlaw bikers that were at the tavern earlier. I'll send the forensic team to the tavern alley and look for fingerprints and other evidence of the assault. Unfortunately, random violent crime is a fact of life these days. I'll file my report in the morning and you can pick up a copy if you like, Mr Hamilton, now if you think of anything thing else here is my card, just give me a call please," Sheriff Carney replied as he closed his notebook and walked out of the emergency room.

A preliminary medical examination revealed that there were no broken bones, missing teeth, fractures or concussions. The tribal medical staff wisely insisted on Wayne having to undergo X-rays and other tests to ensure that no major internal organs were injured. For once in his short life, Wayne had the good sense not to argue with the medical authorities. After taking the requisite x-rays, additional finger probing and blood tests, Wayne was released. The clinic taped up his bruised ribs, cleaned-up and bandaged his cuts and gave him some pain medications.

Wayne was ordered to bed-rest for the next week and he was counselled to get another medical evaluation in a few days to review his lab and X-ray results. The initial conclusion of the tribal paramedics was that nothing was broken and that there were only some serious and painful bruises. Furthermore, Wayne was told to report any blood in his stools or urine.

"Why don't you come home with me, Wayne, my home is nothing fancy, but it's comfortable and my wife cooks up a lot of good hearty food to help get you back on your feet," Chief Joseph generously volunteered. Wayne smiled a grim that was punctuated by the pains caused in his ribs and stomach.

"Thanks a lot, Chief, but I'd rather just retreat back to my motel room for the next few days, I'm in too much pain for eating anything more than coffee and some oatmeal, but thanks a lot for the generous offer," Wayne sighed, as Chief Joseph and Tom slowly led Wayne into Tom's truck for the ride back to Wayne's motel.

"Just take the bumps slowly, my friends, I get the benefit of feeling every damn little bump in the road in my condition," Wayne sighed as he slid painfully into Tom's truck. The hardest part of the journey was getting Wayne up the stairs to his motel room, each step was an agony, so bruised were his tormented muscles. After only a few steps, Chief Joseph and Tom Hawk knew that they had only one option left in this situation. As if on cue, each man took Wayne's arm and leg and cautiously carried him step-by-step up the motel stairway.

Given the width of the narrow stairway, they barely managed to carry Wayne up the stairs of the motel, as the lobby receptionist looked on with horror and curiosity at the sight of two grown men carrying a hurt man up the stairs of the motel. Once in his room, Chief Joseph and Tom carefully undressed Wayne down to his underwear. His midriff was bandaged up like a mummy from a cheap 1930s horror film, while his face appeared as that of a wounded prize fighter, his left eye's blood vessels were broken in some spots, making him appear like a red-eyed vampire.

"Now are you certain that you are going to be alright in this place alone in your condition?" Chief Joseph inquired nervously as Tom looked on in equal concern.

"Sure thing, guys, I'll be fine as long as I have these pain-killer pills, how about you drop-by and check-in on me tomorrow, okay?" Wayne replied in a tired sounding voice.

Both Chief Joseph and Tom Hawk merely nodded to Wayne's fatigued reply. Almost as soon as his head hit the soft pillows, Wayne collapsed into a deep sleep state which would consume the rest of the night and most of the next day. They cautioned the motel clerk to call them if there was any medical issues and that Wayne's room was not to be cleaned or disturbed for the next several days. They also cautioned her that if any suspicious or strange men were asking about Wayne, that she should immediately call Sheriff Dave Carney. Neither Chief Joseph nor Tom discussed the nature of the attack on Wayne, yet both of them agreed that the event was highly suspicious, nothing of this nature had happened to a non-tribal member on the reservation in recent memory.

The next morning, the news of the physical assault on Wayne was making all the talk at Camp Haller. Rumours were that the disgruntled bikers were the culprits, while others thought that it was just a random act of violence, everyone was perplexed that a nice young man like Wayne could be so badly beaten up. The Ready Shack was abuzz with sounds of FM radio chatter and that of the low rumble discussions of the communications staff and the shift supervisors. After completing the morning PT ritual, many of the fire fighters gathered in the Ready Shack to share gossip or got a hot cup of coffee. Within the Ready Shack was posted the personnel 'Ready Board' on which the status of every fire fighter's name was listed. A green check next to a fire fighter's name was indicative of the fact that the person was present and ready for duty. Next to Wayne's name was scribbled the words 'injured/sick' in bold red letters, thus indicating that he was not on firefighting duty.

The only person who seemed not to get the word about Wayne was Robin. She did her fire squad roll-call at 0730 hours and she was most aware that Wayne was not present, just as he was also conspicuously absent for the earlier 0600 hours PT session. After the embarrassing dance that previous evening, she had thought the worst – that he had skipped town and ran out on her, that he was scared of any commitment to her. Wayne's absence still seemed odd to her, it seemed to be 'out of character' for him, even though she had known him only a short time. She gave out the daily training schedule to her squad and requested that a fellow senior fire fighter provide over-sight to her squad while she checked out Wayne's status with the Ready Shack.

"Hey Jeff, where's my Hot Shot Wayne Hamilton?" Robin asked in a hurried voice of her supervisor Jeff Campbell.

"Yeah, good morning to you too, Robin, go take a look at the personnel board," Jeff retorted in a sarcastic tone as he poked his right thumb over his shoulder to indicate the personnel status board. Robin eyed the name of Hamilton and quickly spotted his name in red letters and the ominous words 'injured/sick'; her eyes bugged out with anxiousness and trepidation.

"What the hell is wrong with Wayne? What happened to him? Where is he at?" Robin inquired in quick successive fashion.

He was consumed in performing his tedious supervisor management tasks, yet he finally succumbed to quell Robin's nervous inquiries.

"From what little I know, Robin, Mr Hamilton was beaten up pretty bad by a couple of anonymous thugs the other night in the alleyway behind Indian Joe's tavern, nothing was broken and there's no internal injuries, he'll be out for about the next week or so according to what Chief Joseph told me early this morning," Jeff remarked. Robin was now even more frantic, relieved that he was alive but badly hurt made her even more concerned.

"Where's he at, Jeff? In the hospital?" Robin eagerly inquired.

Jeff turned his back and took a swig of coffee and then he replied in a weary voice, "No hospital, not for that stupid guy, he stubbornly insisted on recuperating at his hotel room. Can you imagine that fortitude? A rich guy like that being holed-up like a mangy dog in a dingy, lonely hotel room? I hear that Chief Joseph and young Tom Hawks have been checking-up on him to make sure that he's all right." In the short time that it took for Jeff to turn around to face Robin, she was gone! She flew out the door and was off to the reservation motel.

Robin frantically ran toward the Camp Haller parking lot to where her truck was located.

"Hey, Robin, can I have a talk with you?" a male voice shouted from a distance. The voice belonged to none other than Rick Conroy. Robin's face betrayed a look of anguish and some anger too.

"What's the matter, Robin? I missed you the other night, it seemed that you were a bit too occupied with 'Boston' to make time for me," Rick smirked.

"Wayne is his proper name, Rick, and he's been beaten up pretty bad, a very convenient situation for you, now isn't it?" Robin remarked with obvious scorn.

"Hey now, wait one fucking minute there, honey! Are you blaming me for this beating, because if you are, I have a witness proving that I was not in that alley," Rick stated defensively and in a scripted manner.

"Just how in the hell did you know that he was beaten up in an alley, Rick?" Robin spat accusedly.

"Well, I mean that's what I heard from the Camp Haller rumour mill, Robin," Rick replied smartly.

"Rumour mill my ass! You're a bad liar, Rick and a lousy friend too! Whatever friendship or relationship that existed between us, Rick is over! I want no part of you! You're mean, self-centred and full of greed – you've changed over the years and it's not been a pretty change either – so good-bye buster!" Robin snapped as she pulled away and left a tail of dust in her rear-view mirror.

"You fucking, little, whoring, bitch! You're going to get nowhere with that no-good 'Boston' jerk – you just wait and see, baby! By summer, he'll be gone and you'll be left with a broken heart, you ignorant bitch-whore!" Rich bitterly shouted out as his fellow co-workers looked on in amazement at a grown man losing his wit over a woman. An unwritten rule of the fire fighters was that summer romances and firefighting did not go well together, it always ended-up badly for those that pursued such liaisons, yet such was the inevitable nature between men and women.

Upon getting into her truck, Robin violently stomped the accelerator to the floorboard, her emotions were running in full throttle. The powerful Dodge Ram reached the motel in short order, as she drove with almost reckless abandon. "Hey you there, what's the room number for Wayne Hamilton?" Robin snapped at the motel receptionist. The receptionist was startled at the rude and demanding request of the inquiring young blonde-haired woman.

"Ma'am I'm afraid that I cannot give out that private information and Mr Hamilton has left instruction not to be disturbed except by Chief Joseph or Tom Hawks," the clerk stated politely to Robin. Instead of physically or verbally continuing to confront the motel clerk, Robin merely took a gander of the room key, pigeon-hole portals that were neatly arrayed behind the receptionist. She spotted the name 'Hamilton' hanging on a spare key and the Room numbered #213, wherein she proceeded to sprint up the stairs to Wayne's room.

"Hey there, Miss, you can't go up there to Mr Hamilton's room unannounced, that man is recuperating!" the clerk yelled as she dialled the phone number to call Chief Joseph and report the incident.

"No worry, I'm his best medicine, honey!" Robin tersely shouted.

Spying down the hallway, Robin looked anxiously at the room numbers before quickly spotting Wayne's room. She knocked firmly, there was no answer, again she knocked and awaited a response – still no answer. A third rapping produced no response either. As she was walking down the hallway toward the stairs, she heard a door deadbolt lock disengage. Anxiously, she ran back to the door, it opened ever so slowly. She peered anxiously to see Wayne; however, as the door cracked open before her, she witnessed a torrid battered face, swollen and bandaged, his body was crumpled over in pain and his eyes were a terrible bloody colour.

Instantly Robin screamed out in utter horror, "My God what the hell have they fucking done to you, Wayne!" she pushed wide open the door and threw her arms around Wayne's neck ever so gently; she tenderly kissed his lips and cheeks in successive waves of affection. Despite his sore face, Wayne cried out too and returned Robin's embraces and kisses the best that he could. Robin closed the motel door behind her. The room was dark and smelled of stale re-circulating air. The distinct scent of antiseptic also tinted the air.

Robin placed her arm around Wayne's neck, helping him into the soft repose of his hotel bed. He was comfortably attired in his pyjamas and white socks. Gently, she lay by his side, softly stroking his hair and kissing his lips and fingers in tender compassion.

Throughout all of her free time, Robin daily ministered to Wayne in his small motel room for the next week, nursing and caring for him. To their unexpected surprise, that week Wayne and Robin became intimate lovers.

* * * * * * * * * * * * * * * * * *

CHAPTER 10

"Baubles, Bangles and Beads"

"The two men now spoke in hushed whispers and plotted the fine details of the plan that was going to allow their mutual dreams to become reality... the vices of greed and revenge made for perfect bedfellows."

"**B**illy, bring up the latest National Weather Service western state regional data, along with the predictive weather model that I have been working on for the past few weeks," Dr Ciellerie dryly noted as he slowly sipped his morning mug of rich, hazelnut-flavoured, black coffee.

"Sure thing, Dr Ciellerie! It looks like it's going to be another hot, dry season in the West again this year," Billy Coffler replied to his senior mentor and employer for this summer season. Dr Ciellerie nodded in mute acknowledgement of Billy's remarks, his mind was concentrated on charts and spreadsheets that appeared within the stroke of a few computer keystrokes from Billy's rapid finger movements.

Billy couldn't help but notice his mentor's face, which seemed to be in a state of utmost concern, if not outright displeasure. The computer screen data clearly had the professor's interest and annoyance – the data looked bad for this year's fire season and as usual, the dry west was going to feel the wrath of the weather patterns, this coupled with a three-year drought. To further aggravate this negative circumstance, the budget for this year's firefighting season was to be even less than the previous year, the recession and the funding cuts were going to make fighting the wildfires ever more challenging. Some fires would get sufficient resources, while others would go wanting. State and local resources were also at an all-time low for fighting fires – only those areas with high value 'jeopardy value' in terms of high property worth, were going to get the bulk of the limited resources. Years of accumulated un-burnt under-growth had made for a natural fire fuel source, old brush, fallen timber and pine needles made for a quick and sustained wildfire.

Any prospect for the idea of merely 'letting a wildfire burn itself out' which had been the prescribed practice in pre-industrial times – was now utterly unthinkable! Once again, money was the driving factor in human affairs. It was difficult to imagine that anyone in their right mind would be foolish enough to build multi-million-dollar homes in these remote wilderness areas, yet the west was increasingly littered with people possessing more money than brains or practical judgment. The rich wanted the world on their own terms, nature and logic be damned. Humans more often than not, did that which only served to immediately please them. The beautiful sedate nature which seemed to be so calmly inviting and serene was in actuality a custom-made tinderbox inferno just waiting to explode. The remote wilderness charm of these forest mega-mansions also meant that these dwellings were remote from established fire- fighting infra-structure, such as water lines and fire stations. Everything that was needed to combat these remote fires had to be shipped in from great distances. The property risk situation was totally insane and unsustainable.

The middle-aged professor took another sip of his black coffee as he continued his stoic gaze upon the scrolling screen of numeric data. His computer-like mind required more data to confirm his hypothesis. He next looked at a different array of multiple computer display screens- these also maintained a dizzying presentation of multi-coloured graphs and numeric data. The doctor's greying hair drooped lazily down from his slightly wrinkled forehead and down onto the rims of his reading glasses. The older man's eyes raced from one computer display to that of another, each glance quickly assimilating the data into his formidable calculating brain. The young meteorological grad student remained silent as the older man gazed silently at the computer screen data.

"Well, that's it, Billy, the data supports my hypothesis, there's no doubt about it, computer data does not lie!" the professor exhaustively sighed. Young Billy also knew exactly what the professor had just confessed. "Unless there was a drastic change to the elements of nature, it's going to be a hot, dry summer plagued with numerous brown-outs, water restrictions and sudden wildfires! God help the western US this summer," the older man noted dryly to his silent young summer intern.

"Hey, Dr Ciellerie, we spoke about the possibility of my going out and getting some field experience this summer, do you think that this is still a possibility for me? Now please don't get me wrong, Doctor, I mean I really like working here with you in the weather forecasting section, but some time spent in the fire camps, even for only for a week or two will mean a lot for me personally and professionally? I am an ex-Army parachutist and maybe I can even make an observer jump with the Smoke Jumpers!" Billy proclaimed in an innocent youthful tone.

The top meteorologist understood his young intern's zeal to get close-up to the real action of the firefighting business, but realities prevailed as well. "Your first obligation is to assist me here, Billy, but go and investigate the protocols for a National Weather Service intern to make a visit to the BLM/USFS camps and if things get slow after the height of the fire season, I'll see if I can spare your absence for the last week of your internship - things should be slower at that time. The field experience will fortify your resume and credibility too!" Dr Ciellerie replied with a fatherly smile.

"Sure thing, Doctor...I'll work my tail off this summer for you and the NWS fire watch centre and I'll represent everyone at the NWS with great professionalism when, I mean if, I get out to one of the fire camps," Billy explained enthusiastically. Both the older and younger man quickly returned back to their critical jobs of trying to scientifically forecast the forthcoming fires for July and August. From all the data which existed thus far, this summer was going to be one of the worst fire seasons in the last 15 years.

* * * * * * * * * * * * * * * * * *

Indeed, things were heating up all over the west this summer and this included the romance department for Robin and Wayne. It seemed Robin's nursing of Wayne after his back-alley confrontation had morphed into a fully-fledged romance that neither of them did anything to discourage. Over the weeks of July and then into August, they had become almost in-separable, never being far from one another in the fire fields or in the bedroom. Robin shared Wayne's motel room continuously, they were indeed 'an item' and everyone was happy for both of them. They made for a natural couple, both of them being young, attractive, and full of energy. They complemented each other's attributes while cancelling out the other's vices.

However, one person was not very happy with the budding romance and that was the jealous Rick Conroy. His hatred of Wayne grew with each passing day. Ever since Robin had ditched him, he was itching for revenge. A man filled with such anger becomes blind to the entire world, yet Rick was a man who cared little for the consequences of his actions; he was an anger-driven man. He acted brashly instead of thinking upon a problem, a romantic trait that was best reserved for novels and the movies.

As the summer season lengthened, so too did the team-bonding among Robin, Wayne, Sammy and Hank – they were like the Four Musketeers – all involved in the same firefighting drama and all sharing their free social time together as well. They had all just returned from fighting a mid-sized high timber fire in the Colorado Rockies about 50 miles northwest of Denver. The actual main fire was contained in three days, but the outlying satellite fires and clean-up took another several days. It was exhausting work that strained the vitality of everyone, the high altitude of over a mile high in elevation made the firefighting doubly difficult. If one wasn't in top physical shape, the work demands would literally exhaust a fire fighter with heat exhaustion. After a few days, they were all again back in Wyoming, recovering their equipment, cleaning it and getting everything in top condition for the next fire call. They maintained their skills with regular PT, new equipment orientation and fire drills. The pace was action-packed, but nowhere near the levels of that encountered in the basic fire training sessions. Life was good and everyone lived for the moment. It was great to be young, healthy and full of life.

"Hey, Robin, can I see you for a moment, boss?" Wayne inquired almost mockingly. Although the two were lovers, a professional decorum needed to be maintained around the other fire fighters, less there become talk of favouritism. Robin sneaked a quick smile when her back was turned away from the other fire camp crew members.

"You bet, handsome, now what can I do for you?" Robin replied in an almost girlish voice.

"Lookie here! I have a little something for you, I know that your birthday is coming up soon in early August and although it's a little premature, I wanted to get you something special," Wayne confessed in an almost embarrassed tone.

Robin noticed that Wayne had taken a small 3" by 5" box from his jacket, it was neatly wrapped in a rich gold foil wrapping and tied with a silk purple coloured ribbon – the entire item seemed almost regal in its appearance and not like some cheap drug store bought item. She was intrigued by the box item and its contents.

"So, what have you got there, Hot Shot? I hope you did not do something foolish, Wayne?" Robin remarked as her girlish grin expanded into a beaming broad white smile.

"Now don't get mad, Robin, I just had a crazy thought about the custom Rolex watch of mine that got damaged when I rode you off the road back there in early summer. Several weeks ago, I had my watch out for repair and it just arrived back along with a companion. So, go ahead and open this…and Happy Birthday Robin," Wayne concluded as he kissed Robin passionately, after which he handed her the small richly attired box. It was heavy and dense, and Robin had always been excited when receiving presents ever since she was a little girl. She stood there in front of Wayne for a few seconds, not knowing if she should open it or politely refuse the token from her lover. Her hesitation didn't last long. In child-like eagerness, she gently and anxiously untied the exquisite fancy ribbon and then nervously proceeded to unwrap the thick metal-like fancy gold coloured gift wrapping.

Lying naked in her hands was a classic black velvet jewellers' box, yet it could not be a ring, for the box was too large and heavy for such a small item. With her heart beating with explosive anticipation, she slowly opened the small black box. Little black boxes were exciting and significant things to the fairer sex.

Unhurriedly and with some trepidation she opened the box and immediately there burst forth many small glittering rays of reflected sparkling white light. She uttered a short cry as she fully opened the box and copiously spied its mysterious contents.

In her trembling hands, she beheld a stunning Ladies' Diamond Platinum Custom Rolex watch, a model that was slightly smaller, yet much more beautiful than its' male counterpart. An array of shiny, flawless one carat diamonds encrusted the entire bevel area as well as on the watch face itself. The platinum metal and diamonds amplified every ray of the sun, the diamonds serving like miniature spectrums, each gem breaking down the sun's rays into multiple colours of the rainbow. If the metal gold was king, then platinum was the Emperor – it was a metal of remarkable beauty, durability, lustre and density. The watch itself cost the equivalent of about $175,000.

"My Lord, it's the most beautiful thing that I have ever seen, Wayne, and it's heavy too! I... I... I can't take it from you! It's far too expensive for me and we haven't known each other long enough!" Robin cried forth with tears of appreciation falling down her face. She hugged Wayne and kissed him passionately. Wayne was taken aback; he thought that his new girl would never reject his gift of friendship.

"No, I want you to have this, Robin; after all, I can afford it, remember I'm that rich tight-ass investment banker from Boston, okay?" Wayne interjected quickly in his defence.

Robin took the watch in her hands, it was indeed a dazzling, dense, and beautiful thing of classic beauty, she confessed to herself. "It's just too damn expensive, Wayne – don't you see, I like you just because of who you are and not for the things that you can buy me," Robin replied and seeing the pain of rejection in his eyes.

"Wealth is worthless unless it is enjoyed and shared! Another thing is that I can't very well take the Rolex back to the jeweller – you see, Robin, the watch is personally engraved to you on the back face of the watch," Wayne exclaimed with a degree of self-assurance in his voice. Robin turned the very ornate and heavy bauble over and looked to see the engraved description.

"To Robin Cynthia Wolf – my best friend forever with love, always – Bradford Wayne Hamilton", the elegant Spencer-scroll writing read. Tears of emotion filled Robin's eyes; she knew that Wayne had genuine feelings for her. She threw her arms around him and gave him a terrific passionate kiss.

"I suppose that means that at least you'll be keeping the watch for at least the foreseeable future – correct?" Wayne exclaimed with some degree of satisfaction and relief.

Robin realized that she had to show some form of reciprocation as well, this was only proper manners in accordance with her strict upbringing. Robin thought quickly of an idea that would satisfy Wayne's pride and her dignity as well.

"Look here, Wayne, I'll make you a deal on this watch, I'll keep and wear it until the end of the summer fire season. After that, we'll re-visit the issue and I also want to buy you a gift as well, now is it a deal?" Robin suggested, while extending out her hand in friendship. Wayne didn't quite know what to make out of this offer, he was uncomfortably perplexed, as no one had ever turned down one of his generous gifts outright and no one ever suggested a temporary mutual gift exchange. Yet this was something that he liked about Robin – it was her unique way of making a practical, novel suggestion to an awkward situation.

"Well, I don't know, maybe we can do something like that, but I'm not sure though," Wayne replied with some hesitation. Robin put her hands on her hips in a commanding fashion and with a big broad smile to boot, as if challenging Wayne's weak toned response. Wayne thought quickly to help diffuse the tension.

"I am curious as to what sort of gift are you going to give to me, Robin? You know that I am a demanding type of guy, right?" Wayne remarked almost in childish inflection.

"Oh no you don't, Mr Big Investment Banker, this is my secret, just like your gift to me was your little secret, but I think you can say that my gift will be unique, beautiful and appreciated, just like this beautiful diamond encrusted Rolex is to me. Now do you have any doubts about my superior tastes in gift giving, Mr Hot Shot?" Robin fired back humorously.

Wayne realized that it was utter folly to argue with a beautiful, smart, and determined lady who he happened to love.

The two smiled at one another then embraced in another passionate kiss and prolonged hug. Afterward, Wayne explained the many features of the Rolex perpetual self-winding watch. With obvious delight, Robin donned the heavy bauble and she was immediately smitten by its beauty and ruggedness. Initially, the Diamond Rolex felt foreign and heavy on her left wrist, yet she knew that she was slowly falling in love with it, just as she had fallen in love with Wayne. She was a girl who was on the top of the world and it felt fabulous.

"Hey there, girlfriend, what's happening over there? That sure does not look like an employer-to-employee counselling session to me! I might have to report both of you lovebirds to the Human Resources representative or Sexual Harassment officer!" Sammy shouted as she hurried up from the Camp Haller airfield and helicopter staging area. Following a few scant yards behind her was Hank. Both of them looked relaxed and care free.

"What's up yourself, Sammy? It looks like you are having a great day also," Robin replied upon seeing her best girlfriend.

"Great is not the right word to use, Hank just gave me a quick ride in his chopper. Boy, he's a great pilot too! We were skimming the trees so low that I thought I was going to catch a bird in mid-air, the flying that is termed as 'Nap-of-the-Earth' flying," Sammy exclaimed with zeal. Before Sammy had a chance to say another word, Robin threw her arms around her and gave her a feminine 'girlfriend-type' hug. While Sammy was always appreciative of Robin's friendship, she was a little bewildered as to the instigation of this present girlish affection.

"Hey girlfriend, what's so special today, Robin?" Sammy inquired innocently. The beam on Robin's face betrayed the fact that this was indeed a special moment. Before Sammy could ask another question, Robin was holding up her left wrist amid a blinding twirl of reflected diamond sparkles. In utter amazement both Robin and Sammy laughed uncontrollably.

"Isn't it just sinfully beautiful, Sammy? It's Wayne's birthday gift to me! It's absolutely over the top and it's the absolute dream gift, girlfriend! I feel like Marilyn Monroe did in that classic movie - Gentlemen Prefer Blondes," Robin giggled uncontrollably.

Hank slowly walked over to Wayne, the two men looking at each other with some facial puzzlement. Each man was wondering about the mystery and dynamics among women and their love for baubles and emotional sharing of which the male of the species would forever remain a stranger. "Hank, can you tell me what it is about diamonds and women that is so seductive and exciting?" Wayne delightfully remarked. Hank too was amazed and still delighted by the two women sharing their feminine delights on Robin's left wrist.

"Wayne, my boy, if I knew the first thing about women, I'd be a wise man rather than the humble old fool who you see standing before you now," Hank dryly remarked. Both men smiled as the two beautiful women discussed Robin's new watch. Both men knew in a mutual and spontaneous thought of just how special and different women were from men and they each appreciated that it was a very pleasant distinction indeed.

To everyone's surprise, a well-weathered pick-up truck came rumbling by the quartet of firefighters, stopping a mere twenty-feet away from the front of the group. Two men emerged from the cabin of the truck; it was none other than young Tom Hawk and Chief Indian Joe.

"Oh, what a pleasant surprise, what are you two guys doing here at Camp Haller?" Robin spurted out in a most honest inquiry.

"Ah, things are dead slow at the bar, we thought that we would come up and visit you brave firefighters and see how everyone was doing today," Chief Joseph sounded off in a slow and resigned tone. "Wow – is that a real, honest to goodness, diamond watch?" young Tom exclaimed in astonishment as both he and Chief Joseph walked up to gaze upon Robin's new bauble.

"Yes, it's a real beauty, now isn't it? It's kind of a temporary summer gift from the overgenerous Wayne Hamilton," Robin explained with obvious abundant admiration and a broad smile.

"Well, that's really some sort of temporary gift, Wayne. Anytime you're feeling generous this summer, please think of me!" Tom remarked with utter hopeful desire.

"Hey, Tom, please go over to Robin's Dodge Ram truck and grab my shoulder bag which is sitting on the front seat," Sammy requested as she handed the keys to the vehicle over to Tom. In a few minutes, he returned back with Sammy's shoulder bag.

"Thanks a million, Tom…I hope what I'm looking for is in here, I seem to have everything in here except the thing that I need. Ah got it!" Sammy exclaimed with excitement, as she withdrew a late model smart phone from her bag. "Wow, that's great, Tom, I finally found it!!" Sammy exclaimed with great satisfaction.

"Listen up, everyone! Let's get some summer photos to capture the good times and that bitching beautiful diamond watch. Now, everyone gather up together and huddle for a few pictures, here you take a few pictures of us," Sammy politely commanded to Tom, who was more than willing to take the photos. Sammy, Hank, Robin Indian Joe and Wayne all huddled together for a group shot. The most prominent star within the camera viewfinder was Robin's watch, which shined brilliantly in the Wyoming summer sun.

"Hey, Robin, please place your hands down in front of you and try to keep that miniature diamond mine on your wrist out of the direct sunlight, that watch has too much sun reflection glitter to get a good photo!" Tom advised. Robin did as she was instructed, this time keeping her left hand out of the direct sunlight. She was keen to make sure that the diamond watch was visually prominent for the pictures.

"Okay everyone, say 'cheese'," Tom commanded. In quick succession he took three rapid shots.

"I want one of those photos to send back to my office in Boston," Wayne shouted to Sammy.

"Sure thing, Wayne honey, I'll send you a copy by e-mail and you can get it printed off today," Sammy exclaimed.

* * * * * * * * * * * * * * * *

If there was merriment at the Wyoming Jeffrey Haller Fire Base camp, then 1,800 miles to the east in Boston, there was no such merriment in the halls and offices of the Hamilton & MacAlister Investment Banking firm. Ever since Brad had left, the 'Ice Princess' was 'on-the-rag' for every little business and personal item that arose; even the Lead Account Managers were not immune from 'Kit Kat's' fury. The weekly business meetings had become a one–way shouting match with 'Kit Kat' spurting out bitterness and loud vocal outrages at the slightest bit of negative report or revenue issues. During one such meeting she yelled continuously for fifteen minutes straight about budget overruns on trivial office supplies, and the meeting abruptly concluded with Katherine throwing the report papers up in the air and storming out of the meeting, leaving everyone aghast at her childish outburst. All of the female office assistants vulgarly gossiped and sneered that Katherine needed 'a piece of man' and that Brad was the only man she would take this from and he had been away several months already.

However, one thing did not change and that was the personal retribution of Katherine against Margie, which continued non-stop every work day. Although Katherine still had the devoted employ of her private Executive Assistant, Joan Peters, with every opportunity, Katherine tried to harass and degrade Margie DeTagelio. Often Katherine would have Margie do low-level errands and other types of demeaning, trivial tasks usually reserved for the mail room or even janitorial staff. Margie could not afford to be bold or antagonistic toward Katherine; besides, her protector Brad was thousands of miles away and 'out of sight, was out of influence.'

The most recent incident occurred when 'Kit Kat' passed by Margie's office desk plant and deliberately knocked over the plant, vase and water contents onto Margie's cluttered desk. In typical 'Kit Kat' fashion, Katherine merely walked by without even making an apology or a delay in her stride. The 'accident' was deliberate, and Katherine amused herself at the misfortunes of her underling upstart. Margie knew that 'Kit Kat' was nothing more than a rich, spoiled bitch, who was used to getting her way in all things. Secretly, Margie was glad that Brad had left to go on his travelling excursion, as Katherine remained alone and personally miserable. It was good to see some cruel women get their comeuppances in this world. Not all women were the automatic friends of every other woman; just as it was with men, women had their natural friends and enemies. The best that Margie could do was try and avoid Katherine and keep a 'low-profile', while quietly managing Brad's office correspondence and related office matters.

"Miss Katherine, excuse me, but I have your daily mail, I have screened out the usual mundane mail and I have separated out the correspondences that require your attention or signatures, oh there's also some personal correspondence as well. Would you like for me to bring these in to you now?" Mrs Peters announced in a genteel and polite voice into the inter-office phone. There was a slight, short reply, which indicated that Miss Katherine had indeed wanted to see her personal mail immediately. Joan Peters politely smiled across to Margie, as she took the small bundle of pre-screened envelopes and papers into Miss Katherine's private office.

As was the usual practice, Joan Peters briefly explained any documents that needed either additional personal review or a signature, thereafter she awaited any further instructions from her boss. Mrs Peters noticed the postcard, but dared not to mention any item of personal correspondence from Katherine's fiancé; 'proper' office manners dictated that workers dare not delve into or mention their superior's personal matters unless the employer brought-up the issue first. Katherine looked over the papers, but said nothing, her eyes eagerly absorbing the details in a fast and furious data gathering manner.

"That will be all, Mrs Peters, thank you," Katherine replied in a short, yet professional, rehearsed tone.

With that, Joan followed her normal procedure and closed Miss Katherine's private office door upon exiting Miss Katherine's office. "Pssst! I think Miss Katherine will be in a good mood today, Margie, I quickly spotted some correspondence from Brad," Mrs Peters conveyed to Margie in a whisper. Intrigued by the news, Margie tried to inquire more, but Mrs Peters had only seen the postcard for a scant second and could give no further details other than that it was a personal picture-type postcard.

Katherine rummaged through the correspondence, when she suddenly noticed that there was a postcard in her stack of mail. Her eyes bulged wide and her heart raced with excitement! She instantly knew that only Brad was corresponding with her by postcards throughout the summer months and his Spencer script styled handwriting was unmistakable. Like an anxious child waiting to open a special gift, she quickly tossed her other papers onto an empty office chair, as she sat down to take a close look at the postcard. For the moment, she ignored the front of the postcard, knowing that Brad's words meant more to her than a mere picture of the typical American scenery that he had been sending to her the past few months.

"Hello Kate: I'm in Wyoming now – a great wide open, beautiful part of the country. I'm having a great time here with the US Forest Service; here's a picture of myself and some of my new-found friends with whom I am working – they're terrific and true friends. Hope to see you in the fall. All My Love, Wayne."

The postcard was short, and it did not say much in terms of details, still Katherine beamed with excitement about hearing from Brad. However, she was a bit perplexed and confused about the way he signed the postcard. He used his middle name of 'Wayne' instead of Brad or Bradford. This was strange in that throughout the summer of correspondence, this was the first time that he had used such a moniker to her.

This seemingly innocent name usage started to arouse Katherine's interest and maybe her suspicions too. 'Mummm, no one starts using their middle name for an unknown reason, especially to his fiancée,' Katherine suspiciously pondered to herself. Her curiosity was keenly aroused, her interest now deepened as she quickly turned over the postcard to reveal its front picture – this was the same picture taken by Tom Hawk just a few days earlier in which Wayne had posed with his four friends at Camp Haller, Wyoming.

Katherine's eyes first focused upon her beloved Brad or now 'Wayne' as he was calling himself apparently. He looked as handsome as ever – probably more so than the previous pasty coloured, thin creature who had left her in the spring. His skin was tanned and taut like fine burnished bronze and his face had the shadow of an emerging beard and moustache – a most rugged, handsome, outdoor-man appearance. His frame was lean, straight and muscular; it was evident that outdoor activity was agreeing with him, Katherine was glad that her man was not getting fat and lazy in his middle-years.

She closely spied at the other four people with a quick scanning stare, hoping for more information from the picture. There was an older rugged African-American man, whose face betrayed both his advanced-age and rough life experiences, both wrinkles and greying hair framed his noble face. Next to him stood a slim, pretty, fair skinned African-

American woman in her late twenties or early thirties. The third person was an older native Indian man with a heavily wrinkled, mahogany-toned face. Like a preying huntress, Katherine's observant eyes quickly focused on the white woman in the photo; this woman appeared to be in her late twenties or early thirties, 'she was an unusually attractive woman, in a 'common girl-next-door manner,' Katherine begrudgingly conceded to herself.

The attractive white woman stood close to her Brad, perhaps too close for Katherine's comfort. Her analysis continued with impeccable discern. Katherine's eyes next focused on Robin's figure and clothing. Katherine appreciated that 'this young woman was well-built, almost athletic in frame and body weight, she had minimal body fat - the result of either self-determination or superior genes', Katherine silently speculated. Her clothing revealed nothing out of the ordinary, aside from the fact that it was worn by the everyday working-class woman- a simple blouse and blue jeans that smartly fitted the woman's slender body like a glove. 'So, this woman was not an office worker or a professional woman by any stretch of the imagination,' Katherine smiled in self-deluded smugness.

Katherine's eyes next focused on the young lady's jewellery. She eyed no visible wedding ring or necklace, yet she was immediately drawn to the elegant watch which was sparkling with radiant abundance even in the questionable production of this amateur-quality postcard photo. If anything, other than that of another potential rival, could draw Katherine's attention, it was that of another woman's jewellery – the two in combination constituted double-trouble! Katherine's eyes bulged with intrigue, as she sub-consciously rubbed her own left wrist and massaged her own wristwatch. In a 'eureka moment' she looked down at her own wrist watch and then she started to squint at the details on the wrist of the pretty young lady pictured on the postcard. A frantic immediate panic of emotion pulsed through Katherine's mind like a sharp pin-prick.

"DeTagelio – get in here! I mean get in here right now, damn it!" Katherine screamed through the closed heavy mahogany doors.

Both Mrs Peters and Margie were startled by the emotional outcry from within Katherine's office. It was almost like a frantic scream of hysteria. Both Margie and Mrs Peters leapt to their feet immediately, they imagined that Katherine had cut herself or suffered some other physical malady. Unfortunately, they were not to be so lucky.

"What's the matter, Miss Katherine? Are you ill or hurt? Do you need a doctor?" Margie innocently inquired with a doe-eyed expression of genuine concern, as she stood in Katherine's office doorframe in utter wonderance as to the emergency that was being pleaded so vocally just a few seconds earlier.

"I don't need any of your stupid questions! Get me a magnifying glass – quickly, girl!" Katherine barked in an obvious upset tone.

"Yes, ma'am," Margie obediently replied, as both she and Mrs Peters scurried through their office drawers frantically looking for the seldom used magnifying glass.

"Where's that damn magnifying glass, DeTagelio… can't you do anything right?" Katherine again shouted out mightily like a loading dock foreman from her open office suite.

"I found it!" Margie yelled-out to Mrs Peters, as she ran into Katherine's office to present her with the requested office item. Margie was now keen to discover the source of Katherine's current crisis. As childish as it seemed, Margie was refreshed by seeing 'Little Miss Perfect' having some real personal life issues like the rest of the human race.

"Give me that damn thing, girl," Katherine snapped back angrily, as she abruptly grabbed the magnifying glass from Margie's hand. Margie glanced over at Katherine and noticed the postcard, remembering that Brad had been sending these correspondences continuously throughout the summer from each location that he had stopped.

"Hey, that looks like Brad, he sure looks great, Miss Katherine, I like that rugged outdoor look too!" Margie remarked innocently as she glanced at the postcard that Katherine was holding in a most clear, unobscured angle.

Katherine threw a frowning glance of visual disapproval at Margie's uninvited remarks; if looks could kill, Margie would be lying on the floor dead already. "This is none of your business or interest. Get the hell out of here, DeTagelio, don't you have your work to do or is unemployment a more attractive prospect?" Katherine thundered out in a very loud and threatening tone.

"Yes, ma'am!" Margie obediently replied as she quickly exited 'Kit Kat's' verbal line-of-fire, while quickly vacating out of the office and gently closing the heavy office door behind her! Mrs Peters, who was not immune from light office gossip, noticed that Margie had a puzzled look on her face.

"Hey, now what in the devil has upset Miss Katherine so much that she screamed at you? What's she doing in there?" Joan inquired in a hushed and muffled tone.

"Beats the hell out of me! She saw Brad's postcard and she's looking it over real closely and now she's in there looking over his postcard with a magnifying glass! Now isn't that kinda spooky to you? Besides, Kit Kat never needs a reason or incident to be angry with me – she simply hates me!" Margie replied as she shrugged her shoulders upwards, expressing a physical pose of puzzlement. The two women looked at one another and merely shook their heads side-to-side in utter amazement.

To her credit, Katherine was neither paranoid nor crazy; she was, in fact, a woman of keen observation and instinct, she could give many professional government imagery analysts a run for their money. Moisture filled Katherine's eyes and a slight trickle of tears rolled down the front of her face. The magnifying glass had confirmed her initial suspicions about the watch on this young woman's wrist – it was an exact duplicate of her own custom Diamond-platinum Rolex wristwatch that she was even now nervously fondling on her own wrist. A cold, calculated thought of personal betrayal entered her thoughts – 'Brad was cheating on her with another woman – the same one in this photograph!' she carefully and accurately concluded.

"Son-of-a-bitch! That frigging son-of-a-bitch! I'll be damned!" Katherine yelled loudly, as her tear-filled voice pierced through her office and out into the office hallway. Both Joan and Margie could clearly hear the profanity spouting forth from Katherine's office and neither woman could hope to guess at the origin of this solitary outrage.

Katherine initially suspected the worst, but she hoped that her fears were totally unfounded…perhaps the result of an over-active imagination. Still, she had to be sure of her suspicions; postcards and phone calls of assurance from Brad were no longer sufficient for her, she needed first-hand, neutral and confirmed information. 'As in any major business decision, top-notch, accurate, complete information was the difference between success or failure, it should be the same for one's private life as well,' she concluded.

Katherine thought prudently. She wiped her eyes and running mascara, pure cold logic now took over quickly from her fleeting initial emotional response. This was a matter that required her own initiative – complete discretion and privacy had to be maintained. Calmly and deliberately, she unlocked one of her desk drawers and withdrew a small, old -fashioned rolodex. Her long, elegant and perfectly manicured fingers quickly flipped through the small paper cards, until she suddenly came to the name 'PD Haster & Dickens'. She noted the number and quickly called the phone number.

"Good afternoon, Haster & Dickens', may I help you?" a deep male voice resounded forcefully over the phone. Katherine immediately recognized the voice and the man behind it.

"Yes, Mr Haster, this is Katherine MacAlister, I have a situation that needs your prompt and personal attention," Katherine replied. After some 20 minutes of private discussions with the mysterious Mr Haster, Katherine's entire demeanour was consoled, if not temporarily vanquished, at least for the rest of this day. She didn't come out of her office until nearly everyone had left the office at the end of the day. Depression and anxiety still haunted her and would continue to do so for the next several weeks. Katherine rarely ventured outside her office and kept her door closed and cancelled most of her weekly staff meetings. Her sombreness and withdrawal were eerie. The only thing more frightening than an outwardly raging Katherine was a self-absorbed, introverted Katherine. So, this drama continued throughout the long, heated summer at Hamilton & MacAlister.

* * * * * * * * * * * * * * * * *

"Open it up! Go ahead, be a man and open it up – I mean now!" Robin cried-out in an anxious voice, as Wayne beheld a medium-sized gift-wrapped box that Robin had just presented to him.

"I simply don't understand this, Robin, I don't think it's right that you are giving me something; after all, it's not my birthday and I really don't need anything," Wayne stuttered in an obvious awkward and nervous voice. She looked at him with a playful, scornful look, then she answered him in an almost threatening voice, "You look here, Mr Boston rich-boy, the way I was brought up, a man doesn't reject a gift offered in friendship, especially when that person is a woman, you hear me, pal?"

"But I really don't understand, Robin, what's this for anyway? I don't deserve or need this!" Wayne replied defensively.

Robin was not to be put-off by Wayne's childish ways. "Remember that we have a deal concerning that super expensive diamond watch! Now look here Wayne, you gave me that beautiful watch to wear for the entire summer and I just thought that I would kinda return the favour..."

except this present does not have to be returned back to me – now do you understand me?"

Wayne knew that he was on the losing side of this argument and that it was better to accept the gift than to engage in further verbal banter with Robin.

"Okay fine, you win, I'll be happy and privileged to accept your gift," Wayne replied with honest acceptance. Robin jumped for joy as she threw her arms around Wayne's neck and piled a large wet kiss on his mouth. After a few seconds that seemed like an eternity, Wayne gently unwrapped Robin's arms from around his neck, as he tried to catch his breath. "Robin sure was a terrific kisser and possessed exceptional lungs," Wayne sinfully thought with delight to himself.

"Here's the big moment, Mr Boston Investment Banker, open up my gift to you!" Robin gleefully toyed with girlish excitement. Emotionally disarmed, Wayne lost all his previous trepidation and began to unwrap the box like a small kid at a birthday party. The box weighed about 12 hefty pounds and it was wrapped in colourful red wrapping paper with a large yellow bow. Both the bow and the wrapping paper were prepared with diligent care and unwrapping the box took several minutes. In his hands he beheld a naked brown carton which gave no visual clues as to its origins or contents. Deftly, he took his Swiss Army pocketknife and slit the final strands of clear shipping tape. A childish excitement filled his heart. Instantly, he smelled a pleasant, almost masculine, yet earthy aroma arising from inside of the box. There was a strange welcoming odor akin to a processed leather-like item, yet this distinct scent was somehow different from that of a modern tanned leather item. As he opened the panels of the parcel and undressed the soft white onionskin inner wrapping paper, there before him lay a beautiful, carefully folded mound of soft, majestic light buckskin. His eyes bulged with obvious delight, as he withdrew an old western frontier styled jacket, the kind that Davy Crockett, Buffalo Bill, Annie Oakley and other old western characters had worn.

The golden, honey-toned coloured jacket was obviously hand-made and adorned with Native American beading and silver work that arrayed the shoulder yoke and jacket seams, while the jacket sleeves had a generous six-inch deerskin fringe. The front of the jacket was of a single-breasted affair that used four steer horn-type buttons to snugly close-up the jacket. Atop the upper left side of the jacket, both silver threads and red beads were artfully crafted to depict a four -inch sized robin bird motif. The back of the buckskin jacket revealed equally intricate handcraft as well, with a back-jacket panel composed of a pure silver threaded wolf figure about six inches square in area, beneath which was arrayed a contrasting, alternating pattern of black buffalo hair braids with that of six-inch long buckskin fringes. The lining of the jacket was of colourful aqua-blue satin. Inside the jacket and sleeves - there was a uniform spaced pattern of small copper-coloured piques, to which one could install an inner fleece sheepskin liner. The entire jacket must have cost a small fortune in both time and materials, costing well over several thousand dollars at the boutique market price. The jacket was as hefty as it was handsome.

Wayne beheld the jacket in his hands for some minutes admiring the fantastic looking garment. He was dumbfounded by the beautiful jacket and he was a bit embarrassed that someone had gone to the time and expense of buying him something this unique and personal. It was obvious that a lot of thought had gone into designing and making this unique jacket and he was touched by what Robin had done for him.

"So, do you like it?" Robin inquired in a manner requesting both affirmation and validation.

"Hell yes, I love it! It's fantastic, Robin…you really should not have gone to the trouble, it's really too much for me!" Wayne pleaded with joy as he gave Robin a big hug and kiss. She was delighted and glad that he had obviously been caught off-guard by her unexpected and unique gift.

"Hey, Wayne, there's more too! There is a set of matching buckskin gauntlets and a sheepskin liner for the times when it starts to get cold" Robin replied as Wayne looked further into the box and examined an equally impressive inner, thick golden-coloured sheepskin liner and richly coloured beaded deerskin gauntlet riding gloves.

"Try it on, let's see how it looks on you, cowboy!" Robin laughed in a devilish tone. She took the jacket and held it open for Wayne to fit his arms through. It was a perfect generous size, fitting most comfortably and with some extra inches to spare, this so as to readily accommodate various under-garments and the sheepskin liner. "So, how does it feel, Wayne?" Robin asked almost rhetorically.

"I feel like some rugged Old West frontiersman! There's nothing like this back east! This custom jacket is simply magnificent! How did you ever get anyone to craft something like this?" Wayne keenly inquired.

"Well, I do know a lot of women who have skills in custom made Native apparel, so I guess you could say that I called in a few 'family favours' and the result is what you're wearing, my friend. I think it's an honest reciprocation for the Rolex, don't you think? Plus, you get your Rolex back at the end of the season, the jacket you get to keep forever, Wayne; after all, I already have one of my own, so you're stuck with my gift – no refunds, okay, buster? I want you to wear it always and when you do, I want you to think of me!" Robin smartly replied and perhaps already anticipating the coming end of summer and with it their relationship. With a smart affirmative nod, Wayne again acknowledged the magnificent gift, one that he was going to treasure; it was not the type of item to be found in the most exclusive stores of Boston or anywhere else either.

* * * * * * * * * * * * * * *

"Hey, Indian Joe, get me a double-scotch on the rocks and a double Yukon Wild Coyote for my thirsty friend here" Jay Blackhawk, Esq jovially heralded out to the barkeep, as he deliberately strolled over to the barstool upon which a sombre Rick Conroy had already perched himself for the evening. Indian Joe merely nodded in quiet acknowledgement of the boisterous order, he tried to remain courteous to all his clients, but somehow, he never managed to hanker to either of these two men, he sensed that something was wrong or twisted in their natures and he wanted minimal social dealings with either man, especially that of Jay Blackhawk. He never trusted him since the time that Jay's legal mis-representation of the tribe had cost the reservation some badly needed State revenues; yet Jay came out smelling like a rose – he made lucrative attorney and consulting fees. As usual, Jay had a fancy legal explanation for the tribe's financial losses, yet Jay had managed to come out on-top. Jay was a 'bad-penny' and a bad Native American too. The tribe was still recovering from his shady deals. Yet no one could prove any wrongdoings against Jay, he was sly and always ended up coming out clean and smelling like a rose, while all other parties came out losers. Indeed, Jay was a man best to be avoided at all costs! He cleverly used people for his own devices and schemes without directly exposing himself.

Rick stared straight ahead, as if in a trance, his mind being preoccupied with 'other concerns'.

"Hey there, buddy, you look down and out, what's the matter?" Jay Blackhawk inquired with only the slightest tone of sincerity in his voice.

"Ah, it's nothing, Jay, it's just been a bad summer for me, that's all, my life sucks at the moment!" Rick replied with his own retort of lying words. Although a very cunning and scheming character, Jay was also a very astute judge of human nature and he could quickly analyse and sum up human relationships quite accurately and always to his own advantage.

"Yeah, Rick old buddy – I know that your life changed when that rich, handsome eastern guy from Boston came here and impressed everyone; he even stole your girl's heart too! You know that I'm right too, don't you?" Jay chided Rick, as he sipped his chilled malt scotch whiskey. As so intended, Jay's words only added resentment and anger to Rick's lamenting heart.

Rick took a big gulp of his drink and spat a challenging remark back to Jay, "So what else is new, what the hell do you want me to do about it, Jay? You just summed it up nicely yourself, the guy's rich and handsome, I'm just a average working stiff trying to keep his job and his gal. I think I might wind up losing both if things continue like they have been this summer! A regular guy just can't get ahead these days! I need a break, a big break at that!"

Just as Rick Conroy had finished up his sentence, Robin and Wayne strolled into the tavern, hand-in-hand and smooching as young lovers often do. Both Robin and Wayne were attired in their matching buckskin fringed jackets and giggling like high school sweethearts. Desiring their own privacy, the pair immediately headed toward a dark and intimate booth far away from the bar area. The young lovers were now quite mutually and exclusively in each other's company, avoiding even their old friends of Sammy and Hank, except for the traditional Friday night fire squad social events. The sight of Wayne and Robin holding hands and kissing in the booth was too much for Rick to bear, as he was forced to look away with obvious disgust and jealousy. A bitter and sober look had imprinted itself upon Rick's face.

Jay knew that he had just planted a seed of action for his long-term financial plans; he knew how to manipulate a person to do his bidding just like a puppet-master could manipulate a wooden dummy. "You know, Rick, the only difference between you and that Hamilton guy is just one thing and one thing only! It's money – he has it and you do not!" Jay remarked with a deliberate smirk.

"You really know how to brighten up a guy's spirit don't you, Blackhawk! I knew that I should have punched that guy's lights out months ago; he's been nothing but trouble for me this past summer! I did everything I could think of to get him to leave, but he's one stubborn and persistent SOB!" Rick remarked bitterly in disgust as he took another sip of the sweet Canadian whisky.

"No, Rick, you got it all wrong!" Jay interjected in a perfectly timed manner. "This Boston guy is just some dude passing through and he'll be gone by the end of the summer; meanwhile, you'll still be poor my old buddy! That's what your gal Robin is really interested in, his money, and money means security to a woman! You know what I'm talking about, Rick. You know what I'm saying is the God's truth," Jay Blackhawk chided.

Rick was more angered than ever after hearing Jay's words. "Well, I was not born rich and I'm not expecting to win the lottery either Jay... like I said, I'm just a middle-aged working stiff," Rick fumed in evident resignation to his blue-collar strife.

Jay had just given Rick the 'stick', now he was going to offer him the 'carrot.' "Well, old buddy, if you don't mind taking a little risk, you could be a rich man, rich enough to get back that girlfriend of yours and to keep her long after that Hamilton guy has beaten tracks out of here...now are you interested in being rich, old buddy or simply staying as a poor working slob?" Jay smiled devilishly as he studied Rick's face which was now filled with undivided curiosity.

Rick said nothing for a few moments before speaking. "Just what do you have in mind, Blackhawk? What do I have to do? And most importantly, how much money is in it for me?" Rick coldly and earnestly inquired.

Jay laughed and patted his new-found partner on the back. He carefully explained his grand plans for the building of a massive new Indian Gambling Casino, amusement park, and resort along with a new major highway project that would bring in at least 100 -250 million dollars a year in profits guaranteed. Rick's initial payment was to be $2 million up front along with an annual payment of $750,000 in addition to a handsomely paid six-figure management position within Jay's corporation. Rick could also be contracted as a construction site program manager and hire out construction contracts to his family's owned construction firm, which would bring in millions of dollars. The deal would make Jay a billionaire and Rick a multi-milionaire. It was a Faustian deal that benefited both parties, especially for Mr Jay Blackhawk.

It took Rick only a few seconds to make his Faustian decision. "Fuck it all! I'm 100% in for the deal, Jay, I'm in it for whatever needs to be done, no price is too high for me! I've got very little to lose! I'm sick and tired of being part of the working poor while other incompetent bastards get ahead of me; besides I'm not getting any younger and my family's construction business is in the toilet as a result of those greedy bankers like that 'Boston' bastard guy over there – those fucking bankers and lawyers have ruined this country for the average working man! This deal is going to solve all of my problems," Rick commented in a bitter voice.

Jay smiled, patted Rick on the shoulder and the two men raised their glasses in a toast, "Here's to being both a business partner and multi-millionaires…we're going to be running this state one day soon, my partner!" Jay declared jubilantly.

"Amen, amen, old buddy – here's to the good life!" Rick responded, as he clinked his glass against Jay's. In just a few seconds, Rick unconsciously sold what was left of his soul to the devil, the die was cast. Rick was determined to go through with any hair-brained scheme and being oblivious to any of the ultimate risks or consequences. "My life can't get much worse," Rick thought to himself in self-pity. The two men now spoke in hushed whispers and plotted the fine details of the plan that was going to allow their mutual dreams to become reality. It seemed that the vices of greed and revenge made for perfect bedfellows.

Indeed, Indian Joe's Tavern was full of interesting characters this late summer's evening. Quietly and without too much fanfare, a beautiful young woman entered the tavern. Like a trained cat burglar, she quickly eyed the tavern area and then strategically positioned herself at the far darkened end of the bar, a spot from which she was obscured from most patrons' attention, yet a point from which afforded her a complete sight of all the activities within the bar room area.

The beautiful stranger wore a stylish light fawn-coloured Stetson cowboy hat that was fashionally adorned with colourful turkey feathers in the headband. Her clothes were of stylish western chic, custom blue jeans, western blouse and Tony Lama cowboy boots; she looked as if she had just stepped out of a Santa Fe Today magazine, yet one thing was for sure, she was no 'local' girl.

Her eyes were the palate of light jade green, her cheek bones were high and distinct, her complexion was of fair alabaster tone, her body was slim, trim and well-toned like that of a fashion model or perhaps a professional trainer.

Confidently taking a seat at the bar, she gently removed her hat to reveal a stunning cascade of beautiful shoulder length light, copper-colorued, strawberry-blonde hair, this lady was indeed a perfect '10'. She placed her stylish almond-coloured Gucci handbag with deliberate care and utmost attention onto the bar, an act that seemed calculatingly deliberate. Yet so subtle and fluid were her movements, that even a trained observer would have had difficulty detecting the least bit of mischief.

"Hi Miss, what'd you like to have to drink tonight?" Jennifer Louise Hawk inquired in a very honest and girlish voice.

The pretty copper-haired lady politely smiled, her perfect straight white teeth further complementing her already abundantly beautiful facial attributes. "I'll have a tall tonic water over crushed ice and a sliver of lemon please," the beautiful, strange lady remarked with a pleasant, yet seemingly detached and almost scripted voice. The mysterious lady's tone was devoid of any noticeable accent, like that of a well-trained actress. Like a wild mountain lioness seeking out its environment, the lady spied out the tavern quickly, looking at each person's face with obvious attention, quickly scanning the entire crowd. Her prowling eyes glazed quickly upon Wayne and Robin and her eyes suddenly stayed focused on them. The huntress had seemingly found her prey.

"How's your drink, Miss? Would you like to see a menu?" the youthful female bartender inquired from the beautiful femme fatale.

"Oh, no thanks, I'm fine for now! I'm just passing through this part of the country, it's quite beautiful. I'm a professional nature photographer and I am wandering about the west to get some scenic pictures for various magazines and advertising print houses. So out of curiosity, what do the folks do around here for fun?" the strange redhead inquired politely from her waitress.

"Well, this is an Indian Reservation establishment, as is most of the surrounding land, so there's not much industry here; you could say that this part of the state is 'deads-ville' except for this time of the year when the fire workers and lumberjacks come in for some seasonal work," Jennifer innocently replied.

The pretty young redhead smiled and ordered another drink from the bartender. "There's some handsome guys around here, a lot of handsome rugged men, I guess it's a romantic season for the fire workers?" the stranger remarked almost casually in an effort to initiate some 'girl talk' with her attending waitress.

"Oh, yes, you bet it is! There is hook-up season here every summer, romances are not encouraged but everyone gets involved sooner or later," the bartender remarked. The two women were soon in eager feminine conversations that lasted well over an hour. They exchanged the local gossip, which naturally included Robin and Wayne.

The strange, beautiful woman drew her focused attention toward where Wayne and Robin were romantically cuddling within the darkened booth. She eyed the couple and carefully re-positioned her handbag atop the bar. She waited and carefully observed the couple for some twenty minutes as she slowly sipped her drink. She said nothing, but she saw everything.

The bartender excused herself, as she moved away to wait on other bar patrons and bussed some of the dinner plates away from the bar area. When Jennifer Louise returned, the nameless redheaded woman had mysteriously vanished. Just as suddenly as the beautiful young woman had arrived, she had suddenly disappeared, leaving only a generous tip of $10 bill tucked neatly beneath her drink coaster.

* * * * * * * * * * * * * * *

The following day unfolded with little fanfare – this was the beginning of the traditional three days of festivities celebrating the Labor Day weekend and the traditional end of the fire season. After this long festive weekend, all the fire camps, including Camp Jeffrey Holler, were going to be placed into caretaker status. A continuous 3-day barbecue celebration was planned and the weather forecast across the state indicated fair-to-good, dry weather conditions Even now, there were fire fighters leaving camp due to previous contracted employment jobs; many of these were teachers or university students who had to get back to their campuses for classes and registration.

The maddening summer was coming to an end and everyone could feel it in their bones, temperament and attitudes. It was normal for the fire season to begin cheerful and optimistic, while it inevitably ended in sadness and resignation. An inevitable casual attitude had descended upon the camp. There was scant activity, even drill training for the fire fighters had ceased. The Ready Shack was quiet; the only activities were those of the weather monitoring crew and several senior fire managers, who were gazing into the cluttered weather data screens and the chatter from the cable TV weather channel announcer. Additionally, there were no 'red or amber' weather alerts charted, aside from a low-pressure system that was forming up in Canada. The weather for the local area was continued high humidity, mild winds and a 15% probability of precipitation. It seemed that the drought for eastern Wyoming was going to continue through the Labor Day weekend. Only the hopeful promise of autumn rains and heavier than normal snows were going to put a dent in the water table for next year.

"Hey – is this place called the Camp Jeffrey Haller Ready Shack? I'm supposed to report in for duty!" a nervous and excited voice of a youthful man squeaked aloud in the almost empty room that still filled with a mass of posted weather reports and muster rosters and assorted equipment tracking charts.

Jeff Campbell, Hank Ransome and Peter Sanchez looked up from their paperwork over to the wide-eyed young man of unknown origins. He was a lanky, slim lad, not the stuff of a well-toned fire fighter. All three men got up from their tables and desks to greet this 'Johnny Come Lately' stranger. The men walked slowly over to the wooden counter that served as a divider between the ranks of the fire fighters and those who managed the fires and all the related activities of Camp Haller.

"Well that all depends, who wants to know, young fella?" Jeff Campbell inquired in a direct manner.

"Sure thing, sir, my name is Billy Coffler, I'm an intern working for Dr Peter Ciellerie from the National Weather Service. Dr Ciellerie and Ms Clarkson from the National Interagency Fire Center in Boise agreed that I could come out to Camp Haller and be an unofficial observer for a few days and you know, kinda get some field training with real field firefighting workers...I'm a post grad meteorology student and I really need some field experience! I guess they call this interning a kind of shadowing of the fire fighters," the young man explained in an almost pleading tone. He proudly presented his ID card and official NIFC authorization letter to the Ready Shack staff.

The older men looked at one another and smiled. "So, you want to be a fire fighter, kid, is that it?" Peter Sanchez remarked with a broad smile.

Still Jeff Campbell was not so amused with this new prospect. "Look here young fella, you sound like a smart, energetic young man, so why would a smart young guy like you want to go around getting all dirtied-up fighting fires? Besides, the season is almost over, almost everyone will be gone after this weekend, I'm afraid you got here too late, kid."

Hank was the last to verbalize his thoughts. "Yeah, sonny, you're getting out here a bit late, young man, the fire season is almost played-out, and as you can see from the activity here, a lot of folks are already gone! I'd say that there ain't much for you to see or do here sonny!" Hank sighed as he looked seriously at the obviously dejected young man.

But Billy Coffler was not going to be dismissed or dissuaded this easily, he had travelled thousands of miles to get to the field and he wasn't going to turn tail and run simply because some middle-aged fire chief wanted no part of him. "Please, Mister, wait just one minute, I'm no kid, I'm a graduate student in meteorology and I was sent here officially by the NWS and NIFC to get some field time, I came late because my eyeballs and brain were busy composing those weather reports that you field workers depend on to fight the fires. Sure, I came here late because it's the only time that the NWS could afford for me to be away from my computers and monitoring instruments, I thought that I could learn something from some old pros like you, gentlemen...but perhaps I was mistaken!"

This young man had very valid points of argument and the older men were embarrassed by their smug attitudes toward this well-meaning, if inexperienced, young man. Billy Coffler had shown some determination and spunk that all of the older men wished that they had seen in other young people, to include their own children. The three old wise men conducted a short huddle as they spoke in hushed tones and muted whispers that Billy could not discern. After only a minute or two, which had seemed like an eternity, the three men turned around to face Billy again.

"Okay, young man, you're right! You do have a right to be out here! Although this is the end of the fire season, you can stay until the camp is fully closed-up in a few weeks; however, we may not have too much to show you in terms of excitement or even actual forest fires," Peter Sanchez confessed in a polite, almost apologetic tone. Peter Sanchez offered young Billy Coffler a strong mug of coffee, while Jeff Campbell explained the layout of the Camp Haller Ready Shack Operations Center, as well as showing him his sleeping and living quarters.

"Geez, that's terrific news, you won't regret it, gentlemen! Did I tell you that I also had Army Airborne jump training and I am free-fall qualified as well, perhaps I can jump with the Smokies!" Billy echoed out in wild excitement.

The three older men said nothing, but merely grinned and rolled their eyes at Billy's wild zeal. The Smoke Jumping skills were far different from military airborne training and he was unqualified as a certified Smokie or Hot Shot. Billy was as excited as a schoolboy! After an entire summer of pleading with Dr Ciellerie to get some real field time, he was finally witnessing a live firefighting operations centre at Camp Haller. Secretly in his heart he wished that the summer fire season would grant him one final wish to witness and maybe even participate in an actual wildfire fighting operation. Unbeknownst to Billy, wishes in life sometimes came true, but not always in the manner as envisioned or desired.

★ ★ ★ ★ ★ ★ ★ ★ ★ ★ ★ ★ ★ ★ ★ ★

Hank had just exited the Ready Shack when he noticed Robin's Dodge Ram thunder into the Camp's parking lot at a reckless speed before coming to a sudden jarring stop. A huge cloud of dry dirt bellowed from the hard friction of the huge tyres stopping against the powder-like dehydrated dirt of the camp parking lot area. Hank squinted furiously through the thick brown cloud of aerial spun dirt, as a feminine figure appeared stomping vigorously toward him. It was Sammy, she possessed a determined, devil-be-damned look in her demeanour. Sammy stormed through the dust cloud and approached Hank in a very aggressive manner, her body was only a few intimidating inches from that of Hank's. She wore an angry confrontational look and her eyes were menacingly cold.

"Okay, you old lying black man, just who the hell are you? What's your family's name? Tell me! You tell me quick before I take a slap to you, old man!" Sammy loudly demanded in very offensive and even challenging tone. Hank was naturally shocked at this affront and hostile verbiage challenge, especially from one who was so much his junior. Yet ever since his closing days in Southeast Asia, Hank had learned to control his anger as well as his past.

"Now you just wait a minute there, Missy, you don't go around talking half nonsense to me, I'm older than you and I demand some respect, now why don't you just simmer down here and tell me what's troubling you?" Hank responded hoping to diffuse the young lady's obvious distress. Yet Sammy was fit to be tied and she was having none of the old man's diversions on her inquiries.

"Respect indeed! That's something you have to earn. You see, I did some talking and investigating on you Hank! I was speaking with some of my mom's old friends from the hood and guess what, 'old man'? I gave them a real good description of you too! They're all saying that you grew up in my Mom's old neighbourhood...that you knew my mom and dad.... that you even served with my dad in Vietnam! So, what in the hell is the big secret, Hank?" I want to know why you never came forward to me this past summer to even say to me that you knew my folks or that you could shed some light on my dead father! You old, fucking bastard, you're holding out on me, what's the big fucking secret, Hank?" Sammy pleaded as she cried and pounded on Hank's chest, yet to no physical avail.

Hank knew that the jig was up! He was tired of keeping secrets from over 40 years ago, he was tired of running from job-to-job, he was tired of the nightmares and the sleepless nights. He had to finally exorcise his demons and the present was as good a time as any.

"Well, it's like this, Miss Sammy, a long time ago two poor black boys from the slums of Chicago went off to serve in a far away, almost forgotten war called Vietnam, we had nothing, neither one of us. We had only distant relatives, no real close kin. For us poor black boys, the Army was our new adoptive family – it fed and clothed us; it provided us with a home and three squares every day; and it provided us with a living and sense of belonging that was lacking in the ghetto. Me and my boyhood friend stayed in the Army and eventually made our way from grunts to chopper pilots. The Army was desperate for chopper pilots in the late 60s, they took both of us in spite of our lack of formal education, but we were young, eager and we took to the choppers like pigs to the mud. We were ferrying some Special Forces and ARVN South Vietnamese soldiers back from the Cambodia's Parrot Beak area back in the 1970 invasion of that enemy held sanctuary area...our UH-1 Huey chopper took enemy fire and we auto-rotated down into a patch of tall elephant grass. Those who weren't killed on impact scattered into the tall grass. Me and my buddy got caught in an enemy ambush – my childhood friend was killed by enemy AK-47 fire. I killed the enemy soldier and thought of an insane idea. I saw my chance to disappear, to start my life over as a new person. I didn't want anyone to know what a failed guy I had become, so I took my dog tags and exchanged them with my boyhood friend. I figured that one black man could be easily substituted for another black man – it was not so hard to do in the chaos of the war zone and it worked! The troop rotations were happening so fast at that late time in the war, that no one knew us on sight in our home unit. I ceased to be Lee Roy Jenks and I became Hank Ransome. That's my story, that's my life, and that's the truth, child!" Hank fully confessed with a sullen embarrassed low tone.

Sammy stood there in wild disbelief, her eyes bulging and her mouth in open aghast at the confession she had just heard. "You old, mother-fucking bastard!" Sammy screamed, as she regained her composure and started to slap wildly at Hank's body and face. In a self-defensive response, Hank instinctively placed up both of his arms against Sammy's slaps, he finally was able to grab both of her arms and throw her back away from himself by several feet.

"You're lying, you're fucking lying, you old bastard! You're not really Lee Roy Jenks, Lee Roy died a hero in Vietnam, my mom told me so, she told me that she and Lee Roy were lovers and that Lee Roy was my Daddy – not you, so you just can't fucking be him! I even visited his grave at Arlington National Cemetery, placed fowers on on his grave and cried for him. You're nothing but a lying old drunken bastard!" Sammy screamed almost hysterically.

The magnitude of Sammy's indictment of Hank's fatherhood suddenly registered upon Hank's brain and emotions. Here before him was the daughter that he had never known or wanted to have known for the past several decades. He knew there was nothing that he could tell her to remove any of the loathing that she saw in him. He was devastated that his only blood kin, his daughter, had found out about his true identity. As so accused, he was a worthless, lying, runaway deadbeat dad! He was out and out guilty for sure, nothing could change the past sins, but he had to try and say something to his disowned offspring.

"Look, Samantha, my precious little child, I know that you can't understand or forgive me right now, but here's my story or you may even say my curse. After my buddy Hank died and I took his identity, I was in an awful mess, you could say that I had some PTSD, that's what they're calling it today. I went to pieces! My best friend had died violently because I was not fast enough on the draw; he took the bullets that should have killed me. I just couldn't cope with it. I assumed Hank's identity because I wanted the world to know me as being dead. I thought that getting myself a new identity would help me start a new life, of course, it solved nothing really. My depression and guilt grew worse, I got hooked on heroin, I kicked the habit before the fall of Saigon and I returned to the States and supported myself by various flying gigs, I stumbled into the firefighting job because I wanted to make a difference and give a little back to others," Hank confessed in a very humble tone.

The horribly confessed words fell upon Sammy's ears like an avalanche. She stood there aghast, her mouth just hung wide open and her eyes were dilated, staring with amazement at the man who had just spoken the unfathomable words of paternalism. It was her turn to speak and she let go with all the anger of her past years.

"So that's just fucking great, Hank, so you suffered a little hurt in Vietnam, you were hooked on drugs, you came back to the US and ended up playing your current flying gig because you wanted to give something back! Well, old man, that's a crock of fucking shit man! What about giving back to Mom and me! You ran away from your identity, you ran away from your husbandly responsibilities and you ran away from me! How'd you think I felt, growing up with a single white mom in the hood and being kidded by all the school kids that that I was an 'Oreo cookie' or that my mom was not a 'soul sister' or that my dad was some bum that got a quickie off my mom! Do you know what it's like for a little girl to hear these things from the older neighbourhood kids? No, you sure as fucking hell don't know, because you're nothing but a cowardly old, drunken, ex-drug addict bastard! You were safe, alive and back in the States and yet you were too much of a coward to come back into our lives. I wanted to be so proud of my daddy and now I find out that he's alive and has lived his entire life a fucking lie! You fucked my head-up, why do you think that I have personal relationship problems? That I have no man in my life? That I'm not married and that I do not have my own family? You screwed my mind up big time and I hate you Hank... I don't want to ever see your sorry old ass anywhere near me! Do I fucking make myself clear?" Sammy screamed as she ran away frantically from the sight of Hank.

Tears filled Hanks eyes too; it seemed that lonely old black men had feelings of pain and regret too. He knew that Sammy's words were true as a bullet striking a metal plate. He knew that it made no sense to say anything more or to try and run after Sammy – he had injured her greatly with the truth, he also realized that all of her words were true. She was right when she accused him of being afraid, in those hazy, mixed-up days of the war, it was so easy to simply 'cop-out' and make excuses. He knew that he was making excuses for the past few decades and now the naked truth was facing him, and it was not a pretty sight. Hank suddenly felt a great guilt draw over his thoughts, he was haunted that he was not the man and father that he could have been to his wife and little girl. He was saddened that he had surrendered both his past and his future because of his own inner guilts and fears. He would go away and sleep this night, a sleep that was for once free of nightmare and alcohol, yet it was to be a sleep of pondering the 'might-have-been' alternatives.

Sammy jumped into Robin's Ram truck, hit the gas and flew down one of the fire camp roads toward a bluff that overlooked Indian Joe's Tavern. She drove fast and determined like a cougar running after its prey. Her emotions were torn to shreds; all the fantasy images and childhood stories that she previously had held about her father dying a hero's death in Vietnam were all suddenly exposed as lies. Her father was nothing more than a Chicago street bum, who happened to take advantage of her poor mother. Emotions of anger and disbelief filled her head, the more she thought about Hank's betrayal to her mother and herself, the faster she drove the huge diesel- powered Dodge Ram truck. A generous light brown cloud of trail dirt followed the path of the monstrous mechanical beast as it raced down the pine tree lined trail.

Sammy squinted desperately to see the road that lay before her, the tears of her eyes made her vision and road perceptions difficult to gauge the traverse of the road ahead. Suddenly before her lay a switch-back curve in the road and a correspondingly steep ravine as well; if she didn't do something immediately, she'd run off the road and kill herself. Road reality won out over raw emotions, as Sammy quickly saw her predicament and struggled to gain control of the massive Dodge Ram. With all her force she slammed onto the massive four-wheel ventilated disk brakes and aimed the vehicle for a straight-line sudden emergency stop. The vehicle's ABS system made an uncomfortable sound and vibration on Sammy's right foot, a definite tactile feedback indication that the brakes were working, yet she was quickly running out of road. She pulled up on the emergency brake and the Dodge truck suddenly yawned to a sudden side-way stop, a massive cloud of dirt and debris eagerly formed in the wake of the truck's rear end.

Sammy hugged the wheel, happy to be alive and yet still heartbroken over learning that Hank Ransome was also her long-lost father. She turned off the ignition and ran furiously from the truck. She felt the need to escape… to go anywhere away from the road and anything that reminded her of the Jeffrey Holler Fire Camp. She ran many yards through the woods until there before her lay a very familiar and very tranquil scene, it was a gentle elevated plateau that she and Robin had come to many times to just talk and hang out. As if by a miracle, she saw Robin standing there off in the distance looking into the horizon and quite oblivious to Sammy's presence.

Robin's recently repaired Custom Harley was parked only a few yards away as well. Alone on a nearby bluff stood Robin, who was gazing over the rich lush green plateau below her. Despite her own tangled personal state of affairs, Sammy seemed to sense that Robin had come to this scenic and desolate spot to be alone. Sammy sensed that Robin had not taken any notice of her presence, as she deftly tried to slowly turn away and discreetly make her way back to the truck.

"Hey there, girlfriend, please wait! Where are you going?" Robin shouted in a friendly tone. Sammy turned about slowly and saw her best friend looking at her with a magnificent cheerful inviting smile. "It's not like you to turn away from my company, Sammy, what's the matter, girlfriend?" Robin inquired politely. Robin knew that something was bothering Sammy and she was determined to find out exactly what the problem was. Sammy raced and threw her arms around Robin, while crying almost hysterically.

"You know that fucking, bastard Hank! Well, that old SOB just told me that he was my father, my long-lost dead father who was supposed to have died in Vietnam decades ago! Do you fucking believe the nerve of that guy! He comes strolling back into my life on the sneak and without any remorse! I wish I had kept my curiosity to myself, it does not pay to find out too much about some people, huh, Robin?" Sammy cried out in a scornful tone.

Robin merely smiled at her friend and brushed away Sammy's tears. Yet she said nothing more, she asked no questions either; it was if Robin had only a passing concern as to her friend's complicated fatherhood issue. "It will be all right girlfriend, you'll be all right I assure you" Robin confided as if she had larger issues of her own. Sammy composed herself and informed Robin of all the scandalous details. At the end of it all, Robin and Sam hugged once again, while Robin withdrew to a distance of several yards away from her friend, as if she wanted to be alone with her thoughts.

"Now, what in the hell is the matter with you, Robin? What big problem could have brought you up here to be all alone?" Sammy frantically inquired in a most direct inquisitive manner. Robin stood with her back to Sammy for some moments before turning around to face Sammy. Sammy drew near as she sensed that Robin had something very personal to say.

"Sammy, I'm pregnant with Wayne's child!" Robin confessed with a tear in her eye and a faint smile on her face.

Sammy was now shaken twice in her boots within the past hour! She couldn't believe what she had just heard. "I don't believe it! Are you sure? What are you going to do, Robin?" Sammy uttered in rapid and unintentional interrogation. Robin's grin quickly morphed into a warm smile as she took Sammy's hand and the two women sat upon a huge boulder which overlooked the majestic tall grass and valley below.

"No worries, Sammy, I'm going to keep my child, I'm going to raise the baby on my own! I'm tired of being alone in this world, I want to share and live my life with someone! For the first time in my life, love has come into my life and I am unsure if it will ever appear to me again. Wayne is not to know anything about this, at least for the present time, do you hear me?" Robin pleaded tearfully to her friend in a confident manner.

"What the hell! Are you crazy, girlfriend? That man has a responsibility to you and the baby, he's filthy rich and he should at least pay you support for his child! Look at how my fucking father walked out on me and my mom! Neither one of us liked it and neither one of us were better women as a result of an absent father! Take it from my personal experience, a child is better off and needs two loving parents around!" Sammy shouted angrily, as she expressed her own feelings of parental abandonment.

"No, Sammy, I don't want Wayne to feel trapped or that he is somehow obligated to me, it took two of us to make this baby and until I find out if he really loves me, I do not want him to know about our child. I can never fit into his society any more than he can abandon Boston and become part of my way of life. Wayne was like a sweet summer wind that breezed happily into my life; when he leaves me, I will know that I will have the best part of him with me forever. Who knows, maybe in time, if I ever see him again, I'll tell him, but not just now!" Robin explained in a very calm and rational manner.

"Will you please keep my secret, Sammy?" Robin pleaded softly.

Sammy couldn't help being kind to Robin, after all, Robin was her best friend. "Sure, Robin, as long as you make me that child's Godparent!" Sammy smiled. The two women hugged and stood up, they both gazed at the majestic valley and emerald green trees that lay before them.

"This sure is God's country and a great place to raise a child," Robin exclaimed.

"Amen sister, Amen," Sammy replied as the two women talked further about the two men in their lives.

★ ★ ★ ★ ★ ★ ★ ★ ★ ★ ★ ★ ★ ★ ★ ★ ★

The Labor Day weekend was a dull and subdued affair at Camp Haller. For most of the fire fighters, it was a weekend of stand-to inspections and stand-down roll calls. Equipment was cleaned, inventoried and turned-in for depot storage. Personal gear was being packed and lockers were cleared out. Presently, there were no fires in the western US which required a fire team response, so most of those still at the camp were preparing for the annual Labor Day barbecue festivities. All, that is, except one anxiously engaged scheming person. While his camp mates were busy getting ready to party or to depart the camp for the end of the fire season, Rick Conroy had more important plans. He lied to the Ready Shack staff when the informed them that he was getting his vehicle repaired over the holiday weekend and that he would be in the local area. The Ready Shack staff noted in their personnel logs that Rick was 'present and accounted for' duty. For his own preverse reasons, Rick needed for everyone to expressly remember that he was physically local to the Camp Haller area for this Labor Day weekend.

Conroy left early in the morning to get a head start on his nefarious journey, a large thermos of hot coffee and half a bag of doughnuts were to be his only travelling companions along with some country western music from his truck's FM radio. Rick determinedly drove down I-25 south past Casper and then down toward Cheyenne. The trip took only a few hours, but he took no stops along the way, as he had many things to accomplish this weekend. Rick was self-absorbed in his thoughts and in his planning. He was careful to make himself non-suspicious and non-descript. No one needed to be able to accurately remember him or his activities. His motel room was paid for in cash for a complete weekend rental. In another strange twist, he rented a very non-descript late model American-made sedan, while leaving his Custom truck parked discreetly outside the back of the motel. All of his numerous phone calls to various parties were enacted using a pre-paid cheap disposable cell phone which did not have a GPS tracking module in it. The rental car would make any of his movements far less suspicious to both the public and the police authorities. All of his bills were paid for in cash and he ensured that any notation of a credit card or temporary receipt - was handed over to him personally and then later burnt. It was important to leave no paper-trail or personal impressions! Finally, to avoid fingerprint remnants, he wore fine woven cotton gloves. At a deserted warehouse area, he met with some strange men, who transferred to him two large non-descript wooden cartons that were loaded with utmost caution and secrecy into the rental vehicle's trunk. There was to be no forensic trails left behind for possible discovery or inquest.

Rick remained isolated in his cloistered motel room; he was too busy and dedicated to his evil tasks to do anything more than to have a few beers which he had purchased earlier in the day. The entire Labor Day weekend was spent making numerous trips to deserted Cheyenne city locations and the writing out of cryptic notes on small pieces of paper that were carefully gathered up and then later destroyed. Rick avoided the motel room phone, this included all in-coming calls as well. No computer or electronic devices existed to betray his presence. He carefully studied topographic maps of the Thunder Basin National Grasslands and those of the Wind River Indian Reservation, taking careful notes of tree density, elevation features, vegetation types and ground contour features. All of his work and planning was being done the 'old way' – prearranged in-person meetings and on paper maps or notepaper. There was to be no electronic fingerprint forensics for the modern-day detective to easily follow his trail of activities. Any hunt for his activities for this weekend would entail the need for a team of old-fashioned gum-shoe detectives, the type of guys who no longer existed in the modern electronic sit-on-my-ass CSI-type analysis world.

For all intents and purposes, Rick was operating like a covert agent or some other perverse character straight out of a 1940s or 1950s crime novel. All of his actions were deliberate and designed for a singular, evil purpose, thus his personal identity, location or activities for this entire weekend needed to be shielded. On the final day of the Labor Day weekend, Rick had to take one gamble to possibly expose his identity and his plan, yet there was no way to conceal this activity, he had to do it by himself or else everything else that he and Jay had planned would come to naught. For this critical part of the plan Rick needed to rent a small private airplane and with the least amount of suspicion possible.

He made a local call from the motel lobby using his anonymous cell phone to a small local airport located in Laramie, a small-town due west of Cheyenne along I-80 west. He called in advance and was informed by Laramie Air Rental that they had a single engine Piper Club aircraft available for a $130 per hour rental. He pulled up to the Air Rental office and showed the agent his Flying licence, driver's licence and credit card. He was most deliberate in spreading about his activities from varied geographic venues, staying in Cheyenne for lodging, while using Laramie as his flight transportation center.

He wore non-descript clothing, sunglasses and a generously brimmed hat to help deflect from his appearance. He avoided direct eye contact and avoided any type of chit-chat conversation with anyone. Purposefully, he ate raw onions and garlic – he did not bathe or shave, he wanted no one to approach him or speak with him any longer than was absolutely necessary. His hygiene plan worked very well! No one bothered long with this strange looking and bad smelling man. He was not a man to be noticed aside from his foul body odours; rather he was a man to be avoided! In this strategy he was most successful – no one took notice or remembered any fine details about this smelly stranger. The genius of evil was indeed powerful!

"So, how long are you going to be needing this aircraft?" the airport clerk inquired with obvious disdain as he tried to wait on this acrid-smelling customer without too much revulsion and contempt.

"Ah, no more than about two or three hours, I need to keep up my flying skills, so I'm just flying local up north and east of the Wind River Indian Reservation then up to the Bighorn National Forest then east toward the Thunder Basin National Grassland – I'll be making a large parabolic circular flight path that I'll outline in my flight plan, okay?" Rick pronounced in a mundane matter-of-passing tone.

The clerk merely nodded as he half-listened to Rick's voice; the clerk was more concerned about avoiding the foul-smelling garlic and raw onion breath of this un-hygienic patron, than he was with jotting down the personal data and flight data of this foul-smelling individual. Every word uttered by Rick was met with dread by the unfortunate airplane rental clerk, he could not even bear to look at Rick directly into the eyes, so foul was this man's dreadful breath.

"Oh, I also want to pay in cash if you don't mind, you see I have to keep my credit card bills down and I'm near my credit card limit, and besides, I don't want my wife to discover that I am spending our hard-earned cash taking a joy ride in an airplane," Rick lied with a devilish smile to convince the standoffish clerk.

"Sure thing, Mister, anything you say, but I'll have to keep your credit card data in my files until the flight is over, you know – just in case there's an accident or something!" the clerk snorted back. The clerk wondered what sort of woman had the misfortune to be married to this wretched, unsanitary, and foul-smelling man. "That poor, unfortunate woman!" the annoyed clerk silently pondered to himself, as he got another whiff of Rick's foul-smelling breath. Rick nodded in affirmation as he took possession of the plane's registration, ignition/starter key and pre-flight checklist. To the sheer delight of the clerk and Rick alike, he was out of the plane rental office in almost record time. Rick's plan was working like a fine Swiss chronometer. No one would investigate or inquire for Rick taking a private flight from this small, remote airfield.

Rick was not lying about his flight route, but he didn't tell all the devious plans that he had in mind. He boarded the plane with a large rectangular flight bag, the olive drab coloured type made of heavy canvas duct material preferred by military personnel for its rugged nature and ability to store a large amount of gear. The bag was also very inconspicuous in appearance and form, thus creating less interest and possible suspicions. He was careful to ensure that no prying eyes saw him place the large cargo bag into the aircraft cabin bay area. The day was bright and clear- it was perfect for the last day of the Labor Day weekend and a perfect day also for low level visible flying. He performed all of his pre-flight duties as prescribed and he made his mandatory radio checks with the flight tower.

"Flight Tower, this is Yankee-Tango-Four requesting permission for take-off," Rick echoed out in a dry, professional mono-tone voice. A reply was not long in coming. "Yankee-Tango-Four this is the Tower, you have permission to take-off on runway Number 2 and proceed with your pre-registered flight plan at an altitude of 5,000 feet, Over," the Laramie Tower Controller replied in an equally dry western tone. Rick proceeded with his instructions and professionally directed his aircraft to the prescribed altitude and along the western vector that he had been directed. Aside from monitoring the radio and making periodic radio checks, in the air Rick was master of his domain and free to do that which he and Jay Blackhawk had deviously contrived some weeks ago.

There was scant turbulence in the warm dry air and the small agile Piper single engine aircraft seemed to float effortlessly in the pale blue azure sky. The plane was above the most eastern part of the flight plan, just due west of the Thunder Basin National Grassland area. Rick placed the plane on auto-pilot and reached down into the large flight bag that he had handled with such steadfast attention and care. He retrieved an odd-looking object, it was the size of a large orange or grapefruit, yet it more aptly resembled a ball from a croquet game except that a small circular lump protruded from atop the brown coloured, orb-shaped object.

The odd-looking object was, in fact, a sophisticated pyrotechnic device that was capable of producing a temperature of several thousand degrees for a period of several minutes. The device's outer shell was composed of compressed wood shavings, similar to that of particle board. The inner part of the device was composed of powdered magnesium, aluminium powder, sulphur and potassium nitrate. The ignition element consisted of a chemical fuse that relied on the chemical nature of the interaction of nitric acid against a fine copper membrane; when the copper membrane was dissolved by the strong acid- a small piece of sterile-protected, potassium metal became heated to the point of ignition which, in turn, produced the chemical heat necessary to ignite the other volatile chemical filler compounds within the wooden composite orb. The wooden pyrotechnic had small holes scattered across a 360-degree pattern throughout the sphere, out of which would shoot a stream of hot particles and gases of over a 3,500-degree Fahrenheit temperature. Regardless of how or where the orb shaped pyrotechnic device fell, it was certain that a fire was generated upon its activation. Once the chemical fuse was activated, the nitric acid was guaranteed to dissolve its way through the thin, copper membrane over a period of the next 24 hours with a 99% certainty of success rate. There were no moving parts to these pyrotechnic devils.

These bomb fuses were the same-type of chemical reaction design, which were used in the failed WW II bomb plot to kill Hitler and also by various British and American saboteur agents to destroy enemy facilities; this type of fuse had worked then and it would work flawlessly again this time. The devices had been tested multiple times and every time the devices ignited without failure. The final beauty of the pyrotechnic device was that it was entirely self-destructive and non-electronic, there would be no trace of it left for any forensic analysis.

Rick threw a dozen pyrotechnics over the thick pine forests which bordered the Thunder Basin National Grassland. Populated among the thick pines, were many multi-million-dollar rural estates and customized millionaire cabins in this affluent area, a factor that greatly increased Rick's calculation that all of the regional and national fire assets would be diverted to protect the life and property of the area's wealthiest citizens, who had foolishly chosen to build their mansions in an obvious fire threat zone. This meant that all the fire assets would be devoted to this fire and given the fact that most of the fire fighters were leaving or had already left after their summer contracts had expired – only added to the confidence that Rick had engineered for his arson plan.

Approximately 90 minutes later, the last leg of Rick's journey placed him over the thick forests located due east of the Wind River Indian Reservation and the lands occupied by Indian Joe's Tavern and its valuable land development potential. Rick spotted out the optimal places in which a fire could best take hold and flourish, he steeply banked the plane and flew back over his mentally noted sites, as he then deftly dropped two dozen of the pyrotechnic orbs in this area to ensure that this part of the forest would burn even more intensely than the first fire planned for the Thunder Basin National Grassland area. 'Start a diversionary arson at the Thunder Basin area, so there would be no fire assets remaining for the primary arson fire at the Wind River reservation' – the plan reeked of pure genius and evil.

Besides this dual location arson strategy, Rick ingeniously crafted another trick to ensure ultimate success, this one based on the element of time. The pyrotechnic devices dropped onto the Wind River Indian Reservation were timed to ignite six hours after the fires on the Thunder Basin National Grassland had started. This time delay between the two separate fires would ensure that the Thunder Basin National Grassland fire was in full fury and thus leave the Wind River Indian Reservation as a secondary fire for firefighting attention; it would either be ignored through sheer distraction or directly suffer devastation from the wild fire through the utter lack of sufficient and available firefighting resources.

One thing was certain, the two massive fires could not be fought equally well at this time of the year with the limited resources that now existed in the post-Labor Day season. Any national fire assets would also take too long to bring into play. The first fire on the Thunder Basin National Grassland would begin in the early dark morning hours of the following day; the second set of fires on the Wind River Indian Reservation would begin in the early afternoon hours. His mission was completed without either incident or suspicion.

Upon landing, Rick made his cash payment on the rental plane and ensured that the clerk destroyed any credit card information concerning the rental of the plane. The plane rental log was a tangible record risk that he had to endure. Next, he ensured that his motel bill and rental car was fully paid in cash. He raced back to Camp Haller in enough time to join the late afternoon barbecue events; no one evidently had even noticed that he had been absent from the Camp.

So secret was his plan that Rick dared not to call or contact Jay Blackhawk by cell phone or any other electronic methods. His plan was set, ready to go and the events were going to unfold precisely as planned. Rick dared not to expose his plan to any possible detection or investigative forensics. He and the plan were to be above all doubt and suspicion. At the Camp Haller Labor Day party, he made an obvious, memorable appearance, so most people naturally thought that he was at Camp Haller the entire weekend! 'Memories are often flawed and easily manipulated,' Rick conjured wisely. He had a few beers and a burger just to be social. He also wanted as many people as possible to see him and remember that he had been at the barbecue just in case he needed an alibi. He made it a short night before hitting a bunk that he kept at the Camp Haller Smoke Jumper sleeping quarters. 'It was all so perfect!' Rick smugly concluded to himself.

Conroy knew that all fires, especially arson-induced fires, were dangerous. In the fire jumper bunkhouse, he lay anxiously awake on his bunk silently in the dark listening to the party music and dreaming about his newfound wealth that he was to get shortly from Jay Blackhawk. He imagined a new house, new vehicles and a new life, maybe a life with Robin and even one without her! His greed was blinding him now even to the woman that he had been yearning over for the past few years. All he could think of now was the power and independence that was soon awaiting him. All he had to do was show up with his fire crew on the Thunder Basin fire and he would be all set. He would ensure that this fire took precedence over the Wind River Basin fire and thus ensure the destruction of Indian Joe's tavern and make way for Jay Blackhawk to build his new casino with Rick as its new General Manager. If he and Jay were especially lucky, perhaps even Indian Joe and some of the other tribal elders would also be killed in the fire and thus prevent any minor Reservation council protests against their future plans.

Rick was going to have more money and power than he had ever dared to dream just several months ago, and he was like a junkie on a drug high envisioning thing of greatness that still merely existed as neurotic synapses in his over-active brain. In the intoxicated stupor of his imagination, Rick laughed loudly from his darkened bunk; in a few hours, he was going to be both a local hero and a very rich man to boot. His plan was brilliant in every planned fine detail and he alone was in a pivotal position to ensure its success. He fell asleep intoxicated in the thoughts and dreams of greatness and grandeur that soon were to be his. All that he had to do now was to patiently await the inevitable fire call alert.

★ ★ ★ ★ ★ ★ ★ ★ ★ ★ ★ ★ ★ ★ ★

CHAPTER 11

The Whirlwind and the Satan's Pitchfork

"Let's call this fire 'Satan's Pitchfork' because this is going to be one hell of a fire and one hell of a day for all of us, over."

The post-Labor Day weekend celebrations had liberally littered Camp Haller with an abundance of trash and assorted celebratory paraphernalia. Everyone was either sound asleep with a hangover or else they had already departed the Camp to return back to their regular civilian lives. However, 100 miles away to the East, the ignition of the first pyrotechnic device was occurring in the wee early hours of the new day and as expected, the device performed flawlessly. The dull brown orb ignited with spectacular results, just like a Fourth of July Roman candle display. There were silent bursts of white-hot chemical fragments of magnesium and aluminium metal ablaze in multiple directions spurting forth many feet in the air like a hellish geyser. In short order the first pyrotechnic had produced a fire several hundred feet in diameter and its rapid spread was made all the more certain by the low humidity, un-cleared dead underbrush and dry forest areas. Within 90 minutes, nature's cauldron was further joined by the ignition of nearly a dozen pyrotechnic devices scattered among the confines of the Thunder Basin National Grasslands.

Nearby multi-million-dollar home owners were nervously awoken by the acrid smell of burning timbers and grasslands, those who ventured forth from their beds could even spot the bright orange and yellow dancing flames approach ever nearer to their beloved wilderness mansions. Panicked phone calls and social media postings from these wealthy concerned citizens soon brought to bear the attention of all the regional fire fighter authorities and the media.

"Hey, get the hell up! Everyone who's still here, get the hell up! Get up off your stinking butts, this is not a frigging joke! We got a fire on our hands and it's looking to be a potential monster!" Peter Sanchez yelled nervously as he ran into the Smoke Jumper quarters hoping to find someone still in their bunks. He turned on the lights and saw only about a dozen bodies curled-up in their bunk beds. Among the sleeping Smoke Jumpers was young Billy Coffer, Dr Ciellerie's National Weather Service innocent, eager intern.

Not unexpectedly, Rick Conroy was the first one onto his feet in reacting to the fire alert. He had been expecting this interruption all night long, lying half-awake in his bunk in a nervous state of expectation. He had spent his bunk hours going over the fire details in every aspect, hoping that he had planned for every detail and contingency. He knew there could be no mistakes. Equally important, no one must ever suspect that either he or Jay was associated or involved with the arson fires. His mind drew a blank slate – nothing had been omitted from the plan, every devious item was planned and going precisely as envisioned – all he had to do now was to let the wildfire events unfold.

"What the hell's going on here, Peter, we're trying to recuperate from the Labor Day festivities; why don't you give us a break and quit yelling! It's too early to be fooling around with us at this hour!" Rick yelled back in a veiled effort to disguise his foreknowledge of the events that were soon to unfold and for which he was the prime instigator.

"This ain't no joke, Rick, this is a real fire, I need every frigging Smoke Jumper here up and ready to go with their gear in ten minutes and that means everyone!" Peter Sanchez snorted back with a serious tone.

"Come on, man! What the hell is going on, Peter?" Rick inquired in the most innocent voice that he could muster.

"There's been a monster wildfire in the Thunder Basin Grassland area, the fire is spreading rapidly and it's endangering numerous luxury homes in the area...in fact, the fire's moving at a rapid pace into the tall dry timbers and we have the makings of a big, dangerous wildfire here, Rick!" Peter announced in a dead-pan voice.

Rick nodded silently as he and all the other Smoke Jumpers got their clothes on and their gear put into proper order.

A young lone voice broke out from the recess darkness of the room. "Hey, Mister Conroy, I'm a qualified jumper, Army Airborne-trained,

I was with the 82nd Airborne in Afghanistan...I want to go with the Smokies," Billy Coffer pleaded.

Rick gave the young innocent Coffer a pathetic look of disdain, then replied frankly, "Hey, look kid, this ain't one of those typical Army jumps that we're going to be doing here, sonny...this is Smoke Jumping, not Army parachuting! Look, kid, I appreciate your enthusiasm, but we don't need any Newbees getting hurt or killed because you were not properly trained as a Smoke Jumper, I'm sorry, kid! Just go and hang out at the Ready Shack and learn something there, kid!'"

Yet the eager young meteorologist was not deterred by Rick's detraction in the least. "Hey look, Mr Conroy, I've been here only a few days and although I am not Smoke Jumper qualified, I am qualified in the square chute and low-level free falls," Billy replied vigorously.

Rick admired the guts and enthusiasm of this young kid, he reminded Rick of himself in his youth. "Fire jumping is not like military jumping, we have special equipment, procedures and there are inherent unique fire dangers – none for which you are the least bit trained! Finally, you are not NFS and BLM certified to do any jumps with us, you are a potential lawsuit liability. Sorry, no way, kid, I cannot take the chance, and this sounds like it is a very dangerous wildfire, maybe next season, that is, once you get fire trained and Smoke Jump qualified!" Rick replied.

Dejected, but not defeated, Billy stomped off to the Ready Shack; he had been rejected by Rick, but maybe he could make an appeal to a higher level of authority.

The phones in the Camp Haller Ready Shack were ringing like fire alarms! Peter Sanchez was the main Operations Chief at the moment, the other Ready Shack leaders being absent for one reason or another. The dedicated private line from the National Interagency Fire Center in Boise was ringing. "This is Camp Haller Command Center, Pete Sanchez speaking," he answered in a dry, calm voice.

"This is Lori Clarkson, National Interagency Coordination Center (NICC) Watch Officer – it looks like we have a blow-up happening in the Thunder Basin area, Pete, I need for you to send everything you have over there ASAP! What are your existing resources?" Lori inquired in a terse, no-nonsense tone.

"Yeah, Lori, I know about the fire from our field reports and the local authorities! I have one helicopter with a water bucket, a few sticks of Smokies and maybe several teams of ground Hot Shots...most folks left yesterday or are not physically at the Camp," Pete explained in a dejected, resigned manner.

Lori thought for a second or two, she knew these were not enough firefighting assets, yet these would have to do, she would have to call up other fire assets from Montana, the Dakotas and maybe even Colorado. With minimal personnel, this was the worst time to resource a wildfire.

"Okay, Pete, get every 'Swinging Dick' and 'Bloody Mary' that you can lay your hands on and deploy these as an initial attack on the Thunder Basin fire, I'll send you the coordinates. I want all the Smoke Jumpers deployed and send the Hot Shots by ground transport. Once the Smokies land give us a SITREP, have the Helicopter ready for water bucket missions and observation reporting. All existing communication SOPs with fire field units are in effect, NICC will be on monitoring mode, ready to react as a reinforcing element as required. I will have a standby recon Predator scrambled from Cheyenne to get us the latest fire disposition and fire direction of travel and you'll have electro-optical Full Motion Video downlink of the Predator along with infra-red heat detection sensor suite data. The Predator will be on a race-track circular course between Thunder Basin and the Wind River Reservation at an altitude between 6,500 - 8,000 feet for a minimum of 10 hours – so alert your aerial assets as to the UAVs altitude, course and duration, Good Copy, Pete?" Lori quickly uttered in a manner worthy of a modern combat warrior. She was a professional, even if she was sometimes a bit rigid bureaucratic and by-the-book type leader. Despite being a seasoned professional, she was shy of taking any undo risks that could not be justified by the rules of the firefighting playbook. "Playing it safe, was playing it right," Lori prudently reasoned to herself.

"Roger...if this Thunder Basin fire expands or explodes faster than our ability to bring assets to bear Lori, we're screwed, I'm out of fire assets after I put forth this initial attack surge," Pete replied dryly into the phone receiver. Clarkson knew of the dire conditions at Camp Haller, in fact, all of the camps were almost depleted of supplies and personnel. It was the end of the fire season and assets were scarce, the vast majority of fire resources having been expended throughout the zenith of the fire months of June through August. By early September, personnel and fire assets were exhausted.

"You're just going to have to do your best with the assets that you have and pray that nothing else pops-up and that the weather and winds do nothing to spread this fire...oh one last thing, Pete, make sure your

Camp evacuation plans are ready to execute! Now do you have anything else, Pete?" Lori replied in a professional and no-nonsense stern manner. Pete knew the situation was bad as soon as the first fire reports started to come in.

"Negative, ma'am, I'll do my best and say a few prayers over a cup of coffee, I'll keep you posted by private line and e-mail. Thank You, Lori...Out," Pete replied as he placed down the phone receiver in silent resignation to the naked facts that he had to try and fight a raging wildfire with just about nothing. Still, he had to try and do his best; everyone was in the same pickle too. Pete Sanchez pushed the Camp Haller audio alarm button, which sounded a shrill fire alert alarm throughout the camp, a Red Flag warning was being sounded. A prominent large Red Flag was also posted outside of the Ready Shack HQ building. Those who were not already awake were soon to be, as the loud piercing audio alarms disturbed even the soundest of sleepers.

Pete Sanchez knew that this wildfire could get out of control really quick unless all his assets were brought to bear, there was no time to waste and all assets had to be deployed within the next 30 minutes. He phoned over to the airport terminal. "Hey, Air Opns, get the Preston's plane and crew alerted and ready to scramble in 20 minutes – this is Sanchez and we have a wildfire near Thunder Basin that needs a stick of Smokies dropped, got it?" he quizzed the air operations chief.

"Roger, sure thing, Pete, anything you say – the entire crew of the 'Icarus' are still all here," the Air Operations duty chief positively replied.

In utter frustration, Pete slammed down the receiver and made another urgent call, this one to the Ground Operations Chief of the Hot Shots. "Hey Frank, this is Pete, I need in 30 minutes every 'Swinging Dick' and 'Bloody Mary' that you can pull out of their bunks – we have a dangerous wildfire at the Thunder Basin area, tell them to get all their gear and be ready to roll – got it?" Pete chattered in an obvious hectic tone. Frank Stanton was the Chief of the ground assets and Hot Shots at Camp Haller and he knew the importance of the frantic early morning phone call.

"Yeah sure, sure thing, Pete, I'll get Ross, Birch, McGuire and Velasquez to get as many of their people that are left, but I'm afraid we may only get a little over a dozen or so Hot Shots, remember that just about everyone's contract was cancelled after Labor Day due to the budget cuts?" Frank replied back in resigned frustration.

"Yeah…yeah sure, I know that, Frank, just get everyone you can get your hands on! We can't wait for any of those fire figthers who reside outside of Camp Haller, so get everyone who is in the Camp and be ready to ship-out with their kits and equipment – got it?" Pete replied with some frustration in his voice.

"Yeah, I got it and we'll be ready to go, Pete," Frank replied as he also slammed down the phone receiver and rushed to get everyone up and ready to go.

While Robin, Wayne and Sammy were not present at Camp Haller when the fire alert sounded, Hank was still there from the weekend Labor Day festivities instead of being in his usual motel room. Recovering from some heavy drinking over his dilemma with Sammy, he was lying in a spare Hot Shot bunk, thinking about the daughter he had just recently discovered and just as quickly had lost. Upon hearing the camp emergency alarm, he quickly dashed from his bunk and dressed. He raced quickly over to the Ready Shack Command & Control room; there he noticed the agitated and frantic Pete Sanchez answering a phone. He waited until Pete had finished his call. "Hey, Pete, what the hell is happening? What's going on?" he inquired nervously.

"Oh boy I'm glad you're still here, Hank, some bad stuff is developing and I need you to get that whirlybird up in the air and provide me with an in-person SITREP! We got ourselves an out-of-control, late-season wildfire. Get a bucket load of water and report back here after you've gotten your pre-flight check done…got it?" Peter snapped in a quick rapid fashion manner.

"Sure thing, Pete, I'll be ready shortly, I'll see you back here and you can give me the mission task," Hank replied as he hurried back to his bunk to finish dressing and get his pre-packed kit of personal equipment. Hank noticed the fear in Pete's face; it was one of desperation, the desperation that came from having to do an impossible mission with inadequate resources. Hank got his chopper pre-checked and all systems were good to go, he was fully-fueled, and his bucket rig was ready as well. He returned back to the Ready Shack for additional instructions.

"Okay, Pete, I'm ready, so what's the mission, boss?" Hank anxiously inquired. Pete quickly turned around and saw that Hank was ready to go and that he was wearing his infamous positive-attitude grin. This confident face broke Pete's nervousness – if Hank could smile by going into harm's way, so could he also mutter through this wildfire.

"That's terrific, Hank, now come over here and take a look at this latest data from the National Inter-Agency Fire Center. The wildfire started at the Thunder Basin region. This fire is unusually intense for some unknown reason. These are infra-red shots from the Predator UAV system like the ones that are fly in the war zones. There are several bright red-hot spots that seem to be the centres of these fires. I need for you to do a bucket drop on as many hot-spots as you can and more importantly, I need you to do a visual recon and give me your impressions from an expert aerial point of view. We're getting pressure from upstairs to get a report about those multi-million-dollar properties in the area. These UAVs are modernized marvels to behold and as you can see the data from the Predator is top-notched, but what I need is for a real human to provide me with an analysis from his vast years of experience. Got it, Hank?" Pete concluded with a deadpan expression.

"Holy shit, man – this is a mission impossible, boss, but I'll try my best! I'll see you later, just give me the flight path and altitude of the Predator, I don't want to be messing and getting tangled up with that flying robotic piece of aircraft," Hank replied as he patted Pete on the back and stuffed an unlit Rocky Patel cigar into his mouth.

"Okay, Hank, the UAVs are flying between 6,500 – 8,000 feet on a race course circuit over the Thunder Basin and Wind River areas, so to be safe, keep your chopper well below their flight elevation envelope, you'll be flying visual and very low...this means be prepared for a shitload of turbulence, my friend!" Pete nervously cautioned to his favourite helicopter flyer.

Hank fired up the engine of the UH-60 and got ready to take off. He normally would have had the company and service of a co-pilot, but his co-pilot was not in the camp and he couldn't afford to grab any other available person, so desperately short was Camp Haller of fire personnel. He was going to have to do the double-duty of flying and spotting the fires. He took off slowly and carefully, being cautious not to damage or to have entangled the large water bucket container that was slung directly below his chopper and which was used to douse pin-point fire spots. Sometimes these small, but precise bucket drops had the effect of changing the course and intensity of a wildfire. Once aloft, Hank manoeuvred his chopper over a nearby lake and filled up the water bucket. He could immediately feel the weight and the drag of the weighted bucket on the choppers speed and manoeuvrability. The new early sunrise was just breaking over the horizon, it promised a new day and hopefully a safe day for everyone fighting the fires. It took less than 30 minutes to reach the Thunder Basin wildfires and was a scene right out of hell. Thick black and yellowish grey clouds engulfed the skies and a black, yellow and red torrent of smouldering earth lay beneath the ferment of the skies.

"Yankee Romeo this is Delta 3, Over," Hank replied into his headset-affixed FM radio, as he tried to contact the Camp Haller Command Post.

"Roger, this is Yankee Romeo, what's the deal with the fire report, Hank?" Pete Sanchez inquired anxiously.

"It's not a positive SITREP, boss! I observe at least half a dozen C and D sized fires, with a good 10-20 mph ground wind whipping up the fires. The fire looks to be heading to the east and northeast – endangering all of those multi-million-dollar residences. If left unchecked, this fire could consume thousands of acres in a day. All the roads are choked-up with the vehicles from the media and those rich-ass yuppies fleeing their mansions too, so getting fire and emergency vehicles into the area is going to be a big problem on those narrow mountain roads. The bottom line is that this is one big fat 'cluster fuck' and you need to get every fire asset and resource here ASAP, Over," Hank voiced with frustration.

There were a few eerie seconds of pregnant silence. "I said 'Good Copy' last transmission, Yankee Romeo, Over," Hank communicated again into his microphone.

"Roger your last transmission…so it's really that bad, Hank?" Pete Sanchez inquired in an unauthorized and open voice communication syntax.

"Yep, I'm afraid it is, Pete!" Hank replied in a similar communication infraction.

"Delta 3, continue your bucket drop missions and report back every 20 minutes with your status and location report, continue SITREPs to this Command as per bucket mission completions and provide fire recon reports as may be practical, Over," Peter Sanchez commanded.

"Good Copy, Wilco, I'm in route for bucket water re-supply and mission attack," Hank replied to indicate that he was going to continually re-fill his water bucket and to fight the raging wildfire.

* * * * * * * * * * * * * * * *

The two sticks of six personnel each comprised the entirety of Smoke Jumpers – hardly adequate for any task of this size of fire. Rick Conroy's

Smoke Jump team landed about one mile from each other, as so intended in the proven tactic of fighting the fire from two directions simultaneously. While Rick led the primary 'Alpha Team' his second group named 'Bravo Team' was led by Steve McGregor, a fine Smoke Jumper with six years of Smoke Jumper experience, Steve was a no-nonsense guy and a capable fire fighter. Being the leader of the entire Smoky fire team, Rick was the first man out of the plane door and the first to land on the ground. His first order of business on the ground was to conduct a head-count of his Alpha Team, then to get the status of Steve's Bravo Team. Rick quickly looked around and counted nine other human figures silhouetted against the bright orange backdrop of burning fields and forests of blazing bright fire. He realized that his stick was of an uneven count. He looked carefully at each of his stick members. 'Fuck me! That blasted stowaway fool kid was there too! What a shame he didn't get lost parachuting into the fire, no one would miss the body of a person who was not manifested or seen on the flight,' Rick thought shamelessly to himself for a split second.

He immediately forgot the devious thought as he saw the fiery marvel of his arson handiwork – this was indeed a killer fire and Rick knew that it was going to get even worse, so that he could call in even more fire assets and then the Tribal Wind River Reservation facilities would be totally unprotected and at the mercy of the second fire that was soon to erupt. As the stick team members immediately spread out to form a fire line, Rick quickly waved Billy over to his location.

Rick had to make an 'on-the-spot' decision about Billy. "Hey look, kid, I should break your fucking foolish neck for this stunt, but I can't afford that luxury now! You are here on the ground and I am going to make your ass useful in fighting this fire – got me?" Rick shouted to the cowering youth.

Rick threw off his Smokie jump gear, rolled it up into a neat tidy ball and quickly dug a shallow, earth-level pit in which to cover his valuable gear from possible fire debris, smoke and burning embers. The other members of his Alpha Team followed the same routine of grounding their gear – this was Smoke Jumper Standard Operating Procedure. Rick's next order of business was to make a communications check with his Bravo Team leader and then to the loitering Icarus aircraft. "Team Bravo, this is Team Alpha Leader, do you read me, Over?" Rick yelled into his portable FM radio. He waited a few seconds for the reply, which seemed like an eternity. A crinkled voice came back in a clear and audible tone, "Good Copy, Team Alpha Leader, I read you Lima-Charlie, how you read me, Over?" Steve McGregor replied in a normal tone.

Although devious and greedy, Rick still cared for his Smoke Jumper Team members, if his plan worked as advertised, none of them would be hurt at all, this would simply be another fire to which they would be responding. "I got all my Bravo Team here, Rick, we're unloading our gear...this looks like a Class D plus fire and it's spreading quickly, you best get some heavier gear like chain saws and water dropped down here ASAP, Over," Steve communicated with an urgent voice. Rick knew that dropping more fire supplies would do no good against this killer fire, yet he had to continue playing the part and order the extra fire drop of supplies just like this was any other fire situation.

"Roger that, Steve, I'll contact the Icarus aircraft and give them our coordinates and inform them about the equipment drop. I'm also going to order more Hot Shot units and aerial tanker assets placed on immediate response alert, we'll need all the fire retardant that we can get! Hey – I want no holding back on the resources for this killer fire! It's 'balls-to-the- wall' on this one!" Rick replied back to Steve and realizing full-well that there would be little fire retardant to go around for a future fire later the same day. The tall pines surrounding the Thunder Basin grasslands were now ablaze, some fires were reaching up into the tops of the 70-tall trees and creating large bursts of fires atop of the trees, these were sometimes called Crown fires, and these were most dangerous as they spread the fires from atop the trees and not at the bottom, making stopping these jumping fires almost impossible.

"Icarus... Icarus, this is Team Alpha Leader, Over," Rick coughed into the radio mike as the thick acrid smoke forced him to cough. There was only silence, so he tried again. "Lima-Juliet, Lima-Juliet, this is Alpha Team, Over," he repeated in a more urgent tone.

This time the receiver cracked back with some life. "Roger, Team Alpha, this is Icarus, give us a SITREP, Over," June Preston requested in her direct feminine professional voice.

"Roger last transmission, Icarus, all Smoky paxes accounted for on the ground safe and sound, we need immediate supply of heavy firefighting equipment, immediate Hot Shot ground support and have aerial tankers with retardant for immediate air attack, Over," Rick shouted as he awaited confirmation of his instructions. Nothing was mentioned as to the presence of Billy Coffer, the stow-away. This conveyance of this information would only complicate the fire fighting operations and lead to all sorts of complicated associated inquiries and maybe even an investigation. Billy's presence could be revealed after the Thunder Basin fire was settled.

"Good Copy, Team Alpha Leader, I copied your signal five-by-five all your traffic, I also have your GPS signals for Team Alpha and Bravo, all souls present and accounted for... I also have five-by-five contact with Team Bravo.... what's the naming for this fire Team Alpha?" June Preston inquired from as a matter of record.

Rick looked out over the burning horizon and he noticed a clump of tall pines in the distance, each group bearing a Crown fire atop the burning trunks. A tall pine stood there majestically aflame with two other slightly smaller pine trees ablaze to the right and the left of the tall flaming middle pine tree. It reminded Rick of a scary childhood tale that his mother had told to him as a boy at bedtime during one of those instances in which he had been behaving quite badly. Suddenly, a devilish smile came to Rick's eyes and he smiled in devilish delight. "Icarus, Icarus, this is Team Alpha Leader...let's call this fire 'Satan's Pitchfork' because this is going to be one hell of a fire and one hell of a day for all of us, Over!" Rick chuckled into the mike.

"Roger, Team Alpha Leader, I have this fire logged as the 'Satan's Pitchfork' named by Fire Team Leader Alpha, Good Copy, Out," June replied as she smartly copied down Rick's data and transmitted it back to the Camp Haller Ready and Operations Shack, where the data and the name 'Satan's Pitchfork' was placed in bold black lettering onto the Operations Board and computer files for the current operations and for record archiving.

Rick's devilish pyrotechnics were still exploding in the Thunder Basin National Grasslands, one every half an hour or so. This made putting out the fires with existing fire assets quite impossible and the weather was only adding to the tempest, a dry northeast wind was now pushing the fires with greater zeal than Rick could ever have hoped for in his planning. At least several multi-million-dollar homes were already ablaze and dozens more were in the path of the fire. As expected, Lori Clarkson was sending in all the aerial fire assets she could find. The Camp Haller Hot Shots were making their way toward the Team Bravo Smoke Jump Team, but these meagre forces could not help to arrest the tempo of this fire. Rick was correct – every frigging firefighting asset from every surrounding state was being employed in this fire – still it was not nearly enough! All he had to do was to keep requesting more and more fire attack assets and he and Jay would be multi-millionaires.

Suddenly, Rick remembered and spotted his young stowaway hiding back and away from the Hot Shot fire line. He motioned with his arms and hands for Billy to approach him. The sound of the fire made verbal commands useless and discretion was key to keeping Billy's presence anonymous. Meanwhile, the other Smoke Jumpers were busily engaged in trying to vanquish the wildfire with dirt in hopes of robbing the fire of its fuel supply. Some Smokies anxiously looked to the sky and impatiently waited for the parachute air drop of chain saws and other logistical gear, to include water containers and portable spray retardant units. They were oblivious to Coffler's presence.

"Hey Coffler, it's bad enough that you're an unwelcome and untrained member of this Alpha Team, the only thing worse is that your sorry young ass gets hurt or killed on my watch. You don't have any training to speak of and you don't have any fire equipment or even an emergency shelter, so you keep your young butt close to me and maybe you'll survive this fire and live to tell your kids a story or two – you got me, Mister?" Rick shouted in a rough and demanding tone to the young upstart.

"Sure thing, Mr Conroy, anything you say, I'll stick to you like glue! Don't worry about anyone noticing me, I have kept myself secluded from the other Smokies," Billy Coffler replied with a slight boyish grin.

Rick admired the guts of this young kid, for in Billy he saw a bit of himself when he was in his early twenties and full of youthful zest and arrogance. "Good boy, now here's a shovel, kid, start attacking that fire right over there to your left by digging up that bush and burying it over with dirt and I mean lots of dirt, you got me? Try to avoid the other Smokies for now, I'll announce your presence after we complete this fire mission," Rick commanded to his new rookie assistant.

Billy dutifully went about his assigned tasks of ploughing away the decayed underbrush that was the fuel for the raging Satan's Pitchfork fire. He was clearing large tracts of earth around the Alpha Team assembly area. The other Smokies took no notice of Billy Coffler's presence, having busied themselves with their intense fire-fighting tasks. Having been satisfied that he had diverted young Billy's attention to mundane, but worthy firefighting tasks, Rick now busily occupied himself with coordinating the air drops and making his SITREP to get more fire assets assigned to the Satan's Pitchfork wildfire.

"Come in, Icarus, this is Team Alpha Leader, Over," Rick dryly broadcasted into his FM radio mike.

"Alpha Team leader, this is 'Icarus' go ahead, ready to receive transmission, Over," June Preston replied back to Rick in quick response.

"Icarus, SITREP to follow...Satan's Pitchfork is spreading rapidly, cannot control the fire with assets on-hand, fire spreading to the north-northeast at 12-15 mph speed of advance, need ASAP at least three aerial attack assets and at least eight Hot Shot Teams, Good Copy, Over," Rick noted in cryptic radio-telephone lingo. Rick needed several aerial air attack retardant platforms and at least 200 ground Hot Shot crews on the double. Such a request, he calculated, would take every remaining fire asset in the surrounding fire camps and leave nothing left for the Wind River Indian Reservation fire that was set to explode shortly.

Without waiting for a response, Rick spoke again. "Hey, Icarus, I want you to tell Sanchez and the NFIC that people's lives are on the line down here, to include my Smokies, not to mention the houses and lives of those millionaire rich shits whose homes are about to catch fire, you got me?" Rick sounded off in a most dramatic tone to emphasize the urgency of getting his request for more fire assets on the Satan's Pitchfork blaze and to make himself more believable too.

June and Bill Preston could clearly hear the urgency in Rick's voice and they well understood the importance and the logic of Rick's urgent request. They were totally convinced of Rick's urgent need for fire support. "Good Copy Alpha Team Leader, we can clearly see from up here that the Satan's Pitchfork is out of control and consuming forest and grasslands at a rapid pace. We'll relay the request to Camp Haller and Boise on your SITREP and add one of ours as well to reinforce your situation. We'll stay on-station as your comms relay, Out," June Preston replied back to Rick and thus ending the transmission session.

Soon June's report and those of Hank Ransome were going to convince Pete Sanchez and Lori Clarkson to gamble every fire camp fighting asset and body to the Satan's Pitchfork fire. In an hour or 90 minutes tops, every fire asset would be deployed to the National Grasslands, exactly where Rick had planned these to be deployed. His plan was working without incident.

Placing his FM radio back onto his belt, Conroy eyed the scene around him. It was like hell's kitchen, there were Crown fires atop the tall Ponderosa pines and spruce trees ablaze and the tall wild grass was smoking and aflame in varying amber tones of consumption. The smoke was thick and non-transparent, it seemed almost as a solid black mass, save for the slowly swirling clouds of dark chocolate and ebony coloured smoke. But something was amiss; that foolish Billy Coffler was nowhere to be seen!

'Where the hell was that stupid young kid?' Rick nervously thought to himself. Although that kid was a pain in the ass, Rick still had a professional duty to look out for the safety of his crew and that even included the foolish Billy Coffler. He walked over to the area where he had ordered Billy to turn-over some smouldering brush and debris. He saw that Billy had done a very professional job and he noticed that the tilting work extended well beyond his visual sight of the Alpha Team Assembly area. "Billy must have taken some self-initiative and worked his fire line far into Team Alpha's far left flank area," Rick correctly guessed. However, self-initiative and daring taken by a novice in a raging wildfire, was a very dangerous and foolish act to attempt.

Indeed, in his youthful zeal, Billy had wandered off to work the left flank fire line to the best of his ability, he was in the process of doing a reconnaissance of his future fire line work, a distance of 100 yards away from the Team Alpha Assembly Area. This area was virgin territory for the fire, not an inch of it was scratched or consumed by fire. The area was a combination of four-foot high wild dry grass and tall dry timber- mostly pine and some spruce. To Billy's immediate front the forest became much denser, a prime ignition point for the roaming fire. It was hard for Billy to conceive how pristine this area was and how soon it could be transformed into a raging mass of black smouldering carbon. He was very foolish to be on his own in a wild fire.

While clearing the un-burnt tall grass, something unexpectedly caught Billy's eye, it was an object that was un-natural and foreign to this natural environment, even its shape was not that of nature. He spied a closer look and picked up the foreign object. It was round and earthen in colour with a rough exterior. Billy had accidentally discovered one of Rick's unexploded pyrotechnic devices. In his innocence of youth, he had forgotten his old Army training motto of 'never to pick up strange objects.' The odd device made no sound, but it had an odd strange smell to it. 'The device was obviously man-made,' Billy astutely concluded, and it was worthy of additional investigation or maybe he would just keep the oddity as a trophy of his first wildfire,' he foolishly thought to himself.

Carelessly taking his 'new trophy' in hand, he slowly and carefully re-traced his steps through the thick acrid smoke to where he had previously been digging his defensive fire line. From the smoky cloud emerged a tall lanky figure. It was Rick, coming to look for his lost lamb.

"Hey there, you damn fool kid, I thought that I had told you to keep close on my ass and not go around and getting lost, or didn't I make myself frigging clear?" Rick yelled out in frustration and ironic relief.

"Hey, Mr Rick, you'd never guess what I discovered in that thick grass over there? It's something I've never seen before! Can I maybe keep it as a fire trophy after we turn it in for examination at Camp Haller?" Billy wildly explained as he handed the unexploded pyrotechnic device to the horrid astonishment of Rick.

An instantaneous frightening chill rushed over Rick; there before him was young Billy holding the sole physical proof of a man-made arson event. To make matters worse, Billy Coffler now knew of the device and, innocent or not, Rick knew that Billy would somehow spill the word to others about finding this strange device. Young Billy was both a potential arson witness and an owner of one of Rick's pyrotechnic devices! It spelled big, immediate trouble for Rick and unfortunately bigger trouble for the innocent Billy!

"Wow, Billy, this sure is a strange device, I'm not sure exactly what it is either, but it does require further examination, maybe it needs to be taken back to Camp Haller for additional examination!" Rick calmly lied and explained nervously as he looked around to see if any of the other Smokies or Hot Shot crews were close at hand. No one but the two of them were present.

"Exactly where did you find this strange thing again, Billy?" Rick inquired in an artificially earnest voice.

Billy turned to his left and pointed with his left arm to the location where the pyrotechnic device was located. There was a sudden thud and Billy went unconscious as he fell to the ground like a dead man. Rick had taken his Pulaski and smashed it squarely across the back of young Billy's skull. Rick's reaction was primal...it was an instant matter of self-preservation. There could be no witnesses or loose string to his master arson plan. He didn't have much time to think, Rick quickly thought to drag Billy's body over to where the fire was spreading, in hope that it would at least be partially consumed by the wildfire. He would simply be listed as a missing stowaway on the Alpha Fire Team, a novice who got lost in his first fire, a young kid who had panicked and died as a result of his inexperience and disobeying of orders. Rick didn't want to kill this fine young man, but Billy was in the way of his plan to become a multi-millionaire and nothing, but nothing was going to stand in Rick's way now. Murder, as well as arson, was now added to Rick's deficient spiritual resume.

Quickly, he pulled Billy's limp body over past the fire line where Billy had just been performing fire reconnaissance. Having placed Billy's limp body where he thought it was most likely to be fire-consumed; Rick bent over and gathered up Billy's personal gear – nothing could be left behind as forensic evidence. He looked around and noticed that the fire pyrotechnic device was still lying on the ground; this item definitely could not be left behind. Carefully Rick looked around, he was questioning in his own mind as to whether or not to toss it into the fire area and hope that the wildfire would consume it or else to take the device with him and run the risk of having the pyrotechnic discovered by another fire crew member.

He wisely concluded that one risk and one murder was enough, he had to ditch the pyrotechnic device. He picked it up and examined it briefly and wondered why this device was a dud, as these pyrotechnic devices were chemically-triggered, and fool-proofed to work every time. As Rick nervously held the device in his hands, it suddenly ignited and white-hot streams of magnesium, aluminium and liquid sodium metals blew into the left side of his face, immediately causing him instant and intolerable pain! Instantly he dropped the pyrotechnic device that continued to ignite and spray white hot streaming gases and particles in a 360-degree fashion.

Rick lay there prostrate and unconscious on the ground. After a period of ten minutes, a fellow Team-A Smoky found Rick and dragged him back to the Team Alpha Assembly area and a Medevac flown by Hank Ransome was ordered in for a 'Dust Off', as was the parlance for a medical evacuation. Billy's body was also discovered and evacuated. Along with that of Billy Coffler, Rick was the second casualty of the Satan's Pitchfork fire. Still, other members of the Smoky crews and Hot Shots would also be counted among the future casualties as well. Rick's soul was now beyond the point of moral redemption, he was totally depraved and corrupted by his self-made evil.

* * * * * * * * * * * * * * *

Some hours had passed since the Satan's Pitchfork wildfire had its un-natural birth and it was now a raging mature inferno consuming thousands of acres. It was now mid-morning at Camp Haller and with all the activity near the National Grasslands, the Camp was virtually a ghost town. Anyone who had been in the camp earlier was now out fighting the Satan's Pitchfork wildfire. Despite this apparent calm, even now the first few of the second series of Rick's deadly pyrotechnic devices were silently exploding at a distance of only a few miles from Camp Haller and the Wind River Indian Reservation. It would take some time for its effects to become manifest, yet this threat would remain silent and unknown for only a short period longer.

Wayne rode into Camp Haller on his spanking new BMW motorcycle, the old one having been totally demolished and beyond repair, this despite the best efforts of the local BMW repair shop technicians. He came to get his gear, officially sign-out, and to bid his farewell to Robin. His firefighting contract was about to expire, and he had greatly enjoyed the physical and mental challenges of being a US Forest Service fire fighter. He had gained a great appreciation for the hard work that these seasonal young men and women did for their country and its great outdoors. He had fallen in love with Robin and he knew that she loved him as well. Ever the pragmatist, he realized that they were from different backgrounds, he couldn't live in Robin's world and she'd never fit into his either. He wasn't sure what he was going to say to Robin when he saw her, as goodbyes were always awkward and bittersweet. His true soul-mate Katherine was nervously waiting for him back home in Boston and he had promises to keep with her, this despite his unfaithfulness to her.

Wayne looked around the Camp and it seemed strange that it was so empty of activity and life. He was totally ignorant that the Satan's Pitchfork fire had sucked every person and asset away from Camp Haller. While waiting for Robin, he thought that he would take a quick walk about the camp and to say farewell to the Ready Shack crew. He noticed the prominent Red Flag flying and this puzzled him. Upon entering the Ready Shack, Wayne was astounded by the activity that Pete Sanchez, Jeff Campbell and the other supervisors were actively engaged in. They were all either monitoring computer screens or anxiously talking on the phone. 'Something big is going on here, maybe it's' a Command Post Exercise (CPX) called by the National Inter-Agency Fire Center. That would make sense, to conduct an exercise when the fire season was finished, and all the fire fighters went home,' Wayne wrongly concluded to himself.

"Hey there, Wayne, get your ass over here, we'll give you a briefing!" Jeff Campbell hollered as he put down his phone receiver.

"What's going on, Jeff, are you having an exercise or something?" Wayne innocently inquired. Wayne could see from the action and faces of those working in the Ready Shack Command Centre, that his hunch about this activity being a test or training exercise was quite wrong. Something seriously real was going on here.

"Hell's Bells, son, we got ourselves one hell of a fire, by coincidence the name of this beast is called the 'Satan's Pitchfork' and it's raising sheer hell in the Thunder Basin area, we already have everything and everyone that we had on-hand to throw at the fire, we've even had some casualities, to include Rick Conroy and that young post-grad intern named, Billy Coffler," Jeff explained slowly.

"Is there anything that I can do to help?" Wayne anxiously inquired.

Jeff was glad to see the enthusiasm of his young protégée; he knew that Wayne had come far from his weaning days as a newbie only some few short months earlier. "Well, get your gear and stand ready, we'll see what resources the NIFC can throw at the Satan's Pitchfork, okay?" Jeff suggested. Wayne took off to his locker area and started to assemble his gear. 'This might be my last hurrah,' he soberly thought to himself as he hurried over to the Hot Shot billeting and locker building.

While Wayne was busy in the Hot Shot barracks, Robin and Sammy also stopped by Camp Haller to get one last look at the camp and to say their farewells to everyone there. Robin was even more disturbed than Wayne regarding their summer fling. For her, the stakes were life-changing, she was pregnant with Wayne's child and she wasn't going to blackmail him into marriage or any sort of child support; for her this was to be their last meeting unless Wayne decided to continue their relationship. She was glad to have known Wayne, he was the only man besides that of her father that she had ever truly loved. Yet she also knew that their social and financial differences were so vast as to make any sort of normal relationship between them all but impossible.

"Now, Robin, are you sure that you want to come back here, to see him again?" Sammy inquired in a compassionate and soft voice that only a true friend's concern could express.

"You bet I want to see Wayne one last time, to see this place one last time too, well at least for a while anyway," Robin sighed with some regret as she parked her massive Dodge Ram just outside the Camp Haller Ready Shack. The two ladies stepped out of the Dodge and took a long, careful look about the camp – a last look one could say.

"Hey, Robin and Sammy – get over here quick!" Wayne exclaimed with obvious glee and anxiousness as he ran forth to see his old friends.

"Well, isn't this great, all of us being here again! All we need now is Hank Ransome to round out the troupe!" Wayne exclaimed as he ran up and gave Robin a kiss and a huge hug to Sammy.

"That's one old, sorry-assed, black man who I don't care to ever see again or to hear about again either, Wayne. Please don't mention his name around me anymore," Sammy rapped out most bitterly.

Wayne was confused about this antagonism, not knowing that Hank had recently confessed to Sammy that he was her long-lost father. Wayne prudently decided not to pursue the comment any further; it was obviously a sore point with his friend and he didn't want to end his last meeting with Sam on a sour note. Some things in life were best left un-said and unknown.

"Did you guys hear the big news?" Wayne excitedly asked. Both Sammy and Robin looked at each other, then back at Wayne with innocent raised brows. "There is a huge blow-up fire at Thunder Basin, they're calling it the 'Satan's Pitchfork' fire, and Pete and Jeff took everyone who was left here and threw them against the fire. They told me to get my gear and to remain on standby to reinforce the fire," Wayne hurriedly exclaimed.

Both Robin and Sammy ran off to their lockers to get their basic fire kit and gear. Sammy took an extra medical bag of equipment. "I guess, we'll just hang out here and wait for the word to go forward," Robin sighed, as she threw her arms around Wayne and embraced him in a long continuous hug. Sammy looked on, hoping that Robin would tell Wayne about her pregnancy. All three of them checked out one another's basic fire-fighting kit of essential equipment and tools. All of their equipment satchels were complete and in good-visible order. Robin and Wayne embraced and kissed for long moments, hoping that the summer was not coming to such a parting end.

Suddenly, Robin and Wayne's embrace was interrupted by the approaching low hum of a helicopter, the rotor sounds of which soon became louder until the noise reached such a whine that the three could barely bear the vibrations of whirling helicopter blades. The helicopter set down about 75 yards from the Ready Shack. Hank soon emerged from the chopper and headed toward the trio of old friends. "Now what does that foolish old black man want?" Sammy remarked bitterly. From his distressed facial expression and breathing, it was clear that the normally composed Hank was anxious about something most important.

"Hello guys, hello Sammy – we got trouble, big trouble out east at the Thunder Basin area, a deadly fire named the 'Satan's Pitchfork' is out of control, it's burning thousands of acres, many multi-million-dollar homes are burned down and a lot more are going to be destroyed. Some Smokies and Hot Shots are causalities as well, to include Rick Conroy and some young scientist kid…I just evacuated their bodies to the hospital about thirty minutes ago!" Hank sputtered out with baited breath.

"Oh my God, is Rick okay? Who else was hurt?" Robin screamed. "I'm not sure at this point… all I know is that this is a killer fire and we don't have enough of anything to fight it, I just got the scoop over the radio from the NIFC in Boise," Hank wearily replied. Robin, Sammy and Hank just looked at one another in disbelief. They were all supposed to be heading for home this day, now they were caught-up in a massive wildfire that none of them could hope to influence or stop. All three of them ran into the Ready Shack to glean the latest fire intelligence reports and to check-in as stand-by emergency back-up crews as required.

The Predator UAV had been making an uninterrupted race-track circular orbit high above the Thunder Basin wildfire area and the visual and infra-red real-time data streams were invaluable in sending down streams of fire information to the primary downlink station at the National Fire Inter-Agency Center in Boise, Idaho. From Boise, the streams were also transmitted via high-speed data relays and servers to other fire and weather centres. Reggie Flowers was Lori Clarkson's lead Subject Matter Expert or SME, on fire video and infra-red data interpretation. He was one of the key NIFC personnel who had located the Thunder Basin hot spots and recommended the aerial direct attack against these intense pockets of fire that fed the other fires. The job required skilful attention to detail, patience, analytical thinking, and keen eyesight.

In order to get the optimal high and oblique angle views of the fire, the Predator was programmed to make a huge loop that took it directly west over the Wind River Indian Reservation before making a gentle loop to head back into an eastern flight path and then over to the Thunder Basin region. The Full Motion Video cameras, or FMV, transmitted all the full-spectrum data that it observed with its multi-million-dollar lens array, which was originally developed to locate key terrorists in Iraq, Afghanistan and other regions of the world. All Predator FMV video and infra-red data was also stored onto off-line data storage farms for later forensic examination and study.

While the UAV was flying over the Wind River area, Reggie's eyes were suddenly distracted to several bright, small flashes – these seemed like a light bulb had exploded and then turning into a fireworks sparkler. There was one flash, then another and still yet another. Reggie seemed to recall a similar flash earlier in the day, when he was examining data from the Predator feed as it overflew the Thunder Basin area. 'Was this a mere coincidence or technical issue perhaps?' Reggie pondered for a moment. 'Nope – there was something similar and eerie about these flashes that could not be ignored…something was un-natural in these fire flashes,' Reggie wisely concluded.

Reggie was on the dedicated private line T-1 point-to-point telephone circuit in a few seconds to Pete Sanchez and Jeff Campbell. "Camp Haller Command Center, this is Reggie NIFC," Reggie sounded with an alarmed voice. Pete and Jeff knew that Reggie was serious about something just by the tone of his voice.

"This is Camp Haller Command Center, Sanchez speaking, so what's going on, Reggie?" Pete anxiously replied.

"Hey, Pete, call me crazy but take a look and see if any of your staff can see anything unusual in the vicinity of the Indian River Reservation at an magnetic azimuth of 179 degrees northeast ASAP!" Reggie pleaded.

"Right, let us have a few minutes to check that location out for you," Pete Sanchez quickly replied.

"Hey, you four over there, go stick your asses out the door and report anything unusual at the azimuth of 179 degrees northeast direction vicinity of the Wind River Reservation and I mean pronto, folks!" Jeff Campbell yelled out to Sammy, Hank, Robin and Wayne. The four dashed out of the Ready Shack Command Center like frightened rats. They all put their gaze to the northeast and saw a terrible sight – there was very dense black smoke that was billowing-up and the tell tail signs of red and yellow hues – clearly indicated that there was another wildfire brewing just north of the Indian Wind River Reservation.

"Fuck me, not another damn fire!" Hank muttered under his breath, having already seen and fought the 'Satan's Pitchfork' earlier, now there was this beast and there was nothing to stop its fury. With horror on their faces, all four of them ran back into the Ready Shack.

"Holy fucking shit, Jeff, we have another killer wildfire brewing at the Wind River Reservation and we have jack-shit to fight it!" Hank quickly surmised in a salty phrase of dire resignation. Both Jeff and Pete were dumb-founded for a few seconds. Pete realized that Reggie Flowers was still awaiting a report back, the bad news could not wait.

"Boise, this is Camp Haller – it looks like we have another wildfire brewing at the Wind River location along the azimuth that you have just described. I think we're in big trouble here, Reggie! We seem to have a second deadly fire aimed squarely at us!" Pete announced with an air of utter despair.

Reggie and the NIFC needed facts and data quickly. The Predator was on a pre-determined course heading out toward the eastern 'Satan's Pitchfork' fire and it could not be diverted, especially given that the nature and size of the Wind River fire was totally unknown. The only thing known for certain was that there was another fire taking shape at the Wind River Reservation.

"Camp Haller this is Reggie; look, we need a visual SITREP from an experienced spotter, our Predator is out of your immediate area. Can you lend us recon fire reporting?" Reggie anxiously pleaded. Hank looked into both Pete's and Jeff's eyes and simply nodded his head up and down to acknowledge his affirmation of this mission.

"Reggie, yes, we got a good experienced man who can do this and this new fire is literally in our own backyard," Pete replied.

Reggie was ecstatic. "Good have him send that SITREP to NIFC ASAP and send it in the clear on the FM spot reporting channel for re-transmittal by your Command Opns section, Reggie directed.

"What on earth is going on, Reggie?" Lori Clarkson demanded as she spied over the data that Reggie was viewing on his Predator video downlink computer screen.

"Hey, boss, I'm glad you're here, do you remember the Predator video earlier in the morning from the 'Satan's Pitchfork' fire?" Reggie asked almost rhetorically to his supervisor. Lori nodded her head and blinked her eyes in silent affirmation.

"For your information, I think I just saw several other similar, if not identical, fire phenomena...these displays were like starbursts or Roman Candles exploding, then producing a fiery stream of white-hot sparkler-like device," Reggie spoke emphatically. He was half-afraid to even speculate in the clear what he was actually thinking: arson!

Lori Clarkson was also thinking the worst of the situation, something fishy was going on with these two massive wildfires, she could sense it in her blood. She had never seen two fires erupt so quickly and in so quick a succession. However, analysis would have to take a back-seat to that of fire containment operations. She was fully cognitive that there were not enough fire resources to fight two fires simultaneously. A Camp Haller evacuation was now a definite possibility

The 'Satan's Pitchfork' was the priority fire problem, it was the first fire and it was a killer fire that was spreading. It was also situated close to valuable private and commercial real estate and lives that needed to be saved. The Wind River fire was born late enough to implement timely evacuation plans and the Indian Reservation buildings were not nearly as valuable as the homes and ski lodges near Thunder Basin. It seemed like the Native American Indian was getting shafted once more, this time by being a low insurance priority.

The naked truths of property trade-offs were difficult to judge, but that's the way things were in the firefighting business: some parties won, while other interests suffered. "Okay, Reggie, enter your SITREP as a Significant Activity report (called SIGACT for short) into the data base and link it with the last Predator feed and your observations thereof... we'll let the analysts and fire forensics experts review the data and final analysis report after the fires are under control."

"Yes, ma'am," Reggie replied as he logged his SIGACT and then busied himself with monitoring and managing two major wildfires.

"Oh, Reggie, inform Camp Haller that the 'Satan's Pitchfork' is our main priority and, that if becomes necessary, the Wind River fire might require the evacuation of the Reservation. Tell Camp Haller to be on stand-by evacuation status and be ready to enter the Camp Fire Bunker! This is an ugly reality...still inform them to perform any possible recon and submit a SITREP with GPS readings; maybe I'll be able to get an aerial attack mission flown to the Wind River fire," Lori instructed in a dead-cold tone. She was not being cold-blooded, she was only being very calculating in a situation in which there was not enough of fire suppression assets to go around.

"Camp Haller Command Center, this is NIFC Command," Reggie announced into his Private Line telephone. He dreaded having to tell a fellow firefighting element that they were getting fucked with their pants on, but that was the situation – no two ways about it! Unless the NWS issued a sweet Hail Mary cold front or there was a sudden shift in wind, the Wind River reservation was going to get fire-roasted very badly!

"This is Camp Haller Command, go ahead and send us the latest good news," Pete barked out sardonically as Jeff Campbell listened intently. Wayne, Robin, Sam and Hank could also discern the transmissions on the private line telephone speaker box that Pete had activated for all the assembled parties to hear.

"This is Reggie, the news is not good, folks; it looks like the Wind River fire has the same making of the 'Satan's Pitchfork' fire, but we have everything committed to the 'Satan's Pitchfork' and I mean everything! That fire beast is chewing up homes and property like a hungry animal, we're throwing everything at it, and so the Wind River comes in second priority. If you can, get an eyewitness, no-shit SITREP with 10-digit grid coordinates, then maybe we can do an aerial tanker attack and nip that little bastard in the bud! Otherwise, be prepared for a general evacuation of the reservation, Camp Haller and get prepared to use your Command Fire Bunker facility. Oh, this evacuation especially includes your favourite hang-out of Indian Joe's, that's it and good luck to you all!" Reggie sighed with inevitable regret.

There was no need to have the message repeated; they all knew that they were being placed in great danger and that there was no cavalry coming to their rescue. They all looked at one another – the look was one of collective despair.

"Good luck, my fucking ass! Yeah, thanks, Reggie – take care, old buddy," Pete exclaimed in a sullen, resigned monotone voice.

There was a ghostly silence that no one wanted to shatter. Hank being the eldest and most life-experienced person present, uttered the obvious, "Well it's up to us – we're the only ones here left to get the job done! I can fly the chopper in, land it in a safe position, and we can hike it out on foot to the edge of the fire for a look-see...We will take our kits and emergency survival packs with us. Does anyone have a better plan than this?"

Not one person uttered a dissenting word in either amplification or objection. The plan was as simple as was their mission – perform an in-person recon of the Wind River fire and provide an accurate FM SITREP immediately back to the Camp Haller Command Post and the NIFC staff. Like all simple plans, Hank's proposal was wrought with unspoken complexities and dangers, anything could go wrong and there was never enough time or resources to cover every safety contingency. Time was of the essence. The mission was given an immediate 'green-to-go' approval.

"Okay, everyone, like Hank just said – get your kit and emergency fire gear loaded on board the chopper and do a communications check before takeoff! I want no hero crap out there either, just do the recon and get the fire SITREP and coordinates and then report back here ASAP, you got me? We might need that chopper to help evacuate Camp Haller and the reservation. I'll send an alert and evacuation order out to the tribal reservation emergency operations centre and police office!" Pete Sanchez replied in a tone that was more out of anxious concern, than anger or frustration.

"Sure thing, Pete, I'll take care of these youngings," Hank winked as he smiled and ran out to do a quick visual flight check of his UH-60 Blackhawk helicopter. The chopper still had over half of its fuel load despite making the bucket runs all morning long.

Straight away, Robin, Sammy and Wayne went to their lockers and gave their survival and field gear a quick visual once-over and everything seemed to be in order. They had plenty of water in their canteens and their FM radios and GPS trackers were 'green to go'. "Okay, we are all ready now, Hank, so how's your personal gear check-out?" Robin dutifully inquired.

Hank looked over his gear – it was as good as the day he drew it from the US Fire Service supply room. Helicopter pilots seldom made use of their basic kit.

"I'm good-to-go, Robin, so how are you and the others doing?" Hank inquired of Wayne and Sammy. Wayne nodded an affirmative up/down vertical nod of his head, while Sammy merely gave Hank a silent and dirty glance. It was evident that she detested him. Hank gave a quick comms check with Pete Sanchez and all comms were good to go.

"Now, Robin, I want you up here in the right seat next to me riding shotgun, you're the most experienced Hot Shot Leader and you can radio in the SITREP and get them the precise GPS coordinates, is that okay, Robin?" Hank requested in a fatherly tone. Robin merely smiled in acknowledgment, as she placed the helicopter's communications headset onto her head. The others also placed on the helicopter helmets and headsets so that they could be kept informed about the fire from both Hank and Robin. In several minutes, the helicopter was several thousand feet above Camp Haller. From this elevation, they could get a bird's eye view of the Wind River blaze – it was in an early, but deadly, phase of development. In the far distance they could also see the faint ash grey clouds that were the product of the 'Satan's Pitchfork' fire.

"Camp Haller Command this is Hotel Whiskey 12 – here's an initial SITREP: we're at 4,000 feet and we're approaching the fire zone for the Wind River blaze, there's too much smoke being generated to see much of the actual fire, there must be a lot of dry brush and green trees down below that are the source of all this smoke. I am guessing that there are multiple Class C and probably Class D+ fires down there, but that's extrapolated from all the smoke being generated; the fires constitute an 800+ acre-sized blaze and this is going to grow quickly. The smoke is moving in a westerly direction toward the Wind River Reservation and Indian Joe's Tavern, I need to get beneath the heavy smoke canopy to get an eyes-on assessment of the actual fire, I can't see anything from this altitude with all this smoke, Good Copy, Over," Hank radioed back to the Camp Haller HQ.

"Hey, Pete, I'm not sure if it's a good idea for those guys to set their asses on the ground in 'harm's way' like that, this may be another 'Satan's Pitchfork' fire in the making and that fire has already inflicted multiple casualties on our fire teams. I'd give this a second thought if I were you!" Jeff Campbell alarmingly voiced out with concern to Pete Sanchez. Pete was concerned about the lives of his fire crew; he had known everyone except Wayne, for several years and none of their lives was equal to any physical property that was in danger of being fire consumed, despite what those bureaucrats at the NIFC thought. Pete knew that Jeff was on the mark with his risk assessment.

"Remember, Hank, you're the adult leader and I am not referring to your age. You've had decades of fighting these fires and you saw heavy combat in Vietnam, so you're a natural survivor or maybe you're just a lucky guy. I want you to shepherd your team to keep everyone safe and alive, this fucking fire ain't worth spit in my book compared to your lives – you fucking got me, Hank? I want my people to come first, fire recon is second! Good Copy, Over!" Pete yelled into the FM radio mic.

Jeff Campbell beamed with pride at the words his friend had just spoken. "You know that the NIFC staff in Boise are not going to like the fact that you just placed your people before the mission, Pete," Jeff announced in a warning tone. Pete took his headset off in frustration and threw it on the table. "You know, Jeff, I don't give a flying fuck what the hell those bureaucratic assholes up in Boise think, these are my people

and I just had some of my Smokies and Hot Shots injured this morning at
the Satan's Pitchfork fire and I'll be damned if I'm going to get any more
killed in the Wind River fire because of some crappy property that can
be rebuilt in a few years! I care more about 'life and death' issues than
I care about some lousy property and insurance' issues," Pete yelled in
frustration. Jeff gave a friendly pat on Pete's shoulders and handed him
a fresh cup of coffee. Jeff was glad that he had a friend like Pete running
Camp Haller and not one of those other US Fire Service or BLM 'pencil
dicks', who did not give a shit about firefighters. 'People over property',
was Pete's philosophy.

Hank understood that he was the 'anchor man' on this team. This
was a time when Hank could not shrink or flee from his responsibility
and he knew it. "Yeah Pete, I got these youngsters here under my wing,
there be no recklessness on my behalf, I am no old fool, Good Copy,
Over," Hank muttered like a parent minding over his children.

"Roger that, Hank, let us have your SITREP when you land on terra
firma, Over," Pete copied back as a mere matter of form. Pete knew that
Hank was the consummate professional and that he would take care of
the young folk.

As they approached the new fire area, everyone in the chopper
suddenly became very quiet, they became enamoured by the danger and
beauty of the raging monster, smoke and fire was everywhere! As the
chopper descended, a pocket of visible air mass emerged before them.
"Okay, folks, there's a ridge up ahead of us which has a reverse-slope, flat-
ledge basin – it's perfectly flat and devoid of any vegetation – it's a perfect
secure and safe spot to land the chopper and perform a quick land recon
of the fire; I hope you're all in great shape because this terrain is going
to be challenging, easy to walk down, but difficult to climb back-up,"
Hank voiced into the helicopter's inter-com. Everyone remained silent,
yet all of them slightly nodded their heads in positive acknowledgment
of Hank's keen observation of the landscape.

Like the professional that he was, Hank deftly placed the chopper
down onto the flat reverse side of a slope that was barren of any
vegetation or trees; this would help preserve the helicopter from any
fire that might spread up into this area and the barren reverse slope
also served as a natural fire break should they be caught in a Blow-Up
wildfire. He kept the engine in a low idle state, just in case a quick
take-off was necessary! Despite these precautions, the situation was still
wrought with danger and it was never recommended that a helicopter

land in a wildfire area, except for the utmost of urgencies. The Wind River fire constituted just such a risk. Hank's reconnaissance group was the only hope for obtaining a NFIA sanctioned aerial fire attack; there was no one else to perform this job. All four of them knew that their very lives were on the line this afternoon and that they could each die before the day was done. Yet none of them shirked from the risk – this was their chosen profession.

"Quickly now, everyone get out and grab your kits and emergency fire packs, I don't want anyone to take any chances on this fire, I think it's a dangerous one, and besides, we don't have to travel that far a distance to hump our gear!" Hank hollered out to the others, after which he gave a quick SITREP back to the Camp Haller Command Post. He also confirmed that the helicopter's GPS unit was active and showing up on the Camp Haller computer tracking screens. This was probably going to be the Team's last transmission until they actually hit the fire line and gave an eye-on of the actual ground fire.

"Remember, everyone, no hero tactics out there today, got it, folks?" Hank warned to prior to their egress from the chopper.

Sammy looked at Hank again with a scornful look. "You're not the one to be warning us about heroics, you're a cowardly old man!" she spat back bitterly as she grabbed her fire kit and emergency fire pack. Fire or no fire, Sammy was still plenty angry about Hank's revelation about being her long-lost father.

The trek up over the reverse end of the ridge was strenuous, even for the young and, harder still on Hank. The terrain was barren, rugged and steep – it was ideal to forestall a fire, yet it was conversely challenging for the frail human body to comfortably and quickly negotiate. Having reached the forward portion of the sloping ridge, the four paused shortly to take their bearings and perform a quick SITREP to Camp Haller. From their high perched view, they squinted down through the smoky haze to view a long sloping tree-lined and grass-filled valley beyond which lay a smoke-filled barrier behind which they could only guess at the threat that lurked therein, yet guessing would not do at all! Where there was smoke, fire existed, but what exact sort of fire existed there? What was its size? Its nature? Its path? Its direction? They had to get these definitive questions answered and this was the reason for their presence on the ground.

"Camp Haller Command, this is Hotel Whiskey 12, we're safe on the ground on a ridge over-looking the Wind River fire, we can't see or report a damn thing with all the smoke, but, I can tell you from the conditions that we see here now, we're going to need at least two large aerial attacks on this area ASAP! There is a lot of heat and smoke up here and all we need now for things to blow here is for this wind to turn on us and we are toast, along with that of the reservation, Over," Hank reported emphatically.

Pete had been sitting nervously by his FM mic waiting for Hank's call. Now that he had heard the bad news, he wished that Hank had not reported his ground SITREP report. "Hey, Hank, it's Pete, I can't promise when I can get that air support for you, that fucking Satan's Pitchfork fire has every frigging fire asset from five states tied up. Lori Clarkson just told me that she'll try and get support for the Wind River fire as soon as possible, but we might have to wait until the aerial assets free-up, Over." This news did not go down well with Hank, he did not like being on a wildfire in which his proverbial dick was hanging out.

"Holy Fuck, we need an aerial fire attack now, not later! You gotta be shitting me, Pete! You can tell Lori Clarkson that we're 'Three Bags Full, ma'am' and that we'll sure be thanking her for her kind support to us poor folks out here at the Wind River' fire, you got my frigging drift, Pete?" Hank replied in a sarcastic tone of African-American southern accent slang that bespoke of their historical second-class, inferior status. Pete knew that the team was in a dangerous predicament, but there was nothing that he could do other than to call Lori Clarkson again and beg for more aerial attack support. Without an urgent and accurate SPOT report, all of Pete's request would be based on mere speculation and thus receive a second-rate priority.

"Hey now, everyone, we got to get better fire data, otherwise we're a second banana for any aerial fire support, the Satan's Pitchfork fire is getting everything! Unless we get that aerial attack support, the reservation and Indian Joe's will be lost!" Hank briefed to the team.

"Well then, let's go and get it, we're wasting time here, Hank," Robin remarked with clarion insight and gung-ho bravado.

"Okay, let's ground our emergency fire packs here, these are of no use to us in the thickets and the fire shelter gear will only slow down our mobility...be sure to clear any debris and to flatten out the ground of any vegetation or fire-prone materials where you place your fire packs!" Robin ordered to everyone. She was the most experienced ground fire-fighter. Wisely, Hank deferred to her decision on this and she was correct too. The portable fire shelters were heavy, and the packs would impede their mobility. The four picked out the most flat and bare ground that they could find near the crest of the ridge. They took their Pulaski tools and cleared the ground for the placement of their survival packs. This was a precaution should they have to do an emergency shelter erection, they needed to have level and cleared ground to make maximum effectiveness of their portable fire shelter tents, which were given the fire fighter's vernacular of 'shake-n-bake' shelters. Within these aluminium and Nomex fire resistant shelters, a firefighter had a better than 50-50 chance of surviving a 'Blow-Up' fire, the biggest danger was not the fire itself, but one of affixation due to oxygen starvation.

"In case we get separated, I want everyone to remember that the route we came down is the same route we exit this fucking place... okay, let's go, everyone and no one gets separated, do you all frigging hear me?" Robin shouted, as she exerted her Hot Shot squad leader traits. They all headed slowly down the steep slope amid the dry wild grass, countless piles of aged pine needles and thick pine trees. The thick smoke soon obscured their vision and their bright yellow Nomex fire blazers became the only visible markers depicting each of the four team members.

Faithful to their training and orders, they stayed close by one another. Deeper and deeper, they waded ever so carefully and slowly into the darkened abyss to be known as the Wind River fire. One hundred yards into the dark smoking forest, they came upon a ghastly sight – the fire beast itself! Roaring directly before them were one-hundred-foot-tall pines and spruce ablaze, their juicy resin and dry barks providing Roman candle-like figures. The tops of the tall trees were ablaze in Crown Fires that were spreading the tree top fires across and down onto other trees and then onto the dry, fuel-laden, forest floor beneath. This was a killer fire for sure.

Suddenly, there was a drastic and strong change in the wind coming from the south, it helped to whip up the Wind River fire even greater than before and the winds had the ability to add to the intensity of the Crown Fires, similar to how a Blast Furnace bellows device stokes a fire to greater intensity and heat category. Hank saw the situation immediately and quickly radioed into his FM radio, "Camp Haller... Camp Haller – this is Hotel Whiskey 12...we have a 'Blow-Up'! I repeat we have a 'Blow-Up', send an immediate aerial attack on my GPS coordinates...we are in serious trouble here, Over," Hank yelled.

Pete and Jeff heard Hank's call and issued an immediate response.

"Hank, we have your coordinates, 'Good Copy', I say again, 'Good Copy','WILCO' – now get the hell out of there now and that's an order, Over," Pete yelled into the mic. Hank knew the situation and did not need any encouragement or additional orders.

"Roger, Pete, we're getting the fuck out of here, just get those frigging aerial tankers here ASAP!" Hank shouted without waiting for the reply. Further communiactions were fruitless.

Hank gave a hand signal over his head to the other team members that indicated a general, immediate retreat back to the helicopter. He yelled to get everyone's attention, instantly everyone got the idea and followed Hank without question. All the trees around them were soon ablaze due to the sudden change in the winds. Entire tree trunks were ablaze and burning pine needles flew through the air like fireflies on a hot summer night. They all moved as fast as they could, the hot air and thick smoke made their breathing difficult and it became challenging to see.

They were finally approaching the hill slope that led up toward the ridge and their personal gear. A sudden roar was heard behind them. They turned to see a massive wall of fire, a literal ball of fire approaching toward them like a consuming beast. They were caught in the beginning of a Blow-Up, a fire term used to describe a fire that literally attacks and advances upon the terrain in an all-consuming manner. The 'Blow-Ups' occur due to a unique combination of topology, fuel, wind, humidity and fuel. Few people survived a Blow-Up in open, unprotected terrain. This was the same type of fire beast which Robin and Wayne had survived earlier at the Hammerhead fire.

Hank, Robin, Sammy and Wayne all looked at the 'Blow-Up' with both fear and awe; in a brief common second, all their memories flashed back to the scene in Indian Joe's bar where Hank was illustrating a burning tilted match being rapidly consumed by fire. They were about to embark on a sloped hill, an incline that was much the same as the tilted match that Hank had held up in demonstration at Indian Joe's tavern. A strong wind also began to develop. A common moment or realization, a shared epiphany, had instantly come to each of them. They either made it up to their shelters or they were all dead in a few minutes.

"Let's get the hell out of here and up into your fire shelters now! We cannot reach the chopper in time! Run for your lives, folks!" Hank yelled as loud as he could. The four immediately started to run for their lives. Their struggle to outpace the Blow-Up just became even more difficult as they started the arduous task of running up inclined terrain with a rushing fire at their backs. The Blow-Up was continually being whipped up by the southerly winds and it could outpace a running human up the slope faster than they could run, yet they had a few minutes of time advantage over the rushing fire. Still, any advantage was fleeting, they all needed to get into those fire shelters as quickly as possible.

Time itself seemed to be dilated. The seconds seemed to be stretched into minutes, as fear and anxiety took primal control over their senses. They could feel the fire temperatures increasing even as they ran desperately up the hill. The heat against their backs was akin to a hot hair dryer. They were only a few yards now from their emergency fire packs and their portable fire. There was a respectable chance that they were going to make it!

"Quickly, folks, get to your packs and get into your shelters ASAP!" Hank yelled to every one of his team members.

Wayne's personal fire pack was closest to the group, so he kindly offered it immediately to Robin. "Hey, Robin, here's my pack, take it and I want no argument from you either - do you hear me?" Wayne commanded in a forceful and yet heartfelt tone.

"Anything you say, boyfriend...this is our second 'shake and bake' event," Robin joked as she instantly agreed and gratefully took out Wayne's fire shelter, erected it and immediately crawled into it. A few yards away, Wayne took Robin's fire pack and quickly erected her shelter and took refuge within it with only a few precious minutes to spare. Sammy and Hank did likewise. Miraculously, they had all made their way into their fire shelters with only several minutes to spare before the 'Blow-Up' descended upon them. They each curled up tight and awaited in anxious anticipation of the fire fury that was soon to descend upon them – no amount of training could simulate or prepare one for this event. The fire roared up the slope with a speed of twenty-five mile per hour hellish winds. Trees were falling along its path and the oxygen levels were dropping as the fire was being fuelled with every ounce of oxygen that was being offered. The fire temperature was nearing 1,000 degrees. The loud roar and crackle of the fire was almost deafening. They all took one last deep breath into their lungs.

All four souls huddled and prayed as they lay motionless in the silver cocoons. The fire tents were ruffled by the strong winds and high temperatures. Everyone struggled with their appendages to keep the light frame of the tent-like canopy from flying away into the Blow-Up fire storm. It took every ounce of strength to keep the base of the fire

shelter on the ground; to do otherwise would result in instant death
from suffocation and burning. Their lungs and nostrils struggled to
ingest the air which they needed to survive and yet which threatened
to burn out their internal breathing organs. The fire seemed to last for
hours, yet it lasted only scant minutes. This portion of the wild fire
'Blow-Up' was finally consumed and exhausted once it had reached the
peak of the hilly crest, where it ran out of both favourable terrain and
fuel, yet on the lower plateau, the wild remained active.

Initially muffled, then louder, and finally frantic coughing echoed
forth from several human. They were coughing up the toxic, hot air
that they had just inhaled. One by one, the team members emerged.
First Hank, then Wayne and Sammy. They each emerged from their
slightly charred aluminium skinned cocoons in unison. It was like
rising from the dead. They coughed and spat up fluids and debris that
had come to rest in their lungs and nostrils. Like a patient awakening
from an operation, each person took personal stock of their individual
bodies. Everything seemed to be working fine, it seemed that no one
was seriously injured.

Slowly they got up from their shelters and looked about. It looked
like a scene from Dante's Inferno – everything was a uniform blackened
mass. Everyone was accounted for except for Robin. Wayne looked
nervously about for her. He got up and took only a few steps before he
screamed out in anguish and dropped immediately to his knees. He
looked down the slope before him and beheld a terrible, gruesome sight.

There lying before him, he saw the twisted mass of a crumpled
and grossly contorted, badly burnt-blackened figure that had once been
a human being. Her body looked like a huge piece of black charcoal.
Robin's right wrist was elevated in a gruesome gesture up above her
head, as it she was in the act of grasping for something in the air.
Somehow patches of her blonde hair remained still intact. Acrid, foul-
smelling smoke was slowly billowing from her charred body and hair.
Her protective clothing had been ripped from her body as the strong,
hot, fiery winds had consumed and stripped her body naked of all her
clothing. The charring of her body was horrific and sickening. The
whole area smelled of pungent, sickening burnt flesh, a distinct aroma
of copper, charcoal, sulfur and burning rubber. Wayne was sickened
by the sight and smell! Instantly he dropped to his knees weeping
uncontrollably like a baby. Sammy screamed and ran to throw her arms
around Hank, temporarily forgetting her feeling of hatred for him.

Although Hank had seen such horrific things before in Vietnam, it unsettled him to see that his friend had died so tragically and so young. Like a veteran combat soldier, he held his composure and slowly moved down to where the body of Robin lay. He would hide away the dreadful memories for a later time and grieve over these in his own private way. The platinum Rolex watch that Wayne had bought for Robin was still affixed to her upraised wrist, its only blemish being a cracked crystal face piece. The platinum metal was true to its noble chemistry – there was no major structural damage to the royal, high-temperature, shock-resistant metal. The Rolex's crystal was cracked, and the time read 2:45 PM; it was the time that Robin had died. Hank knew that it was prudent to remove valuable items from the dead, as even in death, some people would seek to rob personal valuables from the dead. He carefully removed the Custom Rolex Platinum watch from Robin's charred wrist and placed it in his pocket for the time being. Later, at the appropriate time, he would return the item back to Wayne. Wayne could then do with it as he pleased, as it was rightfully his property.

Hank placed his arms gently around Wayne and tried to console him, not with words, but with a fatherly hug. Wayne wept like a baby in Hanks' arms. "Why, why was it her, Hank, we all lived, why did she have to die? She was the best among us, now she's dead!" They all sat quietly together for a few minutes and that same thought now haunted Hank as well. Hank, ever the professional, slowly got up and looked around the top of the ridge area.

In the distance, he spotted the silver-coloured remnants of Robin's emergency fire shelter. He carefully picked-up the tattered item that had been Robin's last refuge on earth. Hank carefully looked at the fire shelter. It contained clear evidence of clean-made, sharp knife cuts at critical points, this indicated this was the act of deliberate, man-made tampering – an act of murder.

"Hey, Wayne, look here, this fire shelter that was meant for you has been deliberately sabotaged by my professional reckoning," Hank correctly analysed. Wayne heard the words, but he placed the words mentally aside for later contemplation. Hank knew that this was now a case of murder in the Wind River fire, he would report it to the sheriff and Federal authorities for investigation. Ever so carefully, Hank rolled up Robin's sabotaged fire shelter and preserved it for official Law Enforcement forensic investigation.

While the wild fire ravaged the lower part of the forest areas, the three of them stood stoically on the front of the ridge, there was a low roar in the distance. Approaching them from the north was the hum of aircraft. The aerial attack planes were on the scene, several of them! Huge waves of red and orange mist flew down from the heavens and poured down like a suffocating rain upon the Wind River fires. It would take a few more aerial attacks, but the force and fury of the Wind River fire was now broken, as was that of Wayne Hamilton.

Hank wearily trekked down to the chopper to make his sad report to the Camp Haller Command Center. He would tell of Robin's death, his suspicion of her being murdered and the status of the Wind River fire. All three of them stayed with Robin's remains until the back-up helicopter arrived. All three of them gently placed her body into a plain black, vinyl body bag and reverently loaded Robin's body onto the back-up helicopter, with Sammy and Wayne acting as her escorts and mourners. From there, Robin's body was to be evacuated back to Camp Haller for processing and delivery to the Medical Examiner. On the helicopter journey back to Camp Haller, Sammy and Wayne cried in utmost remorse over Robin's corpse, while Hank flew solo in his own chopper and mourned throughout the journey to himself.

★ ★ ★ ★ ★ ★ ★ ★ ★ ★ ★ ★ ★ ★ ★

CHAPTER 12

Dead Reckonings

*"His immaturity had been vanquished! As an adult, he
realized that 'in between the gulf of one's limitations
and expectations – therein lay reality".*

"WILDFIRE KILLS BRAVE FIRE FIGHTER, MANY
OTHERS INJURED: ARSON SUSPECTED!" These
were the bold headlines heralded in rich black
bold letters among the various Cheyenne newspapers and Internet
Web headlines highlighting the causalities of the recent tragedies.
"Investigations continue by multiple Federal and State authorities!", the
story line continued, along with the details that outlined the numerous
serious injuries that the other Smoke Jumpers had experienced in the
fire melee that had occurred a few days earlier.

Discreetly eclipsed behind the seductive headlines, there was a buzz
of official activity and serious fire data analysis. The headlines failed
to mention that even now, there were multiple investigations being
conducted by the NFS, NWS, BATF, FBI and State Police officials.
The National Weather Service's Predator UAV Full Motion Video
footage which had overflown and recorded the bursting of multiple
fire pyrotechnic explosions, was a primary objective piece of interest
and forensic evidence for all the investigating agencies. These pictures
presented the imagery analysts with ample reason to conduct further
analysis and investigations into the fire's origin, which was very
suspicious based on existing data and circumstances. As with most
criminal investigations, the officials sought out those parties with

motives, opportunity and capabilities to profit from this arson fire. Yet presently, no individual was suspected.

The Full Motion Video, or FMV, gave even the most ardent sceptic a serious reason to doubt that the fire's origin was of pure act of nature. To both novice and expert alike, the FMV appeared to be an outright case of intentional, man-made arson of a most skilled level coupled with military-like planning. This was definitely not the act of a careless discarded cigarette butt or unattended camp fire. The main investigative focus at this point was concerned with motive and the method employed for the arson. Investigators hoped that some physical evidence and hopefully the in-depth personal interviews of the fire survivors, would provide the final pieces to this puzzle that had claimed so much in forest acreage and human misery. Technical analysis could reveal the method employed, but not that of the parties involved, nor their motives. Personal backgrounds checks taking many weeks or months had to be conducted. The papers also announced the fact that a memorial and funeral service was to be conducted for Robin Wolf later in the day. Many eyes read the story with great interest and also made their own plans accordingly. No chances were being taken!

Robin's funeral was a sombre and sedate affair. It was conducted against the crystal-clear blue skies of Wyoming at the Lakota Wind River Indian Reservation. A cool moderate breeze provided a singular comfort to the mourners. Robin's burial site was located upon a gentle sloping hill encompassed by beautiful majestic conifers of tall majestic pines and evergreens. The site overlooked a valley of rolling, green wild grasses through which ran a small sparkling stream. The beautiful physical venue was the majestic scene from an outdoor magazine layout, save for the solemnity and sadness of the burial ceremony.

All of Robin's friends were present to include, Sammy, Hank and of course Wayne, who was attired in the honey blonde fringed beaded buckskin jacket that Robin had given him only a few short weeks ago. Sammy and Hank stood generously apart from each other, the anger and discord between them had not abated. The acrimony between daughter and father was irreconcilable. Each approach made by Hank to his new-found daughter, was instantly rejected by Sammy with a dead-cold response. Hatred had generously substituted itself in place for that of Hank's 'big lie'.

Wayne was a transformed man, he no longer resembled the innocent, if not arrogant eastern, clean-shaved, investment banker from

Boston, who had arrogantly arrived here only several months earlier. Physically, his hair was bleached with streaks of blonde from the over-bearing, strong summer sun. His face was tanned and adorned with a full and handsome light ash coloured beard and his frame was lean and muscular. Spiritually he was changed too, now being a man possessed of self-enlightenment, introspection, and deliberation. His words were more measured and cautious; he was slower to make either rash or superficial remarks, and he lived comfortably in the moment of things. He reserved his counsel before he spoke, his spirit now ruled over his heart, actions, and his tongue.

Like any man gaining wisdom, he assembled the facts before making judgment and he thought less of superficial appearances and more about behaviors and actions. His eyes were more thoughtful and filled with the presence of a more mature and balanced disposition. When he laughed now, it was with the full roar of delight and when he cried, it would now be with the deepest of remorsefulness. He had reached full maturity in his latter thirties, the cost extracted at the exorbitant price of his family and a girlfriends' premature deaths. The cost of wisdom was mortgaged at a high premium.

Chief Joseph and the tribe had provided a rich array of Native American burial decorations. Robin's casket was made from native mahogany hardwood, which was stained in a rich red-burgundy colour. A colourful Native American floral pattern of various flowers was draped over Robin's closed casket, this was a personal donation from Sammy and Hank. A Celebration of Life collage of pictures depicting Robin in happy times adorned one end of her casket; this substituted for the typical open-casket viewing of her body. Chief Joseph had received tribal council permission to bury Robin, a non-tribal member, on reservation land. The request was made at the bequest of Robin's parents, who thought it only fitting that their only child should be buried on the soil in which she had both loved and died – it was a fitting and beautiful grave site, if such a term could ever be mockingly reconciled with the finality of such a tragic, murderous and youthful death. No type of goodness or positiveness could be resurrected from Robin's senseless death.

The sullen faces of Robin's parents were ashen grey and stoic, the mother's face was modestly camouflaged in a veil of thin black lace that could not disguise the mourns of her sobbing, while her father's hands trembled almost uncontrollably as he slowly guided his grieving wife to a chair that was thoughtfully positioned beside the grave site. The sardonic crackle of birds chirping in the pines provided a wilderness choir that was soon eclipsed by rustic native Lakota drums and burial chants. A Catholic priest provided the formal sacred rites of a Christian burial, even though Robin was not a devout religious member since her youth, still her parents needed the solace and affirmation of their traditional beliefs to lend them courage in the face of life's ultimate tragedies and a parent's worst nightmare – the death of their only child. Their future only promised continued grief and constant depression over all life's possibilities might-have-beens.

After the religious prayers, rituals, and invocations for the dead were consummated, there was an eerie silence which befell over the gravesite – no words could explain or provide solace to those who had witnessed the death of one who was so young. The silence was broken by the words of a friend, as Wayne's voice echoed across the assembled masses.

"Mere words fail to console the heartfelt emotions that we all share here today for our dear Robin and that of her family. No prayers that I can invoke, no actions that I can muster – makes any sense from this useless, senseless tragedy! The pain is so deep that I can hardly stand it. I have lost a lady, whom I had the pleasure of being called her friend, if only for this brief summer, a season that has tragically changed both myself and so many other fine people. I grew to love Robin slowly and with understanding over the past few months, I learned of her great firefighting skills and mentor as a fire team leader, of her love for nature, fondness for children, having the courage of her beliefs and not merely spouting off popular trends. I'll always remember her sense of humour, the determination that sometimes bordered on stubbornness and her serene smile – which captured my heart. She saved my life in the Hammerhead fire. Robin was under no obligation to go the extra mile, but doing that was in her nature, it was she, who led our team to struggle with the Wind River wildfire that threatened the tavern and other reservation buildings, she died trying to save the things in this world that she loved – a most noble act. We, her friends, will grieve for that which was lost in the life of Robin, but I know that I will carry her spirit with me through the journey of my life and that when I think of her, my memories will always be warm and joyful. Perhaps Robin's tragic death only makes sense in the context that although her life was all too short, think of how much emptier our lives would be if she had never come into our lives! I love you, Robin, and I'll love and remember you forever until the day that I die," Wayne concluded sobbingly, as he choked on the tears that had welled-up inside him. Everyone else at the graveside was crying too.

The sobbing was interrupted only by the low gravel voice of Chief Joseph. "Friends and Family, I know that this is a time of grief for all of us, none of us will ever forget Robin, because she still lives in our hearts. We all know that Robin loved teaching children and that one day she wanted little ones of her own, but this was sadly not to be for reasons only known to the Divine Creator. Yet Robin's teaching legacy and dreams will live on! I want to let everyone here know that this spot will mark the future of the Lakota Reservation pre-school and elementary school along with the endowed teaching chairs for 15 teachers, this is a grant from our good friend, Wayne Hamilton and the Hamilton Trust Foundation. Thank you, Wayne, for your generosity, Robin would have appreciated it and we most certainly do, as I am sure those educated in the school will be too. At Wayne's request, the school will be named, 'The Robin Wolf School for Native Americans', so thank you, Wayne."

A flurry of soft respectful smiles and nodes greeted Wayne's tear filled-eyes. He couldn't bear the loss of Robin and his generous gesture was merely one of money, of which he had plenty. He wished as if he had made something more of a personal sacrifice, but maybe his wealth was the only thing that he had to give at this moment. He felt guilty by his thoughts, yet these were true in his heart and he could not exorcise these, nor did he want to either. At this moment he realized that pain and pleasure; acquisition and loss; love and hatred – were all just emotions on the same coin and that nothing in life came without consequences for someone or some party. He always knew this intellectually, it was only now that he lived it emotionally. Life was sometimes good, sometimes bad, but it was life and you either lived it or you died. From here on out, Wayne would choose life, to live it at its fullest and without any second thoughts, regrets or looking backward. Living life was a matter of taking chances, not playing it safe.

"Your attention please everyone! We're having a private reception for those beloved friends and family of Robin Wolf at the reservation tavern for those of you who would like to attend, this was Robin's favourite place and it is where she enjoyed most of her summer nights. I sincerely thank everyone here for their presence at this ceremony, Robin was a great gal and I am sure that she is looking kindly on all of those here; that's all folks," Chief Joseph announced as Robin's friends and family placed small flowers upon the lid of her casket.

"Excuse us, please, Wayne, uh Mr Hamilton that is, sir?" a soft feminine voice echoed as a gentle tap on his shoulder interrupted his morbid solitude.

Wayne turned slowly around, quite surprised to see a gracefully aged couple in their mid-sixties. "Yes, ma'am, I am Wayne Hamilton …and you're Robin's parents, aren't you? I confess my bad manners for not having introduced myself earlier, but I thought it best that in your moment of horrific grief that I respectfully leave you both alone," Wayne confessed with obvious empathy.

"No…no… no…, young man, we are happy to have finally met you!" Mrs Wolf expressed in a most tender, tear-laden voice. "Robin told us that she met someone special this summer and after having seen your generous gift in her memory, I now know how special you must have been to her," Mrs Wolf softly uttered.

Wayne was at a loss for any scripted words, he merely spoke the words that were in his mind and heart. "I loved your daughter Mr and Mrs Wolf, I truly loved her and now she's dead from a senseless fire, none of this makes any sense to me!" Wayne sobbed uncontrollably as he tightly huddled both parents in his arms – as all three wept together several few feet away from Robin's casket.

The three then prayed the 'Our Father' followed by the sign of the cross, then they walked slowly over to Robin's casket, atop of which each placed a flower. Each parent softly kissed and hugged Robin's casket – it was the closest and final parting thing that they could bestow to their beloved little girl. They echoed a soft final prayer, then slowly walked away toward the waiting limousine. "Oh, just one thing before we go, Wayne, the Mrs and I want you to have Robin's Harley and Ram pick-up truck, she'd want you to have these and we'd like to know that you were enjoying her favourite things too…we have no use for these things and these will bring only unhappiness to us every time we look upon these items and we start to think of Robin," Mr Wolf pleaded softly as he lightly clutched Wayne's arm.

"We have no other children, Wayne, please take and enjoy these things, as Robin enjoyed these during her life, maybe think of her when you use them and think of the happy times too! All of the registration papers, vehicle transfers, and titles are in an envelope inside the Ram's glove compartment- please take care and enjoy these things!" Mrs Wolf counselled as tears filled her eyes from beneath the veiled dignity of a black crepe mourning veil. Wayne was dumbfounded, he didn't dare to insult Robin's parents and their sincere, graveside offer.

"Certainly, Mr and Mrs Wolf, it would be my honour to accept these things and yes, I will always think of Robin when I use her cherished possessions," Wayne replied as he softly kissed Mrs Wolf on the cheek in a motherly fashion before shaking Mr Wolf's hand and assisting them into the limousine. The remainder of their hollow lives would now be filled with constant grief, tears, and painful memories. Wayne vowed to stay in contact with them, especially during holidays.

Throughout the funeral service Sammy and Hank stood as far away from one another as possible. Estranged father and daughter remained apart and as distant, anger strangers to one another. It seemed as if their reconciliation was to remain as wide as that of the Grand Canyon.

It was early September now, the days were filled with a shallow soft cool breeze, and the humid, dry days of summer were abating and the fire season was over and soon the cold, damp rains of Autumn would appear, this a mere harbinger to the white mantle blanket of snow that would soon enshrine the western states in just a few months. This summer, like the countless ones before it, would soon be a memory for those who had lived it, and over time, even the memories would fade as well. It was strange and perhaps fitting to be humbled by the majestic and unceasing forces of nature, so it was and so it always would be.

* * * * * * * * * * * * *

"I don't fucking believe it! I really don't buy any of that bullshit rumour talk that either Satan's Pitchfork or Wind River wildfires were mere accidents or a matter of coincidence – it's just too damn convenient if you know what I mean!" Wind River Reservation Sheriff Dave Carney announced to his riding partner, Lt. Dale Buckman of the Casper Metropolitan Police Department.

"You know that there are too damn many inconsistencies, too many coincidences for this fire to have been a mere act of nature – I tell you it was arson and arson of the blackest type!" Sheriff Carney barked forth loudly.

"Listen to me, Dave, your feelings may be righteous, but they do not constitute facts and it's facts that we need to prosecute against anyone involved in this hypothetical arson-fire thing...just let the experts finish their investigations, let them handle it!" Lt. Buckman replied in a defensive tone; his logic was flawless, but not welcome to the ears of the angry emotional Sheriff.

"Let me remind you, that a young friend of mine died in that fire and a lot of other good Smoke Jumpers were hurt, not to mention that poor young scientist! Just how do two huge wildfires suddenly occur out of nowhere and with no specific cause?" Sheriff Carney replied bitterly and with some visible disgust. The two officers were riding together because of an appointment that Sheriff Dave Carney had at the Headquarters of the Casper Police Department. Their consultations were still at the early stages and they were awaiting more data from the other Federal and state investigating authorities. There were no 'smoking guns' as to any prime suspect. They needed someone with the motive, means, opportunity and ability to profit from such an ingenious and sophisticated criminal act. Lt. Buckman had invited Sheriff Carney to his downtown office to get his opinions on the wildfire matter – police investigations were more successful when police departments cooperated with one another, and the two men had known each other for many years and they were close friends as well.

Lt. Buckman decided to use his unmarked undercover Casper police vehicle. This was the most practical choice, since the vehicle was both official, yet visibly discreet. Lt. Buckman was also acting as the gracious host to Sheriff Carney and he knew the city streets well. As the two police officers rode casually to their lunch time appointment, they couldn't help but notice a late model sedan make a right turn at the intersection to their immediate front and it was driven by a very familiar man to both of them: it was the infamous Tribal Attorney Jay Blackhawk. His prominent thick black hair and solid physical profile were immediately evident on-sight to both lawmen.

"Hey, Dale, look over there! It's that no good Tribal lawyer, Jay Blackhawk! Now that's a man with a shady background and a man with a motive for profit," Sheriff Carney barked out with utmost verbal antagonism.

"Oh please, Dave, wait just one darn minute here! This is a free country and Blackhawk can travel as he sees fit. Sure, he's a real dirt bag, Dave, but that does not make him a criminal or someone with a motive," Lt. Buckman replied dryly.

Yet Sheriff Carney was not to be deterred. "Well, let's just follow him a short distance, sometimes a rat can lead you to big cheese!"

"Something is just not right here, Dale, I can feel it in my old police bones! What the hell is rich, vain, superficial Jay Blackhawk doing driving around in that type of mediocre vehicle anyway? It appears to be a rental vehicle from the plates on it," Sheriff Dave Carney snorted furiously, as his police experience provided him with a hunch in this matter.

"I smell a rat, a Tribal Indian rat!" Sheriff Carney fumed.

Nonchalantly, Jay drove slowly through the downtown streets of Casper; he had passed through an intersection on which the traffic light had just turned amber and then red.

"That's our chance to get him!" Sheriff Carney shouted zealously to Lt. Dale Buckman in an elevated and agitated voice.

"Oh, come on now! What's the matter with you, Dave? I know that you personally hate Jay Blackhawk, but the guy just went through an amber light, that's all – it's not like he committed a felony or anything!" Lt. Buckman replied rationally and defensively.

"I have a police premonition, Dale! I feel that damn crooked, Indian shyster, lawyer is up to no good... we have had trouble ever since Blackhawk came back to this state! It's just a hunch that I have, Dale... we have to do something and quick! That Blackhawk is one bad Native American, he would sell-out his own tribe and family to General Custer if the profit was big enough!" Sheriff Carney yelled out in a frantic, emotional voice. Lt Buckman was silent, as he merely drove straight ahead and continued to discreetly follow Jay Blackhawk's vehicle.

Suddenly there was a shrill whining of a police siren and the red & blue 'bubble gum' LED blinking lights from the undercover police cruiser. Dave had just activated the undercover cruiser's grill-mounted light and siren package without the permission of Lt Buckman.

"Damn it to all hell, Dave! What the hell did you do that for? Fuck, I didn't want to pull that Indian lawyer over and besides this isn't even your vehicle or jurisdiction!" Lt Buckman yelled with outright voracity and righteous indignation at his fellow police officer friend. Yet the dirty deed was done. The sedan in which Jay Blackhawk was driving pulled over into a small side street that was totally void of traffic and it was there that Jay Blackhawk waited for the police officers to get out of their police vehicle. Jay was always ready with a quick answer to get out of a possible traffic ticket. The unmarked cruiser followed Jay's sedan as it pulled into a quiet side street, its siren now silenced, along with the eye-catching LED blue and red lights. Sheriff Dave Carney just glanced over at his friend and stared at him with a look that begged out for a favour.

"Okay, Dave, you fucking win on this, but you just remember this is my city and I'll do most of the talking – do you understand me, Dave? I do not want any sort of unlawful citizen harassment or bullying either, do you get my drift? The last thing we need is a police harassment incident and our reputations and careers are in the toilet! This is a prominent citizen and a shrewd lawyer to boot," Lt Buckman replied in a declarative tone.

"Yes sir! Sure, old buddy, anything you say, I'll be on my most charming police behavior too," Dave nodded with a positive wink of his eye.

As with any vehicle stop by law enforcement officers, there was an uneasy delay before the officers approached any suspect vehicle, they were running the vehicle's plates to ensure that there were no outstanding warrants on it or with the owner of the vehicle. In just under two minutes, the results came back, no warrants or other outstanding information on the vehicle. The dispatcher responded that the vehicle was a rental vehicle of a Mr Rick Conroy. Now both officers were very intrigued with this information; it invited further 'official' police inquiry. Rick was one of the fire fighters evacuated and injured in the recent Satan's Pitchfork wildfire. Both lawmen now wondered about the relationship between Jay Blackhawk and Rick Conroy. Jay and Rick were known to be friends, but maybe, just maybe – there was more than just a social connection which existed between the two men. Suddenly, this routine stop was routine no longer.

Jay was annoyed about this unexpected traffic stop – it was the last thing that he needed – as he was eagerly on his way to the hospital to visit Rick Conroy and ensure that his prime partner in the reservation fire arson scheme did not talk to the authorities about their devious plans. Jay knew that Rick could keep his mouth shut, but Jay also knew that people could not be totally relied upon to do the things that they were supposed to do, especially in times of trouble and possible investigations and police inquiry. Better men than Rick were broken by prosecutors and police investigators when placed under interrogation and threats. Another messy fact was the dangling matter of a living witness to boot in the form of the injured Billy Coffler – which only made matters more complicated. Yet Jay Blackhawk did not get this far in his life by being either dimwitted or careless, witnesses were always a problem and he knew how to deal with problems and loose ends.

In customary fashion, Jay withdrew his driver's licence in anticipation that this would be the first item that any policeman wanted of a driver for a stopped car. "Licence, registration and proof of insurance, sir," Lt.

Dale Buckman inquired politely as Sheriff Dave Carney stood a cautious twelve feet away in a back-up and observation position.

"Well, hello, Lt. Buckman, it's Jay Blackhawk, remember me, old buddy?" the Native American lawyer smiled in hope of quickly diffusing the situation harmlessly and quickly.

"Yes, sir, I remember you and a good day to you, sir! I see that you have a valid driver's licence, Mr Blackhawk, but where are the other two pieces of vehicle documentation that I requested, sir?" Lt. Buckman inquired without a smile or indication of a friendly vocal tone. Lt. Buckman wanted to remain 'all business like' when dealing with a slimy character like Jay Blackhawk. This was no mild innocent old lady who was being pulled over.

"Okay, it's like this, Lt Buckman, this is not my vehicle, it belongs to my sick friend Rick Conroy and I don't know where those documents are precisely. You see, I am on my way to the hospital to see how Rick Conroy is doing," Jay Blackhawk explained, as he rummaged through the front seat area and glove compartment for the vehicle registration and proof of insurance.

"Jeez, guys, it looks like I cannot immediately locate those documents, but like I said before – this is not my car and besides, Lt Buckman, you have a visual recognition of me and you know that I am an outstanding member of the Casper Community and that of the State of Wyoming... I am on great terms with the Mayor, Police Commissioner and most of the City Council members," Jay boastfully proclaimed to the police officer. "Besides it's not an arrest offence for me not to have these documents for a vehicle that was loaned to me by my buddy, am I not correct, officer? So, why don't you nice police officers simply cut me a break here?" Jay boastfully exclaimed with obvious command of the traffic law.

"So, you are close buddies with Rick Conroy, the Smoke Jumper survivor of that horrific Satan Pitchfork wildfire?" Lt Buckman dryly inquired.

"Yeah, you got that right, buddy, he's an outright local hero and as I said – I am merely on my way to see my sick friend in the hospital right now! I am going to drop off his car there!" Jay responded almost like he was establishing an alibi. Jay's neat reply sounded too neat and rehearsed for Lt Buckman.

"Hey Blackhawk, so if your buddy Conroy is sick in the hospital, why are you driving his car there? Sick and injured men do not need the use of their automobiles! You could have simply driven your own fancy car to go and visit him today!" Lt Buckman inquired in detective-like fashion to the slightly nervous lawyer.

"Look here now, I am doing this as a favor for my friend, let me explain further, so that you can get this through your thick heads. I'm going to leave Rick's car in the hospital parking lot, so that he will have full access and use of it once he gets well enough to drive it after his hospital discharge! The car will be there ready to go for him!" Jay coyly responded. The explanation sounded as phony as a three-dollar bill, but you couldn't lock someone up for making a second-rate lie which could not be immediately disproved.

Sheriff Dave Carney distinctly overheard the conversation between the crooked lawyer and Lt Buckman, and he instinctively knew that Jay was trying to get out of this dubious traffic stop with another of his sweet-talking, law citing words and prominent name-dropping. Sheriff Carney also knew that the more a guilty man spoke, the greater was the opportunity for the guilty man to slip-up. He needed to find an excuse to keep Jay Blackhawk on the scene there and have him talk some more about his activities.

"Oops, I think that we have a little bit of a problem here, Lt Buckman," Sheriff Carney announced as he discreetly took his right foot and forcefully kicked in the rear end tail light on the vehicle.

Lt. Buckman drew to the back of the car and spotted that the right-side rear tail light was broken, it was obviously the immediate on-the-spot work of Sheriff Carney. Buckman looked at the broken light and gave a rather disgusted look at Sheriff Carney. Lt Buckman was a strict by-the-rules cop and he hated when a fellow police officer twisted the rules to get the bad guys; even scum bags like Jay Blackhawk were to be given the courtesy and benefit of the law. Still the dirty deed was done.

"Please come back here, Mr Blackhawk," Lt. Buckman voiced loudly to the vehicle's driver.

A visibly disgusted Jay Blackhawk got out of the vehicle and walked quickly to the rear of the vehicle.

"Shit, well I did not know that the light was broken and like I stated previously – this is not my car, it belongs to Rick Conroy. After all, fellas, I cannot be held responsible for the integrity of someone else's vehicle, I am merely responsible for the safe and proper operation of the vehicle of which I am presently operating!" Jay shouted back defiantly, as he looked at the broken taillight with disgust and suspicion.

This time Sheriff Carney intervened and did the talking. "You are totally wrong, Jay – you are the operator of this motor vehicle and regardless of vehicle ownership, you are responsible under Wyoming State law to maintain a safe vehicle...so this is a case of probable cause for a vehicle safety inspection, now how about letting us see what's in the trunk, Jay, or do we wait to call in a warrant?"

"Who the hell left you off of the reservation, Sheriff Carney? You have no jurisdiction here! You're just some dim-witted, half-assed, Indian Reservation cop! What the hell is going on here guys, this was a simple traffic stop and now I am being told to submit to a search of a vehicle that is not mine. This is a clear case of police harassment against a very prominent, Native American person! You guys are trying to frame and honest man," Jay protested vocally and with an air of fright in his voice and eyes.

"Quit the dramatics and sidewalk lawyering, Jay, just open-up the frigging trunk!" Sheriff Carney declared with a disgusted tone in his voice. An obvious visible nervousness came over the increasingly agitated attorney.

"Fuck me, why should I open it up? What the hell for, Carney? Like I said before, this is not my vehicle, nor is anything found in it of any direct evidence or association with me; like I said, fellas, this is not my vehicle! You guys are just trying to railroad me! How about if I just abandon Rick's vehicle right here and now? This is outright racial profiling of a hard-working, honest, Native American!" Jay loudly protested and accused most defensively.

"Cut the crap, Jay! You cannot simply walk-away and abandon an operating vehicle on the open streets of Wyoming either! So, what is it exactly 'that does not belong to you', which is contained within this vehicle? Are you trying to run-away or distant yourself from Rick's vehicle for some purpose? Is there something amiss that we might discover in this vehicle, Mr Blackhawk?" Lt Buckman inquired with increasing interest and suspicion. Jay merely shrugged his shoulders in a wild gesture without uttering a word in reply. He knew that further talk was liable to be incriminating to himself.

"Okay, look, guys, I'm a licensed lawyer and you guys have no probable cause, no warrant, and besides like I said, it's not my vehicle and I am not legally responsible for anything discovered in a borrowed vehicle!" Jay replied again in an obvious state of nervousness and outright agitation. The two officers were now very suspicious.

"Well since it's not your vehicle, Mr Blackhawk, then you have no objections or any right of protest either, if we should open it up; like you said, it's not your vehicle, correct, Counsellor? However, to be strictly legal and formal, we can always get a search warrant, if that's what the Counsellor Jay Blackhawk insists upon this situation, correct?" Lt. Buckman announced boldly.

Sheriff Carney merely smiled broadly, as he noticed that his Casper Police friend was finally on the right track with Jay Blackhawk. Both police officers knew that Jay was nervous and perhaps guilty about something particular to this traffic stop. Yet they were on very shaky legal grounds, since this was a rental vehicle of Rick Conroy's and Jay vocally stated multiple times that nothing in the vehicle belonged to him.

Now Jay started to visibly perspire; he knew that the police could get a search warrant in under an hour and have the vehicle impounded on the scene until the warrant came through. Also, a search warrant would mean more outside parties involved in this incident or even a curious citizen, wandering TV crew or nosey reporter might show-up. Experience had wisely taught him that matters of dispute and law could be negotiated best within a small group. A search warrant also meant that an audit or paper trail would be established, not a good thing to have for a guilty man implicated in a guilty act. Realizing that it is in his best interests to deal with just these two police officers on the scene, Jay decided it to be most prudent to defer to the officers' demands.

"Once again, Mr Blackhawk, what's in the trunk?" Sheriff Carney inquired.

"Beats the shit out of me!", Jay replied, as he simply shrugged his shoulders to visibly indicate his ignorance and neutrality of the inquiry.

"Enough of this nonsense! Okay, Jay, up against the vehicle, I'm going to frisk you," Lt. Buckman announced as he padded-down the nervous attorney. The act was done more to un-nerve Mr Blackhawk, he didn't expect to find any weapons on a well-established attorney attired in a $4,000 custom-tailored, Armani suit. Nervous suspects usually had something to hide and more often than not, they usually made mistakes when the appropriate pressure was applied, but Jay was a cool character.

Lt Buckman took the keys that he had taken from Jay and opened up the trunk of the vehicle. There set prominently before their eyes was a large, square, legal attaché case, the kind frequently used to convey large amounts of legal paperwork. Next to the attaché case were two large wooden boxes – each the size of a footlocker – the boxes were without any description or writing.

The trunk smelled afoul with some sort of indescribable odour, it smelled liked something chemical or industrial in nature. This was no longer a simple car-stop harassment of Jay Blackhawk.

"Okay, Blackhawk, what's in those wooden cases? Is it a substance of danger or anything that could harm a Law Enforcement officer or the general public?" Sheriff Carney shouted.

"Once again, fellas, I have to tell you guys that this is not my vehicle; the vehicle, and everything in it, belongs not to me, but to Mr Rick Conroy," Jay pleaded to the two police officers. It was as if Jay was establishing his innocence in anticipation of being formally accused.

Sheriff Carney opened up one of the boxes and it appeared to be half-filled with sphere-like objects that appeared in the form and size of wooden croquet balls, except being much heavier. The outer shell was that of a rough pulp-like material, almost organic and rough in texture. Lt. Buckman grasped one of the items in his hand and examined it in the sunlight. There was a noxious smell to the sphere, it was rough on the exterior, perfectly round in form except for a small round circular mound that sat atop of the grapefruit sized item.

"What in the hell is this thing?" Lt. Buckman exclaimed in amazement.

Sheriff Carney looked at the strange object and remarked in exasperation, "I don't rightly know for certain, but I suspect it is a chemical pyrotechnic device, maybe like the one that an arsonist would use to start a violent wildfire!"

For the first time in his life, Jay Blackhawk was at a loss for words, he knew that saying anything more was self-incrimination. "We'd better put the bomb squad on alert on this one!" Sheriff Dave Carney noted almost rhetorically to his pal Lt Dale Buckman. "Hey Jay, didn't your parents tell you to never play with matches and explosives?" Sheriff Carney commented half-jokingly.

This official 'traffic stop' was becoming all the more interesting with each passing moment. The two officers next directed their attention to the oversized legal attaché' case.

"You are a man full of surprises today, Jay! So now, what's in the attaché case, Mr Blackhawk?" Lt. Buckman asked in a direct, no-nonsense tone.

"Come on, guys! Like I said before all this shit here just beats the hell out of me! Not my car, not my stuff! Not my problem or concern!

I don't know anything, fellas – honestly!" Blackhawk noted in a sour, aggravated tone that was laced with a facial shit-eating grin.

"This thing isn't going to blow up on me if I open it up, now will it, Jay?" Dave Carney smiled as he opened up the top of the large brown leather legal attaché case. Lt Dale Buckman looked on cautiously, as did Jay Blackhawk. All three men looked down into the dark recesses of the car trunk, yet only one man knew the entire attaché case contents, while the other two men soon would.

As the top flaps of the dark brown attaché case were opened, there was the appearance of neat high stacks of new $100 bills over a foot in height and each stack of bills was attired in a $10,000 bank wrapper.

"Whoa! That's a lot of dough fellas," Jay voiced, as he echoed out a long and loud whistle. Dale and Dave's eyes were bulging at the sight of the large amount of cash. "Your money, Mr Blackhawk?" Sheriff Dave inquired after he had regained his composure. Once again, Jay simply shrugged his shoulder and repeated, "Not my car, not my money – go see Rick Conroy…maybe Rick made some good investments!"

The two police officers were not amused by Jay's smart-ass attitudes and cocky comments, but they continued to fish for answers to this incriminating arson evidence that was most likely tied to the Wind River and Satan's Pitchfork wildfire incidents. Both officers were hoping that Jay would either say or do something stupid, but Jay was a clever man, an experienced attorney who would not easily self-incriminate himself, especially to these two local yokels. Jay Blackhawk knew that stupid and careless people can often get a smart guy like himself in trouble, so he quickly thought up a plan to get out of this jam by appealing to one of man's basic instincts – greed!

"Hey, guys, that's a lot of money that we see here! I would estimate, and this is merely an estimate, I'd speculate that there's about two million dollars in there! We just established that no one here really knows where this money has come from, or even who really owns it - this is simply amazing, guys – a rare and great opportunity. This is like finding sunken treasure – finders keepers! Now I assume that neither of you officers called in this stop to the dispatcher or your supervisor, is that correct?" Jay inquired.

The two stunned police officers looked quickly at each other, but they were silent to the accusation as they both glanced at Jay Blackstone. They turned their eyes back to the attaché case full of money only to glance back at Jay Blackhawk as he began to speak once again.

"Well since no one 'officially' knows that there was a search stop here today or even what was discovered in this car trunk, who is to say what the truth is here! If nothing is written down or reported – then it does not really exist – right, guys! No one even knows that you two officers stopped me today and no one except the three of us has seen what is in this car trunk, correct guys?" Jay announced with a convincing, if not logical and argumentative line of seductive reasoning.

Jay continued his diatribe, just like a lawyer pleading a closing-arguments to a jury. "I would carefully counsel to both of you that $2 million in tax free, unaccountable dollars makes for a very attractive nest egg to feather your meagre police pensions. I mean we all know how underpaid you fine civil servants of the law are, especially out in the boonies here in the Casper and on the Indian Reservation, right! Let's face it, guys, how much of any seized contraband ever makes it 100% to the evidence room, officers? I would say that if you guys were smart, you'd make this little unreported stop pay off for yourselves in a very big way – now you know what I mean, right, guys? Now I have an idea, why don't I just start walking down the street here, as if you guys never saw me before! You both take the money, dump those two crates in the river, and we all just walk-away from any incriminating materials, Okay, boys?" Jay smartly concluded. The two police officers just looked at one another with prolonged intrigued stares.

"Hey guys, let all of us be and act, smart here! Don't be dumb cops, instead be smart and rich! These are tough economic times, turn this money and contraband in and you'll be poor, perhaps be given a worthless commendation and some other cops will take a piece of this loot and enjoy themselves! Remember, high morals never left anyone rich in this world; besides, no one will ever be the wiser, this can remain just among us... so don't be chumps," Jay cooly counselled in courtroom persuasive logic fashion. In a twisted way, it all made sense too!

Jay keenly spotted the lingering doubts on the faces of the two police officers and he knew that his proposal had impacted and intrigued both of them. Jay smirked an arrogant smile as he very slowly turned away from the two police officers and started to walk slowly away from the car and down the street. The two officers looked anxiously down at the attaché case filled with the two million dollars. A million dollars apiece tax-free was more money than either officer could ever hope to acquire in several lifetimes. A comfortable retirement was just a remote dream and their chances of living to collect a rather modest pension diminished each day they served on the mean streets. Future ill health, an accident or a bullet could easily terminate both of their lives.

Jay confidently smiled and blew forth a soft whistle tune as he strutted slowly down the street. He could most easily afford this cash loss from his generous personal and business portfolios, it was just the normal expense for doing business and he could afford to pay-off both Rick Conroy and the police without batting an eye. Pay-offs were well worth the price of staying out of jail, the negative publicity and the possibility of a criminal indictment. All he had to do now, was to ensure that Rick Conroy kept his big mouth shut and that he would not 'spill the beans' about starting the reservation wildfire.

Although there was currently no direct evidence linkage between Jay Blackhawk and Rick Conroy, the circumstantial evidence was something that a grand jury could be persuaded to rule against him and this was a chance not worth taking – one inquiry usually begs for yet another inquiry into 'other matters' and Jay's life was a complex web of shady interwoven mutually supporting deals and agreements. Each footstep that he took confirmed his confidence in the frailty of human nature.

"You stop right there, Mr Jay Blackhawk, you're under arrest, stay exactly where you are and do not move! The charges are conspiracy to commit arson and murder, the possession and transportation of hazardous explosive materials without a licence, and operating a motor vehicle without the proper insurance and registration papers," were the unexpected and dreaded words spoken by Lt Buckman to the quite agitated lawyer. The police officer's words that echoed in Jay's ears, were felt like thunderbolts from the heavens. The two policemen cuffed him and read him the Miranda Rights.

True to form, Jay's first words were classic ones, 'I'm not saying one more flipping word until I speak with my attorneys, do you hear me, guys?"

The two police officers merely grinned at one another as they placed Jay Blackhawk into the back seat of the patrol car. They knew that others might have taken the money and kept their mouths shut, yet both officers were simple men couched in classic values, neither of them had the stomach or character for corruption. There were far worse things than being poor in this world; it was a shame that Jay, Rick and others had failed to realize this truth. Besides, once you start taking money from a crook, you can never really stop taking other bribes and someone would always be able to blackmail you in the future.

The District Attorney was going to have to determine the full array of criminal charges and indictment levied against Jay for the arson fires and conspiracy acts, but the present evidence against Jay was circumstantial at this point; he could and would blame everything on Rick Conroy. Under these circumstances, Jay would make bail in several hours and be released on a minimum bail bond.

* * * * * * * * * * * * * * * * *

While Jay Blackhawk was busily engaged in trying to bribe the two police officers, another confrontation and drama was about to happen some ten miles away at the Casper General Hospital – currently the temporary residence for both Rick Conroy and Billy Coffler. On the seventh floor of the hospital Rick was lying motionless in his hospital bed, intravenous tubes were running into his left arm accompanied by an assortment of body replenishing fluids and a pain numbing morphine drip. The entire left side of his face was heavily bandaged from the pyrotechnic bomb that had prematurely exploded in his face several days ago. About 50 feet down the hall was the heavily guarded room of Billy Coffler, his guards were there to prevent entry from the over-eager press and other possible nefarious characters. After all, he was a prime and valuable Federal and State eyewitness to the recent fires.

The hospital room was private, and the TV station was airing news stories about the fire and its tragic results. The TV news story concluded with the status of Billy Coffler and Rick Conroy being among the best eye witnesses of the fire and that an investigation into the tragedy was in its preliminary stages. To date, Rick had given no salient details of the fire to anyone, he kept telling everyone that all of his recollections of the event were 'foggy blurs'. Yet Rick knew that it was only a matter of time before the investigators would come to grill him more intensely, yet he remained confident in his lying abilities; besides, he could always claim that he had simply blacked-out from sheer exposure during the wildfire and not recalling any of the sordid details. He was more worried about that young scientist who had stumbled upon his pyrotechnics and who was only a few dozen yards away down the hospital hallway. If Rick was lucky, this kid would have amnesia or a serious brain injury that would prevent him from remembering anything about the discovery of the fire bombs.

An hour earlier, Rick's old smoke jumper buddies had been around to visit him, one of them had smuggled in a fifth of whiskey – a bottle of Yukon Jack – the drinking favourite of Rick and many of the other fire fighters as well. Despite the doctor's prohibitions against any form of alcohol consumption, Rick was hitting the bottle, which was now only two-thirds filled. His guilt over causing the accidental death of Robin and the injury of several of his Smokie team mates during the arson fire was having its effect on his seemingly cold soul. He drowned his guilty conscious in alcohol. Light headed and a little unsteady, he sat up in his bed and crawled out of the hospital bed and made his way over to the bathroom to empty his bladder. Rick's stubborn independent nature did not cater to asking for the assistance of a hospital orderly or nurse.

While Rick was relieving himself in the toilet, the dim shadow of a man appeared silhouetted on the wall; the shadow was as eerie and cold as the man casting it. Both the shadow and its owner patiently awaited the appearance of the notorious Rick Conroy.

"Well, well, well – if it isn't the infamous Smoke Jumper himself or should I say arsonist and murderer!" Wayne boldly announced and with scornful bitterness as he boldly entered Rick's hospital room unannounced and quite unexpectedly. Wayne's face spit a look of contempt and hatred that could have killed a man by its sheer appearance alone. Yet Wayne's looks of animal vengeance were lost on a guilty man whose soul was as black and desolate as a cold winter's night.

"What the fuck do you want here, 'Boston'! Get the fuck out of here – my visiting hours are over and besides you're not welcome here, pal! Have you come here to gloat or to collect on your stinking bet? Funny, I never thought that you would have made it through the first few weeks of training, you really surprised me, 'Boston', you're tougher than I had thought! You won the frigging bet, don't you know that you are one lucky silver-spooned bastard? I'll mail you your frigging cheque!" Rick bitterly barked out loudly in defiant rage on seeing his nemesis, as he wheeled his hospital medicine dispersing pole around to his hospital bed, where he took up a seat upon its edge.

Wayne took a few more steps into the hospital room; he wanted to get closer to this fiend that had murdered his girlfriend. "That's what I like about you, Rick, you're at the end of your luck and even now you are so filled with hate and envy for me, that you do not have the courtesy to address me by either my first or last names. With all of that hatred and jealousy inside of you, I can guarantee that you will never be lonely in this life!" Rick looked away in obvious revulsion from Wayne's accusations, the sure sign of a guilty soul.

"It's all over for you, Conroy, there's a witness to your little arson job, that young scientist Billy Coffler – that's right, he's that kid who is lying unconscious in a room right down the hall from us and when he talks, both you and that crooked Indian lawyer Jay Blackhawk are finished." Wayne concluded dryly. The accusation was spot-on, yet Rick tried to put a tough face on his inner fears.

"Now you're just guessing and hoping that I will confess or say something stupid, well forget it, rich boy! You fucking got me shaking in my boots, 'Boston', they have nothing on me or anyone else, nothing can be proved and maybe that kid won't wake up to remember anything or maybe he won't wake-up at all!" if you get my drift?" Rick snapped back in a bitter, but certain tone.

Wayne knew that he was dealing with a soulless, desperate man – a true psychopath. "Can't get enough killing, can you! You are all washed-up, Conroy! You not only sold your soul for the almighty dollar, you also tried to kill me, and you also deserted your Smoke Jump team mates, all you ended up accomplishing was injuring a bunch of Smoke Jumpers, almost killed a young intern from the NWS and most of all you ended up killing the woman who I loved! Looking back, it's easy for me to realize that it was you all along, who was behind all those training mishaps, the broken pieces of equipment and accidents that were occurring to me these past months and which I had attributed to freaky luck – it seems like some guys can't stand losing either a bet or their girlfriend. I could easily hire some goons to make your life a living hell, but instead I'm going to let you live each day with the guilt of what you did to Robin! Your jealousy and hatred did this to you, Rick, not the fire! Now you just have yourself a nice recovery, Conroy, and I hope that you are looking forward to the investigations and trial that are coming your way – prison is going to be your next home. You were the brawn and Jay was the brains behind your little arson plan, correct? I want you and Jay Blackhawk to go to trial and to get your legal punishment. The proof of your guilt, you will wear on your face, like the mark of Caine. Every day for the rest of your natural, shitty life, you'll be forced to live with your scarred face! Each look into the mirror, will reflect the scars of anger and envy that led you to kill the one woman in the world that you wanted most," Wayne spluttered out bitterly into Rick's bandaged face.

"You rich, eastern bastard! You fucking spoiled SOB! Born with a silver spoon in your flipping mouth too! You never had to break your ass for a pay cheque or worry about rent or money matters, now did you? Now you get out! You get the fuck out of my room 'Boston'!" Rick shouted loudly, as a nurse and a burly orderly came running down the hallway to uncover the source of the boisterous commotion.

"Sir, what on earth are you doing here! Don't you know that visiting hours are over and you're upsetting this very sick man? I must insist that you leave immediately or do we need to eject you physically?" the startled nurse shouted as she and the orderly went over to Rick and tried to assist him back down into the hospital bed.

"Sure thing, nurse, I was just leaving anyway, I don't have anything left to say to this piece of shit anyway!" Wayne shouted in disgust as a hospital orderly escorted Wayne to the elevator and out of the hospital.

Rick obeyed the nurse and got back into the hospital bed, this as a mere ruse to placate her and get her on her way.

Sombrely, Rick sat down on his bed and pondered his fate as he took another mouthful of Yukon Jack. In a half drunken haze, he pondered Wayne's self-righteous words and strangely enough, he was haunted by the truth. In an act of curiosity and desperation, he carefully scurried out of his bed and walked a few steps into the hospital bathroom and turned on the lights. Desperation and guilt were his constant counsel, yet he needed to know the truth, no matter how ugly, no matter what the cost! He looked into the mirror at the bandaged pitiful creature gazing back at him. Impulsively and defiantly, he quickly ripped off the bandage from the left side of his face! The gross deformed reflection immediately appalled and frightened him. He almost fainted at the horrible image that the mirror reflected back to him.

From the mirror's candid reflection, a hideous unrecognizable blackened mass of swollen and oozing tissue punctuated by a pale blue eye surrounded by bright red ruptured blood vessels, mockingly greeted him. His once handsome face was now like that of a monster from a cheap grade B movie thriller. He wanted to vomit from the gross sickening sight, yet he forced himself to view his face again, this time in a deeper and more prolonged stare. Rick calmly examined the monstrous image for some minutes before turning away in disgust and with resigned acceptance of his future physical fate.

'No fucking amount of plastic surgery was going to make me a whole man again,' he concluded silently. Rick didn't bother to cover up his hideous disfigured face again with the bandage, 'of what use would that be at this point?' he thought. He wearily limped back to his bed, tears running slowly down his blackened disfigured face. He took another full swig of Yukon Jack from the now half-consumed bottle and slumbered off into a twilight dream-state of things that were never to be.

Yet unbeknownst to Rick, Jay Blackhawk's 'Plan B' was even now going into effect. The highly paid and highly skilled pair of assassins were even now in the process of tying up some 'loose ends'. Each assassin was at the top of his craft and both were discreetly attired in pale green hospital orderly uniforms. Only a mere 50 feet down the hallway from Rick's room was Billy Coffler's hospital room. It was there that the assassins made their first move. They created a simple diversion by setting a small fire bomb in the hospital foyer area accompanied along with a loud explosive report device. As calculated, the hospital's emergency siren sounded off loudly. The guards who were placed to guard over Billy's room, rushed out to investigate the commotion.

Immediately after the guards had left, the two assassins entered Billy's room, they each withdrew a .22 calibre Ruger sound suppressed pistol, quickly emptying 20 projectiles into the sheet-covered, curled-up figure. The hapeless figure recoiled slightly from the deadly volley of shots. So accurate were their aim that no other hospital equipment or medical device items were destroyed in the hail of silent deadly bullets. It was a perfect silent killing.

The two assassins each looked at each other, they smiled and nodded to one another, then they re-loaded their pistols, ready to execute their next target – Rick Conroy. Jay Blackhawk had originally only wanted to kill the critical witness, Billy Coffler, but then just this morning, Jay figured that he might be able to get rid himself of all the parties involved for just a few thousands of dollars more and he would not have to pay-out the money with anyone. Rick was to be a second target of opportunity, if the assassins did not kill Rick, then Jay would simply pay him off as originally planned. None of this was personal, it was all just a matter of business and fortunate opportunity.

Just as the two assassins left Billy's room, they were confronted by police officers from the Wyoming State Attorney General's office and the Wyoming State Police. The police officers were covertly posted and lying in-wait for just such an eventuality. Someone in the Wyoming Justice Department was wise enough to suspect that foul play would befall Billy Coffler and ordered the additional guards to be placed in a very discreet hiding location which offered a direct view of Billy's room. The hunch had paid off handsomely.

"Stop right there, you guys! Just hold it right there and drop the guns!" the police shouted loudly. The assassins were true professionals and instead of meekly surrendering to the police as a normal criminal is often inclined to do; they quickly and professionally turned their weapons to the direction of the voices. The assassins knew that if they were quick enough and accurate enough, they might shoot at the police and make a clean get-away. However, as the assassins turned to confront the police, there was a sudden roar from two 12-gauge Benelli automatic shotguns. The thunderous report of the shotguns could be heard all the way down to Rick's room. After the firing had ceased, the two assassins lay motionless and bleeding in the hallway of the hospital in a pool of bright crimson blood, which visually attested to the severity of their wounds and the effectiveness of the shotguns.

One assassin was dead on the spot, while the other was seriously wounded. Buzzers and alarms throughout the hospital went off. An emergency medical team was rushed to render emergency care to the wounded assassin. The police dearly wanted this man alive so that he could testify in court as to who had hired him. It was clear that the State Police and Attorney General's office had set up their own 'sting' operation in anticipation of just such an event. The stories of Billy's presence had deliberately been leaked to the press to ensure that everyone knew of his location and condition. In reality, Billy Coffler was actually located in another state and he was recovering quite nicely. He would be able to make acute testimony in any future trial or legal proceedings.

The roar of shotguns suddenly awakened Rick from his blissful morphine and alcohol induced twilight sleep. He could now hear the screaming of the police officers just a short distance away. Rick became aware that something foul was afoot in the hospital and that he was in imminent danger. Rick wrongly concluded that the assassins were still alive and had killed Billy Coffler with shotguns and that they were even now on their way to kill him too!

In a nervous fit, Rick pulled out all the intravenous tubes that were connected into his arm – causing small spurts of blood and medical fluids to fly wildly into the air and onto his hospital gown and the floor. He quickly took a chair and placed it beneath the door room handle. This crude door-brace would afford him several precious minutes of time.

There was a sudden nudge of the room door. "Let us in, Conroy, open up this door now! This is the police!" a voice echoed through the heavy door. Although the assassins were not coming to kill him, the police would soon have him in custody. He was now facing a situation that in his mind, was as dire as that of being assassinated – indictment, trial and a life-long prison sentence! He needed another way out!

The fact that Billy was alive along with one of the wounded assassins and the discovery of the $2 million in his car trunk – all ensured that Rick was in very deep trouble, even if Rick was unaware of all these proceedings. The combination of morphine and alcohol was making Rick's actions clumsy and uncoordinated. He grabbed the bottle of Yukon Jack and walked unsteadily toward the window. The pounding and pushes made against the door became even more amplified. Rick opened the hospital window and crawled up onto the window sill. Suddenly the sturdy door flung open and several police and a nurse rushed into the room. They were stopped by the horrific sight of a man in a white hospital gown sitting precariously upon the window sill with a horribly blackened, burnt face. Rick was resolved to his fate, it mattered not that it was the police or assassins that found him out - the game was up, and he had no cards left to play, save one.

"Hey fuckers, I want you all to know that it was Jay Blackhawk and me who were responsible for the two massive wildfires... we wanted to get the Wind River Indian reservation land for a casino resort deal. Jay provided the money and the incendiaries, but I alone was responsible for injuring my crew, setting the fires, wounding Billy and killing the woman I loved – Robin. You can consider this the testimony of a dying man...this is my dying confession!" Rick shouted loudly as he took another big swig of whiskey and made a crude sign of the cross across his chest.

"No, don't do it, Conroy! Come down off the ledge Rick, it's not worth it," pleaded the police officer.

"You're 100% correct, officer, it's not worth it, my life is not worth it, none of what I did was worth it! I did it all – I started the fires, I killed Robin and tried to kill 'Boston' too – me and Jay planned it all, we're guilty as sin! May the Lord have mercy on my soul!" Rick sobbed as he passed out and rolled out of the hospital window sill and onto the hard concrete seven storeys below. The police SWAT (Special Weapons And Tactics) team looked on in helpless horror and the on-looking nurse shrieked a blood-curdling scream.

There was an audible low, squashy-like thud which everyone knew was the impact of Rick's body hitting the hard-concrete surface. They all raced to the window to visibly confirm that which they already knew. There Rick lay dead on the concrete sidewalk; his head lay shattered and bleeding by the sudden hard impact. It seems that this dying man's testimony was more than enough information for the prosecution to put all of the pieces of the puzzle together and to get an indictment of murder, arson and conspiracy against Jay Blackhawk. This was now an Iron-Clad legal case.

* * * * * * * * * * * * * * * * *

The intentional confrontation with Rick Conroy had failed for Wayne, it brought neither emotional relief nor spiritual closure for Robin's death. Revenge was an unsatisfying beast! Riding in Robin's massive Dodge Ram pick-up, Wayne drove for many miles with no destination in mind, yet as if on auto-pilot, he discovered that he was driving the same rode that he had driven all summer-long, to Chief Joseph's tavern.

This sweet farewell merited one last visitation! His memories were mostly fond ones! A little over three months had passed since he came to Chief Joseph's Tavern, yet it seemed as if it had been a lifetime. The past summer had amended his life, he had made peace with the passing of his family and the resolution of his prejudices. Additionally, he had forged new diverse friendships, discovered himself, found love, and the meaning of loyalty - all good things that were worth keeping alive in both spirit and in deed.

Driving up to the front of the now seasonally vacated tavern, Wayne spotted his constant summer pals, Chief Joseph, Tom Hawks and Sammy. The crowds and ruckus of fire fighters and strong drinking lumber jacks had faded with the passing of the Labor Day weekend and the sun was setting ever lower and earlier each evening amiss the early cool comfortable September nights.

"Hello, my dear friends, I simply wanted to stop by and say one final goodbye to the people who made my summer so memorable... your friendship has meant a great deal to me, it's in saying farewell to all of you, that I realize how much I am going to miss every one of you enormously... we're all part of each other's lives now!" Wayne confessed with sadness in his voice as his eyes welled up with tears.

"Wayne, you're the lucky one! You made a lot of friends and performed many dangerous, heroic things this past summer. We also know how much Robin's loss is for you and hope that you find peace and happiness again in your life – go and live the life that you were bornn to live," Sammy remarked. Her words echoed the sentiments of everyone present.

"I'll never forget Robin or anyone else here," Wayne tearfully confessed.

"So, I reckon you'll be heading back to Boston, my young son?" Chief Joseph inquired in a fatherly tone.

"Yeah, Chief, I guess so, I have some unfinished business matters and a very impatient and demanding fiancée back there, along with other responsibilities that I need to manage. I've stopped running away from my past, instead I am heading toward my future, Chief," Wayne remarked with a tone of sad resignation.

"Hey Tom, I'm offering to you my BMW motorcycle. The old one that I wrecked was a total loss, so my insurance company compensated me the market value and I added some cash to the deal and received a new bike. Robin's parents have gifted me with her restored Harley Road King, so do you want the BMW?" Wayne asked to the startled youth whose eyes became as big as onions.

"Boy, do I ever! You don't need to ask me twice about that offer! I'd be loco not to take advantage of your generosity, Mr Hamilton, thanks a million."

"All the registration papers are in the BMW saddlebags, we can do the transfer any time that you want, just contact my business assistant, here's my business card," Wayne remarked as he handed Tom Hawk his Hamilton & MacAlister personal business card. "I have left the bike in safekeeping at the BMW dealership, so you can merely pick it up there, I have made all the arrangements myself, Tom," Wayne exclaimed in conclusion.

"Well since we are in the mood for gift giving, I've got a little something for you too, my old friend. Life's a little dangerous on the open roads out here in the West, so an independent man like you needs a little protection." The Chief pulled Wayne aside into the tavern and handed to him a wrapped-up towel from beneath the bar. Wayne unwrapped the heavy towel and discovered an old, but well-preserved Colt 1911 .45 automatic pistol and several ammunition magazines. Wayne was dumbfounded.

"This was my service pistol from Vietnam, it took care of me in the jungle and I hope it will also protect and serve you as well. With my advancing arthritis and slow reactions, a pistol is of little practical use for me, I'll rely on my big old reliable 12-gauge shotgun instead." The old Chief grinned as he patted Wayne gently on the shoulder.

"Thanks, a hell of a lot, Chief, I'll just keep it tucked into my pants when I ride the Harley," Wayne exclaimed as he shook Chief Joseph's hand and patted him on the back.

"Just make sure that you don't go shooting your dick off with that old Colt 1911 tucked into your pants, remember that you got a fiancée back home that's waiting for all the working parts of you!" the old Chief crudely joked as he parted paths with his young friend. The old Chief was going to miss this energetic easterner.

"You know something, Chief, I'd like to send some technical experts out here to the reservation and do a thorough evaluation of the tribe's land holdings and perhaps see what potential exists for the land from both a natural resource and development perspective, I'll pay for the entire cost, the findings will be sent to you and the tribal elders – with your permission of course, sir?" Wayne stated in an earnest rhetorical fashion.

The Chief thought about the proposition, then he broke into a broad smile. "That is very generous, my friend, after all progress itself is not evil, it's more a matter of how someone treats the land and its people that makes a thing either good or bad, correct? Thank you."

The two men smiled and shook hands once more before Wayne made his final farewells and got back into the Dodge Ram. He was leaving in the morning and all he wanted to do now was to get back to his hotel room and get packed for the journey back East the following morning. He hugged Sammy one last time before leaving the reservation for good. Sammy was sorry to see Wayne leave, yet she wisely thought it better not to reveal Robin's pregnancy, this little secret could serve no one for the better and it would only make Wayne's loss all the more bitter. She wisely decided to let the secret remain between herself and her dead girlfriend.

After Wayne had departed from her life, Sammy was wrapped in depression over the loss of her girlfriend and the discovery of an unknown father. She stayed at the tavern until late into the evening hours, doing something that she normally never would have done by herself – getting dead-ass drunk and depressed on hard liquor. Her drink of destruction for the evening was Jack Daniels Black Label; a smooth, silky and somewhat smoky tasting refreshment that packed a punch on a lonely evening. She stopped counting the rounds after her third glass. Sam was feeling mighty lonely this evening, her best girlfriend had been murdered by a fellow co-worker, her friends were all departing, and she had a fiery hatred for a man whom she had believed to be long dead in Vietnam, a virtual stranger who had now suddenly popped back into her adulthood to declare his belated fatherhood to her! Life certainly sucked for her this past fire season, she never wanted to see the pathetic face of that old burned-out Vietnam Viet, Hank Ransome. She couldn't help feeling the lies, cowardice and abandonment that he had done to both herself and her deceased mother.

'That bastard old guy was a real rat fink, PTSD or no-PTSD, he was a man who simply ran away from his family obligations and that was unforgivable,' Sammy cursed silently in her mind as she gulped another mouthful of sour mash whiskey.

"Why don't you go home, Sammy, alcohol will not solve any of your problems," Chief Joseph consoled in a fatherly tone, hoping to get Sammy to quit her drinking and go quietly home.

Sammy simply smiled back and remarked, "Yeah sure, I know that, Chief, but at least the bourbon makes me forget my recently discovered and very worthless 'old man', you know that guy Hank, he's claiming to be my long lost father – now are you buying that shit!"

"Everyone makes mistakes in this life, Sammy, even your parents! You have to forgive and forget in order to move on; it's no good to ponder on the past – it's over and no one can change it," Chief Joseph remarked with a confessing tone. Sammy was not up to hearing any words of advice as she grabbed the bottle of Jack Daniels and re-filled her empty glass once more.

"Amen, Chief! We all make mistakes and mine was in coming to the fire camp this summer, if I hadn't been here and helped to instigate that stupid bet against Wayne, none of this bad shit would have happened! Everything would have been good just as in past summers…I'm not sure if I'll ever come back here again! This place only haunts me now," Sammy lamented as she sipped more of the intoxicating distilled brew.

Chief Joseph was going to say more comforting words to Sammy, when suddenly the roar of motorcycles broke the melody of the evening confessional episode to which he and Sam were engrossed. "Just who in the hell is it that is coming here at this hour at this time of the season?"

the old Chief barked in bewilderment and irritation. The saloon bat wing doors soon exploded with thunderous entrances of six familiar and most unwelcome patrons.

"I told you, old man, that we would be back! This time it's on our terms too and not yours!" bellowed a menacing voice from the recent past. A look of horror and astonishment painted the faces of Chief Joseph and Sammy. The voice belonged to no other than Vic – the bad ass biker and his gang of motorcycle thugs.

"What's the matter, old Indian Chief? You look like you just saw General Custer or something!" Vic laughed insultingly.

"We're closing up here and besides, you're not welcome here, so go away!" Chief Joseph announced in an almost challenging tone. Vic and all his gang smiled and then began to laugh, which then turned to mocking laughter.

"What's the matter, old Indian? Are you prejudiced against African Americans, whites and Hispanics? We're your loyal customers and we want whiskey, right, guys?" Vic yelled as he and the other five gang members walked up to the bar and took control of it. Some of the gang walked up behind the bar and boldly took bottles off the shelves to help themselves.

"Hey, you can't go behind my bar and do that!" the old man yelled. A swift, hard punch in Chief Joseph's face by Vic quickly stopped his vocal protests.

"Hey, old fucking Indian, it looks like you have no big crowds or a crew of lumberjacks to come to your rescue this time, huh!" Vic mockingly teased as he stood astride over the befallen humiliated old man.

"Lookie here, old Indian, you don't look so big now lying there on the floor!" Vic yelled as he kicked Chief Joseph several times in the stomach.

"Stop it, you're hurting him! You're nothing but a fucking bully bastard!" Sammy cried out as she jumped atop of Vic, while frantically trying to slap at his face. Startled by the sudden attack by this young wildcat, Vic spun around from stomping the old man and threw Sammy off of his back. Helpless in pain, Chief Joseph laid on his side, struggling to reach into his pockets for something.

"Well, well…if it isn't Miss Brown Sugar herself! I've been having some nasty dreams about you, girl! My…my…my, now you're in a mighty testy mood this evening and I do like my ladies high strung and frisky," Vic laughed as he quickly bitch-slapped Sammy across the face; the quick meeting of his open hand with Sammy's face, made for aloud audible sound. Vic proceeded to throw Sammy against one of the bar walls. She was caught off-guard by his attack and she had the wind knocked out of her lungs temporarily, leaving her gasping for air and in a weakened state. Vic was determined to have his lustful way with his young filly. Disoriented and hurting, Sammy was in no physical shape to put up much of a fight against her brutal attacker.

"Yo, I'm going to take this mustang bitch into the other room and teach her some loving lessons from a real-man, the rest of you guys go and find any money and valuables around this two-bit joint," Vic remarked to his gang as he pulled Sammy by her hair in to the tavern's adjoining billiard room.

Sammy regained her strength and swung both of her fists at her attacker, she had managed to strike Vic's face and chest, but these had no effect on him except to make him even angrier. "You really are a little tigress," Vic smiled demonically.

"You fucking bastard, stay away from me!" Sammy yelled, but Vic only laughed more. Sammy tried to do a groin-kick, but Vic got one of her legs and flipped Sammy back onto her back. She hit the floor hard and hit her head against the hard-wooden planked floors. There was an audible thud when she hit the floor and she screamed out with pain. Sammy was almost to the point of exhaustion, but she fought to stay awake and to fight off her attacker. Sammy screamed as loud as she could as Vic picked her up off of the floor, slapped her across the mouth and threw her down hard onto the billiard table.

"Hey bitch, I' m going to see now whether or not you're half-white or half-black this evening," Vic yelled as he tore Sammy's blouse and bra off, his hands rubbing her ample breasts in his rough and uninviting hands. Sammy struggled to resist, but she was unable to leverage any of her muscles against this hulking beast of a man. Vic had Sammy pinned spread-eagle atop the billiard table, he was ripping at her jeans and he had her pants down to her ankles.

Suddenly, there was a cold metallic feeling around Vic's throat, a pressure that was sudden, strong and cutting off his oxygen. Vic gasped for air like a fish being angled out of the water. He suddenly jerked back from atop Sammy and down onto the ground in a sudden jerk-like movement.

"So, you like to beat up and rape young women, fella, well how about trying out this old black man for size instead?" a gravelled, deep-throated male voice shouted with vengeance. It was Hank Ransome wielding his infamous German Army entrenching tool, a nasty field entrenching device that was about two-foot long, with a sharp metal top that was half spade, half-pointed pike – it was a deadly instrument that was the equal of a bayonet atop a battle rifle. Vic fell to the floor, as Hank went to the aid of his estranged daughter. Sammy was hurt, but not seriously injured – at least not yet anyway.

"You fight good for a cherry-picking old black man, but you ain't no match for me, you broken-down, old mother fucker! I'm going to kill you slowly, then I'm going to fuck the ass off that half-breed bitch over there, maybe cut her up a bit afterward so that no other man looks at her pretty face no more!" Vic crudely taunted as he arose from the floor with a dagger in one hand and a swinging metal chain in the opposite hand.

Vic sprung on Hank, as the whirling metal chain barely missed his face. Sammy ran to the other side of the room, half naked and terrorized by the attack. Hank quickly tweaked his entrenching tool, so that the sharpened spade blade was in the full-open position, this would afford him a better striking weapon, much like that of an edged weapon.

Vic kept attacking and advancing against his older foe. He threw another lightning-like throw of the swirling chain at the old man, but Hank moved quickly, and the energy of the metal chain ripped into the velour of the green-topped billiard table and exposing the black slate slab beneath. It was another close call for Hank's stamina and he was rapidly fading against the vigour and hatred possessed by the younger man. Hand-to-hand combat was exhausting to the body and a young man's body inherently possessed the fighting advantage.

Vic quickly recovered his attack position and aimed directly for the top of Hank's body. In gladiator-like fashion, Hank defensively raised his entrenching tool, which caught the momentum and whirling chain around the main handle shaft of the entrenching shovel. The whirling metal chain neatly wrapped around the wooden handle like a silver coloured snake. Yet ever so deftly, Vic quickly pulled on his end of the chain and both the chain and the entangled entrenching tool went flying into the air and across the room. Now Hank was left defenceless, but Vic still had a deadly back-up, a double-edged dagger. Vic made quick advances toward Hank to test out the old man's reaction speeds and defensive strategies.

Without missing a beat, Hank quickly threw off his jacket and wrapped it around his left arm as a form of padded defence to block against the impending knife attack. Both men knew that with a dagger weapon, the best mortal wound was to be that of a piercing wound that was thrust into the vital organ of the body, while a slashing wound would produce less lethal cuts to the body, its slim blade not being optimized for inflicting the more serious slashing type knife wounds. In order to get this old man killed quickly, Vic would have to get in close and that would be the time when he was also the most vulnerable.

Like an aggressive wild animal, Vic couched low and with both feet shoulder-length apart, a sound strategy for balance and stability. Craftily, he circled Hank like a preying wolf, keeping his angry eyes all the while on this old cunning black man. Hank knew that he could not match this young buck, muscle-for-muscle or move-for-move; instead he needed to find a way to disarm his opponent without mortally wounding himself and this meant that he would need to employ the tactics of surprise and cunning.

Hank maintained his agility by constantly moving and deflecting each knife slash made to his body. After a few minutes, his former suede jacket was in tattered shreds from the constant dagger slashing. The hand-to-hand assaults had been exhausting and Hank was breathing like an exhausted prize fighter. Vic made a sudden rush at Hank, but Hank deflected the assault by waving his jacket padded arm into Vic's face, temporarily disorienting Vic, while also managing to knock the dagger from Vic's hand and the knife flew across to the other side of the room.

Now weaponless, Vic responded by quickly hitting Hank with a strong left-hook punch, sending Hank to the floor. Sammy quickly seized this opportunity to run to the other side of the room. As Vic ran to get his dagger off the floor, Sammy quickly untangled and grasped the entrenching tool that had been flung aside during the melee. Vic quickly ran and retrieved his knife and with the knife now back in his hand, he quickly turned around to finish off the old black man.

"Time to die, old black man!" Vic spat forth with primal glee. His charge was interrupted by a loud feminine voice.

"Daddy, here, quick!" Sammy shouted as she deftly threw Hank the entrenching tool. Loudly, a murderous scream pierced the room! It was Vic, screaming with venomous rage in a lunging assault toward Hank, but he was stopped dead in his tracks.

Fiercely, Hank threw the sharpened trowel forcefully into Vic's main torso. The entrenching tool impaled itself deeply into Vic's torso; it penetrated at least six inches into the mid-section of the body cavity. Vic fell head forward toward the floor and he fell face-forward with a loud thud, this further impaled the entrenching tool further into his body and fatally rupturing many body organs and arteries. A death gurgle ensured, and a pool of bright crimson blood proliferated the floor ever so slowly and generously so.

Suddenly, the Wind River Police arrived into the melee. Reservation Sheriff Dave Carney led a group of six reservation police officers, each armed with either MP5 sub-machine guns or a Benelli automatic tactical shotguns - deftly into the tavern. Billy Hawk was hiding out in one of the Tavern's more remote areas and he had wisely called the Wind River Police from his cell phone. They first entered the main tavern area and arrested two of the hoodlums in the act of pillaging the cash register; the other motorcycle bandits were caught in the back-office rooms. Upon entering the billiard section of the tavern, Sheriff Carney spotted a dead youthful black man lying in a large scarlet pool of blood with a shorthanded shovel impaled in his centre stomach cavity. The Sheriff turned over Vic's lifeless body. The man's eyes and mouth were wide open, and it was quite obvious that he was dead. There in a darkened corner of the room, he spotted a half-clothed woman and an older man, each sobbing in one another's tearful embrace.

"I still hate you …. why weren't you there for us, Daddy?" Sammy pleaded as she poured out her tears that were decades in the making.

Hank didn't have the right words to justify his actions, but he tried to console his long-lost daughter. "No excuses! Honey child, your dad became a broken man from the war, I too cried for friends killed and maimed, I turned to drugs and before I knew it, I was a drug addict hooked on heroin…by the time I got myself straightened-out, your mom had moved on with her life and I thought it best to do the same with mine. I guess that I was just a coward who couldn't face reality," Hank soberly confessed.

Sammy continued her rage that had built up over the years. "I still can't forgive you. I hate you for what you did to mom and me," Sammy confessed, as she rested her head on Hank's chest; it was a good feeling to be hugged after the malicious attack. Hank said nothing as he tightly held Sammy in his arms, she was his one and only remaining family member that he had left in this world and it was good to feel her trembling embraces.

The old man's tears instantly betrayed the young man's laments and sins. These had been dammed up for decades. Hank's tears flowed in warm streams down his bloodied face.

"That's okay, my little Baby Girl, I'll take your hatred for now, it's more comforting than having no one in my old ass life...I'll take hatred over loneliness any day of the week Baby Girl," Hank asserted as he sobbed and tightly caressed his daughter in his arms.

* * * * * * * * * * * * * * * * * * *

After checking out of his motel and leaving a rather generous tip of $2,000 to the maid staff, Wayne took Robin's massive Dodge Ram along with its bed-nested custom Harley Road King and departed from Wyoming. He was headed home, but this time he was making a slight detour- this made by heading up northeast toward the I-90 Inter-state highway. A lot had happened to him this summer and Wayne thought it wise to start to head back East in a leisurely manner. He hadn't spoken to Katherine for several days and her calls had gone unanswered and he knew that he owed her a call before she called out the State Police or FBI. He thought it ironic, that Katherine was the closest person and friend that he now had left in this world, yet he had thought so infrequently of her these past weeks. It was as if this past summer had existed exclusive of Katherine in Wayne's life. He thought the less of himself for being so self-centred and leaving Kate alone in Boston, he vowed silently to make amends with her.

His hedeonistic summer sojourn had ended, he had to face the reality that his playing games with ordinary working Americans was over, it was a one-time lark and a fiction that could not last, and he appreciated this reality. Robin's death had ended his summer dreams of being an 'everyman', now he had to face the reality of being a proper Boston banker and respected member of the Boston upper-crust community with all the expectations, roles, veneers and phoniness that this role dictated. This conformity was going to be an unwelcome change for him, yet he was now resolved to live his Boston life on his own terms and not those of his social clan, he had finally become his own person.

He started out late, so the daylight was burning fast, this first day's road trip was to be a very short one. He turned on the radio and engulfed himself on an auditory diet of country and western music, along with some classic Rock tunes. After a few short hours, he had left Wyoming behind in his rear-view mirror and in front of him awaited South Dakota and the Great Plains. The road ahead was free of any major traffic. He was getting tired, so he cracked open the windows and allowed a cool gush of air to freshen out the truck's stale air. Even now in early September, the daytime air was getting cooler, with highs only in the mid-70's and nights going down into the 40's and 50's. Wayne pushed the massive Dodge Ram diesel and it responded without hesitation, the mighty vehicle had no problems cruising along at 85 mph and there was little in the way of traffic and road conditions were superior.

By dusk, he had crossed into the state of South Dakota. Road signs boldly announced the names of old west folklore towns of which he had heard of in conversations, but which he had never actually visited. The names of Spearfish, Deadwood, and Sturgis materialized in the form of roadside advertisements for food and shelter. Having driven all day, Wayne wisely decided that 'night-time was right-time' for calling it a day, so he turned the Dodge Ram into the first large town in South Dakota that he came into – Spearfish. He spotted an advertisement for the Ramada Inn. It was as good a place as any to spend a night.

He grabbed a quick, largely unmemorable meal in the hotel's dining room and then prepared himself for a restful sleep. He owed Katherine a call too and she would be miffed at him for not having called her earlier. Sometimes the only thing worse than talking with the narcissist Katherine was not talking to her at all. He threw off his shoes, sat down in a relaxing chair and speed-dialled Katherine's personal phone number. Her phone rang, but Wayne merely received an answering prompt from Katherine's home phone number. He suddenly realized that although it was 6:00 PM central time, it was only 4:00 PM in Boston, so Wayne hung up and re-dialled Katherine's office phone number. The phone rang several times before it was picked up.

"Hello", an attractive feminine voice responded, "this is Katherine MacAlister," the voice echoed. It was at once both a familiar and welcoming voice, something that echoed of home, security and familiarity.

"Hello yourself, Kate, it's Brad…I'm sorry for not calling more frequently, am I forgiven, darling?" Wayne announced almost apologetically.

Kate was both stunned and gratified by both the sound and tone of her fiancé. "Wow it's great to hear from you! Are you all right? Where are you? When are you coming back home to me?" Kate sounded off in her traditional frantic manner. Usually detached and reserved in business matters, she was quite another person in the affairs of the heart, often displaying wells of emotion and almost childlike euphoria. This was a woman who could negotiate a hundred-million dollar deal without exhibiting the slightest trace of emotion, yet who became like an excited child on Christmas morning at the sound of her fiancé. It seemed that everyone was indeed an actor in life, everyone acting like chameleons according to circumstances, people and events.

"Yes, Kate, thanks for asking about me, I'm fine, I'm great...I'm in South Dakota and I am coming home, maybe in a week or less. I miss you and my friends back in Boston, I want to come back home, this trip is finished with me, I'm not running away any more!" Wayne spouted in a sudden explosion of unplanned words. Katherine was elated to say the least.

"Are you really all right, Brad, I mean are you really okay...I mean regarding the past and your family, honey?" Katherine inquired in a gentle prodding manner.

There were a few seconds of pause on the other end of the line, as Wayne thought of a fond memory of his dead family and that of Robin too.

"You bet that I am! I'm fine with my past, I'm all right now, my head is clear for the first time in my life; in fact, I am letting the dead lay in their places of repose," Wayne definitively replied back softly to Katherine.

"Thank God...what a relief to hear, my darling. Honey, I hope that you don't travel back on that crazy, dangerous BMW motorcycle...I almost fainted the last time that I heard you had an accident on that crazy thing...promise me you won't be coming back on that thing, darling?" Katherine pleaded intensely.

"Now that's a promise that I can make and keep, Kate! I no longer have the BMW motorcycle and in fact, I have a four-wheel drive vehicle that I got from a friend out here in Wyoming that I am driving leisurely back to Boston," Wayne responded with a half-truth, not divulging his acquisition of Robin's massive and powerful Harley Davidson Custom Road King.

He felt guilty for not being faithful to Katherine. He was not going to lie to her about his road affairs; then again, he was not volunteering any information either. He had dodged the truth, yet his silence was still dishonest. He relaxed himself into his hotel chair and sipped a scotch before dozing off to a well-deserved sleep. The long drive had exhausted him more than he had anticipated.

Brad's phone call was the emotional elixir that Katherine needed for a late day pick-me-up. Her thoughts became excited about seeing Brad once again and the thoughts of a magnificent New England Autumn wedding once again filled her imagination. Her spirits swelled with the anticipation of a young girl. Her vacant lover was coming back into her life along with her dream wedding to her childhood sweetheart. Her thoughts were interrupted by the all too human necessity to use the powder room. Her private office bathroom was under repair due to a pipe leakage and the work was to last several days. Begrudgingly, Katherine suffered the indignity of having to use the quite elegant, but public ladies' room down the hallway.

The indignity of using the common staff ladies' room at Hamilton & MacAlister did not suit Katherine one damn bit, she cringed each time she had to use the facility. She could tell that the other ladies resented her, and she felt their cold shoulders and silence whenever she entered the ladies' room. It was getting late in the working day and Katherine hoped that there would not be many other ladies using the facility, she was uncomfortable mingling with the common office workers, as she shared little of their activities, concerns or small talk. Life was lonely for a beautiful, intelligent and wealthy woman like Katherine, but her own personality and prejudices had constructed this canyon of genteel partition with the common folks.

As Katherine entered the first door of the Hamilton & MacAlister Ladies' room, she entered into a small, but lushly attired and feminine accented vestibule that then led to the inner door of the women's lavatory. Immediately, she was stopped by a conversation of two women; she waited to overhear the conversation of the two women – they were both talking loudly and joking like giddy schoolgirls. Katherine gave pause to allow the ladies to finish up their social chat before she entered

Although she rarely gossiped at work, Katherine was intrigued by the frank conversation of the women that worked there and whose company she stood distantly apart due to her position at the firm and her formal upbringing. Yet she was intrigued by the conversation, which was clearly audible from the vestibule and she clearly recognized one of the voices as belonging to her office nemesis, Margie DeTagelio. Katherine would prudently wait until this conversation was over, she might even hear something interesting or incriminating too, she cunningly thought to herself.

The two women speaking were indeed that of Margie DeTagelio and her office girlfriend, Gail Meyers, the central receptionist for the firm. The two ladies had been having some 'girl talk' in what they had thought was the privacy of the Ladies room. The chat inevitably revolved around work life and this inevitably meant the subject of Katherine MacAlister.

"That Boston Bitch is really on the rag this week; in fact, she's been on a bitch-tear ever since Brad left a few months ago. I guess some women get really bitchy when they don't get a piece of a man for a while," Margie crudely announced with a broad and self-satisfying smile, as she applied some eye-liner.

"Come on now! Is she really that hard of a woman to work for, she seems okay to me," Gail Meyers replied in a most innocent tone, almost in Katherine's defence.

"Fuck, that rich bitch! 'Kit Kat' is one mean snobby-bitch, she thinks everyone is after her man or after her money or some other shit like that, she just hates me just because I'm younger than she is and that I get along well with everyone around here and she doesn't....I guess money can't buy everything, right? You know that 'Kit Kat' thinks her shit doesn't stink, but her farts give her away," Margie exclaimed with a crude, girlish laughter. Both women were in a fit of hysterical laughter at Katherine's expense.

Unexpectantly, the room was filled with a large banging sound, as the main bathroom door was shoved open wide and Katherine directly walked in on the two ladies' conversation with a menacing, deadly serious expression.

"I don't pay my employees to talk trash in the ladies' room, get the hell back to work now or else!" Katherine shouted in an angry tone. Neither woman knew how much of their conversation that 'Kit Kat' MacAlister had heard, but Katherine had heard the entire crass discourse! 'Kit Kat' was fuming. She was not a woman to be spoken of in rude terms by one of her own employees, especially by DeTagelio.

Embarrassed by Katherine's menacing presence, the two women meekishly started to leave the ladies' room with Gail in the lead. After Gail had passed through into the vestibule area, Margie followed, but suddenly Katherine's arm was raised up to the wall, which blocked Margie's anxious exit. "Now you just stay right here with me, DeTagelio! You and I are going to have a little counselling session about your life here at Hamilton & MacAlister."

Margie looked like a disarmed and guilty schoolchild caught in the act of some elementary schoolyard prank, but this was not elementary school and the lesson to be learned here were livelihood issues. "Now you look here, girlie, you little whore, the game is up for you here at Hamilton & MacAlister...you're nothing but a little fucking office tramp! I've put up with your flirting and ass wiggling antics for far too long, but I'll be damned if I am going to be insulted in my own place of business by the likes of you. Your time here is almost over, Brad's coming back soon and we're getting married. That means that there will be only one woman to distract Brad around here and that's me, honey buns. You're on official notice, I want your flirting ass out of here in two weeks, the sooner the better in fact! Do you understand, DeTagelio?" Katherine sternly demanded as she looked sternly and directly into Margie's tear-filled eyes.

"Yes, Miss Katherine, but I'm sorry for anything that you overheard or misinterpreted, it was just some silly girl-talk, you know!" Margie replied defensively.

"Hah, the only thing that you're sorry about, girlie, is getting caught. Maybe this will teach you some discretion for your next job kiddo, with the job market the way it is today and the reference that you get from my firm - will easily land you a job as a pole or lap dancer at a strip club," Katherine verbally toyed with evident revengeful bitterness.

As she had obviously intended, Katherine's insults cut right to the bone, the attacks were quick, ugly and very personal. Margie ran out of the ladies' room crying uncontrollably. A devilish, cruel grin appeared on Katherine's face; she had finally accomplished her goal of getting Margie the little office tramp- fired!

Katherine had few qualms about firing Margie, who had always been a bit of an obvious flirt, yet Kit Kat had endured Margie only because Brad and the other men seemed to enjoy Margie's company, but now that she was getting married to Brad – things were going to change for the better around the office and that meant Margie was no longer needed as any sort of 'office candy'. Katherine was quite pleased with herself; she coldly consoled herself that she was only being professional and not bitchy, as usual there were no ill conscious afterthoughts on Katherine's mind, and besides, she had her future wedding to think about.

* * * * * * * * * * * * * * * * * *

The next morning broke with an amazing, but welcome quickness. The sleep had been a most peaceful one. The autumn morning glaze of sunshine bespoke that of a fine mild day for the northern Midwest. Wayne awoke to a day of unscheduled events and expectations. After an undistinguished cholesterol laden breakfast and multiple cups of heaping strong coffee from the motel's buffet spread, he journeyed slowly out into the parking lot to gain a personal appraisal of this fine South Dakotan morning. The air was cool, clean and refreshing; the early morning skies slowly surrendered their milky cloak for that of a pale blue azure mantel. 'It was indeed a good day to be alive,' he surmised, as he gasped in each breath of a reviving cool air. Such a day was made for travelling the local roads aimlessly on one's Harley. In a flash, his senses had pre-determined his destiny for this day; he was going riding in the Black Hills country, the stuff of lore and American legend. It was an American biker's 'rite of passage'. Such a serendipitous opportunity might never present itself to him again.

Wayne quickly made his way over to the mighty Dodge Ram and began to unleash Robin's Harley from its blue vinyl protective covering. Within minutes he had deftly lowered the truck ramp and had slid the beast of burden carefully down the ramp and onto the blacktop road. The beautiful chrome encrusted Harley glistened with rays of sunshine as it sat there unleashed like a wild animal ready to make a deadly dash into the wilderness. He performed a pre-inspection check of the Harley to ensure both its mechanical soundness and to re-familiarize himself with its balance and controls, some weeks had passed since he had last ridden a motorcycle and even during this short hiatus from the beast, meant that he was a bit rusty in his riding skills. Nevertheless, everything seemed to be in fine working order, one could not uncover any evidence of any prior road accident from the expertly restored Harley.

He thought for a few minutes, then he quickly dismounted the Harley, went to the Ram's back seat and retrieved the Colt 1911 pistol that Indian Joe had given to him. This was a rugged country with few law enforcement officials around and a man had best be able to take care of himself, so he tucked the pistol into the right side of his pants, so that he could grasped it easily with his left hand, while his strong right hand could manoeuvre the massive Harley frame, throttle and front brake controls. He also had another beautiful item with him, something else that he had also retrieved from the back seat of the Dodge Ram's cabin.

Wayne re-appeared in short order with the beautifully custom beaded fringed honey-coloured buckskin jacket that Robin had generously presented to him. He drew up the jacket to his nose, it still smelled of the rich tanning aroma that it had undergone from the tanning process. He threw on the handsome custom-made threads along with his Nomex riding gloves, he was now set on travelling along the same countryside that had previously been journeyed by the likes of Sitting Bull, Buffalo Bill, Crazy Horse, Calamity Jane and Wild Bill Hickok. The coat fit him perfectly and it richly complemented the nature and history of the landscape of years past, it was practical too in that buckskin was a natural wind deflector. This area of the country wasn't historically called the Badlands for nothing – the men and women who had travelled these parts were either bad people, they came from bad circumstances or they had met with a bad end. Wayne desired no similar notoriety or fate.

He activated the electronic ignition and the Harley instantly roared to life like a demented fire-breathing dragon awakened from its winter-long slumber. There was nothing like the massive thunder from the custom exhaust of a Harley Davidson Big Twin engine. Upon the retraction of the jiffy-stand, Wayne was on his way out of the motel parking lot and onto some of the best motorcycle riding back roads in North America. Riding without a helmet was stupid and even reckless, but somehow logic and safety seemed to be the last things on his mind. He loved the warm rushing wind that ruffled with abandon through his hair, the exhilaration of engine torque through the winding turns and the unfiltered smells of the countryside. He was again, the child of his youth, subject to the simple pleasures of his basic senses, could life be any purer or satisfying than these few stolen moments from nature? Motorcycling was pure fun at its most basic distilled level, it was almost childlike in thrills and activity; it was just this side short of being sinful.

The signs beckoned of towns of great repute, those of Deadwood and Sturgis. It was the latter that drew his attention, it being most noteworthy for its annual sponsorship of the largest Harley Davidson rally in the USA. Since he was now the proud owner of a Harley and thus a member of that fraternity, he thought it only right to visit that town of great motorcycle repute, so off to Sturgis he trekked. He pressed ever so slightly on the right handled throttle and the massive Road King responded to his pressures, as the Harley glided slowly into the right entry ramp onto the road that led to the infamous biker town of Sturgis, South Dakota.

Journeying into the town of Sturgis, Wayne spotted Main Street, which ran directly through the town and which was speckled with bars, tattoo parlours, boutiques and motels – all now empty and without clients, as if from a scene from some cheap Sci-Fi movie or perhaps Ghost Town imagery. In early September, Sturgis was indeed a 'Ghost Town' – it was all but abandoned by the previous surge of several hundreds of thousands of Harley Davidson enthusiasts who had descended upon the small sleepy town in early August. Sturgis was the home of one of the original motorcycle rallies, which had become so very popular in recent years with the re-birth of the Harley-Davidson motorcycling community. During the rally, the town grew from a modest population of several thousand to up to 500,000 hard-drinking, fun-loving men and women motorcycle enthusiasts.

Amidst this gauntlet of urban desolation, he spotted a bar named, the 'Six Shooter' and decided to stop in and quench his thirst. The 'Six Shooter' was a rustic looking two-storey wooden framed building, modelled in a manner depicting a classic Old Western saloon and Cat House. The establishment was adorned with large pane glass windows and ornate 23K gold leaf lettering on the windows.

Like an old western cowboy, he parked and descended from his Harley, there was even the old-fashioned horse hitching post, which was more a salute to times past than the real practicality of actually hitching up one's horse, although one might imagine that in this part of the country, anything was to be expected. There was a mass of motorcycle parking zoned areas, a tribute that the town paid to those late summer visitors on whose visits the town so keenly depended for the rest of the year's revenues.

The designers of this bar had done their homework very well. The atmosphere was one of sheer nostalgia and modern marketing. The bar had old styled gold gilt lettering on the mirrors and glass panels, the floor was of reclaimed American black walnut blanks with an added touch of sawdust shavings that were liberally sprinkled about to deaden the sound of cowboy boots and spilled drinks. The now all too familiar western bat-wing doors, so reminiscent of Chief Joseph's tavern in Wyoming – were there too, as was the old styled yellow-coloured gas lamp lighting. There was the smell of stale beer, distilled spirits and cigar smoke too. With his senses overwhelmed with awe, Wayne slowly entered the bar and thought that he had taken a step back 150 years in time.

He strode into the bar like a ghost from the past; all he was lacking was the metallic sounds of boot spurs. The bat-wing doors creaked as if on cue with the sounds of ancient un-oiled metal-against-metal friction. The smell of old liquor, malt and tobacco permeated the air like a drunkard's breath after a long night of revelry. There wasn't another soul in the bar at this early afternoon hour. A middle-aged and moderately balding man of medium frame with a robust black moustache stood stoutly and with eagle eyes from behind the massive mahogany coloured bar. He too wore the trinkets of the era, attired as he was in a white, barrelled sleeved shirt, blue sleeve garters, gold-coloured waist coat and an elegant silver colored pencil-chord tie. The lighting in the bar was deliberately dim for this hour of the day, the illumination being provided by a massive front plate lead glass window and some stained-glass windows from atop the second storey. From Wayne's singular presence, it was evident that this early afternoon hour was not the time for an abundance of patrons. Still, the mercantile ritual between bartender and patron was to be ceremoniously maintained.

"Good afternoon, sir, may I help you?" the bartender inquired in an earnest, if not enthusiastic, gravel-toned voice. Wayne was oblivious to these mere socially veneer amenities, he had been riding long and living life rich this morning, he was in the mood for some rich, warming distilled spirits, the open, chilly Autumn air had taken its toll of his inner energies and body temperature, this despite the robustness of his heavy buckskin jacket.

"Hey that's a nice jacket there, my friend – it looks very authentic – is it Blackfoot in origin?" the bartender inquired innocently.

"No, pal, actually it's Lakota and do you happen to have any single malt over 12 years old?" Wayne smartly remarked steadfastly without hesitation.

"One moment please, let me take a, look, sir!" the bartender politely replied, as he wandered down the 25-five -foot long mahogany bar, the top of which was adorned with dark green granite, replete with genuine Baldwin brass bar foot rail. In abundance, Classic western Six Shooter styled revolvers attired the scenery behind the bar, a decorative touch that also added to the old western flavour of the establishment. Located behind the bar in big bold letters was a sign announcing the reason behind the name of the saloon: 'For any client or group ordering six drinks, the seventh drink on the house!' – it was clever marketing.

"No, sir, I am terribly sorry, we're still cleaned out from the Sturgis rally, it seems like we had a bunch of classy connoisseurs like yourself drinking the week away. Can't blame them really, it pays to drink the best if you can afford it, life's too short, my friend," the barkeep responded in an anecdotal fashion. "However, I do have some very smooth blended scotch and one eight-year old single malt if you please, sir," the bartender added as an alternative option.

His desire for a classic aged-malt scotch was vanquished, yet an impulsive urge suddenly shot through his psyche. "Hey fella, have you got a bottle of Yukon Jack back there?" Wayne shouted in recollection of the brawling nights at Chief Joseph's tavern throughout the summer and that notorious bastard Rick Conroy.

"I'm sorry, sir, did I hear you correctly that you don't want a malt scotch, but you rather want the Canadian liquor Yukon Jack? Now that's quite a jump in taste, sir, if I may boldly say!" the bartender remarked in a puzzled manner. But Wayne was not taking any guff this morning.

"Think whatever you want, barkeep, but I want a Yukon Jack with a sliver of lime and soda – that's called a 'Rattlesnake', pal," Wayne sparked back in an almost arrogant retorting manner.

The bartender nodded his head in silent indifferent acknowledgment, his pleasant public smile was now erased from his previous friendly demeanour. No one liked a rude customer.

"Here you go, hot-shot, I hope you enjoy yourself," the barkeep remarked with a slight degree of disdain in his voice and quite oblivious to the fact that Wayne was an actual fire-fighting Hot Shot.

"I bet this guy doesn't even know what a real Hot Shot is," Wayne contemptuously uttered in frustration under his breath.

Taking a deep sip of the lightly coloured golden elixir, the distilled spirit went down smoothly and with a sweet, liquorice scented aftertaste, then suddenly the inner warmth of the sweet liquor kicked-in like a hot brush fire. The Yukon Jack packed a punch and he now began to appreciate the reason for why the tough fire workers and lumberjacks of the west preferred this formidable drink over others. The sweet smell of the Yukon Jack instantly brought back the summer memories like a torrent of rain.

He sat there quietly and reminisced about the months earlier when he first came to this vast wilderness, thinking himself superior to it and its people; now he was suddenly humbled. In a very true way, he had become part of the American west and he would forever take a part of this with him wherever he went in this world. Wayne was feeling his oats and he was again in the mood to get back onto his Harley Road King and do a bit more riding before retiring back to his motel for the evening.

"So, Mister, you want another round?" the bartender replied as he saw Wayne sip up the contents of the high ball lead glass shaker.

"Truthfully, I'd like more than that, barkeep, I want a full new bottle!" Wayne quibbled smartly as he withdrew his billfold to pay for both his bar drink and the bottle of Yukon Jack.

The bartender was confused and came closer to Wayne. "You must be a stranger here, my friend, the rules here and in every bar in town is that we don't sell liquor bottles that can be taken out and consumed in public, that's called open-container carrying and it's illegal, sir," the bartender proclaimed in an almost rote-like fashion.

Wayne was having none of the bartender's bullshit this day. "This is supposed to be the wild, not the tamed, west, my friend! Okay, barkeep, how about you just take that bottle of Yukon Jack and place it into one of those brown bags under the counter, wrap the flipping thing up real good and call it a package sale to me. After I get it and walk out of this establishment, it's up to me what happens to it, not you! Sound fair, pal?" Wayne remarked as he slapped three crisp hundred dollar bills vigorously onto the granite bar top.

Wayne opened up his western fringed jacket real wide, the sight of the Colt 1911 pistol butt sticking out of Wayne's pants was evident to the eyes of the bartender, who wasn't sure if this stranger was going to shoot him or simply pay his money and peacefully walk away. The bartender's eyes bulged with both amazement and fear, for here was a man paying $300 for a $24 quart-sized bottle of whiskey and he was packing some serious heat as well.

"Now I don't want any trouble with you, Mister! Sure, anything you say, Mister, just don't you be staying around here after your purchase, neither of us wants any trouble," the barkeep barked out defensively.

"Okay, now my friend, I also want no trouble and no bullshit either, this transaction is called 'getting paid-off under the table money', so do we have an agreement here or do I look elsewhere in town to get satisfaction?" Wayne retorted in a very dry, somber voice.

It was a good bargain for both men. The bartender nodded his head in affirmation of the agreement. Satisfied with the arrangement, Wayne watched carefully as the bartender took a new quart-sized bottle of Yukon Jack from the liquor closet. "Hey barkeep, I also want that bottle 'corked-off' please," Wayne remarked. The bartender looked with increasing trepidation at Wayne, as he wondered about the type of character who wanted a bottle of liquor with a removable cork retaining device.

'Corking-off a bottle' – meant only one thing in this part of the country; it meant that this crazy bastard was going to be drinking from the bottle while riding his motorcycle. Still, it mattered little to the barkeep if this rich, stupid fool wanted to get drunk on his cycle and get himself killed – it was almost $300 in his wallet, regardless of whether or not this guy lived or died.

"Here's your purchase, Mister, now make feet fast out of here like you promised, I want no trouble from you, Mister," the barkeep replied as he handed Wayne the discreetly packed brown paper parcel.

Immediately, Wayne took the paper bag and proceeded from the Six Shooter tavern pronto.

Just as the bartender had correctly suspected, Wayne proceeded to tear off the brown paper wrapping and placed the 'corked' bottle of Yukon Jack into a buckskin beaded pouch that adorned his right-side handlebar. The beaded pouch was meant to carry a generous sized water bottle, but today it had another purpose. The handlebar buckskin water pouch fitted the liquor bottle most neatly, allowing him to quickly and conveniently draw the Yukon Jack quart-sized container from the sack without effort or entanglement.

Again, he left his helmet tied to the rear backrest, adorning himself with only a clear set of riding glasses. In a pinch, he thundered off along the back-winding roads of Sturgis. After riding a good hour, the autumn chill again sneaked back into his body, so he reached into the buckskin handlebar pouch and withdrew the Yukon Jack and with his teeth, he easily uncorked the bottle and took a mouthful of the sweet warming nectar. The taste and warmth were both soothing to the senses and Wayne thought that if Rick Conroy had any redeeming values, it was in his taste of liquor and women. He replaced the bottle into the handlebar sack and thought of more pleasant things than Rick Conroy.

Swiftly coming up fast in his rear-view mirror, Wayne spotted an approaching menacing dark mass. Yet this was not the approach of natural bad weather, it was the approach of bad men and seedy women. Within a few minutes, Wayne was surrounded by a mass of about 25 tough looking renegade bikers. These were not the type of bikers that rode for the weekend outings, these were the infamous '1%-ers' – the outlaw bikers who rode their bikes fast and who skirted the law with abandon. He noticed no 'club patches', club symbols or group affiliation, yet these were clearly bikers who lived life on the verge of civility and the law. Their bikes and bodies were well worn, they had obviously travelled great distances each day, they rode only Harley Davidsons and they were all in their 40s or older. These road denizens had lived a rough and colourful life filled with danger, all of their skin was weathered and burnished in a deep tan from the sun and wind burn, while scars adorned many of their faces and they all wore beards. These were modern day Vikings.

Their women also seemed something fierce, a mix between a low-class stripper and an urban drug user. Both males and females were cloaked in varying shapes and shades of body tattoos, with the women having numerous body piercings. 'A man would be well advised to go visit the health clinic after dating one of these gals,' Wayne thought to himself with some generous level of mental disgust.

After trailing some 20 feet behind him, one of the motorcycles suddenly pulled astride him in the left lane. Aside from Wayne and the biker gang, there was no other traffic on this road. "This would be a bad lonely place to die!" Wayne pondered to himself as he summed up the situation and the odds were not in his favour – there was no law out here, save for that of what the individual could do for himself.

Attired in a faded black leather riding vest and fatigued blue jeans, a mangy-looking, gray-bearded old biker adorned with an eye patch and yellow coloured teeth pulled up beside Wayne and defiantly smiled. "This man must be the gang's leader," Wayne mused since this man gave the appearance of a man who stood outside and apart from the other riders, this old biker rode out front and he rode alone – additional proof that he stood distinct from the other bikers who were bitch-packing their 'old ladies'. The old worn-out biker leader smiled a mocking grin at Wayne, a gesture that was clearly taunting in nature. Wayne decided that it was better to simply look away and stare straight ahead at the road, but this defiant gesture only served to infuriate the old biker; he was not going to be ignored by this upstart weekend yuppie Harley rider dressed in his fancy buckskins and riding the latest model of Harley-Davidson bike.

A few of the biker leader's front teeth were missing and those that remained were yellowish and a few were brown in colour, most probably from years of neglect, fighting, tobacco usage, and dental decay.

The biker shouted something to Wayne, but in the roar of 25 Harley-Davidsons, nothing could be audibly discerned. As Wayne quickly looked over to glance what the old biker was saying, the old biker gave Wayne a mocking wink, then he puckered up his lips and blew Wayne an air kiss. The old biker mentally affirmed this yuppie's good taste in threads and motorcycles and the thought crossed his mind that maybe he could be taking these items from this urban rich-boy before the law had a chance to react. Yes indeed, Wayne's custom new Harley and expensive buckskin jacket would make fine trophy additions to the old biker's attire and stature, not to mention the accrued 'bragging rights' and the tall tale of how these were unceremoniously acquired.

'This rich dude will never miss those threads and the bike, he's probably over-loaded on insurance anyway,' the old biker thought comfortably to himself. To the hard-core biker gang members and especially the 1%-ers, the weekend Harley riders were only passing items of amusement and suitable for taunting, these urbanites yearned to live the biker lifestyle, but were trapped by the conventions and trapping of middle-class consumerism.

With a sudden movement, the old biker started to swerve into Wayne's lane of travel. This intrusion forced Wayne to swerve into the shoulder of the road, before he regained control of his bike. The old biker repeated the scene a several more times, each time Wayne regained control of his bike. The old biker and the other 1%-ers all laughed as they saw this tenderfoot trying to keep control of his bike. Wayne decided to try and outrun the gang, pushing onto the throttle with a fistful of grip, propelling the massive Harley to 80 mph; his bike was quicker and nimbler than the 1%-ers, but they were more determined and soon caught right back up with him.

The old bike leader was furious that this tenderfoot had the audacity to try and outrun him and his gang; he was going to teach this city buck a lesson. As the old biker caught up to Wayne, he withdrew a massive gleaming chain from around his torso; he swung the heavy chain at Wayne, missing his head by only inches. Wayne tried to speed-up, but the old biker kept pace and again whirling his chain at Wayne, this time chipping Wayne's windshield on the extreme left edge.

Wayne knew he had to do something, or he was a dead man. Now in top sixth overdrive gear, Wayne now had his left hand free to do that which needed to be done. His free left hand reached beneath the buckskin jacket, with lightning speed and without any warning, he suddenly produced the .45 Colt 1911 pistol that Chief Joseph had given to him some days earlier. His adrenalin pumping like an anxious animal trying to survive in the wilderness, he acted quickly, decisively and without hesitation. This was a time for action, not mere grandstanding or bluffing! Fighting the wildfires had taught Wayne courage and fortitude in the face of adversity.

In a heated rage that was without any sense of the consequences, Wayne pointed the massive, elegantly forged pistol and fired two shots in quick succession directly behind his left shoulder into the pack of trailing motorcycles that had been following closely behind him. He didn't care who was killed or hurt – these mechanically mounted animals only knew one thing and that was sheer naked violence.

'If I am to die today, some of these bastards will be coming along with me!' he angrily thought, his temper boiling with animal-like ferocity. The two massive .45 calibre bullets broke into the motorcycle pack windshields and rattled off some metal motorcycle engine parts, producing magnificent sparks. All of the trailing bikes immediately slowed down and kept a respectable distance, while Wayne and the gang leader sorted out their differences. Quickly, Wayne next pointed the massive pistol directly at the old biker, who was whirling a chain around his head and was ready to strike again. Wayne fired off a bullet which broke off a link of the chain and metal sparks flew aimlessly about.

The old biker was amazed, then angered at the shot of literal defiance to his manhood and authority. He thought of plunging his bike at this young punk, until Wayne pointed the pistol clearly at the old man's forehead – the shot would have instantly killed the old biker. He saw the look of rage and determination in Wayne's eyes too and he knew that these were 'killer, angry eyes' that would not back down! Wayne pointed and waved the Colt 1911 pistol again in an aggressive manner that indicated the old man needed to back-off.

The old biker was decrepit, crude and dirty, but he was not stupid either! He thought better of the situation and skillfully wrapped the chain again around his torso. After a few seconds, Wayne too lowered and withdrew his weapon, as he placed the Colt 1911 'locked & cocked' back into his waist band. Both men defiantly looked at one another with anger and contempt. The situation could not end in a draw like this. One side needed to bend before the other side conceded.

Wayne looked at his handlebar and noticed the dangling buckskin beaded sack. "An interesting peace offering," he conjured. He placed the

Colt 1911 back into his pants. With his free left hand, he withdrew the bottle of Yukon Jack from its buckskin sheath, pulled the cork with his teeth and took a swig, again it felt like a Godsend especially after this heart pounding confrontation. He corked the bottle and then as if in a gesture from some old western movie, carefully tossed the bottle of Yukon to the old biker, who deftly caught it in midair with the agility of an acrobat – these 1% bikers might have been a nasty lot, but they could sure as hell ride their Harleys with great agility and skill. The old biker was obviously a pro at handling his Harley under any and all road conditions, a testament to his many years in the saddle. The old biker also uncorked the Yukon bottle with those remaining yellowish teeth that he still possessed. He took a swig and then another, he smiled at Wayne, waved his right arms and the remaining members of his gang also followed him forward in the left lane of the highway.

As the gang passed Wayne, the Yukon Jack bottle was tossed into the air from one member to another in quick, efficient succession. One biker even raised the bottle and poured it in the air, allowing the liquor to enter the wind slipstream from which a following biker took a mouthful of liquor in mid-air without missing a drop. As the bottle was tossed down the successive line of bikers, they each passed Wayne and left him in their rear-view mirrors, as just a memory and tale to tell at their final resting place for the evening. The bottle came to the last trail biker and by now the bottle was empty, save for a few precious drops. With a look of utter disgust, the last biker raised the bottle upside down trying to get a few drops for himself and his old lady's libation.

Alas, the Yukon Jack had given up the ghost. In a moment of disgust and true to his biker manner, the angry biker threw the empty liquor bottle up into the air in Wayne's immediate path of travel, the bottle barely missing him by a few feet, then shattering in many pieces. As the last biker rolled on his accelerator throttle, he also gave a 'middle finger' good luck gesture to Wayne and then the biker's girlfriend, pulled something from inside her pants and tossed it up and out in the air directly behind her and straight into Wayne's direction. The object hit his windshield with a solid low thud sound; the impact on his windshield caused an immediate bright crimson-coloured smear. In an act of utter vulgar exhibition and obvious displeasure, the biker-bitch had tossed her well soiled sanitary napkin at Wayne's windshield; she definitely had hit her intended mark.

"You fucking pig, bitch whore!" Wayne screamed out into the wind. Wayne was fuming at this utterly vulgar, filthy act of sleazy female biker defiance. With loud cursing remarks of disgust, he gracefully pulled his Harley onto the side of the road to examine his bike and take stock of his situation.

It felt good to get one's feet onto terra firma after a hectic ride like the one he had just experienced. He was none the worse for the recent encounter; nothing seemed to be broken on either his body or his Harley. He took a slow and careful walk around the massive Road King, its polished chrome glittering in the fading sunlight of the late afternoon. Everything on the bike seemed fine aside for some minor scratches from the old bike leader's chain attack and the filthy sanitary napkin incident. He removed his eyewear and leaned up against the Harley. In that reflective instant, Wayne had his epiphany.

Suddenly for some unknown reason, he remembered his summer sojourn – there sprung a rush of memories of the Copen family, Joyce Miller the waitress, the fire camp experiences and of his summer love, Robin Wolf. These memories instead of being tragic, were entirely joyful and fond. He started to laugh uncontrollably and boisterously in the midst of the utterly quiet and serene wilderness. 'Indeed, it was a good thing to be alive and healthy,' he thought to himself.

After a few minutes his adrenaline dissipated to normal levels, yet he continued to smile at the entire incident with the biker gang. He had just faced down a pack of gangster motorcyclists and had almost gotten himself killed in the process, yet he had gone with his instincts and took a chance, he was alive and oh how great it was to be alive he thought to himself. In one respect it was deadly serious business, yet in another ironic sense, it made little difference to anything that was happening in the world and he began to realize how perishable life was after all and that living for the present was the only true reality.

'Boy that was a tough fucking crowd that I would never want to meet again,' Wayne confessed to himself silently as he pondered the slight brush with death that he had just managed to escape. He checked his Colt 1911 pistol and topped-off the pistol with a fresh magazine of ammunition. It seemed that he owed his life to the Colt 1911 pistol, a bottle of Yukon Jack and some luck too. Later that night, he smiled and laughed to himself about the events and thought what a great story it would be to tell.

His journey was almost complete. He was no longer running from his past; instead, he was going back to fulfil his future. 'Wayne' Hamilton was relegated to the memory of the past summer, while 'Brad' Hamilton was reincarnated for the present. He was going to marry Katherine and get back to the banking business and being the Governor of the Hamilton Trust. His immaturity and prejudices had been vanquished with the fires of Satan's Pitchfork! As an adult, he realized that 'in between the gulf of one's limitations and expectations – therein lay reality'. Kate was his reality and she was waiting anxiously for him to return back home to Boston. Life was filled with both bitterness and sweetness; it was not so bad after all, he rightly concluded.

★ ★ ★ ★ ★ ★ ★ ★ ★ ★ ★ ★ ★ ★ ★ ★ ★ ★

CHAPTER 13

Harvest Time

"No, you're wrong, Kate, you're so very wrong... I'm not like you at all anymore, I've changed...I think of the world and people differently now, Kate"

Progressively, the shortened days were conceding their diminishing faint, golden light to the darkening cloak of the Autumn skies. It was early-September and the massive Dodge Magnum rolled effortlessly across the Massachusetts state line. Carefully nestled within the bed of the Dodge Ram, was Robin's custom Harley Davidson Road King. It was safely covered with a ubiquitous blue vinyl tarp, this to so reduce the wear and tear of the road and weather elements upon the motorcycle, and to keep it from nefarious preying eyes too. His fond boyhood memories of New England were unexpectedly rekindled, as he excitedly spied the lush countryside alive with the vibrant colours of the Autumn. He mused with slight irony, that so much beauty and texture could be enshrined within the throngs of the Fall's tender embrace of natures' annual death throng. He blissfully continued to travel the Interstate Highway 84 which traversed into Massachusetts.

Fond thoughts of the frolicking times that he had experienced over the past summer, magically leapt into his mind. These were now only a cherished memory, like those of his childhood recollections, to be recalled from time to time, especially during the nights when it was quiet, and he was alone. The closer that he came to Boston, the more he began to re-integrate himself as the individual referred to as 'Brad'. The personage coined as 'Wayne' was merely the vanquished vestige of a summer biker vagabond. Besides all of those who had known him as 'Wayne', were either far distanced or dead. The reality of the present circumstances had once again taken dominance of him, he became a geographic persona of wealthy, urban Boston. Yet no person was ever totally free from their history! The past establishes the present, as surely as the present crafts the future.

He exited the Interstate to traverse the scenic secondary roads, this offered breathtaking fiery scenery and a slower pace of travel, after all he was in no hurry and there was no immediate agenda. Along the scenic and meandering back country roads, he sneaked a delightful whiff of burning leaves being unlawfully disposed of by a suburban resident. The whiff instantly transported Brad back to his childhood, as he fondly remembered playing in the Hamilton estate tree fort, the nervous beginning of the school year, and the refreshing briskness of the cool Autumn air. He marvelled at how different and distinct was the aroma of casual burning leaves versus that of a raging wilderness wildfire! The olfactory sense was a funny memory inducer, as it seemed to magically rekindle memories, pleasures, and even pain, that one previously believed to be vanquished forever. The childhood memories flooded back in a torrent of mental flashbacks. He was not merely recalling the scent of Autumn; he was recollecting all of the associations of the season too.

His thoughts soon turned to the memories of family and old Boston, the times when Father would be arriving home from the office for the traditional family dinner. At other all too rarer times, his father would arrive home early to find the children in frolic play. On these rare occasions, Arthur would throw the football to him and his brother Robert, this as a quick unwind from the office drudge before the dinner meal was served. They were together in the spirit of fun and relaxation, if even for a short time. The pain of losing his family reverberated in his mind and forever it would remain so, yet now there was the companion of happy memories too.

He smiled to himself and let the memories play out in his mind, being almost hypnotized by the streaming vivid images. Soon, however, the sights and sounds of metropolitan Boston diffused the rural images of youth and of times long past. Brad's thoughts now turned to Kate and what he would say to her upon their encounter. So much had changed in the past several months for him and yet in many respects, much still remained the same.

A quick stop by the Hamilton Greystone estate presented a golden opportunity to get rested, have a little to eat, and a chance naturally to see Juan and Carla Lopez. The visit provided an opportunity to say hello to his 'second family' and inquire as to any affairs that may need his direct and personal attention. It was still morning, and Brad was eager to see the Lopezes again after his long absence – his visit back to the office could wait a few more hours.

The big diesel Magnum was manoeuvred onto a small, seldom used secondary black-top road that seemed to lead to nowhere, yet after a short distance of 150 yards – there arose a warning sign proclaiming 'Private Property: No Trespassers: Keep Out. Intruders will be prosecuted!' After proceeding a distance of approximately 300 yards along a meandering country road, Brad encountered a huge metal gate that was anchored on both of its sides by six-foot high concrete pillars. These abutments served as the silent sentinels that stood as the first guard to the Hamilton Greystone estate. In decades long past when labour was plenty and cheap, armed guards and patrol dogs would have immediately and sternly confronted any visitors or trespassers.

Stopping the vehicle and deftly reaching onto his trouser belt key fob, he withdrew a robust key ring that was arrayed with multiple keys, one of which unlocked this old estate gate lock. Fiddling for, and then finding the correct key, he unlocked the huge, metal lock. The gate reeked with a moaning cry of metal-on-metal resistance, as rusty metal stubbornly rubbed against itself. With steadfast resistance, the massive and well-balanced wrought iron gate surrendered its static and stoic posture to Brad's concerted muscle strength. He passed the Ram through the old gate and methodically re-locked the dull black metal gate behind him. This was the only estate entry and exit point which did not have a new electronic alarm system integrated into it. The Hamilton estate consisted of approximately 450 acres and Brad had just entered the most obscure and mostly unused southern estate entrance. This place was so remote that even many of the local police did not know of its existence as an actual private estate driveway.

The Dodge Magnum mightily scrambled a path through a gravel-lined series of gentle curves, whereby he decidedly came upon the imposing three-storey edifice of the Hamilton Greystone estate, a magnificent steely mansion of obvious visual grandeur. Stopping the vehicle, he took a long appraisal of the beautiful autumn scenery. This grand estate and home represented all that was stable and tangible in his life, an idyllic place that he had fondly known since childhood. He thought to himself and marvelled at how little his house had changed, yet he realized that everything else of any importance in his life had dramatically changed. He slowly opened the truck door and proceeded to slowly stretch his cramped muscles from the long morning drive.

The rising early morning sun was brilliant, and the maple leaves were transitioning colours of every hue of the spectrum. A slightly cool and periodic breeze brushed across his body. 'Lord, it was a blessing to be alive and be experiencing this fine cool Boston day once again,' he appreciatively pondered. The stark grey appearance of the mansion was sharply contrasted with the turning red and yellow leaves of autumn – it all made for a most memorable and picturesque site. Even now at this very early date, the leaves from the estate's numerous hardwood trees were slowly occupying even more of the lawn with each passing day. It seemed as if the Fall season was arriving just a little bit earlier this year according to Brad's recollection of seasons past. Brad speculated as to Juan and Carla's whereabouts on this fine fall morning and he came upon a sudden urge that would perk their interests.

In a manner that was both vulgarly common and uncouth for his upbringing and class, Brad leaned back into the truck's cab and pushed strenuously on the vehicle's loud signal horn for a few short bursts, enacting the horn intervals every few seconds with a slight modicum of preserved silence. There was no response from the household, no one looked out a window or even opened up the door that led into the kitchen and delivery areas. 'It was possible,' he thought, 'that either Juan or Carla were away performing errands or perhaps they had merely taken a short day off.'

Being away from Greystone for nearly six months, he was unsure of the daily activities of his loyal friends and housekeepers. Undeterred, he made another prolonged attempt before attempting entry with his residence keys. This time, he leaned on the horn for a full minute, followed by another repetition for another two minutes of unrelenting horn blasting, this he figured was enough racket to raise both the deaf and the dead. He dearly wanted to surprise he surrogate parents.

Just then, Carla was ascending the Greystone manor basement stairs, when she heard the racket of a monotonous and very loud vehicle horn blasting obnoxiously just outside the mansion's side kitchen and pantry entrance. Cautiously, Carla peeked out the kitchen window and spotted an unfamiliar fire engine red coloured truck, with a bearded white male pushing on the vehicle's horn. Frightened by the appearance and actions of the stranger, Carla loudly called out for assistance.

"Juan, come quick, there's some strange looking Anglo man in the driveway beeping his horn, come quick I think he's loco or something," Carla shouted out frantically.

Juan was busily engaged in fixing a loose house light fixture, when he heard the pleas of his wife. "Dearest wife, what's the matter? What is it? What the hell is that racket I am hearing outside?" Juan replied, as he came running into the kitchen to see what all the commotion was all about.

Usually, the Greystone mansion was as quiet as a crypt and there were never any unexpected visitors or guests unless Carla or Juan was informed beforehand. "Carla, what is the matter? What is that horrible noise outside?" Juan repeatedly inquired in an anxious tone.

"Juan, can't you hear that awful racket outside? It's some crazy man out there! He's been honking that awful horn for the past few minutes. I think that he is a criminal or a crazy person! Perhaps we should call the police?" Carla wailed fearfully, as she looked desperately into her husband's eyes.

"That bum is definitely trespassing on this private property, maybe he's one of those drug crazed people or a robber trying to lure us outside," Juan exclaimed as he tried to catch a better look at the stranger. Keenly aware that Greystone was in a remote, wealthy area and thus was a prime target for thieves and low-life persons, Juan went over to a nearby cupboard and grabbed a Remington 12-gauge pump shotgun. He quickly loaded five shells into the tube-magazine, then he pumped the action and engaged the shotgun's safety device. 'It was far better to be prepared for danger and besides, the police would take at least 15 minutes to respond to any emergency call, in which time he and Carla could be hurt or worse,' he wisely reasoned.

Juan carefully opened the pantry Dutch-door top and exposed only the upper portion of his torso. "Hey, stranger, who are you? What do you want here? How did you bypass the estate security and gate system? State your business pronto!" Juan yelled outside to the stranger.

"He didn't call into the security system did he, Carla?" Juan muttered to his wife, as he continued to carefully study the suspicious stranger. Carla merely nodded her head in a negative response, while the menacing stranger said nothing.

"Hey man, what the hell are you doing here? Get off that damn horn before I call the police on you...this is private property, Mister, just how in the hell did you get onto this estate property without permission or my knowledge?" Juan repeatedly and forcefully challenged the bearded stranger.

"Juan – he's just smiling at us! Juan... Juan, wait, I think that is Mr Bradford, oh yes I'm certain... it's Mr Brad," Carla screamed almost hysterically.

Juan simply looked at his wife in amazement. Quickly, his old eyes studied the unfamiliar man's features and appearance once again and more carefully.

Carla was right! It was Mr Brad Hamilton, but he looked so strange, so different that neither Juan or Carla initially recognized the man with the short beard, bronze tan, windswept face, and sun-bleached hair.

"Senor Hamilton... Mr Brad, is that really you?" Juan yelled, as he un-chambered all the shells from the shotgun chamber and placed the shotgun aside for the time being.

"You bet it's me! Hello Juan, Greetings Carla! How are you both doing?" he shouted as he ran from the truck with a broad smile and an outstretched hand. Both Juan and Carla exited the mansion and met Brad in the side driveway.

"Mr Brad, we can't believe it's you after all this time, you should have called us," Carla motherly chided, as she gave Brad a huge embrace.

"Yes, I've been away for far too long, I really should have called to let you know of my return, but I headed back East on a spur of the moment decision and I wanted to surprise both of you and I guess it worked too! Well, as you can see, I have physically changed a bit, huh," Brad explained with a broad smile across his tanned and tough face.

"Have you seen Miss Katherine yet?" Carla inquired cheerfully.

"No, not yet. I'm going there later today to see her and the family business. I wanted this to be a surprise for her," Brad whispered.

"Well, I can tell you now, Mr Brad, that Miss Katherine will be very surprised and pleased to see you. You are looking very handsome and strong these days!" Carla proudly proclaimed. "It was a good thing that you stopped by Greystone first to get settled, Mr Brad, we have missed you dearly... have you eaten breakfast yet? Come inside and I will make your favorite Spanish omelette, with bacon, home fried potatoes, wheat toast, and some good strong coffee. Please, no arguments either, do you understand me, Mr Brad?" Carla insisted as she gently, but firmly took a motherly grasp of Brad's arm, as she started to lead Brad into the Greystone mansion's kitchen/pantry area. With such an inviting offer,

Brad could not refuse.

Brad submissively smiled and willingly obliged Carla's efforts to please him and he was a hungry man after having driven since dawn. Juan rushed to get Brad's bags and belongings from the cab of the Dodge Ram truck, while also admiring the rugged beauty of the vehicle, which was seldom to be seen being driven by residents of this county, except for the maintenance and construction labour personnel.

"This is sure a fine, powerful truck that you have here, Mr Brad, it must really eat up the road." Juan took a quick peek under the blue tarp and he whistled loudly at the sight. "Wow, and what a great, big, motorcycle you have in the back, I've never seen one so beautiful and unique," Juan exclaimed, as he admired the styling and amenities of both the Ram truck and the Harley Davidson motorcycle. "Your new motorcycle is certainly more distinguished than the other one that you had, Mr Brad, this one somehow suits your personality," Juan excitedly exclaimed, as Brad smiled and entered into the kitchen with Carla.

Brad was filled with feelings of warmth and security. He fondly eyed the kitchen and its familiarities with the fondness of a lost child returned home safe and sound after a long absence. The rich honey maple styled wood cabinets, parquet wood floors, and rustic red brick oven and fireplace all connoted the style and feel of a Norman Rockwell portrait of traditional Americana. Brad was comforted by his boyhood surroundings and the companionship of Carla and Juan.

"Now you just sit right down there, Mr Brad and I will fix you a breakfast fit for a king!" Carla proclaimed proudly, as she anxiously gathered the utensils and food ingredients necessary for the meal preparation. A big pot of hot, strong coffee was already prepared and waiting. She was very happy to be cooking for someone other than herself and her husband.

"It's sure great to be back at Greystone, Carla; I didn't realize how much I missed this old place. I didn't realize how much I missed you and Juan too," Brad warmly confessed.

Carla's eyes filled with tears and she began to cry. "It's not been good for us, Mr Brad since they died, it's been even worse since you left. Please promise to stay here at Greystone and never leave again."

"It's all right, Carla. Things are going to be okay, Carla, I promise. I miss all of them too. We'll have to continue to live without them, Carla, but at least, we still have our memories and one another," Brad replied. He was a little shocked that he even said these words to Carla, these were the expression of feelings that he had been holding inside himself for the last six months and now that he had openly expressed these, he knew that he was all right.

"Let's get that omelette and bacon cooking, Carla, I'm starving. You might be surprised to know that I did some commercial cooking myself during my travels!" Brad announced to the amazement of both Juan and Carla.

Soon the smell of hickory-smoked bacon filled the kitchen coffers and it tantalized the senses and one's appetite. Carla began the process of dicing the onions, tomatoes, and mild sweet peppers. Brad's omelette was quickly taking form, as Carla began to brown the toast and prepared the setting of the kitchen table.

"Juan and Carla, please come and sit with me!" Brad pleaded softly.

Carla poured Juan, Brad, and herself three generous mugs of strong black coffee. She served Wayne the omelette, bacon, and toast. As they all sat down at the kitchen table embracing their steaming mugs of coffee, Brad eagerly related the experiences of the past several months during which he trekked across America's heartland and western venues. He related most of the factual details of the quest, yet he kept his counsel and silence around his personal liaisons, especially those concerning Robin. These wounds had yet to heal and his heart was not yet an open book to Juan and Carla. These stories would be hidden in his heart and retold at an unknown future date, when the time was appropriate.

"Are you back here at Greystone for good?" Juan added innocently. Carla gave Juan an off-hand dirty look of disapproval, Carla knew that this was not a question that Juan should be asking of his employer.

"I hope so, but I have learned that nothing in this life is for certain, but I do know this, it's that Greystone is my home and you are my friends. My past cannot, and should not be erased, nor should I ever try to run away from my problems or memories, for these can only haunt you. I also realize how important family and friends are to me, but I still might be doing some more travelling; after all, there's more to the world than little old Boston," Brad announced, as he placed his hands into those of both Juan and Carla. The couple smiled and acknowledged Wayne's sincerity, friendship, and vagueness about his future. Brad finished off his second mug of coffee, then he arose from the table and thanked Carla for the excellent breakfast and Juan for maintaining Greystone and its premises.

"Now if you'll excuse me, I want to go upstairs, shower, and change into some new clothes before heading into the city. I think that I'll take the Harley, it's such a nice day for riding the Hog," he announced.

They both just nodded in silent recognition.

"Just let us know if you need anything, Mr Brad and I'll bring up your luggage too?" Juan noted.

"Let me please bring you some fresh towels and linens, Mr Brad," Carla added.

★ ★ ★ ★ ★ ★ ★ ★ ★ ★ ★ ★ ★ ★ ★ ★ ★ ★ ★

The warm and familiar hot steam shower felt like a cleansing renaissance for Brad; he stayed in the soothing warm mist and multi-faucet shower spray for 30 minutes, after which he felt like a fresh cooked lobster and his skin looked like that of a winkled old man. 'Home was indeed a very fine and comforting place,' he contemplated in appreciation of the fine and simple things in life that had been availed to him.

Brad felt like a recharged man after his fine breakfast and refreshing shower. After the austerity of the fire camps, he really appreciated the luxury in which he was raised and still had the opportunity to enjoy. Strangely, he both anticipated and dreaded his trip to Hamilton & MacAlister. He looked forward to his old colleagues and co-workers, yet he dreaded his encounter with Kate. He was uncertain of what he still felt for Kate and what shape their relationship was going to take after his affair with Robin. He still loved Kate, but was it in the same way as before his trip? Was this enough for him now? He knew from experience that running away never solved a problem.

As he dressed for his afternoon journey to Boston, he looked about his bedroom. The familiar images that encompassed his room transformed him back to the days of his youth, when opportunities and dreams appeared endless. Mementoes of childhood and school days gave way to the trophies of adolescence and adulthood, as icons and images of baseball gloves, Varsity letters from rowing, polo trophies and framed degrees - all richly arrayed the walls of his room. These things all seemed so distant and trivial to him now and yet at one time, these relics were so central to him. He slightly smiled to himself, then quickly wondered if he would one day think the same of present events. He began to appreciate his past as being vital events that composed the man of the present. The future he realized could be either mired in the past or liberated by the present.

Looking about his room, Brad spotted the family photo album that his beloved sister Melissa had so diligently kept up to date for him and for each member of the Hamilton family. The photo album resided in a moderately sized bookcase that also contained the leather-bound books of classic works of literature, history, science, and philosophy. He gently grasped the spine of the photo album and contorted himself comfortably in a deep-seated winged leather reading chair and accompanying foot stool. Comfortably, he made himself a king upon this throne, as he crested his lower appendages upon the most obedient leg servant. Most carefully and reverently, Brad methodically leafed-through the family album, with images and memories coming to life with each glimpse and every turn of the page. Pictures of his father, mother, sister, and brother - all sparked his emotions. Yet these feelings were no longer those of sad demons, rather his memories were warm and joyful of the good times passed.

Uncontrollable trickles of tears slowly filled his eyes and gently streamed down his right cheek. 'Robin was quite right and wise,' Brad concluded, 'life truly was a fabric weave of memories that one knitted throughout the course of living; both the good and the bad were framed in a tapestry upon one's soul that was both weaved and worn throughout one's life.'

He looked through the photo album for over an hour, before slowly closing and placing it carefully into its proper place back in the bookshelf. Sitting back down into the comfortable reading chair, he closed his eyes and slowly smiled as he cherished the thoughts of his family and the events of the past several months. It all seemed like a dream and maybe that was what life was supposed to be - one big dream! The images of dirt bikes racing in Ohio, the hash slinging in a hot greasy Kansas diner, and the fighting of raging western wildfires all filled his psyche. Brad realized that in the span of six short months, he had lived fuller than in his previous 36 years.

A sudden knock upon the bedroom door quickly brought Brad back to the present state of reality. "How are you doing, Mr Brad? Is everything okay? Can I get you anything?" Carla graciously inquired in quick succession, as she gently knocked on his bedroom suite door. Not getting an answer after about ten long seconds, Carla again expressed her motherly concern, "Mr Brad, are you okay?"

Quickly Brad awoke from his tranquil trance and groggily responded, "Yes, Carla, I'm fine," Brad replied as he arose and opened up the door.

"Hello Carla, I was just sitting back and enjoying the old photos, I greatly miss those times too!" Brad responded as he smiled broadly at Carla.

"I miss them, too, Mr Brad and so does Juan, pardon the familiarity, but we always thought of the Hamiltons as part of our family, Mr Brad," Carla sighed with emotion.

Brad continued to smile at Carla, giving her a motherly hug and this reunion merely reinforced the feelings that he also felt toward the Lopezes.

"I'll be leaving shortly to head off to the office, Carla," Brad softly stated.

Carla smiled and returned to her household chores, she was both happy and assured that 'her Brad was mentally fine and in a healthy spirit, so unlike that of the man who had left some six months previously. Her remaining wish was that he continued to keep the black dog of depression at bay indefinitely, he still had his whole life in front of him and he had everything to live for, she thought.

He opened up his small travel bag, carefully going through his limited travel gear that had served him so well during his cross-continent motorcycle journey. He smiled briefly as he thought back to how silly he must have appeared to everyone at Hamilton & MacAlister that day when he appeared in his previous garb of highly colourful Kevlar black and yellow, form-fitting jump suit motor clothing. The Harley now at least reflected his new-found maturity, yet it also expressed his youthful zest for life, individuality and urge for adventure.

As he unpacked the summer clothing, the unmistakable smell of smoke scented the air, the burnt aroma immediately reminding him of the western wildfires and Satan's Pitchfork. He selected a set of broken-in blue Levi jeans, tall rustic brown distressed riding boots, and a tightly woven cotton twill red and black checkered shirt. He gently fondled his beloved buckskin beaded embroidered jacket, which Robin had bought for him as a gift. The sterling silver and turquoise wolf beaded figure on the back of the jacket still looked as beautiful and insightful as ever.

Brad completed his dressing by placing his fire fighter identification tags around his neck, this followed by the Indian jewellery ornamentation of the silver wolf figure and neck-chain that Robin had also given to him. He tucked this into his shirt, not desiring to have the precious memento either blow around in the wind or slap across his upper torso. A bright red neckerchief completed the ensemble and assured that Brad's neck area was protected from the elements, in addition to providing a modicum of vivid colour contrast.

He determinedly descended the secondary staircase which led down to the mansion kitchen and pantry area, there upon immediately encountering Juan, who was carrying a dustpan and brush. Juan had just cleaned up on one of the mansions unused rooms, this being part of the constant maintenance tasks that befell Greystone manor. Brad asked Juan top-off the Dodge Ram with diesel and noted that the insurance papers and registration were located in the truck's glove compartment. He added that he expected to be back for dinner about 5:30 PM or thereabout. Juan merely nodded his head in acknowledgment.

Entering the kitchen, he saw Carla busily preparing a salad. "Hello, do you want any lunch, Mr Brad?" Carla smiled and inquired.

"No, not at all Carla, that late breakfast that you made has really finished off my appetite, but thank you for asking" Brad politely responded.

"Is there anything that you want for dinner, Mr Brad?" Carla inquired.

"Well, yes there is, Carla, if it would not be too much trouble, could you please make me the special seafood casserole, the one that you used to make for me with the paper-thin pastry crust, sherry sauce, lobster, shrimp, crab meat, and scallops?" Brad shyly requested.

"That's your boyhood favourite, Mr Brad and it's Juan's favourite meal too," Carla exclaimed. "So, yes, of course I will be happy to prepare this savoury meal for you, Mr Brad, along with some hearty seafood bisque soup, home-made rolls, and perhaps a surprise dessert." Carla smiled as she remembered that Brad and the other Hamilton children often looked forward to this meal that she had prepared for the Hamilton family on an almost weekly basis. Both Juan and Carla followed Brad out to the side driveway where the Dodge Ram was parked.

"That's a very beautiful jacket and outfit that you have there, Mr Brad," Juan exclaimed with fatherly admiration.

"Thank you, Juan, the outfit was given to me by a dear, old friend…a friend who I will never forget!" Brad explained with a tone of sombreness in his voice and sadness in his eyes.

Neither Juan or Carla dared to press him with further inquiries, more details would emerge when he was ready to tell them, they both wisely surmised.

The time was now 1:30 PM and the lunchtime rush had long since abated, the journey would take approximately 50 minutes; however, he was unconcerned with time. "Well, folks, let me get the Harley ready and I'll be on my way, I'm off to see Kate and the family business," he proclaimed proudly.

"Do you need a hand with that big, bad motorcycle, Mr Brad?" Juan cheerfully volunteered.

"No thanks, Juan, it's a job that can be done by one person and I have become adept at loading and unloading the Harley, but thanks for asking anyway!" Brad replied. He proceeded to remove the blue vinyl tarp. Next, he lowered the Ram's tailgate and pried out the aluminium ramp. Meticulously, he removed the four tie-down straps, ensuring that the Harley side jiffy stand was firmly engaged. After the Road King was released from its temporary bondage, he disengaged the kickstand, and carefully guided the Harley down the ramp.

He dismounted the Harley and drew open one of the saddlebags, pulling out his bright orange flame half helmet and clear eyeglass protection. He performed a quick, but thorough inspection of the bike for safety and maintenance purposes; everything seemed well and in order. Brad was ready for the road, as both rider and machine were well fuelled and rested. Juan and Carla both cautiously gathered next to Brad and his Harley.

"Honestly, what do you think of my new machine?" Brad proudly inquired.

"Well, Mr Brad, please pardon the expression, but that is one mean, kick-ass machine!" Juan sighed.

Instantly, Carla looked at Juan with a disapproving nod.

"I wish I were younger, and I would have a machine like this, boy the things that I could do on this motorcycle!" Juan continued with a sparkle in his eyes.

"The only thing you could do, old man, is to get yourself killed!" Carla unabashedly scolded back to Juan in a dismissive voice.

"With all due respect, women just don't know about these things, right, Mr Brad?" Juan exclaimed in exacerbation at his wife's comments.

"Well to tell you both the truth, I indirectly received this Harley from a lady friend of mine and she was one hell of a good rider too!" Brad sighed with a heavy voice.

Both Carla and Juan were speechless at this announcement. They were reluctant to divulge deeper into the private affairs of Mr Brad while he was on his long journey.

"I'll say one thing, it's a very beautiful machine, your lady friend sure had some good taste, Mr Brad, this bike definitely suits you better than that other one that you owned, she sure must have been one heck of a lady!" Carla exclaimed.

Brad smiled and thanked Carla for her compliments of both the bike and the lady who had once owned it. "Yes indeed, she was a very special and great lady too, I'll tell you more about her someday," Brad added as he slowly placed the helmet on his head. "I ride the Harley to respect her memory," Brad added in a sombre voice.

From his belt, he unfastened a barrel key from his key fob to unlock the Harley's ignition switch. He checked to ensure that the Harley's transmission was in neutral position, then he pressed on the ignition switch and waited a moment for the electronic diagnosis sequence to be completed. The sound of the Harley was almost too loud to comfortably bear without hearing protection. The smell of un-burnt high-octane gasoline was both a pleasant and nauseating aroma for both Juan and Carla, as both of them moved away from the bike and its bleaching exhaust and roar. Brad secured his helmet, fastened his gloves, and engaged the clutch into first gear. He slowly drove down the main driveway and waved good-bye to Carla and Juan. The couple warmly embraced each other, as they both silently prayed for his safety and reunion at Hamilton & MacAlister.

* * * * * * * * * * * * * * * * *

Brad expertly man-handled the huge, powerful Harley past the Greystone Main Gate, inserting the magnetic access key that controlled and recorded the time and date of all visitors through both card access recording and video cameras. Security had become a major concern among the ultra-rich, especially on the old vast estates. He eased the lumbering Harley down the colourful lanes of the secondary roads, which liberally crisscrossed the outlying suburbs of Boston and Cambridge. Increasingly, the large landed estates of earlier generations were forfeiting their once mighty acreage to make way to elite subdivisions of the newly-rich class. The old weathered, hand-emplaced stonewalls and converted gatekeeper houses were the telltale architectural testaments that a once grand estate had stood firm on these select sub-divided suburbs.

The sedate and scenic secondary roads soon ceded their colour and genteel serenity to the huge and monotonous double and triple lane highways that indistinguishably and prolifically dotted the landscape from Atlantic to Pacific coasts. As he approached the urban commuter highways of metropolitan Boston, Brad's ride became a more concentrated one, as he sought to safely vanquish both aggressive drivers and meandering huge tractor-trailer trucks with his nimble and reliable Harley. The past several months of riding had rendered Brad a most capable and agile motorcycle rider.

The Harley rumbled down streets bustling with buses and pedestrians, many of whom were returning from an extended or late lunch. At 2:30 PM Brad lumbered the Harley slowly into second gear and down through the financial district and onto Bromfield Street. The colonial red brick building of Hamilton & MacAlister beckoned majestically before him. The reserved parking spot of CEO was still courteously left vacant and reserved for him on the day of his return, this very day in fact.

He slowed the Harley down into first gear and gracefully nestled the bike into the CEO parking slot, manually manoeuvring the bike on a slanted angle with the rear wheel of the cycle braced firmly up against the yellow painted kerb, as this placed the bike for a better departing position and visibility. Brad forcefully throttled the bike's accelerator, thus producing a loud and almost obnoxious thunderous roar from the Harley's substantially modified exhaust system, this he did as much as a matter of habit, as well as deliberately drawing the attentions of any wayward drivers in his immediate area. It also served as his way of announcing his triumphant return back to the office. For several minutes, Wayne repeated this action. He dearly desired that everyone within earshot in the Boston financial district to hear and see his presence and prodigal return. This especially applied to those at his firm.

It was another routine and stressful day for Margie DeTagelio and the rest of the firm's staff, as Katherine continued her petty and scornful outbursts against all of the staff, to especially include Margie. Katherine was now in a perpetual state of 'Brad-PMS'; he hadn't contacted her since he had called her from the Badlands. Katherine was getting more and more nervous; her plans for an October wedding were becoming more precarious with each passing day. She even took the initiative of sending out wedding invitations for a late October ceremony and had made the appropriate reception reservations.

Ever since Margie's earlier caustic ladies' room confrontation with Katherine, their work relationship had gone from cool to ice cold, with Katherine demanding the performance of tedious, petty, and stressful office tasks that frequently caused Margie to work 12-hour days. Margie had to put up with the abuse, as she desperately needed the employment, if even for a terminal period. More importantly, she needed her six months of severance pay and pro-rated annual bonus.

Arriving back from an extended 'coffee- break', she happened to notice the vulgar and intriguing loud roar of a motorcycle, its thunderous bellows were equally repulsive and attractive simultaneously. Not being overly excited about getting back to her desk, she spied a glance out of the main two-storey veranda eyebrow-style window whereby she noticed that some motorcycle vagabond was parked in the reserved space of its CEO and he had the audacity to proclaim his defiance with this loud and continuous exhaust rapture. She thought that this motorcyclist had one hell of a nerve to park in a reserved space that was so evidently marked; after all, there was temporary and visitor parking clearly indicated on the posted signs in front of the building.

'Some people are just damn ignorant pigs, I hope that this guy gets his rude ass ticketed,' Margie casually thought. Harley motorcyclists were a rare sight in front of the Hamilton & MacAlister firm and the scene continued to temporarily eenthral Margie, after all, she'd rather be looking at a grimy biker than Katherine's unsmiling cold puss!

"Hello Margie, what's the big attraction outside? Did someone get run over or have an accident," Leona coarsely stated, as she too gazed out the window to sight the gamely styled Harley motorcycle rider. "That urban cowboy had better watch himself, that's a reserved spot and he's making quite a racket with that iron beast…he had better hope that no one calls the cops on him, especially someone like Miss Katherine," Leona scorned.

"Yeah well, if 'Kit Kat' sees that poor bastard, there'll be no need to call Boston's finest, he'll need the Emergency Medical crew from Boston General Hospital to extract her foot from his ass!" Margie growled, as both ladies laughed.

"Hey now, what's all the commotion around here?" Neal Fowler remarked, as both he and Jim Herrigan also gathered at the window to see what event or activity was drawing the attention and laughter of Margie and Leona.

"Well, it's that mad biker out there, he's illegally parked and he's making quite a stir this afternoon, doesn't he realize that some people are trying to work? Hell, he probably doesn't have a real job, so why should he give a damn! He'd just better hope that Miss Katherine doesn't spot him parking in that reserved spot, she'll sic the cops on that poor fellow," Leona repeated to Jim and Neal.

"Boy, that's a great big beautiful bike that guy has there!" Neal remarked with obvious envious discern and grudging admiration.

"Yeah, a man could sure have some fun on a machine like that, go off and ride off to wherever USA!" Jim dreamily replied.

"Honestly, it's not the machine that I'd like to ride, just look at that well-toned hunk of urban-cowboy down there! You guys can dream about riding that Harley, but I'll dream about riding that hunk down there!" Leona crudely joked, as she girlishly jabbed Margie with her elbow.

"Yes, that sure is a fine specimen of manhood down there," Margie sighed.

"Well, what the hell do we guys up here look like, Elmer Fudd or chopped liver?" Jim shouted back, as Neal gave an affronting glance at the two ladies.

"Oh, don't get me wrong, guys, but you two are just so...so refined ...so civilized...so predictable...so Ivy League and Brooks Brothers suits and well, that guy out there seems so nasty and dangerous...that is nasty in a very sinful way!" Leona crudely joked once again; this time all four of them joined in the laughter.

Brad shut the Harley down and engaged the side jiffy stand, deftly he pulled the ignition key from his belt fob and locked the ignition. He slowly removed his buckskin gauntlets, then his half helmet, and finally his eye protection. His sun-bleached locks of hair blew gently in the wind.

"Wooooo, Weeoooo, Burrrr....Meow.... that's what I want for my birthday!" Leona exhaled in a raunchy low voice and sensually admiring the sexy sun-tanned man adorned with a light golden halo mare.

"Eat your heart out, Brad Pitt," Margie softly muttered.

Jim and Neal just smiled silently and wished to themselves that they too had the good looks and sexual magnetism that their brother-in-arms unquestionably possessed. Every man and woman knew that beauty and handsomeness had the qualities of power unto itself, yet these venial traits were possessed by only a minority of the population. Like money, it was a good thing to have and it had few detractions, still it was also a most fleeting attribute to be used quickly before fading into oblivion.

"I wonder what that sexy hunk wants around this boring place. I doubt if he needs any 'underwriting work'; hell, he's probably unemployed, maybe he's even a drug dealer for some yuppie stockbroker," Margie wily smiled, half wishing that this evaluation was true.

"Hell, whatever it is that he's selling, I'm off work tonight at 5:00 PM," Leona shouted, as she jabbed Margie once again in the same repeated girlish manner.

Margie started to eye Leona with some visual disdain.

"Yeah well, he's probably a delivery man or courier guy or something."

"He'd better drop off whatever stuff he has and then vamoose before he gets cited by the cops or 'Kit Kat' calls the police herself."

In a closing remark, Margie wearily added, "Well that tight ass, Kit Kat, is still on the warpath around here and she's just dying for some fresh meat to chew on and I'd hate for it to be that poor biker bastard out there. If it could be arranged, I'd take half my pay cheque to get 'Miss Kitty' laid, maybe then she would get off our butts! On second thought, no man's ass but Brad's is good enough for Miss Kit Kat!"

Brad looked about and slowly gazed around Bromfield Street, taking a prolonged look at the building of Hamilton & MacAlister. 'Nothing much has changed around here. I wonder how much of the old gang has missed me or if they even missed me at all?' Brad mused. He gazed up to the upper floors of the second floor and there he noticed some familiar faces at the window, he smiled and waved to those looking on with vicarious admiration and attention.

"Hey guys, that motorcycle man…he's looking directly up here and waving to us," Leona shouted in a girlish tone. "Hey folks, I might be having myself a date after all later tonight," Leona added in excitement.

Margie eyed the bearded man more closely and muttered in an almost silent disbelief, "It couldn't…it couldn't be him" she sighed. "Oh… Oh my…Oh my God…Oh my fucking…" Margie shouted to the others.

"What is it, Margie?" Leona cried out.

Both Jim and Neal looked at Margie in amazement.

Traditionally, Margie was the one to always crouch her emotions and vocabulary at the workplace. Her eyes widened, and her mouth opened wide in exacerbation. "I fucking think that Wild West motorcycle man is, Brad! Yes, it's 'our' Brad Hamilton!" Margie wildly screamed in excitement.

They all looked quickly at one another then they all gazed intensely out through the huge window to view the bearded man and study his features more closely.

"Why yes, yes, of course...he does seem to resemble Mr Hamilton a bit, now that you mention it, Margie," Leona exclaimed and still not believing her eyes.

"Yeah, that guy does look familiar," Neal exclaimed in utter disbelief.

Margie and the others all waved back, each with an exacerbated stare of disbelief.

Swiftly and dreadfully, a familiar shrill voice disrupted everyone's composure and attention. "Hey people... and just what in the hell is going on here? Am I paying the employees of Hamilton & MacAlister to stare out the window, when they should be working!" Katherine shouted in a very commanding and annoyed voice, as she spotted four of her workers laughing, talking, and waving out of the large second storey veranda window.

"So, just what in the hell is so damn important or interesting that everyone is away from their work places? I'm not paying anyone here to socialize or look out at the streets of Boston! If you find the view outside so interesting, maybe you'll all find yourselves out there real soon – unemployed, that is! Do you all want to end up like DeTagelio?" Katherine shouted at the four, paying particular acrid attention to Margie and her pending termination status.

Katherine brashly pushed aside the four employees and gazed out the window herself to spy the object of her employees' attention and apparent admiration. She quickly spotted the handsome bearded man and his motorcycle parked conspicuously outside in the firm's reserved parking spaces. "Who's that common biker trash out there? He'd better move his junk before I call the flipping police," Katherine snipped sharply.

"No, wait please! It's Mr Brad, or at least we think it's him, Miss Katherine," Leona wildly exclaimed.

At the utterance of Brad's name, Katherine's facial composure change, as her frown changed immediately into a smile. Katherine's gaze quickly returned to the window, as she intensely gazed at the strange motorcyclist. Slowly Wayne started toward the building entrance. Katherine gazed at the man for a brief few seconds before he entered the Hamilton & MacAlister building and she immediately affirmed the man's familiar smile, piercing blue eyes and familiar stance.

"It's him, he's really back," Kate softly muttered to herself, as a broad smile beamed across her face. "Everyone, back to your work! I mean right now, people! I'm not paying all of you to stand around to gossip and gawk, get your butts back to work, immediately!" Katherine barked as the four scrambled back to their work areas.

"DeTagelio, as soon as Brad comes up those steps, I want you to have him come directly into my office – that means no small talk, no bathroom break, no frigging flirting…he comes directly to my office. Is that clear?" Katherine demanded forcefully.

Margie looked straight into Katherine's menacing eyes. Without waiting for a reply, Katherine continued, "You try anything cute with my Brad and I'll fire your ass right here on the spot and that means no severance pay for you, girlie…now do I make myself frigging clear?"

Margie became quite defensive, but she maintained her professional composure and her dignity. "Yes, of course, whatever you say, Miss Katherine," Margie responded in a mousy and submissive tone.

By now, Margie knew that it was both pointless and unprofitable to discuss anything with 'Kit Kat' on a rational level. She had burnt all of her bridges! Her imminent termination of employment and her bad blood with Kit Kat ensured that her dreams of having a future in the Boston financial sector was slim to none. Katherine's influence and reach in the Boston financial community was indisputable. Kate was not a woman to be either crossed or scorned, unless at one's personal and professional peril. Margie had made an enemy with whom she could not hope to conquer. The best she could hope for at this stage was a modest financial termination package and a less than stellar work recommendation. Without a good reference, Margie was nervous about how she was going to support herself and her aging mother. An undesired relocation to another city was a distinct possibility.

Katherine quickly scurried back to her office, knowing that she had only a few fleeting minutes before she saw her long-lost fiancé. She, of course, wanted to make the best impression possible; after all, the two had left on uneasy terms and it was six months since she had last seen and loved her man. The stranger, who had briefly appeared outside the large foyer window, appeared to be very different in appearance from the man who had left her office that cool spring day. In her brief gaze of the man, she noticed that he was smiling and his movement was one of positive affirmation and personal assertiveness. Oh, how she longed and yearned that her 'old Brad' was back again just as he used to be with her – safe, stable, fun loving and sane.

Katherine quickly retreated to her private office bathroom and scented herself with a quick spray of Chanel #5, she checked in the mirror and quickly combed her hair, next she took a quick gargle, and then finally she reapplied her light pink colour lipstick. Katherine next quickly eyed her office to ensure that nothing was amiss – she checked that the liquor decanters were all filled; that the glasses and ice were ready; and that her office furniture was cleared and ready for sitting or anything else in which they both cared to indulge. These were long, lonely months, during which time Katherine had neither flirted nor entertained the company of other men. Brad was her one and only man. She was faithful and ready for him!

Brad dutifully tucked his eyewear and gauntlets into his helmet, carrying the ensemble by the helmet chinstrap for an easy, natural carry. He slowly made his way up the grand staircase of Hamilton & MacAlister. Reaching into his back pants pocket, he produced a black leather motorcycle wallet, replete with attached security chrome chain. He held the wallet up to a security cipher pad, which was located just outside the imposing main double security glass doors that bore the gold etched name in Old English styled lettering 'Hamilton & MacAlister, Inc.' His security code was good as gold, as a gentle buzz affirmed that validity of the security card held up to the scanner device. A private, secure elevator led him to the exclusive second floor Executive offices. Immediately before him and guarding the access unto all of the Executive areas, was the lead office Executive Manager, Gail Myers.

"Well, hello, Gail, I'm finally back home!" he smiled with outstretched arms of friendship unto his old office friend.

Gail was temporarily startled by Brad's announcement and morphed appearance. She stared admiringly at the strange man, then suddenly cried out, "Oh my dear Lord, you're back...you're really back, Brad!" Tears started to form in Gail's eyes. "It's great to have you back, Brad; after all of these months, everyone will be delighted to see you again... it's been like a wasteland here without you," Gail cried with weighted emotions, as she struggled to believe the strange sight that her eyes beheld. "The boss looked great, like a new man, and with no sign of any depression," she correctly surmised.

He warmly cuddled both of Gail's hands and looked at her intensely in the eyes. "Great, I guess somebody around here missed me after all" he said half-jokingly. Gail merely smiled, as joyful tears trekked down her cheeks.

"You look terrific, Brad, we all missed you and please tell me that you are coming back to stay!" Gail pleaded.

"Well, you see, Gail, I'm taking one day at a time now, that's all that life offers to any one of us," Brad offered softly. "Gail, I'll talk to you later, I want to see some of the others. I'll see you again later," Brad responded as he made his way into the main office corridor and toward the eyebrow window where he had spotted his old office drinking pals.

"Hey guys, how are you all doing? Did anyone miss me?" Brad cheerfully sounded-off to his old friends.

In tandem, they all anxiously ran up to Brad to shake his hands, pat him on the back, or in the case of Leona, just supplant Brad with an affectionate big hug.

"You look great, Brad, really trim and proper," Jim barked, while Leona gave Brad a big kiss on the cheek. "Mr Brad you looked so fine, strapping and unfamiliar that I thought that I had a new date for myself."

Brad smiled and responded in jest, "Well, Leona, don't despair, the day is still young!" The old extraverted, playful Bradford Hamilton was back at last! They all laughed and smiled with one another, with everyone asking a zillion question simultaneously.

"Far too many questions… hey look, let me go see Kate and after that, we'll see…maybe we'll get together at Olde Baileys and discuss the entire sorted adventure," Brad teased the office crew.

They all marvelled at how positive and mature Brad had looked and acted. He sure wasn't the same man that left the office in a deep depression months earlier, they all concluded. Margie was eagerly waiting for Brad at her desk in wild anticipation; she had mixed emotions of both anxiety and redemption.

"Hello Margie! How's my favourite redhead and personal assistant doing these days? I really missed you!" Brad warmingly exclaimed to Margie, as she eagerly arose from her desk chair. Before Margie even had a chance to respond to Brad's presence or remarks, he moved close to her desk and presented to her a long affectionate embrace, one that lasted several long seconds. The two hugged like close friends, yet not as lovers. He whispered softly in her left ear that he had missed her intensely. Margie melted like butter in Brad's embrace, she returned the friendly and affectionate hug, not wanting to let go of the man she secretly loved yet acknowledging in her heart that she could never be Brad's lady. Brad also knew of the hidden crush that Margie had for him, and it was something that he would never reveal or betray to anyone.

Brad loved Margie just as he had loved his own sister Melissa, yet he knew that often in life, desires are not always mutual or reciprocal, that affairs of the heart were never planned, these things just happened or didn't happen. Tears ran like a steady slow stream down Margie's face and she coughed a little from her own tears.

"God, how I missed you! The entire office missed you, Brad... we're so glad that you are finally back among us!" Margie sobbed cheerfully. Margie continued to look intensely at Brad. 'Yes, he was different, physically, emotionally, and spiritually,' she thought. "His depression was gone!" she quickly surmised, yet he was not the 'same old Brad' who had left the office last April. He was somehow different, but it was for the better, she wisely deducted.

"Boy oh boy, you sure do look terrific, Brad. I suspect that western outdoor living agrees with you," Margie exclaimed in admiration of Brad's changed physical features and positive mental demeanour.

"Okay, what do you like the most about the new me?" Brad devilishly inquired.

"Everything...I mean everything," Margie replied as she broadly smiled back at Brad.

"So, how are things going around here, Margie?" Brad inquired anxiously.

Margie looked away for a second, then glanced back to Brad with tears in her eyes. "It's been a living hell around here, Brad. Kit Kat's been on the warpath, in fact, she's terminating my employment – I'm leaving in about a week, Brad." Tears streamed down Margie's face.

Brad gently took Margie in his arms and gave her a brotherly warm hug.

"Not to worry, Margie. You are my personal assistant and only I can fire you; now don't fret about getting fired. I'll make things right for you, so let's have a big smile!" Brad whispered into Margie's ear.

Brad's words of comfort and redemption were most consoling to Margie. Quickly, she remembered the stern charge given to her by Miss Katherine some minutes earlier. Margie quickly composed herself and gave Brad the message that Miss Katherine had directed to her. "So, how is Kate? She must have made life a sheer hell for everyone around here, I imagine! I can taste the tension in the air!" Brad inquired of Margie.

She didn't utter a disparaging word, she just smiled and extended her arm, pointing to Miss Katherine's office.

"Her Highness awaits your presence in her office, good luck in whatever happens," Margie dryly uttered and buzzed Kit Katherine's office.

Wayne merely smiled back to Margie and softly blew her a kiss.

Brad knocked firmly on Katherine's door. Katherine's hands were nervously sweating, and her heart was racing with almost uncontrolled anxiety. Immediately subconscious fears reproached her, "Would Brad still feel the same way about me? Was Brad in love with another woman? Does he still love me the way he used to? Was Brad now ready to settle down and become her husband at last?" – all these things Katherine rapidly self-questioned in her mind, playing 'what if' scenarios like a wild business deal; yet, this was not some cold business deal, it was her life and the stakes were final and personal. The man she loved was about to suddenly re-enter her life and she was unprepared for the encounter. She had always hated surprises as these tended to decrease her control of events and actions. She hoped that she would say and do all the things necessary to confirm Brad's love and get him to stay for good. Desperately she tried to remain cool, collective, and nonchalant, as she sat erect in her high back Louis XV styled desk chair.

Unsure of Brad's mindset or even that of her own, she would try to retain her composure until she was sure that Brad was totally cured of his past depression and that he was back in his old frame of mind. Overexcitement could be devastating to both herself and Brad, especially if he had any vestiges of his 'dark dog' depression.

"Please come in," Katherine replied in a clocked, very business-like tone, not desiring to appear overeager for the person that she knew was beckoning at her office door. Brad slowly peeled open Katherine's door and before him sat a radiant and blushing brunette with luscious green eyes and adoring soft pink lips. This 'Daughter of Venus' had incessantly haunted him throughout his long trek home. Kate was as voluptuous and beautiful as ever, she was arrayed in a pale two-piece light blue business blouse suit and attired in white silk blouse with matching shoes, complemented by a necklace of double strand white pearls accented with 18 karat gold oak leaf styled fasteners.

"Hello Kate, it's good to finally see you again, I hope that I am still welcome here?" Brad smiled, as he warmly cast his gaze onto Kate, while discreetly closing the door behind him. He tossed his helmet and gear aside onto a small blue leather winged chair.

From her short glancing spectacle atop the second storey window, Katherine had insufficient time to fully partake of the 'new Brad' except for a fleeting glance that betrayed the image of a bearded masculine figure and a large Harley Davidson motorcycle. She had no idea of how much Brad had physically changed and she was momentarily, yet pleasantly distracted by his outdoor rugged appearance. Her eyes quickly danced across the image of a handsome man in his mid-thirties; he looked like he had just posed for an issue of Alaska magazine. There before Kate stood a tall, well-toned, sun bleached, bearded man, who possessed the wildly endowed features of her old beau. His clothing was reminiscent of those of the Wild West cowboy, like Buffalo Bill Cody. Brad stood tall and adorned with a broad, flawless smile. He appeared to Katherine eyes to be almost beaming.

Seeing Brad's radiant ivory smile and hearing his warm masculine inviting voice, Katherine's self-control immediately evaporated. "Oh, my sweet Lord, Brad! Is that really you or just a phantom?" Katherine cried out as she jumped up from behind her French styled desk like an eager rabbit emerging from a secret hiding place. With tears of joy and little girl excitement, Katherine madly rushed into Brad's arms and hugged him for dear life, she was afraid that this sweet reality would soon vanish like a mirage before her eyes. Immediately gone were all her illusions of pretence and charade, Brad's muscular embrace had evaporated all of Kate's phony defences. Kate passionately dug her fingers into Brad's buckskin jacket and clung to Brad like a child beholding a newfound puppy dog. After a seemingly eternity of joyful seconds, Kate recoiled from her passionate embrace and started to passionately kiss Brad madly on his lips and face.

"Thank goodness, you're back with me again! I was afraid of the thought that I'd never see you again, Brad! I thought that I'd lost you for good to some low life road tramp or something...I just can't believe that you're back!" Kate passionately sobbed, as she gently whispered the contents of her soul into Brad's receptive ears, all the while continuing to kiss Brad's face and lips with wild abandon. Brad was consumed by Kate's unbridled passions, as their mouths met and joined for seemingly untold moments of eternity. He immediately remembered how soft and warm Kate's kisses and embraces were, the scent of her Chanel #5 perfume released many fond memories of their past amorous encounters. The two embraced in each other's arms and finally they both looked fondly at each other, appraising the physical delight and comfort of the other.

Distance and time really did make their hearts grow fonder.

They gazed into each other's eyes like reunited lovers, which in truth, they were. "Gosh...let me have a look at you, Brad – or is it 'Wayne' this week?" Kate jokingly sighed in a sly hint referring to his signed postcard in which he had mysteriously used his middle name. She took a step back and gave Brad the long feminine twice over, broadly smiling from ear-to-ear all the while.

"Woo my goodness! I do like the hair and I just love the body, and that gorgeous tan – it's to die for, Brad, and that beard, well...I think maybe that I can do without the beard, but for now, keep it for my girlish naughty fantasies. I want to say that I made love to a real mountain man at least once in my life!" Kate sexily purred as she complimented Brad, while running her slim fingers across his well-muscled chest and gently stroking his bronze chiselled tan face. Kate looked tenderly into Brad's eyes once again, this time with a softness and sincerity that was missing during her initial passionate embrace. She looked deeply into Brad's eyes and gently moved her fingers through his sun-bleached, light golden locks.

"Lord how I have waited for this moment, Brad, I've missed you like you can't believe," Kate softly whispered with joyful tears in her eyes, as she gently kissed Brad's lips and cheeks.

His hands gently stroked Kate's soft cheeks tenderly, as he ran his fingers up and down her milky white skin. "I missed you too, Kate... it seems like I have lived a lifetime, since I ran out that door last April," Brad confessed with heartfelt emotion in his voice.

"Hush now...that's all behind us now, darling," she purred and continued to caress his face, then proceeding to gently kiss his rugged fingers and hands. She eagerly scented the rich aroma of newly tanned leather from his buckskin jacket, the masculine aroma only continued to tantalize Katherine's passionate disposition.

"My, oh my...how terrific you look, my dearest Brad, and it seems like everything is right with you now?" Katherine announced as a matter of passive polite inquiry and hopeful affirmation.

"Yes indeed, Kate, I'm fine...better than I have ever been in my entire life!" Brad responded with a faint smile.

Always the keen observer, Kate instinctively knew that Brad was not the same depressed, introspective, grief-stricken guy, who had bolted away from his troubles the previous April, yet he wasn't the same old boyish Brad that she had grown to love either. There was something different in this man, Brad had definitely changed, but she wasn't sure just how and in what particular manner.

Like wildfire, the office was abuzz with talk about the unexpected return of Brad Hamilton. There was anxious speculation among the staff concerning Brad's changed appearance, attitude, and even his future role within the firm. Immediately outside Kate's closed office door, Margie had gathered along with Leona, Jim, and Neal, while Miss Peters stood back several feet.

"So, what do you think is going on inside there?" Margie inquired of her office mates and social drinking buddies.

"I don't know, but I expect that things are not what these used to be and that sparks are going to fly in that office," Leona proclaimed in anxious anticipation.

"Do you think that Brad has found another woman?" Neal speculated.

"I don't know, but standing out here, we're not going to find out anything!" Jim replied with audible frustration.

"I too wish that I was a fly on the wall in Kit Kat's office," the usually aloof and reserved Miss Peters uncharacteristically butted in.

"This may lose us all of our bonuses, but it's worth it, come on!" Margie exclaimed, as she deftly handed out six-inch-long drinking glasses to her partners in crime. Following Margie's lead, each person carefully placed the glass up against Kate MacAlister's office door. It was a crude, almost childish-like intrusion, yet the scheme worked, and each person could clearly hear the echoed conversations of Brad and Katherine from within the adjourning room.

"Okay, let me say again, Brad, you sure do look fine, just like a real mountain man; I'm not sure if a little city girl like me can handle a hunk of man like you," Katherine childishly toyed, as she flirtingly teased her tongue back and forth against her meticulously perfect white teeth. "I really like what I see here, Brad," Katherine added approvingly and in a seductive tone. She approached Brad closely once again and as she smiled, ran her hands and arms across Brad's muscular chest, arms, and back.

"Hummmm...that feels really good, I notice that someone's been working out over the summer! Now tell me, Brad, is my little surprise package as good as it looks?" Katherine sighed as she continued to flirt and caress Brad's upper torso. Brad gently clasped Katherine's hands in his own and looked her stoically and deeply in the eyes.

"Well, Kate, fighting wildfires was never known to fatten anyone's waistline and I don't recommend it as an easier alternative to working out at a gym…it was one of the toughest things that I've done in my cloistered life…it changed me physically and in other ways too, Kate."

Immediately Katherine saw the seriousness in Brad's eyes and she knew instinctively that there was a undisclosed story hiding behind his subtle, veiled declaration. Brad rapidly tried to shift the conversation and tone of their reunion from passionate to serious in the utterance of one short sentence. Yet Katherine was concerned, puzzled, and most intrigued by Brad's revelation, she wanted to know more, despite the dangers and consequences that such knowledge could convey. Serious words portended grave issues.

"Lies, what sort of sweet little lies do we have here, my darling Brad? Fighting wildfires indeed! Well, that's something that you failed to tell me about, my sweetheart. I hope it's not the only thing that you are keeping from me!" Kate toyfully replied back with a smug retort. Brad thought it best to say nothing more about his summer adventures and indiscretions; it would do no one any good.

"Forget it! How about a drink with your future wife?" Katherine smiled.

Brad simply nodded in affirmation, as Kate poured two short, malt scotches liberally heaped with ice cubes. As she prepared their drinks, Katherine passed the seconds by making 'small talk' with Brad, as she casually poured out the aged whiskey into two heavy leaden Tiffany crystal chaser glasses.

"I received all of your little letters and cute memento postcards, Brad, but aren't you going to tell me anything more or do I have to keep on guessing? You have been gone from my life for half a year and I think that I deserve some details about your little adventures! I'm more than just a little bit curious, you know; after all, a future husband and wife should not be keeping secrets from one another!" Katherine coyly proclaimed as she winked a devilish smile while turning her head slightly backward and making a deliberate sardonic glance at Brad.

"Honestly, there isn't that much to tell, Kate, to be quite honest, I just did some odd jobs here and there, but nothing of significance to speak about really!" Brad evasively responded.

Katherine was having none of this cloistered subterfuge.

"Oh, come on now, Brad darling, don't be so modest about your summer adventures! What about Ohio and that Moto Cross racing gig?" Katherine snapped back inquisitively. Brad was surprised and dumbfounded for a moment. "Well then, how about Lawrence, Kansas and your job as a short-order cook?" she inquired rhetorically.

"Ohio... Lawrence?" Brad repeated the words slowly and in self-disbelief.

"Well then, how about Casper and that Indian Reservation Tavern... you know, that rough-neck place where you spent all of that time... the place where you took the bet...the place where you met that girl, now what was her name again...oh yes, her name is Robin...Robin Wolf...that quite common, pretty, half-breed, Native Indian girl, is that correct?" Katherine stated dryly and sarcastically with a slight crease of a sarcastic cruel smile. She was playing high-stakes poker with Brad.

He could not believe his ears – 'just how in the hell did Kate know these very private things?' He appeared visibly disturbed, he now wore a guilty little boy appearance on his face, a look that Katherine immediately noticed as a sign of aversion and deception. As a keen judge of body language, Kate noticed the disturbed and defensive look in Brad's eyes and face, his whole-body posture seemed to tense up at the mention of Robin and his eyes immediately turned away from hers. Katherine knew that she had struck a nerve here. Obviously, there was more about Brad's summer adventure than the innocent looking postcards had seemed to convey.

"Those places and things... were nothing, Kate, just some passing memories of nameless places and faces...so how did you know about these things, Kate?" Brad replied nervously, as he paced the floor and tried to dodge Katherine's embarrassing inquiries.

"Oh, yes my dear, I'm sure there were some innocent moments, but are you telling me the whole truth, my darling, Brad? I think maybe not!" Katherine responded in a sarcastic tone. Katherine moved back over to her desk and placed down her drink. Discreetly, she gazed down at the envelope that was unmarked, save for the prominent words engraved in the upper left hand of the envelope, "Haster & Dickens Private Detectives, Boston, Mass." She played nervously with the large beige envelope.

"Your communications and correspondence with me over the past few months have been rather sparse and irregular to say the least, my darling, and I think that I want to know a little more of what my Bradford has been up to and with whom he has been playing around with this past summer! I had to be a bit pro-active for my own contentment and to protect my most valuable personal asset – which is you," Katherine sounded off justifiably, as she snipped the smooth scotch from her glass.

Totally caught off-guard and morally intimidated by Kate's factual confrontation, he paused for a short moment before tersely replying, "Like I said, Kate, nothing much happened – I met some people, did some odd jobs, had some funny experiences – that's all, nothing else really, nothing that concerns you! I hope this is not some sort of interrogation! I'm not on trial here, Kate!" Brad replied in his awkward defence.

The obvious verbal obfuscation of Brad's oblique responses had hit a raw nerve with Katherine, since she believed that everything Brad did was of a direct concern to herself and her interests... besides it was clear that he was obviously hiding something of importance that he dared not to share with her. Brad was not telling her the complete truth. Distrust between an engaged couple was intolerable, it harkened to future cheating in marriage and Katherine would not have another cheating man in her life.

She became aggressively agitated by Brad's evasiveness of her questions, as he was obviously hiding something important, something personal and secret. "Oh no you don't, Brad, you don't come strutting back here into my office after six months of fucking-around and just pick up things where you left off, I want to hear more...and everything that my fiancé does, interests me and is of my personal concern. I am not starting off my marriage of one that is based on lies and deceit!" Kate replied sharply. She knew that Brad was lying and she wanted the confession from his own lips.

Not knowing when or how to leave well enough alone, Kate pressed Brad on his vague and mysterious adventures. "I know that my beau has changed over the last few months, but I want the truth from you, every detail too!" Katherine smiled as she verbally noted her acute discoveries. "I know that you have a new look, a new motorcycle, some new friends, even a new name – you curiously called yourself 'Wayne', and perhaps maybe you even have a new girlfriend?" Katherine teased as she smilingly looked into Brad's eyes to detect some trace of emotion or personal reaction. Words could lie, but appearances and actions never do!

In an obvious sign of embarrassment and guilt, Brad instinctively looked down and away from Katherine. "We were just a bunch of friends working together, fighting the wildfires, I did not want for you to be overly concerned or nervous about me or the dangerous work that I was doing – that's all, Kate, and that is the truth too!" Brad half-confessed softly.

Katherine detected an evasion, perhaps even guilt in Brad's wavering, low-toned reply and slouched body language. Bitterly looking at the picture postcards that Brad had sent to her the past summer, she angrily and sarcastically muttered out, "Just friends huh...just fighting fires you say...and so was this Robin your summer fling? Were you fucking her all summer long, Brad? Do you love her, Brad? Tell me the truth and tell me now, dammit!", Katherine tearfully pressed Brad, her voice cracking with repressed emotions.

"It's like I told you before, Kate, we were friends.... just a group of firefighters, that's all!" Brad poorly lied defensively, while trying to control the emotions that he still felt for Robin.

"Whose idea was it to use the name 'Wayne', hers or yours? Were you trying to hide your identity or something? You haven't used your middle name since you were a small boy, Brad, so what's really going on here?" Katherine sarcastically accused, yet still wanting to get Brad to admit to her all of his roadside love affairs.

"My affairs...I mean to say, my adventures – were nothing, Kate, nothing, really! Anyway, what's past is past, it's all in my rearview mirror now," Brad poorly lied to Katherine.

Never the fool, she knew a verbal evasion when she heard one and Brad's, sure as hell sounded like a doozy to her.

"Well, well, well, my darling, it seems that we both had some secrets this summer. You know it's really amazing what a little money and a beautiful, tall, red-headed, private detective can uncover," Katherine remarked with a hint of mystery. Katherine smiled and smartly picked up the large manila envelope that she had been fondling. Slowly and smartly, she withdrew a professionally prepared folder from within the manila envelope, the contents of which Brad was not in a position to discern immediately. Aroused with indignation, Katherine proceeded to read aloud in a manner befitting a cost accountant, the various summer episodes that Brad had been living these past six months.

"So, it's nothing...nothing you say...well how about some cheques in the amount of $25, 000 each to five guys in Cincinnati, Ohio and the purchase of ten racing motorcycles for a total of $275,000! How about a Cashier's cheque of $275,000 and a generous tuition stipend to a woman named Joyce in Lawrence, Kansas! There's a multi-million dollar offer to purchase some 'hole-in-the-wall' diner too! Nothing you say... shall I continue for you?" Katherine shouted angrily. "Oh yes, the pièce de résistance, how about a whopping cheque of $17.5 million dollars made out to the Robin Wolf Children's School of the Wind River Indian Reservation, Wyoming! Oh, I have convicting evidence to prove everything that I have just outlined," Katherine shouted forth in a succinct accusatory, bitter-laced, diatribe.

"So, what is all of this charity about, Brad, feeling sorry for the downtrodden working class and Indians or maybe this Robin just had a killer ass, huh Brad?…Well I just hope that she was flipping worth it!… and all this damn time, I am sitting back here in Boston and sucking up the hurt, loneliness, and pulling your weight around the office, while you're out screwing all over the Wild West! I'm mighty glad that we have to get a blood test for our marriage certificate, I don't want to be catching any venereal diseases from your little whore and summer of love!" Katherine screamed loudly.

His demeanour and composure had changed completely with the relentless crude inquiries and personal accusations from Katherine. She had rudely and coarsely peered into his private life and this injured his pride, even if her facts were spot-on! These personal attacks and accusations made his blood pressure and temper begin to boil. She had a right to be angry and deserved the truth, but her entire approach was wrongheaded and most confrontational! Kate was a real tongue-lasher at times.

"First, I don't like being spied upon, Kate, I don't like it one damn bit and what I did on the road with my life was my own business. Second, I don't like that kind of talk – don't you dare to talk like that about her and my friends, Katherine, do you hear me? Third, this is my money and I will spend it on whatever and whoever pleases me!" Brad angrily replied.

"Now you wait just one damn minute there, Brad, honey! I am the wronged party here, not you! I do not like being lied to and being two-timed by my fiancé…just how in the hell can I trust you in the future?" Kate snapped back with equal resolution and justification. Katherine now knew from Brad's reaction and protective tone that he had been romantically involved with this woman Robin, a possibility that she had entertained for some time. Katherine was now afraid that Brad's affair still lingered in his heart and this suspicion she needed to confirm to herself, lest it haunt her future forever. Katherine had no present knowledge of Robin's death, as the pretty female private detective had left Wyoming well before the occurrence of the Satan Pitchfork and Wind River wildfires. Kate needed Brad back with no emotional strings attached to any other woman. Mere casual sex was one thing, love was a different and deeper issue.

Awkwardly, Katherine tried to diffuse the conversation, while still seeking to discover the extent of Brad's romantic liaisons. She rapidly regained her composure, as she smilingly made further inquiries of Brad. "Okay – all right, Brad! Look here, we're both mature adults, I know that you were lonely on the road, that you were under emotional stress. You're a man and you had a fling or two, and that you sowed some 'wild oats' and maybe you even had a few laughs, right, darling?" Katherine smiled with a false veneer of lightheartedness. "Look, I don't approve of what you did, but I do understand why you did it, but that's all behind you now, right, darling? We have a new future from here on out," Katherine definitively and positively announced, while hoping to undo a caustic conversation.

"Look, these were my friends, Kate, they each accepted me for who I was and for what I did, not because of my name, my possessions, or my heritage…this all means something good to me, Kate," Brad stressed in a serious tone.

Katherine looked at Brad in bewilderment, not knowing in the least bit what he was referring to in his silly 'common man' monologue. Katherine picked up one of the picture postcards that Brad had sent to her, it was the one which depicted Robin, Sam, Hank, and Indian Joe. Katherine did not want to further inflame Brad, instead she merely wanted to bring him back to the reality of the world that he had left behind – a world of responsibility, privilege, and traditions, an insular world that was his by right of birth, wealth and upbringing.

Within the neat large manila folder, Katherine had the Private Detective report from the attractive red-headed Jill Sandberg, whose information included a narrative summary of all of Brad's summer activities, cash distributions and photographs of all his intimate contacts. Katherine pulled out one of these from the folder and produced it to him. The picture was taken from the top of Indian Joe's bar, where it showed Brad and Robin kissing and fondling within a secluded booth at Indian Joe's tavern. Pointing and referring to the picture, Katherine further exclaimed, "Look, Brad, I know that you enjoyed seeing how the other side lives, but it's a childish illusion. You could never be one of those common, working-class people, Brad… you were raised as a Hamilton damn it, you're just like me. You can't change that or your basic nature, Brad!"

Undeterred, he valiantly tried to defend his new-found ideals. "Oh no, you're wrong Kate, you're so very wrong... I'm not like you at all anymore, I've changed...I think of the world and people differently now, Kate," he calmly exclaimed.

"Oh, there is another thing, Kate, I hate being investigated! Is this the type of frigging life that I have to expect when we get married as well? Do I have to constantly look over my shoulder for some detective checking me out, Kate? I sure as hell don't want to be looking over my shoulder for a 'private dick' photographer when we are married!" Brad voiced violently. A woman of strong passions, independence and fortitude, Kate wasn't standing still for any of Brad's self-righteous indignation either.

"If you were honest and faithful, my dear Brad, you would have nothing to hide and I would not suspect anything from an honest man. I married a cheating bastard the first time and I will not be married to a cheating man the second time around, Brad! I am not marrying another phony man who cannot keep his dick in his pants! Where was your fidelity to me! Are you seduced so easily by a pretty woman? How on earth can I trust you anymore?" Katherine yelled back in righteous self-defence. Her accusatory points were indisputable.

They were both guilty in their fidelity and trust to one another and each of them secretly knew it. Yet Brad's sin was the graver one, as it was his infidelity which had prompted Katherine's suspicions and actions, yet two wrongs only made relationships twice as fragile. The room grew silent for a few seconds as the two guilty parties sought to find a way out of this verbal combat. The naked truths were fully revealed, now amends needed to be made.

Katherine again tried to reason with Brad. She desperately tried to get him to see things her way, the real way of the world through her discriminating eyes. As true to her nature, Katherine often said the wrong thing at the wrong time. "Look, Brad, you've been hanging out with all the wrong type of people – white trash, Indians, biker bums, blacks, sluts, single moms, and God knows what the hell other type of road vermin...and that's not you, that's not being a Hamilton! You have a responsibility to your social class and peers!" Katherine shouted-out impassionedly in the security of her innate prejudices.

Brad became sullen, distant, and cold in his emotions upon hearing Katherine's prejudiced words. She judged people she did not personally know. A year earlier, he would probably have agreed with her, or at least, never have given her words a second thought. Now her words stung like arrows in his heart, for unknowingly Katherine had attacked Brad's entire last six months on the road across America; he knew in his heart that this was both wrong and inaccurate. 'There was no way for Katherine to either appraise or attack Brad's emotions, experiences, or friends unless she had personally 'been there for the ride' and she had not been!' Brad wisely reasoned to himself.

There was an eerie, uneasy silence between the two resolute parties and it was amazing how such a large office had suddenly become so small; the silence and the emotional friction was suffocating for Katherine and Brad. Both felt the discomfort and emotional tensions of the other. For some seconds, only silence filled the office and all pretences of passion and good will were evaporated. There could only be a definitive conclusion to this discourse, given the words that were spoken and the emotional tones that had enshrined such passions.

By this time, Katherine was very disturbed and frightened by the tone and direction that the conversation was taking and she wished that she had never brought up the entire topic and that it was perhaps wiser to have let 'sleeping dogs lie' where they may lie, but it was already too late for this and the conversation had proceeded too far to be retrieved from the accusatory cauldron. Again, and quickly, Katherine attempted to turn the conversation into another direction.

"Well then, Brad, regarding other more important matters, you know that we had planned for an April wedding that was quite naturally cancelled because of the tragic death of your family, but we did speak about a quiet, little October wedding, now didn't we?" Katherine subtly hinted.

Brad turned up to look at Katherine, still bitter and resentful of her inquiry and attack on his past lover and friends.

"So, given the things that we have said here today, well perhaps it's best, Kate, if…maybe we shouldn't…" Brad sputtered out before he was quickly cut off and confronted angrily by Katherine, who now stood only inches from his face.

At once, Katherine's physical and emotional tone became totally belligerent, as she immediately noticed that the last vestige of her relationship with Brad and her wedding, was rapidly becoming an impossibility. "Son of a bitch! Now you stop right there, Mister…you're not going to arrogantly stand there and tell me that after months of fucking with every little two-bit whore and floozies, that you're backing out of our wedding, are you?" Katherine screamed in a voice to be heard well outside the confines of her office doors. Yet Katherine was only getting started in her personal tirade.

"I have made elaborate and expensive wedding plans to include sending out the invitations! You can't suddenly come back here out of the blue and say that you're not going to marry me while I've been worrying my heart out for you and busting my ass here, covering business affairs in your frigging absence! I've been planning this high society wedding all summer long! You owe me, do you hear me, you fucking owe me, buddy. We had an agreement here, do you understand? I am not about to be made the laughing stock of Boston society again by having you stand me up at the altar. Just who in the hell do you think you are dealing with here? You're a fucking bastard!" Katherine shrieked in a voice that was clearly audible from outside of her office. None of the snooping office staff could believe their ears! This was a total relationship meltdown.

In a primal and uncontrolled fury, Katherine smartly smacked Brad across the face with her open right palm. The face-slap sound was unmistakably heard from outside Katherine's door. Margie and her listening pals heard the smack and couldn't believe the deteriorating tone of the exchange. Quickly recovering from Katherine's face slap, Brad simply looked at Katherine with a look of pity and solace.

Katherine was expecting some emotional response back from Brad, but none was forthcoming. Katherine's failing nature was to never let sleeping dogs lie, so she pressed Brad's buttons even further to get at the truth that he was hiding from her. Katherine's eye quickly noticed the Robin bird design neck piece hanging down around Brad's neck... the same type of design that was embroidered onto the front of his honey-coloured buckskin jacket, given to him some weeks earlier by Robin Wolf. It now served as a keepsake of their relationship and love. Katherine jealously gazed at the neckpiece and the colourful beaded figure on the jacket and then she ran her hand gently over the embroidery.

"So, what's this little damn charming thing? It's Native American, isn't it? It's pretty and so too I bet was the tramp that gave it to you. Is this something that your $17 million-dollar squaw whore gave to you as a memento? Hah, you got the short end of the deal, buddy, she got a $17 million school and you get a fancy jacket and a few weeks of ass," Katherine mockingly and angrily toyed. "Your little whore must have had one hell of a hot ass for $17 million bucks, Brad, I wonder how much your other little tresses will be costing us? I wish I was worth that much to you, Brad, darling," Katherine loudly scolded in evident verbal bitterness and anger.

Without any notice or pretension, a wild emotional rage sprung through Brad's psyche, as he suddenly screamed out to Katherine, "You spoiled, fucking bitch…don't you fucking touch that, don't you say another word about her!" Instantly Brad drew his left hand across his body, then he forcefully bitch-slapped Katherine across her face in a sudden and most audible backslap!

Instantly losing her balance at Brad's sudden emotional and physical outrage, Katherine stumbled down onto the floor and fell onto her hands and knees. The face slap was totally unexpected, Brad had never been prone to violence in his entire life and he had never struck a woman before in his life. Katherine lay embarrassingly sprawled on the office carpet in temporary shock! The slap stung, but only for a few seconds. Brad's violent emotions and actions were totally primal, but primal never lied!

Katherine's true injury was now knowing that Brad had loved another woman, indeed he loved her still even now! Love was a greater rival than that of mere animal sex. As she unceremoniously lay there on the thick red Persian rug, a streak of utter fear filled Katherine's composure – she had lost her only love. Her face cringed with emotional pain, as tears wallowed in her eyes. Ever the tough woman and not wanting to give Brad any sense of emotional satisfaction, Katherine composed herself, as she tried to quickly fight back the tears.

Immediately, Brad realized the wrongful physical and emotional transgressions, which he had just done to Katherine and he instantly sought to help her to her feet and to comfort her. "Oh my God, please forgive me, Kate! I'm so sorry, Kate! I didn't mean to strike you! I never wanted to hurt you in any way!" Brad pleaded as he quickly grasped Katherine's arms and helped her onto her feet. Katherine quickly tried to disguise her agony with a false grin painted onto her face; she instinctively fixed her hair and quickly dried her eyes with her hands.

"No, that's quite all right, Brad, I guess that one good slap rightfully deserves another and that a bitch like me really deserves a 'bitch-slap' every now and again huh!" Katherine replied with a forced mocking, half smile.

Brad tried once again to apologize to Kate, "I'm so sorry Kate, I didn't mean to…" but Katherine quickly cut Brad off in mid-sentence –

"no you hit with your heart and the heart never lies! No apologies are necessary, Brad, I know where the hell I stand with you now. You love another woman, not me! If you want to do me a favour though, Brad, you can," Katherine snipped through her suppressed tears.

"I want you to get out... just get the hell out of my life and stay out...I never want to see your face again...is that fucking clear, Mister?" Katherine shouted loudly.

Brad knew Kate well enough to realize that he could say nothing to alleviate her angry feelings toward him; he just had to let time calm things down. He had done her wrong and he was filled with anguish.

He moved slowly and deliberately toward Katherine's office door and he started to retrieve his helmet and riding gear. Katherine, however, was by no means through with Brad and she wasn't going to let him off the hook that easily. Katherine's passionate verbal venting at Brad was just beginning and she searched for any words that would further hurt him for the betrayal and hurt that she was experiencing. She was hurt and embarrassed and she wanted revenge.

"You know, Brad, I just wish that it were you who had died in that plane crash, not the others of your family, you fucking bastard! I hate you, Brad, do you hear me! The only Hamilton I want to see around this office is the Hamilton on the face-side of a $10 bill!" Katherine vehemently screamed.

Kit Kat was red-hot angry! She looked for an object, any object and there on her desk, she noticed the large Tiffany lead crystal candy dish. Quickly, Katherine picked up the candy dish and poorly threw the lead crystal vessel at Brad as hard as she could. The crystal candy dish sailed through the air and missed Brad by a good one-foot distance; instead, it forcefully struck the heavy oak office door with a loud shattering sound, breaking into several generously sized pieces as it shattered. The noise was heard down the halls of the firm's offices and everyone stopped their work to gather as to what commotion was occurring in the normally sedate office setting. Immediately, the five nosey office spies fell to their knees as the impact of the crystal candy decanter struck their listening plane. In a comedic unison, all five of them crashed onto the floor, rubbing their ears, eyes, arms, and legs.

Katherine threw several other office objects, including a framed picture of Brad and the two crystal drinking glasses, still filled with whiskey and ice. In an act of final desperation, Katherine took off each of her custom Italian-made pump shoes and threw these forcefully at

Brad. Both shoes missed him and harmlessly struck the office wall before dropping harmlessly onto the ornate wood floor.

Brad quite easily dodged all of these assorted flying objects of Katherine's righteous outrage. 'Katherine was still a bad thrower,' he gleefully thought and remembering back to his childhood days when Kate couldn't throw anything well and she was always the handicap player on their childhood teams. Saying not a word, he gave Katherine one final blank pitiful glance, he opened her office door and gazed to see his office friends and employees shutter back away from the doorway, each of them were still readjusting their attire. They all tried to appear innocent and oblivious to the loud outburst that they had secretly overheard. All of them were too dumbfounded to say anything to Brad. They each had a slight feeling of pity for Katherine, but they each knew that she had this reckoning coming to her – the woman just couldn't leave things alone and now she was paying the price for her audacity and poor judgment. They also immediately realized that Brad would no longer be their saviour or mediator with Katherine, and that she was now going to be a full-time angry, frustrated bitch to work for. Life around Hamilton & MacAlister was going to continue to be sheer hell for all of them. Hell had no wrath like Katherine's anger!

He immediately spotted Margie loitering outside his office, and he suddenly remembered that Margie had informed him about her pending termination by Katherine. He walked over to Margie and loudly asked her a question for everyone in the office corridor to hear, including Katherine. "Margie, how much do you make annually?" Brad barked out loudly. Margie was embarrassed and dumbfounded at both Brad's tone and by the very public inquiry of her modest salary. As with most commercial firms, the salary rate paid to employees was deliberately kept confidential, this to keep envy and jealousy away from workplace performance. Margie looked at Brad nervously and with some fear, yet she made no immediate reply to his inquiry. Brad naturally knew how much Margie made in salary, yet he loudly repeated his question again, "Margie, I asked you, how much do you make?"

Slowly and with meek embarrassment, Margie, quietly replied, "I make $48,000 annually without bonus, Mr Hamilton."

Brad smiled and looked decidedly at Katherine. "No Margie, double that, you now make $96,000 a year and you qualify for full bonus status, just like any other fully-vested Hamilton & MacAlister employee, and that starts today! On second thought, make that $175,000 a year! Does everyone hear me?" Brad shouted loudly. Then Brad quickly added, "The salary money is coming directly out of my business account and you are my permanent personal assistant, I alone have personal actions over you!" Brad noted directly to Katherine.

"Thank you most kindly, Mr Hamilton," Margie softly smiled. Brad broadly smiled back in return.

Brad gently pinched Margie's cheek in both affection and friendship. Brad then whispered lightly to Margie, "I need a friend to talk to, Margie, a lot happened out there on the road and I have always kept you as my confidante, you could always keep a secret. Can I call you up and talk from time to time, Margie?"

She blushed a little, as some tears came to her eyes, then she softly replied, "Yes, of course, Brad and you had better call me, now that I'm your personal confidante. Are you going to be okay?" she softly inquired.

Brad smiled then softly kissed Margie's forehead like a beloved sister, "I am fine and I'm going to stay fine too, I'm back from the dead, Margie." Brad then turned and started his slow walk down the main office corridor and saying fond farewells to all friends and co-workers alike.

Still incensed and angry, Katherine shouted to Brad as he slowly walked away down the hall, "Go ahead, Brad, run…run away from me – you cowardly bastard…that's what you do best…you can't face reality, so you just run away from problems and life…why don't you just run to hell…go out there and find yourself another little tramp to spend your time with…and don't bother to come back to me!"

Brad turned briefly to gaze at Katherine, his eyes and facial expression betrayed only sadness, yet he said nothing back to Kate, knowing full-well that his words at this point would fall upon deaf and angry ears. They both had made indiscretions, but Kate was too filled with hatred to listen to any type of logic; maybe there was no place for it in the domain and affairs of the heart.

He smiled, devilishly winked at Kate, then walked briskly through the hallway, down the stairs and out the front door. Kate had never been this angry before, but his actions were not those of a saint; still Kate had no right to say those nasty prejudiced things. Although he felt sad and dejected, he knew Katherine felt even worse. He didn't want things to turn out like this and he had hoped for a happy reunion with Kate, 'but in life, destiny has an odd way of shaping things', he concluded. The best thing option was to simply leave Katherine alone for a period of time.

Everyone's emotions had to simmer down. He made his way down to the Harley, unlocked the ignition, and resurrected the 'Hog' back from the dead. It was sure comforting to get out of that hot, hostile office; the cool autumn air felt very refreshing.

Katherine scornfully eyed the small group of Hamilton & MacAlister employees huddling immediately outside her office doorway. She felt hurt and angry, her emotions were laid bare for all to witness. Even worse, she was publicly humiliated before the primary office staff, they all knew that Brad had 'dumped' her and rejected their future marriage pact, leaving her holding the wedding bag for a second time in less than a year, a definite social 'no no.' Soon all of Boston society would know of her cancelled marriage and engagement. She didn't need money or power, birth had amply bestowed these to her, yet she desired her own selfish dreams and desires! The heart wants, what the heart wants.

Desperately she looked around her office and down the office corridor with tear-filled eyes. "Things were not supposed to work out like this!" she cursed aloud in bitter audible despair. She was supposed to kiss and make up with Brad and be spending the night in passionate lovemaking and preparing for her High Society wedding; however, this night only loneliness and regret were again to be her nightly companions.

Some employees awkwardly gawked down the hallway into Katherine's office, as they silently whispered in hushed tones to one another. In a last gasp of anger, Katherine screamed down the hallway for all the employees to hear, "Everyone get the hell back to work and stop gawking! All of your fucking annual and Christmas bonuses are on the line, do you all frigging hear me?" Katherine angrily shouted at the top of her lungs, as her voiced cracked with emotion and a flood of tears dripped down her cheeks. Her last deposit of self-dignity was finally exorcised.

Everyone in the office made the obstinate illusion that they were busy at their work places and desks, wishing not to incur the wrath of an angry, powerful woman, who was presently prone to violence and financial retribution! Kate hung her head in utter shame and then she commonly sat down upon the floor's plush Persian rug and started to sob like a little girl. In frustration, she grabbed the lead glass decanter and simply chucked down a mouthful of aged malt scotch just like a common street vagabond. The low rumble of Brad's motorcycle filled the air outside her office. 'Why work hard and bust your butt, when there's no one to share your life with?' Katherine bitterly reasoned to herself.

Leona whispered to Margie in a hushed tone, "I'm surprised that 'Kit Kat' didn't ask Brad for a sperm sample before he left!" Margie looked surprised and embarrassed by her co-workers' rude comment.

"Shut up! Just shut the hell up for once, Leona!" Leona was shocked to hear Margie suddenly come to Kit Kat Kate's defence.

"What the hell? What did you say, girlfriend?" Leona spurted out in obvious exacerbation.

Margie replied, "I said, shut up, please!"

Leona was shocked. "So, what the hell gives with you, Margie? The Ice Princess, she ain't your friend, honey!" Leona replied in her own defence and self-justification.

"You see I know how's she's feeling! I've been where she is now. Everyone, even the Ice Princess, has feelings, Leona. We all want things and certain people in this world. We both love the same man, the difference is that she has a chance with Brad, as for myself, I never had a chance with him and I never will!" Margie sadly confessed as she slowly and confidently walked toward Katherine's office doorway. For the first time in her life, Margie was now financially secure and personally confident. The office 'mouse' was now freed to become the savvy 'lioness'.

She boldly peeked into the danger zone of Katherine's office and beheld the pathetic Kit Kat in her bare stocking feet, sobbing against her office table; she was sitting on the floor and crying like a distraught little girl. This was definitely not the image that Katherine had shepherded over the years as being a tough-ass corporate executive, one with ice-cold emotions, keen analytical mind, and few visible feelings. As with most defensive mechanisms, Kate's hard-shell persona was entirely the act of the consummate actress – a wall that was self-erected to keep the world at bay and to keep herself safe away from the everyday world. Yet Katherine had acted too well the part she had crafted, it kept her isolated from her colleagues and it made her no true friends. Margie deliberately cleared her throat, making her presence known to Katherine, yet no response was acknowledged. Margie again repeated her cough, this time it was loud enough to get Katherine's attention.

All thoughts of revenge had been banished from Margie's psyche; now all she felt was pity and remorse. It was bad enough for one person to be unhappy and miserable, yet for two people to be so was doubly tragic, as one of them should at least have grabbed the golden ring. Kate kept sobbing the words, "My mouth, my big fucking, stupid mouth! I could not leave well-enough alone! Why didn't I just keep my fucking mouth quiet?"

Katherine noticed a distinct presence in her office doorway and slowly gazed up to see who in the hell was so rude so as to interrupt her in a moment of personal despair. To Katherine's dismay, she saw Margie and she expected only some well-deserved sarcasm or humiliation.

"What the hell do you want... DeTagelio? You little two-timing, middle-class, scheming bitch! You got exactly what you always wanted! Go take your precious 30 pieces of silver and get the hell out of my office, go have a few laughs with your friends, go celebrate at Olde Bailey's like you always do; make the 'Ice Princess' jokes of which you are so fond of telling! Have yourselves a good laugh on me, kid!" Katherine sobbed. "Brad knows that I can't fire you! Are you happy now, bitch?" Katherine sobbed. Margie continued to stare at Katherine for a few seconds. "So, what is it? Why are you just standing there, DeTagelio?" Katherine inquired as she pitifully sobbed on the office carpet.

Casually lighting a forbidden cigarette, Margie slowly walked over to Katherine; she knelt down and gently placed both of her hands upon Katherine's shoulders and looked into her teary eyes. "Take it from me, no one wants to live a lonely life and you do not have to be alone! You hear that sound of Brad's motorcycle Kate...it's the sound of opportunity and of second chances...so go... go run after him! Be the bigger person in this silly argument!" Margie counselled softly. Katherine looked at Margie with a puzzled look.

"I said, 'go... run for him, go after the man you have loved since your childhood, it's not too late...he's still outside, listen!" Margie exclaimed to Katherine, as the loud purr of the Harley-Davidson Road King accented the air, as Brad throttled the engine loudly, trying to warm up the engine from its cold idle.

"Love is too precious to throw away in a fit of anger or ego trips, Katherine. If Brad was the man who loved me, I'd be running down that hall right now like a mad schoolgirl! I never had a chance with him! Well, what the hell are you waiting for ...go, girl...don't think... just go...run!" Margie shouted at Katherine in an affirmative, almost impertinent tone.

For some strange reason, Katherine took heed to the words of one of her least favourite employees. In a sudden brash emotional rush, Katherine was on her feet and making a mad run down the hallway and then the winding spiral staircase of Hamilton & MacAlister in her bare stocking feet. Katherine was a remarkable sight to behold in her $15,000 custom-made outfit, expensive gold jewellery, swinging pearl necklace, and her mascara-stained eyes. She ran for dear life, hoping to stop the only man she ever loved from running out of her life forever. She didn't know what she would say to him and at this moment she didn't care either; she was tired of being alone. Katherine now realized that they had both said and done some stupid things that neither one of them really meant and now she knew that she was losing everything that she ever wanted because of a fit of childish anger, revenge and pride.

Maybe Brad didn't have the courage to stick around and work things out, but Katherine was strong and now determined to give it a second chance. She would say anything to keep Brad in Boston with her, she would be the one to fall on her sword and admit her failings and complicity. As Katherine finally reached the reserved parking spaces in the front of Hamilton & MacAlister, she saw in her despair the distant image of a motorcycle rear taillight, its roaring exhausts being silenced increasingly by the expanding distance between herself and the motorcycle. The darkened mascara laced tears began to flow down her white rosy cheeks, as she realized that her second chance had just ridden away in the tailpipe exhaust of a Harley-Davidson motorcycle. Her heart sank in despair after realizing that after long months of waiting, she had just thrown away the opportunity to live happily with Brad in just the short span of 15 short lousy minutes. She despised herself now, more than she had hated Brad.

"Why hadn't I just kept my big, stupid, loud mouth shut and say nothing like many other women do?" Katherine bitterly muttered to herself. 'Now I know why I have few friends in this town, I'm a fool of a woman...I'll never fucking learn!' she sobbed scornfully to herself. Katherine was standing on Bromfield Street in utter despair. 'Brad was gone forever,' she cried to herself.

"Hey there, boss lady, now what's this shit all about? A MacAlister bawling her eyes out in the financial district of Boston? We can't have that now, can we?" Margie coolly pronounced proudly to a mouth slobbering Katherine.

Katherine contemptuously turned her head obtusely toward Margie and gave her a dirty look of disgust and hatred. "I've lost him, he's gone...and he's not coming back, does that make you fucking happy, DeTagelio?" Katherine pathetically teared.

The streetwise Margie slowly stalked up behind Katherine. "No way, honey…no it doesn't make me happy and if you keep talking nonsense like that, then you really will have lost him," she remarked calmly.

"What the hell do you know about any of this? Why should you give a damn, he's my fiancé, or at least he used to be my fiancé? He's left me, his heart belongs to another, I saw it in his eyes and with his actions!" Katherine muttered in a low tone.

"That's pure malarkey and pardon my expression and middle-class slang, but that is pure bullshit, honey!" Margie remarked defiantly back at Katherine in an irreverent and authoritative tone.

Katherine was lost for words. She could only defensively look back at Margie with outrage and confusion. Yet Margie explained further.

"Look here, Katherine! Brad, Wayne, or whatever name he's using this week – came back to you across over 1,500 miles of the good old USA. He came to mend fences and to talk to you and what the hell do you do? You throw the entire office at him, slap his face, and call him and his new friends, every flipping name in the book! Just think about it, deary! He could just as easily called you, sent an e-mail or text message , that is, if he didn't give a shit about you. Yeah, I know he's a real gentleman and he has great social breeding, but a man only returns to visit a woman after six long months and many miles under his belt for one thing – love! Both of you have made mistakes here!" Margie wisely counselled.

This little office urchin upstart began to make some sort of sense to her, so Katherine for once, wisely kept her mouth shut and listened further. Margie continued her street-wise counselling.

"Yes, he still loves and cares for you and by the way you still feel the same way too! That's way it hurts so bad. You, your family, and this firm – these are all important things to him. His past and life experiences anchored Brad to Boston. He's no longer running from his hurt, he's running toward his future, he's discovering himself as a full independent individual. Look, take it from a gal who knows from hard experiences, if a guy's going to break-up with you, he does it in the easiest, most cowardly way possible and from what I just saw, that confrontation was by no means easy, you damn near knocked his brains out!" Margie detailed with personal authority.

Margie slowly and gently put her hands-on Katherine's shoulders and looked her in the eyes. Katherine looked like a pathetic, washed-up kitten with ruffled hair, red eyes, and no shoes. "You know that what

I'm telling you is true, don't you? You know what, Kate, he'll be coming back to you too," Margie pronounced confidently.

Katherine looked totally shocked; after all, Brad had just ridden-off to a destination unknown, yet she was also desperate for hope or even seductive lies. "Just how the hell do you know that, Miss DeTagelio" Katherine tearfully inquired with a tone of curiosity and restrained hope.

"You're really something, Katherine… don't you see the way he looks at you? He's a man still in love with you! Yes, I said 'man', because any part of the boy that remained in Brad when he left here last April – has been buried…exorcised from whatever ghosts that have haunted him since his family's death. I noticed the change in him immediately, there is a maturity about him now, it was in his eyes as soon as I looked at him, didn't you see it too?" Margie gently questioned of Katherine.

Katherine just stared at Margie with awe and intent. Katherine seemed to be receptive, so Margie continued her little dissertation. "Sure, Brad has changed and his feelings toward you have evolved too. His feelings are now more developed, more mature. He has now experienced the love of another woman and it's confusing to him. He'll never be the same boyish 'old Brad', but maybe that's a good thing too! Perhaps you cannot continue to be the 'old Kate' either. Maybe you'll need to change a bit too, if you want him back. Not drastic changes mind you, but just enough for some perceptual changes," Margie slyly counselled.

"I don't think that I can do that, I mean I can't change like that, to be somebody I'm not," Katherine defensively muttered.

"Oh, come on now, you're more a natural at it than you think. Just think a minute at how different you can act with clients, friends, and the hired help. Everyone in life is an actor or actress! Frankly, you can turn it on and off like an academy award actress, Kate," Margie frankly spurted.

"Let me tell you a little secret about Brad and me, Miss Katherine," Margie whispered in a low voice to Katherine. With these words, Katherine expected to hear the worst, that Margie and Brad had an affair or something similar. "Remember when the crew from Hamilton & MacAlister went out after work for a few social drinks at Olde Bailey's? Margie inquired rhetorically.

"Now fully intrigued, Katherine passively nodded her head in anxious anticipation and dread. "Well, Brad and I got to know each other well, really well…we became… yes, we became…close friends. Nothing more, Kate…nothing else either. My infatuation with Brad was just that;

it was a romantic schoolgirl crush for me, but he was never mine and he can never be mine – that's because he belongs you. He told me all about your childhood, your dreams, even your moods. He spoke about the great times you both enjoyed and the good times that both your families shared. Every conversation we shared, however, was the same – all of the stories, jokes and dreams centered on you!" Margie confessed softly.

Katherine stood there digesting every word that Margie uttered; desperate to believe anything, even lies, if these could provide her any emotional hope of getting her Brad back. "But...but how do you know he'll be back for certain? You're just guessing, you can't be sure! Brad is off on his middle-life crisis, his Easy Rider crap and who knows what the hell else," Katherine cried out in despair and hoping for some tangible fact to prove herself wrong.

"Oh please, Katherine, I do know and it's a sure thing too," Margie replied before continuing her explanation. Katherine was now totally spellbound by Margie's every utterance.

"So, Katherine, in two, maybe three weeks tops, Brad will be calling me. He always has, and he always will... believe me, he'll call!" Margie responded with a defiant certainty. "Think back carefully. Remember all the times that he has called me in the past? It's like clockwork. Brad and I are pals, Kate, we're just good pals who can confide with one another," Margie quipped.

Katherine became very excited and animated with Margie's revelation and it did seem to make definite sense. "Yes, yes...you are correct, DeTagelio. Brad always calls you first at the office, he will probably not accept my calls anymore. So, you'll let me speak with him on my behalf? I will talk with him, and then... I'll make everything right again. I'll apologize for all the stuff that I said!" Katherine pleaded excitedly to Margie.

Margie paused for a split second in utter horror, her mouth dropping in awe and exacerbation, and then she frankly stated, "Hell no lady! Never! Over my dead body! Not on your life, sister!"

Katherine was dejected and exacerbated and horrified by Margie's negative response. "Why? Why the hell not! You little bitch, you're no damned good!" Katherine screamed in rejection and anger.

"Now hold onto your uppity, Blue Blood temper! You sure don't know a hell of a lot about men and you certainly don't know certain things about Brad, now do you, Kate?" Margie confidently retorted. Katherine, for once, was silenced into confrontational submissive silence by the authoritative personal assistant.

"Now listen to me carefully, you are not going to say any of those crazy, desperate things; in fact, you're not going to even speak to Brad at all. No, lady, I'm going to speak with Brad for you. You see, he still thinks that you are a real rich bitch from hell, the Ice Princess of Boston herself, the witch with the razor-sharp tongue...and you are still this person in Brad's mind and you will still be this woman in his mind when he calls me back. No, Kit Kat, when Brad calls me, I'm going to tell him that you are as cold and bitchy as ever and that you have no desire to speak with him and that you haven't forgiven him for walking out on you and your marriage plans. He will certainly believe this, because it will be true," Margie whispered, as Kate listened with an utter disbelief, but with a keen honed interest.

"What, so how in the hell is that going to get me Brad back?" Katherine replied in utter amazement! "That doesn't sound like any sort of a plan to me, DeTagelio!" Kate quibbled, hoping for a reasonable explanation. Confidently Margie continued her explanation and strategy.

"Later in a couple of weeks or maybe a month or two, Brad will contact me again and he'll naturally inquire about the firm and about you, Katherine. Naturally, I'll explain that you have become detached, even depressed and are becoming withdrawn from daily events, even if ever so slightly. This will slowly start to annoy and disturb Brad and his thoughts will slowly turn back to you, even if just a little bit each day. He knows that this will not be your normal nature to behave like this and he will start to wonder and even worry a bit. Little by little, Brad's thoughts and concerns will turn away from himself and back to you, Kate."

Katherine's eyes started to gleam, and she began to understand the sublime plan. Margie continued, "And in the next call, or maybe two calls, I'll explain that you are also taking a nip or two of scotch every morning and you are arriving late to the office on a regular basis. Brad will become increasingly concerned, even worried about your welfare. By early Spring, I'll be contacting Brad and telling him that you are under a physician's care, maybe even a stay at a private sanatorium, for dehydration and exhaustion – the results of overwork, stress, and depression. I can, or we can, also get Mr and Mrs MacAlister to briefly contact Brad and have them note their concern for their daughter's welfare. By this time, Brad will be pacing the floor with nervousness; he'll naturally want to speak with you, but you will be unable to take his calls, because you are under mild medication and a physician's care. Also, your father will need to meet with Brad to discuss the settlement of the Hamilton estate issues, which will need to be done in person. Soon Brad will be rapidly trekking his way back to Boston again, both to see you and take care of the family business. This will be your opportunity to talk with Brad and mend fences, Kate! Finally, should all that we try still fail to bring Brad back to Boston, we'll inform Brad that Hamilton and MacAlister is a target of a big Wall Street hostile takeover! Now that will certainly bring our boy back running in a hurry for sure!" Margie accurately finished her synopsis of the plan.

Margie's plan was brilliant as it was devious! Katherine was hopeful, but still not fully convinced of Margie's strategy. "It might just work, DeTagelio, but Brad has changed, I haven't! I know who I am all too well. I'm still the self-centred cold, rich bitch that I was and always will be!" Katherine exclaimed in a mocking, depressed, self-confessed tone.

Margie continued with unrivalled confidence, "Getting sick and getting Brad back to Boston is only half of the strategy, Brad will also have to see the 'other Kate', the 'vulnerable Kate', the 'needing Kate'. He needs to see you in a new light, but not as a totally different person."

Katherine nodded in silent agreement, her eyes and heart intent on the entire gambit of dialogue that Margie spoke.

"If I do as you say, Margie, I'll lose control, respect, and position. I just can't do that!" Katherine sounded off defensively.

"Since when does being strong and assertive equate with being a selfish, stiff-assed, butthead?" Margie interrupted. "Men play their games and we will play ours," Margie continued. "We women have always had power over the men that love us, Kate. The secret of the power is never revealing its possession to the eyes of the men we love and using it so very gently and covertly," Margie replied with a wink and a devilish smile.

Margie took a long determined and stern look at Katherine, who seemed like she was in a haze of utter bewilderment. She appeared to hear and acknowledged all the wisdom that Margie spoke, yet her eyes betrayed an ocean of confusion as well. Right then and there, Margie realized that Katherine had not the slightest idea about how to form or implement any plan to get Brad back into her arms.

Kate was very intelligent, yet she lacked the experience for handling interpersonal relations successfully, with either men or women. Margie quickly realized that she had to spoon-feed the entire concept and execution of the plan to Katherine and spell-out the details in excruciating, childlike detail. 'Katherine could be so anal at times,' Margie smartly concluded.

"Now do you mean to stand there and tell me that an intelligent, beautiful, mature woman with the advantage of private schooling, an advanced Ivy League degree and the owner and a manager of a multi-billion dollar business cannot plan out and implement an affair of the heart? So much for the Ethel Walker Finishing School, Vassar, and Harvard," Margie proclaimed in wild exasperation, as she threw up her arms in utter disgust.

"Well…. that was different. That was education and business stuff… this is more difficult, they don't teach this stuff in schools," Katherine retorted in her own defence.

"But maybe you're right, DeTagelio. I'm just not sure what to do," Katherine confessed.

"Listen, I do know what you should do and like I said, I'd like to help you. Follow my advice and by next Summer or Fall, you'll find yourself walking down the church aisle and getting married to Bradford Wayne Hamilton," Margie confided. Both women smiled briefly at one another.

"That's another thing which is bothering me, DeTagelio, so what's in this deal for you? God knows I'm not your friend, I've treated you like shit in front of your friends and the entire office and I've been busting your chops ever since you were assigned as Brad's personal assistant. I've done everything but get you fired and now Brad has removed that option from me as well," Katherine inquired with some honest frustration.

"Spot on, Kate, you forged your reputation as the Ice Princess of Hamilton & MacAlister, you are a real bitch boss lady. Yes, I do want something and the things that I want are simple and reasonable. I want respect for who I am and for the things that I do! I want Brad to be happy, even if it's not with me, because he deserves it! Also, I like working for Hamilton & MacAlister, and I prefer that my work setting be as pleasant as possible! And finally, I want a career, not just a job, at Hamilton & MacAlister! I want to advance and become a working professional in this firm! I am an ambitious, intelligent and hard-working independent woman, who has been supporting her widowed mother and siblings ever since my dad died when I was a teenager. I have earned my associate's degree from Boston College and I am attending night classes for my bachelor's degree in finance… I'm no threat to you, Kate, but with your assistance, I can become a valuable asset to the firm. I can also be a good friend too. Now is all this too much to ask, Miss Katherine?" Margie inquired quite definitively.

Katherine composed herself and thought of the candid words which were just posed to her by Margie. Momentarily Katherine toyed with the idea that this was part of some grand scheme that DeTagelio was concocting for her own advancement, but Katherine dismissed this possibility since Margie was forthcoming with her relationship with Brad. Margie's demands were reasonable and honest. Katherine knew that she needed a friend in the firm and what better person could there be than that of Brad's personal assistant. The personal assistants had the confidences of the executives and the ears of the office workers. Margie could be very valuable to both herself and Brad. Katherine also realized that she could control Margie better with incentives than reprisals. Margie could never assume any title of ownership within the firm and the best that she could hope for was a Junior or Full Account Executive member, this was fine in Katherine's mind.

"You are quite an intelligent, some would say, designing woman, DeTagelio, despite your rather common mannerisms and decor! Both your plans and professional development goals are quite reasonable, even admirable," Katherine replied after a short pause.

"So, DeTagelio, you will help me with Brad?" Katherine inquired with a nervous frown. "First of all, my friends all call me Margie and while at the office it's Miss DeTagelio or simply Margie," DeTagelio responded with a huge inviting smile that indicated both acceptance and friendship.

"So, concerning your employment conditions, I'll go you even one better…You get Brad back here by next Fall and after I walk down that wedding aisle, I'll write you out a cheque in the amount of $1 million, along with all the other items which you have stated!"

Margie thought just a second, scowled and then smiled back to Katherine extending her hand in both a sign of friendship and offer of acceptance.

"Miss Katherine, make it $1.5 million net of taxes and it's a done deal, I have to consider the inflation and time value of money!" Margie quickly retorted, as the two strong willed ladies shook hands in a mutually understanding manner. Both Katherine and Margie then started to laugh, as both were reminded of the formal vernacular that Katherine MacAlister had demanded to be called some months earlier in a heated office showdown between the two women.

"Okay...okay," Katherine wearily sighed. "So, you can call me Kate, but not Kit Kat, when we are alone," Katherine responded.

Both women had finally formed an early, if uneasy, bond of friendship, each realizing their roles and motives in relation to Brad and the firm. The confrontation was anti-climactic, since their antagonism had brewed for many months without meaningful purpose and it finally ended in a whimper on Bromfield Street. The dusk of an early Boston Autumn was rapidly approaching, the sun's rays were very slowly being extinguished by the creeping shroud of grey-purple clouds and these to be replaced by the sphere of a charcoal night. A slight inviting chill began to fill the late afternoon air.

"You know, Miss Katherine, I mean, Kate, you look like hell, in fact, you look like a woman who desperately needs a good, strong drink. How about we continue our girl talk over a few friendly drinks at Olde Bailey's? Let's call it a girls' night out?" Margie suggested to her newfound friend.

"Well...I don't know...I mean I left a lot of stuff back at the office and I really need to..."

Suddenly, Margie quickly cut Kate off in mid-sentence, "The only thing you left back at the office was a bad scene, bad memories, a dirty office, and some nervous financial brokers! Screw it all, Kate!" Margie snapped. "Besides, how many good times did you miss out with the Hamilton staff by staying in that stuffy office?" Margie wisely concluded. Katherine knew that Margie was correct and she had hit a sensitive nerve too.

"So what do you say, Kate, the office or Olde Bailey's?" Margie reiterated.

Kate stonewalled the question slightly, "Well I really don't know, just look at me I'm a frigging mess and I don't like some of the thespians that hang out at Ole Bailey's."

Margie slyly demurred, "Well, I can assure you that no loud-mouthed, pushy, pass-making, blue collar working-stiffs will bother you this evening, not at least while you are with me!"

Katherine's eyes widened with initial surprise, anger, then amusement. "So, Margie, you were the bar bitch that set that ass-grabbing, Neanderthal over to me that night!" Katherine exclaimed.

"Yep, guilty, I'm the very same bitch, Kate. Sorry about that, but you know that you had it coming, especially after what you said to me that day. Just a little girlfriend payback, Kate, you were just lucky that you didn't ask me to get you any coffee or tea that morning, that's all I can tell you," Margie replied.

Kate looked down in embarrassment and guilt.

"Now…now, all that's in the past, forgiven and almost forgotten. We're pals now, let's go get ourselves a drink and talk about Brad and your future wedding," Margie sighed.

Katherine smiled as the two women slowly walked to Olde Bailey's just a block away. Katherine's barefooted walk was slow, she having thrown her high heels at Brad and having left these heels in her office suite.

Immediately, Margie started talking and dominating their conversation once again. "So, Kate, please tell me about the wedding plans of yours! Is it true that rich people don't serve sit-down meals? How many people are coming? Where is it going to be held? Who is in the bridal party? I don't know anything about these high society affairs. Oh dear, running out of the office after you the way I did, I must have forgotten my wallet! Hey Kate, can you vouch for the tab at Olde Baileys, okay?" Margie inquired of Katherine, as she threw a friendly arm around Katherine's shoulder, as the two women slowly headed for 'Olde Bailey's' for some badly needed drinks and mutual feminine bonding.

* * * * * * * * * * * * * * * * *

Brad's trek back from Hamilton & MacAlister to his estate was not relaxed. The thoughts of guilt plagued him throughout his journey back to Greystone. 'Irritated, angry people say things that they usually regret,' he mused with bitterness under his breath.

In sober reflection, he recognized and regretted his brashness and anger. He had been an unfaithful rascal to Kate this past summer, and he had no good excuses for it except for that of self-pity. She had definite expectations for both a marriage and for a shared future together, both of which Brad had unceremoniously destroyed in a moment of outright rejection and physical abuse. He still loved Kate, yet he now despised her prejudiced attitudes and cloistered view of the world, perceptions which only months ago he also boldly shared with her. Unless Kate's attitudes changed, he would never be content and fulfilled in any relationship with her. 'Yet people could and do change given the opportunity and motivation to do so,' he squarely reckoned to himself.

Yet, there was no proper opportunity presented to Kate for a proper chance to repudiate his claims or to appreciate his changed perceptions. Everyone deserves a second chance. She deserved this and so much more from him. He had changed, and Kate needed the opportunity to either live with this change with him or even perhaps make some changes to herself, but she was left with no opportunity to do this, she could only react with revulsion, anger, and despair.

During his solitary ride back to Greystone, he had time to ponder and think, thus he became resolved to give Kate this opportunity that he had experienced, but not now, not at this moment. He wanted Kate's heart to cool off, then he could reason with her and if things then did not work out, they could conclude their relationship on professional terms and both go their own separate ways. Kate's fiery emotions were both her strength and weakness; still, emotions needed to be tempered with virtues of understanding and compassion.

Additionally, being a 50% owner in the firm and having both fiduciary and legal obligations to the firm and its employees, meant that he could not, nor would not, abandon his family's business. Yet these obligations had not yet reached a crescendo stage, he could afford to let Kate 'stew in her emotions' for a short time. He liked travelling the road and seeing America in all of its raw, working man perspective. Of this newfound taste, he yearned for more and he intended to grab his fill; life in the confines of a sheltered office would fill most of his future life and he just wanted to live a little more of life before settling down to the daily drudgery of the 9 to 5 office routine.

"After all, what was another six months out of his young life, the unexplored life was one not worth living," he contemplated to himself. The past road experiences had already broadened his character, outlook, and judgment and this was a good thing! More of the same could only reinforce and increase his perspective on life and it would also serve to make him a better business leader and investment banker as well. In the future, he would be able to relate money and investments in terms of real people, events and character rather than mere dry figures on a balance sheet.

'Yes,' he thought, 'going out on the road again, if even for a short time, was the right decision to make.' He resolved to try and make things right with Katherine when his anger had subsided. Perhaps in a few weeks, he would call her and try to explain things to her. Katherine was bitchy and a snob, but she was also very loving and loyal, still her bitter words stung his soul. The healing would take time and some respectful distance needed to be placed between them. 'A deep, long, frank conversation and confession concerning his travels was required to do proper justice to Kate and to also unburden his soul of any past sins he had committed,' he rightfully concluded.

His thoughts turned to the South with dreams of wintering in Florida. Next, he dreamed of Georgia, Louisiana, Texas, New Mexico, and California – then travelling all the way back again! 'Yes, that sounded like a fine itinerary, it should take him all of six or nine months, if he was lucky,' he gleefully pondered. 'It was sure great to be home again' he thought to himself, 'yet what adventures and characters awaited him on this journey?' There was no true living without consequences and he was determined to live his life on his own terms before conformity, marriage, and family began to place defined obligations and structure upon his ever rapidly fleeting youth.

The Greystone Mansion was now a scant five minutes away. Unexpectedly, he had the almost uncontrollable desire to partake of a healthy portion of Carla's famous homemade seafood melody. The sheer thought of his favourite childhood meal engrossed him totally. "Yes – a good homemade meal, a few days of rest, and then off again across America," he conjured anxiously.

He accessed the main Greystone wrought iron security gate, which alerted Carla and Juan to his imminent arrival. Carefully parking the Harley Road King in the driveway immediately beside the kitchen entrance, he turned off the ignition, and locked the ignition switch. Slowly dismounting his iron horse steed, he removed his helmet and stretched his limbs. A gentle cool air whispered across his face.

"Boy, it was sure good to be back home," he gleefully mused to himself. One journey had ended and if he was very lucky, another one perhaps equally adventurous and challenging, was about to begin for Brad 'Wayne' Hamilton.

* * * * * * * * * * * * * * *

THE END

Edmund Charles has worked in the military, telecommunications, and systems management consulting fields and he has written several defense-related articles. Living in sedate, graceful retirement and contentment, he has written three novels to date. He can be reached via email at *edmundcharles.55@gmail.com*